Fulke gazed upon his wife's face, the dark shadows beneath her eyes, the delicacy of brow and cheekbone and jaw. He knew that most of that delicacy was false, that Maude was usually as robust as a horse, but the bearing of three infants in swift succession and the circumstances of her last travail had drained her strength. How could he ask her to live an outlaw's life now when she needed rest and comfort? How could he trail three small children in his wake, the youngest a baby prematurely born? It would be irresponsible and likely end in tragedy. He gnawed on his thumbnail, already bitten down to the quick, and turning from the bed looked at his two daughters who were playing in a corner with Gracia. He had engendered them. Now it was his responsibility to give them a proper life.

LORDS OF THE WHITE CASTLE

ELIZABETH CHADWICK

sphere

SPHERE

First published in Great Britain in 2000
by Little, Brown and Company
Published in paperback by Warner Books in 2001
Reprinted 1998, 1999, 2001
Reprinted by Time Warner Books in 2005 (twice)
This edition published by Sphere in 2006
Reprinted 2007

A CIP catalogue record for this book
is available from the British Library.

ISBN 978-0-7515-3939-4

Papers used by Sphere are natural, recyclable products made from
wood grown in sustainable forests and certified in accordance with
the rules of the Forest Stewardship Council.

Typeset in Bembo by
Palimpsest Book Production Limited,
Polmont, Stirlingshire
Printed and bound in Great Britain by
Mackays of Chatham plc, Chatham, Kent
Paper supplied by Hellefoss AS, Norway

Sphere
An imprint of
Little, Brown Book Group
Brettenham House
Lancaster Place
London WC2E 7EN

A Member of the Hachette Livre Group of Companies

www.littlebrown.co.uk

ACKNOWLEDGEMENTS

As always my thanks go out to the various people who work behind the scenes, but seldom get their name up in lights. To everyone at the Blake Friedmann Literary Agency, including my wonderful agent Carole Blake, who is now an author in her own right after the publication of her book *From Pitch to Publication* on how to go about selling your manuscript.

I would like to thank everyone at Little, Brown, especially my editor Barbara Boote who always delights me by telling me which bits of the novel made her cry! Also to my desk and copy editors, Emma Gibb and Richenda Todd, for dotting the I's and crossing the T's – not to say sorting out the muddle of dates and seasons that several drafts of *Lords* had left in their wake.

Also I would like to express my gratitude to my family, for putting up with me (although it cuts both ways as I have to put up with them!). To the members of *Regia Anglorum*, Conquest and *Conroi de Burm* for sharing their knowledge and giving me inspiration; the members of Nottingham Writers' Contact for the laughs and support (who can forget Annabel's Antics?); and to the members of Medievalreader@egroups.com and Medievalenthusiasts@egroups.com for chats on my favourite subject!

CHAPTER 1

The Palace of Westminster, December 1184

Although it was not much past midday, the murky winter afternoon was already yielding to dusk. The sleety rain, which had put a stop to weapons practice on the sward, peppered against the shutters like glass needles. Every torch and sconce was ablaze, every brazier in use. Beyond their puddles of light and warmth, in the stairwells and dark walkways of Westminster's sprawl of buildings, a dank chill waited to trap those who were foolish enough to step outside without a cloak.

Seated in a window embrasure of the White Hall, Fulke listened to the growl of the wind and buffed his new shield to smooth the scores and scratches sustained that morning. His father had given it to him at Martinmas when Fulke had turned fifteen, a man's accoutrement bearing the FitzWarin device of twelve wolf's teeth blazoned in red.

'Hah, sixes, I win!' cried a triumphant voice.

Raising his head from the shield Fulke glanced over at the dice game which was occupying Prince John and the other squires of Ranulf de Glanville's retinue. Money jinked as a curly-haired squire swept a pile of coins from the trestle into the palm of his hand. Prince John, who would be seventeen on the Eve of Christmas, scowled and reached into the pouch at his gilded belt to toss more silver on to the board. His stocky frame was given a certain elegance by a tunic of costly blue wool, but the effect was marred by a petulant slouch.

Fulke might have joined them except that he had but half a silver penny between himself and an empty pouch. Had they been arm wrestling he would have succumbed. Unlike Madame Fortune, skill and brawn were dependable and he possessed an abundance of both.

The other lads had called him bumpkin and clod when he arrived from the Welsh Marches nine months ago. They had stolen his clothes, tripped him on the stairs, and emptied a piss-pot over him while he slept. It had taken them a week to learn the hard way that whatever Fulke received was returned twofold. They still called him bumpkin, but these days it was a nickname, a sign of acceptance into their company, if not their rank.

That he had a position in John's retinue at all was by way of a favour to his father from King Henry who valued the loyalty of the FitzWarin family. Fulke knew that John would never have chosen him for a companion, just as he would never have chosen John. Their similar age was the closest the youths came to having anything in common.

Fulke looked again at the dice players. The Prince caught his eye and glowered. 'In Christ's name, stop making love to that accursed shield and bring some more wine.' Raising his empty cup, he waggled it at Fulke. An amethyst ring flashed on his middle finger, and another of heavy gold shone on his thumb.

'Sir.' Fulke laid his shield carefully aside, fetched the flagon from the sideboard and approached the game.

'Fancy your chances, Bumpkin?' asked the curly-haired squire.

Fulke smiled, his flint-hazel eyes brightening. 'I fancy yours more, Girard.' He nodded at the new pile of coins on the trestle. 'I'll arm wrestle you for them if you like.' Pouring the wine into John's cup, he left the flagon for the others to help themselves.

Girard snorted. 'I'm not falling for that one again!'

Fulke's smile broadened into a grin and he flexed his forearm where rapidly developing muscle tightened the sleeve. 'That's a pity.'

Girard made a rude gesture and scooped up the dice. Fulke stayed to watch him throw a total of three and lose his winnings, then sauntered back to the window embrasure and his shield. Two padded benches sat either side of the latched shutters and between them was a gaming table on which John's tutor, Master Glanville, had placed a heavy wooden chessboard.

Leaning on his shield, Fulke contemplated the ivory pieces with a feeling of nostalgia bordering on homesickness. He conjured a vision of the manor at Lambourn; the faces of his brothers etched in firelight as they played knuckle-bones by the hearth. His mother reading by the light of a sconce, her lips silently forming the words. He and his father playing chess in an embrasure just like this one, his father's brow puckering as he toyed with a taken pawn and considered his next move. Fulke knew that he was gilding the image for his present comfort but, even without the veneer, there was still an underlying truth and solidity to the picture. Whilst not wretchedly homesick, he missed the warmth and companionship of his family. He often thought it a pity that his father's next move had been to send him here to learn the skills of knighthood among the highest in the land.

'It is a great honour that King Henry has done our family,' Fulke le Brun had said one day last spring when he returned from attendance at court. Standing in the private chamber at Lambourn, his garments still mired from the road, he had broached the news. 'Not only will Fulke be tutored by Ranulf Glanville the Justiciar, but he will mingle with men of influence who may be able to help us.' Fulke could remember the flush to his father's sallow complexion, the spark of ambition in the deep brown eyes. 'Whittington could be ours again.'

'What's Whittington?' Fulke's youngest brother Alain had piped up. He was only four years old and unlike the older boys had yet to have the FitzWarin *cause célèbre* drummed into him blood and bone.

'It's a castle and lands belonging to us,' said their mother, gathering Alain into her arms. 'Your papa's family held it in the days of the first King Henry, but then it was taken away from them during a war and never restored. Your papa has been trying to get it back for a long time.' It was a tale told in simple terms that a small child could under-stand and her voice was level, omitting the antagonism and bitterness that had built and festered over the years of striving.

'Too long,' said Fulke le Brun. 'It was in my grandsire's lifetime that last we held Whittington. Roger de Powys claims it as his, but he has no right.'

'If King Henry loves you enough to make me Prince John's attendant, why doesn't he give you Whittington?' Fulke had wanted to know.

'It is not as simple as the King's word,' his father had said. 'Our right has to be proven in a court of law and sometimes if a matter is awkward or seen as a mere quibble, it is pushed aside for more pressing concerns. God knows I have tried. Henry has made promises, but it is not as important a matter to him as it is to me.' He had looked intensely at Fulke and gripped his shoulder, man to man. 'Ranulf de Glanville is well positioned to hear our plea, and he will be your tutor. Do your best for him, and he will do his best for you.'

And Fulke had done his best because it was not within his nature to shirk and he had as much pride as his father. His ability to fathom accounts had increased beyond all measure beneath the Justiciar's instruction and he had picked up the broader points of Latin and law. What Master Glanville made of him, however, he did not know for his tutor was a solemn man in late middle age, not much given to open praise.

Fulke pushed his hair off his forehead and grimaced. He was not sure that being educated at court was a grand privilege at all. Being at Prince John's beck and call was a nightmare. At home, Fulke was the heir to his father's lands, cherished, sure of his status, lording it affectionately over his five brothers. Here he was of minor rank, a nobody to be used as John saw fit. More often than not, used translated into abused.

There was a sudden flurry at the dice table as Prince John shot to his feet and the flagon that Fulke had so recently replenished was sent crashing to the floor. 'You thieving sons of whores, get out, all of you!' John gestured wildly at the door. 'You're naught but leeches. There's not one of you worth a pot of piss!'

Fulke slid out of his corner and started to follow the other squires from the chamber.

'Not you, Bumpkin,' John snarled. 'Get me some more wine.'

'Sir.' Expression blank, Fulke stooped to the flagon in the rushes near John's feet. An ugly dent married its silver-gilt belly.

'You shouldn't have left it on the table,' John said petulantly. 'It's all your fault and you can pay for a new one.'

It would have been wiser to keep quiet but Fulke was unable to prevent himself from protesting. 'That is unjust, sir.'

John eyed him through narrowed lids. 'Are you arguing with me?'

Fulke stood up, the damaged flagon in his hand. 'It is true that I left the flagon here when I should have replaced it on the sideboard, but it was not I who knocked it from the table.'

John jabbed a warning forefinger. 'You'll pay and that's an end to it. Now fetch more wine and make haste.'

Scarcely bothering to bow, Fulke strode from the room. Despite the winter chill, he was scalding with fury. 'I won't pay him a single fourthing,' he muttered as he flung into the hall beyond the chamber and marched down its length to the butler's table at the far end.

'For Prince John,' he said woodenly to the attendant.

The butler eyed the damage with pursed disapproval. 'How did this happen?'

'An accident.' Even though Fulke wanted to throttle John, honour and discretion fettered his tongue in front of others. And because he could say nothing, his anger burned the hotter within him, dangerously close to white heat.

'That's the third "accident" this month then.' The butler set the flagon beneath a wine tun and turned the spigot. 'These flagons don't grow on trees, you know. Cost half a mark each, they do.'

Close on seven shillings, Fulke thought grimly: a week's wages for a mounted serjeant and beyond his own reach unless he appealed to his father or spent an entire week arm wrestling for the funds.

Although John had bid him make haste, Fulke took his time to return to the royal apartment, giving his anger time to die down. He was partially successful. By the time he banged on the door and entered with the flagon, his resentment had banked to a smoulder.

John had unlatched the shutters by the chessboard and

was leaning against the window splay, gazing into the stormy dusk. Darts of wind-driven sleet hurled past the embrasure. The courtyards and alleys were in darkness – no torch would remain lit in this weather – but there were glimmers and flickers of light from the occupied halls, and the watchmen had built a brazier in a sheltered corner of the ward. Further away, the windows of the great abbey were darkly bejewelled from within.

John turned, one fist curled around his belt, the other resting on the shutter. 'You took your time.'

'There were others waiting the butler's service, sir,' Fulke lied and poured wine into John's cup. 'Do you want me to leave now?' He tried to keep the hopeful note from his voice but knew he hadn't succeeded when he saw John's expression grow narrow and mean.

'No, you can stay and keep me company. You do little enough to earn your supper.' The Prince gestured to the flagon. 'Pour yourself a measure. I don't like to drink alone.'

Fulke reluctantly tilted a couple of swallows into one of the squires' empty cups. The wind whipped the wall hangings and the candles guttered in the sconces, threatening to blow out and leave them in darkness.

'How many brothers do you have?'

Fulke blinked, unsure what to make of the Prince's mood except to know that it was ugly. 'Five, sir.'

'And what do they inherit?'

'I do not know. That is for my father to say,' Fulke answered cautiously.

'Oh come now. You are his heir. Everything will go to you.'

Fulke shrugged. 'That may be true, but none of my brothers will go wanting.'

'And you think there will be no resentment that you receive the lion's share?' John reached a casual hand to the shield that Fulke had left propped on the bench and ran his fingers over the rawhide edging.

'Not enough to cause a lasting rift between us,' Fulke said. 'Even if I quarrel with my brothers on occasion, blood is still thicker than water.'

John snorted with sour amusement. 'Is it indeed?'

'In my family it is.' Fulke took a mouthful of wine and knew that he was standing on perilous ground. John was the youngest of Henry's children, born after the family inheritance had been apportioned among the other sons, none of whom was willing to give up one iota of what was theirs. John Lackland he was called, often to his face. Glancing at the wild, dark night, feeling the sting of wind-borne sleet against his skin, Fulke began to understand. And that he, in his favoured position of eldest son, his inheritance secure, was being made a scapegoat. 'My father says that we are one body. The head cannot function without a torso or limbs. What you do to one, you do to all.'

'My father says,' John mimicked. 'Christ, do you know how often you trot that out?'

Fulke flushed. 'If I do it is because he speaks sense.'

'Or perhaps because you are a child who has not learned to think for himself.' John cast him a scornful look and closed the shutters on the wildness outside. The candles ceased to gutter and a sudden silence settled over the room, permeated with the smoky scent of burning wax. The Prince sat down moodily at the chessboard and fingered one of the bishops.

Fulke wondered rather desperately how long it would be before the dinner horn sounded. Judging by the advanced state of the dusk, it must be soon.

'What do you say to a wager, Bumpkin?' John gestured to the chessboard.

'A wager?' Fulke's heart sank. Reclaiming his shield, he

laid his hand on the leather-covered lime-wood, exorcising John's touch.

'Defeat me at chess and I'll let you off the price of the flagon.'

Fulke did not miss the taunting note in John's voice. The Prince was an accomplished chess player and his skills had been honed by their tutor Master Glanville, whose incisive intelligence had led to him being appointed Justiciar. Fulke's own skills were erratic, developed not so much from logic and instruction as enjoyment of the game and the ability to think fast on his feet.

'If you wish it, sir,' he said with resignation and sat down.

John gave him a denigrating smile and swivelled the chequered board so that the white pieces were his. 'My move first,' he said.

Fulke touched his shield again for luck. He knew that whatever he did he could not win. If he lost to John then he would have to find the price of the flagon. If he were victorious, John would find other, subtle, malicious ways of punishing him. The safest ploy was to lose as quickly as possible and then lather the Prince in flattery. It was what any of the other squires would do.

Fulke reached to a knight, fully intending to give John the conquest, but against the main tide of his will, a perverse cross-current altered the move, and it became an open challenge.

John narrowed his eyes. 'Where did you learn that one?' he demanded tersely.

'From my father,' Fulke said to be irritating. It was strange. Now that battle was joined, he could feel the certainty and arrogance of that cross-current growing within him, becoming his true self. He was as good as John, but in a different way, that was all. If he played by John's tactics, he would be defeated whatever the outcome. But if he played to his own rules, then he was free and damn the consequences.

John tried to manoeuvre him into a corner but Fulke kept his distance, making little sallies that constantly ruined John's strategy. The Prince grew increasingly frustrated, as much by Fulke's audacious baiting as by the fact that he was unable to pin him down. He downed two more cups of wine; he fiddled with his rings and tugged at the sparse growth of black beard on his chin, his expression growing stormier by the moment.

Fulke moved a bishop. 'Check,' he said. And it would be mate in two moves, neither of which his opponent could circumvent.

John gaped in disbelieving fury. His eyes flickered, calculating the moves just as Fulke had done. A muscle bunched in his jaw. 'I suppose your father taught you to cheat too,' he said in a voice congested with loathing.

Fulke clenched his fists and struggled for the control not to knock John's teeth down his throat. 'I have won fairly. You have no right to missay my family's honour as an excuse for losing.'

John sprang to his feet. A wild swipe of his fist scattered the chess pieces far and wide. 'I have the right to do anything I want!'

'Not to me and mine!' Fulke jumped up too, his eyes dark with fury. 'You're a king's son by birth, but just now I would accord a gutter sweeping more respect than you!'

John roared. Grabbing the chessboard in both hands, he slammed it with all his strength into Fulke's face.

Fulke's nose crunched. He reeled from the sudden violence of the blow, a white numbness spreading from the impact and overlaid by the heat of gushing blood. Raising his hand to his face, he brought it away and looked at his red fingers in astonishment.

John lunged at him again. Fulke ducked the blow and lashed out with his feet. John staggered. The ball of his foot rolled on one of the chess pieces and he crashed backwards, his skull striking the plastered wall with a dull thud. His knees crumpled and he hit the floor like a poled ox.

'Christ, bloody Christ!' Fulke panted and, stanching his nose on his sleeve, staggered over to John's prone body. His first thought was that he had killed him, but then he saw the Prince's chest rise and fall and felt the hard pulse beat against the throat laces of John's shirt.

Anger and shock churned Fulke's gut, making him feel sick. 'Sir, wake up!' He shook the Prince's shoulder in growing fear. Now the fat truly was in the fire.

John groaned but did not open his eyes. Blood splashed from Fulke's nose on to the costly blue tunic and soaked in. Staggering to the sideboard, Fulke poured a measure of wine and drank it down fast, tasting blood. Then he refilled the cup and brought it to John. Raising the Prince's shoulders, he dabbed John's lips with wine.

The latch clicked and the door suddenly swung inwards. Ranulf de Glanville and his nephew Theobald Walter, who was John's tutor in arms, stopped on the threshold and stared.

'God's bones,' declared Theobald Walter, his grey gaze wide with astonishment. 'What goes forth here?'

Fulke swallowed. 'My lord Prince struck his head, and I cannot rouse him.' His voice buzzed in his ears, the intonation thick with the blood that was clotting in his nose.

'And how did he come to do that?' Lord Walter advanced into the room, his tread firm with authority. The practice gambeson of the morning had been replaced by an ankle-length court tunic of crimson wool heavily embroidered with thread of gold. He still wore his sword, but as a mark of rank, not because he expected to use it. Behind him, Ranulf de Glanville prudently closed the door.

'I . . . we . . . there was a disagreement and we had a fight,' Fulke said, feeling wretched. A massive, throbbing pain was beginning to hammer between his eyes.

Lord Walter gave him the same assessing look with which he scrutinised the squires on the practice field. 'A fight,' he repeated. His voice was quiet and pleasant. Theobald Walter never shouted. A single twitch of an eyebrow, a brightening glare was all it took to bring the squires into line. 'About what?' He knelt at Fulke's side, his knees cracking slightly as he bent them. At nine and thirty, he was wearing well, but the English winters took their toll, as they did on every man.

Fulke compressed his lips.

'Don't clam up on me, lad,' Lord Walter said sharply. 'The truth will serve you better than silence.' He turned John's head gently to one side and found the swelling bruise beneath his hair. Then he sniffed the Prince's breath and pulled back with a grimace.

Fulke met the Baron's eyes without evasion. During lessons in weapon play, Theobald had shown himself fair and patient. 'The Prince accused me of cheating at chess and when I denied it, he struck me with the board. I . . .' He jutted his jaw. 'I hit out to defend myself and he fell backwards and struck his head.'

'How bad is it?' Rubbing his neat grey beard, de Glanville came to stand at John's feet. His face wore an incongruous mixture of alarm and distaste.

'There's a lump the size of a baby on the back of his head, but I don't believe there's cause to send for a priest just yet. Part of the reason he's insensible is that he's as soused as a pickled herring.' Theobald glanced briefly at his uncle then back to Fulke. 'This lad's nose is never going to sit as prettily on his face as it did this morn.'

De Glanville stooped to lift the wooden chessboard from

the floor. He studied the crack running through the middle. 'Where is everyone else?' His light blue eyes were glacial.

'The Prince dismissed them, sir.' Fulke faced the Justiciar, feeling like an erring soul before the throne of God on judgement day. 'I would have gone too, but he wanted more wine . . . and then he wanted me to play chess with him.'

John groaned and opened his eyes. They focused precariously on Fulke who was still leaning over him. 'You misbegotten son of a misbegotten whore!' he gasped, then rolled over and vomited the results of an afternoon's drinking into the rushes. 'I'll have your hide for this!'

'You are in no fit state to have anything but a split skull, Lord John,' de Glanville said coldly. He jerked his head at Theobald. 'Take FitzWarin out of here and clean him up. While you're about it, see if you can find His Highness's other attendants. We'll sort this out later.' Twenty years older than Theobald, he chose not to kneel at John's side but sat instead upon one of the padded benches and stared balefully down at the prone youth like an owl in a tree.

Theobald rose, drawing Fulke with him. 'Come,' he said in a brusque but not unkind voice.

'I want to see my father!' John was demanding with vicious petulance as Theobald ushered Fulke from the room.

Fulke shuddered as Theobald led him down the great hall attached to John's chamber. Pain beat in hot rhythm between his eyes and he had to breathe through his mouth, a metallic essence of blood cloying his palate. 'Will he really go to the King?'

Lord Theobald had no comfort for him. 'Knowing Prince John, I do not doubt it.'

Fulke pressed the back of his hand beneath his nose and gazed at the resulting red smudge. 'I suppose I will be dismissed from Prince John's household,' he said gloomily.

'Quite likely.' Theobald gave him a sidelong glance. 'But would you want to stay after this?'

'My father says that being educated at King Henry's court is an opportunity without price, and a great honour for our family.' As the words left his mouth, Fulke realised that John's earlier taunt had substance. He *was* always quoting his father.

'He's right,' Theobald said grimly, 'except about the price.'

'My lord?'

'Nothing.' Theobald suddenly stopped and with a grunt of mingled satisfaction and annoyance, turned sharply to the left.

Within one of the bays formed by the pillars supporting the hall, Fulke saw that the dice game was still in progress. Girard de Malfee was winning again and some noble-woman's attiring maid was watching him with admiring doe eyes.

'That's enough.' Theobald strode among them, his hands fisted around his swordbelt. 'Go and attend your master.'

'But he sent us out, my lord,' Girard objected, his voice overloud with drink.

'Well, I'm sending you back in, and my lord Glanville awaits you there. Go on, all of you, or I'll have you polishing helmets for a sennight. And you can leave that flagon out here. There's been enough damage caused already. You, girl, about your duties.'

The maid gave him a half-frightened, half-resentful look and departed in a swish of green skirts. With bad grace, Girard began pouching his winnings. At one point he looked up to argue with Theobald and caught sight of Fulke standing behind the Baron.

'Holy Christ, Bumpkin.' His jaw dropped with shock. 'What's happened to you?'

All the squires stared.

'I tripped,' Fulke said.

Theobald jerked his thumb. 'Now,' he snapped.

The boys departed in a tipsy clutter and Theobald shook his head like a goaded bull. 'God preserve me in my dotage that I should ever have to rely on wastrels such as them,' he growled.

Attacked by a wave of dizziness, Fulke swayed. Theobald grabbed him. 'Steady, lad. Come on, buck yourself up. You're not a wench to faint on me.'

Fulke's eyes darkened at the jibe. He braced his spine. 'I'm all right, my lord.' It wasn't true, but his pride and the strength of Theobald's arm bore him up.

A glint of approval kindled in the Baron's grey eyes. 'Yes,' he said. 'Amongst those worthless dolts, I think you're the only one who is.'

CHAPTER 2

As Fulke and Theobald crossed the sward, the wind from the river hit them full on with a great sleety smack and Fulke felt as if his face would explode. On reaching the sanctuary of a timber outbuilding behind the hall, he was dimly aware of Theobald being greeted by other lords, of curious looks cast his way and questions asked which the Baron fielded in a manner courteous but short. Then a heavy woollen hanging was drawn aside and Theobald ushered Fulke into a small, makeshift chamber.

A well-stoked brazier gave off welcome heat, the lumps glowing dragon's-eye red on the undersides. Perched on an oak travelling chest, Lord Theobald's squire, whom Fulke knew by sight, was tuning the strings of a Moorish lute. There was a camp bed in the room, made up with blankets and a coverlet of green Flemish cloth. Seated on it, reading a sheet of vellum by the light of a thick wax candle, was a prelate wearing the richly embroidered dalmatic of an archdeacon.

Theobald stared at the man occupying his bed. 'Hubert?' he said, as if not believing his eyes.

The priest looked up and smiled. Two deep creases appeared in his fully fleshed cheeks. 'Surely I haven't changed that much in a year.' He stood up and immediately the room and everyone in it seemed diminished by his height and girth.

'Well, no,' Theobald said, making a good recovery, 'I just wasn't expecting to see you tonight, brother.' With much hugging and shoulder-slapping the men embraced. Close up, the similarities were obvious despite the difference in build. They shared the same brow and nose and had the same way of smiling.

'I arrived in time for the service of nones at the abbey,' said Hubert Walter. 'I have a bed there for the night, but I thought first that I would come and see how you and Uncle Ranulf are faring among the devil's brood. I was about to send young Jean here to find you.'

Theobald gave a short, humourless laugh. 'Devil's brood is the sum of it!' he said. 'God knows what will happen when Richard and Geoffrey arrive.'

'Aye, well, that's why we're all here – to bear witness when Prince John's inheritance is decided.' The Archdeacon gestured to Fulke who stood shivering by the brazier. 'Who is this, Theo, and why does he look as if he has just walked off a battlefield?'

Theobald grimaced. 'In a way he has, and since I'm his tutor in arms, he's my responsibility.' He beckoned Fulke forwards. 'Make your obeisance to the Archdeacon of York,' he commanded. 'This,' he said to Hubert, 'is Fulke FitzWarin of Lambourn, son of Fulke le Brun. He's serving as an attendant to Prince John within Uncle Ranulf's household.'

'Your grace,' Fulke said thickly and knelt to kiss the Archdeacon's ring.

'And he appears to have a broken nose and two black eyes at the least,' observed Hubert. He cupped Fulke's jaw in his large hand and examined the damage. 'What were you doing to get this?'

'Playing chess, your grace.'

Hubert's eyebrows met the brown fringe of his tonsure.

'With Prince John,' Theobald qualified and snapped his fingers at his squire. 'Jean, bring water and a cloth.'

'Sir.' The squire set his lute aside and rose from the coffer.

'Indeed?' the Archdeacon said. 'And might it be politic to enquire who won?'

'Unfortunately that will be for a wider audience to decide – if the Prince has his way,' Theobald said with distaste. 'But for the nonce let us just say that young Fulke here gave as good as he got.'

'I see.' The Archdeacon rolled up the vellum and tucked it in his sleeve. 'Delicate then.'

'Not particularly, but unlikely to advance the Prince's plea that he's sufficiently mature to be let loose on lands of his own – especially following the escapades of the eldest one, and we know how that ended.' Eighteen months ago, King Henry's heir and namesake, a feckless, shallow young man, had died in Aquitaine of dysentery during a petty war with his family over land and influence. Theobald made an irritated sound. 'John has no one to blame but himself.'

'Which is something he never does. It is men like us, Theo, who are the checks and balances to the excesses in the Angevin nature.' He plucked his mantle from the bed and donned it. 'Walk with me back to the abbey,' he requested. 'Your squire can tend the lad, and my lodgings are better than this.'

Theobald considered, then nodded. 'Jean, make up another pallet,' he instructed. 'Let Fulke bed down here for the night.'

'Sir.' The squire turned from rummaging amongst the baggage, his hands occupied by a brass ewer and a linen cloth. 'What about dinner?'

'I will eat with the Archdeacon. You had best bring food to the chamber for yourself and Fulke.'

The squire's mobile features fell.

'That's an order, Jean,' Theobald said sternly. 'God knows there have been enough waves made already today to cause a tempest. Best if you don't dine in the great hall this eve.'

'Sir.' Jean's voice and manner were resigned. Theobald wagged a forefinger in final warning and stepped out of the room with his brother.

Jean swore as the door hanging quivered and was still.

Fulke cleared his throat. 'You go. I'll be all right on my own.'

The other youth snorted down his fine, thin nose. 'Have you ever seen a flayed corpse? It's not a pretty sight.' He tilted his head to one side and his dark eyes gleamed. 'Mind you, neither are you just now.' He approached with the ewer and cloth. 'I take it from what I heard that you've been brawling with Prince John?'

'We had a disagreement,' Fulke said cautiously. Since arriving at court, the generosity of trust in his nature had taken as much of a battering as his body.

'Looks more than that to me.'

Fulke tensed to resist pain, but Jean's touch was surprisingly deft and gentle as he wiped away the caked blood and made an examination.

'You're going to have a rare old kink straight across the bridge,' he pronounced. 'I wouldn't like to play your sort of chess.'

Fulke gingerly raised his hand to feel the damage. The area was swollen and pulpy, more than tender to the touch. He thought it was probably fortunate that there was not a gazing glass in the room. 'It wasn't my sort of chess,' he said wearily. 'It was John's.' In his mind's eye, he relived the moments of the brawl in sickening detail: the crunch of soft bone as the chessboard smacked him in the face, his lashing kick and John's slow reel backwards.

The squire rolled his eyes knowingly. 'I've seen his tactics on the practice field. Lord Theobald says that he has neither discipline nor honour.'

Fulke agreed entirely, but still his brows drew together. 'Is it wise to unbridle your tongue to someone you do not know? What if I go to John and tell him what you have said?'

'Jesu, I wouldn't be Lord Theobald's squire for more than a candle notch if I didn't know when to speak and when to draw rein.' He grinned, displaying a crowd of white teeth. 'I've seen you on the practice field too, remember. You have what John lacks. Here.' He thrust a cup into Fulke's hand. 'Drink this. It might not dull your pain, but it'll certainly pickle it.'

Fulke almost smiled. He took a swallow and heat burned in his gullet while sweetness lingered on his tongue.

'Galwegian heather mead,' said Jean. 'It'll kick you all the way into tomorrow.' He poured a measure for himself and toasted Fulke before downing the drink in a single swallow of his strong young throat. Then, lowering the cup and resting it on his thigh, he extended his other hand.

'I know you are Fulke FitzWarin, but since we have not been formally introduced, I am Jean de Rampaigne, squire and attendant to Lord Theobald Walter. If you think my French strange, it is because I speak with the accent of Aquitaine, my mother's tongue. She was from those parts but married an English knight – like Queen Eleanor married King Henry.' His smile flashed. 'Fortunately I don't have any brothers to dispute my inheritance.' He left a moment's pause for effect before adding, 'Unfortunately, I don't have an inheritance either.'

Fulke shook the proffered hand, a little bemused at the squire's garrulousness of which there had never been a sign on the practice ground. He took another swallow of the mead and felt its warmth spread through his body like liquid gold. Either Jean was right and it was dulling his pain or he was growing accustomed to the persistent throb of his damaged flesh.

'I have brothers,' he said, 'but none like John . . . Well, I don't think so. It's hard to tell with Alain, he's only four years old.'

'Perhaps there's a similarity because John acts like a four-year-old,' Jean said wickedly.

Fulke spluttered, his amusement rapidly cut short by the agony from his nose. 'Don't,' he said.

'But it's true. Lord Theobald's always saying it.'

My father says. Fulke grimaced. It seemed that everyone needed a higher authority to quote, all the way up to the highest authority of all. He drank again and was surprised to find his cup almost down to the lees.

'I did not know that Lord Theobald's brother was the Archdeacon of York,' he said to change the subject.

Jean retreated to the coffer and picked up his lute. 'He'll be more than that one day,' he said as he straightened the red and blue silk ribbons around the neck of the instrument. 'I know for a fact that their uncle Ranulf hopes to bequeath the Justiciar's post to Hubert in the fullness of time.' He coaxed forth a ripple of notes.

'I thought it wasn't hereditary?'

'It isn't, but the one before trains the one to come, and like as not it's usually a relative. Mark me, it will be Hubert. He's had the education for it and he's got the brains.' Jean tapped his head. 'And he'll need them, dealing with King Henry and his sons.'

Fulke nodded agreement. 'He won't need to be an arch-deacon but a saint,' he said. His tongue stumbled on the words. A loud gurgle from the proximity of his belt reminded him that whatever the traumas of the day, he had not eaten since before noon. The strong mead had set his stomach juices churning as well as his head.

Leaping off the coffer, Jean took Fulke's empty cup. 'Food,' he said, 'or never mind the morrow, you'll be kicked well into the middle of next week. Come on.'

Fulke gazed at him owlishly. 'But Lord Theobald said that we weren't to leave and you said you would be flayed alive if you disobeyed him.'

Jean widened his arms. 'My lord meant that he didn't want us making an appearance in the great hall. Unless you have well and truly laid him up, John's likely to be there. My master won't object if we keep out of the way.'

Fulke had doubts, but his hunger and Jean's enthusiasm reasoned them aside. His own nature thrived on challenge and, bruised though he was, Fulke was still capable of rising to meet the occasion. 'Well, where do we go?'

'The kitchens,' Jean said, 'where else?'

Jean was clearly well known in Westminster's kitchens, to judge from the welcome that he and Fulke received. The flustered head cook told the youths to keep out of the way of the preparations for the court banquet in the great hall, but they were found a place in a corner by a more amenable, red-faced woman. Despite their noble rank, she presented them with a bowl of boiled eggs to shell – a delicacy for the high table, eggs being in very short supply this time of year.

'If you want your supper you can work for it like the rest of us,' she said good-humouredly, her French bearing a strong Saxon twang. She tilted Fulke's jaw on her fleshy, onion-scented fist. 'Saints on earth, boy, what have you been doing?'

Before Fulke could give a suitably innocuous reply or tell the woman to mind her own business, a youth who was assembling the dishes ready to be taken to the high table spoke out. 'He's the one I told you about, Marjorie, the one who nearly knocked Prince John's wits from his skull.'

'I didn't,' Fulke protested, wondering with dismay and curiosity how it was possible for news to spread so quickly.

'More's the pity,' Marjorie said acidly. 'And looks like you took a drubbing yourself.'

'I . . .'

'The Prince smashed him in the face with a chessboard,' announced the youth with the relish of one with a tale to tell.

Jean grinned and tapped an egg on the side of the bowl. 'There's no need to listen at doors to hear gossip. You just come and sit here for an hour. They'll tell you everything: whose wife is bedding whom, who's in favour, who's out – even the colour of the King's piss in the morning.' He ducked the playful swipe of Marjorie's hand. 'And they'll feed you better than the royal table, even if you do have to shell eggs for it.'

'Might do Prince John good to shell eggs,' Marjorie said, nodding approval at Fulke. 'I'm sorry for your injuries, but right glad that you've had the courage to answer him back. Someone should have shaken some decency into him long before he left the nursery. If you ask me, Queen Eleanor bore one child too many.'

'Rumour says that Queen Eleanor thinks so too,' Jean remarked. 'She was five and forty when she bore him and King Henry was sporting with a young mistress.'

'Oh aye, small wonder the boy's turned out a rotten apple,' Marjorie sniffed. 'The parents at war, the brothers at war. It's easy to believe that tale about them coming from the devil.' She crossed herself.

'What tale?' Fulke asked.

Marjorie set a trencher before the youths and ladled out two generous helpings of roast boar in a spicy sauce from one of the cauldrons, adding a small wheaten loaf each. Feeling almost nauseous with hunger, Fulke needed no encouragement to take up knife and spoon and set to, the only difficulty being that he could not breathe and chew at the same time.

Marjorie brought a second bowl of eggs to the table and sat down to shell them. 'A long time ago, one of their ancestors, a Count of Anjou, fell in love with a beautiful woman called Melusine.' She pitched her voice so that those around could hear. Songs and storytelling were an integral part of work in the kitchens. They helped to pass the time and made the work more pleasurable. 'She had the palest silver hair as if spun of moonlight and eyes so green and clear that a man could swim in them – or drown. The Count married her and they had two children, a boy and a girl, both as comely as their mother. All was well except that the lady was reluctant to attend church. If she did, she would never stay for the mass, but always slip out of a side door before the raising of the host. Some of the Count's companions became afraid that her beauty and her hold upon their lord was unnatural – that the lovely Countess was using the black arts.' Marjorie paused for dramatic effect. Fulke belched softly into the silence and licked his fingers. Marjorie cracked an egg against the side of the bowl.

'Then what happened?' he prompted.

'They decided to test her by forcing her to stay in chapel throughout the mass. All the doors were barred and armed guards set before them. When the time came for the raising of the host, sure enough, the lady made to depart, but of course, she could not escape. The priest sprinkled her with holy water, whereupon she uttered an unearthly scream. Her cloak became the wings of a huge bat and she flew out of the window, never to be seen again. But she left her children behind and they carried her demon blood in their veins. The boy grew up and became Count of Anjou after his father, and he was our King Henry's great-great-grandsire.' She nodded her head in confirmation.

'You don't believe it?' Fulke said sceptically.

Marjorie swept the eggshells off the table into her apron. 'I only know what I've been told, and there's no smoke without a fire.'

'There's a family legend that my own grandsire fought a giant, but it's only a tale he invented to amuse my father when he was a child.'

'Aye, well, you'll not convince me, young man. You only have to look at them to know they're different. If there's not a demon in Prince John, I'll eat my apron, eggshells and all.'

She went to the midden bucket. Fulke scooped the last morsel of boar and sauce on to the heel of his loaf and demolished it.

Jean took his lute and ran experimental fingers over the strings. 'It would make a good ballad set to music,' he said. '"Fair Melusine".' A silvery cascade of notes like strands of moonlight rippled from the soundbox.

Fulke watched with replete fascination. Although he enjoyed music, particularly rousing battle songs and bardic Welsh sagas, his own skills were negligible. Playing a lute was beyond him. His voice had but recently broken and while it held promise of being deep and resonant when he attained full manhood, his notion of pitch was such that he knew his singing would sound like a dog in a dungeon.

'A lute will open doors that are locked to the booted foot and the sword,' Jean said. 'Men will welcome you for the cheer and entertainment it brings to their hearths. Folk will pay you with your supper; strangers will more readily accept you. And sometimes women will let you enter their sanctuaries.' His eyebrows flashed with innuendo.

Fulke reddened slightly. Women and their sanctuaries were of tremendous interest to his rapidly developing body, but they were a mystery too. The high-born ones were guarded by chaperones and kept at home until they married. Girls of lower degree kept their distance if they were decent. Those who weren't had designs on a royal bed, not the lowly pallet of a squire. The court whores preferred clients with a ready source of income. Other than what fitted where, Fulke had little notion of what to do, and no intention of exposing his ignorance.

Jean leaned over the lute, his fingers plucking a melody to pay for the supper they had just enjoyed. His voice was clear and true, pitched high, but strong as a bell and it chimed above the mélange of kitchen sounds, telling the story of Melusine. Fulke listened in rapt and slightly jealous admiration. It was truly a gift and he found himself wishing that he had it. As his mind absorbed the notes and the words, he studied the reverence with which Jean treated his lute. The sight of the squire's lean fingers on the strings brought to mind another image: his own hands working with an equal reverence to smooth the scars from the surface of his shield.

Suddenly all pleasure and gathering lassitude were gone. As Jean's voice lingered to accompany the lute on the final note of the song, Fulke jerked to his feet and headed for the doorway.

Ignoring the loud applause and demands for more, Jean swept a hasty bow and ran after his charge. 'Where are you going?' He snatched Fulke's sleeve.

'My shield. I left it in John's chamber.'

'You can't go there now.' Jean's voice rose in disbelief.

'The kitchens are one matter, but my lord would certainly have us flayed for going anywhere near John's chamber.'

'It's new,' Fulke said stubbornly. 'My father sent it as a gift to mark my year day.'

'Christ's wounds, are you a little child that you must have it now?' For the first time irritation flashed across Jean's amiable features. 'Leave it until the morrow.'

'You don't understand. It's a matter of honour.'

'Don't be such a fool. I—'

'Come or go as you please,' Fulke interrupted passion-lessly, 'you will not stop me.' He stepped out into the wild night. The sleet had turned to snow as the temperature dropped and they were surrounded in a living, whirling whiteness.

Jean hesitated, then, with an oath, hastened after Fulke. 'John is likely to be at meat in the Rufus Hall, but that's still no reason to tempt fate to the hilt.'

'I'm not tempting fate,' Fulke replied in the same, impassive tone. 'I only desire what is mine to me.' He strode powerfully on, leaving slushy wet footprints on the whitening sward.

Muttering imprecations, Jean ducked his head into the wind and hurried along beside him.

The door to the royal apartments was closed and a soldier stood guard outside. Flickering light from a wall sconce played over his mail and coif, turning the iron rivets to gold. It also caught the wicked edge of his spear tip.

He fixed the youths with a stern eye. 'What are you doing here, lads?'

Fulke had a retentive memory and knew all the guards who did chamber duty. Roger's bark was worse than his bite. 'I left my shield earlier,' he said. 'I'd like to fetch it — sir.'

'I heard all about "earlier".' The guard scrutinised Fulke's injuries. 'Good thing I wasn't on duty then,' he said sourly. 'The man who was is to be whipped for not investigating the commotion.'

'He wouldn't have heard, we weren't near the door,' Fulke said. 'Besides, there had been a commotion all after-noon.'

'Well, someone has to take the blame, don't they?' He gestured with the spear. 'Go on, get you gone before there's more trouble.'

Fulke drew himself up. At fifteen, he stood almost two yards high, taller than many a grown man, and he matched the guard easily. 'I have come for my shield,' he repeated. 'Once I have it, I will leave.'

'Now listen here, I don't take orders from a shaveling like—'

'My lord Walter sent us to fetch it,' Jean interrupted, stepping forwards. 'Master FitzWarin is in his charge for the nonce.'

'Lord Walter sent you?' The guard raised his brows.

'Yes, sir. As you know, he's responsible for training the squires attached to Lord Glanville's retinue. He wants to see the shield.'

'Well, why didn't you say so?' the man growled. He opened the door and gestured Jean to enter. 'Not you,' he said to Fulke. 'It would be more than my life is worth. I've no intention of hanging for a boy's petty squabble.'

Moments later Jean returned. He was holding the shield in a curious fashion so that the blazon faced inwards and all that was visible was the wooden backing and arm straps.

'Satisfied?' The guard closed the door and stood four-square in front of it, making it clear that he would not budge again.

'Thank you, my lord,' Jean said, bowing and using the

inflated form of address to flatter the man's vanity. He started to walk rapidly away.

Fulke hurried along beside him. 'What are you hiding?' He grabbed for his shield. 'Give it to me.'

Very reluctantly, Jean let him have it. 'There's no sense in losing your temper.' He laid a restraining hand on Fulke's sleeve.

Fulke gazed mutely at the shield he had been so carefully tending that afternoon. The smooth, painted leather had been scored repeatedly with the point of a knife, completely obliterating the wolf's teeth blazon. So strong was the malice in the knife that several deep grooves had been cut into the underlying wood.

Rage rose within Fulke like a huge, red bubble. It throbbed behind his eyes, his hatred threatening to blind him. Within that hatred was the knowledge that this was what John must feel for him. To destroy a man's blazon was to insult not only him, but also his entire family and bloodline.

'Whatever you are thinking, he is not worth it,' Jean said, his gaze darting between Fulke's expression and the shield. 'We can have one of the armourers put a new skin on this and no one will know the difference.'

'But I will,' Fulke said in a voice strangled with bile. 'This changes everything.'

'Look, we have to go back to my lord's lodging. We've risked enough as it is.'

Fulke looked at him blankly for a moment, then, with a shudder, controlled himself. He walked stiffly into the adjoining hall, his fist clenched tightly upon his shield strap. There he stopped and stared like a hound spotting its prey. King Henry was talking to a cluster of officials and courtiers. And John was with him, a little pale around the gills, but showing few other signs of damage. His older half-brother

William Longsword stood at his side, and their cousin, Aline de Warenne.

'Don't do anything foolish,' Jean muttered out of the side of his mouth. 'Lord Theobald will not be tender with the shreds of us that remain.'

Fulke could not stop himself from trembling. The force of his rage and the effort it was taking to control it was shaking the flesh from his bones. 'I'll kill him, I swear I will,' he snarled softly.

His glare was like a lance and John must have sensed it, for suddenly he turned his head and their eyes met as if they were on a battlefield. Without taking his attention from Fulke, John spoke to his father, who was deep in conversation with Ranulf de Glanville.

Henry turned somewhat impatiently, bent an ear to his son's swift murmur, and then he too stared across the room at Fulke. Ranulf de Glanville placed his hands behind his back and frowned.

'Christ,' muttered Jean beneath his breath as Henry crooked his finger and beckoned Fulke.

Fulke swallowed, but more with the effort of restraining his fury than with trepidation at approaching the royal party. He strode vigorously over to the group, his head high and the shield brandished to show John that he knew what had been done. Only when he reached the King did he kneel in obeisance and bow his head, his black hair flopping over his brows.

'Get up,' Henry commanded.

Fulke did so and immediately towered over his sovereign who was a little below average height and stockily built. The once flame-red hair was sandy-silver and Henry stood with shoulders braced as if his kingship weighed heavily.

'You have your grandfather de Dinan's size,' Henry said

with a slight narrowing of his eyes. 'And the same propensity for trouble, it would seem. What do you have to say for yourself in answer to my son's accusation that you tried to kill him?'

The tales about Fulke's maternal grandfather, Joscelin de Dinan of Lambourn, were many and legend – and they were told with pride. Fulke was too full of fury and indignation to let him down. 'That his accusation is a lie, sire, and that he struck the first blow.' He raised his hand to indicate his swollen nose and puffy eyes.

John went from ashen to crimson. 'You cheated and you were insolent,' he snarled.

'I have never cheated in my life,' Fulke said hoarsely and swung his shield forwards so hard that he forced a startled William Longsword to take a step back. 'My lord Prince talks of insolence, but what of insult!' He thrust the ruined surface towards Henry and the courtiers.

'You tried to kill me!' John sputtered. 'You threw me against the wall in a fit of rage!' His eyes darted around the circle of barons, seeking sympathy, and lit on Ranulf de Glanville. 'You saw with your own eyes, my lord!'

'I saw the aftermath,' de Glanville said evenly. 'I doubt that whatever the provocation it was Fulke's intention to kill you. He would be stupid to do so, and while he is often rash and hot-headed, he is no fool.'

Fulke gave de Glanville a grateful look. 'I hit out in self-defence,' he said, his shoulders heaving. 'Lord John had already battered me with the chessboard and I had to stop him from doing it again.'

'You stinking whoreson, that's not—'

'Hold your tongue!' Henry snapped, turning on John. 'In truth I have never known you when you are not picking a quarrel over some imagined slight. If Fulke did any harm to you, then I suspect it is no more than you deserve. Come to me for justice, not favouritism.' He turned to the Justiciar. 'Ranulf, see that my son receives a lesson in self-discipline. If the buckle end of a belt is involved, I will not be dismayed.'

De Glanville raised one eyebrow, his aplomb unshaken. 'Yes, sire.'

John turned as white as a table napkin. 'Papa, you would not.' His voice was torn between indignation and pleading.

Henry took hold of John by the shoulders. 'You are my youngest child.' His voice was almost weary now. 'One day soon you must have lands settled upon you, but how can I give you the responsibilities of a ruler when you cannot even play a game of chess without squabbling?'

John pulled away from his father. 'Perhaps if I had the responsibility now, I would not need to squabble at chess,' he spat and, with a furious glare at Fulke that threatened retribution, stalked off in the direction of his chamber.

Fulke looked at the floor, embarrassed, waiting for the King's dismissal and perhaps a flogging of his own. In the aftermath of temper his legs felt weak and he was freshly aware of the pain in his face.

Henry touched the damaged shield. 'Take this to the armoury and have it seen to,' he said. 'Lord John's Privy Purse will meet the cost.'

'Thank you, sire, but I would rather pay for the mending myself.'

Henry drew his finger through his beard. 'Have a care that your pride does not bring you down, Fulke FitzWarin,' he said quietly. 'If it is the be-all, then it can become the end-all.'

Fulke bowed and Henry moved on. William Longsword followed, giving Fulke a look of knowing sympathy, since he too had frequently been on the receiving end of John's unpredictable and vicious temper. De Glanville remained for a brief word.

'I thought Lord Walter would have more sense than to let you wander about near the royal chamber,' he remarked sharply.

'He did sir, but I had to fetch my shield.'

De Glanville looked suspicious. 'He knows you are out then?'

'He's gone to the abbey,' Fulke answered, licking his lips. 'With the Archdeacon of York.'

'I see. In that case you had better hope that he is in a lenient mood when he returns.' The Justiciar flicked one fastidious hand in a gesture of dismissal.

'Sir.' Fulke bowed and prepared to make his escape.

'A word of warning, FitzWarin.'

'Sir?' Fulke stopped and looked over his shoulder.

'The King was right to warn you about pride. If I were you, I would tread very carefully. Prince John will bear you a grudge for today's incident, and he has a very long memory.'

Fulke hefted the ruined shield so that it protected his body from shoulder to shin. 'So do I, sir,' he murmured.

CHAPTER 3

Lambourn Manor,
January 1185

Hawise FitzWarin opened bleary eyes on the morning – at least she assumed it was morning from the stealthy sounds filtering through the bed hangings from the chamber beyond. In winter, it was difficult to tell night from day with all the shutters barred against the weather.

The sharp ache behind her eyes and her dry mouth reproached her for celebrating Twelfth Night too deeply. They had broached a cask of their best Gascon wine and the dancing had made her very thirsty.

'The only thing more potent than that brew is me,' her husband had whispered against her ear as they swirled past each other in a wild carole. He was merry with wine himself, although nowhere near the point of incapacity.

'Prove it,' she had said recklessly, her breath suddenly short and her loins liquid as if the wine she had swallowed was pooling there.

And he had done. Hawise had not been so much in her cups that she could not remember the heat of his mouth on her breasts, the teasing lap of his tongue or the hard masculinity of his body pushing hers into glorious dissolution.

It had ever been thus between them, a fact for which Hawise always remembered to thank God in her prayers. Marriages were made for alliances, for land and wealth and influence, never for love. Fortunately, her father had liked Fulke le Brun sufficiently to welcome his approach, recognising a kindred spirit in the ambitious, black-haired young knight who came courting his daughter.

He was lying on her hair. Underlip caught in her teeth, Hawise gently tugged its masses from beneath his shoulder. He grunted and rolled over, trapping her again. In sleep, he was as warm as a brazier and his heat contrasted pleasantly with the cold air on her exposed shoulder.

'Aren't they awake yet?' demanded an impatient child's voice.

'Ssshhh, no, Master Ivo. You know you cannot disturb your mama and papa when the bed curtains are closed.'

That was the warning voice of Peronelle, Hawise's senior maid.

'But I have to. I've got something important to tell them.'

'Later,' said the maid firmly.

Hawise compressed her lips on a smile. Closed bed curtains were a sacrosanct privacy across which no one in the household was permitted to trespass. It had been a rule instigated on the day after their wedding night when the bloody bedsheet had been displayed to the guests as proof of her virginity and le Brun's ability to take it. Since then, le Brun had insisted that what went forth behind the bed curtains, be it sleeping, talking or coupling, were matters between husband and wife and not for public consumption, even if that public was their own offspring.

'But they're awake, I just heard Papa's voice.'

'God,' muttered le Brun against her throat. He rolled on to his back.

Hawise sat up, her head gently pounding. She fumbled about on the coverlet until she found her shift, heedlessly discarded the night before, and fought her way into it. Then she parted the curtains.

Candlelight illuminated the chamber with a dull, golden flicker and the room was warm. From the ashy glow of the charcoal lumps in the two braziers, Hawise could tell they had been alight for at least an hour. So it must be full morning and she had missed mass.

Ivo and Peronelle were squaring up to each other near the clothing pole, both with hands on their hips and stubborn looks.

'There!' cried Ivo, pointing in triumph. 'They are awake, I told you!'

Peronelle turned to the bed. 'Only because you have disturbed them,' she said irritably and dipped a curtsey. 'Good morrow, my lady.'

Hawise murmured to the maid and pushed her hair out of her eyes. The candlelight shone on the curly strands, burnishing them a wine-auburn. Behind the bed curtains, she heard the muffled rustling of le Brun turning over.

'What is so important that it cannot decently wait?' she demanded of her fourth-born son as she gratefully took the cup of watered wine that Peronelle presented.

Ivo hopped from foot to foot. It was no coincidence that his father had nicknamed him 'flea'. 'Fulke's here,' he announced, a broad grin spreading over his freckled face.

Hawise almost choked on her drink. 'What?'

'I went out to the stables to tend Comet and he was just riding in. He's brought a friend with him called Jean and he's got a lute. They're in the hall, breaking their fast.'

Hawise stared at her son while various thoughts galloped through her aching head. She knew that the court was spending Christmas at Windsor, which was less than 2 days journey, but she had no particular expectation that Fulke would manage a visit. King Henry was notorious for not staying in one place above a few nights and a squire's duties were many. Indeed, she had sent him a new cloak and a box of honey comfits against the likelihood that she would not see him this side of Candlemas. 'What's he doing here?' she wondered aloud.

'Why don't you ask him?' Her husband emerged from the bed curtains and, scratching his beard, ambled over to the latrine shaft.

'He says he's got some news.' Ivo did a handstand and fell over in the rushes.

'I'm sure he has,' le Brun said. He looked down at his stream of urine. 'The question is what.'

'That's why I came to fetch you.' Ivo stood on his hands again. 'He won't say until you come down.'

'Careful of the brazier,' Hawise snapped as Ivo's feet landed perilously close to the wrought-iron stand. She drank the rest of the watered wine and turned to her clothing pole. 'He's like you,' she said to le Brun. 'Never writes a letter and springs surprises like coneys popping out of a warren.' She selected a gown of pine-green wool hemmed with tawny braid.

Le Brun turned round, sharp humour in his eyes. 'And I suppose that your contrary nature is not part of the melting pot?'

Hawise sniffed and raised her arm so that Peronelle could tighten the side lacing of her gown. 'Does not the Church say that it is a man who plants the seed and that woman is just the vessel?'

'Aye, well, wine takes on the taste of the oak in which it's matured,' he retorted.

Hawise pulled a face at him and Ivo giggled. She sent him out to herald their arrival, bundled her hair into a silk net and covered it with a veil and circlet.

Le Brun in the meantime had donned his own clothes. Latching his belt, he went to the door and opened it, ushering Hawise before him. 'Let's find out what that wretched boy has done,' he said.

'You gave him a man's shield for his year day,' Hawise reminded him and laid a cautionary hand on his sleeve. 'Just remember that he is almost an adult. He has been away from us for ten months and the court will have wrought changes.'

Le Brun snorted. 'He's still my son, is he not?'

'Exactly,' Hawise said and led him from their chamber into the hall.

Fulke was sitting on a bench drawn up to the fire, his long legs extended to the warmth and his new cloak still pinned across his shoulders. Seated beside him was a handsome youth whose dark hair, brown eyes and tanned complexion could have made him a family member. As Ivo had said, he carried a lute. However, after one brief glance, it was not at the guest she looked, but at her eldest son, and in shock.

The malleable features of childhood had been pared to the bone and remoulded to leave a hawkish visage, so reminiscent of her father that she almost gasped. All that he possessed of the FitzWarin line was the heavy, crow-black hair and quick brows. The rest was pure de Dinan – even down to the nose where thin, straight symmetry had been replaced by a version that held echoes of his grandfather's war-battered visage.

'Mama.' He drew in his legs and stood up.

'Jesu, what have you been doing!' Hawise cried and threw her arms around him. He had grown again. She was tall for a woman, but the top of her head only reached his collarbone. Pulling his head down, she kissed him heartily on either cheek and then ran her finger down the dent in his nose. 'How came you by this?'

'That's what I've come to tell you, or at least part of it.'

He broke from her grasp to embrace his father. 'We have leave from court to sojourn two days here.'

The word 'we' reminded Hawise of her obligation as hostess and she turned to Fulke's companion who had also risen to his feet. He was somewhat older than her son was, she judged, perhaps seventeen or eighteen. Not as tall, and wirily slender of build.

'Jean de Rampaigne, squire to Lord Theobald Walter,' he said before she could ask, and bowed over her hand with impeccable manners.

'You are welcome,' Hawise responded warmly. ''Tis a pity that both of you could not have been here for the Christmas celebrations.' She gestured around the hall where servants were dismantling the evergreen trimmings and a laundry maid was bundling up the linen tablecloths and napery for washing.

'Why should they want to come here to celebrate when they could roister at court?' her husband asked, only half in jest. 'I know at their age I took my chances.' He greeted Jean de Rampaigne with a brisk handclasp.

'We didn't gain leave until last night, Papa.' Fulke sat down on the bench, then, like a restless dog, stood up again and turned in a circle. One hand rose to push his heavy hair off his brow in a gesture so reminiscent of his father that it sent a pang through Hawise. 'I have so much to tell you that I do not know where to start.'

'The beginning might be a good place,' said le Brun. 'And if it's going to be a long story, we might as well break our fast at the same time.' He gestured to the dais where bread, cheese and ale were being set out on a fresh linen cloth.

The youth nodded. 'It might be for the best,' he said pensively.

★   ★   ★

Fulke watched his father's expression harden as he told him about the incident with the chessboard. Nervously he crumbled a small wastel loaf between his fingers. 'I could not have done anything else,' he said.

'Yes, you could,' le Brun said grimly. 'You could have made sure he stayed down.'

'But I thought you wanted a place in the royal household for me above all else because of Whittington?'

'What do you take me for?' His father pushed his own platter away with a glower and replenished his cup. 'Of course I want Whittington, but in justice and honour. I won't grovel for it and neither will any of my sons.' His gaze swept along the trestle to the five younger boys, all listening agog. 'I would be more angry if you had let him get away with it.'

Fulke looked uncertain. 'I was not sure how you would take the news.'

Le Brun sighed. 'Perhaps I placed too great a burden on your shoulders. Whittington is my responsibility. It won't be yours until I die and, God willing, that will not be until you are a man full seasoned and it is in our hands again.' He raised his cup and drank.

Fulke smiled dutifully. He did not want to think of his father dying. Unlike King Henry's sons, he had no desire to wrench the reins of government from the control of the previous generation. His time would come when it was ripe.

Le Brun set his cup down and wiped his lips. 'You are still at court, so I take it the storm has blown over?'

'After a fashion.' Fulke made a seesawing motion with his hand. 'I'm no longer one of Prince John's close personal attendants, but I still receive lessons with him.' He looked at Jean who had been quietly attending to his meal without taking part in the conversation. 'I'm serving as a squire to

Lord Theobald Walter at the moment. He's nephew to Ranulf de Glanville and Prince John's personal tutor in arms.'

'I know Theobald Walter and his lineage,' his father said, 'although I was unaware he had become a royal tutor. I suppose that's Ranulf's influence. He's in a position to do his relatives great favours. Not that I'm saying Theobald Walter is unworthy of the post,' he added as Jean looked up from his food. 'He's a skilled swordsman with a good brain, but advancement is often a matter of the right connections and fortunate opportunities.' He turned to Fulke. 'At whose instigation did you change your post?'

'Lord Theobald thought it would be a good idea,' Fulke said. 'So did everyone else.' He tensed his jaw, sensing that a storm was brewing.

His father grunted. 'Although no one saw fit to inform me or ask my opinion about my son's future.'

'It is only a few weeks since it happened. I would have written but the opportunity arose to come and tell you myself.' Fulke held his father's gaze. 'I made the decision to join Lord Walter of my own free will.'

'Did you now?' Le Brun's eyes narrowed. 'And what does a stripling of fifteen know about the world?'

'More than he did a month ago,' Fulke replied, refusing to look away although there was a hollow feeling in the pit of his stomach. He knew that he risked a whipping. His father's word had always been the law and he had never challenged it because that was the way the river ran. Honour and obey. 'And,' he continued, 'enough to realise that I have more to gain by serving as Lord Walter's squire than in remaining a companion to Prince John.'

His mother touched le Brun's sleeve and leaned to murmur something against his ear. Fulke thought he heard the words 'shield' and 'manhood'.

For a moment his father's expression remained harsh, but gradually the lines between nose and mouth grew less pronounced and a glint of humour lit in the peat-brown eyes. 'If Lord Walter has chosen you and you have agreed to let him be your mentor, then I suppose I must yield to your judgement, since mine was wrong in securing you a place in John's chamber.'

'Lord Walter is a good master, sir,' Jean spoke up. 'He is strict but he is fair. The King chose him above several others to be Prince John's tutor in arms and he is the Justiciar's nephew.'

'I am not in my dotage or a dullard to be unaware of those points,' said le Brun, the humour still in his eyes, but his voice sharp with warning.

'No, sir.' Jean looked down. 'It is just that I want you to be assured that Fulke will have no reason to regret his change of household.'

The older man nodded. 'That remains to be seen.' He folded his arms. 'Tell me this: would you die for your lord?'

'No, sir,' said Jean without hesitation.

'No?' Le Brun's brows disappeared into his thick fall of hair.

'He wouldn't let me. He would put himself in the way first.'

Fulke's father gave a grunt of amusement at the quick response. 'A regular paragon.' He turned again to his son. 'It seems I should be thanking God on my bended knees for your change of circumstance.'

Fulke reddened at the hint of sarcasm. 'I am pleased to have joined his retinue, Papa, but it is only one of the reasons I've been given leave to visit, and not even the main one at that.'

'Indeed?' Le Brun signalled his squire, Baldwin, to replenish his cup.

Fulke cleared his throat. 'As soon as the winter storms abate, we're going to Ireland.'

'Ireland!' His mother stared at him in consternation. 'Why? What for?'

'King Henry has given John its lordship,' Fulke said. 'He's to go there and take oaths of fealty from the Irish clansmen and the Norman settlers.' He knew what everyone thought of Ireland: a back-of-beyond place across a dangerous expanse of cold, dark water. It always rained and it was infested with bogs and quarrelsome barelegged warriors who were less civilised than beasts. They were half ruled by a group of Norman colonists whose reputation was little better than the savages they were supposed to be governing.

'It was either that or the Holy Land,' said Jean. 'King Henry has been offered the throne of Jerusalem since their King's rotting to death from leprosy and they need a new ruler desperately. He didn't accept it, but Prince John was like a dog who spots a marrow bone just out of reach on a butcher's block.'

'John, King of Jerusalem!' Fulke le Brun choked on the notion and Hawise had to thump his back.

'Henry said that he was too young and inexperienced for the responsibility but that if he wanted a taste of ruling, he could try his hand at Ireland.'

'So he's going to be King there instead, and they're making him a crown of peacock's feathers and gold,' said Fulke expressionlessly. 'Lord Walter is to go with him as part of his household.'

Fulke le Brun took a long drink of wine and wiped his watering eyes. 'I doubt that Prince John is fit to be King of anywhere,' he croaked, 'but it will be good experience for you.'

'You approve then?'

'I do. The Welsh and Irish have many similarities. Their

lands are impenetrable to vast armies; their wealth is of the hoofed and horned variety; and their allegiance is to small and petty chieftains. If you are to inherit and exploit our border fiefs when you are grown, Ireland will do you nothing but good.'

'Why does he have to go to Ireland to learn about the Welsh?' Hawise demanded fretfully.

Le Brun gently covered her hand with his and squeezed. 'Because, as you said to me, all hawks fly the nest. If they cannot test and strengthen their wings first, then how will they manage to soar and hunt?'

Hawise looked down at her platter and broke a wastel roll in two, but made no attempt to eat it.

'Don't you want Fulke to go to Ireland, Mama?' deman- ded William, their second-born son. He was thirteen years old and neither tact nor understanding were facets of his nature.

Hawise was silent for a moment. Then, raising her head, she gazed directly at Fulke and gave him the blind semblance of a smile. 'Of course he must go,' she said. 'Your father is right.'

Fulke eyed his mother curiously. Her reply had been an evasion. Clearly, she did not wish him to go to Ireland. 'Mama?'

'You'll need some more warm tunics before you leave.' Her voice was breathless. 'I'll measure you later this morn. You've grown at least a finger length since I made the one you're wearing.' The catch in her breathing verged on tears. Excusing herself, she fled the trestle.

Fulke looked to his father for explanation, but le Brun spread his hands and shook his head. 'Do not ask me to unravel the mind of a woman,' he said. 'She warns me to tread lightly on your pride for you are almost a man grown, and yet she weeps at the notion of you joining that world.'

'She didn't weep when I went to court,' Fulke pointed out.

'Not in front of you, no, but she shed a few tears in private.' Le Brun frowned thoughtfully. 'I think the first-born and the youngest are the most difficult to send out from the nest. Besides, the royal court might be a dangerous place, but it is ten times safer than an untamed country across the sea.'

'Should I go to her?' Fulke asked, prepared to do so, but not particularly relishing the notion. He had always viewed his mother as stronger than steel, had never thought of her as being prey to fear. She had instilled in him the confidence not to be afraid of new challenges and situations, so he had always assumed she was invulnerable herself. Apart from assuring her that he would come to no harm, he had no idea what to say. Given the chessboard incident with Prince John, he doubted his line of argument would be very convincing.

'No, leave her a while to gather her composure,' his father said, to Fulke's relief. 'Time enough to speak when she measures you for a new tunic.'

'I'm to have a new tunic too,' William announced loudly. 'And I'm going away to be a squire as well.'

Glad of the diversion, Fulke turned to his brother. 'Where?' he asked. As far back as Fulke could remember William had wanted to be a knight, to wear mail and carry a sword at his hip. Not just with a boy's longing, but with a single-minded passion that was almost adult in its determination.

'To Caus, to Robert Corbet,' William said, his chin jutting with pride. 'And I'm to have a new pony too.'

Fulke made an interested sound. Robert Corbet was a neighbouring lord and a man of some influence in the Marches. Indeed, he was their overlord in respect of several manors including one of their major residences at Alberbury, and the Corbets had strong ties with the royal line of Gwynedd. Whilst not acquiring the polish of Henry's court, William would obtain a sound grounding.

'I'm going too,' announced eleven-year-old Philip, not to be outdone. He was somewhat quieter than William and Ivo, more thoughtful and less likely to act upon the goad of the moment. He was also the only one of the brothers to possess the copper-auburn hair of the de Dinan line, everyone else being raven-black.

'Are you indeed?' Fulke raised his brows and smiled.

'Me too, me too!' cried little Alain, plainly not sure what was being discussed but making sure that he was not left out.

'Don't be silly, you're only four,' Ivo scoffed. 'You have to stay in the bower with Mama and her ladies. So does Richard.' He jerked his head at another little boy, who had eaten a gargantuan breakfast and was still quietly stuffing his face.

Adroitly averting the storm, Fulke rose to his feet and plucked young Alain into his arms. 'But he doesn't today,' he said. 'Who wants to come and practise with swords on the tilt ground?'

The yell was unanimous.

Fulke le Brun grinned broadly. 'I'll go and get mine,' he said.

'Your father says that your swordplay has improved beyond all recognition,' Hawise said. She turned Fulke to face the window embrasure and measured him from knob of spine to mid-knee with a length of twine in which she tied knots to mark the length.

'Lord Theobald's a good tutor.' He looked out of the open shutters on the raw January afternoon. William was leading his brothers in a pretend raid across the bailey and berating the youngest two for not keeping up. A midden heap defended by their father's squires, Baldwin and Stephen, was their target.

Weapons practice that morning had fired William's enthusiasm to a state of near frenzy. It was as if he believed that the harder he battled, the sooner the time would pass to his attainment of knighthood – if he didn't get himself killed first. Lord Theobald said that superior fighting ability was a blend of instinct and intelligence. A good leader had to be one thought ahead of his opponent all the time.

'Stretch your arm.'

Obediently he complied and she measured him from armpit to wrist.

'I won't come to any harm in Ireland,' he said. 'Lord Theobald will not put his squires at risk.'

Hawise knotted the cord. 'If you trust Lord Walter, then so do I.'

'Then what is wrong, Mama? Why don't you want me to go?'

Hawise took another measure from armpit to knee. Then, stepping back, she sighed. 'I have striven never to hold you or your brothers back, by word or by deed. With my heart in my mouth I have encouraged you to gallop your pony bareback, to climb to the top of a wall, to fly a falcon that could gouge out your eyes with one strike of its talons.' She turned away to place the lengths of knotted cord in her sewing basket. 'I have hidden my fear because it is mine, not yours, and I never wanted you to become infected by it.'

'And you fear Ireland?' Fulke looked puzzled.

'No.' She shook her head a trifle impatiently. 'I have heard it is a wild place where it constantly rains and the people are untamed half-heathens, but in that respect it is little different to certain parts of Wales.'

'Then what?'

His mother bit her lip. 'When I was a small child, we had reason to make a river crossing on a ferry, but in midstream the boat capsized and I was almost drowned. It was winter, the water was very cold and my clothes dragged me under. By the time my father pulled me out, I was more than half dead.' Her voice wobbled. 'Since that time I have harboured a dread of crossing water. I think of the river that almost claimed me, how I was dying even though I could see dry land on the other side.' She swallowed and compressed her lips, fighting for control. 'When I think of the ocean you must cross, my heart dies inside me.'

'I do not fear crossing water, Mama,' Fulke said. 'I have travelled on the great River Thames often enough these past months without mishap and I can swim.' He did not add that on more than one occasion he had played at water jousting, where opposing boats would come at each other and a pole bearer at the prow would try to knock his counterpart into the water. Then, of course, there was the exhilarating but more dangerous sport of shooting the arches of London Bridge at high tide. What she did not know could do her no harm.

From around her neck Hawise removed a small reliquary cross and, with shaking hands, gave it to him. 'Will you wear this for me when you go? It contains a lock of St Elmo's hair and it is proof against drowning.'

'Of course I will, Mama.' Fulke kissed the cross and placed it around his own neck, tucking it down inside his tunic.

She forced a smile. 'I might sleep a little easier now. I only wish I had something for Jean too.'

'Oh, he wears a token of St Christopher in his cap, and I've yet to see him not land on his feet whatever the situation,' Fulke said lightly in an attempt to ease the atmosphere. He was more than relieved as footsteps hammered outside and a panting William burst into the room.

'Are you still being measured or do you want to come and join us at ambushes?' He was pink with exertion and the joy of play. 'Jean says he'll take the part of Roger de Powys. We're using the midden as Whittington keep.'

'I've finished for the nonce,' Hawise said quickly and gave Fulke a gentle push. 'The tunic won't be ready for trying until late this evening.'

Fulke did not require a second bidding. The boy in him clamoured to be out with his brothers, and the man did too. He needed to release the tensions raised with a bout of vigorous activity.

Hawise drifted to the window and watched him as he emerged into the winter afternoon. The wind ruffled his dark hair. She saw how the other boys clamoured around him, William foremost and clearly full of worship; she watched the way he organised them, including the little ones. He had always possessed those abilities, but life at court was honing and polishing them, taking and changing him. If Whittington was to be theirs again one day, then he was their brightest hope. She touched her throat, feeling for a cord that was no longer there. With a sigh of self-irritation, she turned abruptly from the window and approached the bolt of fabric waiting on her sewing trestle. Worry only bred more worry. With six sons, she had cause enough to know.

CHAPTER 4

The Irish Sea was a deep, cold green, topped with crests of white foam that broke and marbled in the steep troughs. A hard east wind strained the canvas sails of the ships that climbed and fell the mountain range of waves, their prows pointed towards the Irish coast and the port of Waterford.

Fulke's belly quietly churned as their vessel plunged down the small hillside and surged up the slope of the next. He was one of the fortunate ones, his nausea being mild. He had only been sick once at the outset of their journey. Lord Theobald, Jean de Rampaigne and other members of John's entourage were incapacitated in the deck shelter; all of them as green as new cheese and puking like pregnant women. Apart from the crew and a Welsh archdeacon, Fulke was the only one still upright, and he much preferred the wildness of the open deck to the groaning stench of the shelter.

The size of the waves made Fulke slightly apprehensive; it would only take one slip of the helm or one swoop of water larger than the rest to send their vessel to the bottom of the Irish Sea. He could well understand his mother's terror and even feel an echo of it in the churn of his belly. In his arrogance, he had thought that playing games on the River Thames was sufficient preparation, but rough water on the Thames was like a caress compared to the hammering fists of the Hibernian Sea. He touched the cross on his breast and murmured a prayer to St Elmo, seeking reassurance.

The Welsh Achdeacon staggered over to him, fists tightly clutching his cloak to his body. He was a small man in early middle age with sandy tonsured hair and a round face whose genial features were marred by an air of petulance. 'If they have no stomach for it now, they might as well turn round and head home,' he said scornfully. 'It will get no better.'

While on attendance duty at Milford Haven before they embarked, Fulke had served the Archdeacon at Lord Theobald's table. He was Gerald de Barry of Manorbier and he was accompanying this venture because he was one of the few people acquainted with the Irish and their customs. Wherever he went, he carried a wooden book containing pages of waxed tablets. The only reason he was not writing his tart and gossipy observances just now was that the sea was too rough for him to control his stylo.

'You mean the weather will grow worse?' Fulke glanced anxiously at the scudding fleece of grey and white clouds and then at the next glass wall of sea menacing their bows.

'It might at that; only God can say. Their sea is as contrary as the Irish themselves.' Malicious amusement filled Archdeacon Gerald's sloe-berry eyes. 'Why, lad, are you afraid?'

Fulke clutched his little cross. 'I have faith in God,' he said, reluctant to admit his doubts to the small, acerbic churchman.

'Very proper too, and you will need it. King Henry is sending a spoiled child to do a man's task. I have no doubt that blood will flow in direct proportion to the amount of wine consumed.'

Fulke said nothing. In all likelihood, Gerald was right – if the inebriated state of John and his immediate companions when they boarded ship at Milford was any indicator.

'Nor,' continued Gerald, wagging his forefinger like an Old Testament prophet, 'do I think that those barrels of silver we loaded will ever reach the troops he's supposed to buy. Mark my words, we're in for a stormy passage.' The Archdeacon staggered across the deck to look out over the side.

In the short time he had known him, Fulke had quickly realised that Gerald had a tendency to exaggerate. Some of his tales about the Irish were clearly preposterous, such as the one about stones that could speak prophecy if a corpse was passed over them; but beneath the extravagance and fabrication, there was occasionally a kernel of truth – no reassurance to Fulke.

From his precarious position on the cross spar, the lookout bellowed warning of land. Fulke joined the Archdeacon at the side and squinted through spray-stung eyes. As they crested a wave, he saw the hazy outline of grey-green hummocks that did not move.

'The Wicklow Mountains,' said Gerald. 'We'll be in Waterford before nightfall.'

A trifle battered, but unharmed beyond the odd torn sail and leaky caulking, Prince John's fleet sailed into Waterford to be greeted by a handful of Norman–Irish settler barons who had put down conquering roots a generation before. Groggy, reeling from the effects of seasickness and wine, John and his entourage were escorted to the stronghold of Waterford, known as Reginald's Tower after the Norse leader who had originally built it.

Lord Theobald had been violently ill throughout the crossing and only a tremendous effort of will kept him upright as a groom led forward a bay gelding. He grasped the reins and swayed, his forehead clammy with sweat.

'Boost me up,' he commanded Fulke, the last word ending on a swallowed gag.

Fulke hastened to comply, fitting Theobald's foot in the stirrup and thrusting up as the Baron pressed down and heaved himself across his mount's saddle. A muffled oath escaped between Theobald's clenched teeth and he retched dryly into the horse's mane. Jean grasped the reins as the gelding sidled. His own normally golden complexion was sallow and his feet unsteady, but he was in far better case than their master.

'My lord?' He gave a concerned look upwards.

'Just keep the beast quiet,' Theobald gulped.

'Yes, lord.' Jean exchanged a wry glance with Fulke and clicked his tongue, urging the horse to a gentle walk. From the direction of the saddle, there came a suffering moan. Fulke paced at Lord Theobald's stirrup and carried his banner. The moist sea breeze rippled through the embroidered silks and caused a pleasant snapping sound. Ahead of them the Angevin leopards blazed in thread of gold on their blood-red background. John's dark head bobbed in and out of view, crowned by a golden circlet and surrounded by a protective forest of spears and banners. Naturally, he rode on a white horse. After a single, sour glance, Fulke ignored him. There were more interesting sights to see.

The Irish of the town looked little different to the ordinary folk of England and Wales. They wore the same simple tunics in muted shades of brown, tawny and green. Here and there, an occasional blue garment or a richer dye marked out someone of wealth. The older men cultivated long hair and wore full, heavy beards that put Fulke in mind of a hermit he had once encountered living wild in the forest beyond Alberbury. The sound of Gaelic filled his ears with its strange, musical harshness. He had a smattering of the Welsh tongue, garnered from Alain's nurse

Ceridwen. Irish had a difference cadence, less lilting but strangely hypnotic.

He noticed that neither the native Gaels nor the Norman settlers were smiling. People bowed in deference to the spectacle of royalty, but their faces were wary and in some eyes Fulke was sure he detected a glimmer of scorn. He had an itchy feeling between his shoulder blades, a sensation of vulnerability that only diminished when they reached the safety of Reginald's Tower.

'Are you able to dismount, my lord?' Grasping the stirrup strap, he looked anxiously at Theobald whose hands were white-knuckled on the reins.

Theobald nodded wordlessly, lips tightly compressed. Leaning forward, he swung his right leg over the saddle and slid down the bay's side. For an instant, Fulke bore Theobald's full weight. He braced his shoulder and locked his thighs.

Swaying, Theobald pushed himself upright. 'Why do I feel as if I'm still on board a ship?' he demanded, then, uttering a groan, staggered to a corner of the bailey where he doubled up, retching once more.

'You have the same effect on me, FitzWarin,' Prince John paused to taunt him on his way into the tower. 'You make me sick as a dog.' His companions sniggered. At the back of their party, Archdeacon Gerald frowned with disapproval.

Fulke faced the Prince in polite but stony silence. Since the incident with the chessboard, John had taken every opportunity to bait him, although never when Ranulf de Glanville or Theobald Walter were within earshot. Now, with power to wield and Theobald incapacitated, he obviously felt safe to do so. The best remedy was to ignore him and hope that he would quickly grow bored with bouncing insults off a blank wall.

'Your Highness, will you come within? Everything is

prepared for you,' said Philip of Worcester with an ushering gesture. He had been sent ahead of the main party to make ready for John's arrival.

John inclined his head. 'I certainly have no desire to remain out here with dolts and bumpkins,' he said. 'Perhaps you will see to it that my lord Walter receives adequate attention for his purging. I doubt his squires will be of much assistance.' He moved on and Fulke carefully let out the breath he had been holding.

'Pay no heed,' Jean muttered.

Fulke glowered. 'There is a tally in my mind and each time he goads me, I add another notch.' He went to Theobald who was leaning against the wall, his complexion the unhealthy hue of lime mortar. 'Can you walk, my lord?'

Clutching his stomach, Theobald slowly straightened. 'I'll be damned if I'll be carried,' he said hoarsely, and took the banner Fulke was holding to use as a crutch. A squire on either side, he made his slow way into the tower.

Philip of Worcester had managed to find a wall chamber where Theobald was able to lie down and nurse his churning stomach. Jean went in search of a hot tisane for his lord to sip, leaving Fulke to see to the arrangement and unpacking of the travelling chests. Lord Theobald lay like an effigy on his travelling pallet. Fulke suspected that not only was his master suffering from the effects of *mal de mer*, but that he had eaten something that had disagreed with his gut. On board a ship, it was not difficult.

He went to the narrow window splay and peered out on a rainy April dusk. His constricted view yielded him the sight of a handful of the bailey buildings. He could have been anywhere from Westminster to Lambourn. The smell of woodsmoke drifted to his nose, and on it, the appetising aroma of roasting meat. On the bed, Theobald caught the scent too, and moaned.

The heavy curtain screening the chamber from the stairs rattled on its pole. Fulke turned, expecting to see Jean with the tisane. Instead, his eyes met the astonishing sight of a beautiful woman, accompanied by the hugest dog he had ever seen, bigger even than his father's deerhound, Griff. It had paws the size of trenchers, a shaggy, silver-grey coat, and his youngest brother could have ridden it as a pony. The woman wore a gown of rose-coloured wool in the Norman style, and a white veil bound in position with a woven band. Two heavy braids, glossy black as Fulke's own hair, hung to her waist.

'My lady?' His voice rose and cracked as it had not done in over half a year.

A swift word in Gaelic, a pointed finger, and the dog lay down across the threshold like a giant rug. She came forward, her step sure and confident. 'I was told that one of Prince John's lords was sick and in need of tending?' She spoke the Norman French of the court, but with a lilting cadence that curled around the words and made them seductive. Her eyes were a stunning hyssop-flower blue and the colour of her lips matched the deep rose of her gown. Advancing to the pallet, she looked down at the supine Theobald.

Fulke swallowed. 'He has the seasickness but it won't abate. Who are you?' The question blurted out of him like a splash of ink on a clean vellum page. All the blood in his body seemed to have left his head and travelled rapidly south.

As if aware of his discomfort, she gave him a slow, knowing smile: a little scornful, gently amused. 'My name is Oonagh FitzGerald, widow of Robert FitzGerald of Docionell in Limerick. Since my husband died in the winter, my home has been here, and since I also have some small knowledge of healing, it has fallen my duty to tend the unwell.' She wrapped one of her braids around her fore-finger and considered him. 'And who are you?'

Fulke managed a clumsy bow. 'Fulke FitzWarin of Lambourn and Whittington, squire to Lord Walter.' She looked far too young to be a widow. Her skin bore the flawless bloom and rounded outline that spoke of a girlhood still recent. He wondered if he should offer condolences on her husband's death, then decided it was better not to say anything.

'And you did not suffer the seasickness yourself, Fulke FitzWarin?' Approaching the bed she laid her hand across Theobald's brow and gave him a reassuring murmur.

'No, my lady, or only a little at the beginning.'

'You are one of the fortunate ones then, like your liege lord the Prince.'

'You have met him, my lady?' Fulke spoke without inflection.

'Indeed I have.' Her own voice too was neutral, revealing nothing of her thoughts. 'He was in the hall when I was bade attend upon your master.' Reaching into the satchel slung from her shoulder, she withdrew a small linen pouch. 'Give him as much as will cover your thumbnail dissolved in hot wine. One cup now, another at compline and a third in the morning.'

Theobald weakly lifted his head. 'How soon can I rise from my bed?'

'As soon as the room ceases to sway and you stop vomiting,' she said. 'Although I think you could have answered that for yourself, my lord,' she added as Theobald lay back, his colour ashen and his throat working as he swallowed a retch.

'I feel like a puling infant,' he groaned.

'Aye, well, 'tis the state of man from cradle to grave.' Her smile took the sting from the words. 'You must eat only dry bread and light broth for two days after you rise, lest the purging begins again.'

Fulke opened the pouch, sniffed the contents, and turned aside to sneeze.

'Mint and ginger, not suitable for inhaling,' she laughed and went to the door. Another word in Gaelic brought the massive dog to its feet.

'How much does it eat?' Fulke asked.

Oonagh gave him a teasing look. 'That depends on how hungry she is, and if anyone has been foolhardy enough to take liberties.' She gestured. 'Go on, stroke her if you wish. She won't bite unless I say.'

Fulke was fond of dogs. Indeed, he was more afraid that Oonagh would bite him than the bitch. He went forward confidently, let the dog sniff his hand and swipe it with a long, pink tongue. He scratched her beneath the chin and braced his knees as she leaned on him, an expression of canine bliss in her eyes.

Oonagh watched him thoughtfully. 'You have gentle hands,' she said.

Fulke felt his ears begin to burn. 'I don't know about that, my lady.'

'I do. There are not many men who have gentle hands.' She stepped over the threshold. Another command in Gaelic brought the dog from her ecstatic trance to instant obedience and she followed her mistress.

'Doubtless I will see you again, Fulke FitzWarin,' Oonagh FitzGerald said and, with a brief nod, went on her way.

Moments later there was a warning snarl and the sound of her voice sharply raised as she called the bitch to heel. Fulke ran out to see what was happening and met Jean on his way up the stairs, a steaming jug in his hand and an expression of recovering shock on his face.

'Jesu, have you seen the size of that brute?' he cried. 'It's bigger than a pack pony and it's got teeth like palings!' He looked over his shoulder as if expecting to see the wolf-hound padding up the stairs after him.

'Yes, we've met.' Fulke smiled, an air of smugness hovering at his mouth corners. 'Its mistress came to tend Lord Theobald.'

Jean cocked a curious eyebrow. 'You look highly pleased about something. It can't be that dreadful dog. What's her name?'

'The dog or the woman?'

'You know what I mean.'

Fulke grinned. 'The lady's name is Oonagh FitzGerald and she's a widow.'

'Do you think her loneliness needs comforting, perchance?'

The notion of comforting Oonagh FitzGerald was one that had a direct effect on Fulke's nether regions. The remark about his gentle hands still scorched his blood. 'I think that is why she keeps the dog so close,' he said. 'To afford her comfort and protect her from unwelcome approaches.'

'Ah, but your approach obviously wasn't unwelcome or your eyes wouldn't be gleaming like that and your ears wouldn't be so red!'

'God on the Cross!' groaned Theobald from his pallet. 'Will both of you put your pricks back in your braies and be about your duties. I could die of thirst or purging while you prate nonsense!'

Fulke and Jean exchanged wry glances. 'Yes, my lord,' both said in unison and strove not to set each other off laughing.

Theobald's sickness gradually abated, but he had purged so much that he was as weak as a kitten and unable to attend the state sessions in the great hall until the end of the week. By that time, much of the damage had been done. Taking the bit between his teeth, John ruled as he chose. He had not wanted to come to Ireland. It was a mere crumb thrown from the largesse of his father's table, a sop to keep him quiet, and he had neither the will nor the experience to do the task he had been set.

While Theobald slept his way back to strength, Jean and Fulke had long periods when they were free of obligation. As always, Jean eased his way into the community of kitchen and stables, slaughter shed and dairy. His ear for language quickly rewarded him with a smattering of Gaelic and access to the groundswell of general opinion, none of it good where John was concerned. To the Gaels, he was just another booted foot to crush them. To the Norman colonists, he was an interfering boy who was already bearing out his odious reputation for ill manners and petulance.

Other information was forthcoming too, and of particular interest to Fulke.

'Lady Oonagh FitzGerald,' said the castle butcher as he scraped the last shreds of meat from a beef leg and slapped the marrowbone into Fulke's hand with a wet smack. 'Now there's a name to conjure with.' He nodded at the bone. 'Going courting are you? It's always a good idea to sweeten the chaperone.'

Fulke laughed. 'It would take more than this, I think.' He looked curiously at the butcher. 'Why is it a name to conjure with?'

'You're pitting yourself against fifty others, all with the same notion. The lady Oonagh's an heiress and a rare beauty. Not often you find both together. Mind you, perhaps you'll get further than the rest. You're the first who's come to ask me for a bone. Of course,' he added, 'you'd best play while the sun shines. Prince John will sell her off to the highest bidder.'

Fulke stared. The marrowbone in his hand felt slimy and wet. The powerful smell of butchered steer coiled in the air. It was the law that a widow could not be remarried unless she chose, but it was a law frequently ignored and vastly open to abuse.

'Not a pretty thought, is it?' The butcher turned away to his block and picked up his cleaver. 'But it's the way of the world. You can't give a dog a bone without killing a cow.'

Fulke winced at the comparison and walked off across the ward. A sudden shout and the close thunder of hooves caused him to spin round and leap aside just in time to avoid being ridden down by a group of horsemen. They drew to a chaotic halt in the centre of the bailey, their mounts barging each other, plunging, circling. The short, bright tunics and plaid cloaks would have marked them as Gaelic lords even if their beards had not. Each man sported a magnificent set of whiskers. Some let their facial hair flow loose to the waist. Others had plaited their whiskers and one or two had divided their beards and waxed the ends heavily so that they were as stiff as spindles.

Fulke gaped at the sight, his eyes huge with astonishment.

'A fine sight, do you not think so, Fulke FitzWarin?' murmured Oonagh, who had walked quietly up beside him, her dog at her heels.

He gave a slight start and his pulse quickened. 'Who are they?'

'The first Irish lords coming to pay their respects to Prince John and claim his support for their cause.'

'What cause?' He felt sufficiently emboldened this time to fondle the bitch's silky ears. The hound raised her nose and snuffled the air, but had the manners not to snatch at the marrowbone in his other hand.

'Their fight against other Irish lords who will also come

and try to win your Prince's influence. It has always been the same in this land. No single man is strong enough to hold the rest, and because they all have a similar power, they spend their time waging futile war.' She looked up at him. 'Your Prince has mercenaries, your Prince has barrels of silver pennies to buy weapons and men; therefore he is to be courted.'

Fulke thought about what Archdeacon Gerald had said on the crossing about those barrels of pennies. 'I do not believe he will make much of a bridegroom,' he said and, hearing the last word in his ears, flushed slightly. While his mind had been considering what she had said, his body had been responding to hers. He had the uncomfortable suspicion she was aware of the fact.

'Does any man?' she replied with the flicker of a smile. 'Are you betrothed?'

Fulke swallowed. 'Not as yet, my lady.'

'No.' Her expression hardened. 'It is the girls who are bargained away before they are scarce out of childhood. How old are you, Fulke?'

'Fifteen summers,' he said, wishing that the answer were more.

'I had been wed for two years by the time I turned fifteen,' she murmured. 'But then girls grow up faster than boys. They have to.'

Fulke asked if he could give the marrowbone to the dog. Oonagh nodded and spoke in Gaelic. The bitch wagged her tail and, opening her formidable jaws, took the offering from Fulke's hand with a ladylike dignity. 'Someone told me that Prince John would sell you in marriage to the highest bidder.'

Oonagh laughed and the sound sent a chill down Fulke's spine. 'He can try,' she said, and laid her hand on his sleeve. 'Would you offer for me?'

Fulke coughed. Gauche and naïve he might be, but he knew she was playing with him. 'If I did, he would refuse it. Prince John does not look kindly on me.'

'The kindness would be in his refusal, I promise you. You would not want me for a wife.'

'I—'

'Fulke, we're needed in the hall!' Jean came running across the ward. 'William de Burgh wants attendants for the Irish lords and we're to do duty.' Arriving, he bowed breathlessly to Oonagh and eyed with interest the way that her hand rested on Fulke's sleeve.

'And do your duty you must.' Oonagh released Fulke's arm and gave him a look through her lashes. 'Thank you for the bone.'

As the youths hurried towards the hall, Jean said enviously, 'I do not know how you do it.'

'Do what?'

'Make a woman like that take notice of you. God knows, half the squires in camp would give their eye teeth to have her touch them and gaze at them the way she gazes at you.'

Fulke looked embarrassed. 'She was just teasing.'

'Aye, well, you're fortunate to be so teased.'

On reaching the hall they were immediately directed to the high table and commanded to bring wine. The Gael lords were clustered around the hearth, muttering amongst themselves and fingering their impressive beards. A couple of Norman colonist barons had joined them, their own facial hair clipped within orderly bounds and their dress less flamboyant. Of John and his retinue, there was no sign, although de Burgh was doing his best to play the welcoming host. There was a grim expression on his face and he kept casting expectant glances in the direction of the stairs to the private apartments.

'He'll be lucky,' Jean said from the side of his mouth.

'The Prince swallowed enough wine last night to sink a cog. Even if he does appear, he'll be in no fit state to greet important guests.'

Jean's words were borne out. As he and Fulke presented wine to the guests, there was a fanfare of trumpets from the far end of the room and two guards emerged from the stair entrance to flank the arrival of the royal retinue.

Fulke almost overflowed the cup he was pouring for the Irish lord, but the chieftain did not notice for his own attention was fixed on the group emerging from the darkness of the stairway into the daylit great hall. He muttered something low, guttural and, from the tone, uncomplimentary.

John was plainly still suffering from the excesses of the previous evening. His tread was unsteady and if he had been to bed, it was in his clothes, which were rumpled and stained. His dark hair stood up in spikes around the gold circlet binding his brow. He resembled a beggar in borrowed robes, or a boy masquerading as a man, trying to hide his inexperience behind a keg of wine. His companions were in no better case, all of them lurching and red-eyed.

Ignoring the group by the hearth, John tottered over to the dais and slumped down in the high-backed chair that stood behind a napery-covered dining trestle. His retinue arranged themselves around him like a throng of half-dead butterflies.

'Wine,' John snarled and clicked his fingers.

Fulke watched a hapless junior squire scurry to the Prince's bidding and felt great sympathy for the youth and contempt for John. To avoid the royal eye and with it the royal malice, he busied himself among the guests where John's blatant bad manners and ignorance had caused the muttering to grow more vociferous.

'I'll not bow the knee in homage to a conceited little arsewipe like that,' growled one of the Gael lords in laboured

French to a Norman settler. 'I'd rather give King Dermot the kiss of peace first.'

The Norman lord looked uneasy. 'The Prince is in his cups,' he excused. 'I do not imagine he was expecting our arrival.'

'That's pigswill, man.' The Irish chief made a casting gesture and Fulke had to step smartly backwards before the flagon was knocked from his hand. 'He knows that the lords of Ireland are riding to Waterford to greet his landing – to see for themselves what manner of man has been sent to rule over us.' He jutted his beard contemptuously in the direction of the dais. 'I don't see a man; I see a spoiled and useless child. How will he exert control when he cannot control himself?'

Striving to soothe ruffled feathers, William de Burgh brought the Irish and Norman lords to the dais to present them to the Prince.

One elbow resting on the board, jaw propped on his hand, John watched them approach and gave a theatrical yawn behind his other hand. Then he looked round to meet grinning approbation from his companions.

'Can this charade not wait?' he demanded over loudly of de Burgh. 'My brains are fit to split from my skull and I'll never remember their names. They all sound like someone being punched in the gut anyway, and God knows what's nesting in those beards.'

One of John's companions choked on a guffaw. Fulke winced. In private, the remark would have been amusing, but ridiculing allies and vassals in public was stupid, danger-ous and shameful. A good host saw to his guests' comfort. A good ruler ensured that their loyalty remained staunch.

'What's nesting will be a serious rebellion unless you mend your attitude,' de Burgh murmured. 'Your Highness, you cannot afford to antagonise these men.'

'I can afford anything I want,' John slurred.

'Including a bloody war when you could have peace?' de Burgh hissed. 'Many of them speak French. You have already caused untold damage.'

'Oh, in the name of Christ's cods! You prate like an old woman!' John drew himself upright and affected an air of regal dignity. 'Kneel and do your homage to me,' he commanded in a raised voice. 'Then you can go.'

After a long hesitation, Robert FitzAlan, one of the settler Normans, came forward to bend the knee and take his oath of allegiance. He spoke as if he had a constriction in his throat but somehow managed the declaration. But he was alone. To a man the Irish lords turned round and walked out, their acknowledgement of John's right to rule ungiven. They collected their weapons from the steward at the door and they were gone.

A cursing William de Burgh ran after them to try to persuade them to stay, but returned empty handed. Expression thunderous, he strode towards the dais.

John lurched to his feet. 'Whatever you are going to say, you can keep it behind your teeth,' he said. 'You forced me to attend on them. You take the consequences.' He swayed down the dais steps. 'I'm retiring to my chamber and you will not disturb me again.'

De Burgh stopped as if he had been struck with a poleaxe. The Norman lord who had sworn allegiance looked sick. Fulke eyed the flagon in his hand and thought of the one in Westminster, and how John had blamed him and ordered him to pay. And in the end he thought, everyone *would* pay for John's wilful conceit, perhaps with their lives. He was no longer playing petty games of chess and dice. The board was larger, the stakes higher, and the only way to win was by ruthless commitment.

CHAPTER 5

Theobald came down to the hall on the third evening following Prince John's arrival in Waterford. His stomach, although still tender, had settled sufficiently to allow him to rise from his bed and he could consume bread and watered wine without being sick.

The evening meal and festivities were marked by a significant absence of Gael lords, although there were a reasonable number of colonist Normans and their families. Theobald had been horrified at what his squires had told him of John's behaviour towards the chieftains who had come to pay him homage. One of the barons, John de Courcy, had written to King Henry, informing him of the Prince's conduct and other senior lords, worried at the behaviour of the younger element, had signed the letter.

Theobald was not so optimistic as to believe that a single letter would bring a solution. Henry was notoriously blind to the antics of his youngest son and unlikely to act until the situation became so damning that it could not be ignored.

Breaking a morsel from the wastel loaf on his trencher, Theobald dipped it in the bowl of chicken broth at his right hand, and mindful of the lady Oonagh's advice, ate slowly. John had invited her to dine at the high table and she sat not far from Theobald, her eyes modestly downcast.

He had enjoyed her sick-room visits for she was as intelligent as she was alluring. Theobald was not married, but, looking at her, he thought he might like to be. So did every other man present – and youth. He cast an amused glance at his younger squire. The lad hadn't taken his gaze off her once.

It did no harm to dream. Fulke must know that she was not for him. Her wealth was here in Ireland and her next husband would be a man who intended to settle here, not a raw squire with a future rooted firmly on the Welsh borders. Theobald was aware that he could fit himself for the post. Given his abilities it would be simple enough to convince John, and there would be the advantage of not having to face a sea crossing back to England. Theobald shook his head and gave a smile of self-mockery. He was as foolish as the rest of her admirers.

Below the dais, the trestles were being dismantled to make space for dancing and entertainment. Even as the musicians changed the tempo and cadence of their playing from soft accompaniment to toe-tapping jig, men were on their feet and seeking partners. Oonagh was immediately surrounded, but not for long as there was a sudden flurry of snaps and snarls from the protective dog. Oonagh sharply bade the hound lie down.

John was laughing as he waved her admirers away. He murmured close to Oonagh's ear and, linking her hand in his, claimed her for himself. As he drew her to the cleared space in the main part of the hall, she gave him a coquettish look and said something in reply that brought a flush of lust to his face. When they began to dance, it was with a symmetry that was hypnotic to watch. John might be small and stocky, but he was light on his feet and fluid of movement.

Leaning to replenish Theobald's cup, Fulke almost knocked

it over. The older man could sense the agitation coming off his squire in waves.

'You're better off out of it, lad,' Theobald murmured. 'I am not saying that her character is like his, but they share similar traits. When it comes to matters of the heart, or should I say lusts of the body, they are both predators.'

'She doesn't know what he is like,' Fulke said grimly.

'Oh, I think she does, and she is very clever,' Theobald contradicted him. 'If she had agreed to dance with one of the others, they would have taken it as preferment to their suit. By going with John, she has put herself above them. If I am right, the next man she partners will be an older one and firmly wed.' He lifted his gaze to his squire. 'Long for her if you want, Fulke, but curb your jealousy: it's a waste of time. She is not for you.'

Fulke flushed. 'John's a lecher,' he said.

'John's an opportunist, and he exerts an attraction for women, but Lady FitzGerald can take care of herself. She is no innocent. If she was, do you think she would be flirting with the Prince as she is? Open your eyes, lad.'

Fulke's colour darkened and, for a moment, Theobald thought that he was going to be treated to a furious outburst. To his credit, however, the boy contained his anger. His flint-hazel eyes dwelled briefly on the swirl of dancers as Oonagh and John changed partners in a figure of eight and returned to each other. Then he looked away. 'Yes, sir,' he said stiffly.

'Ah, God, you're so young. What can I tell you? Women are not as strong as we are in the physical sense. We use our bodies to shoulder aside whatever lies in our way. They use theirs to bribe and persuade, but it has the same result – they get where they want to go.' Theobald wondered if he should arrange for one of the more decent women among the camp followers to endow Fulke with a little education and in the same thought decided against it. The lad was inordinately proud and it would only cause awkwardness where there should be trust and camaraderie. He would not dream of sending Fulke or Jean to procure a woman for his own use, so it behoved him to uphold moral standards, even if they were crumbling all around him.

The dance ended and, as Theobald had predicted, Oonagh partnered an older man and then a settler lord who was known to be devoted to his wife. Then, to Theobald's dismay, as another lively tune struck up and the men began to cluster, she approached Fulke and asked him to lead her among the dancers.

'My lady?' Fulke looked as if he could believe neither his ears nor his luck.

'Unless you would rather decline?' A dazzling look through her lashes. The hand on his sleeve. Theobald could understand her reason: Fulke would never be a contender for her hand in marriage. But whilst it was safe for her to dance with him, Theobald was not sure that such a move was in Fulke's best interests.

'Perhaps you would honour me instead.' Rising from the bench, Theobald extended his hand. 'I have yet to thank you for your care while I was sick.'

Oonagh looked briefly surprised, then she smiled. 'Of course, my lord.' She transferred her hand from Fulke's sleeve to Theobald's. As he led her to dance, she looked over her shoulder to the stricken Fulke. 'Will you take Tara outside for me?' she asked sweetly.

'My lady.' Fulke gave Theobald an aggrieved look, bowed tersely and turned on his heel.

Theobald led her among the dancers. The heady smell of attar of roses wafted from her wrists and throat. Her warmth and suppleness were alluring. 'Leave the boy alone,' he murmured. 'He's too young.'

She arched her thin, glossy brows. 'Implying that you are not, my lord?'

They completed a half-circle and turned. 'Implying nothing of the kind. I suspect that you would be too much of a handful for me,' Theobald said wryly. 'I am asking you as a favour not to play games with Fulke, especially if you are going to involve Prince John in them.'

'May I know why?' She looked half annoyed and half amused.

'The details are unimportant. Suffice to say that the Prince and my squire are already on hostile terms. Adding you to the brew will only make the pot boil over again.'

They changed partners and returned to each other. 'I like Fulke,' she said, a contrary set to her lips.

'Then in pity's name let him be.'

'Have you never played the game of courtly love, my lord?'

'I always had more sense,' Theobald said curtly. Queen Eleanor had brought the convention with her from Aquitaine: a fashionable ideal of unrequited love where a man would worship an unattainable woman and strive to win the favour of her glance by composing songs and performing heroic deeds in her honour. Where the pain of denial was viewed as pleasure. Even if the lover did attain the possession of his lady's body, he was not permitted the satisfaction of spilling his seed, but must hold himself back for her honour. 'Play where you will,' he said softly, 'but do no damage to Fulke, because if you do, I will kill you.'

She narrowed her eyes. 'You speak plainly, my lord.'

'I know of no other way. You may not like what you hear from me, but you will never have to sift my words for hidden meanings.'

The dance ended and he swept her a bow. Oonagh returned it with a curtsey. 'Not because you threaten me,

but for Fulke's sake, I will do as you say,' she murmured.
'But first I must find him and my dog. You will grant me
that moment at least?'

Not particularly sanguine at the thought, but relieved
that she had been reasonable, Theobald nodded and returned
to his seat.

Fulke took the bitch on a circuit of the ward, pacing with
her in the grey wash of the moonlight. He kicked at the
ground. A pebble skittered from underfoot, struck the wall
and rebounded with a click. He knew that Lord Theobald
had partnered Oonagh because he wanted to warn her to
keep her distance. As if Fulke could not make up his own
mind, as if he were a child. A dance, he thought, angrily,
would have cost and meant nothing. It would have salved
his smarting masculine pride and redressed the balance of
watching her flirt with John. He kicked the ground again,
and Tara growled.

Suddenly the bitch abandoned him and loped across the
ward, her tail wagging furiously. The greeting could only
be for one person and Fulke's stomach churned as he saw
Oonagh emerge from the hall. She was wearing her cloak
over her gown and the moonlight caught glints of the silver
braid woven down its edge. He followed more slowly in
the dog's wake, feeling foolish and not a little resentful.

She gave a small sigh and shook her head. 'You should
not be angry,' she said. 'Your lord has your interests at heart
and in truth he is right. If I had known of your quarrel
with Prince John, I would not have asked you to partner
me in the dance at all.'

'It would not have mattered, my lady,' Fulke answered
woodenly.

'I do not believe that, and neither do you.' She looked
at him sidelong. 'He thinks that I am toying with you . . .

and perchance I am, a little. I like to flirt. But I meant what I said about your hands – they are gentle.' She moved closer, the moonlight drenching her in shades of silver, blue and grey. Her fingers meshed through his and as his body rippled at the contact, she stood on tiptoe and kissed him.

Fulke would have gasped except that she had stolen his breath. A wordless groan was trapped in his throat. The tightness of apprehension in his belly descended to his groin. His other hand swept around her waist. For an instant she resisted, and he was just about to drop his hand when she melted against him. He closed his eyes. If this was toying, she could play with him for ever. The softness of her breasts, the litheness of flank and thigh. The honeyed warmth of her mouth.

And then she broke the kiss and her lips were at his ear. 'I have to go. Think of me when you stand thus with another woman, and remember what I said about gentle hands. A man has need of them to be a good lover.'

Fulke swallowed. 'Don't go,' he pleaded.

'God keep you.' She turned away. The bitch growled, her hackles bristling in a ridge down her spine. Stiff-legged, she began to advance on a figure concealed in the shadows of the tower wall.

'Call your dog off, madam,' said Prince John, stepping into the moonlight.

Fulke went rigid. So did Oonagh, but the reaction was brief. A swift command brought the bitch circling to heel. Leaving Fulke without a backward glance, she went to John, the hand that had so recently been meshed in Fulke's now outstretched in greeting. John said something to her and scowled at Fulke from beneath his brows. She answered with a dismissive laugh and together they went within.

Fulke did not follow them. Had there been a flagon to hand he would have drained it to the lees; had there been another squire he would have picked a fight; and had there been a woman . . . He swore aloud and took himself on another circuit of the ward while his anger, if not his agitation, diminished. He was still too pent up to enter company, however, and finally took himself off to the stables to bed down with his roan gelding. The most a horse could do was kick him in the teeth, which was eminently better than the backhand blow dealt by the pleasure of 'toying'.

Excusing himself from his dining companions, Theobald eased to his feet and quietly left the hall. There was no sign of Fulke in the ward, or in any of the garderobes. The kitchens and dairy yielded only servants. He found Jean in the guardhouse with some mercenaries, entertaining them with a bawdy drinking song, but the youth had not seen Fulke. Theobald dissuaded him from joining the search, saying it was of no matter, and continued doggedly.

Finally he came to the stables and found the lad asleep beside his horse. The roan cob swung its head and snorted at Theobald with sweet, hay-scented breath, then lowered its head to snuffle at the lad. Fulke muttered and turned over, his sword hand curling as vulnerably as an infant's. Theobald deliberated, turned around, and quietly walked away.

'Did you hear that Oonagh FitzGerald shared the Prince's bed last night?' Jean asked.

Fulke grimly shook his head and concentrated on harnessing Lord Theobald's chestnut stallion. The court was going hunting and the bailey was filled with the excited yelping of dogs. Their owners stood in groups waiting for their mounts and discussing the likelihood of good sport.

'Well, everyone else did. They said it sounded like a cat being skinned.'

'Do you think I'm interested?'

'Aren't you?'

'No,' Fulke snapped.

'God knows what's got into you this morn. I could understand if you'd been drinking with me in the guard-room, I've got a head like a thundercloud, but you've no excuse.'

'Do I need one?'

'Suit yourself.' Jean poked at a front tooth with his thumbnail. 'I suppose you won't be interested either in the news that she's to wed Guy de Chaumont. It was announced this morn at the breaking of fast. That's quick work even for John. Beds her one night and sells her off by dawn.'

Fulke cinched the girth and dropped his hands. De Chaumont was one of John's drinking cronies. He was slightly older than the Prince with a minor career on the French tourney circuit to boast of as experience. Loud-mouthed and brash, but with a grounding of education and a glimmer of intelligence. Fulke disliked him, but not as much as he disliked John. 'Did she agree to it?'

'Well, she went very pale, but she curtseyed to John and thanked him in a loud, clear voice for the honour he had bestowed on her.' Jean pursed his lips consideringly. 'I suppose it was a shock, but not too terrible. De Chaumont's an arrogant swine, but handsome with it. Of course, there was a disturbance,' Jean added as Fulke led the courser in a circle to prevent its muscles from stiffening. 'One of the Irish lords, Niall O'Donnel, had already offered John fifty marks as a marriage relief to take the lady to wife. So when John gave her to one of his favourites instead, there was uproar.'

'What did John do?' Despite his intention to sulk, Fulke's curiosity got the better of him.

'Threatened to imprison O'Donnel if he didn't hold his

tongue. O'Donnel did, but you could slice a roast with the looks he's been casting at John ever since. His lands march with hers and the rumour is that he and Oonagh FitzGerald know each other well.' His words were heavy with meaning.

'I've never seen her with anyone,' Fulke muttered sullenly.

'Well, that's because O'Donnel only rode in today. He's been fighting rebels in the field. He's as big and blond as a lion with muscles to match.'

Fulke scowled. Salt was being well and truly rubbed into a smarting wound. Before he could decide whether to retaliate or ignore it, Lord Theobald arrived, his short hunting cloak pinned at his shoulder and his fist curled around the haft of a boar spear.

Taking the courser's reins from Fulke, he made no comment on Fulke's absence of the previous night, except to enquire if he had broken his fast.

'Yes, my lord.' Fulke eyed the ground which was suddenly of great interest.

Theobald swung into the saddle. 'A good gallop in the fresh air,' he said, his gaze both sharp and sympathetic, 'that will cleanse your blood. Make haste and mount up, lad. You too, Jean.'

Fulke went to his roan cob. He had saddled the gelding earlier and left it tethered to a bridle ring in the wall. Girard de Malfee stood nearby, adjusting the girth of his own mount. He darted Fulke a sly glance from beneath his brown curls, then looked to the right where a smiling Prince John had just gained the saddle of a handsome dappled courser with tasselled harness.

Fulke untied the roan and, ignoring the stirrup, leaped for the saddle and swung his leg over. As his weight came down, the horse flung upwards in a spectacular rear. Fulke clawed for the reins, squeezed with his knees and brought his mount jolting down to all fours. The roan squealed and bucked, arching its back, bunching its quarters, lashing out. It careered into two other horses and sent them skittering and bucking too. The dogs yammered and snapped and men dived for cover. Whinnying in pain and fear, the roan fought from one end of the bailey to the other, eyes rolling, bloody foam flecking the bit rings. Fulke clung like a limpet to its back. Then, in mid-plunge, the horse staggered and its back legs began to buckle.

'Fulke, in Christ's name, let go!' Jean roared, his voice cracking at full bellow.

Fulke heard the warning as if from a distance. He had bitten his tongue and the taste of blood filled his mouth. He felt as if the flesh was being jarred from his bones. It was instinct that saved him as the horse lurched and crumpled. Lashing his feet from the stirrups, he flung from the roan's back and hit the bailey floor with a jarring thud. Pain shot through his rib cage like a massive kick. The roan struck the ground in a threshing tangle of legs and tail, shuddered violently and was still.

Curled up, clutching himself, Fulke's eyes met the glazing stare of his mount's. The world swam, sparkled and went out of focus. He was vaguely aware of Lord Theobald asking him if he was all right, of someone forcing him to drink strong wine laced with mead, of the roan being dragged to one side, the curious dogs being whipped off the corpse, and the hunt spurring out of the gates to the halloo of the hunting horn.

When Fulke returned fully to his senses, he was lying on a pallet in Lord Theobald's chamber. Oonagh was leaning over him, her satchel of nostrums at her shoulder and the wolfhound bitch at her side. He tried to sit up, but a searing pain prevented him. Oonagh hastened to his aid, plumping the pillows and bolsters at his back. 'I saw what happened from a chamber window,' she said. 'You have some cracked ribs for certain.'

'Is that why you're here, to tend my cracked ribs?' Fulke glowered, wishing that she would leave him alone.

'Yes, in part.' Rummaging in her satchel she produced several lengths of linen bandage. 'Raise your arms.'

Fulke did so and in seconds she had whisked off his tunic and shirt without him quite knowing what had happened. He looked obdurately at the wall. Last night he had slept in the stable beside his horse and now it was dead. Moreover, she had slept with Prince John, thus slaughtering his fragile dream. 'And the other part?'

She leaned in close and began wrapping the bandage around his chest. 'To ask a boon of you.'

'A boon?' His glance flickered. 'I fail to see what I can do for you, my lady, that Prince John cannot,' he said rudely.

'Then you must be blind, for Prince John does very little for me.' She wrapped and pulled. 'Is that too tight?'

Fulke shook his head in bewilderment. 'But I thought . . . I was told that you went to his bed last night.'

Oonagh smiled acidly. 'That was pleasurable enough,' she said, 'but what I received in exchange was hardly worth the bargain. I suppose you were also told that I am to wed one of his drinking cronies?'

'Yes, my lady.'

'I asked John to promise me my choice of husband. He said he would think about it.' She sucked a breath through her teeth and secured the end of the bandage with a small circular pin. 'Obviously he came to a swift decision. Not that it matters to me. I will be a most loving and dutiful wife to Guy de Chaumont.'

Fulke blinked at her in bafflement.

'Or what remains of him in six months' time.'

The purr in her voice sent a ripple of apprehension down Fulke's spine. 'You mean you'll kill him?'

Oonagh laughed and shook her head. 'What would that gain for me except another husband of John's choosing? But if my lord de Chaumont was to meet with an accident – perhaps take a knock on the head whilst hunting and be rendered witless, the rule of the lands would fall to me, and whoever I appointed as administrator in my poor husband's stead.'

Fulke swallowed. She was ruthless. Theobald, with his greater experience, had been quicker than he to see it, but now his own eyes were wide open. 'So what do you want of me?' There was a nasty, prickling sensation between his shoulder blades. What if she asked him to arrange the 'accident' to de Chaumont?

'I want you to take Tara.' She gestured over her shoulder at the dog. 'As I said, a dead husband is of no use to me. Either Tara would rip out de Chaumont's throat, or he would have her killed for her aggression. She does not growl at you. Take her back to England. She will serve you well.'

Fulke eyed the dog. As if sensing his stare, the bitch raised her head and thumped her tail on the floor. He wondered what Lord Theobald would say about the presence of a pony-sized hound snoring on his chamber floor. 'Gladly, my lady,' he said, relieved to have escaped so lightly. Then he frowned. She had said 'back to England' as if the journey was imminent. 'What makes you think I will not be remaining in Ireland for some time yet?'

'Your Prince.' Her blue eyes were suddenly as hard as glass. 'When the silver is spent and the wine all drunk, then the game will end. There are good men in his retinue. Your own lord is one of them, William de Burgh another, but they can do nothing when they are fettered by the

Prince's command over them. I give you until the winds of autumn.' Leaning over him, she brushed her lips against his cheek, then stepped back.

'A pity you are not ten years older,' she murmured. 'Or perhaps a blessing?' Going to the door, she stooped to the dog, put her arms around her and murmured soft love words in Gaelic. Then, bidding the bitch stay, she left briskly and did not turn round.

Fulke let out the breath he had been holding on a gasp of relief and regret, then clutched his ribs at the pain. After a moment the dog padded over to him and licked his hand.

'This was under your saddle cloth.' Seating himself on the end of Fulke's pallet, Jean presented him with a shard of glass that had come from a broken goblet. Only the nobles who sat at the high table drank out of glass because it was expensive and difficult to carry between households without being broken. 'The moment you set your weight in the saddle, it would have pressed into Russet's flesh like a sharp spur.'

Fulke took the piece of glass and turned it in his fingers. Green light smudged his skin. A thick line of opaque red with roan hairs adhered to the vicious point at one end. It was not long enough to kill on its own, but sufficient to drive an animal mad with pain and make it burst its heart. He remembered de Malfee's sly glance and Prince John's smirk of pleasure. Doubtless they had thought it a fine jest.

'I know where to lay the blame for this,' he said grimly. 'My father was right.'

Jean raised his brows in question.

'I should have made sure that the whoreson stayed down.'

* * *

In September a galley arrived from England, bearing letters and emissaries from King Henry; and Oonagh's words were borne out.

'We're sailing for England,' said Theobald as he dressed in his wall chamber for the evening meal after attending a private discussion in John's solar. 'The travelling chests must be packed by dawn.'

Fulke had known that it was coming. Even without Oonagh's prophecy the signs had been present in the steady trickle of deserting mercenaries and the arguments of the townspeople over lack of payment for their produce.

'King Henry did not send more silver then?' He helped Theobald don his long court tunic of crimson wool edged with gold braid.

Theobald shook his head. 'If silver has arrived, lad, it is not for John. He might be Henry's favourite son, but even favouritism has its limits. More silver would just buy more wine and Henry's coffers are not bottomless. I suspect that John will go home to a scolding and then be treated like a prodigal son.'

Fulke knew what Theobald meant. The Prince had been chastised over the incident with the chessboard, but the whipping had somehow never been administered.

Theobald latched his belt and checked that his scabbard was securely attached. 'It is not all John's fault,' he said as he ran a comb through his cropped tawny curls. 'You cannot expect a spoiled stripling to do a man's work. Still,' he added as he set the comb down on the coffer. 'I suppose that lessons have been learned.' Reaching for his cloak, he smiled at Fulke. 'You are not disappointed to leave, I warrant?'

'No, my lord.' Fulke lifted his shoulders. 'It is not that I have hated my time here, and I have learned much, but . . .' He flushed slightly beneath his lord's quiet grey gaze. 'But I want to see my family again and my home.'

'It is always good to wander,' Theobald said, and his eyes left Fulke and swept towards the window embrasure and an arch of wintry grey light. 'And always good to return.'

They sailed from Waterford on the morning's tide. There was a bitter wind to blow them home and a choppy grey sea that Theobald eyed with alarm and Fulke with resignation.

As the last coffers were being loaded on to the ships, Jean returned from one of his kitchen forays with a mutton pudding, a flask of mead, and the news for Fulke that Oonagh FitzGerald's new husband, Guy de Chaumont, had been severely injured in a hunting accident.

CHAPTER 6

The Welsh Borders,
Summer 1189

The older FitzWarin boys and the de Hodnet brothers, Baldwin and Stephen, had spent the morning at the booths in Oswestry, examining the wares of the harness-maker, horse-coper and swordsmith. Fulke had a mended bridle to collect, William was looking for a new mount, and all the young men were passionate about the sleek blades displayed on the cloth outside the swordsmith's booth.

Some were fashioned from a single bar of steel; others were made in the old way, from several layers of iron, beaten and hammered until they formed intricate ripple designs on the surface of the weapon. It was said that these pattern-welded blades possessed less strength than the plain ones, but for visual beauty, they were unsurpassed.

'I'm going to have one of these when I'm knighted.' William's brown eyes gleamed covetously. He was eighteen now; slender, fiery and desperate for the ceremony that would confer on him the badge of warrior manhood.

Fulke admired William's choice. It would have been his own selection too, except that when it came his time to be knighted, the gift of his sword had been promised by Lord Theobald. The ceremony was likely to take place when Lord Theobald returned to England. For the nonce, he was fighting across the Narrow Sea in Anjou. King Henry and Prince Richard were at each other's throats again. Prince John was with his father, opposing Richard, and from what news came to them here in the Marches, the situation was ugly and acrimonious.

Fulke was glad not to be attending Theobald. Instead of crossing the Narrow Sea, he had been summoned home when his father had fallen dangerously sick. Although le Brun had recovered from the high fever that had briefly threatened his life, Fulke had not returned to court. His father had deemed it better for him to learn the obligations of governance at home for a while rather than become involved in the vicissitudes of Angevin family warfare.

Today, however, Fulke had his freedom to enjoy the perfect Lammastide weather and the booths in Oswestry. English and Welsh folk mingled, intent on barter and purchase. Their languages blended, mixed with more than a seasoning of Norman French. Fulke watched the trading with pleasure, knowing that it was not always this peaceful. Frequently the Welsh and English were at war with each other and Oswestry was a battleground, claimed by both sides and sacked by both too as a result.

Last time they had been in the town was the Whitsuntide of the previous year. Granted leave by Lord Theobald to visit his family, Fulke had been in Oswestry to hear the Bishop of St David and his deacon, the irrepressible Gerald de Barry, preach the need for a new crusade to restore the Holy Land to Christian rule. Gerald had been so eloquent and passionate that several folk had joined the crusade on the spot and been handed red crosses to sew on to their cloaks. Fulke had felt the tug of the sermon but abjured, knowing that his own family's Jerusalem was Whittington and his future already mapped out. William had stepped forward like a speeding arrow and been hauled back by le Brun's hand on the scruff of his neck.

'Too young and so hot-headed you'll burn yourself up,' their father had snapped with a jaundiced glare at Gerald and the Bishop. 'You were ever one to hear tales of a dragon at your nurse's knee and straight away run off in pursuit of one.'

Prince Richard had sworn to take the Cross and ride for Jerusalem as soon as the matter of his inheritance was resolved. Lord Theobald's brother Hubert had sworn too, and their uncle, Ranulf de Glanville. Theobald himself was to remain behind in John's retinue. It was a sensible move and made the best of both worlds for the Walter family. If and when the crusade departed, they would have influence both in the field and at home.

'I like this one.' Philip lifted one of the plain steel swords. It suited his nature, which was sturdy and cautious despite his unruly cloud of auburn curls.

Both de Hodnet boys opted for pattern-welded blades. Finally growing tired of their penniless enthusiasm the swordsmith waved them away, grumbling that sweaty finger-prints would damage the steel.

The young men repaired to the alehouse where at least their purses could afford the price of two jugs between them. They sat at a trestle under the shade of an oak tree and took it in turns to drink. Tara, Fulke's wolfhound, flopped nose on paws at his side and watched the world from beneath her brows. He combed his fingers through her harsh pelt, stiff as fine silver wire.

'It don't bite, do it?' One of the alehouse girls paused warily to admire the massive dog. Moistening her lips, she darted her gaze over the assembled young men in similar wise.

William grinned broadly and raised the jug in toast. 'No, but I do, sweetheart, if you want to sit on my lap and try me.'

'No, she doesn't bite.' Fulke gave his brother a nudge and removed the jug from his hands. William was always boasting about the conquests he had made, but Fulke suspected that most were imagined in order to increase William's standing among his peers.

Fulke's own experience of women had considerably expanded since his return from Ireland. Hanild, one of the court whores, had taken a fancy to broaden his education beyond the arts of weapon play and ciphering – teaching him 'the differences between a knight and an oaf' as she had put it. Her instruction had been vastly pleasurable and more than a little enlightening, not to say a welcome release from the frustrations that now seemed to be plaguing William.

'Can I stroke her?'

'Of course.' Fulke spoke gently to the dog and studied the girl through his lashes as she tentatively patted Tara's head. Small, curvaceous, with a winsome, kissable smile. When William began talking about his own willingness to be stroked, Fulke bade him somewhat curtly to hold his peace.

William reddened with indignation. 'I saw her first!' he cried. 'Find your own wench!'

'If you desire to be a knight, then act like one,' Fulke said tersely.

'What's that supposed to mean?'

'It means holding your tongue until you have something worthwhile to say . . . either to me or the girl.'

She was looking fearfully at the young men, clearly not following the rapid French, but understanding enough from the tone to realise a quarrel was brewing.

William jerked to his feet. 'You think that because you've been to court, you can lord it over us all, play the master. Well, you're not mine, and I'll do as I please.'

'Go on then,' Fulke said with a sweep of his arm. 'Make a fool of yourself.'

The brothers stared at each other, William breathing jerkily, Fulke maintaining an air of superior calm, although the shudder of his tunic neckline against his throat revealed how hard and swiftly his heart was beating.

'Will, sit down, you're making a mountain from an ant mound.' Ever the peace-maker, Philip tugged at his brother's sleeve.

William shook him off. 'I don't want to sit down. I'm sick of being told what to do.' He stalked away in the direction of their tethered horses.

Fulke stared after him, bemused at the speed with which the quarrel had hit. He had always thought himself fond of William, and the feelings of irritation and anger were unsettling. So too was the notion that William was clearly resentful of him.

'You have trampled on his pride,' Philip murmured. 'And you have taken his place as king of the castle. While you were at court, Will was the oldest and strongest, the one who led. Now you are home and it is clear to all that he cannot hope to compete.'

'I don't want to compete.' Fulke watched William swing into the saddle and tug on the reins. 'God's bones, I've seen enough fraternal squabbling at court to last me a lifetime. Heaven forbid that we should ever come to be like King Henry's sons.'

'He'll come round,' said Baldwin de Hodnet stoutly as William rode away. 'His temper's all blaze and no substance.'

Philip pulled a face. 'But heaven help those who get in its way while it's burning.'

The girl had retreated as the quarrel sparked, but only as far as the alehouse door, and it was her cry that slewed Fulke and his companions on the bench to see that

William's path was blocked by a belligerent group of horsemen.

Fulke's gaze narrowed on the banners fluttering from their spears. 'Morys FitzRoger,' he hissed, and the instant he spoke the name, was on his feet and running to his horse. Morys commonly titled himself lord of Whittington and was their sworn enemy. He was accompanied by his adolescent sons, Weren and Gwyn, and five men-at-arms. As Fulke swung astride, his mind was racing. Even for honour or pride, they could not afford a fight. What he had to do was extricate his hot-headed brother before one began.

He was too late. There was a sudden flurry and scuffle as William launched his brown cob at FitzRoger's stallion and was immediately tipped from the saddle. He sprawled in the road to the accompaniment of jeers and laughter. FitzRoger playfully prodded the tip of the spear he carried against the hollow of William's throat.

'Let him be,' Fulke commanded, riding up and drawing rein.

'Well, well, not just one FitzWarin whelp, but three,' smiled FitzRoger as Philip arrived on Fulke's heels with the de Hodnet brothers. 'And far out of your territory.' He kept the spear at William's throat while his other hand effortlessly controlled his bay destrier.

'Not as far out of it as you are out of yours!' William snarled from the ground with rash bravado.

'How so?' FitzRoger raised his brows in mock surprise. 'Surely Whittington is closer to Oswestry than Alberbury.'

'Yes, and it's ours!'

The smile broadened, but with threat, not friendliness. 'Yap all you want, you ignorant pup, but it won't get you any further than the stink of your own kennel. You say Whittington is yours. Come and take it then.' He leaned with precision on the spear edge, drawing the smallest bead of blood like a jewel stitched on a tunic.

'Let him go,' Fulke repeated. With an effort, he succeeded in keeping his voice calm and level.

FitzRoger laughed. 'Or else what, child? You will assault me with your eating knife like this purblind idiot was about to do?'

'As you say, he is of no importance. Why waste your time on him?'

'Oh, it isn't time wasted,' FitzRoger said blithely. 'I am more than willing to spend a few moments teaching him a lesson he will not forget in a hurry. Indeed, I have a notion to widen the education of all of you, since Fulke le Brun has plainly failed to teach you to mind your betters.'

On the ground, William choked, as much from rage as from the pressure of the spear against his windpipe. Fitz-Roger's men shifted in their saddles, easing their weapons, flexing their muscles. Behind the nasal bars of their helms, FitzRoger's sons smirked at each other. Fulke's hackles rose but he knew that he could not afford to lose his temper.

'My father has always taught us to give respect where respect is due, so we have never had cause to be polite to the house of FitzRoger,' Fulke retorted, and with a glance sidelong and down, uttered a sharp command.

A ripple of silver-grey fur and the slash of fangs on his spear hand were the first that Morys FitzRoger knew of the wolfhound's attack. He bellowed and snatched his arm away, dropping the spear. In a blur of speed, Fulke seized the weapon, hooked it in the mesh of FitzRoger's mail coif and brought him crashing out of the saddle. The bitch went for his face and Fulke roared her off just before her teeth snapped shut on FitzRoger's nose.

As swords hissed from scabbards, Fulke laid the spear edge against FitzRoger's throat. 'Do not believe me too soft to do it, for I will.' He glared at FitzRoger's men, his eyes the hard deep grey of flint. 'I have fought in Ireland and I have been blooded. If my brother is a whelp, then I am a wolf.'

FitzRoger's men stared, transfixed by shock at the speed with which the tables had turned.

'William, mount up.' Fulke jerked his head.

The youth scrambled to his feet and straddled his horse. Against his pallor, the trickle of blood at his throat was bright crimson.

'You will pay,' Morys FitzRoger wheezed from the ground. 'I swear on my soul that you will.'

Glaring down into the hate-filled eyes, Fulke's own animosity and contempt grew. The temptation to lean on the spear trembled through his hands and he had to remind himself that his aim was to get himself and his small company clear of the situation.

Without taking his attention from FitzRoger, he snapped at his companions to spur for home. 'Do it!' he roared, as he felt rather than saw William hesitate. As he heard the receding drum of hooves, he applied the slightest pressure to the spear, drawing blood as FitzRoger had drawn blood from William.

'You are right,' he said hoarsely, 'I will pay. I will give you everything you deserve. On my soul, before God, I swear it.' Removing the lance from the hollow of Fitz-Roger's throat, he couched it lightly and wheeled his mount one-handed. A terse command brought the bitch to his stirrup and he galloped after the others.

'Fulke, I'm sorry,' William said in a crestfallen voice as they slowed their blowing mounts to a trot and cut across an old drover's track to avoid the next village.

'God on the Cross, you ought to be!' Fulke snapped. He

was still not sure they were safe and his temper was ragged. 'You could have got us all thrown into a cell or tied to our horses' tails and whipped from one end of Oswestry to the other! Morys FitzRoger, however much we revile him, is still a man of influence in the town while we are just visiting squires – raw boys with eating knives at our hips in place of swords and scarce enough silver between us for a firkin of ale.'

'I said I was sorry. Besides, it's not all my fault. FitzRoger wouldn't let me pass.'

'And it didn't occur to you to stand aside.' Fulke knew the answer to that even as he spoke. William would hold his ground even if confronted by all the fiends of hell.

'Would you have done so?'

'To avoid trouble, yes. I would.'

William's look was disbelieving. A smile suddenly twitched his mouth corners. 'After what I saw you do to FitzRoger, even if it was to save my hide, I don't believe you.'

'It's the truth. And if you had used your wits and stood aside, I would not have been forced to set the dog on him and we wouldn't be fleeing across the fields like outlaws.' Fulke gazed over his shoulder but the track behind them stretched empty until cut off by the upward slope of the land.

'It was worth it though, wasn't it?' The beginnings of an incorrigible grin deepened William's smile.

Despite his determination to remain angry, Fulke found his lips curling with reluctant humour. 'That's a question you'll have to ask Papa when he lifts your hide with his belt,' he said.

William grimaced at that. Then he shrugged. 'It won't be the first time. Can I carry the spear?' He held out his hand.

'If it's not the first time, then plainly you do not learn by your mistakes,' Fulke said, handing the weapon across.

William grasped it, bunching his fist around the smooth ash haft until the tendons stood out like whipcords on his wrist. Fulke saw from the look on William's face that his brother had opted to be deaf to the remark.

When they rode into Alberbury several hours later, their horses lathered from the punishing pace Fulke had set, le Brun was waiting for them in the courtyard, his hands folded around his belt and his features grim.

Although he knew it was impossible, Fulke thought for a moment that news of the incident at Oswestry had outflown them. But then le Brun took a pace forward and, without asking why the horses had been ridden so hard in the summer's burn, or what William was doing with a spear, said, 'A messenger rode in at noon. King Henry is dead and we are summoned to swear allegiance to Richard at Winchester.'

CHAPTER 7

Palace and environs of Westminster, September 1189

'Fulke!' Theobald Walter engulfed his erstwhile squire in a bear hug, then held him away to look him up and down. 'Holy Christ, have you grown again?' He shook his head. 'No, it's the dark colour of that tunic making you look taller, and you've lost the puppy flesh.' He drew Fulke into the striped canvas pavilion that was serving as his lodging. 'Are you ready for your knighting?'

'Yes, my lord,' Fulke said eagerly. 'Two of my brothers are to receive their spurs too.'

'Excellent!' Theobald declared. 'Your father must be proud. Three sons knighted by Coeur de Lion is a true mark of favour.'

Fulke agreed for form's sake that it was. His father had been pleased but not ecstatic at the news. 'Richard may do me the honour of conferring knighthood on my sons, but it would be a greater honour by far if he would recognise our claim to Whittington, and that remains to be seen,' he had said somewhat testily.

'Is your mother here too?'

Fulke nodded and grinned. 'And my aunt and the rest of my brothers. A coronation and a knighting are occasions too rare and grand to be missed. Women might not be permitted to attend the crowning, but my mother has plans to empty the family strongbox in the markets and look up other wives who have come to trawl the booths and gossip.'

Theobald returned the grin. 'Doubtless there will be some boasting too.' He signalled his junior squire, Adam, to pour wine. Fulke reddened with pleasure and embarrassment. It would be the first time that he and Theobald would drink man to man instead of as master and equerry.

'To King Richard.' Theobald raised his cup. 'And to the glory of knighthood.' If there was any cynicism in the toast, he kept it well hidden.

'Amen.' Fulke echoed Theobald's gesture before taking a swallow.

Lowering his cup, Theobald rested one haunch on his clothing coffer. 'I suppose you came looking for Jean too.'

A smile lit in Fulke's eyes. 'In part, my lord, but I came to pay my respects to you first. Knowing Jean, he's as likely to be in the kitchens or stables as here.'

Theobald threw back his head and laughed. 'Indeed, you know him well. Knighthood certainly has not bestowed any airs and graces on him.'

'Does he still intend taking the Cross?'

Theobald sobered. 'Yes, he does. I shall miss him, but my brother Hubert will gain, since Jean is to travel in his retinue.' A note of exasperation entered Theobald's voice. 'The lad isn't fired up with religious zeal like many of them – it's that accursed wanderlust of his. He wants to see other lands and other customs; that's his appetite in life.' Theobald looked at Fulke from beneath his thick, fair brows. 'You weren't tempted yourself?'

'A little, sir, but not enough to stitch a cross to my cloak. My brother William was all for going, but my father sat on him.'

Theobald snorted. 'But in his youth, I think that your father would have gone. He was renowned for being a fire-eater. No one ever went up against Fulke le Brun with a lance if they could help it.'

Fulke felt a small glow of pride on his father's behalf. 'They still don't.' He took another drink of wine. It was smooth as red silk and reminded him that Theobald's tastes were impeccable. A little of the best rather than a largesse of dross. 'He always claims that my mother put a stop to his adventurous wandering – that he found what he was looking for: a handsome, spirited woman with a dowry larger than her capacity to nag.'

Theobald chuckled. 'One way of putting it, I suppose,' he said and then shook his head. 'I doubt that the Queen Mother or Richard's betrothed, the Princess Alais, could keep Richard from this great enterprise of his, whatever the size of the bribe.'

'Well, Richard's different to most men.'

Theobald gave him a sharp look.

Fulke reddened, suddenly feeling that he had spoken out of turn. 'I mean that he lives for war. As you said about Jean's wanderlust, war is King Richard's appetite for life. He doesn't have the time or inclination for gentler pursuits.'

'True,' Theobald nodded. Certain ugly rumours abounded concerning Richard's sexual preferences but he was not about to voice them to a young man of nineteen on the verge of knighthood. Besides, he was aware that his own bachelor state might be cause for gossip in some quarters, yet he liked women well enough. It was just that the time had never been ripe to take a wife and there were women at court who were paid by the Crown to see to the comforts of retainers such as him.

The tent flap was pushed aside and Theobald's brother Hubert entered in the company of a slender, balding man whom Fulke did not know. The latter was introduced to him as Robert le Vavasour, lord of Shipley and Warrington, a baron sharing similar interests to Theobald in their northern holdings. In common with other tenants-in-chief of the Crown, he was here to witness the coronation and renew his oath of fealty.

'FitzWarin?' He looked Fulke up and down, a strange, almost envious expression in his eyes. 'You must be one of le Brun's whelps then.'

'You know my father, sir?' Fulke was discomforted by the man's stare.

Le Vavasour's smile twisted. 'We were rivals in passing for your mother's hand in marriage. He won – to be expected, I suppose, when he had once been her father's body squire. It gave him an unfair advantage.'

Fulke said nothing, unsure how to respond.

Le Vavasour's lip curled. 'I wed Jonetta de Birkyn instead. Unfortunately she did not vouchsafe me a crop of sons the like of your mother's. Between all the miscarriages and failures before she died, she bore me a single daughter.' His tone rang with bitterness.

'May your lady's soul rest in peace,' Theobald said, crossing himself and bringing a measure of compassion to the conversation. Fulke followed his example, signing his breast and murmuring appropriately.

Le Vavasour merely grunted and folded his arms, affecting a stance that said he was a man to be reckoned with. 'It had better,' he said brusquely. 'I've spent good silver to have masses said in her name.' Thus dismissing his late wife, he turned to the subject of his daughter.

'I've brought young Maude with me,' he said. 'It's never too soon to start looking for a likely match. She's well dowered. No telling whether or not she'll be a beauty when she grows into her looks, but she's got her mother's hair and the Vavasour spirit.' He rubbed his jaw and watched Theobald slyly beneath his lids. 'I'm open to offers, Lord Walter.'

Theobald looked slightly taken aback. 'Are you indeed? And how old is the lass? Surely she's still a child?'

'Of legal age to wed,' le Vavasour responded with a thrust of his jaw. 'It was her twelfth year day at the Midsummer feast.'

'Jesu, Rob, I'm nearly old enough to be her grandsire!'

'There's scarcely a grey hair in your head, and I'd rather have her wed a man who knows the ways of the world, who can fight and govern, rather than squander her on a stripling. Give me age and experience over the prettiness of youth any day.' He glanced at Fulke, without intending insult but emphasising a point. 'Our interests run together in the north. It would be a profitable union.'

Theobald shook his head. 'I'm not looking to marry.'

'You should. Your brother's not going to provide any legitimate offspring, is he?' Le Vavasour nodded at Hubert.

'Neither would I with a twelve-year-old,' Theobald said shortly.

Le Vavasour unfolded his arms. 'Well, if you should have a change of heart, I'm open to offers for the wench from a man of your standing and means.' Smoothly he altered the subject, talking more generally of the coronation.

Fulke politely excused himself and threaded his way through the mass of tents and buildings towards the kitchens in search of Jean. He decided that he did not much care for Robert le Vavasour. The man had too high an opinion of himself and too vociferous an opinion on everything else.

Fulke finally found his friend in the kitchens being loudly berated by fat Marjorie.

'A thousand extra cups and two thousand pitchers!' she cried, her face pink and sweat-streaked from toiling over three cauldrons at once. 'And that's just the start. The old King would be turning in his grave if he could see the extravagance!' She waved a wooden ladle at Jean, then at Fulke, as if she thought it was their fault.

To Fulke the kitchens resembled how he imagined a hall in the court of hell would look. Fires blazed beneath cauldrons, fireboxes full of charcoal gave off a simmering heat over which sauces were being stirred and pie fillings prepared. A mountain of dead chickens, ducks and partridges obscured Fulke's view of the oven where yet another batch of bread was being baked for the banquet. Several maids sat plucking the fowl and filling sacks with feathers. To one side, a huge wild boar awaited a butcher's attention. Since the weather was fine, even the area outside the kitchens had been utilised and servants toiled by ragged torchlight to chop and stir and mould. No one was going to sleep tonight, and certainly not on the morrow.

'Richard knows the value of display,' Jean said to the woman as he acknowledged Fulke with a wave. 'Give a man a full belly, make him feel important and he will be more disposed to respond generously.'

'So we can expect an increase in our wages then?' Marjorie demanded sourly. Then with an impatient sound she relented enough to toss the young men a large cobble of gingerbread each from a pile that was cooling on a wooden tray. 'Away with you.' She made a flicking gesture at the open door. 'I ain't got time to gossip tonight and you're more hindrance than help.'

Jean swept a bow. 'I'll consider my ears boxed, mistress.'

She mockingly shook her fist at him but found a preoccupied smile before returning to her row of cauldrons simmering on a grid over one of the fireboxes.

Jean clapped Fulke's shoulder. 'It's good to see you.'

'And you.' Fulke chewed on the gingerbread, relishing the honeyed spiciness of the sweetmeat. Between rotations of his jaw, he told Jean about his forthcoming knighthood.

'No longer Fulke, but "Sir" Fulke,' Jean teased with a white grin. His own knighthood had taken place two years earlier, but, unlike Fulke, he had no inheritance and he served the Walter family for his daily bread.

Fulke laughed. 'I doubt that anyone will grace me with that title.'

'Aren't you going to have a squire then?'

'Yes, my brother Ivo, and he certainly won't address me as "sir".'

Outside the kitchens, they paused beside a cauldron of wine and water into which a kitchen boy was scattering cups of wheat and barley to make a jellied frumenty.

'What will you do once you're knighted?'

'Mayhap I will spend a season on the tourney circuit.' It was the occupation of many a newly knighted young man. Those without lands took to the tourney field in the hopes of gaining employment or a fief of their own. Those who had an inheritance but time to kill before it came to them joined the tourneys in order to broaden their experience of warfare and stave off boredom. It was an excellent if somewhat dangerous training ground.

'You do not desire to take the Cross then?' Jean indicated the red linen insignia stitched to his cloak in token of the vow he had taken to join King Richard on crusade.

'A little, but I am no burning zealot, and my family lands come first.' Fulke looked at his friend. 'For you it does not matter so much, and I know how much your feet itch if they stay in one place too long.'

Jean grinned at the assessment. 'I need to know what lies on the other side of the hill, be it grass or desert.'

'Usually it's just another hill,' Fulke said.

By unspoken and mutual consent, they set off in the direction of one of the alehouses that served the palace workers and off-duty guards. Finding a recently vacated trestle, they sat down and ordered a jug of mead to wash down the heat of the gingerbread.

'My father says that Richard is going to put England up for sale,' Fulke said as they filled their cups. 'That every office, lordship and sheriffdom will be taken from its present holder and sold to the highest bidder.'

'That is likely true,' Jean nodded. 'Lord Theobald's Uncle Ranulf has been stripped of the shrievalty of Yorkshire and made to pay a fine of fifteen thousand pounds for abuses of the office.'

'Abuses?' Fulke thought of the dignified grey-haired man. 'That's a contrived accusation, surely!'

'In part, yes. Ranulf cannot be everywhere at once and he deputised most of the work to his steward – who's been fined hard too. Minor difficulties have been inflated out of all proportion.' Jean rubbed his thumb over the lines incised round the fat belly of his cup. 'All Ranulf's power came from King Henry and Richard wants to show that his word is now the law of the land. The de Glanville family is not to be flattened, but it has been warned not to flaunt its power.'

'What does Lord Theobald say to all this?'

Jean shrugged. 'Very little. He's astute enough to know when to hold his peace. His brother Hubert dwells in Richard's camp and he remains with John's retinue – keeping the family's eggs in more than one basket. Until King Richard marries and begets an heir, Prince John is his successor.'

Fulke grimaced at the notion. Richard was already two and thirty. He had been betrothed to Princess Alais of France for more than Fulke's lifetime and still there was no sign that a wedding was imminent, much less a dynasty. Moreover, going on crusade was scarcely a guarantee of longevity. 'What about Prince Arthur?' he asked, grasping at straws.

Geoffrey, who had been next in line to Richard, had died in an accident at a tourney soon after John's ignominious return from Ireland. However, he had left a son growing in his wife's belly.

Jean shook his head. 'Arthur of Brittany is only two years old. The lords will not choose a foreign-raised infant above John. Whatever his faults, he is still Richard's brother. Richard might threaten John by naming Arthur his heir, but when it comes to the sticking point, he will not do it.'

'Then I wish Richard a long and fruitful reign,' Fulke said vehemently and signed his breast to give the intention more weight. 'What worries me is who will have control of Richard's lands while Richard is away saving Jerusalem? Who will save England from John?'

'Lord Theobald says that Queen Eleanor will be made a regent for certain. Hubert told him that Richard will not give John any power because he does not trust him to hold steady to any ambition but his own.'

'I hope that is true,' Fulke said grimly, remembering how it had been in Ireland and imagining John's vindictiveness and tyranny let loose on a wider scale with larger funds. And if Richard should die on crusade . . . an involuntary shudder rippled down Fulke's spine.

From the alehouse, they strolled companionably to the tents that housed the FitzWarin retinue. There was not a patch of green to be seen between the host of canvas shelters belonging to the lords and vassals who had come to Westminster for the coronation ceremony and to swear allegiance to the new King.

'Will your father appeal for Whittington?' Jean asked as they approached the FitzWarin pavilions. The canvas had been gaily painted with the wolf's teeth device and his father's banner fluttered from a spear planted in the ground outside the larger of the two tents.

Fulke nodded. 'It was his first thought as soon as he heard that King Henry was dead. He's been counting the silver ever since because he knows as well as every man here that Richard needs money for the crusade, and he's open to all offers.' His expression clouded. 'But it rankles with him more than I can tell, Jean, that what is ours by honour and by right should have to be bought like a bolt of cloth at a market.'

Their conversation was interrupted by an unholy shriek as a girl raced past them, a ball of stitched leather clutched in her hands. Fulke received an impression of flying silver-gilt plaits and a blue dress kilted through her belt to allow for running. Dainty shoes of tan goatskin adorned her flashing feet and she was laughing as she ran.

'Give it back!' Round the corner of the tents pounded three boys in full indignant cry: Fulke's youngest brothers Alain and Richard with their friend Audulf de Bracy.

'Not unless you let me play!' She whirled round, the ball tucked under her arm, and flicked her plaits out of her face. Her flat chest was heaving. A pretty silver brooch adorned the neck opening of her gown and a border of exquisite embroidery spoke of a rank at least as high as Fulke's.

'You're a girl!' Alain's voice rang with self-explanatory indignation.

'That means I'm a match for any turnip-witted boys!'

'You're not. Give me that ball!' Alain launched himself at her. She screamed and made to run, but she was not quite swift enough and the boy brought her down in a flying tackle that sent her sprawling in the grass. But instead of bursting into tears or throwing a tantrum like most little girls that Fulke had encountered, she kept tight hold of the ball and used it to belabour Alain until for his own preservation he was forced to let her go. Richard and Audulf gaped like a couple of landed codfish.

Dishevelled but triumphant, she scrambled to her feet, the ball still firmly in her possession. A long grass stain marred her blue gown and one of the garters holding up her hose had come untied so that there was an unseemly wrinkle of fabric around her skinny left leg.

'Let her play, lads,' Fulke said through his laughter. 'She deserves it.'

The girl flashed a glance at Fulke, obviously seeing him for the first time. He had expected blue eyes to go with hair so blonde, but they were a clear, pale green like expensive glass and fringed by heavy lashes a few shades darker than her hair.

'I don't want to any more,' she said with a regal tilt of her neat little nose and tossed the ball at a red-faced Alain as if it were a crust to a beggar. 'Is he your squire? He has no manners.'

Fulke smothered a grin. 'He's my brother.' At his side, Jean was making small spluttering noises.

She eyed Fulke suspiciously. 'He's a lot younger than you.'

'Eleven years,' Fulke said with a warning glance at Alain who looked as if he was about to explode like a barrel of overheated pitch. 'And you are, my lady?'

She flicked at her plaits again and fixed him with an imperious stare, made all the more touching and amusing by her disorderly appearance. 'I am Maude le Vavasour,' she announced proudly. 'My papa is a great lord and the under-sheriff of Lancashire.'

Fulke's gaze widened. 'Yes, I've met him.'

A nervous look entered her eyes, but she jutted her chin. 'No, you haven't,' she said.

'I have. His name is Robert and he's wearing a red tunic and blue chausses with leg bindings of scarlet braid.' *And he's offering you in marriage to Theobald Walter or anyone else of likely blood who's prepared to pay the fee.* A spark of pity entered Fulke's gaze. She was a child, a skinny, kipper-chested little girl running away with his brother's ball. He couldn't imagine her married to anyone. 'He's a friend of the lord to whom I was squire,' he continued when she said nothing, just stared at him with those strange, clear eyes while shifting awkwardly from leg to leg. 'Does he know you're here?'

She nodded. 'He knows I've gone visiting with my grand-mother.'

Fulke glanced around. 'And where is your grandmother?'

'In there.' Maude pointed to the FitzWarin tent. 'She said I could watch the boys at play — but I wanted to join in.'

'And no blame if you did.' Fulke wondered whether to enter the tent and introduce himself, or beat a hasty retreat. He was certain that le Brun and his two other brothers William and Ivo had made themselves scarce. The notion was borne out by the fact that the dogs had not rushed out to greet him. The excuse of taking them for some exercise and clearing the tent of their size and smell was too fortuitous to miss when his mother had the company of a gossip.

Before he had made up his mind to follow their absent example, however, there was a flurry of tent flap and the sound of female voices raised in farewell. A slender, sharp-featured woman, elegantly gowned, stepped outside, followed by his mother.

'Now,' said the visitor, 'where's that child?' As she spoke, her eyes lit on Maude and her thin features grew pinched with horror. 'By St Mary and the Virgin, what have you been doing?' she gasped, hurrying to the girl with the little mincing steps of someone who has been taught their manners in high-born company. 'I told you not to dirty your dress. What will your father say? You look like a little hoyden!'

'I wanted to play, but the boy was rude and said I couldn't join in because I was a girl.' Indignation filled the child's voice. 'Then when I tried, he chased after me and knocked me down.'

There was no sign of Alain, nor the two other boys, who, at the first indication of trouble, had hastily sloped off.

'Never trust a woman,' Jean muttered out of the side of his mouth. 'Even at this age they're deadly.'

'It's all right, Mathilda, bring her within and we'll soon mend the damage,' soothed Hawise. 'It's not so bad.'

'Her father wants her to make a good impression, especially when he's looking to make a match for her.' Taking her charge's arm in a firm grip as if fearing that the girl would otherwise abscond, the older woman marched her inside the tent and dropped the flap.

'I feel sorry for the lass,' Fulke said wryly, 'but I cannot help wondering if I am a dupe for doing so. I think if my mother had borne any girls, my sister would have been just like that.'

'Thank heaven for small mercies that she didn't, else you'd all be wound tightly round the wench's smallest finger,' Jean said prophetically.

Theobald Walter slowly became aware that he was being addressed. 'What?' he said to his brother.

Hubert gave an exasperated sigh. 'I said you could do worse than to consider le Vavasour's suggestion.'

They were sitting in Theobald's tent, drinking a final cup of wine before retiring. It was late, although before the hour of midnight matins. For the final time, Hubert was wearing the robes of office that marked him Archdeacon of York. On the morrow he would be consecrated Bishop of Salisbury and would don a mantle embroidered with thread of gold and the gilded mitre of his office.

'What, and sue for the hand of a twelve-year-old girl? Do you think I'm a depraved lecher?' Because Hubert's words had caught him on the raw, Theobald's tone rang with indignation.

'No, you lack-wit, sue for her lands!' Hubert snapped. 'She comes with a rich dowry and that's worth a moment of anyone's consideration, even someone as righteous as you! Edlington, Shipley, Hazelwood, Wragby! Whoever takes the girl to wife is going to inherit a fortune!'

Theobald eyed his brother with a feeling very close to distaste. Hubert might be a priest, but he was far from holy. His fiscal acumen was not just renowned, it was notorious. 'She is twelve years old,' he reiterated.

Hubert shrugged. 'What does that have to do with the colour of silver? By the time the daughter is, say, fourteen or fifteen and fit for breeding, you'll hardly be in your dotage, will you?'

Theobald waved his hand. 'Get out before I throw you out,' he snapped, but with impatience rather than acrimony. He was uncomfortably aware that from a family viewpoint, Hubert was speaking a lot of sense.

'I was leaving anyway.' Hubert levered himself to his feet and went to the tent flap, treading lightly for all his height and bulk. 'Think on it, Theo. It's a good offer and if you don't make wedding arrangements soon, you never will. Perhaps of the two of us, you should have been the priest.'

'I don't have the avarice for it,' Theobald growled.

Shaking his head but smiling, Hubert departed.

Theobald glared at the tent flap. The land would indeed be useful since it dovetailed with his own northern estates and interests. But did he really want a bride of twelve? Even fifteen seemed perilously young. Fulke had been fifteen when he had taken him on in the winter before they went to Ireland. He tried to imagine a girl of that age and grimaced. The image was too tempting and too appalling to bear. Leaping from the campstool, he took himself off to his narrow, solitary bed, its sheets made up with the tight precision of a pallet in a monastic cell.

CHAPTER 8

The gold silk of Fulke's surcoat was as nothing compared to the garments in which the great magnates and bishops were decked for the coronation. Vibrant hues of scarlet and blue, encrusted with jewels and embroidery, made the abbey floor glow like a living stained-glass window. So great was the quantity of seed pearls frosting Archbishop Baldwin's cope that it was a wonder he could walk.

Prince John was resplendent in a robe of blue wool the colour of a midnight sky. Small gemstones decorated throat and cuff and an enormous circular brooch of exquisitely worked gold fastened his sable-lined cloak. He looked every inch a prince, but all eyes were on Richard. Even clad in a tunic of plain russet wool, no one could mistake him for anything other than a king. The lack of adornment only emphasised his athletic build and the severe beauty of his bone structure.

With great ceremony, attendants stripped Richard of his tunic, shoes and chausses, to leave him standing in his shirt and braies. The lacings on the shirt were unfastened and the royal chest laid bare, revealing an expanse of virile, ruddy curls. Archbishop Baldwin anointed Richard's head, chest and hands with holy oil, thus conferring on him the divine sanction for his kingship.

The solemnity of the moment, the silence in the great

vault of King Edward's abbey church, sent cold sparkles down Fulke's spine. From the expressions on the faces of those pressing around him, he knew they shared his sense of awe and wonder.

Following the anointing, Richard was dressed in the robes of kingship. A gown of purple silk replaced the russet tunic and instead of plain chausses there came a pair embroidered with tiny golden leopards.

Richard approached the altar and, lifting the crown in both hands, presented it to the Archbishop. Fulke exchanged a glance with his father who quirked a wry eyebrow at Richard's gesture of helping himself to the crown instead of waiting for Baldwin's sanction. The Archbishop maintained a dignified countenance, whatever his private thoughts on the matter. Smoothly he accepted the diadem and placed it upon Richard's brow, thereby binding Richard to his sacred position as ruler of England.

After the coronation came the banquet over which Marjorie and the other kitchen attendants had been slaving for the past three days. As in the abbey, there were no women present, even as servers. The wives and daughters of the men who had attended the crowning were gathered for their own feast in the Rufus Hall, presided over by Queen Eleanor.

Mindful of his knighting on the morrow and the fact that he had to keep vigil in the chapel overnight, Fulke drank sparingly of the wine even though it was excellent and plentiful. It would be a sacrilege to fall into a drunken slumber over his prayers. Even William, who was the most susceptible of the brothers to the pleasures of wine, managed to abstain.

Throughout the feast, nobles approached the high table, bearing gifts for the new King, among them Morys FitzRoger de Powys.

William went as rigid as a dog preparing to fight over a bone. 'How dare he?' he whispered, gripping the haft of his eating knife.

'Peace,' le Brun warned. 'It is his right as much as it is the right of any man present to bear gifts to the new King. Think you if we mar this feast with a brawl that Richard will regard us with favour?'

'But he will let him do homage for Whittington and it will never be ours!' William cried furiously.

'Hold your tongue!' le Brun hissed with equal fury. 'Now is neither the time nor the place. It galls me as much as it does you, but I swallow it. On the morrow, you become a knight. Make sure that you also become a man.'

William glowered but subsided with an angry slouch and flicked his eating knife to one side.

Fulke watched FitzRoger bow and return to his place. Whatever he had said to King Richard, he had not lingered to wheedle favours – probably wise while Coeur de Lion was beset on all sides by men vying for his attention and goodwill. The King was unlikely to remember one minor plea amongst the many.

While William continued to glower murderously at FitzRoger, Fulke's glance swept up the hall to the high dais and rested on Prince John who sat in a position of honour close to the King. Richard had been generous and given his younger brother Isabella of Gloucester to wife, thereby securing John's right to some very rich lands in the south-west, the Marches and the Midlands. John had every reason to look smug, although his expression still managed to contain a whisper of petulance. Then again, Isabella was known to be a raucous shrew with two chins and a smudge of dark hair on her upper lip. Since John's preference had always tended towards flaxen-haired girls with sharp hipbones and taut buttocks, Fulke doubted that the Prince's marriage bed was going to be a place of delight.

John turned his head and his gaze encountered Fulke's. It was as if two blades had clashed together, naked steel striking sparks. Fulke held his ground for a moment then lowered his eyes as etiquette dictated. But not in submission. John made a comment out of the side of his mouth to his nearest companion and the man laughed. Fulke's fists clenched, much as William's had done at the sight of Morys FitzRoger. Carefully he relaxed them and told himself that John was not worth it. But unconsciously, a moment later, he raised his hand and ran his forefinger over the kink in his nose.

Maude le Vavasour sat beside her grandmother in the Rufus Hall and poked at the portion of porpoise on her trencher. It was supposed to be a great delicacy but Maude hated fish of any variety, even when it was surrounded in a sea of pretty green aspic with a decoration of whelk shells. The whelks still occupied their dwellings and silver pins had been provided to drag them out. Maude watched in revolted fascination as her grandmother pried one of the greyish-brown creatures from its lodging, dipped it in a bowl of piquant dressing, and conveyed it to her mouth.

After an interval of chewing, Mathilda dabbed her lips delicately with her linen napkin. 'Delicious,' she pronounced.

Maude shuddered. She wondered how long it would be before the sweetmeats were served. She was very partial to fruits steeped in honey and fried fig pastries, but such fare had not yet been forthcoming and the feast seemed to have gone on for ever.

Queen Eleanor and various noble ladies of the court occupied the high table. The bovine Isabella of Gloucester, recently betrothed to Prince John. Isabelle of Pembroke,

William Marshal's half-Irish bride. Alais of France, supposedly soon to be married to King Richard, although her grandmother had muttered something on that score about pigs roosting in treetops. It was an interesting notion and Maude conjured with the image of a razor-backed hog swaying perilously to and fro in a high elm tree during a gale. You'd have to be careful walking underneath; squirrels and crows were bad enough. She almost giggled, but managed to turn the sound into a cough before she was reprimanded for unseemly behaviour.

Yesterday her grandmother had dealt her a severe scolding about her hoydenish ways, about staining her dress and behaving disgracefully in front of Lady FitzWarin and her sons. 'How will your father ever find you a decent husband if you are going to act in so shameful a manner?' she had demanded. 'If your poor mother could see you, it would make her weep!'

Maude pushed again at the thick slice of porpoise, all urge to laugh dissipating more swiftly than the heat from the congealing food. Her grandmother was trying to make her feel guilty, and succeeding, but beneath the chagrin, anger and resentment simmered. Her mother had always been weeping, either because she was unwell, or because life was too full of challenges and difficulties that she did not have the strength to meet.

Besides, Maude knew that Lady FitzWarin had been neither shocked nor disapproving. There had been a twinkle in her eyes and her mouth had twitched as she fought not to let her amusement show. She had also minimised the fuss over the stained gown, saying that it was a common hazard of childhood play, not an overwhelming disaster. Her grandmother said that Lady FitzWarin was just being polite, but Maude knew differently. Despite the wide age gap, she had recognised a kindred spirit.

Unfortunately, Lady FitzWarin and her younger sons were sitting at a trestle on the other side of the hall. Alain and Richard FitzWarin might be ignorant swine but their age was similar to her own and their company would have helped to alleviate the boredom of this interminable feast. At least people were not assessing them as if they were nags at a horse fair and deciding whether or not they were of good bloodstock. Maude had heard other women with sons whispering to Mathilda, enquiring about her granddaughter's age and dowry and disposition. Maude had stuck her tongue out at the last one, thereby earning herself a furious reproof and the threat of a beating.

Not for the first time, Maude wished that she had been born male. It would solve everything. Her father would have an heir. She would not have to stay in the women's quarters at home cared for by nurses and reluctant relatives, but would already have been sent for fostering as a junior squire in some great household. She swung her legs beneath the trestle, kicking in irritation at the hampering folds of her best blue gown. Male clothes were far more practical. She had often longed to pose with a sword at her hip like her father. The weapon spoke to her of power and rank, of the mystique of the warrior and the voice of authority. It was a power she knew that she would never have. Even Queen Eleanor was not permitted to attend her own son's coronation and feast with him afterwards. It wasn't fair.

'Sit still,' Mathilda snapped irritably, 'and stop playing with your food.'

'I don't like it.'

Her grandmother cast her gaze heavenwards. 'You would if you tried,' she said impatiently. Removing one of the whelks from Maude's trencher, she gouged it from its shell and popped it in her mouth. 'See?'

Revolted, Maude looked away.

The older woman sighed. 'What am I going to do with you?'

It was a question repeated so often and to so little effect that Maude took no notice.

'I need to visit the privy,' she said plaintively.

'Can't you wait?' Mathilda hissed. 'Are you two years old that you cannot hold yourself for a minute?'

'But it's going to be a lot longer than a minute.' Maude wriggled further to emphasise her need.

'Oh, very well,' her grandmother capitulated, 'but don't make a show of yourself and mind that you hurry back.'

Maude left her place at the trestle with the demureness of a gently bred young lady. It was hard, for she was yearning to run, but as her grandmother had pointed out she did not want to call attention to herself. However, she had not the slightest intention of hurrying back. She could plausibly claim that she had lost her way among Westminster's labyrinth of buildings.

She found the privy easily enough and it was the work of seconds to ease her bladder, which was nowhere near as full as she had pleaded. Instead of returning to the women's hall, however, she went towards the White Hall where King Richard was feasting with his magnates, her father among them.

Servants hastened hither and yon with platters, either heaped and steaming or congealed with remains. Maude recognised the ubiquitous portions of porpoise garnished with oysters and whelks. The fishy smell wafted on the evening air. So did the sound of laughter and music from the interior of the hall. She crept nearer, longing for a peek into the masculine world from which she was barred.

Following a man laden with a salver containing an enormous stuffed pike, she entered a world that was astonishingly familiar, but alien too. The voices were louder and more boisterous – the guests mostly being grown men – but the finery of the clothing, the opulent colours crowding the trestles and the formal manner of seating exactly mirrored the women's hall. King Richard sat at the centre of the high table in precisely the same position as Queen Eleanor. His hair blazed like flame and, in his ceremonial robes of white, purple and gold, he was incandescent. The Bishops of the realm strung away from him on either side like jewels on a glittering necklace. Beneath the high table sat the magnates and nobles, all gleaming with silk and hard, yellow gold. If each gathering was a mirror of the other, then the affair in the women's hall was a dull reflection of this peacock brilliance.

Maude stood against the side door, her eyes at full stretch and still not wide enough to take in the gorgeous array. Her small figure was dwarfed by the hall's hugeness and the great gathering it contained.

'I think you are about to be in trouble again, Mistress le Vavasour,' said a rich voice, pleasant with humour.

Maude jumped and switched her scrutiny from the eye-aching scene before her to Alain FitzWarin's older brother. She knew that his name was Fulke because her grandmother and Lady Hawise had been talking about him and how he was to be knighted.

'I went to the privy and I got lost,' she said defensively and tilted her head to gaze up at him. He was much taller than her papa with a wealth of glossy black hair and smiling eyes that in the haze of torchlight were a dark, indeterminate colour. His nose would have been fine and straight, were it not for a misshapen kink to the bridge.

He folded his arms. 'That's not true, is it? You wanted to look, didn't you?'

'And if I did?' The amusement in his eyes annoyed her.

She had the suspicion that she was being mocked, that her action was providing him with entertainment. 'What business is it of yours?'

'None, mistress, since I am leaving to take up my vigil, but others might not be so inclined to turn a blind eye. What will your father do if he sees you?'

'He won't mind.' Despite her brave words, panic flickered beneath Maude's ribs. She could recall with uncomfortable clarity the lash of her father's riding crop on the back of her legs and desired no fresher reminders of the sensation. She glared at Fulke, wanting to fight, wanting to hide and cry.

'You know him best, I suppose, but I doubt that he will welcome you with petting and smiles.' He took her arm. 'Come, Mistress le Vavasour, let me escort you back to the women's hall.'

'I don't need escorting,' she snapped gracelessly and shook him off. 'I can find my own way.'

'I'm sure you can, and I'm also sure that it would be very long and meandering. It is not safe for a girl-child to be wandering around Westminster alone.'

'If I was a boy you wouldn't say that!' Maude cried, feeling belittled.

'No, well, the dangers for boys are different.'

'Fulke? I thought you were going with your brothers to the chapel?'

Maude looked up at an older man, only a little less tall than her tormentor. He had a full head of cropped tawny curls just beginning to thread with silver, and piercing light grey eyes.

'I was, my lord, but then I encountered Mistress le Vavasour snatching a glimpse of the feast.' He spoke her name with a meaningful inflection and a look passed between the two men.

A frown caused two deep creases to appear between the older man's flaxen brows, but his tone was kindly enough when he spoke. 'Child, you should not be here. Do you wish to speak to your father?' He cast a glance around, searching the hall.

Alarmed, Maude shook her head. 'I only wanted to look,' she repeated, but in a voice that was filled with wistful pathos now, not defiance.

The man grunted and tilted her chin on his forefinger, examining her face. Then he looked at Fulke. 'I will take her back to the women. Go to your vigil, lad.'

'You are sure, my lord? It will be no trouble.'

The man nodded. 'I am sure.'

Somewhat reluctantly, she thought, Fulke FitzWarin inclined his head and went on his way.

A servant scurried past with a steaming boar piglet on a silver salver, its crisp-skinned corpse surrounded by a field of green parsley sprigs. The aroma of roast pork hung succulently on the air.

'Come.' The man held out his arm in formal court fashion for her to take.

'I don't know who you are,' Maude said.

'It is a little late to be concerned with propriety,' he answered drily, 'but I will humour you. My name is Theobald Walter, lord of Amounderness, and your father is known to me.'

After a brief hesitation, Maude laid her hand on his sleeve. He was wearing a tunic of bright blue wool and it had been so expertly woven and clipped that it was as soft as thistledown to the touch. His face bore lines and creases like her father's, but they were less harsh and he seemed kindly disposed. Many of the barons in the hall would have gone straight to her father and demand that he administer a sound thrashing.

'You do not resemble your father,' he said curiously, 'except that perhaps you have his way of looking.'

She wrinkled her nose. 'People say I am like my mother, but I'm not.' A hint of rebellion returned to her voice.

'You are angry with that comparison?'

Maude gave a graceless little shrug. She could feel him looking at her, could feel his silent demand for a reply, and she squirmed. 'Mama used to keep to her chamber. Even when she wasn't sick, she acted as if she was. Papa got so angry that he used to shout at her but that only made her worse.' The words emerged like a blurt of ink on a clean page. She had not meant to say them, but he had pulled them from her by the perception of his question.

Lord Walter's eyelids tensed. He quickened his pace. 'Does he shout at you?'

'Sometimes. Not as much while my grandmother's looking after me. She shouts instead.' She looked up at him. He was frowning now and his jaw was tight, emphasising the hollows beneath his cheekbones. 'Why are you asking me these things?'

He did not reply immediately. By the time he did speak, they had reached the women's hall. 'Because no battle captain leaps into an engagement without knowing what he is up against,' he said a trifle grimly.

Maude stared at him blankly. The torchlight outside the hall wavered and guttered, making him look very tall. The gold braid at the throat of his gown and his ornate belt buckle picked up the twinkles of light from the flames. He looked like a figure in a night-lit stained-glass window.

'Go on, child,' he said gently, 'get you within, and make sure you stay. Heaven knows what you might surprise out of the darkness.' He made a shooing motion, not unlike her grandmother.

Maude stared an instant longer, then whirled and ran into the hall, almost colliding with a servant bearing a platter of fried fig pastries. She had arrived just in time for the sweetmeat course.

Her grandmother delivered her a furious scolding, but as Maude nibbled the crisp, golden pastry with its sticky sweet filling, her mind was busy with the matter of Lord Theobald Walter and what a strange, but oddly comforting manner he had.

The chapel of St Peter held the darkness of night transformed by the illumination of hundreds of wax candles and tapers. No daylight made jewels of the stained-glass windows, but the flamelight reflected on every surface like watered gold. Before the high altar, the Confessor's tomb drew the eye to the skill and magnificence of the stone-carver's art.

Fulke bowed his head and softly murmured the words of the *Pater Noster*. Beside him he could hear others whispering too, attempting to stave off sleep as they knelt in vigil on the eve of being knighted. There were a dozen young men, gathered together for the same purpose, his brothers among them. William's gaze was fixed in shining determination on the altar beyond the tomb, his fists clasped one upon the other in fervent prayer. Philip, in contrast, was murmuring quietly to himself, taking the moment in his equable stride.

Fulke gave a self-deprecatory smile. And he was taking the moment by observing others when he should be communing with God and praying for the grace to be worthy of knighthood. He made himself concentrate, and for a time succeeded. When he came to awareness again, he was surprised to see Theobald Walter praying amongst the novice knights, his head bowed and eyes closed with a tightness of concentration at their corners that gave him a pained expression.

It was against custom to speak unless in prayer, and Fulke received the distinct impression that Theobald desired to be ignored. He was not here to bolster the young men in their vigil, but for reasons of his own. Respecting the silence, Fulke said nothing and pretended that he was unaware of Theobald's presence. He focused on the cross gleaming upon the altar and the world narrowed down to a shining cruciform of gold. When he looked round again, Theobald had gone.

The interminable hours passed. Fulke's eyes ached with staring and burned for want of sleep. William's head kept sagging towards his clasped hands and he would suddenly jerk, his eyelids fluttering as if striving to hold aloft a great weight. At one point, Fulke could have sworn he saw Whittington keep floating in the air before the altar. A woman stood in one of the window embrasures, her silver-blonde hair tugged outwards by the wind like a rippling silk banner. He could not see her face, but he received the impression of an allure so strong that it pierced him to the core, melting his heart and loins. As he watched, she climbed through the embrasure, impossibly narrow though it was, and for a moment stood on the ledge, poised between air and ground. He wanted to call out, to stop her from throwing herself that last measure, but as he drew breath, she flung out her arms and he saw that her dark-coloured cloak was in fact a pair of wide, leathery wings. When she leaped, they bore her easily, the light shining through the membranes. She circled the keep once, then flew away until she was naught but a small dot in the distance.

Fulke snapped to awareness, a cry locked in his throat and the hair prickling at his nape. His heart was thundering and there was a fading pulse of sensation at his crotch. Yet he was not aware of having slept. His eyes were so dry with staring that they had started to water. Visions on the eve of knighthood were viewed as prophetic, but if so, what had it meant?

Fulke had little time to puzzle over the event, for daylight was finally greying the east window and attendants were arriving to take the postulants away to receive the ritual bath and donning of fresh raiment in preparation for the knighting ceremony.

Fulke stepped into a steaming barrel tub, and the last vestiges of the disturbing image were washed away as he was deluged by a jugful of hot water borne by a squire.

Maude screwed up her face and yelped as her grandmother yanked on her hair.

'Oh, stand still, child, it's nothing,' Mathilda said irritably. 'I'll never be done if you don't stop wriggling.' She gripped the half-woven braid and continued to plait it tightly. 'You must look your best for today.'

'Why?' Maude clenched both fists and teeth in an effort not to flinch.

'That is for your father to tell you.' Reaching the end of the braid, Mathilda secured it with a silver fillet. 'He has some very important news,' she said as she set about a similar torture on the left-hand side.

Maude frowned. It must be news that concerned her, or why else should her neat appearance matter so much? Unless her father had been given a huge barony by the King and she was to sit at the high table.

'Is my father to be honoured by the King?' She tried to look at her grandmother, but the tight grip on her hair as Mathilda plaited the braid prevented her.

'Now why on earth should you think that, child?'

'Because you're making me dress up like one of those marchpane subtleties at the feast last night.'

'Don't be impertinent.' Mathilda tugged and wove, her lips tightly pursed. 'Don't you want to look like a beautiful lady?'

Maude pulled a face but withheld the retort that not if it meant having the hair twisted on her scalp until it was almost torn from its roots.

Her grandmother threaded the second fillet on to the braid. 'Your father will tell you everything as soon as he arrives.' She stepped back to consider the finished result. 'Holy Virgin, Maude, you look just like your mother when she was your age.' Suddenly the older woman's voice wobbled with emotion and tears filled her eyes.

Maude scowled and shuffled her feet. People were always telling her that she resembled her mother and she hated it.

'Look at me.' Her grandmother laughed tremulously, and wiped away her tears on the side of her hand. 'I'm an old fool.'

The tent flap parted, admitting Robert le Vavasour. A brisk September breeze had lifted the strands of hair he so carefully cultivated over the balding patch on the crown of his head. His eyes were bright with pleasure and there was a smile on his lips. Taking Maude by the shoulders, he turned her round for inspection. 'You've arrayed her proudly, madam,' he said to Mathilda. 'She looks like a princess.' He gave a stiff nod of acknowledgement to his former mother-in-law. Maude knew that they were not fond of each other, that it was only for her sake that her grandmother had agreed to look after her at court.

Mathilda de Chauz smiled tepidly. 'She has taken a notion into her head that the reason she is to look her best is because you are set to be granted an earldom by the King.'

He threw back his head and laughed, a bitter edge to

the sound. 'To be granted that I'd need a fortune. The most I can hope to buy is a shrievalty.'

'And suitably reimburse yourself from the revenues,' Mathilda said sweetly.

Apart from a scowl, le Vavasour ignored her; still holding Maude's shoulders, he stooped to speak to his daughter. 'I have some good news for you, sweeting. Late last night I received an offer of marriage for you from none other than Theobald Walter, lord of Amounderness, and I have decided to accept. You are to exchange pledges of betrothal this morning in the chapel after the knighting ceremonies.' He gave her a smile that was supposed to reassure, but only made her want to run away. 'Of course, there will be no wedding until you have grown a little more. There would be no point now, and you still have much to learn before you can run Lord Walter's household.' He pinched her cheek encouragingly.

Maude stared at her father. She felt like a puppy, dragged from a corner and thrown in front of the wolves.

'Well, child, have you nothing to say?'

Mutely, Maude shook her head. She looked at her grandmother, but Mathilda's expression was so rigidly controlled it was as if the tearful emotion of a moment since had never been.

'It is a fine match,' her father enthused. 'His uncle is the great Ranulf Glanville and his brother the Bishop of Salisbury. Theobald Walter is to be granted lands, privileges and a shrievalty. His lands march close to ours and we have interests in common. So much the better if our families are bound in marriage.' He turned her head on his palm, forcing her to look at him, and his tone grew stern. 'Now, I expect you to do your best for me. No sulks and tantrums. You are a Vavasour and you will bear that name with pride. I'll not have Theobald Walter reneging on this match because you act like a sulky infant. Do you understand?'

'Yes, Papa,' Maude whispered, her pupils so dilated that they almost masked the clear, pale-green iris.

'Good.' Her father nodded, clearly satisfied, and opened the tent flap. 'Come, we do not want to be late.'

Maude felt as if her legs were made of melting lead. How could they bear her up and carry the burden of her family name without stumbling? When she did not move, her father made an impatient sound and grabbed her arm, drawing her with him. Unresisting, numb with astonishment and shock, she followed him into the bright, brisk morning.

The abbey was not as packed as it had been for the coronation, but still a substantial number crowded into the nave to witness the knighting ceremony. There were women present today and the atmosphere, although formal, was more relaxed than the previous day.

Fulke's sword lay across the altar beside the swords of his brothers and the other nine young men who were to receive their knighthood from King Richard. Fulke's pattern-welded blade was a gift from Theobald Walter. The gilded belt and scabbard had been furnished from Lambourn's wool clip. His father had laughed, saying ruefully that while he did not have any daughters to drain his wealth in dowries, furnishing his sons' helms was an expense almost as ruinous. However, when knighthood came at the hands of Richard, Coeur de Lion, in the great abbey church of Westminster itself, it was an event worth every last fleece in family prestige.

Archbishop Baldwin blessed the swords with holy water, asking God that their owners might use them justly in defence of churches, widows and orphans and as a scourge against all evil-doers. Royal attendants girded the swordbelts around the waists of the postulants and each young man was presented with a pair of gilded spurs.

Richard, who had been standing a little to one side, now came forward. His eyes were bleary from the pageantry and feasting of the previous day, but his hair still glowed like spun gold and he wore the royal crown of England on his brow.

The postulants knelt before him, heads bowed. Fulke, first in line, gazed at the King's shoes. They were delicately embroidered in gold thread, the workmanship sitting somewhat at odds with the enormous size of Richard's feet.

There was a soft hiss of steel against fleece-lined scabbard as Richard drew the polished steel blade and laid it first upon Fulke's right shoulder, then his left.

'Fulke, son of Fulke, be thou a knight,' Richard declared in a ringing baritone and, sliding the sword back into the sheath, bade him rise. Facing the King, Fulke braced himself for the accolade, the final act that would confer knighthood upon him. By tradition it was a hefty clout to the shoulder, a symbol of the last blow a postulant would ever receive without the right to answer back as a full-fledged warrior. When it came, Fulke reeled because Richard did not pull the force of the blow, and the bright blue eyes were fierce.

While Fulke recovered, Richard moved on down the line, drawing the sword, speaking the words, striking vigorously. William had planted his feet wide in anticipation and when his turn came, he swayed at the accolade, but remained firmly grounded. Richard acknowledged the bravery with a nod and a faint smile that made William flush with pleasure.

Following the ceremony and the celebration of mass, the brothers turned to receive the hugs and congratulations of their family. Hawise was sniffing into a kerchief. Ivo wanted to look at the spurs and the sword and was sternly warned not to mar the steel with sweaty fingerprints. Alain demanded to know if the accolade had hurt.

'Not much,' Fulke said, 'but I would hate to face the King blade on blade in battle.'

'Wouldn't you like to fight with him on your side though, blade *by* blade,' said William, the glory still shining in his deep brown eyes.

'If you could keep up with him,' Philip said, rubbing his abused shoulder.

Theobald Walter came forward to congratulate Fulke and his brothers but after a moment took Fulke to one side. 'I have a boon to ask of you.' He clasped his hands together and wiped them one over the other, plainly ill at ease.

'Name it and it is yours,' Fulke said, his voice full of pleasure and high spirit.

Theobald gave a pained smile. 'You had best hear what it is first: I want you to stand witness to my betrothal to Maude le Vavasour.'

Fulke's eyed widened and his lips silently repeated the name.

'It is not what is seems,' Theobald said hastily, hot colour flushing his face and throat. 'I am not an old goat suddenly taken with lust for a lass not yet into womanhood.'

'I know that, sir.' Fulke continued to stare in disbelief. 'When I served as your squire, I sometimes wondered if you were human, all the temptations you resisted. Indeed, behind your back, we used to call you "the monk".'

'I know you did, and it amused me. Youths are easily led by their loins. Twenty years on it grows easier to resist the tug – so to speak.'

Fulke rubbed his palm over his freshly barbered jaw. 'So, does Maude le Vavasour have vast lands or important family connections?' He was thoroughly curious to know what would drive a confirmed bachelor into a match with a girl who was almost young enough to be his granddaughter. Although he had quickly agreed with Theobald that lust was not the motive, he could not help remembering how Theobald had offered to return the lass to the women's hall last night.

'Not vast lands, but large enough and they march next to mine. Her father and I have interests in common.'

Fulke nodded expressionlessly, but something of what he was thinking must have percolated through, for Theobald bared his teeth.

'Taking a wife has always been something I said I would do one day when I found the right woman and the right lands. Well, I'm four and forty now and still waiting. The girl's dowry is more than acceptable, as are her connections. If I ignore le Vavasour's offer he will sell her else-where and I might not approve of the man who becomes my neighbour by right of her dowry.' He looked at Fulke, his gaze hard and clear. 'I am not the kind of man who enjoys unripe fruit,' he said. 'I can give the lass the time she needs to grow into a woman and I will treat her well. You have seen how it is with some men, Fulke. They stroke their hunting dogs and beat their wives. The lass touched a tenderness in me last night, and I want to protect her.'

Fulke said nothing, feeling intensely uncomfortable.

'It matters to me that you give your consent to be a witness without a shred of doubt in my honour.' Theobald laid his hand on Fulke's sleeve to emphasise the point. 'You are a new-fledged knight and you have promised to protect the weak and stand firm for justice. I want that integrity at my betrothal.'

Fulke was embarrassed at the turn his thoughts had taken and the way that Theobald had seen straight through them. He was also ashamed that he should harbour such doubts about his former mentor, a man whose honour and moral code had always been impeccable.

'I am not worthy.' He clasped Theobald's hand. 'But I will stand witness, gladly.'

Hubert Walter, Bishop of Salisbury, was waiting in a side chapel with Maude le Vavasour, her grandmother, her father, and a small knot of witnesses. Fulke almost turned round and walked out again when he saw that one of the witnesses was a smiling Prince John, but Theobald propelled him forward, the flat of his hand firmly pressed into Fulke's twitching shoulder blade.

'For better or worse, he is my liege lord for Amounderness and my Irish lands,' Theobald muttered. 'It would be a grave discourtesy not to ask him to stand witness.'

Fulke continued to walk, but his spine was rigid and if he had been a dog, his hackles would have stood on end.

John was standing beside his illegitimate half-brother William Longsword. The Prince glanced up as Fulke entered the chapel and his face darkened. However, suddenly he smiled, his eyes meeting Fulke's in open malice. 'You *are* making an auspicious occasion of your betrothal, Theo,' he drawled. 'A prince, a bishop, a bastard, a child, and Parsifal the fool who became a knight – all gathered in one holy place.'

Fulke curbed the urge to retort. They were, as John said, in a holy place and present to witness a betrothal. Beginning a verbal brawl would *not* be auspicious in the least. 'I am pleased to be of service,' he said lightly, 'and flattered at your reference, Your Highness, since Parsifal was the foremost of Arthur's knights in purity.'

John gave Fulke a narrow-eyed scowl, then ignored him as if he was of no consequence.

Bishop Hubert raised his arms, spread them, exposing

the gorgeous embroidery in his cope, and bade Maude and Theobald stand before him.

Feigning indifference to John, Fulke fixed his gaze on the couple. Theobald was a tall man, active and powerfully built. Maude came up to his armpit and his size and vigour made her seem by contrast as delicate as a faery child. Against the deep blue wool of her best gown, her little face was bleached of colour. White skin, pale hair braided as tight as a stay rope, eyes wide and glassy with fear.

She gave her responses in a faint but clear voice, repeating the words that Hubert Walter put in her mouth, holding out her small hand so that Theobald could engulf it in his tough, swordsman's grip whilst Hubert wound his stole over and around the link. Now they were bound together almost as closely as a husband and wife. The union could not be put asunder except by appeal to the Church.

Theobald sealed the promise by the bestowal of a ring set with a square-cut amethyst. Since the betrothal had been agreed in a hurry, there had not been time to have one made and although the ring had been a snug fit on Theobald's little finger, it was still too large for Maude.

Everything was too big for her, Fulke thought, watching her leave the chapel with her grandmother, her head modestly lowered in contemplation of the loose gleaming gold.

'Congratulations, Theo,' John declared, giving Theobald a hearty slap on the back. 'You'll enjoy teaching her to be a wife.' He winked salaciously.

Theobald's smile was strained. 'I am not intending to wed until she is ready,' he said.

'Sometimes women don't know when they're ready. You have to show them.' John gave him another slap and went on his way. William Longsword spread his hands in a gesture that apologised for his half-brother, and hastened after him.

Theobald stood for a moment, opening and closing his fists. So too did Fulke, until he had composed himself sufficiently to go forward and offer his own congratulations.

Theobald accepted them with a preoccupied expression. 'Have I done the right thing?' he asked.

Fulke did not reply. It was not his place, and besides, he was not sure that Theobald would like the answer.

CHAPTER 9

Normandy, May 1193

Under a flawless azure sky, the array of brightly coloured pavilions glowed like a field of exotic flowers: red and yellow, blue and green and white. Tournaments in early summer always attracted hordes of young men, drawn by the lure of sport and the prospect of achieving fame and fortune. Already the field was full of activity as jousters sparred with one another or took practice runs at the quintain.

It was the fourth season that Fulke and his brothers had crossed the Narrow Sea to follow the tourney circuit. For four months they could hone their warrior skills, practise their horsemanship and keep their bodies tough and lean.

King Richard had vanished during his return from the crusade. Rumour, abetted by Prince John, said that Richard was dead, likely murdered by brigands, but without hard fact, no one was going to yield John the power he so craved. There had been spats and small skirmishes, but neither side was yet prepared for all-out war. Fulke le Brun had kept his head down and minded his own business, prudently sending his sons of fighting age away from the bickering factions.

Mounting his horse and gathering the reins, Fulke smiled to think that his father had viewed sporting at tourneys as a safer occupation than becoming embroiled in the dispute at home. Already this season, William had suffered two broken fingers and lost a front tooth. And Philip was using his second string destrier because his best horse had been kicked in a fight and was lame. Still, they had won several useful ransoms and their reputation had grown over the seasons to the point where they were spoken of with respect in most quarters and awe in some. Raw novices were warned not to go up against the FitzWarin brothers unless they wanted to lose all save the modesty of their shirts.

Their success was due in part to their individual fighting abilities, but what made them so formidable was Fulke's leadership. They were a cohesive team, not individuals fighting for their own glory. Fulke positioned each man to make the best of his skills. Thus William was always at the forefront of the attack because it would have been impossible to ask him to bide his time and keep a calm head. Baldwin de Hodnet, who was strong and large-boned, usually joined him, leaving Stephen de Hodnet and Philip, lighter but steadier, to follow through. Fulke's role was to lend his aid wherever it was needed and keep a weather eye on the overall position.

Slinging his shield on its long strap behind his back Fulke touched his heels to his destrier's flanks. Ivo joined him, the FitzWarin wolf banner fluttering on the haft of his spear. Still a squire, but on the verge of knighthood, he always rode at Fulke's left shoulder where he could both protect and be protected.

Together the brothers trotted out to warm up their horses and were joined by the other members of the group, William looking slightly the worse for wear after a night's carousing.

'Sure you're fit to fight?' Fulke asked.

'Course I am!' William snapped. 'Have I ever failed you on the field?'

'No, but I wouldn't want you to do so now for wine-fuddled wits.'

'Don't lecture me. I won't let you down.'

'It's not wine that's fuddled his wits,' grinned Baldwin de Hodnet, pointing at a telltale red bruise on William's throat.

Fulke fought to keep a straight face and act the stern commander. 'Well, he shouldn't keep his wits in his braies,' he said acidly. 'Any of a dozen women could find them there and addle them beyond repair.'

'Lead me to them this instant!' Stephen guffawed.

Fulke could see that the conversation was likely to degenerate. 'You need money first,' he said, 'and to earn the sort of money to attract that kind of attention, you have to capture at least two ransoms. Besides,' he added, 'the only thing that's getting stiff between my legs just now is my horse.'

The remark had the required effect. Amid good-natured jeers and whistles, Fulke's small band rode off to warm up.

There were five Flemish knights on the field, intent on making a name for themselves with their heavy horses and equally heavy mail – mercenaries looking for an enterprising Norman lord to employ them. There were many such soldiers on the circuit since the return of the crusaders.

William, as usual, was all for surging into the fray, but although Fulke allowed him to cry a challenge, he restrained him from wading in. 'They're heavier and stronger,' he warned. 'Don't engage for all you're worth or else I'll be ransoming you. Draw their blows, lead them on until they tire.'

William fretted his horse. 'I know what to do; you don't need to lecture.'

Fulke swallowed his irritation. 'Go,' he said tersely. 'And mind yourself.'

William spurred his mount. Fulke directed Baldwin to follow William and peeled off to the right taking Ivo. To the left came Philip and Stephen.

The five Flemings drew up in battle formation and, stirrup to stirrup, levelled their lances. Unhurriedly Fulke slipped his shield on to his left shoulder and threaded forearm and fist through the short straps. Blaze sidled and the bridle rubbed lines of foam on the slick liver-chestnut hide. 'Steady,' Fulke murmured, 'steady.'

The Flemish commander yelled a battle cry, the sound emerging somewhat indistinctly through his full-face helm. His men spurred their destriers and William shot forward like a bolt from a crossbow, roaring his own response.

'Fitz Warin!'

Clods of soil flew from pounding stallion hooves and the ground shuddered beneath the force of the charge. Judging his moment, Fulke echoed his brother's shout and spurred forwards.

The sport was rough and hard, but no worse than Fulke had expected. William took the Fleming on the far right, neatly inserting the blunted point of his spear between the man's fashionable crusader surcoat and mail hauberk. It was a speciality of William's, a move he had practised to perfection and the unfortunate Fleming was tipped neatly out of the saddle. William could not sustain the weight and had to relinquish his spear, but since the latter was no good for close fighting anyway, it didn't matter. As the mercenary hit the ground on a winded grunt, William laughed and drew his sword.

What the Flemish knights possessed in weight and power, they lacked in speed and manoeuvrability. By the time the fallen man's companion had turned to deal with William, it was too late. A single clash of blade on shield was all he managed before he was jabbed in the ribs by the blunt spear of another knight sporting a close-cropped auburn beard.

'Your life is mine, yield,' declared Philip cheerfully before ducking under the blow of an incoming mace and galloping out of reach. When Philip's victim chose to ignore the rules of combat and continue to fight, Philip repeated the move. And this time he did not have to duck and retreat because Fulke had neatly unhorsed the third man and confiscated the mace.

The rest was sheer pleasure. Fulke stood back and let his brothers play until the Flemings had all yielded with varying degrees of grudging reluctance.

In high spirits Fulke and his companions returned to their camp, discussing each blow and countermove as they rode. William was more than full of himself, but Fulke allowed him to prattle, recognising his brother's need to release his tension. Besides, he had done well and worked as part of a team instead of tearing off on his own, as was his weakness.

William joined Fulke, his eyes gleaming. 'I told you.'

'Yes, you did,' Fulke acknowledged generously. 'Next time, you can decide the tactics in order to gain some experience.'

William's look of pleasure became tempered with apprehension, making Fulke smile. He suspected that William enjoyed playing wild because he knew his excesses would be regulated by others more responsible. However, being accountable for himself was an entirely different prospect.

Dismounting at their horse line, Fulke handed Blaze to Ivo and headed towards their pavilion.

'Tell your fortune for a penny, m'lord.' A swarthy, black-bearded figure stepped across Fulke's path. He was strangely clad in a loose-fitting tunic and even baggier chausses. There was a sickle-shaped knife in his belt, and an embroidered cloak was fastened across his shoulders by a loop of gold braid. A turban of bright red silk was wrapped round his head as a hat.

'I have no need of fortune tellers,' Fulke said gruffly, and gestured the stranger aside. 'I'll carve my own future.' He was used to being accosted by all manner of hucksters, peddlers, chirugeons and whores, determined to make a living out of the knights who frequented the tourney route.

'That you will, sir, but be not too hasty to dismiss me out of hand. I can be of great use to you.'

'Indeed?' Fulke raised a sceptical eyebrow. 'For how much?'

'A short while of your time; a meal at your fire.'

Fulke studied the man, tempted to kick him out of the way, but stayed by a puzzling sense of familiarity. 'Tell me something then,' he challenged. 'Prove yourself.'

The fortune teller rubbed his black beard with a lean, brown hand. A gold ring flashed, proclaiming that his trade, whatever its vagaries, was a profitable one. 'That scar on the bridge of your nose was caused in a fight with Prince John of England over a game of chess.'

Fulke refused to be impressed. 'That is a tale known to many,' he said loftily.

'It was a night in December and it was sleeting. You dined on roast boar in the castle kitchens in the company of Theobald Walter's squire, Jean de Rampaigne.'

Fulke's gaze narrowed. 'How did you . . . you rogue!' he cried, and pouncing upon the 'fortune teller', embraced him ferociously. 'Christ, you had me convinced for a moment!'

'Then I have failed.' The white teeth flashed. 'I was hoping to keep you convinced all night!'

Fulke thrust Jean away and looked him up and down. His face was thinner and the rich black beard and moustache disguised its contours. 'And so you would if you had not made mention of your own name! What are you doing here and dressed in such garb? No. Be seated and have some wine.' He gestured to one of the wooden stools set around the banked cooking fire. 'Never mind fortunes, you can sing for your dinner once I've shed the weight of this hauberk. There'll be no more bouts until the heat goes out of the sky.'

'You wouldn't call this hot if you had fried in your mail on the road to Arsuf under Muslim attack,' Jean said.

'Likely not,' Fulke agreed wryly. 'And for small mercies I am glad.'

Jean turned to greet Fulke's brothers and the de Hodnets as they too arrived in camp and set about stripping off their accoutrements. Curiosity and suspicion quickly turned to dclight as they realised their guest's identity.

William wanted to know everything about the crusade, each blow and tactic, each moment of heroic suffering.

'It was not a game like this tourney is a game,' Jean said with a contemptuous gesture at the field beyond. 'When I set out I was a boy like you and I thought it was. Then I watched Ranulf de Glanville die of a bloody flux at the siege of Acre. Never before have I seen living flesh melt down to the bones of mortality in so short and foul a time. He was a man who set great store by his dignity and yet he died with none.' Jean cupped his hands around the horn of wine he had been given, cradling it to his breast as if for comfort. 'I watched our soldiers kill three thousand hostages when Saladin broke his pledge. Three thousand.' He stared round the circle of listeners, holding each man's gaze for an uncomfortable moment before moving on. 'Can you imagine what that kind of butchery looks or smells like in the burning heat? Can you feel the tragedy and the waste of it all in no matter whose name?'

There was an uneasy silence, no one sure how to respond, and all disturbed by the notions and images that Jean had loosed upon them.

'Mayhap some day I will compose rousing songs to honour the dead, both ours and theirs,' Jean said with a grimace. 'I will sing the praises of Coeur de Lion as the greatest general since Alexander. I will tell stories of glory and heroism to quicken the blood and fill the eyes, but not now. I could not bear it.'

Fulke refilled Jean's cup. The young man drank and a humourless smile twisted his lips. 'Jesu, I'm sorry. I was the one lusting to go with King Richard after all, and you are forbearing not to remind me of the fact.'

Fulke acknowledged the remark with raised shoulders. 'And you are the one who has gained in wisdom and experience,' he said tactfully. 'I can see that it is hard for you to speak of that time but will you not tell us what you are doing here disguised as a foreign fortune teller?'

'I'm acting as a messenger for Hubert Walter. I'm on my way to him now from the court of the German Emperor. As to the disguise . . .' Jean plucked at his over-sized tunic. 'There are certain factions who would give their eye teeth to intercept any messages between Richard and Lord Hubert. But they won't be watching for a tourney huckster.'

'No, but you look outlandish enough for a local baron to cast you in his prison or punish you for a heretic,' Fulke pointed out dubiously.

Jean flashed a true grin. 'I admit I am a little over-dressed, but that was for your benefit. Usually I travel as a charcoal burner or peasant.' Unwinding the turban, he raked his hands through his flattened hair and gave his scalp a thorough scratch. 'I heard about this tourney and I had a notion that some of you might be here. Seems I'm in luck.' He looked around the circle. 'If any of you have a mind, an armed escort would be useful for the last part of my journey.'

'Nothing would please me more,' Fulke responded. He glanced to the side. 'Will, I said I would give you the responsibility of leadership. Now you can have it while I accompany Jean to England.'

William inhaled to protest, then obviously thought the better of it and closed his mouth. Riding escort was a dull duty when compared to the hurly burly of the tourney, and even if he did go, he would be subordinate to Fulke. His bluff had just been very neatly called.

Fulke turned to Jean. 'Now, or the morrow?'

'The sooner the better.'

Fulke rose from his stool. 'I'll put my mail back on then,' he said with resignation. 'You can borrow my spare gambeson.' Gesturing Stephen to arm up, he told Ivo to ready the horses.

Jean followed Fulke into the tent. 'Aren't you going to ask what the message is?'

'It's none of my business.' Fulke rummaged in a chest and produced a thickly quilted tunic. The unbleached linen was marked with black streaks from being worn beneath a greased hauberk and there was a tear under one arm, allowing some of the wool stuffing to poke out, but it was still in serviceable condition.

'It is, since you are putting yourself out to accommodate me.' Jean took the gambeson and with Fulke's help wriggled his way into it. 'The terms of the King's release have been agreed and although he has yet to be set free, that moment will not be long in coming. I've been sent ahead by Chancellor Longchamps with the news. For the nonce, it is not common information, although it soon will be. Philip of France has his spies at the German court. When he learns that Richard is to be set free, he will not hesitate to warn John and, between them, they will try to prevent it from happening. The news needs to reach Hubert Walter first so that he can act on it with advantage.'

'I take it from all that you have said that Hubert Walter is more than just the Bishop of Salisbury these days,' Fulke said drily.

'Richard has given him the powers of a Justiciar and entrusted him with guarding the realm and raising a ransom.' Jean tugged the gambeson into place and took the spare belt and scabbarded hunting knife that Fulke handed him. 'Also Richard has promised to sponsor Hubert for the post of Archbishop of Canterbury.'

Fulke uttered a low whistle and looked impressed.

'It was Hubert who held the troops together at Acre after the deaths of Ranulf de Glanville and Archbishop Baldwin. He's been with Richard every step of the way and not faltered once.'

'It is strange that Hubert Walter is so loyal in Richard's service but that Theobald cleaves to John,' Fulke commented as he donned his mail shirt.

'What else can he do? He is beholden to John for his Irish lands and he holds Lancaster Castle at the Prince's pleasure. Being John's man does not mean that he is John's creature,' Jean retorted.

Scowling, Fulke jumped up and down to jolt the iron mesh over his body until the split hem swished at his knees. 'No, and that makes it even harder to understand.' He donned his surcoat and latched his swordbelt with rapid, jerky movements that betrayed his irritation.

'He has given his oath and he is a man of honour.' John raised a forefinger in warning. 'Richard has no children. His brother is likely to be the next King, and then we must all give our oaths. I think my lord Walter bears that in mind also. Biting the hand that feeds is never wise.'

'Then that makes me a lack-wit immediately,' Fulke said curtly and, settling the sword at his hip, strode outside into the burning summer heat.

CHAPTER 10

Lancaster Castle, Summer 1193

The comb and mirror were exquisitely carved out of cream ivory set with tiny garnets and pearls. The mirror in its dainty hinged case was so rare an item that it was the first time Maude had ever seen one, although she knew they existed from listening to troubadours' songs of fair ladies admiring themselves as they dwelt in their sweetly scented bowers.

Maude gazed briefly at her image in the glass. She had sufficient vanity to acknowledge the pleasing effect of her thick silver-gilt hair and clear green eyes, and sufficient common sense to know that her looks were the only facet of her life that mirrored the beguilement of a story.

It was her wedding day and the mirror and comb were presents from the guest of honour, Prince John. Maude knew that he had not come for the simple pleasure of celebrating the nuptials of one of his vassals. With all the unrest and rumour concerning King Richard, the Prince was here to bolster Theobald's loyalty to his own cause.

John had arrived late the previous evening. Since Maude had already retired, the gift had been brought to her chamber this morning, together with other bride gifts. There was a cloak brooch and a veil of the sheerest aquamarine silk, whip-hemmed in thread of gold, from Theobald; and from her father, a belt sewn with seed pearls and finished with strap ends of solid gold. The men themselves had stayed away as tradition dictated, and were in another chamber of the keep, preparing for the marriage.

Maude gently closed the mirror and set it down on her coffer. Her hand shook slightly and her stomach gave a sudden flutter. She was not ready to be a wife, but time had run out.

'You had your first bleed more than a year ago,' her father had said brusquely when informing her that the date of the marriage had been set for the midsummer feast of St John. 'Theobald Walter said he wanted to wait until you were old enough to breed, and you're more than old enough now.'

Today she was to marry a man three times her age. That she liked him, that he was kinder than her father and would be a good provider, weighed little in the balance when she thought of her own part of the bargain. Nine months from now she could be a mother. Indeed, her father expected it of her. Nine months from now she could be dead. The thought galvanised her to her feet, but there was nowhere to go, except back and forth across the chamber like a trapped animal, and she refused to show her anxiety to the other women guests crowding the room.

Immediately her grandmother was at her, smoothing creases from the panels of the costly teal-coloured gown, pinning a stray wisp of hair into place, adjusting the marriage chaplet of dog roses and musk-scented lilies twined with greenery and silver wire. Maude bore the fiddling and primping with rapidly fraying patience. She dug her well-tended nails into her palms and clenched her teeth, knowing that she was on the verge of screaming.

'Let the girl be, Mathilda.' Hawise FitzWarin detached herself from the other women. 'Can't you see that she's wound as tightly as an overspun thread?'

Mathilda de Chauz inhaled to retort, but Hawise stole the space. 'You have already worked wonders. Whatever you do, you cannot make her look more perfect than she does now . . . save perhaps that she needs more colour in her face.' Hawise took Maude's light cloak from the bench where it was draped. 'Come, child, fresh air will do you a world more good than pinching your cheeks or dusting them with red powder.'

'But the men will be here at any moment!' Mathilda protested.

Hawise cast a glance beyond the open window to the courtyard below. 'They're not coming yet,' she said reasonably. 'You don't want her fainting in the middle of the wedding mass, do you?' Not giving Mathilda time to answer, Hawise whisked Maude out of the room and down the turret stairs. Behind them came sounds reminiscent of a disturbed hen house, rapidly fading as they descended.

'I remember being driven half-mad on my own wedding day by sage advice and fussing,' Hawise said sympathetically. 'My hair would not lie tamely beneath my veil and you would have thought it the end of the world to hear the other women.' She smiled. 'I did not give a bean for their opinions because I knew that even if I came to the altar barefoot in my shift with my hair in eldritch tangles, le Brun would still take me.'

They emerged from the tower into glorious sunshine. Between the service buildings, the sward was as green as emeralds and the smell of roasting meats for the marriage feast carried on the breeze. Maude's stomach was hollow with hunger and nauseous with fear. She swallowed a retch.

'I know that Theobald Walter is not the man of your choosing,' Hawise murmured, 'but he is decent and honourable and you will not be ill treated.'

Maude compressed her lips, then forced herself to speak. 'I know that, my lady.'

'And for the moment it makes no difference.' With an understanding nod Hawise led Maude to the peace of the small garden tucked against the corner of the keep wall.

'What was . . . what was it like on your wedding night?' Maude blurted out as Hawise opened the gate of oak laths leading to a series of herb- and flowerbeds, already heavy with scent in the mid-morning heat.

'What was mine has no bearing on what will be yours.' Hawise refastened the gate behind them. 'Fulke le Brun was my father's choice, but I wanted him desperately and there was less than ten years between us.' She looked sharply at Maude. 'Has your grandmother said anything to you on the matter?'

Maude shook her head. 'Only that I must be led by my husband and do my duty.' Her skin flushed crimson. 'I know what that duty is, my lady, I am not entirely ignorant.'

'Only enough to be afraid,' Hawise said shrewdly and began to walk amongst the beds and borders, drawing Maude with her. 'You ask about my wedding night. I would be lying if I said there was no discomfort, but the pleasure more than compensated.' She laughed softly. 'I think that Fulke was more worried than I, because he was afraid of hurting me.' She lightly squeezed Maude's shoulder. 'Theobald Walter is no green boy to cause you pain through clumsiness or lack of consideration. This may not be a love match, but I promise that you will be cherished. Lord Walter cares for those who belong to him. My eldest son was a squire in his household for several years and could not have had a better mentor.'

Maude clung to the positive note in the older woman's voice. She had to believe that it was going to be all right, that her life within marriage was going to be better than the one she led beneath the strictures of her father's roof. It wasn't just the wedding night that filled her with apprehension. It was the anxiety of what might follow.

The gate latch clicked and the women turned. Standing in the entrance was Theobald Walter himself. His tawny, greying curls had been trimmed and combed back so that they resembled rippled water. The badger-striped beard hugged his jawline which was still strong and taut. In honour of his marriage, his lean frame was clad in a long court tunic of deep blue wool and his belt was tooled with gold leaf.

'The women said that you had gone outside for a moment,' he said with a husky catch in his voice. 'I thought I would find you here. It is the most peaceful part of the keep.'

Maude gazed at him and the initial jolt of panic she had felt at his appearance subsided to a queasy flutter.

'Are you ready to come to chapel, my lady?' He held out his seamed, war-scarred hand. It was trembling slightly and Maude realised that he was probably as nervous as she was.

'Yes,' Maude whispered and, leaving Hawise's side, went forward to put her own hand, and her trust, in Theobald's.

The wedding ceremony itself was an affair not much longer than the betrothal. Theobald pledged his life to Maude as she pledged him hers in the keep's small but elegantly appointed chapel. He placed a gold ring set with a ruby for constancy on her heart finger and this time the fit was perfect. She gazed at the blood-red stone with a strange sense of detachment. It was as if she were watching herself from a distance. It was her voice making the vows, her hand extending to receive the ring, but there was no reality to the moment, no connection between action and mind.

The wedding mass followed the pledging and it was a long ritual with prayers chanted in sonorous Latin. Maude knelt and stood in the right places, murmured the responses, opened her mouth for the wafer, sipped the red wine of Christ's blood, all without feeling. Behind her, from the place where Prince John stood, she heard an exaggerated sigh and the impatient shuffle of feet. John had a reputation for giving religious observance short measure. She had heard it said that he chose his household chaplains by the speed with which they were able to say mass and no other criteria.

The priest, able to take a hint himself, bustled through the remainder of the ceremony and finished it with a blessing upon Maude and Theobald. The guests crowded around to offer their congratulations. Maude was embraced by people she scarcely knew, the soft cheeks of women pressing to hers, the harsher rasp of masculine moustaches and beards. And then hands at her waist in a more intimate grip and hot eyes that pierced the shell of her numbness.

'Theobald certainly knew what he was doing when he chose you for his bride,' said John. 'You were a pale little bud at your betrothal, but now you're like ripe blossom on the bough.' A grin exposed his fine, white teeth. 'And it's my privilege to sup the nectar.'

Other guests had kissed her cheek. One or two had claimed her lips, but only in a salutary peck. John pulled her against him as no man had ever done and brought his mouth down on hers. The pressure of his lips made hers part and, swift as a darting fish, his tongue slipped inside.

Maude's eyes widened in shock and she bucked within John's embrace like a wild colt. Her teeth snapped together and if he had not removed his tongue smartly, he would have been well bitten.

Panting with outrage and revulsion, she glared at him,

but John merely smiled and dabbed his wet lips with the back of his hand.

'Given time, you'll learn what pleases,' he murmured. 'It's rather a pity I cannot teach you, though. I fear your innocence will be wasted on Theobald.'

Maude's instinct was to kick him in the groin and run, but she was constrained by circumstance to hold her ground. She thought that she was going to be sick, and it would serve John right if she vomited all over his fine gilded shoes.

'Your Highness, give me leave to congratulate your bride.' Hawise FitzWarin swept a deep curtsey to John and gave him an alluring look through her lashes, which said that younger women had their charms, but older ones had had much more time to practise them.

John's lips curved with amusement. 'Of a certainty, Lady . . . ?'

'FitzWarin,' said Hawise sweetly. 'My eldest son was trained in Lord Walter's household – and for a time in yours.'

John's smile withered at the corners but Hawise had already turned to Maude and, with a protective arm around her shoulders, was leading her towards Theobald.

'Bitch,' John muttered softly.

Maude was grateful to lean on the strength of Hawise's arm. 'Thank you, my lady.'

'It was a pleasure,' Hawise said with more than a hint of relish.

'He put his tongue in my mouth.' Maude shuddered.

Hawise made a low sound, conveying sympathy and outrage. 'I would have bitten him,' she said vehemently.

'I tried, but he was too swift.' Maude looked nervously at Theobald whom they were fast approaching. 'Do . . . do all men do that?'

'Not like John, no,' Hawise said diplomatically. 'And your husband is neither a lecher, nor a boor.'

Maude swallowed. She still felt queasy but she managed a wan smile for Theobald. When he smiled in response and stooped to kiss her lips, she kept them closed and only flinched a little.

The messenger arrived late into the evening just as the newlyweds were about to be conducted from the hall to their bedchamber. The women had gathered around Maude to escort her, and the men had surrounded Theobald. Bawdy suggestions and advice flew from wine-loosened tongues, most of them masculine.

'Pay no heed,' Hawise murmured in Maude's ear. 'It's just drunken foolery and they'll be gone soon.'

'But not before I have to stand naked before them,' Maude whispered. As part of the ceremony, she and Theobald would be stripped so that all could witness that there was no physical reason for one to repudiate the other. The thought of standing unclothed and vulnerable beneath Prince John's predatory stare made her shudder.

'Your grandmother and I will make sure that part is over as quickly as possible.' Hawise patted Maude's shoulder. 'And so, I think, will Theobald. He is no lover of exhibition.'

But Prince John was. With dragging feet, Maude went unwillingly to the turret stair. As she set her foot on the first step, the messenger entered the hall, accompanied by one of John's squires. The man's boots and the hem of his cloak were powdered with dust and his eyes were dark-shadowed for want of sleep.

The masculine group ceased its progress. Theobald pushed his way out of the centre and beckoned to the messenger. The news he bore was clearly important to be delivered at this time of night and the man had obviously ridden hard to reach Lancaster.

'I bear letters for His Highness, Prince John.' The messenger knelt at Theobald's feet – more out of exhaustion than reverence.

Frowning, John left the guests, his hand held out for the sealed packet that the man had withdrawn from his leather satchel. 'No, stay,' he commanded as Theobald made to leave. 'I may need you.'

'Sire.' Theobald inclined his head and signalled the women to continue to the bridal chamber.

Hair combed until it shone like a silver mirror, her otherwise naked body wrapped in a warm, fur-lined cloak, Maude waited for her husband and watched the night candle burn down on its iron pricket. She was no longer afraid. That mood had passed into a numb daze, enhanced by the spiced wine with which Lady FitzWarin had been liberally plying her. Her eyelids had begun to feel heavy and sore with the effort of staying awake. Clenching a yawn between her teeth, Maude glanced over her shoulder at the bed, its coverlet thrown back to show an inviting expanse of crisp linen sheet. If only she could lie down and go to sleep. But no one was going to allow her to do that.

The sound of male voices echoing in the stairwell pierced her numbness with a small, sharp arrow of unease. The women guests who had been desultorily chatting and eating small fig pastries from a large salver, dusted crumbs from their gowns, finished their wine, and stood ready.

Still fully clothed, the groom was ushered into the room. With a flood of relief that almost buckled her knees, Maude saw that Prince John and the knights of his entourage were not present. Theobald's visage was drawn with tiredness, the creases fanning from his eye corners no longer lifted by a smile. His companions too were more subdued than earlier, although it did not stop William Reinfred from nudging the groom and offering five hundred marks of silver to take his place.

'Not for all the wealth in England,' Theobald said, and sent Maude a reassuring look as the men began disrobing him.

'A pity you did not come to me with that offer when you had the chance, Reinfred!' jested Maude's father. 'I'd have let you have her for that sum!'

He probably would at that, Maude thought. She felt the eyes of the men upon her like horse-traders assessing the points of a young brood mare at market. Their salacious curiosity as the women unfastened the heavy cloak and lifted it from her shoulders, filled her with unease and revulsion. She could not even hide beneath the cloak of her hair because her grandmother gathered it in her hands and lifted it up to show that there was no flaw concealed under its silken heaviness.

'See,' said her father proudly, 'not a blemish on her.'

'I am satisfied,' Theobald said in a somewhat congested voice and gestured at Mathilda de Chauz. 'Let her put the cloak back on.'

Maude threw him a grateful look and was not slow to answer his bidding.

'And you, my lady?' asked the priest who was present to bless the couple and the bed. 'Are you satisfied?'

Given his age, it could not be said that Theobald was without flaw, but such as existed were minor and not a barrier to the marriage contract. His body, although not lean and narrow through the hips like a younger man's, was still firm and the muscles of his upper arms were powerful and glossy. His teeth were sound and his hair, although well mingled with grey, was thick and strong.

'Yes, she is,' said le Vavasour with an impatient wave.

Maude lifted her chin, determined to answer for herself, her courage enhanced by the protective presence of the cloak around her shoulders. After a swift glance at Theobald's nakedness, she confined her eyes to his face. 'I am.'

The priest made them stand side by side and sprinkled them with holy water from a vial in his hand. He intoned words of blessing in Latin, asking God that the marriage be long, prosperous and fruitful. Then he instructed Theobald and Maude to get into bed. Again they were sprinkled, and the bed itself was blessed.

'Remember your duty, Daughter,' le Vavasour said as he leaned over and kissed Maude's cheek in parting.

'Yes, Papa.' The words emerged cold and stilted. Her father had always been a stranger, but never more than now.

'God bless you, child.' Her grandmother embraced her tightly, a hint of moisture glinting in her eyes, as if she were making a final farewell.

Perhaps she was, Maude thought. Between tonight and the morrow, there surged a vast sea of experience, and once it was crossed, there was no returning. Either she would know what her grandmother and her unfortunate mother had known, or she would gain the knowledge that made Hawise FitzWarin smile and squeeze her hand.

'I wish you joy,' said Hawise, and was one of the few female guests to speak to Theobald too and kiss his cheek.

There were a few parting jests consisting of weak innuendo about ploughing furrows, sowing seed and sheathing swords, but finally the door closed behind the last guest and Maude and Theobald were alone.

'I swear never to tease a bride and groom again in my life,' Theobald declared. 'Wine?' Donning his cloak, he left the bed and poured spiced morap from the flagon that had been left conveniently on the coffer.

Maude nodded. She had already drunk beyond her limit. One more measure was not going to make a great difference and it would stave off the moment of dread for a while longer.

Returning to the bed, Theobald handed her a brimming cup of the mulberry wine. He climbed in beside her but did not attempt to touch her or press close. 'I don't know what you have been told, either in jest or a genuine attempt to help you tonight,' he said, 'but I have no intention of leaping on you like a wild beast.' His lip curled with distaste. 'Rape appeals to some men, especially when sanctioned by marriage, but it has never appealed to me.'

'No, my lord.' Maude looked down at her cup.

'Call me Theo. Formal address is for formal places.' He touched her then, but only to tilt her chin on his forefinger and make her look at him. 'You need not fear me. I don't want a wife who cowers from my voice and is afraid to speak out lest she is chastised.'

Maude met his grey eyes doubtfully. Such fair words sounded too good to be true. No one, man or woman had ever dared contradict her father's wishes. 'I do not fear you my . . . Theo.'

'I am glad that you do not.' He removed his finger and drank his wine. Then he cursed softly. 'Jesu,' he said and she saw that his hands were trembling. 'If I were still unwed, I would not dream of seeking out a girl so young for my pleasure.'

Maude did not know how to respond to that; probably he did not expect her to do so. To fill the unbearable tension in the air, she asked with nervous abruptness, 'Was Prince John's news bad?'

He gave her a distracted look. 'What?'

'The messenger. He looked as if he had ridden far and

hard. And the Prince was not among the guests at the bedding ceremony.'

He shook his head and at first said nothing. Maude wondered if she had overstepped her bounds. Her father said that affairs of state should not concern women, whose occupation was the keeping of the hearth and the bed-chamber. He conveniently ignored such contradictions as the fact that King Richard's mother had been appoint-ed Regent of England in her son's absence. Unfamiliar as she was with Theobald, she had small inkling of his opinions.

'I did not mean—' she began, but, as she started to speak, he let out his breath on a long sigh and answered her.

'The news was a setback, yes,' he said. 'And the Prince has retired to his chamber to consider its implications. Also he is leaving at first light, so he needs to rest.' He looked at her sombrely over his cup and she received the impres-sion that he was measuring her character, delving beneath the physical surface and the shallows of wedding-night anxiety to the underlying backbone.

'The messenger brought a letter from King Philip of France, telling John to beware – that the "Devil is loosed".'

Maude wound a tendril of hair around her forefinger. 'Does he mean that King Richard has been freed?'

'Not quite. But the terms of his ransom have been agreed and he will be released as soon as a substantial instalment has been paid.'

'Is that bad news for you too?' she enquired with a frown.

Theobald finished his wine in several long swallows. 'For better or worse I am John's man. I hold lands by his will, and he has entrusted me with the security of this keep because it is within the heartland of my northern hold-ings.' He spoke with a wry mouth as if the words tasted bitter on his tongue. 'But I am Richard's man too, for he is the King, and he has the ultimate authority.'

'Then you are torn both ways.'

He nodded. 'Whatever I do, I cannot win. If I hold out for John, I am guilty of treason. If I yield to Richard, I am guilty of betraying John's trust. Our wedding was not the reason he came to Lancaster, but the excuse. He wants to bind me more tightly to his cause, to make me renew my oath to him. I was supposed to do it on the morrow in the great hall, but I had to take it tonight, because at dawn he will be gone.' Theobald lifted his cup again, stared at the dregs, then rose to replenish it. 'I knelt and put my hands between his and swore him fealty, which means that I will defend this place come hell or high water . . . but come Richard . . .' He swung round and rubbed his hand over his face. 'Not only torn both ways, but torn apart. Murdered honour is never a pretty sight.'

Maude hugged her knees and watched him, wishing she could offer comfort or wisdom, and possessing neither. Wishing too that she had not been presumptuous and asked the question in the first place. 'Can't John be persuaded to yield to Richard?'

Theobald returned to the bed and eased in beside her. She moved slightly, as if making room for him, but also preserving the distance between them.

'There is that hope,' he said, 'but while Richard remains imprisoned, John will scheme to strengthen his own position. He will try and delay the ransom and likely even offer payment to Emperor Henry to keep Richard under lock and key. He will do all in his power to keep the power that he has.'

'And yet you serve him?'

The note of censure in her voice caught him on the raw, for he turned on her a look that was fierce and defensive. 'Yes, knowing him for what he is, I still serve him. He lies, he cheats, he is petulant, lecherous, and would not know the meaning of honour if it walked up to him and hit him over the head. But that is only the dark side of the coin. He has a fine mind beneath the mire; and when he is not engaged in a self-destructive war with Coeur de Lion's shadow, he is perhaps the most able statesman amongst all of Henry's sons.' He paused to draw a slightly ragged breath.

Maude accepted his defence but could not prevent an instinctive shiver of distaste when she thought of the way John had mauled her at the wedding ceremony.

'There is no one else,' her new husband said wearily. 'Arthur of Brittany is a child and he has never set foot on English soil, whereas John knows England and likes it well.' He rotated his cup and gave a snort of grim humour. 'I cannot believe that I am sitting here on my wedding night talking affairs of state with a sixteen-year-old girl.'

Maude felt a rush of panic. If he stopped talking then he would snuff the night candle and they would set about the bloody act of consummation. 'But I am interested,' she said, wondering how much longer she could postpone the inevitable. 'I want to learn these things. The more I understand, the more I will be able to help you.'

'You, help me?' He smiled, but the grimness remained. Carefully he set his cup aside and turned to her. 'How could you do that?'

'If I know things, then I won't speak out of turn in my ignorance.'

'Some would say that knowledge is dangerous.' He took a coil of her hair and twined it around his fingers, admiring the shine in the candlelight.

'So is ignorance, my lord.' She bit her lower lip, wondering if she had gone too far, but Theobald did not seem annoyed. His breathing had quickened and there was a heavy look in his eyes, but it was not anger.

'Well then,' he said softly, and wound the coil of hair tighter, bringing her towards him. 'If you desire to learn, I suppose I must teach you.' His other hand lightly cupped her jaw. 'My knowledge and your ignorance.' Theobald's breathing shook and he gave a tremulous laugh. 'Lord, girl, there lies danger indeed.'

CHAPTER 11

The pleasure of riding through the cool of the early morning birdsong was only small compensation for the heat that would later stew the men inside their armour. At least, Fulke thought, being grateful for small mercies, they should reach Lancaster before the full burn of the sun's midsummer rays hit them. The last few days had been a purgatory of sweat-chafed skin and permanent thirst as he took his troop northwards under cloudless skies. The country lay quiet but uneasy beneath the rule of Queen Eleanor and her Justiciars, and wise men took the precaution of travelling in their mail, despite the discomfort.

Having successfully delivered the letters from the German court to Hubert Walter, Fulke and Jean were travelling to Lancaster, this time with missives from Hubert to Theobald, together with the Archbishop's wedding gifts for the couple. On the return journey, Fulke was to bring his mother safe to Alberbury, then return to his brothers in Normandy.

'I wonder what Maude le Vavasour looks like now,' Jean mused. He had opted for folly and wore a bright red tunic which would have been horrendously garish had not his dark colouring suited it so well. His lute was slung on a leather baldric across his back and his dark curls were crowned with a dashing red hat sporting a peacock's tail feather. He was a minstrel today and overflowing with the joys of summer.

Fulke shrugged and studied the road. It had been empty for some time, but now he could see a puff of dust ahead. 'I had not thought,' he said with only half his attention.

'Mark me, with those eyes and that hair, she'll be a rare beauty by now.'

Fulke grunted. His mind filled with the image of a little girl, striking rather than pretty and full of volatile contrariness as she held his brother's ball to ransom. He remembered her wilful curiosity as she peeked at Richard's coronation banquet, and then thought of her standing beside Theobald Walter in the abbey, her expression glassy with fear and her spine rigid as she sought the courage not to run. By turns, he had been amused, irritated and pitying. To imagine her as a beautiful young woman was so incongruous as to be beyond him.

The cloud of dust was greater now, and the pace it was travelling suggested a horseback troop of some size. Fulke drew rein and signalled his own small conroi to pull aside into the dusty verge.

The first horseman into view was a knight riding a pied stallion and bearing a spear crowned with a rippling red and gold banner. The Angevin lions snarled in appliquéd silk across the background and the knight's surcoat was red and gold too. Then came more knights, similarly accoutred and riding at a rapid, mile-eating trot. In their midst, astride a Spanish stallion, was Prince John, his expression furious. On seeing Fulke and his troop, the fury became thunder. He jerked on the reins, sawing his horse to an abrupt halt that almost caused a collision amongst the knights at his back.

'Your Highness.' Fulke inclined his head in grudging obeisance.

'Off your horses and kneel to me!' John ground out. 'I will have proper respect.'

For a long moment Fulke stared at John, making it clear what he thought of the command. Behind him, not one of his men moved.

'I said off your horses, you gutter sweepings, and kneel!' John's voice was a hoarse whisper.

Without taking his gaze from the Prince, Fulke swung from the saddle and bent his knee. At a brief gesture, his men dismounted too, but it was clear that it was at Fulke's command, not John's.

The Prince glared, almost steaming with rage. 'One day your insolence will destroy you.'

Fulke raised his head. 'Were you the anointed King of England and my sovereign, I would have knelt immediately, Your Highness. As it is, you claim that which is not yours.'

John made a choking sound. His horse sidled, its hide twitching, and then began to buck and plunge. Girard de Malfee quickly reached to grab the reins and steady the beast.

John drew a breath through his teeth. 'I will show you what I can and cannot claim,' he hissed. 'If I give you your life, FitzWarin, it is only so that you will learn to rue this day.' Jabbing his spurs into the grey's flanks, he surged forwards, causing de Malfee to lose his grip.

The royal troop clattered on its way and Fulke slowly stood up. His legs were suddenly weak and he had to grip his mount's bridle.

'Well,' said Jean de Rampaigne, 'there is not much difference between you and your brother William after all. You both go stamping roughshod over ground where angels fear to tread. What are you going to do when John wears the crown of England?'

'If and when, I will kneel to him because it is his right.'
Fulke scowled at Jean. 'You did not have to follow me. You
could have knelt of your own accord.'

'Then I suppose I must be at least as foolhardy as you,'
Jean said and remounted. Waiting for Fulke to swing into
the saddle, he studied the settling cloud of dust. 'It looks
as if the news of Richard's release has reached him.'

'I scarcely believe that he is rushing south to organise a
ransom,' Fulke said grimly. 'Hinder it, mayhap.' He slapped
the reins on the chestnut's neck.

Maude turned over, thrust her hand beneath the soft feather
pillow and courted the deep slumber that moments ago
had been hers. Stealthy sounds intruded on her vague
consciousness and although she kept her eyes closed, they
grew louder and the dark peace of sleep receded.

A hand touched her bare shoulder; the palm, the fingers
were warm, broad and masculine. 'Good morrow, my lady
wife. Your women are here to tend you.'

She raised her lids to find Theobald leaning over her.
He was dressed and, beyond the haven of the bed curtains,
it was full, glorious morning. 'Good morrow, my lord.' Her
voice emerged on a dry croak and her mouth tasted of
stale wine. A headache thumped behind her lids and a
sensation of raw discomfort twinged within the cleft
between her thighs. 'What hour is it?'

'Nigh on terce,' Theobald said. There was a slightly
anxious expression in his eyes. 'I left you to sleep as long
as I could, but the guests are all assembled in the hall. Are
you well?'

Maude wanted to cover her head with the bolster and
groan at him to go away. 'Yes, my lord.' She struggled
upright. The light hurt her eyes and made her squint.

'Your women are here to tend you.' He gestured over

his shoulder towards the sound of whispering and cleared his throat. 'I am sorry if I hurt you last night.'

'It was only a little my lor . . . Theo.' She remembered what he had said about using his name in the informal setting of their chamber, and saw his gaze soften with tenderness.

'Even so, I would not have hurt you at all,' he murmured and stroked her cheek. 'I am afraid, sweetling, that you will have to make haste. The wedding sheet is needed in the great hall so that the guests can bear witness.'

Maude made a wry face at the thought of having the proof of her virginity hoisted aloft for all to see.

'I'll leave you to your preparations.' Somewhat awkwardly, Theobald backed away from the bed, murmured to the waiting women and made himself scarce.

Immediately Maude's grandmother and the maids surrounded the bed. One of the women handed her a hot herbal tisane. Maude cupped the steaming mazer in her hands and gratefully sipped.

'You have done well,' Mathilda de Chauz said with a brusque nod that was as close to praise as she was going to get. 'Your husband seems very pleased.'

Maude continued to drink the brew. The act of consummation had not been the pleasure of which Hawise FitzWarin had spoken, but neither had it been the dreadful ordeal that her grandmother had hinted at. There had been pain, for which Theobald had gasped an apology while he was still capable of speech. There was still pain now, but not beyond bearing, and after last night, Maude realised that she now had power and influence beyond anything she had possessed in her father's household. She was Lady Walter, and Theobald had entrusted his thoughts to her. It was that, as much as anything else, which compensated her for the physical discomfort he had inflicted.

'Here's water to wash yourself, Lady Maude,' said Barbette, one of the maids assigned to her at Lancaster. 'And some soothing balm if you have need.'

Maude shook her head. 'Lord Walter was good to me,' she said.

Immediately her grandmother looked anxious. 'He did consummate the marriage?' Throwing back the covers, she gestured Maude to leave the bed and heaved a sigh of relief when she saw the blood-smeared sheets and the red streaks bedaubing Maude's inner thighs. 'I am proud of your bravery,' she said. Turning to the maids, she ordered them to strip the sheet and take it to the great hall.

'I wasn't brave,' Maude admitted. 'I drank so much I scarcely knew what was happening, and now my head aches.'

Barbette laughed, the sound quickly smothered as Mathilda scowled.

'You need willow bark powder, my lady,' the young woman said. 'I'll fetch you some.' She whisked out of the door, and the two remaining maids set about stripping the bloodied sheet, proof of Maude's virginity. Should she bear a child nine months from now, it could be none other than Theobald's.

Maude washed the blood from her thighs. When he had penetrated her, she had clenched her teeth to hold back the scream. Theobald had apologised, but pushed deeper, whispering raggedly that to withdraw again would only cause her worse pain. The first time was always difficult. It would grow easier. She had to trust him. And trust him she had, throwing her arms around his neck, clinging to him for dear life as he hurt her twice more and then shuddered in her arms like a dying man. In those sticky, bloody moments as she held him, the vulnerability had been transferred and she had been given an inkling of the power a woman might hold over a man.

With her grandmother's help, Maude donned an under-tunic and gown of pale and dark green linen. Mathilda braided Maude's heavy blonde hair in two thick plaits and dressed it with a veil of light silk. The tug of the plaits, the tightness of the silver circlet securing the wimple, intensified her headache. Barbette returned with another steaming cup, this time containing an infusion of powdered willow bark.

Maude drank it down, grateful for the sweetening of honey that took away the bitter aftertaste. She risked a glance at her reflection in her new mirror. The ravages of the night showed in the dark rings beneath her eyes, but otherwise her face was unchanged. To look at her, no one would know the bridge she had crossed last night.

Down in the hall they were waiting for her. Some of the younger men, still gilded from the wedding feast, raised a cheer when she appeared, her arrival preceded with great ceremony by the wedding sheet. She affected to ignore them but was betrayed by a blush. She knew that they were looking upon the bloodstained linen and imagining her defloration – not necessarily by Theobald.

The wedding sheet, as custom demanded, was opened out and pegged on the wall behind the high table like a banner. After a single glance, Maude averted her eyes and took her place at Theobald's side. He kissed her hand and greeted her formally, addressing her as 'my lady wife'. He too avoided looking at the sheet.

His squire served her with bread and cheese. She declined the wine that was offered and contented herself with a cup of buttermilk. Her head was still throbbing but the willow-bark potion was slowly beginning to take effect. She noticed that Theobald drank sparingly of the wine and surmised from the way he occasionally rubbed his brow that he too was suffering for last night's indulgence.

Once they had eaten, Theobald rose to his feet and called for silence. 'As you know,' he declared in a powerful voice, 'it is customary for a groom to give his bride a gift on their wedding morn in token of his esteem. This is a true gift, hers alone, and cannot be given or sold without her yeasay.'

Turning to Maude, he presented her with a vellum scroll, tied with red ribbon and sealed with his device. 'I call you all to witness the gift I bestow upon my new wife, namely the incomes from five manors, two fisheries and two mills in my honour of Amounderness, and in Norfolk, these incomes to be disposed of as she chooses.' With a flourish he presented her with the scroll, adding to it a small ivory casket containing a rope of seed pearls and, suspended from it, a gold cross set with rubies to match the one in her wedding ring.

Maude was overwhelmed. Despite her noble status, she had never been showered with as much largesse as in these last two days. In addition, Theobald had chosen wisely and kindly. The jewellery was a symbol to all of the store he set by her and the grants of income gave her a source of personal independence. 'Thank you, my lord,' she said breathlessly.

'It is little enough.' His tone was gruff. Taking the pearls, he set them around her neck, arranging the cross so that it hung straight.

'She is overly young to be entrusted with such wealth,' her father said from her other side where he had been observing the proceedings with a critical eye.

Theobald turned to his father-in-law. 'But not overly young to become a wife or be entrusted with the well-being of myself and everyone in this keep,' he said curtly. 'If she is ready for one, then she is ready for the other.'

Robert le Vavasour thrust out his heavy lower lip.

'Whatever their skills, women need firm guidance if they are not to stray.'

'Maude will receive all the guidance she needs from me,' Theobald said, laying a gentle hand on his bride's shoulder, the gesture nevertheless indicating possession. 'All she has to do is ask.'

Le Vavasour made a gruff sound in his throat and his complexion darkened slightly. 'I would not like to see my son-in-law make a rod for his own back.'

Theobald inclined his head, showing that he was aware of le Vavasour's concern. 'We reap what we sow,' he said pleasantly.

Maude had been silent during the exchange, but her emotion was one of pleasure that Theobald was taking her part. Here was a man she could respect of her own accord, not out of duty.

'My lord husband, give me leave to stow this vellum safely,' she requested. She could have sent a maid on the errand, but it was a way of escaping the situation. Whether Theobald defended her or not, it was still like being a bone between two dogs.

'By all means.' He met her gaze in perfect understanding. She curtseyed deeply to him, gave a small dip of her head to her father, and made her escape.

'She's a fine, spirited lass,' Theobald said, admiring her lissom figure as she made her way to the stairs. And that spirit must be very strong, he thought, to withstand her father's bullying and emerge relatively unscathed, except for a certain nervous manner of glancing. 'She is my bride; I'm entitled to indulge her a little.'

'Aye, well, for your own sake, make sure a little does not become too much,' le Vavasour growled. 'Women spoil very easily.'

Somehow, Theobald managed to bite his tongue on the

remark that Robert le Vavasour had certainly spoiled Maude's mother with his treatment. Indeed, he had likely killed the poor woman. Theobald intended to keep her daughter safe from any such spoiling.

A short time later, Maude returned to the great hall, driven from her chamber by the presence of her grandmother and the other female guests and their insatiable quest for gossip. It was like being a young pullet in a hen house, pecked and harassed by the older birds who knew their place and wanted to show her hers.

Her father was no longer at the high table and a young, raven-haired knight had taken his seat. He looked vaguely familiar but she could not immediately place him. Certainly, he had not been present at the previous day's nuptials. She would have remembered the striking, hawkish looks. He was eating bread and cheese with gusto and nodding vigorously to Theobald's conversation. His recent arrival was clear from the helm and sword laid to one side of his platter and from the dust clinging to the surcoat he wore over his mail. On her husband's other side sat another young man, his attire more suited to that of celebration. Instead of a sword and helm, a handsome lute lay at his right hand, and, unlike his companion, he wore neither mail nor surcoat. Nearby were several more armour-clad young men, hungrily breaking their fast.

Maude considered turning round and retiring to her chamber again, but quickly dismissed the notion. Rather the unknown than the hen coop. Putting on a welcoming smile, she went forward.

The knight raised his head and his jaw ceased in mid-chew as their eyes met. The hair prickled at Maude's nape and she felt as if a fist had punched inside her rib cage and squeezed. She put her hand to her midriff and, beneath her palm, drew a short, congested breath.

Theobald beckoned her to come and sit with them on the bench. 'Do you remember Fulke FitzWarin?' He gestured to the knight.

'No. I . . . I mean yes,' Maude stammered and tore her gaze from the young man's smoke-hazel eyes. In his turn, FitzWarin broke the contact by lifting his cup to wash down his food.

'I am not sure that I remember you,' he said ruefully. 'Jean warned me that you would have grown into a rare beauty, but his words do not do you justice.'

The young man in the fine clothes smiled. 'They do not, my lady,' he agreed.

Theobald introduced him as Jean de Rampaigne, his former squire. With an effort, Maude gathered her scattered wits and responded. He was more handsome than FitzWarin if neatness and regularity of feature was a consideration, but with his roguish grin and merry eyes he was endearing without Fulke's smouldering attraction.

She took her place beside Theobald, squeezing up against him so that no part of her touched Fulke. His mail-clad arm rested on the board. She looked at the shine of light on the rivets, her eyes travelling its length to the cuff of gambeson and tunic and following by natural progression the tanned contours of his hand. The lean, strong fingers were quite beautiful. A narrow white scar across the knuckles and a newer pink one curving around the base of the thumb, only served to enhance the appeal by suggesting that here was both experience and vulnerability.

'So, what brings you from the jousting circuit?' Theobald enquired.

Fulke drew in his arm and, leaning back, folded it inside

the other. 'Jean had errands for Lord Hubert and I offered to ride escort.'

'If I had known you were in England, you would have been welcome at my wedding.'

'I know that, my lord, but considering your other guests, it was for the best that my mother represented our family.'

'Perhaps so.' Theobald looked slightly embarrassed. He waved his arm. 'But I insist you stay for tonight. I've missed your company and there are years of tales to tell. You'll want to wash away the dust of the road and be rid of your weight of mail.' He glanced at Maude and cleared his throat.

She realised with a jolt of panic that it was now her duty as lady of the castle to see to the comfort of their guests. Oh, Jesu! she thought. She might have lost her fleshly maidenhead last night, but there were still many areas of virginity to be broached. What would her grandmother do? Maude rose unsteadily to her feet and then looked desperately at her husband.

'I believe there is an empty wall chamber now that Prince John has departed,' Theobald prompted.

'Oh yes, indeed.' She smiled gratefully at him and turned to his guests. 'I'll show you where it is and the maids will fill some tubs so that you can bathe.'

Fulke collected sword and helm from the trestle. Maude watched the motion of his hands and then tore her gaze from them.

Fulke was looking at Theobald, wry amusement in his eyes. 'I am to occupy Prince John's chamber? I do not know whether that says something about your sensibilities, or your sense of humour.'

Theobald waved him away. 'Just my sense, since we are sore-pressed for space. Go on with you.'

Fulke gave Theobald an amiably sarcastic salute and turned to Maude. 'Lead on, my lady.'

Her face flaming, she led Fulke and his small entourage from the hall. At least, she thought with relief, she had not caught his gaze in speculation on that damned bridal sheet. Indeed, he had seemed at pains to avoid looking at it, and for his chivalry she was glad.

Actually, it was not chivalry, but a broil of far less worthy considerations that had caused Fulke to avert his eyes from the wedding sheet. At first he had not looked because he had been raised in a slightly eccentric household where the deeds of the bed were viewed as something between man and wife and not the rest of the world. Although he knew the sound reason for the display, it was still a little obscene. When Maude had entered the hall, he had almost choked on his bread. Gone was the thin, huge-eyed waif of his memory, replaced by a young woman, still coltish and slender, but certainly not a child. The eyes, a clear cat-green, the braids heavy white-gold falling beyond her veil, the cheekbone and jaw finely wrought, and, God in heaven, that wide, cushion-soft mouth.

Their eyes had met and the incandescence of his thoughts must have hit her, for she had not been flustered before. No, he dared not look at the sheet because he was already overwhelmed and struggling to come to terms with the notion that far from being a skinny child to whom he could relate as brother to sister, or his former tutor's wife to be treated with passing courtesy, Maude le Vavasour was quite simply the most alluring young woman he had ever seen.

She showed them the chambers that had recently been vacated by Prince John, then excused herself to chivvy the maids and summon Lady FitzWarin from the women's chambers. Fulke watched her leave, his gaze lingering on the doorway even when she was gone from sight.

'I told you, didn't I?' Jean boasted with cheerful

superiority. He gave Fulke a hearty nudge. 'I've seen poled oxen with less glazed expressions.'

'What?' Shaking his head, Fulke turned around.

'Maude le Vav— I mean Maude Walter. I told you she'd be a rare beauty.' Jean grinned. 'It's not very diplomatic to fall head over heels in love – or in lust – with your mentor's wife, you know.' He ducked beneath the blow that Fulke aimed at him and danced out of reach. 'Admit it, she's a peach.'

Fulke glared at him, then turned to prop his sword in a corner and lean his helm against it. 'She is indeed lovely,' he shrugged. 'But you exaggerate my response. Besides, even if she is of marriageable age, she is yet little more than a child.' It was a discomforting thought to add to the turmoil in his mind. Not since the days of Oonagh FitzGerald had he been so instantly affected by a woman. Except this one wasn't yet a woman and as far from his reach as the stars. Desiring her was both dangerous and morally wrong. So said reason. His body, however, was less inclined to be persuaded, and in that, he suspected, he was in the same case as every red-blooded man in the keep.

Jean flourished his lute. 'True, but not for long. Give her a short span of years to learn her power and she'll be another Melusine.'

'You mean she'll fly out of the chapel window like a bat?' Fulke's tone was deliberately light and sarcastic.

Jean rolled his eyes. 'No, I mean she'll take your soul and you'll be glad to give it.'

Fortunately Fulke was prevented from making an answer, either verbal or physical, by the appearance of two manservants bearing bathtubs, several maids with fresh pallets and bedding, and, hard on their heels, his mother. For the moment at least, all jesting, both frivolous and serious, stopped.

*   *   *

That evening the wedding celebrations continued, albeit in a less fulsome vein than those of the previous day. Fulke found himself obliged to dance with the bride, for he would have seemed churlish otherwise.

'You must be more comfortable now that you have shed your mail,' she said as they took their positions in the open space framed by a rectangle of dining trestles.

'And much lighter too, my lady,' he replied with a smile.

They grasped each other's wrists and turned in a slow figure of eight. It was a traditional carole, always danced at weddings and symbolised the eternal bond between man and woman. In the smoky, candlelit darkness, the clear green of her eyes was almost obliterated by the wideness of her pupils. *Theobald's wife*, in Christ's name, he told himself. *A child*. But it was not a child's body that turned and moved with supple grace beneath his hands. The slender waist; the brush of her braids as she stepped past him and round; the curve of breast. He had to do something.

'I remember you stealing my brother's ball because he would not let you play,' he said, trying to re-establish the connection with the child she had been.

Maude wrinkled her nose. As a little girl, the mannerism had been endearing. Now it sent a chill of pure lust down Fulke's spine. 'My grandmother was furious,' she said, 'but I cared not.'

'And are you still the same?'

'Only on the inside,' she replied with a demure flicker of her lashes. 'Outwardly I am learning to be a lady.'

The dance finished. Bowing to her, Fulke made his escape, letting another knight take his place. It did not help matters when there was a break in the dancing and Jean took up his lute to sing the ballad of Melusine. First composed in Westminster's kitchen on a snowy December evening, Jean had honed the song until it was a work of art. The listeners could almost see the witch standing before them with her shimmering hair and eyes.

'Are you ailing, my son?' Hawise laid a gentle hand on Fulke's sleeve, her voice filled with concern.

He forced a smile. 'Not in the least, Mother, but I've heard that damned lay of Jean's so often that it drives me half mad.' Abruptly he jerked to his feet and stalked from the hall, leaving her to gaze after him in consternation.

Standing outside, Fulke took several deep breaths to clear his head of the cloying fumes of smoke and song and wine. Theobald's young wife was only affecting him because he had been too long without a woman, he told himself. Abstaining from tourney whores was a simple matter of self-preservation and besides, most of them were about as appetising as a bowl of cold porridge. Nevertheless, abstinence meant that he was very susceptible to the charms of sweetly scented almost-virgins like the delectable Maude le Vav— Maude Walter.

There were watch fires in the ward for the cheer of the guards on duty. A woman, who had been talking to the men, detached herself from their company and sauntered towards Fulke. She wore the panelled dress of a wealthy woman, the sleeves so long that they almost trailed the ground, but the low curve of the neckline had no modesty of laced undershift to conceal her cleavage and her glossy dark braids were brazenly exposed.

Fulke recognised her immediately. Hanild was a courtesan whom he knew from general acquaintance and a long-ago closer intimacy. She was neither the youngest nor the prettiest of the court whores, but she had an earthy allure that went beyond mere looks and she was known to be barren. No man – or youth as he had been then – was going to bed her and then find her knocking at his door with a swollen belly.

'A long time since I've seen you, Fulke FitzWarin,' she said, her hands on her hips and a speculative look in her slanting dark eyes.

'I've been following the tourneys,' he replied with a dismissive gesture. 'You didn't leave with John's retinue then?'

Her teeth flashed. 'Oh no. There's more money to be made at a celebration than a wake. When Prince John is in a filthy mood he takes it out on his followers, and, in their turn, they take it out on me.' Her voice softened to a purr. 'I'd rather earn my living in pleasure, than in pain.' She moved closer, tilting her head to look up at him. 'Do you know why John is in such a temper?'

'No idea,' he lied. 'I am only here to escort my mother home, and of course to honour Lord Walter's nuptials.'

'Oh.' Hanild looked disappointed. In her experience, men were somewhat cagey of being seen with her if their respectable womenfolk were in the vicinity.

'But she's in the hall.' He took her hand, preventing her from withdrawing. 'And I'm . . . I want . . .'

Her breath caught. Sometimes it was for money alone. On rarer occasions business and pleasure mixed. She smiled. 'I know what you want,' she said throatily. 'Fortunate indeed that I did not leave with John.'

To get to her own chamber, Maude had to climb past the one that had been given to John and now housed Fulke FitzWarin and his troop. She had not seen Fulke for the latter part of the evening and wondered if he had retired early. He had seemed somewhat distracted and there had been an air of constraint about him when they danced.

The chamber door was firmly closed. Maude imagined him asleep on his pallet and her stomach fluttered. She should not be thinking about him. She should be going straight up to bed to prepare for her duty to Theobald.

Suddenly, through the wood, she heard Fulke speak, and a woman answer, her reply ending on a husky laugh. Before Maude could move on, the door opened and the owner of the laugh emerged, fingers busy braiding her loose dark hair, her expression one of sated languor.

The woman stopped short as she encountered Maude and, stifling an oath, dipped a curtsey. 'Lady Walter,' she gasped.

'I do not believe I know you,' Maude said stiffly.

'My . . . my name is Hanild de Bruges. I arrived with Prince John's entourage.'

'But you did not leave with them.' Maude realised with a rush of chagrin that the woman must be one of the court whores. It was difficult not to feel intimidated by her. Hanild was tall for a woman and positively towered over Maude who had yet to attain her full growth. A musky, feral scent wafted from her body.

A masculine hand gripped the door and pulled it wider to reveal Fulke FitzWarin, clad in naught but shirt and chausses. After last night's initiation, Maude well recognised the glazed look in his eyes. 'Mistress Hanild is an old friend,' he said impassively. 'I invited her to come and talk a while.' His hand left the door and descended lightly to the whore's shoulder in a gesture of reassurance.

Maude coloured to the roots of her hair. It was quite plain that the last thing they had been doing was talking. She wanted to snap that her household was not a brothel, that his manners were execrable to bring a whore to his chamber, but she bit her tongue on the words. He was, after all, a guest. Besides, the sight of him standing there in disarray, his eyes hazy in the aftermath of recent pleasure, was unnerving.

'Then I'll bid you goodnight,' she said stiffly and left

them at a dignified walk, but once out of sight, she gathered her skirts and ran, feeling the world's greatest fool.

Fulke groaned and struck the doorpost.

'It's all right,' Hanild murmured, rubbing her cheek against the back of his hand. 'She's only a child. She won't make trouble for you.'

'She already has,' Fulke said wryly.

'I encountered Fulke FitzWarin with one of John's whores,' Maude told Theobald with indignation as her maid curt-seyed and left the room with his squire. 'She's called Hanild and she has remained behind to ply her trade among the men.' Although Barbette had already combed Maude's hair, she began to groom it again like an angry cat sleeking down ruffled fur.

Theobald pillowed his hands behind his head and regarded her, a trace of amusement in his eyes. 'Yes, I know Hanild,' he said.

She looked up sharply.

'Not in that sense, of course,' he added hastily. 'But since she dwells in John's retinue, our paths sometimes cross. Indeed, her services are paid for by the exchequer. Men become lonely away from their wives. Some, like Fulke, are bachelors, and women like Hanild serve as a vent for a young man's heat. Still,' he mused, 'it is unlike him. He's no prude, but he's usually discreet these days, and discreet is not a trait you can claim for Hanild.' He looked askance at his bride. 'Where did you see her and Fulke?'

'She was leaving his chamber as I climbed the stairs.' Abandoning the comb, she came to join him in the bed. Theobald put his arm around her and drew her against him, but companionably so. 'I felt foolish,' she admitted, 'and also angry at his lack of manners in bringing her to the private quarters.'

He ran a silky tress of her hair through his fingers. 'I'll speak to him,' he said.

'No!' She shot away from him, her eyes wide with alarm. 'Say nothing. I would feel more foolish yet — like a child carrying tales. Now I have told you, I am not as angry.'

'As you wish,' he soothed. 'Belike the spirit of celebration got the better of Fulke's senses. We all make mistakes.'

Maude did not feel as forgiving as her husband. It was one matter for Prince John to bring a courtesan as part of his retinue; quite another when she lingered to solicit after John's departure and the guests took every advantage.

Fulke FitzWarin was no better than the other ignorant oafs who had raised bawdy cheers at the presentation of the bridal sheet. As she snuggled back against Theobald's chest, she felt anger, humiliation . . . and relief. The pedestal she had been in danger of building had tumbled. Fulke FitzWarin was nothing.

CHAPTER 12

Winchester, April 1194

Fulke stroked Blaze's white muzzle and held him steady while his youngest brother Alain threw the saddle across his back. The stallion's coat shone like dark blood in the spring sunshine now that the last of the thick winter hair had been teased out.

The broad tourney field on Winchester's outskirts was filled with knights and combatants warming themselves and their mounts for the coming fray. All weapons were blunt today, the tourney being as much for show as to display serious prowess. The spectacle had been organised to celebrate King Richard's safe return from imprisonment in Germany. Yesterday there had been a grand crown-wearing ceremony attended by all the nobles in the land. Oaths of fealty had been renewed, pardons granted to those whose loyalty had wavered, and generous rewards given to men who had held firm. Even Prince John, the most serious instigator of the troubles, had been let off lightly, if humiliatingly. Richard had forgiven him, declaring that, owing to his youth and inexperience, John had been gulled by the wilier Philip of France. And John could do no more than bow his head and swallow his bile, for Richard was still without an heir of his loins and all was still to play for.

'Think you'll carry off the prize?' Alain demanded. His voice grated in the space between boy and man.

'Not with William Marshal in the field,' Fulke said with a glance in the direction of the new Earl of Pembroke who was putting a powerful bay destrier through its paces at the quintain rings. Marshal was several inches taller than Fulke, a couple of stones heavier and had half a lifetime's experience under his belt. Fulke had occasionally jousted against him and knew him for a formidable opponent.

Alain checked that the girths were secure and Fulke swung into the saddle. Leaning to take the blunted lance from Alain and the kite shield from his companion Audulf de Bracy, Fulke rode out to join the rest of his troop who were already warming up on the field. His brother William came cantering to greet him; his lance aimed at the centre of Fulke's shield. Fulke brought his own lance down and across and dug in his heels. Their meeting was a polite rap of metal on wood, nothing to endanger or unseat, but still a slightly flamboyant show for the audience assembling in the stepped lodges to view the sport.

'I'm going to enjoy today,' William announced. He had yet to don his helm and he turned in the saddle to view the crowd gathering in the lodges. 'There'll be some rich ransoms on offer and an admiring audience. Look at that one in the green dress. Do you think she'll give me her favour to wear?'

Looking amused, Fulke shook his head. 'That's Eustace de Vesci's wife,' he warned. 'Her husband would carve out your liver.'

William shrugged. 'Well, that one over there with the red veil.'

Fulke laughed at his brother's audacity. He did not know the young woman in the red veil but she would be some rich baron's wife or daughter. Only the most privileged were permitted a seat in the central lodge near the royal panoply.

Then he saw Maude Walter taking her place upon the benches with her maid. Her gown was a deep ocean-green. A paler green veil threaded with gold framed her face but left her throat exposed and showed the heavy gleam of her braids.

William uttered a soft growl of appreciation. 'No, I think I'll have her,' he said.

Fulke's amusement evaporated. 'She's married to Theobald Walter.'

William's jaw dropped. 'That's Maude le Vavasour?' he demanded. 'The brat who was in Mama's tent at Richard's coronation?'

'The very same.'

His brother gave a low whistle. 'Still,' he rallied, 'I do not suppose that an apple pip much resembles an apple. Jesu, she's a beauty.'

Fulke rubbed his hand over his face. In the ten months since his visit to Lancaster, he had tried to put Maude Walter from his mind. She was very young, she was someone else's wife and it was no more than the hammer of lust because he knew nothing of her personality. Most of the time he succeeded. There were matters of greater importance to occupy him and he was no slave to appetites of the flesh. But seeing her again made him realise that the hunger had not goneaway.

'You were her husband's squire,' William said. 'Go over and ask if you can carry her favour on your lance.'

'That would not be wise.' Remembering the incident at Lancaster when she had caught Hanild emerging from his chamber, Fulke intended to keep his distance.

'Why? Surely Theobald Walter won't carve out your liver?'

'You know what a hive of gossip the court is. Folk would read all the wrong reasons into such a request.'

William shook his head sadly. 'You're becoming an old man, brother. It's harmless and the wives expect it – gives their lives a little savour.'

'Not that particular wife,' Fulke said grimly.

Even as they were speaking, Theobald Walter himself rode up to them. His horse was barded in the red and gold colours of the King and he wore a surcoat bearing the same to show that he was Richard's man.

'Well met,' he greeted them cheerfully. 'I trust you have paid your fees?' There was a lightness in his bearing and a gleam in his eye. Part of the change was due to having a young wife to keep him lively, but the main difference was because he had succeeded in keeping his lands despite his divided loyalties. Unlike John, Richard did not harbour grudges. He had pardoned all those who had held castles for John and had even bestowed increased privileges on some. Thus, Theobald (not without a little influence from his brother Hubert who was both the Justiciar and Archbishop of Canterbury) had been confirmed in all his lands. He had also been granted the office of gathering licence fees from all tourneys held in England, including this one.

'Yes, we've paid,' Fulke said, 'although we hope to re-imburse ourselves handsomely.'

'I have no doubt you will, and you have an appreciative audience.' Smiling, he gestured to the lodges, his voice warm with affection. 'It's the first time that Maude has ever attended a tourney and she's as excited as a dog with two tails, bless her.' He looked at the brothers. 'As an official, I'm not fighting today. Fulke, as a boon, I ask you to bear Maude's favour in the tourney. I know you are skilled and that you will do her proud.'

Fulke started to shake his head, but before he could refuse, Theobald raised his hand and interrupted.

'I am aware of the awkwardness caused between you by what happened at Lancaster, but it is time it was put aside. It was nothing, a storm in a pitkin.'

Conscious of William's avid curiosity, Fulke cleared his throat. 'Some might misconstrue the sight of me wearing her colours,' he said.

Theobald looked amused. 'If I am present when she bestows her favour, then no one can see mischief in the motive. Besides, the sooner she gives it, the less she will be importuned by other men of considerably less honour.'

Fulke gave an uncomfortable shrug. 'I do not think that your lady believes my own honour to be much above the gutter.'

'I have reassured her on those grounds. What happened at Lancaster was unfortunate, but not your customary behaviour.'

Cornered, Fulke could only incline his head and yield with grace.

'What did happen at Lancaster?' William demanded as he, Fulke and Theobald trotted towards the lodges.

'Nothing that need concern you,' Fulke said irritably.

'Oh come on, tell me. I'm always dragged over the coals for *my* sins.' William rode closer.

'If you must know,' Fulke said tersely, 'I bedded one of John's whores under the bride's roof. Satisfied?'

'Astonished,' William said.

They arrived at the lodges and faced the growing audience. Theobald beckoned and, with a quickening of pink in her cheeks, Maude rose from her seat and came down to the men, her maid discreetly following a few paces behind.

'My lord?' The way she looked at Theobald revealed to Fulke that there was a genuine and strong affection between them.

'You remember Fulke FitzWarin?' Theobald said. 'And this is his brother, William.'

Her colour heightened, making her eyes the translucent green of sea shallows. 'Of course I remember.' Her tone was neutral but left him in no doubt of her opinion. To William she murmured a polite greeting as he bowed over his saddle in return.

'Fulke has won much renown on the tourney field,' Theobald said to her. 'I have asked him to bear your favour in battle today, and he has agreed.'

The flush faded from her cheeks. 'My favour?' she repeated in a brittle voice.

Fulke could see that she too was cornered. Theobald plainly intended his wife and his former squire, now his friend, to be on good terms with each other, whatever their personal notions on the matter.

'Come now, wife,' he said, an edge to his voice. 'Smile for me and give him a ribbon.'

She bit her lip. In his mind's eye, Fulke saw her standing her ground, his brother's ball clutched fiercely to her chest as she refused to yield because it wasn't fair.

'She doesn't have to,' he said. 'I won't be offended.'

'No . . . no, I want to.' She fumbled at her braid and unwound one of the green silk bindings. The way she looked at her husband told Fulke that she was only complying because Theobald had asked it of her.

Fulke dipped his lance and, in silence, she wound the green ribbon around the shaft. Trapped in the silk, two filaments of silver-blonde hair glittered in the sunlight.

'Be lucky, ride well,' she said flatly.

'For your honour, Lady Walter,' Fulke replied in a similar tone and, saluting her with a dip of the lance, reined about and rode away.

'Christ's body!' William exclaimed, cantering at his side,

'the air between you and her just then would make hell seem cold by comparison!'

'Let it be, Will,' Fulke snapped.

'She doesn't like you much, does she?'

Fulke rounded on his brother with a snarl. 'I said let it be!' He spurred Blaze to a burst of speed that left William grinning, but baffled, in his dust.

In the lodges, Maude reseated herself on the bench and pressed her palms to her burning cheeks. The moment had been awful. She had wanted to run and hide, or alternatively to slap the look of stony courtesy from FitzWarin's face. He had no more desired to carry her favour than she had desired to give it.

She was determined to ignore his presence on the field but as the moments passed her concentration slipped and curiosity overrode her intention. She found herself following Fulke FitzWarin's progress. He was polished in the saddle and each move seemed smooth and effortless, although she knew from observing Theobald that such skill came not only from talent but also from long hours of practice. She had seen Fulke's athletic body in repose, had seen him half-clad in the company of a notorious whore. Now she watched him play at war and felt an unsettling flutter in her mid-section. There was beauty in the co-ordination of hand and arm and eye, the flash of blade, the masculine grace and power. Shivering, she watched the lance strike and unhorse with unerring accuracy, the silk pennon flying and her green ribbon shimmering on the haft. She saw the way he manipulated each encounter, forcing his opponent to fight on the terms he dictated. Time and again he brought her favour to glory and her grudging admiration grew until her heart swelled with treacherous pride and she leaned forward on the bench, willing him on.

'Enjoying the sport, Lady Walter?'

She looked up at the sound of the cultured, masculine voice. Again, her stomach jolted, but far less pleasantly. 'Sire,' she murmured and rose to sweep a curtsey at the feet of Prince John.

Stooping, he raised her to her feet, retaining her hand in his. In the months since her marriage, she had grown a little more and stood almost on a level with him, for he was not a tall man. He had fine eyes and his dark beard suited him, making him look saturnine and worldly wise rather than merely petulant. But his grip was a little too firm and predatory and she could still remember that wedding-day kiss with revolting clarity. 'Yes, sire,' she replied, scarcely moving her lips, and gave an experimental tug.

Smiling, and thoroughly aware of her discomfort, he held on to her. 'I've never seen much point in the joust myself,' he said. 'But Richard's always been one for bread and circuses.' His glance darted to the awning where his brother was seated in full royal splendour, eagerly watching the sport. 'I prefer gentler pursuits myself.' He rubbed his thumbnail lightly along the inside of her wrist and Maude gave an involuntary shiver.

A crack of lances made him turn in time to see Fulke FitzWarin tip his opponent cleanly out of the saddle. John's jaw tightened beneath his beard. The fallen man was Girard de Malfee, one of his own retainers. Maude used the distraction to snatch her hand out of John's. He looked at her and smiled. 'The thing to remember when hunting a bird in the bushes is to bide your time,' he said. 'Sooner or later it will fly to your hand.' A gleam in his eyes, he inclined his head to her and then, mercifully, he was gone.

Maude glared after him. 'Hell will freeze over first,' she spat. Trembling with shock and a growing rage, she sat down on the bench.

'My lady?' Barbette touched her shoulder in concern. 'Shall I fetch Lord Theobald?'

'No,' Maude said swiftly. 'It was nothing.' Theobald was beholden to Prince John for his lands and she did not want to start a quarrel.

'You are sure, my lady?'

She nodded at her maid. 'The Prince was merely teasing me because I am a new wife.' Everyone knew about John's predilection for seducing the wives and daughters of his barons. Maude swore grimly to herself that she was not about to join their ranks.

She gazed blankly at the tourney field until her focus was sharply restored by the sight of Fulke FitzWarin and his troop engaging in a mock battle with the Earl of Pembroke and his household knights directly in front of her.

William Marshal was no easy conquest as Girard de Malfee had been. Indeed, the sides seemed evenly matched, Marshal's greater experience and slight edge of expertise offset by Fulke's youth and the swiftness of his reactions. If he made a mistake, his correction was so quick that Marshal had no opportunity to take advantage. But neither was he able to win past Marshal's impenetrable guard. Finally they declared a draw and rode off to seek different adversaries before they exhausted each other to the benefit of neither. Maude stared, her knuckles clenched tightly in her lap. As Fulke and the Marshal disengaged, she let out her breath and felt the chill of drying sweat on her body.

She was still recovering from the ordeal of watching Fulke and being accosted by John when Theobald arrived to take her around the booths that had been set up to one side of the lodges and tourney ground.

Theobald gave her a fond look and led her among the stalls. 'There is no need to look so worried,' he said, giving her a squeeze. 'I told you that Fulke would do you proud. Why, he even held his own against William Marshal, which takes no small degree of skill.' There was pride in his voice, for the part he had played in tutoring Fulke.

Maude murmured a suitable response and tried to sound enthusiastic.

'You still bear a grudge, don't you?'

'No, my lord. As you say, it is in the past.' Not looking at him, Maude pretended to examine some silk veils tied to the corner of a draper's booth. 'I have no doubt that Fulke FitzWarin is a *preux chevalier*.' She cast him a side-long look, seeking to distract him from a subject about which she did not want to talk . . . seeking to distract herself too, if the truth were known. 'I need new ribbons for my hair,' she told him and indicated her denuded plait.

Smiling, shaking his head, Theobald indulged her. His woman, his child.

In the great hall that evening, Fulke and his troop were the toast of the trestles for carrying off the most prizes on the tourney field. King Richard presented them each with a fine hunting knife and a gallon keg of wine to celebrate their success. It was a popular result and men pounded the tables with their fists and eating knives to show their appreciation. William Marshal, Earl of Pembroke congratulated Fulke with a hefty slap as he approached the dais to receive his own prize of a golden, horse-shaped aquamanile.

Waiting until the furore had abated, Fulke left his trestle, and approached Maude where she sat among the gathered noblewomen. She reddened and her glance met his before she lowered her gaze to the crumb-strewn trestle.

'My lady,' Fulke said, and with a courtly bow – he could not quite bring himself to play out the charade by kneeling – presented her with the green hair ribbon, somewhat frayed and muddied from the clashes on the field. 'I thank you for your favour and the good fortune it has brought me.'

'If it has brought you good fortune, then keep it,' she said unsteadily without looking up.

Fulke inclined his head. 'I am honoured,' he said impassively. Duty done, he returned to his place and tucked the length of green silk into his pouch with ambivalent feelings of disappointment and relief. He pushed them impatiently from his mind as he joined his companions. There was a gallon of wine to drink and an arm wrestling contest had just begun. Far better to opt for the safe shallows of honest masculine camaraderie than to drown in the murky depths of courtly love.

Maude watched the men at their sport, laughing, drinking, still play-fighting with each other as they had done on the tourney field. They were like children, she thought scornfully, and within that scorn was aware of more than a tinge of envy. Had she been male, she would have been there in the thick of it, powerful and confident. She imagined her elbow resting on the board, her hand clasping Fulke's, saw herself forcing him down into defeat and felt the heat in the pit of her belly.

CHAPTER 13

Alberbury, Shropshire, September 1195

Hawise FitzWarin was in the bailey, talking to a peddler who was laying out his wares on a red cloth, when the guard on duty shouted that Lord le Brun had returned.

'I have silver needles,' the man said. 'So fine that they will pass through silk and leave no hole.'

Hawise shaded her eyes in the direction of the gate.

Sensing that he was losing her attention, the peddler raised his voice. 'See this white rose-petal unguent, guaranteed to make your hands so soft and smooth that no man will be able to resist kissing them.'

'I'll have some then,' said Hawise's maid with a giggle, 'but only if you refund my coin if it doesn't work.'

'There's no question of that, mistress. You'll be desired all the way to Land's End, I promise you.'

Ignoring their banter, Hawise went to the gate. It was almost three weeks since her husband and sons had set out for London to press their case for the return of Whittington. They had been loyal supporters of King Richard, had contributed funds to the crusade and sacrificed a year's wool clip towards his ransom. In return, their case deserved a fair hearing. With Hubert Walter as Justiciar, Fulke le Brun had a firm hope that their plea would succeed.

Two serjeants unbarred the gates and swung them

ponderously inwards to admit the troop. From experience, Hawise stood well back from the horses and the dust raised by their trammelling hooves. Autumn might be on the threshold, but the softness of rain had yet to damp down the heavy summer dust. Her heart swelled with pride as she watched her menfolk draw rein and begin dismounting. They were so vital, so handsome, and now, for a short time at least, they were hers.

Fulke le Brun swung down from his courser and immediately turned to search for her. There were shadows of fatigue beneath his fine dark eyes and he was favouring his left leg where an old injury always plagued him when he was tired. But beneath the dust, beneath the exhaustion, he was glowing.

'We have it!' he cried fiercely as he saw her. 'Beloved, we have it!'

She ran into his arms. Gripping her as tightly as his shield in battle, le Brun swung her round and kissed her. She tasted dust on his lips and felt the salt moisture of either sweat or tears on his stubbled cheek. 'Oh, that is wonderful news, my love! You should have sent word ahead so that we could have a feast in celebration!'

'No, I wanted to tell you myself,' he said against her ear. 'I wanted to give it to you whole.' He thrust his hand inside his tunic and brought out a vellum packet mounted with the Justiciar's seal.

'What's this?' Hawise took it from him.

'Hubert Walter's adjudication that Whittington is ours.'

Hawise looked from the package to her husband. She laughed, more than half of her humour derived from disbelief. 'Just like that? You were not made to jump through burning hoops like a tumbler's dog?'

'Not one.'

It seemed too good to be true, but she did not want to

be a killjoy and dilute the euphoria of the moment by expressing doubts. Perhaps Hubert Walter truly had given them Whittington on the strength of their abiding loyalty. After hugging her husband again, she turned to greet her sons. Engulfed in half a dozen sweaty embraces, she saw that they shared their father's optimism. Even Philip, the quietest of the brood, wore a smug smile. William was positively gloating, and Fulke sported an ear-to-ear grin – as well he might since he was the heir and the one who would reap the full benefit of their gain.

'So what happens now?' Hawise asked as le Brun's squire finished unarming his lord and took the mail hauberk away for scouring and greasing. In a corner of the chamber, the maids were preparing an oval bathtub. Hawise had been raised with the rule that travellers, whether guests or family, should always be greeted with the offer of water for washing, clean clothes and refreshment. While the boys could do for themselves, using the laundry tubs if they so required, Hawise observed the formalities with her husband. A bath in their chamber gave them an opportunity to be alone and allowed him to soothe his aching joints and muscles without admitting weakness.

Moving stiffly to the tub, he eased himself into the steaming water with a groan of pleasure. 'What do you mean?'

'Do you just ride up to Whittington's gates with that judgement in your hands and command FitzRoger to leave?'

'Not unless I want an arrow through my throat.' He swilled his face and scooped his hands through his hair. With a pang of regret, Hawise saw that there was a greater amount of grey than black these days. 'I have to wait for the official writ from the Justiciar, for which I must pay the privilege of forty marks.' Le Brun grimaced at her. 'Yes,

I know, one more expense to bleed us dry, but once I have that writ in my hands, I have recourse to demand that royal officials evict Morys FitzRoger.'

'He will resist that, surely.' There was a note of anxiety in her voice. Although le Brun was skilled in battle, he was no longer young and it worried her to think of him with a sword in his hand.

'No doubt,' said le Brun with a wintry smile, 'but he will be offered suitable compensation. The royal manor of Worfield, so Hubert Walter suggests.'

Hawise brought him a cup of spiced wine. He drank it swiftly, his free arm resting on the edge of the tub, his knees slightly bent to accommodate his length. 'And when will you have the writ?' she asked.

'In the due course of judiciary business.' The gleam in his eyes dulled a little and weariness deepened the natural lines of ageing in his face. 'However long that might take. But our true right to Whittington has been recognised. It has taken more than forty years to come this far, but I know that my sons will reap the reward. There will be a Fulke FitzWarin at Whittington again. I feel it in my bones, and they never lie.' She saw him force a smile. 'Just now they are telling me that I'm no longer young enough to keep up with my sons and not pay for it.'

'Wine and a bath will refresh you,' Hawise said, concealing another pang at his words, which were an uncanny reflection of her thoughts. His health was not as robust as it had once been and he was much quicker to tire these days. 'Doubtless our sons are counting their saddle sores in trying to keep up with their father.'

'"*Fulco filius Warini debet xl m. pro habendo castello de Witinton sicut ei adiuticatum fuit in curia regis*,"' read the scribe in a nasal voice. 'Fulke FitzWarin pays a fine of forty marks to have the castle of Whittington as adjudged in the King's court.'

Morys FitzRoger gripped the lion's head finials on the lord's chair in Whittington's great hall and ground his teeth. His complexion darkened and the veins in his throat and temple bulged like whipcords. The scribe, recognising the signs, laid the scroll carefully down and began edging away. The messenger who had brought the letter from Morys's contact in the Justiciar's department had already made himself scarce.

'I will see the shit-eating son of a whore in hell first,' Morys wheezed. 'Let him pay as many fines as he wants. Those words aren't even worth wiping my arse upon.' Leaping suddenly to his feet, he snatched the vellum off the trestle, spat copiously upon the careful brown lettering, and then thrust the document into the flame of a wall cresset. 'Whittington belongs to my bloodline and it always will.'

The flame hissed on his spittle as the vellum was consumed. Drips of red wax splashed on the floor like blood.

'I don't understand,' said Weren, his eldest son. 'Why, after all this time, has the judgement gone in his favour?'

'Why?' Morys's upper lip curled. 'Because he's a lick-arse, and where his tongue cannot reach, his eldest son's does – right up the Archbishop of Canterbury's backside. They have Hubert Walter's favour, and his word is the law of the land.' He dropped the last twist of vellum before the flames scorched his fingers, then stamped on the burning fragment, grinding it beneath his heel.

'Then what can we do?'

Morys glared at the young man. 'What can we do?' he parodied in cruel imitation of Weren's light voice. 'You're like a mewling infant still in tail clouts. Have you no mind of your own?'

Weren turned crimson. 'Yes, Papa, but I defer to you.'

Morys gave an impatient growl and bit at a ragged strip of skin beside his thumbnail. 'Then set aside your deference for a moment. Tell me what you would do.' His voice was filled with challenge and scorn.

Weren frowned, clearly struggling. 'Fight?' he said.

'With the judgement in FitzWarin's favour?' Morys spat. 'Do you have pottage for brains? Why do you think the FitzWarins have never sought to take Whittington by force of arms in all the time that they have disputed it?'

'Because they are not strong enough?'

Morys bared his teeth. 'Because, boy, any use of arms would have made them outlaws and destroyed their claim. If we take up weapons against them, then we become the outlaws and it won't just be the FitzWarins evicting us, but the entire feudal host of Shropshire. And we are certainly not strong enough to withstand that.'

'I would submit a counter-claim,' Morys's second son Gwyn spoke out. 'Even if the FitzWarins are as thick as thieves with Hubert Walter, he is a man of high importance and to him the ownership of Whittington is but a small matter and easily forgotten. Fulke le Brun may be his friend, but we can make friends too – with the clerks who administer his commands.' To emphasise his point, he patted the money pouch at his belt.

Morys eyed Gwyn with shrewd approval. The only thing the lad had ever done wrong was to be born second. The older man sometimes thought that Weren's brains had been left behind in the womb and Gwyn had collected them on the way out. 'Indeed we can,' he said. 'Hubert Walter is not always going to be the King's Justiciar. He is already Archbishop of Canterbury and a papal legate. A man can only stretch himself so far before he fails.'

Gwyn stroked his sparse sandy beard. 'If the FitzWarins

are in high favour with Hubert Walter, perhaps there are other great men upon whose toes they have stepped. Was there not a rumour concerning le Brun's heir and a quarrel with Prince John?'

Morys chewed his lip and considered. 'Yes,' he said after a moment, 'I believe there was. I cannot remember the details, except that much of it was rumour, but it bears investigating. Prince John has lands in the Marches and if he does harbour a grudge against the FitzWarin family, then perhaps we can put it to good use.'

Gwyn nodded and looked at his father through thoughtfully narrowed lids. 'It would be fortunate for us if Fulke le Brun were to meet with an accident of some sort?' He phrased the statement as a question.

Not just brains, thought Morys, but underhand cunning. He did not know whether to be proud or disgusted. Sometimes cunning was a milder way of saying dishonour. 'From a point of personal satisfaction, yes,' he agreed. Returning to the board, he poured himself a cup of wine from the flagon. 'Other than that, it would be of no benefit to us. Le Brun has six sons, all of them dyed in the same wool as their sire.' He grimaced, remembering the incident in Oswestry. 'We would be rid of one devil only to land ourselves with another, and then another.'

'But we have to stop them, for if they gain possession, we have nothing.'

Morys nodded. 'Believe me, lad,' he said fiercely, 'there is naught I would like better than to take my sword and hew the entire brood of them limb from limb and stuff the pieces into the maw of hell, but we would destroy ourselves into the bargain. No, we play a waiting game.' He gave a wintry smile. 'After all, possession is nine-tenths of the law.'

CHAPTER 14

Winchester, Summer 1198

Maude approached the bedside and knelt to kiss her brother-in-law's episcopal ring.

'Daughter,' he croaked and gave her a tired smile. His lips were cracked and his breath was sour. Sweat shone in the slack folds of his jowls and soaked the hair surrounding his tonsure so that it stood up in spiky brown clumps.

Maude wondered if he was dying. Certainly it was in Theobald's mind. They had received an urgent message from a clerk of the judiciary household to say that Hubert had been taken ill with an ague.

'Hubert.' Theobald too kissed the ring of office, and then embraced his brother.

A glimmer of amusement appeared in the sunken eyes. 'Don't fret, Theo, you're the eldest and I have no intention of dying before you. I've too much to do here on earth to give my spirit to heaven just yet.' Hubert struggled to prop himself up against the bolsters and was taken with a bout of harsh coughing that left him gasping for breath.

Theobald helped him to sit and Maude brought him watered wine. Hubert drank greedily, then laid his head back with a gasp. 'It was good of you to come though.'

'You fool,' Theobald said fiercely. 'You'll work yourself into the grave.'

'And that's a skillet calling a cauldron black,' Hubert retorted. 'You scarcely sit at home with your feet on the hearth yourself.'

'But I'm not the Archbishop of Canterbury, the papal legate, the Justiciar *and* the Chancellor either,' Theobald snapped. 'Collecting coin for tourneys, being a travelling judiciary and administering a few chosen estates hardly compares. And don't tell me that I'm nagging like an old woman. Whatever you say, you would not have sent for me unless you believed you were very sick indeed.'

Hubert fiddled with the open strings on the neck of his nightshift. 'I admit I have been very ill, Theo, but I do truly believe that with God's aid I will recover.'

'And then what? Make yourself ill again?'

Hubert cast a commiserating gaze to Maude. 'Is he harsh like this with you?'

Maude looked from one to the other. Theobald's expression was exasperated. She knew how worried he was about Hubert. She also knew that railing at the sick man would achieve nothing beyond more exasperation. The mood had to be kept light. 'Only for my own good, so he claims,' she replied with demurely lowered lashes.

Theobald gave a splutter of indignation and Hubert chuckled, started coughing, and once more had to resort to the wine. When he had recovered, he reached out a febrile hand to pat his brother's shoulder.

'I'll put you out of your misery, Theo. You'll be pleased to know that even now one of my scribes is copying out a letter of resignation to King Richard. I am yielding the post of Justiciar. As you rightly say, I cannot be all things to all men, and, in truth, God should come first.'

'I am glad to hear it.' Theobald folded his arms and tried to look stern.

'The notion has been in my mind for some time. Indeed,

I have been grooming Geoffrey FitzPeter to take on the responsibility.'

Theobald grunted. 'I'll be even more pleased when you are well enough to leave your bed. Until you are, I am going to be your watchdog and ensure that you lift not so much as a little finger.'

'Then I will die of boredom instead of overwork!' Hubert protested, looking dismayed.

'You think my company boring?'

'Of course not, don't put words in my mouth, Theo.'

Maude left the brothers to their argument, which she knew they were both secretly enjoying. Theobald would know to stop before Hubert grew too tired.

Servants had brought their travelling baggage within the palace, the brass-bound clothing coffer, the pieces of their bed which would be assembled in a guest chamber, her embroidery frame and braid loom. She did not know how long they would be staying. There was no denying that Hubert was very sick, but he was bright enough to argue, and indeed did seem to be on the mend.

Theobald's interests had fared well while Hubert was Justiciar, but it had meant more responsibility and more time spent travelling the country. The increased pace had taken its toll on her husband too.

Of late Theobald had spoken of his wish for a quieter life. The revenues that had come to him as a result of Hubert's powerful position had been put towards founding various religious establishments. There was an Augustinian abbey at Cockersand in Amounderness, and several monasteries in Ireland. He spoke often of returning there, as if the place was drawing him. Sudden, dangerous illness had caused Hubert to evaluate his life, but Maude felt that Theobald had been unobtrusively putting his own house in order for the past year and more.

She gazed at the pieces of their bed. They still shared its broad, feather mattress when he was home or when she travelled with him, but mostly for the purpose of sleep. Occasionally he would wrap her in his embrace and, murmuring love words, enter her body with his, but it was an infrequent demand and not one that she sought to encourage. The pain of that first time had diminished, but the act was still uncomfortable. Mostly, Theobald treated her as a sexless companion. He would talk to her, using her to explore his ideas, to grumble or expound theories in the closeness of their bed where there were only her ears to hear. And for that she loved him and granted him the use of her body ungrudgingly on the rare occasions that he hungered.

Younger men tried to tempt her, believing that she could not possibly be satisfied with Theobald, but Maude rejected their advances with icy disdain. All they wanted was to get their hands beneath her gown and she had no time for their tawdry lusts. When she attended tourneys with Theobald, they would clamour to wear her favour, and sometimes she had to give it for goodwill, since Theobald was responsible for collecting the fees of those hoping to make their mark on the field. She now had a store of purpose-bought ribbons to distribute. Not since that first tourney, when she had given Fulke FitzWarin her plait binding, had she bestowed a personal piece of apparel on any knight.

Sometimes Fulke would attend the tourneys, but he kept his distance and she kept hers. A polite nod in passing was as much as each gave in acknowledgement of the other. If by chance they sat close at the tourney feast, their conversation was courteous but stilted and without eye contact.

The reputation of Fulke and his troop drew large

audiences and the revenues from the tourneys they attended were satisfyingly high, delighting Theobald. Such was the level of expertise, there were even murmurs that Fulke's talent rivalled that of the great William Marshal in his youth. His skill in the saddle brought other rewards too, Maude had noticed with a jaundiced eye. Not just from women like Hanild, but others of more refined birth whose blood was stirred by his performance in the field. They wanted him to perform heroically in their beds too. Her cheeks flushed at the notion and she turned abruptly from studying her own bed.

'Lady Walter?' A wiry, handsome young man with an olive complexion and dancing dark eyes was addressing her from the doorway. He bowed. 'I do not know if you remember me. We were introduced at your wedding. My name is Jean de Rampaigne and I'm one of His Grace's retainers.'

'Yes, of course I remember,' Maude said. It was a half-truth but in her position she had quickly learned the courtesies that greased the wheels. She had been introduced to many people and although he looked familiar, she could place it in no particular context.

'I am glad that Lord Theobald has arrived,' the young knight said. 'He is family and His Grace will recover the swifter for seeing him. I think that Lord Theobald is one of the few people to whom my master will listen. If his older brother tells him to stay abed and rest, he might do so.' He looked wry. 'When he summoned you, he did truly believe that he was at death's door, and so did we. He takes too much upon himself.'

'So he has admitted. I suppose it must be a family trait.'

'He has told you that he is to resign the post of Justiciar to Geoffrey FitzPeter?'

She nodded.

'I'm to carry the message to King Richard as soon as the scribe has made fair copies.'

Giving him a more thorough scrutiny, Maude replaced his clean-shaven visage with a cropped black beard and dressed him in a tunic of bright red wool instead of the plainer tawny robe he wore now. She snapped her fingers. 'I remember you at Lancaster! You played a lute and you sang a song about a woman called Melusine.' She smiled at him. 'I thought you were very accomplished.'

'Thank you, my lady.' The white flash of his smile gave him the face of a handsome rogue. 'I do sometimes travel in the guise of a troubadour. Singing for my supper is a useful skill to have.'

'I did not realise you were a member of Hubert's household.'

He shrugged. 'No reason for you to do so. I served as a squire with your lord husband, but I took the Cross with Lord Hubert.' He tilted his head to one side and a gleam that was almost mischievous entered his eyes. 'When I came to Lancaster it was in the company of Fulke FitzWarin. He was once one of your husband's squires too.'

'Yes, I know.' Maude's tone lost its warmth and she drew herself up.

'He's a good friend, but I haven't seen him in a while.'

She gave him a stony look. 'Then perhaps you should ride the tourney circuits and frequent the taverns,' she said, and then closed her mouth, realising that she must sound censorious and angry when it was none of her concern what Fulke FitzWarin did with his life.

His smiled widened. 'Ah no, my lady. I have enough excitement in my life as it is.'

The door opened and Theobald emerged from the sick

room. Maude was pleased to see that he had cast off the anxiety he had worn when they arrived. Clearly, he too was convinced that Hubert would live.

'Jean!' With a cry of delight, he strode forward to embrace the young knight. 'How are you faring?'

'Well, my lord. And you?'

Murmuring her excuses, feeling unsettled, Maude went to organise her maids and begin sorting the baggage coffers.

Mounted on his dun cob, Fulke le Brun listened to the whistle of the autumn wind and felt its sharpness not only about his face, but also in the right arm holding the reins. There was a tight band across his chest, constricting his breathing. The autumn woods surrounding the keep at Whittington wore a dying treasure of gold, bronze and verdigris copper against a sky of knife-blue and the beauty was so powerful that it cut him to the core. But still the pain was not as great as that engendered by the sight of the castle, his birthright, standing on the marshy ground beyond the woods. Close enough to touch, unattainable as a star. He gazed upon the limewashed timber palisade and gatehouse, on the roofs of the wooden structures within its outer defences; the smug twirls of blue domestic smoke rising through its louvres; the guards pacing the wall walks, sharp sunlight reflecting off their spear tips.

'My lord, it is not safe,' said the knight Ralf Gras, whom he had brought for company. His father was a FitzWarin tenant and Ralf had served his apprenticeship as one of le Brun's squires.

Le Brun smiled bleakly, without taking his eyes from the keep. The pain had eased a little, becoming a dull ache. 'I'll take the risk.'

The young man said nothing, but le Brun sensed the unspoken question. 'A messenger arrived from the court yester eve,' he said. 'Hubert Walter has yielded the post of Justiciar to Geoffrey FitzPeter.'

Ralf raised his brows. 'Is that bad news, my lord?'

Le Brun grimaced. 'Hubert Walter granted me the right to Whittington in the royal court, pending the granting of an alternative estate to Morys FitzRoger in compensation for his loss, but now I doubt how much further it will go. I have no rapport with FitzPeter and, as John's man, he will not be interested in advancing the judgement.' He spoke quietly, the bitterness present but controlled.

The night before he had not been as restrained. Fortunately, owing to the lateness of the hour, the messenger had delivered the letter in his private solar and only Hawise had been present to witness the destructive force of his rage.

'A lifetime of waiting and lies and broken promises,' he had snarled, hurling a goblet across the room, following it with the flagon, kicking a coffer so hard that he had almost broken his toes. 'It is over three years since Whittington was adjudged to me, and still I am made to wait for it and look like a fool!' He had sent the candlestand crashing over to accompany that remark and Hawise had shrieked at him to stop. He had roared at her like a goaded bull, raised his fist, stared at it in horror and all the fury remaining in him had imploded across his chest in a band of fiery lead. He had a vague recollection of sitting on their bed, doubled over with pain, of Hawise's arms around him and the terror in her voice. Mercifully, the pain had ebbed, but the undertow had dragged something of himself with it, leaving him hollow with loss.

Hawise had not wanted him to ride out from Alberbury this morning, but she could not stop him any more than he could stop himself. The need to see Whittington was a compulsion that drove all other considerations from his mind. Now, from the shelter of the trees, he sat and gazed until his eyes watered with the staring.

'My father spent all his life in dispute over this place,' he murmured. 'I was fourteen years old when we lost it, but I can still remember standing on the wall walk and looking out towards Wales.'

'How did you come to lose it?' Ralf asked curiously.

Le Brun spoke with the flatness of a tale told so often that it emerged by rote. 'The Welsh raided Whittington in the last years of King Stephen's reign while we were at Alberbury. By the time my father arrived with our soldiers, they had taken the keep and slaughtered the garrison.' Le Brun's lip curled as if the tale was souring his mouth. 'Roger de Powys was their leader. He was half-Norman, half-Welsh with a few scattered holdings, but gaining Whittington gave him prestige.' He made an angry gesture and his horse sidled. Le Brun drew the reins in tight, controlling himself as much as his mount.

'King Stephen and Prince Henry had no time to spare for war in Wales as well as war with each other. De Powys was left in possession of Whittington and we were given Alveston as a temporary measure with the unwritten promise that Whittington would be restored to us when Roger died.' He looked at Ralf. 'All men on whatever side they fought were supposed to have the lands that had been theirs in the time of the first Henry before the conflict began. But a royal promise is not worth the quill with which it is written.' Le Brun almost spat the last word. 'So now I come to look at what is mine by right and held in the hands of a thief at the behest of an oath-breaker.' For an instant longer he gazed upon the timbered keep and the banners fluttering from its battlements then pivoted his horse and dug in his heels.

They trotted single file through the woods, intending to

meet the road that linked Oswestry to Shrewsbury. But as they crossed a small charcoal burner's clearing, a party of huntsmen with dogs and hawks barred their path. The wind roared through the trees like an ocean on the turn and le Brun felt its surge within his body. Pounding, taking and threshing him in its tumult.

A beautiful peregrine falcon perched on the gloved fist of Morys FitzRoger, preventing him from drawing his sword. His companions, however, including his sons, freed theirs from their scabbards with alacrity. Morys held up his left hand to stop them, the movement slow and controlled to avoid frightening the hawk.

'I presume you have come to look at what you cannot have,' he said to le Brun in a contemptuous voice. 'For a man who bears the teeth of a wolf on his shield, you have nothing left with which to bite.'

Le Brun had reached to his own sword hilt but refrained from drawing the weapon. Partly it was because they were two against ten, but mostly in response to the terrible pain that was ripening in his chest. 'Whittington is mine, as adjudged in the King's court,' he gasped through clenched teeth. It was hard to breathe, as if he were sucking air through a cushion.

'Face the truth,' Morys sneered. 'That judgement was a sop from Hubert Walter's office to keep you quiet and off the Justiciar's back. They've forgotten you and they've abandoned the judgement. You are trespassing on land that is not yours and never will be.'

'This is not the end.' It took all le Brun's determination, all his stubborn pride to keep him in the saddle. A grey haze veiled his eyes.

'Oh, I think it is. If ever you trespass on my territory again, I will kill you out of hand. Go home, old man, and nurse your bones by your own hearth instead of coveting another's,' sneered FitzRoger, as if the ten years by which Le Brun was older than him was a lifetime. He gestured. The knights in the hunting party closed around le Brun and Ralf Gras, disarming them while two of the huntsmen set out with dogs to make sure that there were no hostile troops hiding in the forest. Finally, FitzRoger had le Brun and his companion escorted through the woods to the Oswestry road.

Le Brun leaned over his saddle as the pain crashed over him, wave upon wave, surging, grabbing him, dragging him away from the shore and out to sea.

'Sir?' In consternation, Ralf grabbed the bridle of his lord's mount.

With a last conscious effort, le Brun exerted pressure on the reins and brought his horse round so that he was facing the road to Whittington. 'Tell Hawise . . .' he said, fighting for breath, 'tell Hawise that I'm sorry.'

Ralf's instincts and reflexes were swift. He was off his horse and managed to catch Fulke le Brun as he toppled from the saddle.

But there was nothing he could do.

Snow had covered the land in a white shroud, and in the bitterly cold air a leaden sky threatened to turn the light covering into a full blanket. The peasants huddled close to their hearths and housed their beasts in a partitioned section of the same room for warmth and shelter. Folk obliged to be out in the weather wore their warmest cloaks and hoods, and travellers made haste to reach their destinations.

Fulke rode into Canterbury on a freezing December dusk to seek shelter and audience with Archbishop Hubert. His Grace, however, was absent on business, although his elder brother and wife were in residence.

'It grieved me to hear of your father's death.' Theobald

Walter offered Fulke his hand in sympathy. 'He was a fine man and, as I came to know him, a good friend.'

Fulke returned the handclasp. Theobald's fingers were warm. His own were frozen claws from gripping the reins. Even with gloves, the cold still penetrated. 'It was a full month before the messenger found us with the news,' Fulke said grimly, his eyes dark with pain. 'The tourney season was good and the weather held so fine that we stayed longer than usual. If we had come home at the appointed time, I might have been able to prevent what happened.'

'I thought your father died because his body failed him.'

Fulke gratefully took the hot wine that Theobald offered. They were alone in the warmth of the private solar, the shutters barred against the inclement weather and several charcoal braziers giving off a luxurious heat. There was no sign of Maude, and he assumed that she was keeping to the women's chamber since a high proportion of celibate – and supposedly chaste – clergy occupied the Archbishop's residence.

'That is partly true,' he said. 'But I believe that his heart not so much failed as broke within him. He could neither eat nor sleep for thinking of the injustice done to us over Whittington. The knight who brought him home to my mother said that my father was humiliated by FitzRoger and it was the final blow to shatter him.'

'Humiliated?' Theobald's gaze sharpened.

Fulke told him about le Brun's visit to Whittington and the incident in Babbin's Wood. 'Perhaps my father was foolish to go there, but I can understand the frustration that drove – and eventually killed – him.'

Theobald sat down with his wine and lapped his fur-lined cloak over his knees. 'I cannot say that I understand the depths of your father's striving for I have never been deprived of something I consider my birthright, but nevertheless I sympathise.' He looked shrewdly at Fulke who had remained on his feet, his tension palpable. 'We are all driven by our demons – ambition, hatred, love.'

Fulke took a swallow of wine. 'He wanted Whittington above all things, perhaps even above my mother who was the light of his life. I have often wondered if Whittington was his darkness. Certainly it destroyed him.'

'You must not let it destroy you,' Theobald said, his gaze troubled.

Fulke paced to the shutters, stopped and swung round. Candlelight shone on his hair like a reflection in black water. 'I have no intention of letting it do so, but still it is my legacy. For my father's sake I have to see this matter through to the end.'

Theobald was silent, considering. 'Can you not just let it drop?' he said at last.

Fulke shook his head. 'The Curia Regis has granted our entitlement to Whittington. We have a ruling that confirms our claim, but the order commanding FitzRoger to quit has never gone out from the Justiciar's bench. The matter has to be settled and, as head of my family, it falls my duty. Besides, Whittington is not some small, insignificant manor. It encompasses more than seventeen geldable hides, including more than a league of woodland, and land for twenty-five ploughs.'

'So that is why you are here to see my brother?'

'He was the Justiciar at the time of the ruling, and he still has contact with that office and the officials. He trained Geoffrey FitzPeter as his successor.'

'Do not expect miracles,' Theobald warned. 'Hubert does have a certain influence, but Geoffrey FitzPeter is not a man to be pushed without strong reason.'

'Is justice not a strong enough reason?' Fulke demanded on a rising note.

Theobald gave a slight shake of his head. 'You know the world of court politics as well as I do. Justice is always subject to personal loyalties, favours owing, debts called in and bribery. None of us is exempt.'

Fulke swore and paced the room. He had to move. If he remained still his emotions would explode like a barrel of hot pitch. 'Do you know,' he said, 'my brother William wanted to ride straight to Whittington, lay siege to the keep and slaughter Morys FitzRoger and his sons out of hand? Ivo and Alain were all for it too. They said the only way we would ever get Whittington back was over Morys's dead body.'

'What was your answer?'

'I said that to get to Morys we would have to step over my father's dead body too, and that I had at least to try a final time to obtain Whittington through the King's court.' He rubbed the back of his neck. 'Now I wonder if William was right. Perhaps I should have followed my gut and theirs and gone to Whittington with fire and sword.'

'You would have been foolish to do so,' Theobald murmured. 'Two wrongs do not make a right.'

'Then what does?' Fulke demanded bitterly. He drained his wine. 'If I do not succeed in wringing a notice from Geoffrey FitzPeter to take seisin of Whittington, then two wrongs or not, I swear on God's holy name that I will go to war and damn the consequences.'

Despite the bone-chilling wintry conditions, Maude had been thoroughly enjoying herself among Canterbury's merchants and traders. Wrapped in a cosy, fur-lined cloak and hood, her shoes lined with fleece, she was insulated against the cold. Shopping was not only pleasurable, it helped to fill the hollow feeling that sometimes disturbed her sense of wellbeing. Although he had not the slightest interest in trailing around the booths himself, Theobald was quite content to let her go out with her maid, two serjeants and a purse full of silver to purchase whatever she desired. She did not know whether to be flattered by his trust in her common sense and good taste, or irritated by his lack of enthusiasm.

She had bought him a beechwood cross intricately carved with a knotwork design that the trader had assured her was Irish. It was strung on a simple leather cord and she thought that Theobald would like it. The rusticity of the wood combined with the beauty of the carving could not fail to appeal since his mind was often on Ireland and his foundations there.

For herself she had purchased several belt lengths of braid, some linen to make a chemise and fine silver needles that would not leave great stitch holes in the fabric. She had enjoyed the stalls, their colours bright and brave in the winter chill, and the haggling had roused her competitive spirit.

As she made her way back to the palace, the snow that had been threatening all day began to sprinkle down like fine ground almonds through the mesh of a hair sieve, dusting the ground, outlining the contours of the houses. Chunky wax candle flames shone golden through the thick window glass of the Archbishop's palace, drawing Maude towards their cheering warmth. She walked briskly across the courtyard, her nose and cheeks numb with the cold, her eyes sparkling.

The environs of the Archbishop's palace were always busy with couriers, supplicants, guests and clerics, so Maude paid no heed to the two horses that a groom was tending until one of the animals threw up its head and whinnied as something startled it. Maude turned instinctively to look. Cursing, the attendant dodged the sudden flail of hooves to grab the headstall and bring the horse under control. It was a striking liver-chestnut stallion with distinctive white face markings. She knew the animal well, even if she did not recognise the nondescript dun rouncey at its side. Blaze, Fulke FitzWarin's destrier. Her heart rose, plummeted, and rose again.

'What is he doing here?' she said with agitation.

'My lady?' Barbette hunched over her folded arms and looked longingly towards the palace.

Biting her lip, Maude shook her head. He did not appear to have arrived with a great retinue. Obviously, he was making a personal visit, which meant that, with Hubert absent, he would be closeted with Theobald. She drew a deep breath, steeled herself and went within.

Once in her chamber, she wondered if she should change her gown for something more becoming than the plain brown wool she was wearing and immediately berated herself for being vain and foolish. The brown wool was her warmest dress. What would be the point in shivering in her green linen gown with the gores and gold braid in order to impress a knight whom she did not even particularly like? Besides, his father had recently died and it would be tasteless to commiserate whilst robed in her court finery.

Finally, as a sop to her feminine vanity which refused to be entirely silenced, she donned her new goatskin shoes and exchanged her plain belt for one of the pretty braid ones she had bought at the booths. Then, feeling armed if not suitably girded for battle, she left the safety of her chamber for the danger of the solar.

Opening the door tentatively, she gazed around. There was no sign of Theobald. Fulke FitzWarin sat in a curule chair near the brazier, his elbows on his knees, his head braced in his hands and his entire posture one of utter weariness. He looked so vulnerable, so different from the brash tourney knight of her experience whose traits she had exaggerated in self-defence, that she had no protection.

He must have sensed the draught from the door, for he raised his head and looked round. Immediately he lowered his hands and sprang to his feet. 'Lady Walter,' he said and bowed. The weariness remained but the vulnerability retreated behind a polite mask. The smoke-hazel eyes gave nothing away, except by the dark smudges beneath them, yet his jaw was taut with the effort of appearing impassive.

'Lord FitzWarin,' she returned, using the title that was now his by right. There was a moment's uncomfortable silence. Maude considered muttering an excuse and leaving him, but that was the coward's way out and even if she and Fulke had never been at ease with each other, it would still have been unforgivably rude. Gathering her courage, she entered the room and came to him.

'I was sorry to hear of your father's death,' she murmured. 'He and your mother extended me every kindness when I was at Westminster. I have written to Lady Hawise, and I will visit her when I can.'

'That is good of you, my lady,' Fulke replied, avoiding her gaze.

'How is she?'

'Grieving — as we all are.'

He was shunning her, each reply given grudgingly with scarcely a movement of his lips. She felt a niggle of irritation. 'More wine, my lord?' She picked up his empty cup.

He shook his head. 'My skull already feels as if it is stuffed with a whole fleece. Another cup and I would be on the floor.' He cleared his throat and moved away to stand before the shutters. A chessboard stood on a low table and he toyed with one of the squat ivory pieces. 'Your husband was called away by one of the stewards, but he said he would not be long. If you have duties, do not let me keep you.'

Maude flushed. 'I have the duty of seeing to your comfort,' she almost snapped.

'I doubt anything you could do would improve that,' he said, then dug his hands through his heavy black hair and flashed her a look in which she saw her own irritation mirrored. 'I am not good company at the moment, Lady Walter, and best left to my own devices. By all means, find me a sleeping space and a pallet on which to lay my head. I would be grateful even if my gratitude does not show.' He gave her the semblance of a smile, the merest curve of his lips that did not reach his eyes.

'Of course. You will excuse me.' Glad that he had given her a reason to retreat, Maude briskly left the room and did not return. Having survived one encounter, she was not going to risk a second.

Fulke slumped against the wall and put his face in his hands. Theobald arrived to find him standing by the chess-board, shuddering with dry rigors. Wrapping him in a paternal embrace, murmuring words of comfort, the older man brought him back to the warmth of the brazier.

Hubert Walter took a large bite out of his portion of chicken in verjuice and, chewing, considered Fulke's request. 'I agree the matter of Whittington should have been settled long ago – one way or the other,' he said. 'But the course of justice does not often run as smoothly as we would wish.'

It was Hubert the royal official speaking and Fulke had to struggle with his patience. A raw headache pounded behind his eyes and he had barely touched his food. He had no time for all the delicate spices, the little touches and fripperies that graced the Archbishop's rich and

Epicurean table – not tonight anyway. His need was for the plain and simple, without gilding or embellishment.

'I know your family lost Whittington when the Welsh overran it and the de Powys family took possession. What was temporary became permanent because the de Powys family had their feet in both camps and restoring Whittington to your family would have upset the delicate balance at the time.' Hubert smiled without humour. 'Henry trusted the FitzWarins not to rebel more than he trusted the Welsh.' He wagged a salutary forefinger. 'You were given Alveston to compensate.'

'As a sop,' Fulke snorted, unimpressed. 'Alveston is a quarter the size of Whittington. And I am not so sure that King Richard can have the same trust in me as he had in my father and grandfather.'

'Is that a threat?' Hubert's eyebrows rose.

'A threat, a warning, call it what you will. There are two sides to the bargain when an oath of loyalty is sworn. We have kept our side, answered calls to arms and performed feudal service on demand. It seems to me that all we have received in return is a pouchful of nothing.'

Hubert dabbed his lips with a fine linen napkin. 'Those are harsh words, Fulke, and dangerous too.'

'It is a grief for me that I should have to speak them, your grace, but they are true. I do not want to spend the rest of my life fighting this dispute as my father did and die bequeathing it to sons of my own. It must be finished now.'

Hubert Walter leaned his head against the hard back of his chair and studied Fulke, as if by gazing he could draw out his character and examine its workings. 'I can promise nothing,' he said at last, 'but I will do what I can. Since Whittington was adjudged to your father, and it belonged to your family in the time of the first King Henry, I would

say that you have a reasonable case. You have a death duty
to pay to inherit your father's estates.'

'A hundred marks,' Fulke said on a slightly aggrieved
note. It was the standard payment for the relief on a barony,
but still it would absorb this year's wool clip and more
besides.

Hubert nodded, ignoring Fulke's tone. 'Then let Whittington be included in the list of lands for which you pay
your fine. I will ask Geoffrey FitzPeter to have a document
drafted and when I go to King Richard in Normandy after
the Christmas season, I will see that he lends a sympathetic
ear to your case.'

Knowing the many occasions when hope had turned to
disappointment for his father, Fulke's expression did not
light with joy, but he was nevertheless grateful. If matters
had gone the wrong way, he might have found himself an
excommunicate. 'Thank you, your grace.' He bowed his
head.

Hubert eased his bulk in the chair. He reminded Fulke
of an overfed tawny lion. Sleepy, flabby, but still powerful
enough to kill with an indolent flash of claw. 'Do not thank
me,' he said with a wave of his hand. 'I know your capa-
bilities and Richard needs men like you to take his part,
not act against him. I would hate to see your playing on
the tourney field become a thing of deadly earnest.'

'Indeed, your grace, so would I.'

Hubert raised his cup in toast. 'To peace then.'

'To peace,' Fulke said, and crossed himself.

'His father's death has hit him hard,' Theobald remarked
to Maude as they prepared for bed that night. 'It was strange
to see him like that. He reminded me of the youth he was
when he first became my squire, and at the same time all
trace of the youth had gone.'

Maude drew her antler-work comb through her hair. 'He has responsibility now, where he had none before,' she said.

'Mayhap.' Theobald looked up from examining the knotwork cross she had given him. 'But it is more that he loved his father dearly. I held him in my arms and he wept for him.'

'Fulke FitzWarin wept?' Maude ceased combing and turned to stare at Theobald. She thought of the moment she had opened the door and seen Fulke sitting with his head in his hands, of his attempt to be civil, her own frosty courtesy. Chagrin washed over her. She felt small and mean.

'Why do you persist in thinking of him as a manner-less boor?' Theobald demanded with exasperation. 'Fulke can be as stubborn as an ox, I admit, and once set on a course it's impossible to deflect him. He lacks diplomacy. With Fulke there are no sugared words, just the blunt truth, but that does not mean he lacks finer feelings.'

'I did not say that.' Mathilda jutted her chin at him defensively. She was in the wrong, but, as always, admitting it was hard. 'He just seems so . . . so impervious!'

'I think he is like that in front of you because of his pride. Few men will open themselves to a woman, even if it be their mother or their wife.'

'You do.'

'In certain matters, yes, but only God has seen the true baring of my soul.' He looked at the little cross and tucked it down inside his linen shirt so that it lay against his skin.

This was why he was so keen to found his monasteries, she thought. God, being masculine, would understand a man's soul and make allowances. It was a somewhat blas-phemous notion and she kept it to herself.

Coming to the bed, Theobald took the comb out of her hand and gently began to run it through her hair, smoothing out the tangles, making the silvery waterfall sparkle with life. 'Besides,' he said gently, 'Fulke deliberately keeps you at arm's length. You are his mentor's wife and the age gap between you and me is so large that tongues will wag about the state of our marriage at the slightest opportunity.'

Maude rounded on him with flashing eyes. 'That is wicked. I have never so much as looked at another man since our wedding day!' Her face was bright with indignation. 'And certainly not at Fulke FitzWarin!'

'Hush now, be not so wroth.' Theobald drew her back to him, an indulgent smile in his eyes. 'I know that you are faithful and I know that your eyes do not stray – or if they do it is only in the manner that they would to admire a fine horse or a meadow of flowers. I do the same myself. But Fulke has known the ways of the court and the tourney and therefore he is careful.'

'He has no reason to be,' she snapped, folding her arms vigorously. 'I am not some simple-witted tourney slut to be devastated by his charm!'

Behind her, Theobald shook his head and with an exasperated half-smile abandoned that particular strand of the conversation. While he would have liked to foster a decent friendship between Maude and Fulke, he was also aware of the inherent jeopardy. They were both young and volatile. 'I am glad that my brother agreed to help him,' he remarked instead. 'It was the right thing to do.'

Maude was just as glad to leave talk of her relationship with Fulke FitzWarin. There were too many conflicting emotions to make sense of any of them. She was horribly aware of having protested too vehemently about the faith of her marriage vow. Theobald might be growing old, but his perceptions remained as sharp as an awl. 'You know Fulke FitzWarin better than I,' she said. 'Do you think he truly will rebel if the decision goes against him?'

Unseen by his wife, the fine lines around Theobald's eyes tightened, but she did not miss the sudden hesitation of his hand in mid-stroke. 'It takes a great deal to push Fulke over the line, but once it is done, he will not go back. I hope that he receives his wish because yes, in the wrong circumstances, he is quite capable of rebelling with a vengeance.'

It was a warm evening at the end of March 1199 when Richard Coeur de Lion rode beneath the walls of the fortress of Châlus Chabrol in Aquitaine to urge on his soldiers. They were besieging the keep which belonged to his enemy, the Vicomte de Limoges. The defenders were pinned down by fire from Richard's archers, but one crossbowman, using a frying pan as a shield, stood up on the castle walls, took aim and loosed a shot. Richard had been laughing with admiration at the man's boldness, but that stopped abruptly as the bolt skimmed the top of the red and gold shield and lodged in Richard's collar bone.

At first it seemed a superficial injury, but the bolt was in deep and the surgeon had to probe the wound to extract the iron head. Fever quickly developed and the festering wound turned gangrenous.

On the sixth of April, as the world basked in the renewal of spring, Richard Coeur de Lion died, bequeathing his soul to God and his throne to his brother, John. And to John's care were consigned all the charters and documents, all the writs that were awaiting Richard's attention. Among them, close to the top of the pile, was a request from Hubert Walter, Archbishop of Canterbury, that Fulke FitzWarin be given full seisin of his father's lands, including the keep of Whittington and all its environs and appurtenances.

Roscelin, the clerk responsible, gathered the vellum scrolls, slammed them back in their coffer and sent them on to their new master to be sanctioned.

CHAPTER 15

Alberbury, The Welsh Marches, Summer 1199

Fulke studied the roll of vellum that the messenger had recently presented to him and grimly broke the seal. He had known it was coming, but even so, he could feel a knot of anger and apprehension tightening in his belly.

'What is it?' Hawise rose from her tapestry frame by the window and came across to him.

'What I've been expecting. A summons to pay homage to John at Castle Baldwin in two weeks' time.' He could not keep the distaste from his voice and the wolfhound dozing beneath the dais table raised his head and whined.

His mother took the document and screwed up her eyes to study the royal seal.

'He might be the anointed King of England and due my homage,' Fulke growled, 'but kneeling at his feet and swearing loyalty will be a bitter draught to swallow.'

Hawise raised her eyes from the letter and looked anxiously at him. 'You will do it?'

Fulke winced. 'What other choice do I have? There is no one else. John's nephew Prince Arthur is only a child of twelve — and a spoiled French brat, so I've heard from those who have met him.' He shrugged. 'The devil you know, or the devil you don't. I warrant a long spoon's needed to sup with either.'

'What of Whittington?'

'John must honour the judgement,' he said grimly.

'And if he does not?'

He looked at his mother. In the year since his father's death she had grown old before his eyes. It was as if she had half died when they buried le Brun. The hollows beneath her cheekbones were cadaverous, the angle of her jaw so sharp that it was almost a blade. 'I will cross that bridge if it arises,' he said.

'It was your father's dearest and dying wish that we regain Whittington.' Her voice faltered slightly and her hand trembled on the vellum.

'I know that, Mama.' So dear that it had killed him and turned his mother from a beautiful, vivacious woman into a crone overnight. 'I will do all within my power to honour his memory.' He set his arm around her shoulders and kissed her cheek.

Hawise leaned against him briefly, then, with a shaky breath, drew away and stiffened her spine. 'Sometimes I think that it would have been better if my father had arranged my marriage to a man I did not love, then the pain of loss would not be so great.' Her eyes glittered with tears. 'But then I tell myself that I would never have known the joy either, or borne sons who fill me with such pride. All of you honour his memory.'

Fulke said nothing. Words, no matter how comforting, were just words and he found himself awkward in the face of his mother's life-consuming grief. Clearing his throat, he pivoted on his heel and headed towards the door.

'Where are you going?'

He heard the lost cry in her voice and his own throat tightened and swelled in response. She had been so strong and vibrant when his father was alive that her disintegration now was all the harder to bear.

'To find my brothers and tell them,' he said, taking refuge from emotion in practicality. 'I will not be gone long. Finn, come.' He snapped his fingers to the dozing wolfhound, a great-grandson of the bitch that Oonagh FitzGerald had given him. Tail wagging, the dog rose and followed him.

Outside the door, he encountered his aunt Emmeline bearing a jug of wine. She was his father's widowed sister and had the FitzWarin dark brown eyes and warm olive complexion.

'Was the news good?' she asked.

'I'm to go and pay homage to John for my lands,' Fulke said neutrally. He nodded over his shoulder towards the interior of the room. 'Look after her. She needs you.'

'Aye, we're all grieving, but she's finding it hard to move on,' Emmeline replied sympathetically and pointed at the jug. 'Third one today. She's like a soldier with a battle wound, drinking to numb the pain.' Then with a little sigh, she entered the room and drew the curtain pole across. Fulke heard Emmeline's soothing murmur and his mother's reply, the sound rising and cracking on a sob. Clenching his fists, he strode away in search of his brothers.

King John sat in state in Castle Baldwin's great hall and gently stroked the breast feathers of the white gerfalcon that perched on his gloved wrist, its talons gleaming like scimitars. It had just been presented to him as a gift. Such birds, the fastest and fiercest of the longwings, were rare and beautiful. Grey ones fetched a high price, but the expense of the white lay in the realm of magnates and kings, of which he was now one.

Through eyelids narrow with suspicion, John surveyed the kneeling man who had presented him with the bird. Morys FitzRoger was a minor border baron who could ill afford so costly a gift unless he expected high favour in return. John could think of no reason why he should wish to grant this man a boon, even if he was pleased with the gerfalcon. He had learned from a very young age that everything and everyone had a price, either material or emotional.

'There is a war horse too, sire,' FitzRoger announced, 'a destrier bred from the line of the de Bellême greys. I ask you to receive it as a token of my loyalty.'

A murmur went round the gathered courtiers. The de Bellême greys were renowned for their looks, their stamina – and their cost. John's suspicion increased, and so did his curiosity. The man was clearly desperate to buy his good favour. Perhaps FitzRoger had committed some heinous crime in Richard's reign and desired to wipe the slate clean. Alternatively, perhaps he was trying to divert suspicion from rebellious tendencies by proving how 'loyal' he truly was. John knew that there were many barons who begrudged him the Crown and were not to be trusted out of his sight.

'Your generosity does you credit,' he murmured with a regal tilt of his head. He looked at the bird, its fierce eyes and beak covered by an exquisitely stitched hood of scarlet silk. His forefinger gently dipped amongst the gleaming breast feathers and stroked with sensual slowness. 'But then I ask myself what you hope to gain. No man beggars himself just for the joy of presenting a gift.'

FitzRoger's head remained bowed. 'My only desire is to serve you to the best of my ability, sire.'

'Well, that's refreshing to hear.' John shot a barbed look at his courtiers. He was reasonably sure of William Marshal, Hubert Walter and de Braose. William Ferrers, Eustace de Vesci and Ranulf of Chester were more suspect and would bear watching. 'Remind me, what lands do you hold?'

Now Morys FitzRoger looked up and John saw him flush and his breathing quicken. Here then was the meat of the matter. 'I hold the honour of Whittington, sire, as it

was held by my father when your own sire bestowed it
upon him.'

'Whittington.'The name tugged at John's memory. What
was it about Whittington?

'If it be your pleasure, I would request that you confirm
the lands to me and my heirs by your charter,' FitzRoger
plunged on and in the Baron's eyes John saw a hunger that
verged on desperation. John's vision suddenly filled with the
image of another man kneeling at his feet in the cloudy
dust of a summer highway, not in homage but in resentment. Hard on the heels of that came the recollection of a
raw winter's evening at Westminster and a splintered chessboard. 'Surely the lordship of Whittington is in dispute?' he
said silkily. 'Does not the FitzWarin family possess a claim?'

FitzRoger's flush darkened and he lifted his head. 'A false
claim, sire. Once they held the land from Lord Peverel, but
they lost it during the war between Stephen and Empress
Mathilda. It has been ours since that time, and so granted
by the settlement between King Stephen and your father.'

John handed the hawk to a courtier and motioned
FitzRoger to rise. Then he leaned back on the carved oak
throne and lightly tugged at the dark beard on the point
of his chin. 'So you say. Do you have a charter?'

'It . . . It was always a verbal understanding, sire.' FitzRoger
looked as if he might choke.

'And the FitzWarins: do they have written evidence to
back their claim?'

Morys shook his head emphatically. 'They do not, sire.'

He would say that anyway, John thought. 'So it is your
word against theirs, but you have the advantage of possession.' He continued to toy with his beard. Clearly,
FitzRoger desired passionately to hold on to the land and
the castle – as well he might, given its important position
and the accompanying estate. Likely he could wring more

from him than a gerfalcon and a Bellême stallion and still be avenged on the FitzWarins for past humiliations. John began to smile with malicious delight. 'Have your claim written down by a scribe and copies made.' He gave a gracious waft of his hand. 'Bring them to me when you have done so and I will put my seal to them.'

Morys stared and swallowed, plainly unable to believe his good fortune. He began to stammer his gratitude and John cut him off with a silencing gesture. 'Of course, the fee for a barony usually stands at a hundred marks,' he said pleasantly, knowing that in all likelihood the fool had beggared himself or gone into debt to buy the falcon and destrier.

Morys blanched. 'I would need a little time to raise such a sum, sire.'

'I think you would need more than a little, but since you please me, I am disposed to be generous. You may have Whittington in perpetuity for fifty marks, and I will make you a warden of the March.'

FitzRoger's eyes widened. 'Thank you, sire,' he said in a voice drenched with astonishment and relief.

John eyed him with scornful amusement. If the Baron had not been such a thorn in FitzWarin's side, he would have dismissed him out of hand. As it was, he would nurture him for the sheer pleasure of making Fulke FitzWarin grind his teeth.

Fulke stood by the farrier's forge attached to the lodging house at Castle Baldwin, and broke his fast on a fragrant crust of new bread smeared with honey. The smith's son held Blaze firmly by the cheek strap while his father stooped over the stallion's hind leg, fitting a new shoe. The stink of hot metal and burning horn joined the heavy waft of woodsmoke on the morning air.

'A fine beast, my lord,' said the smith, Blaze's hoof clamped between his knees. He set about banging in the nails. 'Some of 'em have to be shod in a frame the way they bite and kick, but this 'un's got the manners of a prince.'

Fulke's lip curled at the comparison. The princes of his acquaintance had not been renowned for their manners – unless it be lack of them. 'He's trained to stand while being shod.' Sauntering over to the stallion, he patted the muscular liver-coloured hide before offering Blaze the remnants of his bread and honey on the flat of his palm. 'Try and mount him without permission and it's a different matter. He'll buck you off in the midden before you've even hit the saddle.'

'You got him well schooled then, my lord?'

Fulke smiled. 'You can't afford not to with a tourney mount.' The stallion whiffled up the bread and chewed it with obvious relish. 'No one's going to steal him if I'm unhorsed during a mêlée, because he won't let them.'

Iron nails gripped between his teeth, the smith secured the shoe and releasing Blaze's hoof, straightened up. 'Saw a fine beast through here earlier this morn,' he said. 'Going as a gift to King John I'll warrant.' He jerked his thumb in the direction of the castle brooding above the village. Fulke followed the man's gesture to the red and gold banners fluttering on the limewashed walls, the three Angevin leopards proclaiming that King John was in residence. The village was bursting with men like himself who were here to tender their homage to the new King. Fulke glowered and bit his thumbnail. As duties went it was one of the more onerous.

'A fine grey,' the smith continued, 'with a great arched crest and a rump you could dine off for a month. If I'd been his owner, I wouldn't have parted with him.'

'Neither would I,' said William FitzWarin, emerging from

the lodging house to hear the end of the conversation. His brown eyes were still bleary with sleep. 'Not to a swine like John.' Yawning and stretching, leaving a whiff of stale wine and armpit in his wake, he went to sluice himself at the trough.

Fulke glanced at the smith and his lad. 'Watch your tongue, Will.'

'Why? It's the truth. By all accounts you've said and done far worse where our beloved sovereign is concerned.' William plunged his hands into the trough and splashed his face.

'You need not fear that I or young Hal will carry tales,' the smith said. 'I know when to mind my own business.' He took the payment of a silver halfpenny and scrutinised it carefully to make sure that the rim had not been clipped.

Alain and Philip tottered out of the lodging house, squinting like moles at the bright morning light and obviously suffering the effects of last night's conviviality. Fulke shook his head with exasperation, but he was grinning too. 'Best get yourselves spruced up and break your fast if you can bear to eat,' he called. 'We've an appointment with His Grace the King. Where are Ivo and Richard?'

'Still snoring.'

'I'll kick them up,' William volunteered, sleeking back his wet hair.

'I—' Fulke spun at the thunder of hooves in the smithy yard and stared as Jean de Rampaigne drew his bay courser to a dancing halt.

'Christ in hell, Fulke, get to the castle,' he panted. 'John's just promised Whittington to Morys FitzRoger for fifty marks.'

'What?'

'I saw and heard the entire exchange. FitzRoger is to write himself a charter and for the payment of fifty marks John will put his seal to the claim.'

'The whoring son of a leprous gong farmer!' Fulke snarled, completely forgetting his reprimand to William. Snatching Blaze's bridle out of the lad's hands he vaulted into the saddle without recourse to stirrup and plunged the horse around.

'Wait!' cried William. 'I'm coming with you!' He sprinted off to saddle his own horse.

Fulke was so consumed by rage that he heard nothing but the hot pounding of blood in his ears. He slammed his heels into Blaze's flanks and with a leap of surprise the horse went from stand to flat-out gallop. Jean reined his courser around and spurred after him.

Fulke reached the keep only to find his way barred by the guards on duty who were dubious about admitting a raging madman.

'I demand to see the King, it is my right!' Fulke roared. Affected by his rider's mood, Blaze danced and circled. Fulke drew the reins in tight and gripped with his thighs, swinging the destrier to confront the crossed spears. He fought the urge to draw his sword and hew his way through, knowing that if he so much as bared a blade he would be dead. Still, his right hand twitched on the reins with the need. His chest heaved as he struggled for control.

'My name is Fulke FitzWarin,' he said, his voice shaking. 'I have come to pay homage to King John for my lands.'

Jean de Rampaigne rode up, William galloping at his heels. 'Let him through, Alaric,' Jean cried to the larger of the guards. 'I will go surety for him. He's well known to my master the Archbishop.'

The guards hesitated, exchanging looks. A crowd was beginning to gather as others waited their turn to enter the keep.

Alaric withdrew and beckoned with his spear. 'Very well

then, enter,' he said. 'But leave your weapons here. You too,' he said to William.

The brothers unlaced their scabbards and handed them over. Fulke's hands were trembling so hard that he doubted he could have used a weapon anyway.

'I told you that we should have ridden straight to Whittington when Papa died and taken FitzRoger then,' William muttered as they led their horses across the ward and found a boy to tend them.

'Hindsight is a wondrous thing,' Fulke sneered. 'Likely we'd have ended our lives swinging from a gibbet.'

'Well, if you think there's going to be a happy outcome from this, you're a greater fool than you've ever taken me for!'

Fulke rounded on him with bunched fists and Jean hastily put his wiry frame between them. 'Peace!' he hissed. 'We're not clear of the guards yet, and you do yourselves no favours by this childish brangling. If you cannot handle yourselves, then what use are you going to be before John?'

Fulke clamped his jaw until the muscles showed in two rigid grooves below his cheekbones. 'You do well to remind me, Jean,' he said with a stiff nod. He looked at William. 'We need to be united by our brotherhood, not split by our differences of opinion. Are you ready to go within?'

William wriggled his shoulders within the thickly padded gambeson. 'No point in coming just to stay outside.' It was the nearest he would come to conciliation.

Fulke leading, they mounted the wooden forebuilding stairs and again were challenged by a pair of guards. This time Fulke managed to give his name in a courteous if curt fashion and the small party was allowed into the hall.

John was seated on a raised dais at the far end, on a throne cushioned and draped with embroidered purple cloth. He was chewing his index finger in a slightly bored fashion as a baron knelt to pay him homage. Fulke glanced impatiently around the rest of the hall, taking in the gathering of marcher lords, both the great and the insignificant. He saw looks and whispers cast his way. Hubert Walter detached himself from a conversation with Ranulf of Chester and William Marshal and hastened across the hall, his Archbishop's robes glittering stiffly.

Fulke knelt to kiss his ring, then immediately stood and looked Hubert Walter hard in the eye. 'Do you remember when we drank to peace?' he asked bitterly. 'It was futile from the beginning.'

Hubert met his stare without flinching. 'I said that I would do what I could, not that I would succeed. I was elsewhere when the King made a bargain with FitzRoger, otherwise I would have intervened.'

'Then what is stopping you from intervening now . . . your grace?'

The Archbishop's eyelids tensed at the way Fulke spoke the title. He shook his head. 'It is not too late to make your peace, and I advise you to do so. Naught but bloodshed and heartache will come of this matter.'

'So you will do nothing?'

'I did not say that. I will try my best for you, Fulke, but sometimes it is easier to go around a stone wall than butt through it with your skull.'

'Tell that to our father,' William muttered, perfunctorily kissing the air above the Archbishop's ring. 'All his life he abided by the rules and it bought him nothing but a shroud.'

The conversation had not gone unnoticed on the dais and a squire, summoning them to attend upon John, escorted the brothers up the hall.

Fulke paused at the foot of the platform and looked up at John. The royal gaze gleamed with malice and the hint of a smile curved the bearded mouth corners. The King leaned back in his chair, affecting an air of indolence but Fulke could sense his tension. John was like a spectator at a cockfight, awaiting the first flurry, the drawing of blood. The King's gaze flickered to the group of courtiers standing around his throne. Following the glance, Fulke saw Morys FitzRoger standing among them, his thin face wearing an expression of fear mingled with exultation.

With great reluctance, Fulke bent his knee and bowed his head to pay homage. Anger simmered within him, controlled but still far too close to the surface. His skin felt raw with it. Beside him, William knelt too, muttering softly beneath his breath.

'This is a sight to gladden my eyes,' John purred. 'Fulke FitzWarin on his knees at my feet.'

'I owe you my fealty now, sire. Before, I did not,' Fulke said curtly.

John merely smiled. 'So you have come to do me homage for your lands? To put your hands between mine, swear your loyalty and receive the kiss of peace?'

It was like drinking bitter poison. Fulke swallowed his gorge. 'Yes, sire. I have come today to do homage . . . for all my lands.'

John shifted in the chair. The curl of his smile deepened. 'You mean those to which you are entitled,' he said.

Fulke stood up. His heart was pounding and his mouth was dry. Do not do anything foolish, he told himself. The words were waiting to fire off his tongue like swift-loosed arrows but he made himself speak slowly, enunciating each one, so that those around could hear and not mistake. 'By the benefit of common law, the castle, the lands and appurtenances of Whittington are mine by right and reason of my inheritance from my father. In respect of this, I offer you a hundred marks as the relief on the barony, including

Whittington which in the time of your great-grandfather the first King Henry was settled as the head of the FitzWarin family seat.'

John considered Fulke narrowly and fiddled with a large amethyst ring on his forefinger. Hubert Walter stepped forward, raising his arms to show the glittering goldwork on his cope, making his appearance as commanding as possible. 'May I speak?'

John waved his hand in assent, but looked irritated.

'King Richard, your brother, adjudged that the FitzWarin family had the right to hold Whittington and that another estate should be settled upon Morys FitzRoger and his heirs in compensation. The final documents were never sealed, but only because of his untimely death. I have those documents to hand in proof of the decision, which I myself approved as King Richard's Justiciar.'

John's look of irritation increased. 'Richard is dead,' he said bluntly, 'and you are no longer my Justiciar. I have already granted Whittington to my good servant Morys FitzRoger de Powys for fifty marks, and my decision stands whether men are angered or not. Fulke FitzWarin will do homage for the fiefs that were held at the time of his father's death. No more and no less.'

Fulke clenched his fists and battled against a scalding wave of fury. 'I am within the right of the law,' he said hoarsely. 'You murder justice for the sake of a petty grudge.'

'Mind your words, FitzWarin, or you will find yourself without any lands at all,' John warned, triumph glowing in his eyes.

At Fulke's side, William shot to his feet and put his hand to his non-existent scabbard. At the same time, Morys FitzRoger stepped from the group of courtiers. He was plainly delighted at John's decision and could not resist gloating.

'You are foolish to try and make a claim on my lands. If you say you have a right to Whittington you are lying through your teeth and if not for the King's presence, I would knock them down your throat and choke you.'

It was William who broke. With a howl of fury, he launched himself at Morys and punched him in the face with his bunched fist. Morys reeled with a cry, blood bursting from his nose. William went after him, intent on beating him to a pulp, but was dragged off his victim by Hubert Walter and John's half-brother Will Longsword, Earl of Salisbury. William struggled against their restraint but was held fast. Morys FitzRoger staggered to his feet and stanched his bleeding nose and cut lip on the fine woollen sleeve of his court tunic. His expression was one of dazed astonishment. 'You misbegotten whelp!' he gasped.

Fulke swung round to John who was leaning forward, the excitement of a bloodsport enthusiast gleaming in his eyes. 'Sire,' he said icily, 'you are my liege lord and I am bound by fealty to you whilst I am in your service and as long as I hold lands from you. You ought to maintain my rights, and yet you fail me both in rights and in common law. You have denied justice to your freeborn tenant in your court, and for this reason I hereby relinquish my homage.' He turned to Hubert and Salisbury. 'Let my brother go.' The molten heat of his rage had solidified and was now as cold and hard as polished granite. The command in his voice, the look in his eyes caused the men to slacken their hold and William was able to wrench free.

Fulke grabbed William by his gambeson sleeve and marched him out of the great hall. In the bailey, he collected their weapons from the gate guards, their horses from an attendant. All in grim silence, for there was nothing to say. It had all been said – and done.

Jean de Rampaigne sprinted out of the hall as Fulke set his foot in the stirrup.

'Fulke, go!' He waved his arms wildly. 'Morys FitzRoger is demanding your blood and John's asking who is prepared to go out and hunt you down for an outlaw! Lord Hubert's doing what he can, and Chester and Salisbury, but John's mercenaries will do as John bids!'

Fulke gathered up the reins. 'If they pursue me, they will receive all that they deserve,' he snarled.

'Well then, God speed you, and lend strength to your sword arm.'

Fulke leaned down from the saddle to clasp Jean's arm. 'At least I still have friendship amongst all the falsehood,' he said, and then spurred for the gate.

Back at the smithy his troop was waiting, Philip and Alain galvanised into sobriety by de Rampaigne's earlier appearance and Ivo and Richard groggy but awake after a thorough dunking in the trough.

'Mount up,' Fulke snapped. 'We're riding for Alberbury. I'll tell you why as we go.'

'We're outlaws!' William cried as his brothers and the other knights of Fulke's company ran to their horses. 'Fulke's renounced his homage to the King – and more than time too!' He showed his teeth in a wolfish grin. 'And I've struck a blow for our family pride.'

'You'll have more blows to strike soon,' Fulke said furiously, 'and you had best make every one count. This isn't a tourney or an escapade.'

'I know.' William's voice continued to gleam with relish and Fulke knew that his words had fallen on stony ground. He wondered if William understood the magnitude of what they had done. They were outlaws, landless men, game to be hunted down like wolves and their hides presented to the King for a bounty payment. And there was no retreat.

Their path was set. God on the Cross, what price family pride?

They were no more than a mile and a half from Castle Baldwin, on the Welshpool road, when a band of John's mercenaries, riding hard, caught up with them. Fulke knew immediately that there was to be no negotiation. Every man was fully armed and they were led by Pierre d'Avignon, who was one of John's hard-bitten mercenaries, known more for his acts of chevauchée than his skills as a diplomat.

Fulke signalled his own troop to turn and face their pursuers. The road was dusty and rutted. There was no room for a charge of more than four abreast, but that suited Fulke who was outnumbered.

'I have promised the King that I will return with your heads for the insult you have caused to him and his vassal!' d'Avignon bellowed, the words emerging somewhat muffled through the vents in his helm. There was no sign of Morys FitzRoger.

Fulke drew his sword. A lance was fine for the first charge providing you could keep it straight, but for serious close-in work on horseback, the best weapons were sword and mace and it paid to shorten the stirrup leathers. 'Then you are more than foolish to promise what you cannot have,' he shouted in reply, his own voice clear and powerful because he was wearing the older style of helm with an open face and just a nasal bar for protection.

The sun beat down, glancing on mail rivets, turning them to fire. Fulke watched d'Avignon drive in his spurs and slap the reins down on his destrier's wet neck. He saw himself respond, heard the stretched-out echo as he roared a command to his troop. He felt the bunch and surge of Blaze's muscles and the sudden cool stream of air over the burning links of his hauberk. Then the shock of meeting, the clash of blade on shield, of blade screaming and sparking on mail. Fulke knew the tactics. So did d'Avignon. Go for the collarbone and shoulder. Even if the sword could not part the mail, the force of the blow would break bones and disable. Once a man lost the use of his shield, he was easy prey.

Sweat stung in Fulke's eyes, but he was in better case than d'Avignon whose closed helm was acting as a cooking pot in the day's heat. Fulke thrust with his shield and swung his sword, urging Blaze with his knees. D'Avignon recoiled and his blow of retaliation went wide. Fulke pressed his advantage, chopping in hard beneath d'Avignon's shield. The mercenary gave an involuntary howl of pain; his guard went down and Fulke attacked in full earnest.

The battle in the road was ferocious but brief. Trained by their seasons on the tourney field, Fulke's troop fought as a cohesive team. Skilled though their opponents were, they were not accustomed to fighting in partnership. It was each man for himself and thus they were easy to pick off. Having dealt with d'Avignon, Fulke spurred to help Philip and Stephen who were fighting two against three. A swift blow brought one man out of the saddle and a backhand slash disabled the second, leaving his brother and companion well able to finish the task.

Crying the FitzWarin name at the top of his lungs, William had joined with Ivo in despatching two more opponents. A third mercenary pulled himself out of the fight and, digging in his spurs, fled back down the road towards Castle Baldwin.

'I cry quarter, I yield!' screamed a knight mounted on a black Friesian destrier as Fulke cut off his path of retreat. He threw down his sword, cast off his shield, and raised his hands in the air. His surrender was quickly echoed by the remaining half-dozen men. While they served John for pay, they couldn't collect it if they were dead.

'Hold your sword!' Fulke snapped at William, who was so consumed with the fire of combat that he was all for continuing to the death. 'There's naught to be gained in slaughter and we're wasting time that could be better spent.'

Blood was running down William's chin from a split lip where a sword hilt had struck him. 'They rode out intending to kill us.' He spat out a mouthful of red saliva and his eyes burned. 'Do we just let them go unscathed?'

'Hardly unscathed.' Philip gestured at the bruises, swellings and cuts sported by the soldiers. Some, like those sustained by the FitzWarin troop, were superficial; others would take more healing and leave permanent scars and disfigurement. And four of their pursuers were dead.

'Don't worry, they'll pay a price,' Fulke growled. He ordered the surrendered men to dismount. 'Take their horses,' he said curtly, 'and their weapons.' He pointed with his sword. 'Your mail, gentlemen. We'll have that too. I would hate you to have the discomfort of walking all the way back to Castle Baldwin in this heat wearing those heavy hauberks. Your spurs also, so you don't trip.' He rotated the blade in his hand, causing the steel to flash with sunbursts. 'Make haste before I change my mind, or my brother loses his patience.'

Clearly reluctant, but driven by fear of death, the mercenaries did as they were bid. Soon two of their former mounts were laden with an assortment of hauberks and weaponry.

Fulke saluted them, an ironic grin, devoid of humour, curling his lips. 'Now you are free to go,' he said, 'and I trust we'll not meet again.'

Without waiting to see the soldiers start on their walk, he kicked Blaze to a trot. His brothers and the rest of the troop followed, the captured horses on lead reins, the sound of their booty making soft clinking sounds with each stride of the packhorses. His first deed as an outlaw leader. Fulke did not know whether to laugh or weep.

'Well,' John addressed the quivering soldier kneeling at his feet, 'where is Fulke FitzWarin?'

'I know not, sire.' The mercenary wiped a persistent trickle of blood from a cut across his eyebrow. 'When Pierre d'Avignon fell, I was forced to ride for my life.'

'Pierre d'Avignon is dead?' John stared in furious disbelief.

'Yes, sire, and Amys le Marquis.'

John swore and clenched his fists. Every encounter with Fulke FitzWarin brought him back to the humiliation of that adolescent chess game where he had lost on all counts. And he was still losing. Morys FitzRoger looked shocked and disbelieving too. He was sitting in the window embrasure, head tilted while the blood clotted in his nose.

'I could have told you the outcome.' Hubert Walter spoke quietly so that the words would not carry, but they were heavy with emphasis. 'Fulke possesses warrior skills almost the equal of my lord Pembroke's and you have ground his family pride in the dust. I know that you have quarrelled with him in the past, but perhaps you should have been more conciliatory. Your brother Richard acknowledged his family's rights in the matter of Whittington. For the price of setting aside your grievance, you could have yoked a very useful man to your side.'

'There is truth in what His Grace says,' agreed Ranulf of Chester, and received a nod of approbation from William Longsword too.

'It's not too late to revoke your decision, sire.' Hubert opened his hand in a gesture of appeal. 'Return the gerfalcon and the horse and give FitzRoger alternative lands.'

John glared at his magnates, feeling a suffocating sense of betrayal. 'Are you telling me how to rule?' he spat, glaring at his half–brother and then the Archbishop.

'No, sire.' Leaning on his staff, Hubert bowed. 'Merely offering sound advice.'

John ground his teeth. 'I do not need your advice to deal with a traitor,' he said venomously. He pointed towards the embrasure. 'Morys FitzRoger is my sworn vassal for Whittington and that is my last word.'

'And my last word is that you are making a mistake,' Hubert said.

There was a sudden commotion at the far end of the hall as the remnants of John's posse made their entrance: limping, staggering, beaten, their armour stripped, their bravado in rags. His expression thunderous, John flung from the dais to meet them.

'FitzWarin took our horses and our armour, sire,' their spokesman gasped. A section of his surcoat had been torn off and wrapped around a bloody wound on his hand. 'He said to tell you that he would wage war against you until you gave him the justice of common law in the matter of Whittington.'

John's incensed bellow echoed around the hall, bringing immediate, shocked silence. 'By God on the Cross and the Devil in the pit of hell, I will give Fulke FitzWarin and his brothers the justice of common law,' he choked. 'I will have them strung from a gibbet on Whittington's battlements and they can gaze on their land from there!' Spittle gathered at the corners of his mouth. The urge to cast himself down amidst the rushes and drum his heels was almost overwhelming. In lieu, he flung to the nearest trestle and, in a single swipe, sent cups and trenchers crashing to the floor. With a tremendous heave that tore the muscles in his arms, but gave him a pang of dark satisfaction, he upended the trestle itself. Panting, he staggered away from his handiwork and looked around, but none would meet his gaze. He felt their shock and contempt.

'Satan's piss on the lot of you!' he roared and stormed from the hall, leaving Hubert Walter and Salisbury to the task of succouring the wounded knights.

'You cannot stay here, you know that,' Hawise said as she bathed a superficial cut on Fulke's hand with lotion of woundwort. 'They will pursue you in force after this.'

'Yes, Mama, I know.' Fulke's weary gaze fell on the window where the open shutters revealed the glimmer of a fine summer dawn. They had ridden through the night to reach Alberbury on drovers' paths, their ears cocked for the sound of pursuit.

By candlelight a chirugeon leaned over William, attempting to extract the broken remnants of two teeth from his gum. William, half-drunk on mead, was making a determined effort to remain still and not leap out of his skin at each probe. Now he turned his head. 'We'll not run away,' he declared in a voice blurred by blood and drink. 'Whittington is ours and we'll fight for it to the death!'

'And your death it would indeed be, you fool!' Hawise snapped. 'John will send out every baron, knight and serjeant along the March to hunt you down.'

'I don't care about that.'

'I can see that,' Hawise said waspishly, 'but I do. You would die for no more purpose than to increase the burden of my grief. Sometimes I think that you have no wit beyond the desire to lift a sword.'

'Mama.' Fulke laid a restraining hand on her arm and felt her tremors through his palm. He could see by the set of her jaw that she was striving not to weep.

William's expression was both hurt and incredulous. 'I

am fighting for our family's honour,' he said indignantly. 'I won't just crawl under a stone and hide like a louse.'

She shook her head at him. 'Did I say that was what I wanted you to do? By all means fight back, my son, but not now. You have to wait for the right moment.'

'Mama's right,' Fulke said as William prepared to continue the argument. 'John will raise the hue and cry throughout the borders. If we stay, we'll sell our lives dearly, but it will be small recompense for letting John win.'

'Then what?' William said sulkily.

'We cross the Narrow Sea until the furore has died down. John can't afford to keep men in the field just to lie in wait for us. There will come a time when vigilance relaxes and the soldiers are sent to other tasks. It is then that we return and make him pay.' He looked at his mother, speaking to her as much as his brother. 'I intend to make myself so much of a thorn in John's side that in the end he will be glad to give me Whittington in order to have peace.'

William grunted, declaring acceptance if not outright approval. 'And what of Morys FitzRoger?'

Fulke shrugged. 'Let him enjoy the fruits of his treachery while he is still able,' he said implacably. 'It won't be for long.'

CHAPTER 16

Alberbury, Shropshire, Spring 1200

Maude was shocked at the change in Hawise FitzWarin. Gone was the vivacious red-haired woman who had caused heads to turn as she passed. Now if heads turned it was in pity, or unease. In her dark widow's weeds, her face framed by the severity of a full wimple, Hawise could have been a nun – except that there was no sustaining spiritual glow. Maude thought that it was like looking through a window into an empty room; she wondered if she had done the right thing in coming to Alberbury.

'I will not trouble you above one night,' she said awkwardly as she exchanged a kiss of greeting with Hawise. A groom appeared to take her dappled mare and show the serjeants of her escort where they could stable their mounts.

'One night?' Hawise's lovely, ravaged face fell with disappointment. 'Can you not stay longer?

'I do not want to impose on your hospitality.'

'Tush!' Hawise waved her hand. 'It will do me good to have company, especially young company. This place is too full of silence where voices should be. Where are you bound?' She gestured and her maid came forward to take Maude's travelling cloak.

'To visit my father.' Maude heard the desperation in Hawise's tone. She doesn't want to be alone, she thought.

'Theo's in Normandy with King John, seeking his permission to go to Ireland. If he receives it I will go with him, but for the nonce I am performing my duty as a daughter.' She placed heavy emphasis on the word 'duty'. 'If it will not burden you, I will be glad to remain for a sennight.'

Hawise's smile was an incongruous mingling of delight and sadness. 'Of course it will not burden me, although perhaps I will burden you.' She linked her arm through Maude's and drew her within the keep. 'Ireland, you say?'

Hawise's touch was bird-like and Maude noticed how loose the rings were on the older woman's fingers. 'Theo wants to inspect his religious foundations,' she said, wrinkling her nose. 'He says he wants to be buried at the monastery at Wotheney.'

'He's not ailing?' Hawise said quickly.

Again that strange, almost desperate note. 'Not that I can tell,' Maude said, 'but he doesn't smile much these days. You know that John confiscated the rights of Amounderness, took away his shrievalty and threatened to deprive him of his Irish lands?'

'No, but nothing that monster does would surprise me,' Hawise said, sudden fire in her eyes. 'I had to pay a fine of thirty marks when my husband died in order not to have another man forced upon me by our beloved King!'

Maude made a shocked sound in her throat, but she was not surprised. To raise revenue both John and Richard had sold lands, offices and people as if they were hot cakes off a cookstall.

'I suppose you heard about the matter of my sons,' Hawise added. 'Not only has John deprived them of their inheritance, he has deprived me of their comfort and support . . .' Her voice wavered. 'At least while our overlord for this place is Robert Corbet, I am assured the tenancy. He and my husband were good friends. John cannot touch the lands that I hold in dower, or which are held of others.'

Maude patted her arm in sympathy, unsure what else to do. 'Hubert Walter told us what happened at Castle Baldwin,' she said. 'Have you heard from your sons since they . . . left?' She had been about to say fled but caught herself in time.

Hawise nodded and sniffed back the threatening tears. 'A messenger travels between us regularly. They are sheltering in Brittany with distant de Dinan kin – earning their keep as castle guards and household knights – biding their time.' Her mouth corners tightened as if pulled by a drawstring. 'But for John's ill temper and grudge-bearing, my sons would be here now. Fulke would have taken seisin of Whittington and likely a wife as well.' Her pursed mouth softened in a bleak smile. 'I know that mothers are notorious for clinging to their sons, but I would welcome another woman into the household, and the opportunity to dandle a grandchild in my lap.'

She led Maude into the solar, to the warmth of a brazier and an oak bench padded with an embroidered bolster. 'It is too late now. That time has been squandered.' With the slow effort of an old woman, she sat on the bench, one hand pressed to her left side.

When Maude murmured in concern, Hawise shook her head. 'I will be all right presently.' She signalled a maid to bring wine and when it arrived, drank with shaking hands. Her colour improved as if the redness of the wine had gone straight to her cheeks, but her face remained drawn. With a visible effort she gathered herself and patted Maude's knee. 'Divert me a little. Tell me how you and Theobald are faring.'

Maude searched her mind for matters that Hawise might find amusing or interesting. To tell her that Hubert was using his influence to have Theobald's lands restored would not be tactful, and to talk of Theobald's obsession with his monasteries was enough to put even a dedicated cleric to sleep.

'Well,' she said dubiously, 'Theobald and I have been kept apart recently because he has followed John into Normandy, but I hope to go with him to Ireland.' She sighed. 'You are not the only one who desires grandchildren to dandle in their lap. My father is constantly reminding me that it is my duty to provide Theobald with an heir and that I should encourage him to play his part at every opportunity.'

'And you do not welcome these reminders?'

'I do not need them.' Maude toyed with her wedding ring. 'I know my duty and I love Theo dearly. When we are together, we live as man and wife in every sense of the word — except it be a holy day.' It was not entirely true but there was righteous comfort in the delusion. Their relationship was comfortable and loving, but it was more father and daughter than husband and wife. She had to think hard to remember the last time that they had lain together in the carnal sense. 'What will be, will be.' She gave a dismissive shake of her head, reached for her wine and smiled. 'In Theobald's absence I have been honing other skills.'

'Indeed?' Hawise raised her brows.

Maude giggled. 'Do you remember how I was forever running off and playing tomboy games to my grandmother's despair?'

Hawise smiled. 'Only too well,' she said wryly.

'Well' — and a slow smile spread across her face — 'I have taken to archery,' Maude said. 'It's a sport permitted to women, so my grandmother cannot complain, and I have discovered a certain degree of skill.'

'Archery!' Hawise repeated, her expression intrigued. 'I

would not have thought you had the strength to pull a bow.'

'A great deal lies in the technique,' Maude said, 'and I'm stronger than I look.' Her eyes brightened. 'It gives me pleasure to see the men's astonishment when I match them at the target. Every time I hit the centre, I'm striking a blow for the girl-child who wasn't allowed to run about with the same freedom as a boy.'

'What does Theobald say?'

'He encourages me.' She laughed. 'He says that if ever the day comes when we have to withstand a siege, he will put me up on the battlements with his other archers. I told him I would hold him to it.'

'I could imagine you doing so,' Hawise said. 'And having skill in embroidery, you could stitch wounds as well as inflict them.' She had been smiling as she spoke, but the curve suddenly left her lips as if she had been slapped.

'Lady Hawise?' Maude gently touched her hand.

The older woman's eyes had filled with tears. 'My sons,' she said with a painful swallow. 'Who is going to bind their injuries and watch out for them from the battlements?'

Maude bit back the reply that they were grown men who could fend for themselves. She thought of how protective she felt towards Theobald, imagined him wounded and in need. 'Surely they will be cared for by their kin in Brittany?'

Hawise shook her head and did not answer. She fumbled a linen kerchief from her sleeve, dabbed her eyes and blew her nose. 'I am being foolish,' she sniffed, 'and all the tears in the world will make no difference.' Pink-nosed with emotion, she straightened her shoulders. 'Enough. Do you have this bow of yours with you? I would like to see it.'

* * *

Maude spent the next hour out on the sward, demonstrating her new skill to Hawise at the large, straw-stuffed butt. Time after time the goose-fletched arrow flew to the centre. Maude was rapt with concentration. She moistened her lips; her eyes shone with the pleasure of accomplishment. One of the household guards who reckoned himself a good archer came to match shots with her, and was beaten.

'You do indeed have a skill,' Hawise murmured.

'It is like any discipline, you have to practise.' Maude held out the bow, offering Hawise a shot. 'You could learn.'

The older woman refused with a sad shake of her head. 'It is too late.'

'It's never too late.'

'For me it is.'

They went within shortly after that for the sun had lost its warmth and a cold breeze had sprung up. Hawise shivered and huddled inside her cloak, her face grey and drawn.

In the hall, they dined on almond pottage and saffron squab pie. Maude ate with the healthy, ravenous appetite of active youth. She had been hungry when she went out to shoot and now her stomach felt like an empty cavern. While she devoured the pottage, the pie, and the bread that accompanied the dishes, Hawise just poked at her own food and scarcely touched a morsel.

'Are you not hungry?' Maude asked, thinking it small wonder that Hawise was so thin.

'I have no appetite these days,' Hawise confessed, looking at the few scraps on her trencher with distaste. 'Sometimes even the smell of food makes me feel sick.'

'Have you consulted a physician or a wise woman?'

Hawise shook her head. 'For thirty years I have tended to the ills of all within my household. I do not need a physician to tell me what is wrong.' She did not elaborate, merely toyed with her goblet. The set of her face discouraged Maude from enquiring further.

Later that evening, however, as they sat over a game of merels by the hearth, Hawise pushed one of her pieces with her forefinger and said softly, 'Maude, I cannot keep it to myself any longer. I have to tell you that I believe I am dying.'

The fire spat and crackled on a knot in the wood. It was the only sound in the room. Maude looked at Hawise, lost for words. Although the room was warm, a shiver rippled down her spine, as if drawn by the tip of a scythe.

'I feel as though I am being eaten alive and it grows daily worse.' Hawise bit her lip. 'When my sons left, I thought it was the grief of seeing them go following so hard on the heels of their father's death.'

'Mayhap that is so,' Maude said quickly, clutching at a straw of comfort.

Hawise shook her head and laid her palm to her belly. 'I have a lump here and it grows with the pain. When I am being fanciful, I tell myself that it is my broken heart pushing against my skin. But I have seen such growths before, and I know that they foretell death.'

Maude's swallow was audible. 'I am sorry,' she whispered, knowing that it sounded inadequate, but what else was there to say, except to wish Hawise's confidence unspoken? She did not want the burden that was being laid upon her.

The corners of Hawise's eyes crinkled in a travesty of a smile. 'There is no need to be, although I will be glad if you pray for my soul. Death, when it comes, will be a welcome release . . . and at least I have time to prepare. It is the waiting that is the hardest part – and the daily grind of the pain.'

'But it's not fair!' cried the rebellious child in Maude's nature, the violence of her own emotion taking her by surprise. Her eyes filled with tears of frustration and anger and she dashed the merels pieces from the pegged wooden board with a swipe of her hand.

Hawise rose and hastened around the board to take Maude in her arms. 'If life was fair,' she said, 'my husband would still be alive, my sons would be here, not exiled in Brittany, and Whittington would be ours.' She stroked Maude's cheek tenderly. 'If life was fair, I would have borne at least one daughter and she would have been like you.'

Her words made Maude want to cry even harder and rage against her helplessness. There was nothing she could do to make things right – no matter how many times her arrows hit the centre of the target.

CHAPTER 17

Manor of Higford, Shropshire, Summer 1200

As Fulke and his brothers dismounted in Higford's bailey, his aunt Emmeline ran out to greet them. Putting her arms around Fulke she kissed him on either cheek in greeting, and then she hugged him fiercely. 'I am so sorry.' She moved on to his brothers, doing the same to each one. 'At first she would not let us send a message. She thought that while you were in Brittany you were safe, but Lady Walter said that you should know. Your mother gave in . . . but too late for you to see her. She died little more than a week after the messenger left.'

Fulke stared at his aunt. The sun beat down fiercely as only it could in July. Hot and overhead for much of the day. 'Lady Walter said?'

Emmeline nodded. 'She came to visit your mother and stayed with her until the end, God bless her. Your mother was much comforted by her presence.'

'Is she here now?'

'No, she's gone to her father, but she did say that she would return this way on her journey south.'

Fulke did not know whether to be pleased or relieved. At least it was one less portion on his trencher which was already piled with a detritus of worries and demands. He was not sure that he would have been able to cope with Maude Walter too. 'We have come from my mother's grave at Alberbury,' he said. He cleared his throat. 'There is a deal of unfinished business before she or our father can truly be laid to rest.'

'I know that,' his aunt murmured and took his arm. 'But you can suspend it at least until you've removed that armour and refreshed yourselves.'

Fulke resisted her tug. 'If you take us in, Aunt Emmeline, you will be guilty of aiding hunted rebels,' he warned.

She drew herself up to her full height, which brought her eyes level with his chest. 'I am almost insulted enough to order you out of Higford's gates,' she snapped. 'How dare you! I am a FitzWarin too; your father's own sister. Even if I did not take you in for loyalty's sake, I would do so for love.'

'Then thank you.' Fulke stooped to kiss her burning cheek. 'We are grateful.' But he still resisted her insistent pull on his sleeve. 'There is one more thing.'

She lifted her brows.

'My troop.' He gestured towards the castle gates. 'I bade them wait behind in case you would rather not succour them too. Many have joined my retinue since my banishment. There are in excess of fifty knights, all with horses.'

His aunt Emmeline blinked once and then recovered. 'By all means admit them,' she said with a beckoning gesture. 'I might as well be hanged for a sheep as a lamb and with such a troop inside its walls, no one will dare to assault Higford.'

'We won't trespass on you for long, I promise.' Fulke gestured Alain to fetch the men. 'Just long enough to plan our campaign.'

'So, you won't return to Brittany. There is nothing I can do to persuade you to dwell in safety there?'

'Nothing,' he confirmed. Brittany had been necessary at the time. It had given him space to think, to decide whether to live out his life as a hearth knight and mercenary, a servant and dependant of his distant relatives, or to risk all and fight for his own lands. 'My choice is made – and if I die in the attempt, then so be it. At least I'll be in good company.'

They stayed a night and a day with Emmeline FitzWarin, and, late the following afternoon, as the heat cooled from the air, donned their mail and buckled on their swords.

'I do not know whether to wish you God speed, or beg you not to go,' his aunt said as Fulke set his foot in the stirrup and swung into the saddle. The shadows in the bailey were beginning to lengthen, blocks of grey encroaching on intense sunlit gold.

'Stay with the first,' Fulke advised with a humourless smile. 'You know that none of us will heed the second.' He leaned down to take the traditional farewell cup of wine from her, drank and passed it on to William.

'Higford's gates are open if you have need.'

'I know, and I can never thank you enough.'

'You do not need to thank me, I have told you.' Emmeline made a shooing motion and then dabbed her eyes with the trailing edge of her sleeve. 'Just return in one piece, that is all I ask.'

'If I can.' He gave her a smile that was more reassuring than his answer, turned the horse and, with Blaze on a lead rein, headed for the gateway. It was a good three hours' ride to Whittington, longer if they took circuitous roads and byways to avoid being seen. By moonrise he wanted to be secure in Babbin's Wood, which was the nearest hunting preserve to Whittington – the lord's game larder. This time, however, the prey was to be two-legged and the hunter was going to become the hunted.

★   ★   ★

In the grey light of early morning, Gwyn FitzMorys opened his eyes and lay listening to the bird song while he gathered his wits. Beside him on the pallet, Alfrun the forester's widow snored gently, her breath heavy with the taint of stale wine. She was past thirty years old, but still handsome with masses of coarse black hair and full, red lips. She was also, for a consideration in silver, very accommodating to a young man's lust and Gwyn found his way to her door at least twice a week. His father was amused, his brother scornful – but only because he was jealous.

Quietly Gwyn reached for and donned his clothes, then slipped outside the small timber-framed cottage to sluice his face in the water barrel. Alfrun's chained dog growled at him, realised who he was, and wagged its feathery tail. Gwyn scooped the water from his face, palmed it through his hair and, having patted the dog, went to his horse which was tethered on the other side of the cottage. A night of bed sport had made him ravenous. At the keep they would be paddling the day's bread from the oven about now. Quietly he harnessed the cob and swung across its back, then with a click of his tongue urged it on to the track. Alfrun would not expect a goodbye. She knew well enough that he would be back.

He had travelled less than a quarter of a mile when he thought he heard voices. He drew rein to listen, head cocked, ears straining. The sound came again, soft and elusive. His horse pricked its ears in that direction, making Gwyn positive that it was not imagination. Heeling about, he guided the cob through the tangled undergrowth of ivy suckers, brambles and moss-grown dead branches. Perhaps a peasant family was abroad early and gathering wood, he thought, but the notion did not ring true. Wood-gatherers were usually women and children. Faint though the voices had been, they were definitely masculine.

Gwyn touched the dagger on his hip for reassurance. Surely not outlaws, he thought. They would not dare with the keep so close. And surely not Llewelyn's Welsh either for they would cross the border at King Offa's Dyke and raid from the direction of Gobowen – unless of course they were lying up and waiting their chance. The fine hairs at the base of his neck began to prickle. Or perhaps . . .

Gwyn's fears were confirmed as he saw the dull flash of mail through the trees and, to his right, a man standing sentry duty, his posture slouched as if he had been there some hours, but his eyes nevertheless watchful. Gwyn stared at William FitzWarin in shock, and William FitzWarin stared back at him while raising and blowing on the hunting horn slung from his shoulder.

Gwyn whipped the cob around, dug in his heels and, uncaring of the danger posed by tree roots and low branches, raced hell for leather in the direction of the keep.

Cursing, Fulke ordered his troop to mount up, but not because he intended to pursue Gwyn FitzMorys. The young man had far too great a start on them. It had always been a danger that someone would chance into the woods and see them.

'God knows what he was doing in the middle of the woods at this hour,' William said with bared teeth. 'Christ, I wish I'd had a bow with me. I'd have shot him straight out of the saddle. Now he'll raise the hue and cry and they'll come into the forest after us.'

'What do we do, fight or flee?' Philip FitzWarin drew up his mail coif, concealing his copper-bright hair.

'We fight,' Fulke said tersely. 'I know we have lost the element of surprise, but that was always a chance we had to take. Now Morys will come to the hunt a little more prepared, but all is not lost. Gwyn only saw William and our perimeter guard post. It is my belief that he will underestimate both our numbers and our fighting ability.'

'You think he will come out?' William untethered his horse from the low branch of an oak tree. 'Is it not more likely that he'll skulk behind the keep walls and keep his yellow liver safe?'

'Oh yes, he'll come out,' Fulke said softly. 'And you are wrong about him being a coward, Will. His ways might be sly and conniving, but he will fight if he thinks he can win.' He narrowed his lids. 'John granted him Whittington and forced us into exile. That will make FitzRoger feel self-righteous with anger and make him over-confident that he can defeat us.' Untying Blaze, he mounted up. A short command, a swift twist on the reins, and he was out of their campsite and heading for the forest track that led to the castle not half a mile away.

Fulke and his troop reached the edge of the woods as the rising sun turned the morning from pearl to streaming gold and the leaves on the trees shivered as if breathed on by the rippling light of dawn. Metallic dazzles winked on the armour of the troop approaching the wood at a fair canter from the direction of the keep.

'See,' said Fulke to William, pointing at FitzRoger's bold green shield with its device of two golden boars.

'Let me take him,' William begged. 'Fulke, if you love me, give him to me!'

Fulke bared his teeth in a savage grin. 'I love you well, but not well enough to yield him to you when he's mine!' He tugged the morning star flail from his belt and wrapped his fingers around the leather grip. The spiked ball swung gently on its chain. It was so destructive a weapon and its technique so time-consuming to perfect that only the most skilled knights used it, and seldom in a tourney where there were set rules. The morning star was a weapon for battle, not courtesy.

Fulke turned in the saddle to address his troop who were fretting their horses, adjusting their shields, checking their weapons. He saw excitement, tension, a little fear – all his own emotions except perhaps for the deeper bite of anger, the need for revenge.

'You have all ridden and trained with me long enough to know your part,' he cried. 'The only difference between this and a tourney are the rules of engagement. 'À outrance. Sharp weapons and no ransoms taken unless it be your particular desire. The land is flat, no advantage to either. Keep your wits in the midst of valour and victory is ours.'

'Victory!' William echoed, punching his sword into the air, his lips parted in a snarl.

'Victory!' came the response from more than fifty throats and, on that resounding note, Fulke sprang his troop from the woods at a fierce and focused gallop. Morys's own troop had been cantering towards the woods in a haste of anxiety rather than an organised charge and there was consternation as Fulke and his men broke suddenly from the cover of the trees and thundered towards them.

Fulke's mouth was dry; his hand slick with cold sweat as Blaze carried him towards the point of impact. The ground throbbed beneath the galloping hooves and the vibration carried up through his saddle and coursed in his body like a wild heartbeat. Closer and closer. Sunlight flashing on armour, its dazzle on a sword blade, the rapid breathing of his horse and the thump of its stride. His own voice shattering inside his helm as he roared his battle cry and swung the flail.

The clash of the two lines meeting was a solid whump of sound that expanded and splintered into numerous indi-vidual battles. The morning star wrapped around a knight's helm with stunning force and knocked him senseless from the saddle. Fulke pivoted Blaze with his knees and urged him into the depth of the fray in search of the green shield and gold boars of Morys FitzRoger. Several times he drew close, only to be engaged by one or other of Morys's body-guard. Frustrated, he forced himself to remain focused and not lose his temper. Somewhere off to the right he could hear William's voice roaring out the FitzWarin name as he always did in battle, using it as a talisman to anchor him to the task in hand and to intimidate his enemy. Ivo's lighter voice replied, followed almost simultaneously by Alain's ox-like bellow. '*FitzWarin!*' Fulke howled, not to be outdone, and redoubled his attempts to reach Morys FitzRoger.

There was a sudden gap and at the end of it the green and gold shield. Fulke spurred Blaze into the space, the flail already on the back swing. Over and down, hard and swift. Morys's eyes flickered with horror as too late he realised the danger. His shield flashed high, but not swiftly enough and the ball of the morning star struck down on his shoulder, smashing the mail links into the quilted tunic beneath, bruising flesh and cracking bone. Morys's shield dropped as he lost the use of his left arm. Fulke drew back to strike again. Screaming the retreat in a voice torn with pain and urgency, Morys reined his destrier away and spurred for the keep walls. Fulke's second blow came down instead on the horse's crupper. The animal squealed and stumbled, but quickly regained momentum and, beneath Morys's desperate urging, was soon galloping flat out.

Blaze's stride faltered as one of Morys's knights cut across Fulke's path and launched a sword blow. Fulke warded it on his shield and struck with the morning star, then swerved Blaze to one side and again took up the pursuit. He had to catch Morys before he gained the safety of the castle.

Morys and his fleeing troops hurtled into the village,

scattering poultry in all directions. The bridge over the ditch was down and there were archers on the palisade walls. As Fulke made one final effort, Morys waved a frantic command and a storm of arrows hailed down on their pursuers.

Cursing, Fulke reined Blaze to a skidding halt and turned to spur out of missile range.

He was almost clear when the crossbow quarrel hit him, the vicious point piercing through his mail and gambeson to lodge in the flesh of his thigh.

William and Ivo were quickly at his side, the latter grabbing Blaze's rein and drawing the horse well out of harm's way.

'Fulke?' William's face was white.

Fulke clenched his teeth. Blood was seeping from the wound but he could tell it was not mortal – or not mortal as yet. 'I'm all right,' he managed to gasp. 'It's only a flesh wound, not in the bone.'

'Can you ride?'

Fulke laughed mirthlessly. 'I can scarcely walk, can I?' He looked over his shoulder. Desultory arrows still hissed at them, falling far short. All the doors in the village remained firmly closed, the ruffled hens and geese the only signs of occupation. No one was going to challenge them. 'One more moment and we would have had FitzRoger.' He ground his fist against his saddle.

'We could always surround the keep,' William speculated. 'He lost several men back there, and he's obviously on the defensive now.'

Fulke shook his head. 'If we sat down to a siege, it would be our last deed on this earth. Someone in the village will go running for aid and I have no desire to be trapped if reinforcements arrive from Shrewsbury.' He looked at William to see if his point was hitting home. 'To succeed we have to be swift. We have to practise chevauchée and make ourselves such a nuisance to John that he will be desperate for peace on our terms.'

William scowled, obviously seeing the sense in Fulke's words but reluctant to give in.

'There will be other opportunities,' Fulke said through a fire of pain. 'We have given notice of our intention. Let FitzRoger stew in fear for the nonce.'

'I don't—'

A loud scream from the direction of the village made the brothers turn. One of Fulke's knights had found a young peasant woman hiding behind a byre and with a grinning companion in tow was set upon having some sport. They had pinned her against the daub and wattle wall of the byre, and were dragging her dress from her shoulders.

Fulke swore. Despite the hot agony spearing his leg, he kicked Blaze to a trot, crossed the road, and forced his way through a gathering crowd of his knights, some watching uneasily, others sheepishly grinning. He drew his sword. The sound of it clearing the scabbard caused both men to look up from what they were doing.

'If that is your need,' Fulke said icily, 'there are whores enough in Oswestry and Shrewsbury to give you service. Any man who has a taste for rape has no place in my retinue. He also has no bollocks.' He flourished the sword. 'Let her go, mount up, and either learn your lesson or leave.'

'It was only a bit of fun, my lord,' one of them tried to defend himself, sidling towards his horse. His companion lowered his eyes and shuffled away from the weeping, half-hysterical girl.

'For whom?' Fulke bit out. 'Do you not have a mother and sisters? What would they think if they could see you now?'

In silence, shamed, the young men mounted up. Fulke

glared at them, and then round at the other soldiers. 'Whittington is mine,' he said, laying down each word like a blow. 'Every stick and stone, every cow and calf and person. Harm one and you harm me. Those who cannot live with that notion can leave my service now.'

There was some shuffling, some cleared throats, but no one moved. Fulke held them with the blaze of his stare for a moment longer then turned to the weeping girl. 'Go home,' he commanded brusquely. 'No one will harm you further.' He tossed her a silver penny. The coin landed in the dust at her feet. She looked at it, wiped her hand beneath her nose, streaking a trail of mucus and tears, then snatched up the silver and fled.

Fulke twitched on the reins and swung Blaze on to the road that led out of Whittington and back into the woods, his thigh pulsing and jabbing with each stride that the stallion took.

CHAPTER 18

Maude enjoyed riding, especially when she could be astride a horse of her own rather than having to sit pillion behind a groom. She liked controlling the reins and feeling the response between herself and her palfrey. To protect her skin from the midday sun, she wore a broad-brimmed pilgrim hat over her light linen wimple. This was the third day of her journey from Theobald's abbey at Cockersand near Lancaster to Higford. The weather had grown progressively stickier as they moved inland away from the cooling sea breeze of the coast and down through Cheshire.

She had stayed with her father at Edlington for the briefest time that duty permitted. As usual he had been patronising and brusque, his main concern not for her welfare, but for her position on fortune's wheel. 'I made you a good marriage,' he had said, fists clutched importantly at his belt. 'You are kin to Hubert Walter, perhaps the most powerful man in the land. Why is it that your husband has no more now than he had on your wedding day — less in fact, since King John has removed many of his privileges?' He spoke as if it was her fault. Perhaps in a way it was. Doubtless if she had lain with John like so many baronial wives and daughters, the King's favour would have been easy to obtain.

Maude shuddered at the notion and the palfrey responded with a flicker of her ears and a sideways prance. She had told her father that Theobald would not curry favour at the price of his honour. Robert le Vavasour had snorted rudely and said that his son-in-law's honour was an expensive luxury that would eventually ruin him. At the end of a week, she had left Edlington without looking back.

It was common knowledge that a man's seed was stronger than a woman's, that what he planted in the womb was mainly of his essence. God help her, it couldn't be true. She didn't want to be made in the image of Robert le Vavasour: greedy, so obsessed with status and power that he was like a man with his face pressed up to an impenetrable wall.

Another week had been spent with her grandmother at Bolton, but that too had been raw with friction. Mathilda de Chauz said with pursed lips that Maude should settle to her needle and distaff and produce some children instead of spending hours at the archery butts. It was neither womanly nor decent. How did she expect to attract her husband to her bed when she behaved like a hoyden?

Maude had borne the clucking, her gritted teeth masquerading as a smile. Obligation discharged, she had ridden on to Theobald's manor and abbey at Cockersand. The salt tang of the wind, the wide view of sandy mud flats reddening in the sunset, the hiss of the ocean curling on the shore had given her the space she needed to recover from the ordeal of duty.

Theobald's messenger had found her there and given her his letter. The court would soon be returning from Normandy and she was to meet him in London. He did not say whether he had been successful in gaining permission to visit his Irish lands. The main item of news was that King John, having divorced his first wife, had taken another bride, a girl of twelve years old. Her name was Isobel of Angoulême and Theobald had written laconically that not only was she a great heiress, but that John was fond of her.

Maude grimaced, not venturing to wonder what that fondness might entail. Twelve was, after all, the age at which a girl could legally be married — even if she had not yet attained her physical womanhood. Maude remembered the fears and anxieties of her own wedding day. And she had had nothing to fear from Theo. What would it be like to be married to John? It was said that he was good to his mistresses, providing for them generously and acknowledging his bastard children, but that did not change the fact that he was a lecher, cruel and selfish in his lusts. Maude suspected that for every woman to benefit from his generosity, there were half a dozen others who paid the price — their families too.

Maude and her escort rounded a curve and the road widened, yielding a view of the daub and wattle houses of Higford. She had promised Emmeline FitzWarin that she would return this way and although it was a slightly longer route, the journey was pleasant and it was no chore. She liked Emmeline, she wanted to pray at Hawise FitzWarin's tomb, and the horses could be rested for a couple of nights before she continued down to London.

She rode past the shingle-roofed mill at the riverside and was curtseyed to and gazed at by the women waiting to have their wheatsheaves ground into flour. The mill wheel turned ponderously, the water of the race rippling like translucent green silk. A fisherman was emptying his wicker eel trap of its wriggling, glittering catch. Maude smiled. Likely she had just seen her dinner.

Rounding another turn, she came upon the manor. Lulled by the scenes of pleasant industry in the village, she was startled to find the place frenetic with activity as if someone had thrust their arm into a hive of bees. The courtyard was filled with horses and armed men, recently arrived to judge by the chaos. Emmeline's grooms were busy amongst them and the knights themselves were unsaddling their mounts. Maude felt a selfish rush of dismay and irritation, swiftly followed by a burst of curiosity.

'Shall I find out what is happening, my lady?' asked Wimarc of Amounderness, who was in charge of her escort.

Maude nodded. 'Do so.'

Wimarc dismounted and went to speak to the men within. Maude watched him join a group, saw him listen and nod. Glancing beyond, her gaze lit on two young men in conversation, one as tall and thin as a jousting lance, the other smaller and stockier with a head of cropped red curls. Alain and Philip FitzWarin. And where Philip and Alain went, Fulke was likely to be ahead of them. She scanned the crowd, her stomach suddenly turning like the mill wheel.

Wimarc returned and told her what she already knew. 'Lady Emmeline's nephews are here to rest up for a short while,' he said. He gave her a shrewd look. 'Do you want to ride on, my lady?'

Usually decisive, Maude did not give him an answer straight away, but looked at the activity in the courtyard and gnawed her lip. It would be for the best, she thought. Accommodation would be horrendously crowded and the thought of seeing Fulke made the wheel in her stomach churn and surge. The thought of not seeing him filled her with flat disappointment. She had promised Emmeline that she would return this way and she owed Fulke the courtesy telling him how sorry she was for his mother's death. But with so many men, his purpose was obviously not just to visit his aunt.

Wimarc rubbed his palm over his bearded jaw and, as if reading her thoughts, said, 'They tried to lay an ambush for Morys FitzRoger and Lord Fulke came away from it with a quarrel in his leg. Lady Emmeline's tending him now.'

'A quarrel?' Maude stared at Wimarc in horror. King Richard had died of a crossbow bolt in the shoulder – a minor battle wound that had festered and poisoned his blood so that a week later he died in agony. 'Lady Emmeline will need aid if she is to tend Lord Fulke and see to all these men,' she said, her decisiveness returning. Gathering the reins, she nudged Doucette through the gateway into the frantic business of the yard.

Maude quietly parted the thick woollen curtain and entered Emmeline's bedchamber. It was a large, well appointed room at the top of the manor with limewashed walls that had been warmed and decorated by colourful hangings.

Fulke was in Emmeline's bed, propped up against a collection of bolsters. There were dark circles beneath his eyes, his mouth was thin with pain and weariness, and his nose had caught the sun so that he looked more hawkish than ever. Although battle-worn, he scarcely appeared to be at death's door and the fist of fear beneath Maude's ribs ceased to clench quite so hard.

The covers were flapped back and Emmeline was leaning over his lower body, her own complexion the colour of whey. As Maude advanced to the bed, Fulke looked up. Alarm flickered in his eyes and he lashed the covers back over himself so swiftly that he almost took out his aunt's eye on the corner of a sheet.

'What are you doing here?' he snarled in a voice that was as far from the grave as Maude had ever heard. 'Get out!'

Hand over her eye, Emmeline turned. 'Maude?' Behind

the half-mask of her fingers, a look of relief swept over her features.

'I said I would return this way.' Maude looked angrily at Fulke. His rejection made her all the more determined to stand her ground. 'With an invalid to nurse' – here a disparaging curl of her lip at Fulke – 'and a passel of hungry men to feed, you are in need of help.'

Emmeline rose and wiped her streaming eye on her cuff. 'Bless you, child,' she said in a heartfelt voice.

'What do you want me to do?'

'You're not going to do anything,' Fulke snapped, drawing himself up on the bolsters and glowering furiously. 'I'm a rebel, and if you so much as associate with me, you'll be tainted too.'

Maude shrugged. 'Who's to know?' she said. 'Theo would be more angry with me for riding away than for staying to help.'

Emmeline looked uncertainly between them. 'It is true that I will be very glad for you to stay, but not if it is going to put you in danger.'

'No more danger than you are in yourself,' Maude said to the older woman. 'My brother-in-law is the Archbishop of Canterbury and the King's Chancellor. That surely must bestow some protection.'

'His support never did us any good,' Fulke growled.

Emmeline turned round, her sallow cheeks flushing. 'Has your wound bled the courtesy from your body?' she demanded. 'What is wrong with you that you should behave like a thwarted small child?'

'Aren't all men like that when they are injured?' Maude gave Emmeline a wry woman-to-woman smile.

Emmeline snorted down her nose. 'Some of them are like it all the time,' she said darkly.

Clearly annoyed, but recognising that a retort would only

lead to more ridicule, Fulke clamped his jaw and thrust his spine against the bolsters. 'If you can remove this arrow from my leg, I won't trouble your hospitality above a couple of days,' he said.

'I've sent for the priest. He'll be here as soon as he can.'

'The priest?' Maude thought of the agitated note in Emmeline's voice and linked it with her pallor as she leaned over Fulke's wound.

Her horror must have shown on her face because for the first time since she had entered the room, Fulke smiled, albeit savagely and without humour. 'You need not concern yourself, Lady Walter, I am not about to be administered the last rites.'

'I . . .'

'Someone has to cut this arrow out of my leg. Having seen the mess William makes gutting a hare, I don't trust him to do the deed, and I won't ask any of the men. It's too great a responsibility. If aught should go wrong, I do not want one of them to carry an unnecessary burden of guilt.'

The speech had begun with defensive, sardonic humour, and ended in sincerity. Maude's throat tightened as she was yielded a glimpse behind his shield.

'I am afraid I cannot play the healer's part,' Emmeline said, unconsciously wringing her hands. 'Even the sight of blood makes me faint. My father always said that it was a good thing that I wasn't born male.'

'And can the priest?'

Emmeline nodded, although there was a spark of doubt in her eyes. 'He set Alwin Shepherd's broken arm last year and it has healed cleanly.'

'But he has never removed an arrow?'

Emmeline shook her head. 'Not that I'm aware,' she said.

Maude pushed up her sleeves, exposing slender forearms, and advanced to the bed. 'How deep is it in?'

Fulke's fist clenched on the bedclothes, holding them firmly down over his leg, and in his face there was fear, anger, and stubborn mutiny. Maude looked at him and then down at his hand, remembering how the sight of it had affected her as Theobald's new bride. Now the long fingers were curled in tight and the raised knuckles were bleached.

'Let me see,' she said, laying hold of the sheet's edge.

'Why?' he challenged. 'I warrant you have never removed an arrow from flesh either.'

'No,' Maude admitted, 'but I have seen it done. One of Theo's knights received a quarrel in the leg during a hunt, and we were fortunate enough to have a Salerno-trained chirugeon claiming hospitality in Lancaster at the time.' She held Fulke's gaze steadily. 'Me, or the priest. The choice is yours.'

He returned her stare, then with a sigh capitulated, raising his hand and looking away. 'Do as you will.'

Maude lifted the covers and folded them aside. He wore a loincloth for modesty, but still she had never been as close to any man's intimate area save Theobald's. Fulke's thighs were long, powerful, and surprisingly hairless given his dark colouring. On the nearside one, the stump of a quarrel protruded from the skin like the stalk of a pear. The full length of the shaft had been snapped off to leave about two inches standing proud.

'I'll need a thin wedge of wood,' Maude murmured as she gently prodded and felt Fulke tense like a wound bow.

'I don't need anything to bite on,' he said indignantly.

'Oh, stop being so proud, you fool,' Maude snapped. 'And it's not for you to bite on anyway. The way you're behaving it might be a good thing if you used your own tongue as a clamp.' She raised her head to Emmeline and gestured with forefinger and thumb. 'A wedge of wood about this thickness, no more. I'll also need two wide goose quills, a small sharp knife and needle and thread.'

Emmeline nodded and turned away.

'Oh, and in my baggage there's a small leather costrel. Ask my maid to find it.'

Fulke's aunt vanished on her errand.

Maude sat down at the bedside. One half of her mind was studying the other half in astonishment. Had she really given orders so briskly and with such confidence? Any moment now the façade would desert her and leave a trembling wreck, no more capable than Emmeline of doing what had to be done.

'I am sorry that your mother has died,' she murmured. 'I came to see her at Alberbury when she was ailing and I stayed with her.'

Fulke stared obdurately at the wall hangings directly opposite his line of vision. 'That was kind of you,' he said stiffly as if the words were being forced out of him. 'My aunt did tell me.'

Maude pleated the coverlet in her fingers. 'We became good friends,' she said. Some instinct held her back from telling him how close. She did not think he would want to hear that Hawise considered her the daughter she had never had. At least not now, when it might seem like a rejection of the sons she had borne.

'Did she suffer?'

Maude busied herself with the coverlet. 'No. At the end she went peacefully in her sleep.'

'You're not a very good liar, are you?' He turned his head so that their eyes met on the level instead of from a side glance.

'What do you want me to say?' Maude demanded. 'Will it make any difference to know that she was in terrible pain? Will it ease you to know that she only died in her sleep because we dosed her with Alberbury's entire supply of poppy syrup to calm her agony?' She blinked and scrubbed angrily at her lashes. 'I loved her, and I didn't want her to go, but for her own sake I prayed harder than I have ever done in my life for God in his mercy to take her.'

There was a quivering silence. Then she saw his throat work and the betraying glitter in his own eyes. He turned his head again, this time looking away, and muttered indistinctly beneath his breath. Of its own volition, her hand crept from its pleating to cover his on the bedclothes. Even while she made the move in compassion and the need to offer comfort and be comforted, a part of her mind acknowledged that it was something she had wanted to do ever since her wedding breakfast.

He tensed, his face remained averted, but he did not withdraw from the light pressure.

The curtain rattled on its pole as Emmeline returned with Barbette in tow and the requested articles. Resisting the impulse born of guilt to snatch her hand away, Maude tightened her grip.

'How good are you at ignoring pain?' she asked Fulke.

He shrugged and looked at her, his expression restored to one of sardonic humour. 'That is hard to say since I have never had an arrow taken from my flesh before. How much are you going to inflict?'

Maude briefly compressed her lips while she pondered how to reply, finally deciding that in kind was as good a way as any. 'That is hard to say also, since I have never taken an arrow from anyone's flesh before.'

Fulke eyed her fingers upon his. 'Then we are well matched,' he said.

Maude reddened. 'In this matter, yes,' she said, trying to appear unruffled and in her own time removed her hand.

'Do you want me to stay?'

Maude glanced over her shoulder. Emmeline's voice had been thready with fear. 'No, there is nothing you can do, but if you could send two of the men in, I would be grateful.'

Emmeline nodded and scurried out, her relief obvious.

'Two men?' Fulke raised his brow. 'You think it is going to be that difficult to hold me down?'

'You may well buck like a branded colt, and do serious damage to yourself.'

She took the knife, examined its edge, then went to the brazier burning in the middle of the room and thrust the instrument among the glowing lumps of charcoal. Fulke stared, and she saw sweat spring on his brow. She had no doubt that if he had been sound in limb he would have run from the room.

'Good Christ, woman, what do you think you're doing?'

'The chirugeon who showed me his art said that fire purifies. To stop a wound from festering you must use instruments that have been tempered in its heat. Don't worry: I'll quench it first.'

'I think I need to be drunk,' he said weakly.

Maude gave a brisk nod. 'It would be a good idea.' Leaving the knife in the glowing charcoal, she went to the costrel and removed the stopper. 'Are you familiar with uisge beatha?'

Fulke managed a grim smile. 'I was introduced to it as a squire in Ireland with Theobald – vile stuff, but useful if you crave to get drunk without bursting your bladder.' He held out his hand for the costrel. Before she gave it to him, Maude poured off some of the almost colourless liquor into a large pottery beaker.

'Are you going to drink that before or after you cut out the arrow?'

'Neither,' she said. He was jesting, trying to be light and flippant, but she knew that he must be feeling sick with apprehension and fear. Even if the operation of removing the arrowhead was simple, it was still no small undertaking and she knew without a doubt that for a brief time at least he was going to be in agony.

The curtain pole rattled again as two of Fulke's brothers entered. Not William, who was nursing cracked ribs and heavy bruises, but Ivo and Richard who were both big and strong. The latter was cramming the last of a griddle scone into his mouth and dusting his hands on his tunic.

'Is there ever a time when you're not eating?' Fulke demanded from the bed.

Richard patted his solid stomach. 'Extra flesh acts like another layer on your gambeson,' he said.

'It's no wonder your horse sags in the middle.' Fulke took a swig from the costrel, and his repartee was immediately silenced by a glottal wheeze.

Maude waited until he had drunk more than half the remaining uisge beatha in the costrel then gestured Ivo and Richard into position. Fetching the knife, she quenched it in a jar of water standing nearby and then, with a prayer on her lips, picked up the mead cup and sloshed some of its contents over Fulke's wounded thigh.

Although he was well on the way to being gilded, Fulke still arched and yowled like a scalded cat and there was nothing his brothers could do to hold him. 'Bitch!' he gasped. 'Vixen, bitch!' He fell back on to the bed, his lids squeezed tightly shut and moisture leaking out between them.

'That is the worst over,' Maude said tremulously. Her heart was pounding in her throat at both Fulke's reaction and what she was about to do.

His voice was ragged. 'Christ, just do what you must, and be quick about it!'

Faces grim, Ivo and Richard pinned him. Maude took the knife. 'I have to open the wound to reach the arrow head. With good fortune it will not be barbed and can be eased out.'

'And if it is barbed?' Ivo gave her a searching look from beneath his brows.

'That is what the goose quills are for. They are set over the tines so that when the arrow head is drawn out, the flesh is not ripped.'

Both brothers winced. Fulke made an inarticulate sound conveying drunken, angry impatience.

Maude took a deep breath, entreated God to steady her hand, and set to work. To his credit, Fulke tried hard not to tense his leg and she was able to cut down to the arrow head reasonably quickly. There was plenty of superficial blood, but she could tell from the way it welled around the wound that no major vessel was involved. A gentle probe revealed that mercifully the arrow head was not barbed. She took the thin wedge of wood, slid it carefully into the side of the slit and eased the iron arrow out.

'Here,' she said, presenting it to Fulke in her bloody fingers. 'A talisman for luck.'

'Luck!' he laughed weakly. His complexion was ashen and his pupils huge and dark with pain. 'What kind of luck is that?'

'The kind that lets you off lightly. It was only in your flesh, no damage to bone or major vessels. If you do not suffer the wound fever or stiffening sickness, you will live with naught but a scar to show for it.'

While he was still looking at the bloodied arrow, she removed the wedge and doused the wound in uisge beatha a second time. Once again he reacted like a scalded cat, this time almost losing consciousness. Maude quickly packed the wound with a greased bandage and then wrapped it in strips of linen swaddling band.

'How long before he is able to ride again?' Ivo asked. His look was a little reproachful and she could tell that he thought her unnecessarily cruel. 'When can we leave?'

'A week at least, but better two. You'll need to do some hunting for your suppers if you are not to strip Higford of its supplies.'

'Oh yes, we'll hunt,' Ivo said. The way he looked at Richard made Maude decide not to ask the kind of prey they had in mind, although she suspected that any royal manors within the vicinity might soon find themselves receiving a visit. So she merely nodded and changed the subject.

'He needs peace and quiet to sleep and recover,' she murmured. 'One of you can sit with him and make sure he needs for nothing. I will speak to your aunt – reassure her that all is well.' She grimaced at the dried blood caking her fingers. 'Although I had best wash my hands first, or she will never believe me!'

That raised half-smiles from Fulke's brothers. She took the costrel bottle and swigged down the dregs. The fire of the brew hit the back of her throat and shot in a line of liquid flame to her belly. She gasped, first with shock, then with relief. Fulke half opened his eyes and looked at her mazily. 'I don't know whether to kiss or kill you,' he slurred.

He was out of his wits with drink and pain, but his words still sent a jolt through her that almost rivalled the uisge beatha for effect. 'Perhaps you should just thank me,' she said, and left the bedside before he could say anything else.

Three days later, Maude was able to pronounce that Fulke's wound was healing cleanly, without signs of the dreaded wound fever. At first she had not been sure and had had to wait out the raging headache, the thirst and sickness caused by the after-effects of his drinking such a large quantity of uisge beatha. Now, however, she was certain. Already he was proving to be a restless, irritable patient, refusing to stay abed and swallow his nostrums as instructed.

'I'm not a puling infant,' he snarled at the sight of Maude armed with a bowl of oxtail broth. 'It's my thigh that's injured, not my stomach.'

He was fully dressed and sitting in the window embrasure, his leg stretched out in front of him. His tangled hair and a four-day growth of beard made him look like the outlaw he was rather than a polished knight.

Maude narrowed her eyes. He had already sent one of the maids out in tears that morning, and had been thoroughly insufferable ever since William had taken the men out on a 'hunt' after the breaking of fast. She knew that he saw it as his responsibility to lead them, and was not happy at being forced to delegate, but that did not mean he should take his ire out on those around him.

'It's the state of your manners that concerns me the most,' she answered tartly as she set the bowl down in front of him together with a small loaf. 'Since everyone else is dining on oxtail broth, I do not see that you should object. You cannot bring fifty fighting men into a small manor like this and expect to dine like a king every day.'

He gave her an angry scowl and drew himself up. 'I will pay my way. The men have gone out foraging, as you well know.'

'Stealing from John, you mean.'

'Much less than he steals from me.' Grudgingly he tore a piece off the bread and dipped it in the broth. 'Why bring it to my chamber?' he demanded. 'I am quite capable of sitting in the hall with my aunt and whoever else remains.'

'Partly because I hoped you might still be abed,' Maude snapped, 'and partly because no one wants to sit at table with a boor.' She had intended staying with him to make sure he ate his broth. Since he seemed to have every intention of doing so and she found his behaviour objectionable, she abandoned her plan and stalked out. She would examine his leg later, and if she hurt him, she would not be contrite.

Too angry and exasperated to sit at table in the hall and make conversation with Emmeline, Maude fetched her bow and quiver from her chamber and went to practise her archery at the butts.

Fulke drank the broth, which was excellent and full flavoured. He ate the bread and knew with annoyance at Maude and irritation at himself that she was right. He was being petulant, but only because he was bored, shut away in this chamber and treated as if his wits had bled out of the hole in his leg. He was a proud, active man, healthy and vigorous, and not within his living memory had he been confined to bed for more than a day. The thought of William out foraging at the head of the troop was enough to make him bite his nails ragged. It was true that his brother had learned a little more prudence along the tourney road, but not so much that Fulke trusted him without qualm.

Still, he should not have taken his frustration out on Maude. He owed her more than he could repay. Perhaps that was part of the reason that he had lashed out. He made an impatient sound at the thought, and decided on the instant to do something to amend both his behaviour and the situation.

Pulling himself up by the angle of the embrasure wall, he limped slowly and painfully to the entrance curtain. His lance was propped against a coffer nearby and he grasped it to use as a prop. His chamber was part of a large room divided by the curtain, the other section containing his aunt's solar. A maid was busy weaving braid on a small loom, but his aunt was nowhere to be seen. Likely she was in the hall dining on her own broth and being regaled by Maude with the tale of his execrable behaviour.

It was that thought rather than the pain in his leg that made him grimace as he limped to the embrasure. The maid had opened the lower shutters to allow daylight into the chamber. Fulke gazed out on herb-beds and a green area beyond, which the manor's retainers used for battle training and archery practice.

A single bowman faced the straw butts, drawing and releasing with fluid ease. He narrowed his eyes, the better to focus on the distant figure. A *bow woman*, he amended with surprise and admiration. Even from where he stood, he could see that Maude Walter was good.

Not without a little difficulty, Fulke negotiated the wooden external stairs at the end of the solar and descended to the courtyard below. There was a slight breeze, enough to ruffle his hair, but not sufficient to blow the arrows off their course as Maude sent them winging into the butt. He watched the sharp angle of her arm, the tilt of her head, the way her lips pursed on the draw and then released in an expression that was almost a kiss as she loosed all the pent-up tension and let the arrow fly. Beauty controlling power. He felt the hair lift on the nape of his neck.

He limped between the herb-beds until he reached the edge of the sward, then paused to gain his breath and recover from the pain.

She must have seen him from the corner of her eye, for she turned. Angry colour burned her cheeks and she lowered the bow, her next arrow un-nocked.

'I am glad that it was not you shooting at me from the walls of Whittington,' he said, 'for I know I would be dead. You have a better eye than Alain, and he's by far the keenest marksman among us.'

She shrugged. 'I shoot finest when I'm angry.'

Fulke stirred his toe in the soft, thick pile of the grass. A beetle was toiling amongst the short blades, its body as glossy as polished dark leather. 'As you have every right to be.' A glance at Maude from beneath his brows revealed that she was eyeing him warily, anger still apparent in the set of her lips and the slight narrowing of her lids. Christ, she was lovely. It was all too easy to imagine her long-limbed and wild in his bed. He cleared his throat and quashed the thought. 'Even since being bound in swaddling bands as an infant I have chafed at confinement. I am sorry if I railed at you for what is none of your fault. Indeed, I owe you and my aunt a debt beyond all paying. I would not have you think me ungrateful.'

Her look told him that while she was a little mollified, she was not yet prepared to let him off the hook. 'I don't.' She walked up to the butt and tugged her arrows out. He looked at her straight back, the ripple of her linen veil at each jerk of effort. 'But you're still a mannerless boor,' she said on her return.

'If you gave me another chance, I could prove otherwise.'

Her lips curved. 'How many chances do you want?' she asked sweetly.

Fulke gave her a questioning frown.

'On my wedding morn,' she said, 'you took a whore beneath my bridal roof.'

'What?'

'Hanild. Was that her name?' She nocked an arrow and let fly into the heart of the target. Thud. As if it were her enemy's heart.

He stared in astonishment. 'And that has rankled with you all this time?'

'Should it not? I was a new bride, and you humiliated me!'

'I didn't do it to humiliate you,' Fulke said on a rising note, 'I did it because I—' He dug his fingers through his hair and bit back the rest of the sentence.

'Because what?'

He shook his head.

'No, tell me, I want to know.' A new arrow sat between the leather guards on her fingers.

Fulke swallowed. 'Because, as you say, you were a new bride – Theobald's wife. And, God help me, I wanted you.'

She lowered her eyes and studied the goose-feather fletching as if it were of vast importance.

'Every man present was imagining himself in Theobald's place – claiming your virginity, creating that bloody sheet, and I was no different.' He smiled, although the gesture did not reach his eyes. 'I had no intention of insulting you when I took Hanild to my bed. She was there; I was in need; and at the time it seemed like a reasonable idea to a man who had almost lost his reason.'

It was her turn to swallow. He saw the ripple of her throat, the way she drew a sharp, small breath, and he realised that the incident must have meant far more to her than a brief moment of chagrin. Why else would she remember so small a detail as Hanild's name? Why else hold it against him for so long? Perhaps the attraction was mutual. Perhaps that was why she was so hostile.

'The wanting has not gone away,' he said softly. 'If anything, it is worse now than it was before because it has grown as we have done. But whatever you think of my manners, I honour you and I honour Theobald.' He drew a line of darker green in the moist grass with the haft of the lance, bisecting the yard of ground between him and Maude. 'I will not step beyond the line, and neither will you,' he said. 'But we both know it exists . . . don't we?'

Trembling, she lifted her chin, her eyes as clear and hard as green glass. He saw the denial, the preparation of an angry rebuff.

'Or am I more honest than you?' he asked.

She put the arrow to the string and raised the bow. 'I love Theobald dearly, and my loyalty to him is firm as a rock,' she said in a quivering voice. 'How dare you!'

'Because you wanted to know.' He spread his hands. 'I love Theobald too, and I would not do anything to betray his trust in me.'

'Is lusting after his wife not a betrayal of his trust?'

'Not while neither of us crosses this line.' He smiled again, still without humour. 'Call it courtly love. The giving of a token for the breaking of a tourney lance in the season. If you are going to shoot me, do it now. Pierce my heart a second time.'

'Go away!' Maude hissed, tears glittering in her eyes.

Fulke regarded her sombrely. 'I came to make my peace,' he said. 'I did not intend this to happen, I swear it.'

'Please . . . just go!'

He did as she asked, but slowly. His leg was throbbing with the strain of standing for so long, and although the burden of confession had been taken off his mind, the weight of its consequence had just been added. Behind him, blind of all but instinct, Maude sent fletch after fletch into the heart of the straw butt.

Later that evening she came to his chamber. This time there was no bowl of broth in her hand for he had taken his evening meal of salt fish in the hall with his aunt, amid the constraints of propriety. It was Maude who had eaten in her own tiny chamber, pleading a headache.

He was briefly surprised to see her now, but then realised that he should have known. Running away was not in her nature. Right or wrong, she would rather stand and fight.

She approached the bench in the embrasure where he was sitting, and he saw that she was carrying a clay ointment pot and fresh swaddling bands.

'Is your headache improved, my lady?' he enquired politely, casting a glance to the curtain, which she had left open for propriety's sake, nipping in the bud any gossip that might arise from her being alone with him.

'A little. Your leg needs tending, and my head will bear up to the task better than your aunt's stomach.'

She hooked up a footstool with her ankle and, sitting down beside him, unfastened the pin securing his bandage. Obviously she was not going to ask him to lie down on the bed. Too dangerous, he thought with a bleak and private smile. Who was to say she was not right?

With brisk competence, she tended the wound, remarking that it was healing well. Fulke had cautioned himself against reacting to her touch but there was no need. Her cold tone and practicality were so powerful a barrier that there was not the slightest reaction from his groin, lest it be a slight tightening and shrinking away. God knew what she might do with those sewing shears at her belt.

She refastened the bandage and sat back, folding her hands in her lap like a staid matron. Then she drew a deep breath and looked at him, her expression a heart-rending mingling of fear and courage.

'I have come to make my peace with you,' she announced. 'And to be as truthful with you as you have been with me.'

He wondered how long she had sat alone with her

'headache', wrestling with what she was going to do and say. Suddenly he was almost afraid to hear it, but he had to listen, had to know.

'I do love Theo,' she said. 'He is kind and generous and honourable, and I never think of the years between us, except to hope that he remains in good health.' Her tone grew vehement. 'He is my friend, my companion, and I would give my life for him. I would not hurt or harm him in any way.'

'Neither would I.' But he could scarcely imagine Theobald being delighted at this conversation, or the one that had taken place at the archery butts. It was dangerous ground, thin, thin ice, offering no retreat.

'You are right about the line, though,' she said, her voice now scarcely above a whisper. 'And I am so afraid that one of us will step across and destroy everything. Theobald knows that something is wrong between you and me. He cannot understand why we avoid each other's company, but one day I fear that he will see and know.' She folded her arms tightly across her breasts, protecting her body. 'Is it love or lust? I do not know, because I do not know you. Perhaps it is no more than wishing after what you cannot have.'

He eyed her sombrely. Mayhap that was the way she felt; until today he had been good at keeping her out, but he had seen facets of Maude since her late childhood that made him certain of his own commitment. 'Since the only way to find out is to cross the line and neither of us will do so, there is no remedy save to keep apart,' he said.

'Well, that is simple enough,' she said with false brightness. 'I am to join Theo at court and then we're going to Ireland.'

He smiled grimly in response. 'And I am going back into the forests, seeking thorns to put in King John's side.'

They looked at each other, the unspoken knowledge between them that he was treading a hazardous path, possibly towards his own death. The keeping apart might be as final as eternity.

There was sudden noise in the courtyard, a groom shouting for torches and the clattering of many shod hooves. In the chamber doorway, Emmeline called excitedly to Fulke and Maude that the troop was home from its foray.

'I have to go.' She rose so quickly that she stumbled on the full hem of her gown. He grasped her hand to steady her, the force pulling her momentarily towards him, and now her touch streaked through him like fire. Teetering on the line, one hair-fire strand remaining. Another tug and she would be in his lap.

He snatched his hand away and waved it hard. 'Go!' His voice was ragged. 'You'll be safe. I can't run after you, can I?'

With a gasp, she fled.

Leaning back, Fulke closed his eyes and tried to summon the will necessary to greet and question his brothers.

CHAPTER 19

Marlborough, Wiltshire,
Autumn 1200

'I am going to ask John for an outright answer.' Theobald's voice was firm with determination as he changed from the day's practical hunting gear into a sumptuous court robe of blue wool embroidered with thread of gold. Despite his new-found piety he still enjoyed clothes and could gild the lily with the best of them. 'He cannot keep dangling me like this.' He thrust one leg forwards so that his squire could wind the decorative tablet-weave bindings from ankle to knee. 'What does he think I am going to do — foment a wild rebellion?'

'Perhaps he does,' Maude murmured, standing still while Barbette floated a light silk veil on to her head and secured it with a circlet of silver wire. 'How many of the barons truly serve him out of love and respect?' Outside the rain was drumming on the roof of their tent. Now and then, the striped canvas rippled alarmingly as it was buffeted by sudden gusts of wind. She would be glad to cross the wet sward and enter the warmth of the palace for the afternoon's feasting and entertainment. At least she would be warm and dry.

'Very few,' Theobald said bleakly, 'but the majority give him their loyalty. He is our rightful King.' He sighed. 'I just wish he trusted me enough to let me go, but that is one of his flaws. He trusts no one. He keeps us within his sights not out of love or need, but out of a fear that we are going to stab him in the back.' He scowled with frustration. 'I want to see my monasteries in Ireland again before I die. Is it so much to ask?'

Task finished, Barbette stepped back and Maude came over to Theobald. Waving the squire aside she continued with the task of securing his leg bindings. 'You speak as if you are a doddering ancient,' she said as she knelt. 'You're not going to widow me for a long time yet, I hope.' It was a hope bolstered by fervent and guilty prayer. At the back of her mind, sealed away in shame that it existed at all, was the vision of a line drawn by a lance point in dew-wet grass.

Her head was bent to her efforts and she felt his hand descend lightly to her shoulder. 'I am five and fifty years old,' he said. 'At that age a man's mind turns easily to thoughts of his own mortality. When I look around, I do not see many who are more than ten years older than me. I must think to the future of my soul. No man wants to die, but it is best if he is prepared.'

Maude's movements grew abrupt. 'And what of the future of your wife?' she demanded. Selfish though it might be, she felt that her fleshly life was currently of more interest to her than the good of the soul. 'Have you prepared for that?'

'I have left you well provided for,' he said in a tone that was slightly puzzled, slightly hurt. 'Why are you angry?'

Breathless from the constriction of kneeling, Maude stood up and glared at him. 'Well enough to make me a valuable marriage prize for one of John's cronies?' she snapped.

Theobald blinked and shook his head. 'Of course not. You will have Hubert to guide and protect you. No one will dare to harm you if you are under the wing of the Archbishop of Canterbury.'

'Who is younger than you by what, two or three years? He has already been sick. I will be sold to the highest bidder.'

Theobald looked perplexed, like a small boy who expected to be praised and was receiving a scolding instead. 'I have taken what precautions I can,' he said, trying to lighten his tone. 'I promise to do my best to live to be as old as Methuselah. Come, sweetheart, don't frown.' He set his hand to her brow and smoothed it gently with the pad of his thumb. 'I've seen too many glum looks on your face since you arrived at court.'

For his sake, Maude forced a smile. 'I am pleased to be at your side, but you know I hate these great gatherings.'

'There is nothing else troubling your spirit?'

She shook her head and hoped that God would forgive her for the lie. 'Nothing,' she said. 'Indeed, if you think upon it, I did not begin to frown until you spoke of dying.'

'Ah, so it's my fault.'

'Don't be foolish.' The words emerged more sharply than she had intended and he raised his brows. 'Oh, pay me no heed, Theo.' She gave him a hug of contrition. 'If I'm in a crotchet it is of my own making. Come, are you ready?' She linked her arm through his.

He was as eager to dismiss the moment as she and gestured his squire to draw back the tent flap on the rain-laden dusk. As they moved to the entrance, he looked down at her and the graven seams at his eye corners deepened in a smile. 'You will be the most beautiful woman there, Maude, and whatever John metes out to me, I will still be the most fortunate of men.'

'Flatterer.' She nudged him, her throat suddenly tight with tears.

★   ★   ★

The food was rich and elaborate as befitted a royal banquet to honour John's new Queen. There was roast boar and venison from the royal forests, attended by numerous colourful and piquant sauces; there were small pies, their crusts shaped like castle turrets; and there were sugared plums and marchpane sweetmeats for the child bride's delight.

Isobel of Angoulême had to sit on a large cushion to make her the right height for the arched marble table. She was fey and dainty with a cloud of pale blonde hair and eyes the deep, true blue of cornflowers. Twelve years old, her breasts scarcely beginning to bud, the bones of her face still tender and malleable, she was already a rare beauty. Rumours abounded. John was infatuated by her, it was said. Apparently he had broken her betrothal to another man in order to have her. The more prosaic explanation was that the original betrothal had been between two powerful families opposed to John. By marrying the girl, he had neatly kept the factions divided and gained an excellent dowry as well as a beautiful, biddable wife.

Remembering her anxiety at the time of her own marriage, Maude sought to befriend the girl and offer her a shoulder to lean on. It quickly became apparent, however, that despite the similarity of circumstance, Isobel was a creature cut from a very different cloth. Whereas Maude had worn her childhood scrapes and escapades like badges of honour, Isobel's pride was in her possessions, in her clothes and jewels, in dressing exquisitely and receiving the adulation of the smitten. John had ordered some bolts of fabric to make winter gowns for his child bride. A merchant train was expected to arrive before the court left for Gloucester and Isobel was petulant because dark had fallen and the cloth had not arrived. That was a matter over which Maude could empathise. The arrival of a merchant train was always of interest, particularly when the content was fabric. There was nothing quite like an ell of expertly woven blue broadcloth or a splash of scarlet Italian silk to draw a crowd of admirers and that was just the men.

The many courses of the meal were separated by entertainments: jugglers, tumblers, musicians. Jean de Rampaigne dazzled them all with his skill at the lute and the soaring range of his voice. And there was dancing. Isobel loved to dance. She was light on her feet with grace and natural ability. She partnered John and she partnered his barons, her movements quicksilver, her face sparkling and animated.

Theobald went to speak with John about Ireland and Maude sought the garderobe as Falco de Breauté, one of John's mercenary bodyguards, approached her with the obvious intention of asking her to partner him. She could not abide him, although he seemed to think that he was God's gift to women.

Having visited the garderobe, she lingered, giving de Breauté time to fix his attentions elsewhere, and then made her way slowly back. Perhaps if Theo had finished talking to John, they could retire to their pavilion for the night. As she entered a walkway lit by a guttering torch, a figure walked from the opposite direction, blocking her path, and made no move to step aside. When Maude paused to let him by, her heart thumping, he stopped too, and she drew a sharp, involuntary breath.

'Lady Walter,' purred John with a feline smile. 'You should not be lingering out here, you'll catch a chill.'

Maude mangled a curtsey. 'I was returning to the hall, sire.'

'That is as may be, but I am glad to find you here, for I wish to speak to you.'

'About what, sire?' She wondered how easy it would be

to duck around his bulk and run for the bright, smoky safety of the hall.

John's eyes were darker than darkness. He parted his lips and she saw the feral gleam of his teeth. 'I thought you would be pleased to know that I have granted your husband's request. He is free to go and dwell in his Irish bog with his monks if that be his desire.'

'That is indeed generous of you, sire,' Maude murmured. She wondered what he wanted in return. Something for nothing was not within the lexicon of John's nature. Theobald's gratitude might suffice, but she doubted it unless the King was in an exceptionally expansive mood.

'And trusting, after the way he behaved over Lancaster,' John remarked nastily, revealing that Theobald's yielding to Richard six years ago still rankled in his memory.

'He has always served you well, sire,' she defended him.

'Whilst serving himself at the same time. I know his ilk, my lady. Honourable, upright, devout.' Each word was spoken like an insult. 'If I am letting him go, it is to prevent that brother of his from carping at me on the matter. Besides, I doubt that Theobald has the vitality to foment rebellion these days!'

Maude compressed her lips to contain the hot words that filled her mouth, reminding herself that tomorrow she and Theobald could leave the court and breathe clean air.

'A young and lovely woman like you must find it a trial dwelling with a man whose sap has ceased to rise,' John said provocatively and moved closer, the intention obvious in the glint of his eyes. 'Surely you cannot be pleased at the thought of dwelling in the midst of nowhere while your husband practises his religious chants with a group of celibate monks?'

'There are many worse ways to fill my days.' Maude tried to step back and sideways.

'And many better.' John stepped with her. She felt the heat emanating from his body, and even as she was being repulsed, was aware of a treacherous undercurrent of attraction. His masculinity was a hot, raw thread, drawing her flesh towards his. John had often been accused of pursuing the wives and daughters of his barons, of seducing them and causing great scandal and dishonour, but he had never once been accused of rape. 'You could remain here as one of the Queen's attendants, or you could amuse yourself and travel with the court.'

'You are generous, sire,' she said frostily, 'but my place is with my husband.'

John's expression twisted and the customary cruelty showed through. 'Honourable, upright, devout,' he sneered. 'How well you suit each other. But it's superficial, isn't it, Lady Walter? What you hide beneath your self-righteousness is what every woman hides beneath her skirts, and I should know. I've pleasured enough of your kind.' His hand shot out, grasped her wrist and dragged her against him. His mouth plunged at her throat like a striking snake and his other hand rammed down between their bodies, fingers seeking and probing through the fabric of her gown.

There was terror and a betraying thrill of sensation; there was heat and shame. For an instant Maude was immobilised by the shock of the assault. Then her free hand came up. She grabbed a fistful of his hair and yanked his head back, at the same time bringing her knee viciously forward and up.

John uttered a choked wheeze and folded over. He staggered a few steps and clutched the wall, his hands cupping his abused genitals. Maude fled. Bile rose in her throat and when she came to the garderobe pit serving the great hall, she turned aside to be wretchedly sick over and above anything that she had eaten.

One of the other women discovered her crouched there. At first she thought Maude was drunk, but when she realised that her condition was caused by distress, she fetched Theobald from the hall where he was in conversation with Hubert.

Maude felt strong arms folding around her, and heard Theobald's voice warm and reassuring, asking her what was wrong. She weakly gulped out what had happened and clung to him, hiding her face against his breast.

Theobald's expression set like stone. 'I will renounce my fealty,' he said through his teeth.

'No!' Maude jerked her head from the safety of his chest. 'Why should you be punished for what is his doing? Do you want him to make of you an outlaw as he did to Fulke FitzWarin? No, let us leave now – dismantle and pack. Ride out and never return.'

He hesitated, frowning.

She clutched his tunic, her eyes glistening with tears. 'You will gain nothing from confronting him and it will only make a public scandal.'

'I am not such a weak reed that I am swayed by the hot air of scandalmongers,' he said with a curl of his lip.

'He is not worth it. Theo . . . please.'

He looked at her and after a long pause, sighed heavily. 'You are right,' he capitulated. 'He is not worth it and I have wasted too much of my life already.' He turned to the hall. 'I will say my farewell to Hubert and we will leave.'

She came with him, holding on to him like a child afraid of the dark, but also to make sure that he did not act foolishly in his anger. He was not a man to stamp or rage, but the calm of his attitude was deceptive. She knew that he was furious.

When they entered the hall, however, Hubert was with John at the high table. The music had ceased, the dancing had stopped and everyone was staring at the bedraggled party of men kneeling before the royal chair. John was sitting at a peculiar angle that spoke of deep pain. He was patently irate, but clearly in too much discomfort to vent his rage in bellowing. Maude felt a rush of satisfaction and fiercely hoped that she had damaged him for life.

A terse question by Theobald to a baron standing nearby yielded the reply that the awaited merchant train had just arrived.

'Half their mounts gone and all the King's goods,' said the noble with a hint of relish that spoke of a yen for a good tale, no matter that it was someone else's misfortune. 'Robbed in Braydon Forest by outlaws.'

Theobald frowned in dismay, wondering if such news boded ill for his imminent journey. 'Fortunate that they kept their lives.'

One of the merchants mumbled a response to a question fired at him. John suddenly bolted to his feet. 'Fulke FitzWarin?' he roared, then paid for it as he hunched over with a gasp. 'Are you telling me this is the work of Fulke FitzWarin?'

The man nodded. 'He told us to greet you on his behalf, sire, and thank you for your generous gift of fine robes.'

John's eyes bulged and the sounds that emerged through his clenched teeth were incoherent. His body shuddered as if the flesh was leaping from his bones. Theobald grabbed a squire, gave him a message for Hubert, and hurried Maude away. 'Best that we go now,' he said. 'If they were robbed by Fulke, then we have nothing to fear.'

Maude hurried along at his side. 'He is a fool. He will be killed!' She could not keep the anguish out of her voice.

Theobald gave her a quizzical look. 'Mayhap but if I were making wagers, my money would be on him, not his pursuers.' He bared his teeth. 'I know in part how Fulke must feel, and I wish him good hunting.'

She said nothing. The stakes were too high to make wagers. Three months ago, it would have mattered, but not so much. Now she could feel the cold sweat of fear in her armpits.

Once in their tent, Theobald gave the order to begin packing. They would leave at first light and head down to Bristol to take ship for Ireland. Maude made herself busy, working harder than her maid, knowing that if she sat and did nothing, she would go mad. She was aware of Theobald watching her with curiosity. She felt his gaze, the unspoken questions, and turned away in shame.

An hour later, Hubert Walter arrived with Jean de Rampaigne in tow.

'Well,' he said without preamble as he looked around the tent, by now bare of all save the essential sleeping pallets and blankets. 'There is more than one cat among the pigeons tonight.'

The years since the crusade had not been kind to Hubert. Whereas Theobald's bones had sharpened with age, Hubert's had melted into the flesh of good living. His corpulence was concealed to some extent beneath his gorgeously bejewelled and embroidered cope, but nothing could hide the lapped folds of his numerous chins.

Theobald gave him a narrow look. 'Meaning?'

'Meaning that the King's body is in as much discomfort as his mind. An attendant found him doubled up in the walkway between the hall and the private chambers, swearing that he would "kill the bitch" for what she had done. By the time he was escorted back to the hall, he was claiming that he had walked into a pillar, but of course, no one believes him. There are wagers and speculation aplenty, and Maude's name is on too many lips.' His glance flickered to his sister-by-marriage.

'Let them speculate,' Theobald said icily. 'I have been given leave to retire to Ireland, and I see no reason to stay.'

'You will not renounce your fealty?' It was the royal servant speaking rather than the brother – the Chancellor and Archbishop who had to know men's hearts and minds.

'Would I tell you even if it was my intention?' Theobald sat down on a campstool that had yet to be dismantled and pushed one hand through his iron-grey curls. 'Jesu, Hubert, if blood is thicker than water, then power is thicker than blood.'

If the remark stung Hubert, he did not show it. 'It is my duty to know your frame of mind,' he said evenly.

'If you do not know it by now, then you are not my brother.'

Hubert sighed, the sound wheezing in his chest. 'I have to do more than know; I have to hear your loyalty declared lest John should ask me.'

'And rub salt deep into an open cut?' Theobald's upper lip curled back. 'John insults my wife, insults my honour, and then demands my oath of fealty! God's sweet wounds, you are asking too much!'

'It is a price you have to afford if you don't want to be arraigned for treason.'

'Treason!' Theobald almost choked on the word. He shot to his feet, paced the two steps to the rear of the tent where Maude stood, and paused, breathing hard, summoning control. At last, turning round, he glared at his brother. 'Very well,' he said with bitter contempt. 'I swear my alle-giance to John as King of England and lord of Normandy and Ireland, saving only my honour and the honour of my wife.' He slipped his arm around Maude's shoulder. 'Do not push me for more, Hubert, you will be wasting your time and, my brother or not, I will drive you from my presence on the edge of my blade.'

'No, what you have said will suffice,' Hubert replied, thinking that in the interests of diplomacy he could omit the last part.

As if reading his mind, Theobald gave his brother a glacial look. 'If he touches Maude again, I swear I will cut off his balls and stuff them in his mouth. You can tell him that too.'

'I doubt that necessity. You will both be out of sight and mind in Ireland, and just now John has other prey to hunt.'

'Meaning Fulke?' Theobald relaxed slightly and a hint of grim pleasure curved his lips. 'I know where my sympathies lie.'

'And so they should,' Hubert said, his own expression sombre. 'John's ordered a full pursuit and nothing will satisfy him save Fulke's hacked corpse thrown at his feet for him to trample.'

Maude gasped. She clapped her hand across her mouth to stifle the sound and gazed in horror at Hubert. 'You have to warn him!' Her eyes flew to Jean de Rampaigne who had been standing unobtrusively near the tent flap throughout the exchanges.

'He's a rebel, an outlaw, and he has just robbed the King of England of more than a hundred marks' worth of merchandise. Not only that but recently he attacked and sought to kill Morys FitzRoger, the lawful vassal of Whittington.'

'Morys FitzRoger is no more a lawful vassal of Whittington than John's an honourable king!' Maude spat. 'And since John has robbed Fulke of his inheritance and denied him the justice of the common law he has no recourse to complaint!'

Hubert blinked rapidly, obviously surprised at her vehemence. 'Whatever the argument, it does not alter the fact that the King is sending troops to hunt him down,' he said.

Maude shuddered. She felt Theobald's hand tighten on her shoulder. 'There must be something you can do,' she whispered.

'My hands are tied,' Hubert said, but at the same time spread them open, palm up, in a contradictory gesture. 'I know that you have much to do if you are to leave with the morrow's dawn, Theo. Perhaps you would like to borrow your former squire for a time. I have no pressing need of him at the moment, and he will likely be of great use to you.'

A look passed between the brothers, acknowledging the words that went unspoken. Maude realised that Hubert had come here with the intention of helping Fulke without being seen to do so.

'Thank you; indeed he will.' Theobald's tone thawed slightly. 'If you want a drink there's wine in that flagon.'

Hubert shook his head. 'I cannot stay,' he said. 'Other than my official business, I came to wish you a good voyage and to ask you to pray for me in a less worldly place than this.'

Theobald went to him and the brothers embraced, at first in a constrained manner, and then with the bearhug reminiscent of their young manhood when neither had much more to their dignity than the family name.

Maude came forward. 'Sister.' Hubert embraced her too and she was engulfed in the mingled scents of sweat and incense. When she drew away and looked into his eyes, she saw warmth, intelligence, and a terrifying shrewdness that overrode both.

Hubert departed into the wet evening, and there was a brief silence, punctuated by the drip of water on the canvas roof and the muted sound of rain on grass.

Theobald handed the wine flagon to Jean. 'Collect what you need for your journey and go,' he said. 'I trust you to find Fulke before John's men do.' Reaching in his pouch, he drew forth a handful of silver pennies and handed them to the knight.

'You can count on me, Lord Walter, my lady. I have no more desire to see him captured than you.' Jean took a full swallow of wine and then flashed his smile. 'Mayhap for my pains Fulke will give me a bolt of cloth.' Setting the flagon down, he pouched the coins, drew up the hood of his cloak and ducked out into the dusk.

Maude sat down on the campstool, her stomach churning so badly that she thought she might be sick again.

She had used their supply of uisge beatha on Fulke's wound, but Theobald had a small, personal flask of his own, and now he brought it to her and bade her drink. 'Jean will reach him in time,' he said. 'And Fulke has more skill and cunning than any man the King will send against him.'

'I know. But you did not see the arrow I dug out of his leg. Even the skilled and cunning are not immortal.' Maude gratefully took the flask and swallowed deeply. As usual, the brew robbed her of her voice and set her gullet on fire. It also brought tears to her eyes. She dashed them away on the back of an impatient hand.

'Strange the ways of love,' Theobald mused, taking the wine flagon and leaning against the tent pole. 'We strew the paths we tread with thorns, do we not?'

It would have been easier to keep her back to him: the coward's way out. Maude forced herself to turn on the stool and look him in the eyes. 'My love is for you,' she said steadily. 'I would never betray you or dishonour your name.'

'I doubt neither your love, nor your honour.' Theobald took a long swallow straight from the flagon's rim without bothering to find his drinking horn. 'But I have seen the care that you and Fulke take in each other's company — the cold courtesy, the avoidance of touch. At first I thought that it was because you harboured a grudge over that incident with the whore, but I grew to realise that it was not in your nature to allow a petty quarrel to fester. Not once have I seen a lover's look pass between you, and that is because you will not look each other in the eye.'

Maude felt the heat of tears behind her lids. There was no point in denial. Theobald's perception was sword sharp. Her voice wavered. 'I do not deny that he attracts me, but I have fought it as hard as I know how. I do not want to feel sick at the thought of his danger; I do not want to be on edge when I know he is by – craning for a look at him and frightened that others will notice, or that he will turn and our eyes will meet. Sometimes I imagine—' She broke off, biting her lip, and looked at her husband. There was compassion in his eyes, and sadness. If there was jealousy, it was well hidden. She swallowed. 'Your love is like a warm cloak around me, Theo. His would be like riding an untamed horse. I need . . . I need your shelter.' She went into his arms and they folded around her, as she had known they would.

Theobald kissed the top of her head and felt a tightness in his throat. To be told that she compared his love to a sheltering blanket was a tender, touching compliment but no consolation when matched against riding an untamed horse – by implication a stallion. Against his better nature, he felt hurt and possessive.

'We do not have to stay until morning,' he said. 'We can leave now if you desire.'

'Please,' she said and buried her face in the dry, sagey scent of his tunic.

CHAPTER 20

A pale thread of smoke dallied from the fire towards a leaf canopy of lamellar gold and the breeze sent flickers of changing light through the branches like fingers rifling a jewel box.

'Fine day,' remarked Jean de Rampaigne, joining Fulke on a fallen log that had been draped with a saddle blanket. 'Pity there won't be many more of them this side of winter.'

Fulke rubbed his thigh. 'We have friends enough to give us shelter or look the other way.' His mouth curved in a grim smile. 'And we have the means to pay for our keep.' He glanced around the camp they had made the previous night after the raid on John's merchant train. Several laden pack ponies attested to their success. He had distributed most of the bolts of cloth amongst his knights but had retained for himself a cloak of heavy blue wool with a beaver lining. As Jean said, the fine weather would soon end and while red and gold silk was a wonderful luxury, it would not keep him warm on a winter's night.

Jean nodded. 'But a thousand pounds' worth of silver for your hide might sway the odds in the King's favour.'

'The odds were already in his favour. This raid will not alter that balance, but it will show him that an underdog can still have sharp teeth.' Continuing to rub his thigh, Fulke rose and walked to the fire. Men were breaking their fast on unleavened barley cakes smeared with honey or bacon fat and the horses were champing on rations of oats.

They couldn't stay here. Even without Jean's arrival at first light, he had known that they would be hunted for this. John had been made a laughing stock before the entire court and nothing less than death would punish the perpetrators. He stroked the crooked bridge of his nose with the tip of his index finger. They were still playing chess and neither of them had learned the lessons of the past. Fulke had expected John to be fair and John had expected to win.

'So where do we go now?' Jean asked.

Fulke swung round. 'We?'

Jean grinned. 'His Grace the Archbishop likes to have a foot in each camp.'

'As long as he doesn't get caught by the bollocks straddling both,' Fulke said acidly, and then gave an answering grin. 'But you are more than welcome to stay. There is no one I would rather have at my side.' He waved away Jean's flippant gesture of acknowledgement. 'Next, we go to Higford to repay my aunt for her generosity. After that, we divide our time between Morys FitzRoger and John. I'm going to burn them so badly that they'll be glad to make peace on my terms.'

Jean helped himself to a barley cake from a pile that Richard FitzWarin was just sliding off the griddle. Throwing it from hand to hand like a tickled trout, blowing on the crusted dark surface, he said with eyes firmly on the morsel, 'John attempted Maude Walter yester evening in between the roast and the subtleties.'

Fulke's hand closed over his sword hilt. 'What?'

'Oh, it was all kept quiet and besides, the arrival of your merchants put all other happenings in the shade. Apparently he granted Theobald leave to go to Ireland and suggested that Lady Maude might be better "served" by remaining behind and following the court.' With perfect dramatic timing, Jean bit into the barley cake then fanned his hand in front of his mouth. 'Hot,' he mumbled.

Fulke stared at him. A few merchants, a hundred marks' worth of damage. He had found pleasure in the deed, but now it seemed not nearly enough. 'And?' His voice was dangerously hoarse.

'And Lady Maude "served" him,' Jean said, drawing it out like the skilled storyteller he was while he observed the effect on his audience. 'But not as he expected, only as he deserved.' Jean polished off the rest of the barley cake and dusted his hands. 'She kicked him in the bollocks so hard that he was almost bent double when he received those merchants you robbed. Then she and Lord Theobald made preparations to leave the court. They'll be halfway to Bristol by now, heading to take ship for Ireland.'

Fulke let out the breath he had been holding.

'Don't worry; she's safe.' Jean folded his arms and looked shrewdly at Fulke. 'Her main concern was for you and the danger you were courting.'

'The danger *I* was courting!' Fulke laughed harshly. 'That is a case of a griddle calling a cauldron black if ever I heard one.' Then he sobered. What other choices could either of them have made except unnacceptable ones?

'I never thought when I teased you at her wedding that she would indeed become your "Melusine",' Jean murmured.

Fulke made a wry face. 'Even if I am hers, she is not mine,' he said. 'And likely safer because of it. I think that—' He stopped speaking as a hunting horn sounded in the distance to the south, and then another one, a little to the east of the first. Swearing, he shouted the command to saddle up.

'They'll be riding from Marlborough to hunt you,' Jean

said as he hastened to his own mount and unrolled his mail shirt from its waxed wrappings on the crupper. 'John will have alerted all the villages too. With a reward of a thousand pounds of silver on your head, you're worth the chase.'

With the speed born of long practice, Fulke and Richard had the fire kicked out and the griddle dismantled in moments, the hot iron plate cooled with a splash of water from a leather costrel. By the time Jean had struggled into his hauberk, the packhorse was loaded and Fulke was swinging into the saddle. 'Well then,' he said with a wolfish grin. 'Let's lead them a merry dance.'

'A merry dance eh?' Jean gasped as he wiped his sword on his cloak and briefly removed his helm to blot his brow on his sleeve. 'I tell you, the steps are too fast for my liking. There must be more folk hunting you in this forest than there are trees.'

An attempt to break out on the eastern side had failed. A contingent of knights had been waiting for them and although Fulke might have won through, it was by no means certain. He had turned around, headed back into the woods and been met by a smaller hunting party. A difficult skirmish had brought them out free, but not unscathed. Blood was streaming from Ivo's brow where the edge of a spear had slashed up the side of his helm, narrowly missing his eye, and several other members of the company had been wounded.

'I cannot help that!' Fulke panted in return. 'If we are to win, then the steps have to grow faster yet!' He reined his sweating horse about. 'East!' he said. 'They won't be heavily guarding the south road because they won't expect us to head back towards Marlborough!'

'And when we get there?'

'There's Savernake Forest to give us succour, and Stanley

Abbey.' Fulke wheeled Blaze and slapped the reins on the stallion's neck.

They followed the deer trails, leaping streams, thudding along moist paths, autumn leaves flickering down on them like golden feathers. The sound of hunting horns came close at times, at others diminished as they played a game of catch as catch can with their pursuers.

'Halt in the King's name!' A trembling lone huntsman barred their path, clearly a local villager rather than a soldier, for the only weapon he had about him was a reaper's sickle. He did, however, have a pair of powerful lungs, and a polished hunting horn, which he frantically set to his lips. William spurred forward and with a blow from the flat of his sword, struck the horn from the man's hands. It was the work of a moment to seize and bind him to a tree, gagging him with his leg bindings.

No one came to his aid; he was indeed the single outpost of the rearguard and the fleeing men were able to clear the forest. Fulke was in no doubt that they would still be hard pursued. Someone would soon realise they had doubled back. They could not take refuge in Marlborough and Ivo's wound needed tending. Stanley Abbey was their best option for it would buy them time and sanctuary if necessary.

As they approached the abbey, the porter saw them coming and ran to close the heavy oak gates of the lodge.

'Open in the name of Hubert, Archbishop of Canterbury!' Jean bellowed, thudding his sword hilt on the iron-studded wood.

The only response was the sound of a key grating ponderously in the huge lock.

Fulke turned in the saddle and gestured to Alain. 'You're the tallest,' he said. 'Make haste and have a word with that porter.'

Alain manoeuvred his mount up to the wall, then, while

Richard held the bridle, he stood on the destrier's back, secured hand and footholds in the gritty stone, and hauled himself upwards and over. There was a quavery shout, the sounds of a scuffle and once again the key grated in the lock.

'Enter, brethren,' declared Alain, grinning at his own joke as he swung the gate open and ushered them within. The porter sat dazed on the ground, his head in his hands and a great graze on his forearm where Alain had wrestled him down.

He glared balefully at the dismounting knights. 'You will be declared excommunicate for this!'

'Let God judge as he finds,' Fulke snapped. He gestured Baldwin de Hodnet to help Ivo into the lodge. Philip, the best at tending wounds, followed.

Fulke turned back to the monk. 'Give me your robe.'

'I'll give you nothing but God's curse!'

Fulke's patience, already strung gossamer thin, snapped. Striding to the porter, he seized a handful of the dark grey habit and hauled him to his feet. With William's help and the victim's considerable hindrance, Fulke finally succeeded in divesting the porter of his gown. Shivering in his white alb, the man cursed them in the language of a street trader rather than a holy monk until William and Richard bore him squawking inside the lodge and parked him under guard in the corner. Removing his helm, Fulke donned the monk's voluminous garment and secured it at his waist with a rope girdle, then drew up the hood of the habit so that his features were cowled in shadow.

'What in God's name are you doing?' demanded Jean who had watched the entire incident with a mingling of amusement and disapproval.

'Trying on your clothes for size.'

'What?'

'Disguising my appearance to change the perceptions of others.' Seizing the porter's quarterstaff, Fulke went to the gates. 'Keep your ears open and be vigilant lest I need help,' he commanded. 'But do not come out unless I shout.'

Jean eyed him dubiously. 'I hope you know what you're doing.'

'What I must,' Fulke said shortly. 'What the outcome will be remains in God's hands.' He crossed himself and went out on to the highway, leaning on the quarterstaff for support as if he were injured.

He did not have long to wait before a group of pursuing knights came hurtling towards the abbey in a cloud of dust. Their leader halted his lathered mount and, scarlet with the exertion of the chase, leaned down to speak to Fulke. 'Tell me, brother, have any armed knights passed this way?' he demanded.

'Indeed they have, and in a mighty flurry.' Fulke pointed down the road with the quarterstaff. 'Almost rode me down in their haste, the villains. I pray you bring them to justice, but I fear you will have to belabour your horses.'

'Their horses will be tired too,' the knight replied and Fulke saw the glint of battle in his eyes, the hope of glory at being the one to bring the FitzWarin brothers to account. 'We're so close I can smell the victory. My thanks, brother, for your help.' He clapped spurs to his mount's flanks and rode on with his troop, the autumn sun dazzling on mail and weapons.

Fulke inhaled and his nostrils were filled with the rank smell of the habit's customary occupant. The porter, he deduced, had a penchant for garlic. Having bought them a small amount of time, he turned to go back inside the abbey, but as he laid his hand to the door, more riders arrived, obviously stragglers from the party that had just galloped off. Their leader was Girard de Malfee, whom

Fulke knew well from his squirehood. The cowl preserved Fulke's anonymity, but he was still vulnerable to being discovered as de Malfee quickly proved. Levelling his spear, the knight poked it through Fulke's habit, where it grated on the telltale resistance of mail shirt and gambeson. 'Well, well,' grinned Girard. 'Here's a well-stuffed monk. I wonder what will happen if I prick him to make him leak.' He leaned on the spear haft.

'You'll regret it more than I.' Raising his voice in a cry for aid, Fulke lashed the quarterstaff round in an arc to deflect the spear, and gave de Malfee a tremendous buffet beneath his helm.

As de Malfee reeled, the Abbey gates swung open. Fulke's own men poured out, brandishing weapons, and, after a brief, bloody skirmish, took the stragglers prisoner.

'No killing,' Fulke warned as he put down the hood of his tunic. 'Not on holy ground.'

'We could always take them back outside to finish them,' William declared as he tied a victim's hands with vicious thoroughness.

Fulke shook his head. 'That would be obeying only the law, not its spirit. Girard, if you've any sense left in your skull, greet King John for me and thank him for the morning's entertainment.'

De Malfee glared at him, one eye framed by rapidly swelling flesh. 'It is not a game, FitzWarin,' he snarled.

'It is, and I'm winning,' Fulke retorted. 'If John doesn't want to play any more all he has to do is yield. You can tell him that I was always better at chess.'

'Tell him yourself!' Girard snarled.

Fulke gently rubbed the bump on his nose. 'I will, when he's prepared to listen. For the nonce I think it safer to communicate like this.'

Trussed up like bedraggled fowl, de Malfee and his

companions were dumped in the porter's lodge where the porter too had been tied to prevent him from raising the alarm. Fulke instructed his men to take the best of their victims' mounts and weapons.

'Are you fit to ride?' Fulke asked Ivo as they prepared to leave. Philip had stuffed a makeshift linen bandage between Ivo's helm and cheek, concealing the wound on the left side from view.

'Since the alternative is staying here to be tended by the monks, I'll manage to be fit,' Ivo answered with a mirthless grin. 'I doubt that the Abbot is going to be much impressed by the gift you're leaving in his lodge.' He jerked his chin in the direction of the monks, who were pouring out of the chapel.

'That cannot be helped,' Fulke said, 'but perhaps we can offer him some compensation. I'll make sure he receives a fine bolt of silk damask for his altar.' He smiled with savage humour. 'After all, it is cloth fit for a king.'

CHAPTER 21

Limerick, Ireland, Spring 1201

The rain whispered down, soft as the touch of cobwebs, shrouding the green of the land in swathes of clinging grey. Maude had grown accustomed to the damp climate, to the clouds that constantly swept in, heavy and moist, off the Irish Sea. She had become used to hearing the soft, guttural tongue of the native Gaels in place of French and the stretched vowels of the English; to feeling as if she was living on the edge of the world, where the seasons moved, but time stood still. And always it rained.

Rising from her bed, Maude glanced to the window embrasure where the soft patter of rain was like a song on the shutters. She found herself longing for just a moment's kindness of sunshine; a warm sparkle to light a pattern on the floor rushes and banish the smell of must from the wooden walls of the keep. In the cold, wet winter, she had kept to the hearth, sewing by the light of candles and rush dips, weaving braid, listening to the harps of bards and the long tales they sung of the history of their land. She had practised with her bow, rain notwithstanding, until she could almost hit the centre of a target with her eyes closed.

The occasional times when there was a gap in the weather, she and Theobald had gone riding together in the wild and beautiful country, green as Eden. With pride and humility, he had shown her his religious foundations: the monasteries at Wotheney, Arklow and Nenagh. And he had voiced his intention of taking the cowl before he died. Not, he said, that he intended to die yet. But when the time came, as it must come to all men . . .

Last night in the hall, the bard had sung a new ballad that had crossed the sea from England and travelled with peddlers and entertainers to Limerick on the Shannon. A song of the outlaw Fulke FitzWarin, who had robbed King John of a treasure in rich cloth and jewels, and then outwitted his pursuers by disguising himself as a monk and tying them up in the porter's lodge of a nearby abbey.

Theobald had dismissed the latter part of the story as disreputable embroidery, but Maude wondered. Fulke was living on a knife-edge and mayhap that made a difference to what he would and would not do.

Barbette appeared to help her dress in an undertunic of bleached linen topped by a gown of warm green wool and a mantle of the checked fabric such as the Gaels wore. The pattern was attractive, the emerald and blue enhancing the clear green of Maude's eyes.

'There are visitors below, my lady,' Barbette murmured as she positioned a circular silver brooch high on the mantle. 'An Irish lady, but she speaks passable French, and she seems to know your lord husband.'

'Her name?'

Barbette shrugged. 'I do not know, my lady. It sounded like the kind of noise men make when they're practising with swords.'

Maude's lips twitched. 'That is not very kind.'

'I cannot help it, my lady. Perhaps I am not very kind because she is very beautiful and, when I left, all the men were hanging on her every word. Do they not say that

St Patrick banished all the snakes from Ireland? Well, I do wonder if he left one behind.'

Maude was intrigued and the *ennui* of another soft grey day receded as it was overtaken by curiosity and anticipation. Any woman who could make Theobald sit up and take notice was bound to be interesting, especially if she had a name that sounded like the noise men made in battle practice . . . which was also the sort of noise they made in bed.

Maude arrived in the hall to find Theobald still seated at the high table, lingering over the breaking of fast as he very seldom did these days. He was wearing his customary long robe, bereft of embellishment, charcoal-dark in colour so that it appeared little different from a monastic habit, save that there was a gilded leather belt at his waist and a fine hunting dagger slung from it.

He was listening intently to a woman seated at his left-hand side. She was elegantly clad in the Norman fashion, her gown of rose-coloured wool laced to show the curve of breast and hip, and her veil worn in a style that exposed her white throat and her glossy black braids. The woman's hand rested on Theobald's sleeve and her manner, even from a distance, seemed distinctly flirtatious.

As Maude came closer, she realised that their guest was older than she first appeared. Fine lines radiated from her eye corners and two small creases tracked between her nose and mouth.

'My lord.' Maude curtseyed formally to her husband, a question in her eyes.

Clearing his throat, Theobald rose to his feet, kissed her hand and sat her on his other side. 'My lady. This is Oonagh O'Donnel who is here to bring her son as an oblate to Wotheney.'

Maude murmured a courteous greeting. So that was why

Theobald had been hanging on her every word. Her son was to take the cowl.

'I knew your husband many years ago when he came with Prince John to try and tame the Irish,' said the woman in a husky purr. 'Indeed, it was even possible that we might have wed.'

Maude made a sound of polite interest and accepted the bread, cheese and wine that the squire on duty served at her place. Oonagh. It did sound like a name that men shouted in battle or in bed. Theobald, she could see, was at a loss. 'Then why did you not?'

Oonagh laughed. 'He wasn't the sort to be wrapped around my little finger,' she said. 'Even though I tried. Do you remember?' Playfully she tapped Theobald's arm.

Mute, a little dusky of colour, Theobald shook his head.

'Ah, but you were a good dancer in those days.'

'He still is,' Maude said with a glance at her husband, who was clearly wishing himself elsewhere.

'Indeed, so am I.' Oonagh took a swallow from her cup. 'But I don't dance as often as I used to, and with far fewer partners.' She shrugged. 'I suppose it comes to us all.'

Maude decided it was time to change the subject. 'Your son is to enter the noviciate?' she enquired.

The woman smiled, although the gesture did not reach her eyes, which narrowed slightly. 'Ruadri, my middle child.' She gestured to two handsome boys sitting at the trestle just below the high table. They were large, fair-haired adolescents. 'Adam has come to bear me company. Collum, the youngest, is at home.' She looked at Theobald and smiled. 'Sadly my second husband died almost seven years ago, but he had been in poor health for some time before that.'

Maude wondered why the woman was smiling as she spoke, then decided she did not want to know.

'Yes, we heard,' Theobald said without inflection and

began to toy with a scrap of bread on the board.

Oonagh finished the wine in her cup and dabbed her lips with the napkin, leaving a faint pink stain. 'Tell me, my lord Walter, what happened to that strapping young squire of yours? What kind of man has he made?'

'A fine one,' Theobald said tersely.

'I'm sure he has. Even without his antlers, he was a handsome young stag. I was very tempted to go after him and bring him down – and I could have done, you know.' She leaned back in the chair and ran a finger sensuously up and down the stem of the goblet. 'Sometimes I still call myself a fool for letting him go.'

'I scarcely think that this is talk worthy of the mother of a postulant,' Theobald snapped, openly agitated now. He rubbed his forehead and frowned.

'Ruadri's the one entering your monastery, not me,' Oonagh replied without heat. 'Save your sermons for him and let me live my life as I choose.'

A muscle ticked in Theobald's cheek, but he held grimly on to his composure.

Oonagh eyed him sidelong and a hint of a smile curled her mouth corners. 'Very well, I admit I spoke out of turn. I hope that Fulke fares well, and that he remembers me with as much affection as I remember him.' She set the cup down and rose to her feet in a swish of expensively heavy cloth and musky perfume. 'Now, my lord Walter, are you going to sit there all day, or are you going to show me this monastery of yours?'

Maude was effectively pushed aside, Lady O'Donnel treating her as if she were of no consequence. A chit of a girl, Maude read in the other woman's eyes, a minor threat to be summarily dismissed. Silently she fumed.

Theobald, who was never clumsy, almost lurched to his feet at her question. 'I can show you the guest house, my lady,' he said. 'Women are not permitted further, but your son is welcome to see everything.'

'Then that will have to suffice.'

Maude watched them leave with the two boys. She could have been awkward and declared that she was coming too, but saw no point. Oonagh O'Donnel clearly did not desire her presence, and although Theobald was obviously discomforted by the woman and found her attractive into the bargain, he was hardly going to strike up a liaison in a monastery. Beckoning a squire, she told him to fetch her bow and quiver, and hoped that Oonagh's stay was not going to be a protracted one.

Theobald rubbed his thumb knuckle across his forehead, his expression tight with pain.

Maude eyed him with concern. Lately he had become susceptible to debilitating headaches and their frequency had been increasing. After a day like today, it was no surprise that he was suffering. She told Barbette to fetch some willow bark in wine and went to lay her palm against his brow.

'I am glad she's gone,' she murmured. Oonagh O'Donnel had departed shortly after noon, leaving her son in the care of Wotheney's Abbot.

Theobald closed his eyes. 'She always liked to cause trouble,' he said. 'Today she wanted to prove that despite having sons on the verge of manhood she could still outdo any woman in the vicinity.' He found a smile. 'I suppose it would be true if the contest was for harlotry. There is a rumour that she had her second husband mutilated so that she could have her freedom.'

Maude gazed at him in shock. 'Mutilated?'

'Aye.' He gave her a wry look. 'She didn't have him killed outright, because that would only have brought her another Norman husband to govern her land. He was "injured" in a hunting accident, so we heard – a knock on the skull that rendered him witless. Obviously she kept him alive until interest waned and when he died, she married Niall O'Donnel, the man of her choice – and there is no doubt those lads are of his siring, not Guy de Chaumont's.'

Theobald was not one to indulge in idle gossip. What he had told her was sordid enough, but it was the implications lurking behind the words that made Maude shiver and cross herself.

Theobald noticed her gesture. 'Yes,' he said, 'Oonagh O'Donnel is ruthless and self-seeking. She bedded John when I was here last and, if I had not prevented her, she would have sunk her talons into Fulke too.'

'And how did you do that?' Maude's hand remained at her breast. She felt like crossing herself again.

'Told her I would kill her if she did. He was no more than a green lad at the time.'

'And she obeyed you?'

Theobald rose and went to lie on the bed. 'Not from fear. I think she had a genuine liking for Fulke and thus chose to spare him. You've seen those great dogs of his?'

Maude nodded.

'They're bred from a bitch she gave him as a leaving gift. That is why I think her regard for him went beyond lust.'

'And his regard for her?' Maude's voice was neutral. She would not permit a note of jealousy to enter.

Theobald gave a smile, wry and tight through the pain. 'He was a squire with a youth's interest in women made all the more intense by lack of experience. She was about your age but a hundredfold less innocent. You saw how she was in the hall, the way she talked and touched. Imagine the effect she would have on a young lad.'

Maude said nothing. She could imagine the effect all

too well. Silently she agreed with Barbette that St Patrick had not rid Ireland of all its vipers. She was glad that Fulke was in England and had no cause to cross the sea and renew old acquaintances.

In the morning, despite liberal doses of willow bark in wine, Theobald's headache was worse and he complained that his vision was strange and blurred. Shaking his head in a vain attempt to clear the difficulty only exacerbated the symptoms. Maude wanted him to spend the day abed. Theobald insisted he would rise. Finally they compromised, and those who had business with him came to his bedchamber. Despite the pain, Theobald was busy. Messengers came and went throughout the day and he dictated a plethora of letters and writs.

'You should slow down,' Maude said with troubled eyes.

'Some matters will not wait,' he answered. She could not argue or send those around his bedside away, because he had specifically requested their company.

Again, she went outside with her bow to practise at the targets and ease her worry. Theobald was past his prime, she knew that, but he was not yet in his dotage. He was her buffer from the world, her safe enclosure, and the sight of him ill made her feel vulnerable.

Two hours later, she was in the hall talking to one of the knight's wives when a panicking squire summoned her to the bedchamber. Theobald had complained that the pain was intolerable, had vomited several times and then collapsed. He was still breathing and his eyes were open, but no one could rouse him.

With a terrible foreboding, Maude sped to the chamber and went straight to the bed. It and Theobald had been tidied and cleaned while the squire went to fetch her. The tight, crisp sheets, the man flat upon it, his chest barely moving, put her in mind of a corpse on a bier.

'Theo?' She leaned over him and took his hand. It was cold in her grasp and limp. The pupil of one eye was wide and dark. The other expanded as her shadow took away the light from the embrasure. 'Theo, can you hear me?'

Nothing. She looked round at the sombre audience and fought the wave of panic that was threatening to rise and engulf her.

The Abbot arrived and with him the infirmarian, Brother Cormac, a rotund monk of cheerful disposition. Palm at her mouth, Maude watched him examine Theobald with gentle competence. The Abbot stood gravely to one side, his own hands tucked within his habit sleeves.

'I am afraid that he has suffered a seizure.' Brother Cormac spoke in French, but with a strong Gaelic accent. His brown eyes were sorrowful. 'I would be holding out false hope if I said that he would recover, although sometimes it does happen. But I think you should be prepared for the fact that God might take him to his bosom tonight.'

'There must be something you can do for him!' Maude cried.

'Daughter, his life is in God's hands,' the monk said gently.

'But he can't die, I need him!' She turned away, her hands covering her face, her body shaking. Suddenly she was no longer the archer, loosing flight after flight, but the target, struck and struck again. Barbette set a comforting arm around her shoulders. A cup of uisge beatha was pressed into her hands, but she thrust it aside. Tearing from her maid, she rushed into the garderobe and leaned over the pit, retching violently.

The first shock receded, but the pain remained, as if an iron fist was squeezing her core. She braced herself against the wall and breathed deeply. There would be time and too much of it to wallow in her fears. She must arrest her selfishness; Theobald's needs were uppermost.

Drawing herself upright, lifting her chin, she returned to the chamber and came to the bed. Theobald had not moved and they had closed his eyes to prevent them from drying.

'Can he hear what we say?' she asked.

Brother Cormac shrugged. 'Who can tell? It is as likely as not, my lady.' He stood back a little way.

Maude bit her lip. Kneeling at the bedside, she took Theobald's hand in hers. His skin was limp and cold. There was no answering squeeze of strength and reassurance. Terror stalked her, biding its time. She swallowed against the breath-constricting lump in her throat and raised her eyes to the Abbot. 'My husband wished to end his days as a member of your order. I beg that you ordain him as a monk – and if he is to die, then bury him here among your brethren.'

The Abbot inclined his head. 'It shall be done, daughter.'

She pressed her cheek to Theobald's unresponsing hand. 'Let it be now,' she said and managed to speak firmly without the wobble of tears, although inside she was crying an ocean. Tucking her husband's chilled hand beneath the covers, she kissed his cheek. 'God speed,' she whispered. 'Know that I love you and that your love has meant everything to me.'

His stare was like a blank sheet of vellum and she could not tell if he had heard her, or if his soul was already beyond such mortal concerns. Biting back tears, she rose and stood aside to let the monks take her place.

Theobald died as a watery sun set over the Shannon, his passing marked by the soft chanting of monks and the mournful cry of gulls in the estuary channel. Candles flickered on the holy oil anointing his forehead and his hands clasped a silver reliquary cross.

Maude found that her tears had dried and she could not weep. The mantle of security that had protected her was gone, replaced by a threadbare, desolate uncertainty. Theobald had been granted his peace. She did not begrudge him that. What she did begrudge him was the fact that he had left her naked to the world; to the greed of men who would devour Theobald Walter's widow in a single voracious gulp.

CHAPTER 22

Higford, Shropshire,
May 1201

Fulke was seated on a bench in Higford's sunlit courtyard, smoothing a nick from his sword on a whetstone when Jean de Rampaigne rode in.

'Christ, you're harder to find than a virgin in a brothel!'
Jean declared as he dismounted and led his horse to the
stone trough outside the stable block. The sun had reddened
his cheeks and the bridge of his nose. His padded gambeson
bore dark patches of sweat beneath the arms and around
the upper chest. His hair was gently dripping.

Fulke sheathed his sword and strode across the courtyard to greet his friend, whom he had not seen since the
late autumn when Jean had returned to Hubert Walter.
'That is intentional,' he said with a smile. 'Let John and his
minions chase me up hill and down dale. They'll only waste
their breath and resources.'

'Yes, well, it's my breath and resources that have been
wasted this time, and in your cause,' Jean replied a trifle
irritably. As his horse ruffled the water with its muzzle, he
stooped to the trough, cupped his hands and splashed his
face. 'I've been through every forest between Canterbury
and Carlisle hunting for you. Came here twelve days ago
and your aunt had no idea where you were apart from she
thought you had gone north.'

'I am sorry for your trouble, but glad that even you have

found me so elusive.' Fulke slapped Jean across his damp shoulders. 'Come. A pitcher of ale and one of Emmeline's chicken pasties will improve your temper.'

'God, and still the optimist after all this time,' Jean said acidly. 'Don't you want my news?'

'Indeed I do, but since it's been simmering in your pack for at least a twelve-night, I dare say it can hold a moment longer.' He snapped his fingers at a stable lad who was trundling a barrow of soiled straw to the midden heap, and told him to take care of Jean's courser.

'Simmering is the word,' Jean said darkly as he followed Fulke within the cool of the manor.

Jean greeted Fulke's brothers, kissed Emmeline, and sat down at the dais table to eat and drink. Delving inside his tunic, he presented Fulke with a packet bearing the seal of Hubert Walter, Archbishop of Canterbury. 'To add to your troubles,' he said, then attacked the pasty.

Fulke broke the red sealing wax and unrolled the sheet of scraped vellum. The scribe's writing was neat, brown and legible, every word clear as daylight, stringing together into phrases as sharp as the point of a bodkin arrow. His lips moved silently and his scalp began to crawl.

'Theobald is dead,' he said.

Jean nodded. 'I was present when the news reached His Grace and also when he dictated that letter. Apparently when Lord Theobald was ailing, he wrote to his brother with explicit wishes that you be informed in the event of his death.'

Fulke swallowed. 'She is being fought over like a bone between a pack of dogs.' He stared at the letter again. Hubert of Canterbury had set out the facts with stark simplicity. Maude had returned to England and gone to Canterbury for protection only for her father to arrive claiming that, as her closest kin, he was responsible for her. 'Le Vavasour will milk her lands and then sell her to the highest bidder,' Fulke said in a tone heavy with loathing.

'I think he will trade her for royal favour too,' Jean said between rotations of his jaw. 'It is no bad thing to have your daughter in the King of England's bed. Go through the King's cock to get at his ear, so to speak, and then marry her off once lust has been sated and rewards reaped.'

Fulke lunged to his feet and paced to the far end of the dais. The words presented him with a vision that was all too clear. John and Maude in bed together. Sheets rumpled in the struggle for supremacy. Her spirit pushed to the edge and broken on the wheel of John's lust. He crumpled the vellum in his fist.

He swung round. 'Is she still in Canterbury?'

Jean washed down the remnants of his pasty with several swallows of ale. 'Well, she was when I left, but, as I said, I've been on the road for more than two weeks trying to find you, and it's a full four days' ride back to Canterbury. Doubtless my lord Hubert will do his utmost to keep her with him, but he can only procrastinate for so long.'

Fulke was silent for a dozen heartbeats while he thought, and then that silence was replaced by the energy of decision. 'There's enough of the day remaining to make a start. We can be on the road in an hour and if we take torches we can ride into the night.'

'No feather mattress then,' Jean said flippantly, but he was already on his feet. 'I knew the moment you set eyes on that letter you'd be like a scalded cat. I'll need a fresh horse. Mine's footsore and unfit for anything but a meadow for at least a week.'

'You can use one of my remounts.' Fulke left the dais and prepared to issue commands.

Jean stayed him with a hand to the elbow. 'Lord Theobald knew about you and Maude.'

'Knew what?' Fulke's smoke-hazel eyes were suddenly wary.

'That you were both faithful to him.'

'Then I hope by the same token that he never knew how close we came to breaking that faith,' Fulke said and, just in case Jean had the answer, strode down the hall and out of earshot.

Maude stared coldly at her father. 'I do not wish to dwell in your household,' she said. Dressed in a gown of sombre charcoal colour, wearing a wimple of plain, bleached linen, she both looked and felt like a nun. A severe nun who would hold to her faith come martyrdom or the fires of hell.

'I did not ask what your wishes were,' answered Robert le Vavasour testily. 'It is your duty to do as you are bid. I know that he is but recently in his grave and I am sorry to say it, but your husband was far too lenient with you. Indeed, he has made a rod for the backs of others.'

'His Grace the Archbishop is content for me to remain here beneath his protection.' Maude was determined not to lose her temper. If she did, it would only add credence to her father's belief that she was a hysterical female, incapable of running her own affairs.

'His Grace the Archbishop has a vested interest in your dower lands,' her father sneered. 'He wants to keep them under his control.'

'And your own interest is only that of a concerned father for his grieving daughter?' she retorted bitterly.

He thrust his hands into his belt. 'It is because of that concern that I must ensure your wealth is properly administered.'

Maude compressed her lips. 'I can take care of my own wealth and, I say again, I will not be governed by you.'

'Your dower lands are in my custody until you should marry again, and so are you.' His bald patch gleamed red. 'You will do as I say.'

Father and daughter glared at each other. They were standing in a small side chamber of the Archbishop's palace, the curtain drawn across, but although the heavy fabric served to muffle conversation, it could not conceal an outright argument from the clerics, officials and monks going about their business in the corridors of power outside.

The knowledge that she was cornered made Maude all the more defiant. 'I will claim the right of sanctuary,' she threatened.

Robert spluttered. 'You will do no such thing.'

There was no point in staying to argue. Maude started towards the curtain, but her father seized her arm in a bruising grip and spun her round to face him.

'I will have respect from you, daughter,' he hissed, 'even if I have to beat it into you!' He raised his fist.

Maude whitened. 'You cannot have what does not exist,' she spat. 'You ground my mother beneath your heel until she died. I might have been a child, but I was never blind. My only mistake was in thinking it was the way of the world, but Theobald showed me that not all men abuse those who cannot fight for themselves. He opened the door of the cage and I am not about to step back inside it.' With a sharp movement, she wrenched herself free, and tearing aside the curtain almost ran into the main room, surrounding herself with the protection of others. There were curious looks, sidelong flickers of disapproval. Even if this was the secular part of the Archbishop's palace, many of its officials were clerics and monks who saw women as a disruptive influence.

Maude choked down a sob that was half anger, half self-pity. Despite having Hubert Walter as a bulwark, she was reluctant to lean on him. True, he was her husband's brother and had been close to Theobald, but he was ambitious too and had motives of his own that did not necessarily march well with loyalty to the deceased. She could not be sure what lurked beyond the bland, flesh-lapped features. He was John's man to a degree, but above all served his own ambitions. Probably her father was right and Hubert Walter wanted the control of her lands for himself. She was like a grain of corn trapped between two huge millstones.

Her father emerged from the small chamber, his expression still thunderous. Maude walked briskly away, setting more distance between them. He would not dare strike her in the open, she told herself, but still felt afraid and intimidated. There was a guest chamber for women attached to the hall and she hurried towards it.

'Maude, come here,' her father summoned her as if she were a dog, his voice choked with suppressed fury. She ignored him and continued forwards.

A fanfare suddenly echoed through the room and a herald cried that all were to kneel for the King and Queen of England. As everyone dropped to their knees, Maude sped the last few yards to the women's guest chamber and gained its sanctuary. Closing the door, she leaned against it, panting. The iron studs in the oak pressed into her spine. She felt as if she were surrounded by wolves. Everyone wanted to devour her and, because of it, she found herself hating Theobald for dying, and herself for feeling that hatred.

Having discussed matters of state with Hubert Walter, chief among them the pressing need to return to Anjou where rebellion was brewing, John decided to pursue another issue for a moment of light relief.

'I was sorry to hear of your brother's death,' he murmured. 'He served me well, and I was fond of him.'

'It is indeed a great grief to me,' Hubert said. 'Theobald and I were very close. It still seems not a moment since we were boys together in Norfolk, and then attendants in Ranulf de Glanville's household.'

John nodded. He was sitting on a cushioned bench in Hubert's private apartment, the thick grey glass in the windows giving a distorted view of the building work going forth at a rapid pace. A new aisled hall of grandiose proportions was being built to house the Archbishop's household, and no expense was being spared. John had arrived at the same time as a cartload of Purbeck marble columns: black and pink like a blood pudding. Sometimes he wondered who was the King of England, himself or Hubert Walter.

'I understand that his widow has sought succour beneath your roof,' he said silkily as he reached for the silver goblet of wine that had been poured for him. The taste and pale gold colour said Rhenish and expensive.

'That is true. Lady Maude is currently a guest here at Canterbury.' Hubert's voice made a calm statement, giving nothing away.

'She must be worth enough to make a tempting marriage prize.' John rolled the wine around his mouth, enjoying the mingling of tart and smooth.

'Indeed, sire. But it is less than two months since my brother's death and she is still in deep mourning.'

'Deep mourning?' John snorted in disparagement. 'Christ, he was almost old enough to be her grandsire!'

'Would you not hope that your own wife would mourn you decently if that unhappy time ever arose?' Hubert Walter asked gently.

John scowled. He had been hoist with his own petard

since Isobel was only thirteen to his thirty-three. Indeed, she had yet to begin her fluxes and he frequently used other women to ease his lust. The memory of his last encounter with Maude Walter made his genitals cramp. 'Deep mourning or not,' he said shortly, 'life goes on and your sister-by-marriage has need of a protector.'

'She has two of them in myself and her father. Of course, sire, it is desirable that she should remarry in the fullness of time – but to a suitable man.'

John stroked his beard and inwardly smiled at the heavy emphasis Hubert Walter had placed on the last two words. 'I agree. There are several barons in my own household who would prove likely mates for Lady Walter.' He saw the flicker of apprehension in the Archbishop's eyes and felt malicious satisfaction. Hubert Walter thought that he could have his own way in everything. Taking Theobald's widow from beneath his nose and giving her to a man of John's own choosing would be a salutary lesson to the old lard barrel. The coin for the marriage fine would go into John's personal coffers, not Canterbury's. 'At the appropriate time, of course,' he added with a decidedly lupine smile.

The women's quarters proved to be less of a haven than Maude had anticipated. Queen Isobel descended upon them with her entourage and effectively took them over. Her greeting to Maude was perfunctory and she made it apparent that she found her presence irksome, although she had the grace to murmur scant condolences on Theobald's death.

'Still,' she added, tossing a butter-blonde braid over her shoulder, 'he was an old man and very dull. Mayhap you will have better fortune next time.'

'I loved my husband dearly, madam,' Maude replied, striving not to strike the self-satisfied expression from the brat's kitten features. 'If you had known him as I did, you would not have called him dull. I doubt that I will ever find better, whatever my "fortune".'

Isobel gave a small shrug of her silk-clad shoulders. 'I was merely trying to comfort you,' she said and turned away, dismissing Maude as off-handedly as she would flick a speck of dust from her clothes.

Fighting tears, Maude retired to a seat in the window embrasure. She leaned her head wearily against the wall and gazed out through the open shutters on the bustle of building work. The metallic chink of a stone chisel and the joyful banter of the masons and labourers rang in her ears.

Two merchants rode into the courtyard and asked directions of one of the clerics. Their tunics bore the sober, deep dyes of respectability and wealth: fir green and dark plum trimmed with braid. Both wore wide-brimmed pilgrim hats to protect them against the sun and both carried leather drinking costrels and square satchels. She watched them until they rode from sight and not for the first time in her life wished that she had been born to the freedom of being male.

Hubert Walter was poring over a heap of documents when the two 'merchants' were shown into his private solar. He looked from one to the other and clucked his tongue.

'You took your time.'

Fulke knelt and kissed the Archbishop's ring, then rose and stepped back. 'I am here now,' he said, and beat at the gritty dust on his tunic. 'Where is she?'

Hubert Walter's brows rose towards the high fringe of his tonsure. 'With the Queen and her ladies in the women's chambers, I should imagine,' he answered as bluntly as Fulke had asked, gesturing the two men to be seated. 'The King and Queen arrived shortly after noon. I need not tell you how dangerous it is for us both that you should be here. Even disguised as you are, there are those who will recognise your face.'

Fulke knew that Hubert was taking a risk as great as his own. If it became known that the Archbishop had entertained a wanted rebel in his rooms, the latter's career as Chancellor would be in jeopardy. 'I do not plan to remain a moment longer than I need,' he said. 'But since you summoned me, I assume that you are willing to help.'

'Not exactly willing,' Hubert said with a dark look, 'but I have a duty to my brother's last wishes, and I am fond of my sister-by-marriage. I have no desire to see her sold off in order to further her father's ambitions or fulfil the King's lusts.'

'That will not—' Fulke began, but was silenced by the Archbishop's raised hand.

'Yet I do not wish to encourage a man who desecrates abbeys, trusses blameless brethren like Christmas capons and blasphemously masquerades as a monk,' Hubert added severely.

'I have confessed and done penance for that sin,' Fulke answered, trying to sound sincere even though he was lying through his teeth. 'I know it is not an excuse, but at the time I was cornered and there was no other course.' He leaned forward and spread his hands, showing that he was being open with the Archbishop. 'I am deeply sorry for your brother's death and I grieve for him myself. He was my friend and mentor.'

Hubert's expression softened slightly. 'I know there was a longstanding bond between you and that Theobald regarded you highly.' He sighed and shook his head. 'Perhaps too highly. On the day that he died, he wrote to me with the express request that if Maude was put in a position where she had to remarry, that I do all in my power to ensure it was to you. He also seemed to think that you would be willing.' He gave Fulke an assessing look. 'Did he ever discuss the matter with you?'

Fulke flushed beneath the other's scrutiny. 'He did not,' he said and cleared his throat. Had Maude told Theobald what had happened at Higford? Likely she had.

'Were his thoughts correct?'

Judgement day would be easier than this, Fulke thought, suppressing the urge to squirm in his seat. 'Yes,' he said and decided to leave it at that. Either Hubert Walter knew him by now, or he never would. Explanations would only tangle the web.

Hubert's gaze, shrewd and incisive, nailed him for a moment longer and then lowered without conclusion. The Archbishop exhaled wearily. 'As Maude's nearest kin, her father has the right to pay a fine to take her and her dower lands under his control until he finds her a suitable husband. The man who weds her will need le Vavasour's permission and have to pay for it dearly.'

'With what?' Fulke snorted.

Hubert rubbed his chins in thought. 'A promissory note might suffice if le Vavasour thought that his son-by-marriage could repay him at a future date in land and prestige. He respects powerful men.'

There was emphasis placed on the last four words and Hubert Walter's look was charged with meaning. He would not say the words directly but Fulke understood the impli-cations. If he wanted Maude, he was going to have to brow-beat Robert le Vavasour into agreeing. Curious how many languages there were underlying the common one. Charm, diplomacy, aggression, violence. He wondered what kind of language he was going to use towards Maude and how she would respond. What if she refused him? Struck him across the face and called him a thief at the graveside, her face filled with revulsion? But surely he had to be a better option than her father or John.

'I need to meet with him, and I need to speak with Maude,' he said.

'That can be arranged.'

'And mayhap after that I will need the services of a priest.'

Hubert Walter smiled bleakly. 'That too can be arranged,' he said.

Shortly after the dinner hour, Robert le Vavasour came to Hubert Walter's private solar to discuss the matter of his daughter's value in the marriage market. It was a subject that Hubert had briefly raised as the diners assembled, requesting le Vavasour attend him in private so that they could discuss the young woman's future and come to an agreement.

'If Maude has been pleading with you to keep her under your wing, you can save your breath,' le Vavasour snapped as he stepped over the threshold. 'I am her father and her custody belongs to me.' His manner so perfunctory it was almost an insult, he dipped his knee and kissed the air over Hubert's ring of office.

'I do not dispute your rights,' Hubert said mildly. 'You must do as you see fit in the matter.'

'Hah, well, you've suddenly changed your tune. Only two days since you were insisting she should stay with you.'

'Only because I was concerned for her.'

'And now you're not?' Without being invited, le Vavasour prowled further into the chamber and sat down on a padded bench.

'Oh no. She is still very much in my thoughts.' Hubert went to a coffer at the side of the room and, in the absence of any servants, poured wine into three goblets. 'I was wondering how much you would consider a reasonable sum to let her marry where she chose?'

Le Vavasour's eyes narrowed. 'Why do you ask?'

'Let us say for curiosity's sake.'

'It would depend on the bridegroom.' The baron took the cup that Hubert offered him and drank greedily of the fine red wine. 'You're not the first to broach the subject today.'

'Oh?'

Le Vavasour took another mouthful of wine and pouched it in his cheeks, savouring its richness. Hubert waited patiently, his expression impassive.

'Falco de Breauté approached me with an offer for Maude just before we sat down to dinner.' Le Vavasour scowled at the Archbishop. 'Not of your doing, I hope. You've not invited me here to talk about him?'

'Indeed not!' Hubert's nostrils flared at the very notion. He knew Falco de Breauté was one of John's mercenaries and renowned for his complete lack of qualm or sensibility. Tell him to spit a baby on his spear, pay him the right fee, and he would do it. He was, however, utterly loyal to John – who had obviously been busy since their conversation earlier.

'No, I thought not.' Le Vavasour rubbed the side of his jaw. 'But I ask myself where a common mercenary, a baker's son, could have obtained a sum to buy my daughter, and the only answer that comes to mind is the King himself.'

'That would seem likely,' Hubert said. 'An heiress of sound family is as good a way as any for him to reward loyalty.'

'Not with my daughter, it isn't,' le Vavasour growled. 'I'll not have my grandchildren bearing the blood of a common French baker – even for a thousand marks!' He wafted his hand angrily. 'I'm not a fool. I know that the girl is pretty and biddable when she chooses not to sulk and make a parade of her contrariness. I've seen the way that John looks at her. He won't bed his wife because she's too young, hasn't even begun her fluxes yet, so he seeks substitutes. I know that if I give my consent, my first grandchild could be half royal.' He snorted and drank off the rest of the wine. 'But then the King's thrice-great-grandmother was a plain tanner's daughter from Falaise and bore the Conqueror out of wedlock.'

'So you have refused?' Hubert kept the eagerness out of his tone.

'I said I would think on the matter, but it will take more than the sum de Breauté is offering to wipe out the stain of his lowly birth. I know he would rule Maude's estates with an iron hand and give her some of the discipline she lacks with the buckle end of his belt, but that's not enough to commend the bastard by far.'

'Indeed not,' Hubert said without inflection.

'So.' Le Vavasour spread his arms across the back of the bench and crossed his legs. 'I assume you have some sort of proposition to put to me − a man of your choosing, or a bribe to pay me off.' He jutted his chin in the direction of the third goblet. 'The first, I suspect, although I have not seen anyone in the hall today whom I would remotely consider making my kin.'

'You are shrewd, my lord,' Hubert said wryly, wondering if perhaps le Vavasour was going to be too cautious to take the bait. Going to the door, he opened it, and spoke quietly to one of the two knights on duty, then ushered him into the chamber, leaving Jean de Rampaigne on sole watch. Dressed in full mail, borrowed from the armoury, clad in a face-obscuring helm with long nasal bar, and a mail aventail covering his jaw, Fulke was as anonymous as any household guard.

Robert le Vavasour stared. 'What trick is this?' He reached to his belt, instinctively grasping for his sword, but he was not wearing it since no man came armed into the presence of the Archbishop of Canterbury.

'There is no trick, my lord.' Fulke propped his spear against the wall, removed his helm and pushed down his mail coif. He raked the fingers of one hand through his flattened raven hair and with the other unfastened his aventail. 'This is a guise to keep me safe rather than to threaten you.'

Le Vavasour continued to stare. 'Are you mad?' he choked at Hubert without taking his eyes off Fulke. 'You want my daughter to wed an outlaw?'

Fulke went to the coffer and took the wine that had been poured for him. Turning in a jingle of mail, he raised his cup in a slightly sardonic toast to Maude's father. 'Think how valuable I am,' he said before Hubert could answer. 'John has offered a thousand pounds of silver for my hide and put a hundred knights in the field to acquire it.'

'That is hardly a reason for me to give my daughter to you!' le Vavasour spluttered.

'No, but you are a man who respects personal worth,' Fulke said.

'What Fulke means,' Hubert said hastily, 'is that his breach with the King is a temporary one.'

'In the end, John will see that he could save himself considerable expense and aggravation by restoring my lands.' Fulke sat down opposite le Vavasour. Beneath the borrowed mail shirt and gambeson, he wore his merchant's tunic, the plum-coloured wool and edging of blue and gold braid revealing that its wearer could afford to dress expensively. There were rings on his fingers too, and a gold cross secured to the mail rivets of his hauberk. Fulke well knew how much store le Vavasour set by wealth and outward appearance. The raid on John's baggage train in the autumn had been worth every moment of danger.

'I will not be dragged into your petty rebellion,' le Vavasour snapped.

'It is not petty,' Fulke said quietly, although there was a sudden gleam of anger in his eyes. 'But I am not asking you to join me, only that you give your consent to a match between myself and your daughter.'

'I'd rather—'

'Give her to a baker's son?' Hubert Walter interrupted. 'A common mercenary? Buy the King's favour with her body and see her used and passed on?' He pointed at Fulke. 'His grandsire was lord of Ludlow and his line is descended from the Counts of Brittany.'

Le Vavasour ground his teeth. Fists clenched, he took two paces towards the door and then swung round and glared at Fulke. 'Why do you want her? What's the advantage to you?'

Fulke knew he was treading on dangerous ground. Mooting loyalty and love would only earn a snort of derision from a man of le Vavasour's ilk. Fortunately, whilst awaiting his summons to the arena, there had been ample opportunity to think.

'I admired the way your daughter conducted herself as my lord Walter's wife,' he said. 'She was gracious with others but never familiar, and she always appeared to enjoy robust health as well as being pleasing to look upon. Such qualities are frequently difficult to find in one woman. Also she has some experience of life. I have no particular desire to take a virgin child into my bed.' 'Of course,' he added, 'there is also the matter of her lands. Yorkshire, Lancashire, Leicestershire, Ireland. Plant those acres with my own, plough and sow them – think of the harvest they would yield.'

'But you haven't got any lands.' Le Vavasour's response was automatic. Fulke could see that he had captured the man's interest.

'The King will have no choice but to restore them,' he said confidently. 'Already he has too much on his trencher. Normandy and Anjou set for rebellion. The Welsh making inroads. He needs every fighting man he has. I should be among his warriors, not whining in his ear and stinging his flesh like an angry gnat.'

Le Vavasour pursed his lips and looked at Fulke, appraisal in his stare. Fulke knew that the Baron would be aware of his skills in the field, and his athletic appearance spoke for itself. Le Vavasour would also know that he was born the eldest of six sons, all hale and strong like himself. A bloodline predisposed to healthy males was a great advantage in the marriage stakes. Not to mention the qualities of his famous grandsire Joscelin de Dinan and the links with high Breton nobility.

'I have been offered a thousand marks for her,' le Vavasour said. 'How much are you prepared to bid?'

Fulke shrugged. 'A fair price.' He pondered for a moment. Obviously, le Vavasour would want more than a thousand marks. There would be no advantage to him in accepting Fulke's suit otherwise. 'Does a thousand pounds of silver instead seem appropriate?' he asked. There was a difference in the measures, a mark being seven shillings less than a pound.

Le Vavasour's lips curved in an arid smile. 'Would that be now, or when your lands are restored?'

'A deposit of two hundred pounds now, the rest in later instalments,' Fulke said briskly as if he was very certain.

'And if you renege?'

'Is it likely?'

Maude's father considered, holding Fulke with an

unblinking stare that reminded him unnervingly of a snake. At last, he gave an almost imperceptible nod of the head. 'So be it. The girl is yours for the sum of a thousand pounds of silver. Let the Archbishop draw up a contract.'

Fulke let out his breath on a sigh of relief.

'Of course,' le Vavasour mused, 'I need not go to the trouble of giving you my daughter in marriage. I could as easily gain a thousand pounds of silver by handing you over to the King.'

'You would not live long enough to enjoy the fruits of your betrayal,' Fulke said dispassionately. 'Nor would it make any difference to my claim. Even if I die, I have five brothers to succeed me. Besides, you are implicated, as the Archbishop of Canterbury will himself attest.'

'Not worth my while then,' said le Vavasour with a humourless smile.

Hubert Walter lifted a scroll of vellum from the trestle. 'I took the liberty of drawing up a draft contract earlier. Only the details need to be added. With Jean de Rampaigne as witness there is no reason why the wedding cannot be performed now.'

Le Vavasour's smile remained, but his eyes narrowed. 'Do not take me for granted,' he said. 'I am no tame or stupid dog to trot to heel.'

No, Fulke thought, you are vicious and cunning, and you would not be doing this unless it suited your purpose.

'That was never my intention, my lord,' Hubert Walter said evenly. 'But this saves us time. There are safer places for Fulke to be than Canterbury.'

The Baron grunted. 'You have a sound reason for every-thing you do, your Grace,' he said in a less than compli-mentary tone. 'Or at least sound excuses.'

Hubert Walter chose to ignore the jibe and went to the door. A murmured request sent Jean de Rampaigne on an errand to the women's chambers. 'Now all we have to do is wait for the bride,' Hubert said as he turned back into the room.

Maude was dozing miserably on her pallet when the maid came to summon her with the news that Hubert Walter was seeking her presence and an attendant was waiting to escort her to him.

Maude rose and washed her face in the ewer, blotting away the stains of her earlier tears. Her stomach was queasy. Why did Hubert Walter want to see her? Having argued with her father this morning, she had no desire for another confrontation, another mauling at the hands of a man who was 'acting in her best interests'. Unfortunately, she could not turn down a summons from an archbishop, especially when he was her host.

As she gestured Barbette to accompany her, Queen Isobel flashed her a look full of malice. 'Likely it is about your proposed marriage,' she said with a feline smile. She was sitting near the brazier, eating honey nougat while a maid dressed her hair with red ribbons.

'What marriage?' Maude stared at Isobel and felt as if she had swallowed a bucket of ice.

The Queen put a small white hand across her mouth. 'Oh, have I spoken out of turn? Didn't you know?'

You little bitch, Maude thought. 'What marriage?' she repeated.

Isobel lowered her hand, revealing that the cat smile had grown to a near grin. 'Falco de Breauté has offered your father a thousand marks for you.'

Maude swallowed and felt sick. She had seen how Falco de Breauté treated women in public and knew that in domestic privacy it would be far worse. The bruise on her arm where her father had gripped her was as nothing compared to what awaited her if she became de Breauté's wife. The man was a wealthy mercenary, but not to the tune of a thousand marks. Therefore, it followed that he must have obtained the coin from somewhere – in all likelihood from John, or why else would Isobel be so well informed?

'Falco de Breauté can go piss in the wind,' she said furiously, and stalked to the door, her mind racing frantically with thoughts of running away.

'Lady Walter,' said the guard and, as he swept her and Barbette a bow, he cast a twinkling glance from beneath his brows.

Maude was buffeted by another shock, this time more pleasurable. She had not seen Jean de Rampaigne since her arrival in Canterbury, but now here he was in the full armour and surcoat of the Archbishop's guard. 'Why am I summoned?' she demanded as he ushered her before him and the door to the women's chambers closed with what seemed like a far too final thud. 'Is it about my proposed marriage?' The last words were spoken scathingly.

Jean looked taken aback. 'You know about it?'

'The Queen has just taken great pleasure in enlightening me. I hope that your master has plans to thwart it. I will scream my refusal all the way to the altar.'

From looking taken aback, Jean's expression changed to one of dismay. 'The Queen knows? How?'

'I suppose John must have told her.'

De Rampaigne halted in the corridor and faced Maude. 'Either we are talking at cross purposes or there is an entire plot here about which I am ignorant. Just who have you been told you must wed?'

'Falco de Breauté has offered my father a thousand marks for the right to take me to wife,' Maude answered, frowning. 'Is that not why the Archbishop has summoned me?'

'No, that is not why,' he said and began walking again, striding out so that Maude had almost to run to keep up with him.

'Then what?'

Jean did not answer for their rapid progress had brought them to the door of the Archbishop's rooms. He knocked and shouted his name to request entry.

Maude fought the urge to turn tail and run as she heard the scrape of footsteps and the clunk of the draw bar. Then it was too late. The door swung inwards on silent hinges and she let out a gasp of shock as she found herself standing mere inches from Fulke. He was clad in the mail of a warrior, the iron rivets making his eyes as dark as stormy sea. His expression was one of self-containment overlaid by wariness.

Her father stood a little to one side, nervously rubbing his hands and the Archbishop was busily preparing seals for two sheets of vellum. Maude took all this in at a glance and heard Jean close and bolt the door.

'What are you doing here?' she managed to ask in a voice that was hoarse with shock. 'If you are caught, you will be killed!'

He shrugged. 'But only if,' he said, 'and I have no intention of giving John that satisfaction.' The mail rivets on his hauberk flashed as he drew a deep breath. 'I am here because I have come for you . . .'

'For me?' Maude returned his gaze blankly.

Before Fulke could speak, le Vavasour stepped forward. 'FitzWarin has offered me a thousand pounds of silver for your hand in marriage, daughter, and I have agreed.'

'What?' Maude's stare shifted to encompass all of the men. She began to tremble. 'Am I to be bought and sold like a brood mare in the ring?'

'Maude—' Her father's voice was a warning growl. 'Curb that tongue of yours before I curb it for you.'

'As you would have done this morn?' she spat and was all too aware of the closed door at her back. 'Is there not a spark of decency in any of you?'

Le Vavasour reddened. 'God's blood, girl, you try me sorely. I'll have you bitted and bridled like a mare indeed to cure your insolence . . .'

'Peace,' Fulke said with a curt gesture. He turned to the fuming le Vavasour. 'Will you grant me leave for a private word with your daughter?' The calm tone of his voice was belied by the rapid beat of the pulse in his throat. Maude wondered at whom his anger was directed.

Her father glowered, but nodded brusque consent. 'You have my permission to thrash her if she oversteps her bounds,' he said. 'Unfortunately she has not learned the difference between being spirited and being obstinate.'

Hubert Walter's expression was inscrutable. He gestured towards the small curtained-off antechamber beyond. 'You may speak in there,' he said.

Maude was in half a mind to refuse just to be contrary, but when Fulke held out his arm in a courtly gesture and gave her the look of a conspirator, she took it and went with him.

He drew the curtain and crossed to the far side of the chamber. It was only a matter of a few yards, but it would make all the difference as far as being overheard was concerned. Then he faced her.

'Do you have any objections to marrying me?' His voice was pitched low, but it was not a whisper – that too would have carried and mayhap conveyed the wrong impression to those beyond the curtain.

They stood two feet apart, but she could feel him without touching. The hair rose on the nape of her neck and her stomach fluttered. 'I object to being passed around like an item of furniture or . . . or a prize milch cow. John wants my body, Falco de Breauté wants my land, my father wants me to do as I'm bid and you want to save me from all of them by taking me for yourself.' She paused to draw an indignant breath. 'What I want matters not one whit.'

'Then what do you want?'

'To be left alone to mourn decently for my husband.' Her eyes began to sting again.

'You cannot have that except in your dreams.' He gave a pragmatic shrug. 'You have to make a choice, no matter how reluctant you are.'

She had a desire to lash out, to rage and kick at the corner into which she was being forced. But there was another desire too. Take his offer, it said. Take him and cling on tight for the wild ride.

'I grieve for Theobald too,' he said softly.

Her tears brimmed and spilled over. 'I know that,' she sniffed.

'I held him in high esteem. He was my mentor; the man who brought me from gauche squirehood to the full stature of knight.'

Maude wiped her eyes on her sleeve, swallowing and swallowing again to try and dispel the aching lump in her throat.

'I swear that I will honour his memory and I will honour you.'

She gazed at him through her swimming vision. 'It is just that I do not trust my own judgement where you are concerned.' A self-mocking smile glimmered through her tears. 'I look at you and my reason flies out of the window.'

'Like a bat at mass,' he said. 'My own reason does the same.'

Maude raised her brows at him. 'What?'

'You've heard the song of Melusine with her silver hair and sea-water eyes?' He came closer and reached to her hand. 'Collected men's hearts and wore them as a necklace, still beating?' His thumb stroked her palm. 'Is it not better to be reasonless together than apart?'

'Seduced out of my wits instead of beaten, you mean?' she said rallying now, the curve of her lips growing almost mischievous.

His arm lightly encircled her waist and he drew her against the cold iron rivets of his hauberk. 'Surely you would rather the first?' he murmured. With the armour and padding between them, there was little physical sensation, but the symbolism was enough to add fuel to the spark that had kindled.

Maude hesitated, knowing that she stood on the brink. One more move and the battle would be over. She had nothing to lose but herself, and, in recompense, Fulke had sworn her his heart. He bent his head to claim a kiss, but she twisted out of his arms.

'You may seduce me as much as I like,' she declared with a wrinkle of her nose, 'but not until we are wed.'

The wary expression that had crossed his face as she thrust him away, was replaced by one of rueful amusement. He lightly touched her cheek with his forefinger. 'Well then,' he said, 'let us go and kneel before the Archbishop, and make our vows in the sight of God forthwith.'

Seduction of any kind had to wait. The wedding ceremony was a brief, simple affair. Their hands bound by Hubert Walter's purple stole, they gave their oaths. Fulke produced a ring of simple braided gold, which the Archbishop blessed, and as Fulke slipped it on to Maude's finger, pronounced them man and wife unto death.

Unto death. Maude shivered at the thought. How long would that be? A few hours, a few days, or a lifetime? Fulke kissed her, but it was a formality before witnesses and there was none of the breathless pleasure she had experienced in the antechamber. After Fulke came her father, and Jean, and finally Hubert. As he kissed her on both cheeks, she experienced a sudden rush of affection, followed by a melancholy lump in her throat and a sparkle of tears, because he reminded her of Theobald and all the safety and gentle affection she had left behind on a windswept Irish shore.

'If you set out now while the court is readying to dine, you'll have several hours of daylight on your side and very few witnesses to see you leave,' Hubert said practically.

Barbette was sent to the women's quarters to fetch cloaks and her mistress's bow and quiver. If questioned she was to say that Lady Maude was going to practise her archery. Ideally Maude would have liked to take her coffer and her favourite green dress, but could not do so without rousing suspicion. Besides, she was aware of the necessity of travelling light.

Fulke was not riding Blaze, but a grey rouncy of high quality with a fluid pacing motion to eat up ground and carry the rider for long distances in comfort. Fulke mounted up and, leaning from the saddle, held out his hand. Maude grasped his strong, tanned fingers and swung up behind him on the leather grid of the crupper. Jean de Rampaigne offered his own hand to Barbette.

Maude turned to her maid. 'My danger does not have to be yours, Barbette,' she said quickly. 'Stay here if you wish. The Archbishop will find you another household.'

The young woman shook her head decisively. 'I have served you since your marriage to Lord Theobald, my lady. I know that I could not be comfortable with any of those women we are leaving behind.' Pulling a face to add emphasis to her words, Barbette settled at Jean's back and gave a mischievous smile. 'Well, not as comfortable as this anyway.' She put her arms around Jean's waist.

'I agree,' Jean grinned.

Maude laughed and her spirits lightened. Suddenly there was a feeling of camaraderie and adventure. It was them against the world, and they were fearless.

Fulke clicked his tongue and Maude put her hand through his belt, taking a firm grip. Occasionally she had ridden like this with Theobald, but the emotions had been different. She had been more interested in her surroundings than the closeness of the man guiding the horse. Now the landscape had changed. She was aware of every fibre of Fulke's cloak. The way his hair grew, the sleek black layering like the folded wing pinions of a raven. The glimpsed line of cheekbone and the flicker of dark-lashed lid at the slight turn of his head. His strong, lean hands on the reins. The thought of them placed in possession on her body sent a small shimmer of sensation through her, part fear, part anticipation.

They rode out of Canterbury as the cathedral rang the hour of vespers. It being nearly midsummer, several hours of daylight travelling remained and Fulke urged the rouncy into a smooth, fluid trot. After about half a mile they met a merchant riding towards the city, his pack mule laden with chaplets of fresh flowers twisted together with fine wire and hemp string. News that the court was at Canterbury had spread like wildfire and traders were taking every advantage.

Fulke drew rein and reached to the leather pouch at his waist. A quarter-penny was exchanged and the merchant unfastened a chaplet fashioned of woodland greenery and dog roses, delicately fragrant.

Turning in the saddle as the man moved on, Fulke crowned Maude's plain white wimple with the circle of flowers.

'Every bride needs a chaplet and a ring,' he said.

Maude felt silly tears fill her eyes and had to bite her lip.

He would have kissed her then and she would have kissed him back, but at that moment a troop of armed horsemen arrived, heading for Canterbury, and Fulke pulled aside to make way rather than call attention to themselves. One of the last riders in the party, a serjeant in quilted gambeson, eyed the four travellers curiously, and even as the troop rode on, looked over his shoulder, frowning.

'I think he knows us,' Jean muttered. 'Have you seen him before, Fulke?'

'No, I—'

'He served under Theobald for a while, but he was dismissed because he was always brawling and causing trouble.' Maude watched the receding horsemen with troubled eyes. 'But he knows me and he knows Barbette.' Her grip tightened in Fulke's belt. 'He entered Theo's service in the days when he was collecting tourney fees. It may be that his memory will tell him who you are too. I know he will not think twice about making enquiries and earning himself some Judas silver.'

'Then we had best be on our way.' Fulke guided the grey back on to the road and urged it to a rapid trot to put distance between themselves and any pursuit that might come of the chance encounter. The moment of romantic pleasure was lost.

CHAPTER 23

It was dusk when Fulke and his companions entered the great forest of the Andreadswald and almost dark by the time he arrived at the place where he had left his men. The Andreadswald stretched from the outskirts of Canterbury westwards to Chichester. It was ancient woodland and its sparse population was governed by the harsh forest laws, laid down by Norman and Angevin kings jealous of their hunting privileges. All dogs were to have three claws extracted from their front paws so that they could not chase game, and any man caught 'red-handed' over the body of a slain deer was liable to be hanged. The royal foresters responsible for capturing miscreants were feared and hated. No one was going to tell them there were outlaws in the vicinity. Let them discover for themselves.

The men had felt safe enough to build themselves a fire for cooking and comfort, but Fulke ordered them to kick it out and be prepared to ride at a moment's notice if need be.

'Christ, unless they're following right on your tails, they're not going to burst into this clearing and overwhelm us,' William objected, although he did as Fulke bade. 'No one but a complete idiot would take to fighting in the midst of a wood at night.'

'I agree,' Fulke said shortly. 'If I were commanding a

troop in pursuit, I'd follow the smell of smoke and the sound of voices until I found the fire. I'd wait until the dawn and strike then.' Sometimes he wondered if William was ever going to learn – to see more than the nose in front of his face. 'Still,' he said as William flushed with chagrin, 'whatever you've been cooking smells good and my stomach is nigh clamped to my spine with starvation. And my lady wife's too, I should not wonder.'

'Wife?' William's voice rose a notch as Fulke swung from the saddle, thrust the reins into his brother's hands and lifted his arms to Maude. She came down lightly into them; he could feel her slenderness through the concealing layers of the unbecoming woollen gown, and the suppleness of muscle tone. He could not quite believe that she was his, that despite the danger she was here with him, a brightness in her look that answered his own and threatened incandescence.

'We were married by the Archbishop himself in the presence of her father with Jean and Barbette for witnesses,' Fulke said.

'And under King John's nose,' Maude added with a hint of mischief as she stepped forward to kiss William on the cheek. 'I have been an only child, but now I've to become accustomed to a passel of brothers.'

William looked slightly nonplussed, but managed a bow. 'And none of us has ever had a sister,' he said. Suddenly his brown eyes gleamed. 'I hope you're good at sewing tears and stitching wounds.'

Maude laughed. 'Not when I'm as ravenous as a she-bear and my backside feels as if it has been used as a threshing floor!' She rubbed her rump. 'Saddle-sore!' she added quickly as William's eyebrows rose towards his parting.

'Aye, well, too much hard riding will do that,' he said, and ducked beneath Fulke's swipe.

Fulke's other brothers welcomed her into the family and congratulations followed from the rest of the troop. Fulke was slapped heartily on the back and robust, not to say ribald comments flew. He took them in good part but was a little uneasy as to how the rough jocularity of his men would sit with Maude. She was, after all, the former sister-by-marriage of the Archbishop of Canterbury and Theobald in his last years had been of monkish tendencies. These men were young bachelors and the women in camp consisted of four 'laundresses' whose morals were as grimy as some of the shirts and braies they beat on stones in passing streams.

Maude, however, seemed equable enough. She ate an enormous bowl of hare stew and polished off as much bread as a grown man. Fulke gazed in astonishment at her slender frame and enquired if she had hollow legs.

'I told you I was hungry.' She licked her fingers daintily like a cat.

'I'll make sure we load an extra pack pony with rations for your personal use,' Fulke grinned. 'I never realised that you had the appetite of a gannet.'

'There are many things you do not know about me,' Maude said and gave him a sidelong look that made his breath catch and an urgent warmth surge in his groin.

'I intend to find out.'

Suddenly the atmosphere between them was charged like the air at the heart of a thunderstorm. Their eyes met and held, the connection sparking between them. Maude licked her final finger, and then her lips. Fulke struggled against the urge to grab her hand, drag her into the darkness of the trees and take her without any consideration but the driving need of lust. One minute, two, was all it would take. He was as hard as a bone sword hilt and he could tell by her dilated pupils that she was as moist as honey.

The moment was broken by William who joined them, seating himself on the ivy-covered tree trunk and adding the light of his own candle lantern to the small one that had illuminated their meal. He presented Maude with a leg from a pair of linen chausses. There was a three-cornered tear at the knee. 'Do you feel able to do some sewing now?' he enquired.

Fulke did not know whether to be angry or relieved at William's intervention. 'Surely you can do that yourself, or plead with a woman of your own,' he said irritably.

William gave a disarming shrug. 'The laundry girls are too busy and . . . and they're not family. Our mother made these chausses for me. I want the stitches to be set in by another woman of the family.' He looked pleadingly at Maude.

'I am not a skilled sempstress, especially by this light,' she laughed, but, moved by his words, accepted the garment and the needle and thread he took from his pouch.

'I have heard some excuses . . .' Fulke growled, giving William a narrow look.

'It's the truth.' William spread his hands. By the flicker of the lantern-light, his features were a mingling of woodland faun and lost child. 'You think I live for adventure, that I'm reckless and wild. In part it is true, but there is another part of me that remembers how it was. When a day's hunting was as wild as we got and when Mama sat at her sewing in the embrasure and told us stories about serpents and gold.'

Fulke's expression mellowed slightly. 'We all remember,' he said softly. 'I know we can never go back, but one day I hope to do nothing wilder than go hunting for the table or listen to my children's mother tell tales of serpents and gold to our offspring.'

Maude raised her head from the chausses to give him a

luminous look. 'What need of tales when the truth will keep them occupied for all the years of their childhood?' she said.

Her remark led on to the manner of their marriage and escape. Between them, they told the tale in full to William, but soon had a larger audience. Fulke's pride in Maude increased. She was no haughty lady who regarded the gilded trappings of a keep as her natural habitat but was as resilient and adaptable as good sword steel. Whatever he asked of her, she was capable of performing. He wondered if he was as worthy of her.

She finished stitching William's chausses and presented them to him with a flourish. 'The first and last piece of sewing I do for you, brother,' she said, her eyes sparkling, her lips slightly pursed with amusement and yet with a hint of warning that she had no intention of being taken for granted.

William took the chausses from her and clutched them to his breast. 'Thank you,' he said, 'this means a deal to me.' He cleared his throat. 'In token of my appreciation, I would like to present you and Fulke with a marriage bed.' He gestured off into the darkness.

Fulke raised his eyebrows. 'What have you been up to?'

'Nothing,' William said nonchalantly. 'I just organised something while you were eating. After all, before you can tell tales to your offspring, you have to beget them. Come and look.'

He led them to the edge of the clearing. Green boughs had been cut from a nearby beech and curved to form an arbour. Sheepskins lined the base of the shelter and blankets were draped across the entrance forming a crude screen.

'Troubadours are always singing songs about leafy arbours in the woods – aren't they, Jean?' William looked over his shoulder for approval.

The knight smiled. 'It is a constant theme,' he said.

Fulke was touched. William's scapegrace antics were often ill conceived, but not this one. 'Our marriage bed could not be better even if it was a feather mattress in a royal palace,' he said.

'That's a lie,' William retorted, but he looked pleased. 'We've put dry ferns under the skins so it should be soft.' He cleared his throat and looked slightly embarrassed. Normally at wedding celebrations wine flowed freely, loosening inhibitions. There were ribald jests and a boisterous bedding ceremony before the bride and groom were left in peace and the guests returned to the feast. Here there were no such conventions to follow, no priest to bless the bed. Maude was a great lady, and a recent widow.

'Thank you, that was thoughtful.' Maude took the moment into her own hands by kissing William's cheek affectionately before vanishing inside the shelter and lowering the blanket screen behind her.

'I promise we won't listen outside,' William said.

'I will kill you if you do,' Fulke vowed. He looked at the dropped screen, wondering if it was an invitation or a rebuffal. Should he join her, or return to his men? He compromised, spending half an hour talking to the knights on matters of strategy so that all knew their part should they be pursued on the morrow. He made sure that guards were posted and alert, then removed his mail and gambeson, knowing that the task would be impossible within the confines of the 'arbour'. At last, a wine costrel in his possession, he went to join Maude.

She was sitting on the blankets and had spread her cloak on top of them. Although still fully clothed, she had removed her wimple and in the light cast by a single candle lantern, her braids shimmered like silver on gold. Christ, she was lovely, Fulke thought as he ducked within and sat down. There was no room to stand, although plenty to lie side by side. Once he had drawn a line in the dew between them, but there was no barrier now.

In the silence that fell, he handed her the costrel and laid his sword to one side. 'I do not need to be drunk,' she said with a wry smile. 'I know what to expect.'

He accepted the return of the flask and took several swallows himself. It was not politic to ask what kind of a lover Theobald had been. A considerate one, clearly, because she was not cowering and there was no distaste in her expression. Likely an infrequent one too, given his advancing years and his interest in religion.

The onus was on him to find out what she expected and to exceed it. But he was not sure that he could. An outlaw's leafy bower might lend a wild and romantic ambience to a mating, but there were drawbacks. They had an audience even if the men pretended to be deaf, and with the threat of pursuit so close, it would be foolhardy to remove their clothes and indulge in naked abandon. The latter would have to wait, pity though it was. They could, of course, just chastely kiss and go to sleep, but Fulke was not that much of a martyr and it was a long time since he had taken pleasure in lying with a woman. Besides, an unconsummated marriage was one that could be dissolved.

He touched her braid, entranced by its sheen, then laid his fingers tentatively on the delicate skin of her throat. He felt the sudden leap of her pulse, heard the rush of indrawn breath. Outside someone laughed loudly at the fire, and was silenced by a terse warning from William.

He tried to ignore the sound and covered her mouth with his. Her lips parted willingly and her arms encircled his neck. They rolled together among the fern-cushioned sheepskins. Heat surged into Fulke's groin so hard and tight that it was as much a physical pain as pleasure. He cupped her breast, seeking the sensitive centre with his thumb, circling and rubbing, feeling her nipple bud against his touch. Maude made a sound in her throat and pressed against him, arching and rubbing like a cat. Even through various layers of clothing, the sensation was so intense that Fulke tore his lips from hers and muffled a groan in the silk of her hair.

Knowing he would be finished before he began at this pace, he tried distracting himself by thinking of other matters: the morrow's journey; the likelihood of reaching safety and of keeping his prize. Such thoughts, however, only made the urgency keener. There was naught to do but endure for as long as he could.

He set his hand beneath her skirt on her hose and slowly smoothed his palm over the fine silk. She shuddered as he reached the soft skin of her thigh between hose and loincloth and so did he. Christ Jesu, this was torture. Unfastening her loincloth, he caressed higher, feathering his touch upon the springy hair of her pubic bush, seeking, parting. At the questing touch of his finger, she arched against him with a muffled oath. She was as slippery and hot as molten honey and as he stroked her, he heard her breathing become a disjointed sob and felt the muscles of her belly tensing.

He kissed her, and she returned his kisses fiercely until they were breathless. Her hands sought beneath his tunic and shirt to find his skin. She rubbed her palms over his ribs, then smoothed them down over the small of his back, and under the drawstring of his braies to the curve of his buttocks. Then she pulled him over on top of her and tilted her pelvis in a wordless, primordial demand.

Fulke unfastened his braies, pushed her skirts out of the way and, closing his eyes, thrust into her. It could not last for long; it was too intense. Fulke strove to hold back, both desperate and reluctant for release, but Maude's whimpering, her stifled gasps of pleasure and the way she writhed down on him, forcing him deeper, were goads he could not resist. When she stiffened and clasped him with her legs, her nails digging into his spine, he was lost. Claiming her mouth, so that neither of them would cry out for the entertainment of his men, he pushed forward a final time and shuddered in a spark-shower of release.

The rush was blinding: pure pleasure followed by a moment of oblivion. He lay on her, his eyes closed, lassitude stealing through his limbs. She lowered her legs and her fingers smoothed through his hair in a caress. After a moment, she gave him a gentle push.

'You weigh as much as an ox,' she murmured.

He rolled over, pulling her with him. 'I feel like a poled one,' he said. 'Chastity and desire make for a potent brew, not to mention the spice of danger and some hard travelling.' He laughed softly. 'I doubt I could fight my way out of a flour sack just now.'

She sat up, straddling him. There was an expression on her face he had never seen before. Her eyes were heavy-lidded, her lips swollen and red from their kisses. Strands of silver-blonde hair had wisped loose from her braids and clung to her brow and throat. She looked so wanton and sultry that, despite his weariness, he felt a stray spark of desire flicker in his loins. There was something else in her expression too. Surprise, and curiosity, he thought, as if she were assimilating a new experience.

'I hope I did not fail to live up to your expectations,' he said.

She tucked a stray tendril of hair behind her ear and her lips curved. 'No, you didn't fail,' she said consideringly and her nose wrinkled. 'Theobald used to fall asleep too.'

Fulke shifted uncomfortably beneath her. He did not

want to think of Theobald, but it was his own fault for seeking reassurance. He had not mistaken her pleasure; he should have left it at that.

Leaning forward, she kissed him softly on the mouth. 'You did not fail,' she repeated. 'You exceeded them, and I am not going to say anything more lest your head swells and becomes too great to put through your hauberk.'

The kiss, the words, ignited the spark; and although five minutes since Fulke had not believed himself capable of anything but flat-out sleep, he felt the urgency surge through him again. 'I don't think my head is the problem,' he declared as he stiffened inside her and cupped her haunches. 'But I know the remedy.'

Maude woke before dawn and for a moment wondered where she was. Prompted by the weight of Fulke's arm across her waist, she remembered and smiled. The darkness held the scent of leaves and compressed bracken, of man and woman. He was breathing slowly and deeply, still sound asleep.

She lay still to avoid disturbing him and thought about their wedding night. About the difference between what she had expected and what had happened. She knew that she should not make comparisons between Fulke and Theo, but it was impossible to avoid. In their last year together, Theo had slept with her, but they had not coupled. Even in the time before that, Theo had viewed lying with her as a routine duty, never particularly high on his list of priorities. He had always been gentle with her and a little apologetic. She had not realised that the act of procreation could be filled with irreverence and laughter and such sheer, raw lust that it left her breathless. She had not guessed at a pleasure so intense that it made her want to scream. Even the thought of it now brought a tingling warmth to the place between her legs, accompanied by a slight soreness. She smiled. Riding a horse for mile upon mile and then riding a husband for the time it took to bring about a second pleasuring were not to be recommended in the same day and night.

The languorous drift of her thoughts was rudely interrupted as their screen of blankets was flung back and William's head appeared, illuminated like a demon's by the flicker of a hand-held lantern. Maude stifled a shriek and shot to a sitting position. So did Fulke, already groping for his sword despite the fact that his eyes were still closed.

'Fulke, there're horsemen in the wood. We have to leave,' William hissed urgently. 'One of the outpost men saw their torches, and they've got dogs with them.'

Fulke swore. 'All right. You know what to do.'

William nodded. 'I've brought your hauberk,' he said, indicating a bundle on the ground, and, leaving the lantern, he went.

Fulke rapidly tied one of the lacings on his chausses that had come adrift from his braies. 'Good morrow, wife,' he said, baring his teeth with savage humour. 'I'm afraid our wedding breakfast must wait.'

'At least we had our wedding night,' she said. 'They cannot part us on the grounds of non-consummation now.' Wrapping her arms around his neck, she kissed him. He pulled her close for a moment and she savoured the rasp of his beard stubble and the strength of his arms.

'No regrets then?' he asked.

'Only that we haven't the leisure to lie abed this morn.'

They kissed again, hard, but fleetingly. Fulke broke from her embrace to go outside and don his padded gambeson and mail hauberk. Maude hastily bundled her hair into the confines of a silk net and covered it with her wimple. The crown of roses, slightly crushed and wilted, flickered at her in the dim lantern light. Lifting it carefully, she placed it on her head and secured it with a couple of hairpins. She was not going to leave her bridal chaplet for their pursuers to find and desecrate.

By the time Fulke was ready for his hauberk, Maude was there to help him. The weight of the mail shirt almost made her stagger as she helped position the neck and sleeve holes. Once the garment was over his head, it was only a matter of tugging it down over the snug-fitting gambeson. There was no time to indulge in the palaver of donning mail chausses. Maude brought him his sword belt and watched him gird it on with nimble efficiency, no sign that only moments ago he had been deeply asleep, his arm across her breasts. Was it the result of living on a knife-edge, or was it habitual? There was so much she had to discover – if they lived.

She took her bow and quiver from the bottom of their makeshift bed where it had lain with his sword. 'I am as good a shot as any man,' she said with a defensive jut of her chin when she saw his expression.

'I know you are, but I am hoping you won't have to prove it by driving an arrow through someone's throat.' Grasping her hand, he ran across the clearing to the tethered horses and boosted her across the grey's back before mounting Blaze. As he adjusted his stirrup, he spoke rapidly with his brothers and the man on outpost duty who had sped back to tell the camp of the enemy's approach. Satisfied, he nodded, and turned to a knight who was waiting on the periphery, mounted on a light, slender-legged horse. He held a length of rope to which was attached the butchered head and forequarters of a decomposing roe deer.

'You know what to do, Ralf. Take them westwards.'

The knight nodded and a smile flashed amid the darkness of his beard. Reining about, he set off, the decaying carcass bumping and bouncing behind.

Fulke led the rest of the troop at right angles to the north. The dawn was just beginning to break and the foliage of the trees turning from black to a heavy green. 'I can see you are using Ralf as a decoy,' Maude said, 'but will that be enough to put them "off the scent"?'

'For a time at least.' He grinned at her over his shoulder. 'The dogs will latch on to the stench of the meat and Ralf's riding one of the swiftest horses so they're unlikely to catch up with him.'

'But surely they will notice only one set of tracks going Ralf's way and more than two score going this?'

'I'm hoping they'll follow the dogs at first and not think about the number of horses. Even if they do, it's still too dark to see tracks properly. By the time they retrace their path, we will be that much further away and I took the precaution last night of having our horses' shoes re-nailed back to front. They won't find any tracks going in this direction.' He waved his hand. 'You can see too how the men have spread out a little. There is not going to be a worn trail. I know there are signs such as snapped twigs, but even a skilled tracker has to stop and examine, and that again gives us more time.'

His speech drove home to Maude that this was not so much an escapade for Fulke as a way of life. Her life now also. 'You have done this before,' she said.

He guided Blaze around a bramble thicket. 'I haven't, but a commander should always have something up his sleeve in case of necessity. If I had done it before, they would know which trail to follow straight away.'

'How do you know it will work?'

'I don't.' He shrugged and stared straight ahead. 'It's not too late. You can turn around and go back to Canterbury – claim you were abducted.'

She eyed the defensive set of his shoulders. He had

complete confidence in himself as a commander, but not in his ability to hold on to her. Perhaps he thought that he had not so much rescued as 'stolen' her, and the notion was jabbing at his conscience.

'I would rather walk in rags from one end of England to the other than go back now,' she said fiercely. 'Before the Archbishop of Canterbury himself I pledged myself to you until death should us part. Does your own pledge mean so little that on our wedding morn you suggest I go back?'

'You are twisting my words!' he said indignantly.

'Am I?'

He did not answer immediately and his shoulders remained tense. Finally, he looked at her. 'If you turned back, it would break me,' he said huskily, 'but I need to know that you are here of your own free will. I never could bear to see a creature in a cage.'

'Do you think I would have any free will of my own if I went back?' she demanded, her voice rising. 'If I was going to refuse, I would have spared you this difficulty and done so in Canterbury. Have my lips said no? Has my body? Could you not read the language of the night?' She glared at him in exasperation. 'For a man of supposedly quick wits, you are being remarkably dull.'

His eyes narrowed. 'I made a reasonable suggestion. I did not expect your tongue to become a sword because of it.'

'You call sending me back to Canterbury a reasonable suggestion?' Maude drew herself up. A tiny part of her was actually enjoying the exchange. Sparks had never flown between her and Theobald. The sexual tension generated between herself and Fulke was promising a conflagration that would burn white hot in their bed.

'More reasonable than your attitude.'

'*My* attitude!' Maude gave her mount a kick in the flanks, making it skitter and snort in surprise. 'This is not the time, nor the place, but when we are free and clear of our pursuers, I will show you what reason is, Fulke FitzWarin, and then I will take it from you.' She gave him a narrow look, the strengthening dawn and the light from the trees enhancing the green of her eyes.

'I think you already have,' he said wryly.

CHAPTER 24

'Not far now,' Fulke looked at Maude, who was drooping in the saddle. 'We'll be at Higford by compline.'

Immediately her spine straightened. 'I am all right,' she said defensively as she drew herself up. 'The warmth of the day has made me sleepy, that's all.'

It was a lie. She was exhausted. He only had to look at the dark shadows beneath her eyes to know that. They had been travelling hard, making sure that they had left any pursuit far behind. The weather had been kind in that it had not rained, but the heat was draining and they had been avoiding the towns which meant taking lesser-known paths through frequently rough terrain.

Maude had not complained, but Fulke knew the enforced travelling had taken its toll. When she had accompanied Theobald to Ireland, the pace had been protracted with comfortable stops in abbey guest houses and friendly keeps along the way. She had not been forced to live on siege rations and camp out on the hard ground every night. Nor had she been hunted.

Fulke thrust his feelings of guilt aside. It was unwise to keep chewing at that particular bone. She had agreed to the marriage, had gone with him willingly, and, as she had said, going back would be like returning to a prison.

But seeing her suffer filled him with remorse.

'I am not as frail as I look,' she said, as if reading his thoughts. 'You keep gazing at me as if I'm made of glass, but I'm not. I can stay in the saddle as long as you, or any of your men. I won't be treated differently.'

'I only said that it wasn't far to Higford,' he replied. 'I know full well that you are no fragile creature. In truth, you remind me of a hedgepig. Certainly you have the spines.'

Her eyes flashed, as he had known they would. They were indeed like glass, he thought, a green so clear and light that they gave the illusion of being translucent.

'Like always mates with like, so they say, and you have the bristles to prove it,' she retorted, touching her cheek where her skin was marked with a pink rash of stubble burn.

Fulke rubbed the dark four days' growth of beard on his chin. 'I'll barber this off the moment we reach Higford,' he promised. During the winter, he would have let his beard grow, but in the summer, it was too hot and prickly, especially if worn with a mail coif or closed helm.

'You think we'll be safe at Higford?'

'For a time at least. William FitzAlan is sheriff of Shropshire and I number the sons of many of his tenants among my men. He's sympathetic to my cause and, thus far, he's turned a blind eye. My Wiltshire lands are accessible too since William of Salisbury is the sheriff.'

'He's John's half-brother!' Maude exclaimed. 'Are you wise to trust him?'

'He's also my friend. If he is forced to move against me then he will give sufficient warning. I would not abuse his hospitality, but I know I could claim it if I had to, and not be betrayed. He loves John, but he does not swim in the same murk.'

Maude chewed her lip and looked doubtful.

'Besides,' Fulke added, 'there are barons of the northern counties who will succour us. Eustace de Vesci hates John, and there is your father too.'

'You cannot rely on him,' she warned with a shake of her head.

'I would not want to dwell in his pocket,' Fulke shrugged, 'but we understand each other.'

'Do you?' Her expression was filled with distaste. 'Before you arrived in Canterbury, he threatened to use his fists on me to beat me into obeying. You heard him say that he would bind my tongue with bit and bridle.'

'I said that we understood each other, not that we were the same,' he said a trifle impatiently. 'I swear that he will never threaten you again.'

'Of course not. He gave that right to you at our wedding.'

'A man who beats a woman emasculates himself.' Fulke's voice was husky with revulsion.

Maude exhaled down her nose. 'My father would say that such an attitude is storing up trouble.'

'And the other way is not? I might bellow myself hoarse or burst with temper, but if ever I strike you, I grant you leave to divorce me.'

'If ever you strike me,' Maude said sweetly 'you will find your dagger in your ribs instead of at your belt.'

He laughed. 'You see what I mean about your spines?'

All thoughts of banter and dalliance were thrust from their minds as they rounded a curve in the road and saw a troop of horsemen advancing from the opposite direction. Fulke narrowed his eyes to try and focus on their banners. Then he cursed fluently and, swinging his shield round and down on to his left arm, unlooped the morning star flail from his saddle.

'Get to the back of the line,' he said urgently to Maude. 'Go, now! Alain, take her!'

'What is it?' Maude demanded, her stomach plummeting.

'Morys FitzRoger and his sons,' Fulke snarled. 'In Christ's name, go. If he charges, you'll be killed!'

White-faced, Maude swung her mare and dug in her heels.

Twenty yards from Fulke, Morys reined to a halt, clearly as surprised as Fulke by the encounter, but fully prepared to fight instead of avoid. With a slow flourish, he drew his sword for close-in fighting, the move copied by his men in a threatening rattle of sound. Then came the moment of silence, of held breath and building tension as both groups assessed each other and mentally selected their targets.

'FitzWarin, you're naught but a thieving outlaw!' Morys bellowed across the space where in moments the battle would fall. 'Tonight the heads of you and your brothers will be paraded on spears from Shrewsbury's walls where they can gaze on all the land they want!'

'You'll have to take us first!' William rose in his stirrups to retort, his own sword glittering in his hand. He was fretting the bridle and the horse circled and pranced, foam churning the bit.

Morys raised his hand, but Fulke pre-empted him and with a roar to his troop he dug in his spurs, gaining that important hair's breadth of advantage.

The shock of the two lines meeting was like the ripple of a giant serpent: a shuddering undulation. Dust boiled up around the struggling combatants. Desperate to protect Maude, terrified lest Morys's men broke the line, Fulke fought out of his skin. At some point in the frantic battle, he lost the morning star around the handle of an enemy's hand axe.

He managed to draw his sword. A flicker in his side vision warned him to duck and the blow aimed at him by FitzRoger that would have broken his collarbone clanged on the side of his helm instead. Stars dazzled in front of his eyes. He saw the heave of FitzRoger's shield as the Baron tried to manoeuvre his horse in for a second strike. Gritting his teeth, Fulke responded, his aim driven by years of training and practice rather than conscious effort. The sword edge sparked upon the mail rivets of FitzRoger's aventail and the power of the blow was only partially deadened by the padded leather beneath. Morys gave a choking grunt and folded over his saddle, gagging for breath. As the stars cleared from Fulke's vision, he saw that his blow had crushed Morys FitzRoger's throat.

FitzRoger lurched and toppled from his horse, striking the ground with a heavy thud. He clawed at his throat, convulsed and was still. As if the battle had been channelled through his body alone, the fighting ceased and men on both sides fell back.

'Papa!' Weren FitzMorys flung down from his horse and knelt at his father's side. 'Papa!' He shook the man in the dust, then turned him over, frantically seeking signs of life. 'You've killed him,' he said in a tear-choked voice, raising hate-filled eyes to Fulke.

'As he would have killed me,' Fulke retorted, chest heaving with effort. 'As he killed my father. It was a fair battle, and God has decided.' He gestured with his sword, the steel still clean and mirror bright. 'Take him and go while you are able.'

'You will pay for this!' Gwyn snarled, joining his brother.

'Do not waste your time with threats you cannot fulfil.' Fulke's tone was weary with distaste. 'I have given you mercy to take your father's body and go. Do it now, or let the bloodshed continue.'

The young men exchanged glances. Fulke saw their nervous uncertainty. Their only tempering had been the skirmishes of minor border battles. They were outclassed and they knew it. 'This isn't finished,' Gwyn warned as he and Weren raised their father's body from the dust and laid it across his horse.

'No,' Fulke said savagely. 'But it will be soon.'

The FitzRoger troop rode away, taking their dead and injured with them. Fulke turned to his own men. There were no fatalities, although there were several nasty wounds, including the loss of a finger and two broken collarbones. Ivo had been hit in the ribs by a flanged mace and was in considerable pain. Maude was busy with the victims, binding up, reassuring. Relief and weakness flooded Fulke's limbs when he saw that she had come to no harm.

He dismounted, and she ran to him, flinging her arms around his neck. He felt the tremors ripple through her body.

'Jesu,' she half sobbed. 'I thought you would be killed!'

'Hush, I'm all right.' He rubbed her back and suppressed the urge to crush her against the iron links of his mail. 'I've endured hard fighting before.' The words mocked him with their shallow bravado.

'But men are dead, and do not tell me they were green to warfare. It could have been you.' She gulped and bit her lip, struggling for control.

'But it wasn't.' He tilted her chin on his thumb. 'If I was worried, it was for you, all soft and unprotected in the midst of a mêlée. You feared for me, but how much more did I fear for you.'

They kissed briefly, but with fire. Mindful of his duty to his troop, Fulke broke away to talk to the injured. Shaking, but aware of her own duty, Maude tended them.

William caught Fulke's arm. 'If we ride for Whittington

now, what chance is there of taking it?' he demanded with gleaming eyes.

His fierce urgency kindled a momentary response in Fulke, but he forced himself to think with his head instead of his gut. 'The garrison won't open the gates for us while his sons still live, and we can hardly sit down for a siege without becoming victims ourselves.'

'Then what are we going to do?'

Fulke glanced over his shoulder. 'Get Maude and the injured men to Higford and consider from there,' he said, then lowered his voice. 'It is in my mind to cross the border into Wales.'

William's brows shot up. 'Wales?'

'Morys FitzRoger was kin to Prince Gwenwynwyn of Powys. You know how seriously the Welsh pursue blood feuds.'

'You think Gwenwynwyn will come after us?'

'I think it likely. Even without the fact that I've killed his distant cousin, Whittington is an important border fortress and Gwenwynwyn is John's ally on the borders. They both want to curb Prince Llewelyn of Gwynedd.'

William frowned, and then his brow cleared in understanding. 'So we are going to pay a visit to Llewelyn and offer our services to him?'

'I think it the best course of action in the circumstances.'

William nodded and even looked pleased. Inwardly Fulke grimaced. His brother was amenable to the notion of going into Wales because it promised new experiences and adventures. He was also buoyed up by Morys's death and doubtless would make others suffer his ebullience for several days. Fulke wondered if he should feel more euphoric himself. Perhaps it would come. Perhaps it would pierce the numbness of fatigue and he would manage to smile and raise a goblet in celebration – and perhaps it was the price for leading that he might not.

★   ★   ★

'What were you saying to William about Wales?' In the aftermath of lovemaking, Maude leaned over Fulke and studied him by the light of the thick wax candle burning on the pricket. There were few marks of the afternoon's battle on his body, the occasional red blotch of a bruise the only evidence that he had been fighting for his life. The memory of the attack would dwell in her mind for as long as she lived. Watching a tourney was completely different to being in the thick of a kill-or-be-killed struggle. No courtesy given, no second chances or blunted blades. The metallic smell of blood mingling with the gritty taste of dust.

She had overheard only part of the muttered conversation between Fulke and William while tending the wounded, but the furtive way that Fulke glanced at her had made her suspicious. They had the great bed to themselves in Higford's upper chamber and the rare luxury of being alone. Fulke's aunt Emmeline had insisted that everyone but the newly-weds should bed down around the hearth in the hall below.

Fulke twined his forefinger around a silver tendril of her hair then released it and gazed at the curl he had made. 'I have to visit Prince Llewelyn ap Iorwerth,' he said. 'Morys FitzRoger was kin to Prince Gwenwynwyn, and Llewelyn is his rival. Llewelyn understands all about making alliances as well as war with marcher lords.'

Maude narrowed her eyes, not impressed. 'When were you going to tell me?' she demanded. 'As you rode out of the gates? Or perhaps not at all?'

He shifted uncomfortably. 'I was just awaiting the right moment,' he said. 'This is the first time we have been alone all day . . . and the subject of Llewelyn, no matter how important, was not the first thing on my mind.'

'You should have told me before.'

He shrugged. 'Mayhap I should. Are you going to sulk and scold because of it?'

'Am I not entitled to do so?' Maude demanded crossly. 'How would you respond if I suddenly announced that I was taking off without so much as a fare-you-well?'

'It's not the same,' he said in a mildly exasperated tone.

'Why not?'

'Because if you took off it would be on a visit to your family or to a confinement of a friend or some such. Where I am going, there is mortal danger. If I did not tell you straight away, it is because I did not want to worry you.'

Maude sat up, her eyes blazing. 'You think I am some frail milksop to stumble over obstacles?'

'I have never known anyone less like a milksop in my life,' Fulke said. 'I thought I was being considerate.'

'Considerate be damned,' Maude snapped. 'You knew that telling me was going to be difficult, so you put it off.'

'I won't make that mistake again,' he said wryly.

She leaned over and bit him, not entirely in play and certainly not in forgiveness. He yelped, grabbed her wrists and rolled her beneath him. They tussled back and forth, her hair tangling about them. She scratched him and he pinned her down and thrust into her. She cried out and clasped him with her thighs, but instead of the hard, fast surge that her desiring craved, he held still above her, braced on his forearms, black hair tangling at his brows. 'Now,' he panted, 'shall I be a considerate husband or not, my lady? It is for you to say.'

'Damn you,' Maude gasped. 'Damn you!' And dragged his mouth down to hers.

'Take me with you on the morrow,' she requested a few moments later when the shock waves of pleasure had receded sufficiently to give her coherent thought again.

Gasping harshly, eyes closed, Fulke shook his head. 'Too dangerous,' he got out between breaths. 'I don't know for sure how Llewelyn will respond.'

'But it's dangerous here too.'

'Not as bad as across the border.'

'So you wed me and then abandon me.' She pushed at him.

'Oh Christ, Maude, I don't have the strength for another fight.' Rolling over, he looked at the rafters. 'I need to parley with Llewelyn. The likelihood is that I can make an agreement with him, but there is always a danger that he will turn on me or take me hostage to win favour with John. I cannot bring you with me for these early negotiations. Better to stay here with a picked number of my men. If all goes well, then I will come for you.'

'And if it doesn't? Am I supposed to sit here, wringing my hands and wondering if I am a wife still or a grieving widow?'

'I know it will be hard . . . sometimes I think that the waiting is worse than the doing, but you must see that you are safer here for the immediate future.' He reached for her hand and took it in a sweat-warm grip. Maude fought the urge to rebuff him. These might be the last moments they had together; if they were, she would be smothered in a burden of guilt, had she turned her back on him.

'If it comes to a fight, I need to have my wits about me,' he said. 'If I have to look out for you, my attention will be split and it will be more dangerous for us both — could mean the difference between life and death.' He squeezed her hand. 'I came for you at Canterbury; I will come for you at Higford, I swear on my soul.'

'Indeed you do swear on your soul,' Maude said with intensity, 'for if you do not keep your word, may you be damned in hell.' She threw herself against him, clinging to the damp, taut flesh, wanting him inside her again. To possess and be possessed.

And because he had made a promise on his soul and he knew that to fail her now would be to put a tarnish on his oath, Fulke somehow managed to rise to the occasion a third time.

The goblet was fashioned of silver, inlaid with a hunting scene in black niello. Oblivious of its beauty or cost, John seized it from the table and hurled it against the chamber wall. William of Salisbury ducked. Sticky wine dregs splattered his tunic. Hubert Walter stood his ground and narrowly missed being brained.

'Fulke FitzWarin!' John roared like a curse. 'I am sick to the back teeth of hearing his name in connection with outlawry and murder! And you are his accomplice!' He stabbed his forefinger at the Archbishop. 'You had him in your grasp and you let him go. Now Morys FitzRoger is dead and his sons clamour for vengeance!'

Hubert's pale complexion flushed slightly, but he maintained his composure. 'Sire, whatever his failings and wrongdoings, Fulke served my brother diligently and well. Since we are speaking plainly, it seems to me that you did him an injustice when you refused him Whittington. Some folk would say that your denial smacked of vindictiveness.'

John looked around for something else to throw, but there was only the chessboard within reach and the sight of the object, with all its associations, made him feel physically ill. 'So there are different rules for different people?' He bared his teeth. 'I deny him land and I am vindictive. He slaughters Morys FitzRoger and he's justified? Christ, Hubert, you're sailing dangerously close to the wind.'

'We only have his son's word as to what happened,' Hubert

said. 'I doubt that Fulke would go out of his way to lay an ambush on the Shrewsbury road when he had women with him.'

'Yes, let's talk about the "women", shall we, or one woman in particular. Maude Walter.' John's fists opened and closed. 'For that alone, I ought to dismiss you as Chancellor and confiscate Robert le Vavasour's lands.'

'It was my brother's dying wish that Maude and Fulke be brought together. An outlaw Fulke FitzWarin may be, but that does not make him excommunicate and you know as well as I that the matter of his inheritance could have been settled amicably long ago. Besides, Robert le Vavasour would never have accepted his daughter's match to Falco de Breauté.'

John's chest heaved. 'You let him walk in and out of Canterbury without raising the hue and cry.'

'I am a man of God as well as your servant,' Hubert said.

'When it suits you.'

William of Salisbury, who had been silent thus far, stooped to pick up the goblet. He turned it round in his large hands and said slowly, 'Why don't you pardon him, John? You need fighting men of sound ability, and no one can deny Fitz-Warin's prowess. Better with you than against you.'

'I'd sooner wipe my arse with a leper's loincloth,' John sneered, and the simmering anger inside him came dangerously close to boiling point again. As if it wasn't enough that Fulke FitzWarin was a thorn in his side, his own circle of kin and advisers were sympathetic towards the son of a whore. He could not tolerate a betrayal, particularly from his half-brother. Will was sheriff of Wiltshire, but he wore a blindfold when FitzWarin was active in the county. It was like having a favourite dog turn and bite off the hand that fed it.

'I want FitzWarin brought to justice,' John seethed. 'And now.'

'I agree with Will, conciliation is the wisest path,' said Hubert. 'You have been set on bringing Fulke to justice for two years and nothing has come of it but expense and humiliation.'

John showed his teeth. They were white and strong and his smile when genuine was his best asset. He was not, however, smiling now. 'For a start, the sheriff of Shropshire can go. FitzAlan's far too sympathetic. Henry Furnel can take his place. Gwyn FitzMorys is to be given a hundred marks from the treasury to increase his troop and pursue his father's murderers, and the hundred men I have already assigned to the task are to be kept in place.' He glared at his half-brother. 'And if you do not look to the laxness in your own shrievalty, Will, I will replace you too.'

Salisbury flushed but said nothing.

'All for one outlaw?' Hubert raised his brows. 'Surely the resources would be better spent in Normandy?'

'I want Fulke FitzWarin brought to his knees,' John said obstinately. 'He's more vulnerable now that he has a wife.' The thought, as he spoke it, gave him a brief surge of pleasure. Fulke would not move as fast or be as daring with a wife to consider. He must either bring her with him or leave her in a place of protection. It would be worth sending out spies as well as soldiers. Maude Walter had lessons to learn too. FitzWarin had not abducted her across his saddle; the bitch had gone willingly. As John thought what he would do to her when she came into his custody it soothed the gripe in his belly. He turned to pace the room, each step flaring the crimson wool of his court gown.

Part of what he was thinking must have shown on his face for Hubert Walter exchanged glances with Will Salisbury.

'You will need to tread carefully where Lady Maude is concerned,' the Archbishop said on a warning note.

'Meaning?' John sneered.

'Meaning that her father is powerful in his own sphere and has alliances with neighbouring lords of similar stature who need little excuse to foment unrest at the best of times. Meaning that she was my sister-by-marriage. I know you have certain "preferences" where women are concerned. I would hate to see her become one of them because you hold a grudge.'

John was beginning to realise how his father had come to the murder of Thomas Becket. A meddling Archbishop of Canterbury was a bane. When that Archbishop was also the papal legate and the Chancellor, and had been responsible for training all the senior civil servants upon whom John's administration depended, the contest was frustrating and unfair. Worse still, John needed Hubert Walter's experience and incisive mind to keep afloat the treasury that his beloved, chivalrous brother Richard had drained to the lees.

'If you had closed your fist on FitzWarin when he came to Canterbury, Morys FitzRoger would still be alive and I would not have the worry of a dangerous outlaw at large when I'm about to sail for Normandy,' he snapped, passing the blame.

Hubert Walter spread his arms. 'He came under a truce to talk of my brother. He was a guest in my house. Arrest me if you want.'

John gave him a hostile stare. 'Thomas Becket looked the part,' he said snidely. 'Your jowls proclaim that the only thing you are a martyr to is food.'

Hubert ignored the jibe. 'When I was Justiciar I recommended that Fulke FitzWarin be given Whittington and that FitzRoger be compensated with a different fief. If that had happened, you would now have a warrior of William Marshal's ability waiting to sail with you. As it is, he's ranged against you instead.'

'I will not be held to ransom by the likes of Fulke FitzWarin,' John hissed. The discussion was going round in circles. His pacing had brought him back to the chessboard. Using forefinger and thumb, John flicked the bishop on its side with a spurt of malicious pleasure. 'It will be as I say. Let him be hunted down and brought before me in chains like the common thief and murderer he is.' He flashed a glance at Hubert and did not miss the distaste in the older man's eyes. 'You warn him, old man, and, archbishop or not, I will see you in chains too. And you, Will, take heed. I've been generous, but that can stop in an instant.' He snapped his fingers to emphasise the control he had over his half-brother's purse strings.

Salisbury shook his head sorrowfully. 'You are making a grave mistake.'

John moodily flicked over a knight to join the bishop. 'Time will tell, won't it?' he said.

CHAPTER 25

'They say that the Welsh can move so quietly and track with such skill that you do not know they are upon you until you receive a spear in your back.'

Fulke smiled at the apprehension in Ivo's voice. Put his brother in the midst of a mêlée or ask him to charge across open ground at opposing cavalry and he would not balk. But give him the massive greenery of the Welsh mountain forests and the possibility of wild Welshmen lurking in ambush and he became as anxious as a nun in a brothel.

'They are men like us, not the faery folk they would have us believe,' Fulke said. 'If we are being watched, they will see that I carry a white banner on my spear and that there are not enough of us to begin a war.'

'But we could be a raiding party,' William said, glancing around as if he could pierce the heavy, green silence.

'If we stay to the worn roads, we won't be molested.' Fulke hoped that he was right. It was unlikely that Llewelyn's men would attack first and ask questions later, but not impossible. The relationship between the Welsh and the English was a delicate one. As often as truces were made they were broken. The Welsh would come raiding and seize on lands that they claimed were theirs by ancestry. Oswestry had been Welsh and English so many times that it was like the oche on a tug of war. The English would try to village-hop, taking a bite out of the fertile Welsh settlements on the border and pushing the Welsh back into the forest. Fulke's own family was as guilty as any. Much of the land surrounding Whittington had as much claim to be Welsh as English.

The track narrowed and Fulke's troop had to ride single file. A fine drizzle set in, misting the air like cobwebs and laying a fine grey haze upon the wool of their cloaks.

'What if we don't find Llewelyn?' Ivo said. 'What if we just wander round in these woods for days on end?'

Fulke cast his brother an exasperated glance. 'Either we're being watched, or we're being left to our own devices. It cannot be both. If I had known how edgy you were, I would have bid you stay at Higford to guard Maude and brought Philip instead.'

They continued through the trees, the green gloom thickening around them and the smell of the forest floor catching pungently in their nostrils. A pair of wood pigeons took flight from a huge beech tree at the side of the track, the clap of their wings so loud that it had the men reaching for their swords and staring nervously around.

'This is a Godforsaken place,' Ivo muttered, surreptitiously crossing himself.

'It's a forest,' Fulke said. 'Like any other forest.' He made himself sound indifferent, as if the heaviness and the gathering gloom were not affecting him. The drizzle increased to a soft patter and runnels of water dripped off the nasal bar of his helm. All the mail and harness would be as rusty as a monk's cock after this and take hours of cleaning, he thought dismally. The path became slippery and difficult with a steep, wooded bank to their right. Awkward, Fulke noted, if one had to swing a sword.

Suddenly there was movement in the trees. William

snatched at his sword and Fulke held out his hand in a warning motion. 'They're not attacking,' he said. 'This isn't an ambush. God help us if it were.'

The men who appeared and blocked the path were dressed in the garments typical of Welsh infantry. Each warrior carried a spear and shield and a long knife at his belt. Most of them were either barelegged or wore short woollen hose reaching to the knee. The youngest members of the troop were clean-shaven, but all those old enough to grow facial hair sported impressive moustaches.

Their ranks parted to allow their leader through, and Fulke found himself looking at a man in his middle years, slight of build and dark of visage. Unlike his troop, he was wearing armour in the form of a slightly old-fashioned mail shirt with short sleeve pieces – probably handed down from father to son.

Fulke gestured to William. Having been raised as a squire in the Corbet household where connections with Prince Llewelyn were strong, his brother spoke enough Welsh to make a conversation. 'Tell them who we are and whom we are seeking.'

William raised his hand in greeting. '*Cyfarch I, Fulke FitzWarin a ei brawd, rydyn ni'n ceisio Llewellyn Tywysog Gwynedd.*'

A slightly scornful look passed across the Welsh leader's face and one or two of his younger men lowered their heads to conceal smirks. 'Fortunately, I speak better French than you do Welsh,' the warrior said, his cadence lilting, but the flow of the words confident and smooth. 'I am Madoc ap Rhys, and I am responsible for ensuring the safety of travellers through these woods.'

Fulke raised one brow. He knew what that meant. 'My name is Fulke FitzWarin,' he responded, 'and I am journeying in the hope of finding Prince Llewelyn ap Iorwerth. I have heard that he is at Deganwy. Mayhap you can take me to him?'

'Why should I do that?'

'I have news for him,' Fulke said. 'News that I would deliver in person.'

Madoc ap Rhys looked thoughtfully at the banner of truce. 'Then you must want something,' he said. 'The only time that a marcher lord comes into Wales under such a flag is when he has trouble on his own territory.'

'Let Prince Llewelyn be the judge of that.' Rain was now sluicing off Fulke's helmet and soaking through his mail to the gambeson beneath. Beyond the creak and jingle of harness, the sound of the dripping forest was like a monotonous conversation.

Madoc eyed him narrowly, weighing him up. Then, abruptly, he gestured. 'Come,' he said. 'We will escort you to him.'

Built upon two hills guarding the estuary of the River Conwy, Deganwy Castle was a fitting stronghold for a prince. Although not as magnificent as keeps such as the Tower of London or the fortifications at Windsor or Nottingham, it nevertheless held its own with most of the baronial castles belonging to its wealthier English neighbours. Through the tipping rain, Fulke saw the dragon of Wales snapping from the battlements, revealing that Prince Llewelyn was in residence. Beyond the crenellations, the sea lay like a flat grey blanket and it was difficult to judge where water ended and sky began.

Madoc ap Rhys led them through the iron-clad castle gates into the courtyard and bade them wait while he went within and sought audience with Prince Llewelyn. Fulke began biting his thumbnail, caught himself and lowered his hand. It was too late now for worrying to be of much use. Llewelyn had the reputation of being an honourable host, which was more than could be said of many Norman lords of Fulke's acquaintance.

Moments later, Madoc returned. 'The Prince will see you and your brothers,' he said. 'The others are to hand their weapons to the duty guard and go to the hall where they'll be given food and they can dry out by the fire.'

Fulke inclined his head and gave charge of his men to Baldwin de Hodnet. 'See that no one starts a fight,' he muttered, 'or I will personally wrap their entrails around my shield.'

'My lord.'

Madoc grinned. 'I do not expect you have problems of discipline?'

'Once and never again,' Fulke replied and with William and Ivo followed the Welshman across the ward and up some narrow, twisting stairs to the private rooms on the upper floors.

At the door, Madoc stopped and held out his hand apologetically. 'I must take your weapons too.'

Fulke had been expecting it. Even valued guests at the English court were not permitted to go armed in the presence of the King. Although he felt uneasy without the comforting weight of a sword at his hip, he unfastened his scabbard without demur and, behind him, heard the clink and shuffle of his brothers doing the same. Once that formality was completed and the weapons handed to a guard, Madoc ushered the men into Llewelyn's private chamber.

Fulke immediately felt more at home, for the room reminded him of the bedchamber at Lambourn or Alberbury. There was wealth, but not the silk opulence of which John was so fond. Bright embroideries coloured the walls. The floors were carpeted with scented rushes, and wax candles burned in various holders to augment the light that showed dull grey sky through the arrowslits.

Llewelyn was using his bedchamber as his state room, an arrangement common to most magnates. Away from the bed, with its discreetly closed hangings, stood an ornate chair, a throne Fulke supposed, although no one was sitting on it. A group of courtiers clustered near a brazier, talking animatedly in Welsh. Madoc went and murmured to one of them – a slender, brown-haired man of about Fulke's own age. The courtier nodded, said something to the others that raised a laugh, and, breaking from their company, came over to Fulke and his brothers.

William, who recognised Llewelyn from his squirehood days in the Corbet household, quickly knelt. Fulke and Ivo followed.

'It's a pleasant surprise to have marcher lords kneeling to me,' declared Llewelyn ap Iorwerth with barbed lightness. He bade them rise. 'Despite my opinion of what you Normans would like to do to Wales, you are welcome at my court.' A raised finger sent a servant to bring mead. 'I have heard all about your activities in England. Some I've dismissed as a minstrel's fancy, but others bear the ring of truth. I suppose that is why you are here – seeking a bolt hole from King John's wrath?'

'That is one of the reasons, my lord.'

'One of them?' Llewelyn raised his brows. 'I do not know why else you should seek me out. Unless of course you want to hire your sword to me.'

'I should be glad to fight for you, my lord, but it is more than that.'

The servant arrived with the mead and once it was poured, bowed and stepped out of earshot. Llewelyn looked expectantly at Fulke.

Fulke took a swallow of mead. It was sweet and potent

with an underlying tang of heather. He drew a deep breath. 'A few days since, I encountered Morys FitzRoger on the Shrewsbury road. There was a skirmish and I killed him.'

The Prince's eyebrows rose.

'He was Gwenwynwyn's man and King John's vassal in the matter of Whittington. By the law of the land, Whittington should be a FitzWarin fief.'

Llewelyn swirled the drink in his cup, his expression thoughtful. 'I know of your longstanding dispute, but I wonder why you think it should interest me?'

The Prince's indifference was feigned. Fulke knew that Llewelyn had every reason to be interested in the news.

'You are right that I am here to request shelter at your court for myself and my retinue. In exchange I can give you fifty knights, all battle trained. I know that there is no love lost between yourself and Gwenwynwyn and that King John is your enemy, as he is mine.'

'So, you are proposing an alliance?' A glint of amusement lit in Llewelyn's peat-brown eyes. 'In return for succour, you fight for me?'

Fulke smiled too. 'No, sire. I fight for myself, but to your benefit. We have mutual interests.' He looked directly at Llewelyn. 'It would be easy for you to take Whittington while Weren and Gwyn FitzMorys are in disarray. And if you did, you would need a seasoned military man to hold it for you.'

Llewelyn exhaled down his nose. 'You want me to take Whittington for you?'

'In return for feudal service, sire.'

'You are audacious.' Llewelyn's eyes narrowed. 'Are you also foolish?'

'No, sire,' Fulke replied, his voice remaining calm, although he felt as if he were walking on a blade's edge. 'I may gamble, but I always try to ensure the odds are in my favour. Whittington is a valuable keep. It guards the valleys of the Dee and the Vyrnwy. You have an opportunity to take that control from John and Gwenwynwyn and use it to your own advantage.'

The Welsh Prince considered him. 'I shall think on the matter,' he said. 'In the meantime, you and your men are welcome under my roof for the price of your swords.'

'Thank you, sire. I—'

Llewelyn raised a forefinger. 'Do not be too effusive in your gratitude,' he said. 'Odds in your favour do not mean that you will win. If we are allies, it is because we share a common enemy, not because we are friends.'

CHAPTER 26

Maude hung over the chamber pot and retched. She felt terrible. Weak as a newborn kitten and as fatigued as an old woman.

Emmeline clucked her tongue in sympathy and whisked out of the room. When she returned, it was with a cup of sweet mead and a wooden platter containing two dry oatcakes.

Maude had staggered back to the bed and was sitting on its edge, clutching her aching stomach and wondering what she had done to deserve such a malady. Every morning for the past three days she had been as sick as a dog and she felt so tired that it was as if she had not slept at all.

'Here, eat these slowly and ease them down with mead,' Emmeline said. 'They'll help stop the sickness.'

Maude took the bowl and looked at the oatcakes. Strangely, the sight of food did not make her feel ill, unless it be queasily ravenous. 'What is wrong with me?' she demanded in a voice querulous with worry and took a tentative bite.

Emmeline sat down beside her and smoothed Maude's hair with a maternal hand. 'I would say, my love, that you are likely with child. Can you remember the time of your last flux?'

Maude frowned. That was hard, especially when half of

her mind seemed to be wrapped in a woolly fog. 'It would have ended the week before Fulke came to Canterbury,' she said at length. 'I know because I told Barbette that my old linens would not stand another washing, and that I must buy some new.'

Emmeline counted on her fingers. 'That was almost seven weeks ago,' she said.

'With child.' Maude spoke the words and considered the notion with a mingling of fear, surprise and delight. The fist that had been clenched at her belly now opened and she spread her palm protectively. She had vague memories of her mother's pregnancies, of the constant sickness and the way her mother had dragged herself around as if at death's door. Indeed, the last confinement had killed her and the baby had been stillborn like all the others except Maude.

'You and Fulke will be just like his parents.' Emmeline gave her a huge hug, clearly delighted at the prospect. 'Six healthy sons, not a weakling among them.'

Maude almost choked on the dry piece of oatcake she was trying to force down. Six! She could not even imagine herself the mother of one just now. Impossible to think of a child growing inside her. Impossible to reconcile the exquisite pleasure of the act of procreation with the malaise that followed.

'The sickness will pass,' Emmeline said, as if reading her thoughts. She kissed Maude heartily on the cheek. 'Fulke will be overjoyed.'

Maude made a wry face. 'Wherever he is,' she said and wondered if she had become a typical baronial wife, fertilised and then abandoned, naught but a breeder of children. Of the seven weeks that Emmeline had counted on her fingers, Fulke had been gone for almost five of them, and no word. She had no idea what had happened to him, whether his plea to Prince Llewelyn had succeeded or whether his bones were bleaching in some Welsh forest. Surely not the latter, because he had been leading a large enough troop. Someone would have escaped to carry the tale home. Alternately she cursed at him in anger, and wept for him in fear. Theobald would never have treated her thus, but then Theobald had been a man of balance, of even-handed flatness. There had been no hell – and there had been no star-shining heaven either.

'He will come,' Emmeline said, giving her a reassuring pat.

'And perhaps I won't be here,' Maude could not help but snap. The mead coursed through her veins, invigorating her, and the oatcake was doing its work. Her stomach, although queasy, no longer threatened to turn itself inside out.

'Oh, come now.' Emmeline clucked her tongue. 'I know you fret for him, and he's inconsiderate not to send word, but men are like that. You do the best with what you have.'

'Except when you haven't got it,' Maude said crossly, but found the glimmer of a smile. It wasn't Emmeline's fault and Fulke's aunt had been so kind that she did not deserve to bear the brunt of Maude's ill temper.

Leaving the bed, she went to her clothing pole. She had left Canterbury without spare garments. Emmeline had lent her one of her gowns and, in the last fortnight, the women had sewn two new undertunics and a dress from the fabric that was to hand. None of the garments were fitted except for the gown in which she had arrived, so at least she had some accommodation for when her belly began to grow.

Once dressed, she repaired to the main hall. Richard and Alain had taken a dozen men out on patrol, leaving Philip at Higford in command of the other ten. Maude wondered whether to tell him that she was with child. It was Fulke who should know first, but he wasn't here, and the news would be common knowledge soon anyway. Yet she bit her tongue. She needed time to come to terms with the fact herself.

'Do you think Fulke's safe?' she asked Philip instead.

Having been up and active since first light, Philip was sitting amongst the crumbs of a demolished loaf and the remnants of a new cheese. He took a drink of buttermilk from the wooden cup at his side and offered a crust to Fulke's wolfhound, Finn, who was lying beneath the trestle, eyebrows cocked, jaws at the ready. 'Yes, I do,' he said after a moment. 'Sending a messenger all the way back through Wales would be dangerous and a waste of a man unless the matter was urgent. I can well understand why we have not heard from him.'

'But surely he should have returned by now.' She shook her head at the offer of bread and cheese, but accepted another dry oatcake and a small cup of buttermilk.

'That depends how far he had to travel to find Llewelyn and what happened when he got there. You do not just appear at the court of a Prince, say your piece and ride out again.' Philip rubbed his thumb along his close-cropped auburn beard. 'You have to await the Prince's pleasure.'

'But what if that pleasure is to throw him in prison or kill him?'

Philip looked at her and his expression softened. Maude's heart turned over for he had the same eyes as Fulke, deep smoke-grey, striated with gold. 'Llewelyn is not a vindictive man, and he has a powerful streak of common sense. He has everything to lose and nothing to gain by rejecting Fulke. Nothing will happen to him, Maude, I promise. I know my brother.' He laid his hand lightly over hers in re-assurance, then rose and left.

'It is more than I do,' Maude murmured softly.

With Barbette in dutiful tow, and Finn at her side, she left the keep to walk in the glorious sunny morning. She was tempted to have a groom saddle a horse, but was unsure if her settling stomach would bear the jolting. Women in the later stages of pregnancy were not supposed to ride or even travel in a cart. She did not think it would make much difference to her current state, but it was better to be safe. It was June now. Count back to conception in May. The child would likely be born around the feast of the Virgin in February's cold. As to where, she did not know. Perhaps they could go to her father's lands in the north, to Wragby or Hazelwood. Or to Ireland, where John's writ was weakened by the wild Hibernian Sea.

Maude strolled down to the riverbank. The water level was low in the summer heat and the brown outlines of fish could be seen shimmying among the ribbons of weed. She seated herself on an area of turf that had been cut by a fisherman and folded her arms around her knees. Reed buntings warbled their territory claims from the tall stems of cow parsley and the manor's herd of long-horned cattle grazed in the lush meadow, flicking their ears and switching their tails at the irritation of tiny flies.

Finn trotted through the grass in search of hares, but avoided the cows. Maude inhaled the sunshine and peace of the morning. It was the first time she had been out of the manor on her own since her arrival. Once or twice she had ridden out, but always hemmed around by an escort of Fulke's men, armed to the teeth. It was only by saying nothing to Philip of her intentions that she was here now with only Barbette for company. Philip would have sent along at least four soldiers to protect her at each point of the compass. She grimaced, knowing that the gate guard would run and tell him, and she would have company soon enough. Unfortunately, not the company she craved.

Lying back, she pillowed her head on her arms in a decidedly unladylike manner and closed her eyes. The distant shush of the water in the mill race was soothing. She dreamed that Fulke came for her on a white horse, a bridal chaplet of red flowers in his hands and there was no one in the world but the two of them, riding through the summer morning for ever.

Finn rudely curtailed her idyll as he came tearing out of the meadow and launched himself into the river with a tremendous smack and splash of water. Barbette screamed and Maude shot upright, her gown covered in dark blots of water.

'Finn!'

Plainly deciding that Maude's screech was a command to come, the dog circled in the water, paddled to the bank and heaved himself out.

'Finn, no!'

It was too late. Starting at his head and twisting down to his tail, a massive shudder rippled through the wolfhound and the women were drenched in a spray of silver droplets.

'Bad dog!'

Anxious to make amends, Finn advanced on Maude, tongue at the ready to lick his way back into favour. Maude struggled to her feet, tripped on her gown and fell over. Immediately Finn was upon her, anxiously washing her face as if she were a stray member of the pack, his belly hair gathered in points and dripping river water all over her gown.

Barbette moved to haul him off by his broad leather collar. Suddenly the dog went rigid in her grip and stared at the path that led between river and village. His lips curled away from his teeth in a snarl. Stiff-legged, his ruff raised and the hair standing erect along his spine, Finn took several warning paces towards the two men leading their horses from the direction of the houses.

Filled with alarm, Maude scrambled to her feet. She knew neither of them. They were dressed as travellers with cloaks and satchels, but the long hunting knives at their belts and the way they carried themselves made her think of men trained in warfare.

'Call off your dog!' one of them shouted. 'We mean no harm.'

The language was the Norman French of the court, which did nothing to set Maude's mind at ease. 'I do not know that,' she replied. 'Who are you and what do you want?'

The men exchanged glances as if silently corroborating a tale. 'We are seeking Fulke FitzWarin in order to join him. Mayhap you ladies know of his whereabouts.'

The words were too glib. Maude wished she had not indulged her whim to step outside for a walk. 'Your journey is wasted,' she said, backing away. 'He is not here.'

'Then may we claim hospitality at the manor until he comes? We have been told that this is where we will find him.'

'Then you have been misinformed. I cannot help you.'

One of the men put his hand to the hilt of his dagger. 'But I think you can, since we know you are his wife,' he said.

Maude's heart was pounding. She wondered whether to set Finn on them, but the sight of the knife made her hesitate. She had no doubt that the man would plunge it into the dog if he were attacked.

Behind her, there was a sudden shout and the thud of hooves quickening to a gallop. Turning, Maude felt weak relief flood through her as she saw Philip at the head of a conroi of six knights.

The strangers took one look, mounted up and fled. Philip spurred after them but an instant later reined back with a curse. Their mounts were too fast and they were not bearing the weight of mail. Chase would be fruitless. Behind the nasal bar of his helm, his expression was furious. 'What in God's name are you doing here?' he roared at Maude. 'Don't you realise what easy meat you are?'

'I thought a stroll by the river was safe enough,' Maude replied, standing her ground but feeling distinctly unwell. 'I am not a hen to be kept in a coop.'

'Yes, you are, and they were a pair of foxes,' Philip said tersely.

'If I am not safe here, then I am not safe inside the manor.'

Philip removed his helm and wiped his brow on his gambeson sleeve. 'Do you think I do not know that?' he said with a mingling of anger and weariness. 'What did they want?'

'To join Fulke, so they said, but they also knew I was his wife — so I suppose they had been spying on me.' Suddenly the shock of what had happened robbed her legs of strength. Barbette's cry of consternation was lost on Maude as her vision blurred and a strange buzzing sensation made her feel as if her skull was filled with a swarm of bees.

Maude came to her senses in the main chamber at Higford. The smell of lavender invaded her nostrils. She was propped up against several feather bolsters and Emmeline was bathing her temples with a cold cloth.

'Will she be all right?' The masculine voice was full of anxiety. It sounded like Fulke's and when her lids fluttered open, she saw him gazing at her from the bedside, his expression one of intense worry.

'No thanks to you, if I am,' she muttered, wondering if he was real or a result of the strange symptoms being visited on her body. The former, she quickly decided, because he was wearing his mail and it bore flecks of rust. There was a stripe of rust on his nose too, where the nasal bar of his helm had rubbed, and he was tanned as brown as Jean de Rampaigne in one of his disguises. A figment of her imagination would not have appeared so rumpled.

He knelt quickly at her side and took her hand in a warm, tough grip. She looked down at their linked fingers and fought the urge to burst into tears.

'I arrived as they were bearing you in,' he said. 'Jesu, Maude, I have never been so afraid in all my life. Philip said you were walking by the river and were accosted by two strangers.'

She nodded and swallowed. 'They were looking for you.'

'They did not harm you?'

'No.' Maude bit her lip. 'I was frightened and angry, that is all. I had Finn with me and he would have ripped out their throats.'

His eyes darkened. 'You should not have gone out alone. Surely you must have realised the dangers.'

'I have been lectured once already,' she snapped. 'Philip compared me to a hen in a chicken coop. Do not you dare to do the same.'

He inhaled to speak, but let his breath out on a sigh, and rubbed his hand over his face. The action smeared the helm rust across his cheekbones. After a moment he said, 'Those men were likely John's spies, here to look for me and report back to my pursuers. Philip says they had been asking questions in the village and around about. Obviously when they saw you out alone, they realised that if they could take you, they would have a valuable pawn to bait a trap.'

'I did not think that I would be in such danger from taking a simple stroll within view of the manor.' It was the nearest she would come to an apology. Pushing her other hand through his lank, black hair, she curved it around his neck and fiercely drew him down to her. 'I've been so lonely and afraid. Where have you been?'

For a while there was no answer as they kissed. Emmeline quietly and tactfully retreated.

'Where I told you, at the court of Llewelyn ap Iorwerth,' he said as their lips parted. 'I'm more concerned about you.'

'Then why did you not come sooner?' She could not help herself, she had to say the words although she had promised herself that she would not cling.

'Because I offered Llewelyn my sword and he accepted. I've been in the field, chasing his enemy Gwenwynwyn for the past fortnight.'

Maude eyed him sidelong. 'So you will serve Llewelyn as a mercenary?'

'As far more than that,' he said, and now there was a glow in his eyes. 'He is going to help me regain Whittington, and then I will hold it for him as his vassal.'

'Is that wise?'

He made a wry face. 'Since I have renounced my fealty to John, I am free to give it elsewhere.' Bleak humour flashed in his eyes. 'Marcher barons are a law unto themselves. There have always been alliances between the Welsh and the border Normans when it has suited both parties.' Leaving the bed, he paced restlessly to the window and looked out. 'I've brought sufficient men with me from Wales to take Whittington.'

She studied the straight set of his spine, the way he braced one arm on the wall and clasped his sword hilt with the other, fingers tapping an unconscious rhythm. The room seemed too small to contain his energy. Emotions surged through her: fear, love and pride. She concealed the former, pushing it firmly to the back of her mind, and allowed the latter two to shine in her voice as she threw back the covers and came to him.

'That is good news,' she said softly, her hand on her belly. 'Our first child will be born there.'

He swung round and stared with widening eyes. 'You are with child?'

'So Emmeline says, and I cannot doubt her since I have all the signs.'

He reached out and gathered her into his arms. Then, as she gasped at being squashed against the hard metal rivets of his hauberk, he let her go as if she were scalding him. He looked down at her belly as if expecting to see it swell before his eyes. 'When?' he asked.

'Around Candlemas, I think. Are you not pleased?'

He swallowed. 'Of course I am pleased,' he said huskily. 'And terrified too.'

'Terrified?' Maude suppressed the reply that it was she who should be terrified since the burden of carrying and bearing fell to her.

He laughed without humour. 'A few months ago my responsibility was to my brothers and myself. Then I married you, and now you are with child.'

Maude folded her arms beneath her breasts. The movement made her realise how tender and sore they were. 'You could have chosen not to do so,' she said huffily.

'Oh Christ, I didn't mean that. I have no regrets on that score, nor ever will.' He went to grab her again, gazed at his hands as if they were clumsy appendages, and lowered them. 'I want to protect you, I want to keep you safe from all harm, and, so fierce is the desire, I am afraid I am not equal to upholding it.'

'I have told you I am not made of glass,' she said, going

into his arms and drawing them around her waist. 'The only mistake you make is in underestimating us both. I am as strong as sword steel; you are my shield. We will not fail.' She pulled him down to her and kissed him. The smell of horse and sweat engulfed her but she revelled in it, the pungency reinforcing the joy of having him back.

'Are you going to unarm, or is this a fleeting visit before you abandon me again?' she asked a trifle waspishly, and nipped his ear.

'I didn't abandon you!' he protested.

'It felt as though you had.' Maude deftly unlatched his sword belt. 'I expect you to make amends.' Her breath grew pleasantly short with anticipation.

'Amends,' he repeated softly, and his glance flickered to the bed, the covers invitingly pushed back where Maude had left them. He began to smile. 'I do not think that will be too difficult a task.'

Maude narrowed her eyes. 'Do you not?' she said softly. 'We shall see.'

'Well,' Fulke said, tugging on a strand of Maude's hair, 'you are right. I have never met a woman so abandoned in all my life.' He yelped as she poked him in the ribs. The bedclothes were rumpled and half strewn on the floor, and tangled amongst them were various items of discarded clothing. 'Have amends been made to your satisfaction, my lady?'

She stretched sinuously and gave him a wicked look through her lids. 'What if I say no?'

'I will consider you the greediest woman alive.'

'I am,' she murmured, and ran a finger down his bicep. 'I do not think you know the depth of my appetite.'

As if in response, her stomach rumbled loudly. She had eaten nothing but oatcakes that morning and it was past noon now. Queasiness lurked in the background, but it was a minor discomfort compared to the ravening hunger brought on by the relief of Fulke's return and a bout of intense lovemaking.

Fulke laughed. 'Well, if I cannot satisfy it, I'd best find you a man who can,' he said. Drawing on shirt and tunic, poking his feet into his shoes, he headed for the door.

'Where are you going?' Maude propped herself up on her elbows.

'To see the cook, of course. What do you think I meant?'

Maude threw a bolster at him. Rising, she drew on her chemise and began to comb her hair, going over to the window. The courtyard was full of soldiers making camp: Fulke's men and Llewelyn's, the latter barelegged, the older ones amongst them sporting impressive moustaches. Many of them carried longbows of yew and ash, formidable weapons that were little enough to look at, but deadly in use. She shivered at the thought of the fighting likely to come.

Fulke returned with a large wooden platter of roast hen, bread, cheese and wine. Maude's mouth watered. Suddenly the hunger was too much to bear and almost before he had put the platter down she pounced, grabbed a portion of hen and bit into it ravenously.

Fulke eyed her with mock trepidation. 'Thank Christ that you did not bite me like that,' he said.

'You escaped lightly,' she retorted through a mouthful, then paused, her gaze switching to the door where Philip was hovering on the threshold.

Fulke followed her look and beckoned. Hesitantly Philip entered the room, his glance tactfully avoiding the story told by the strewn bedclothes and Fulke and Maude's state of undress.

'What is it?' Fulke asked.

'I thought you should know. Arfin Marnur's below – just returned from Shrewsbury with some interesting news.'

A gleam of interest lit in Fulke's eyes. Even as Henry Furnel had his henchmen and spies everywhere, so Fulke had his own sources of gathering information and Arfin was one of them. 'I'll come down,' he said. 'What sort of news?'

Philip's rather thin mouth softened in a smile. 'Apparently Gwyn FitzMorys is in Shrewsbury to see Furnel the undersheriff. He's got half the knights of the Whittington garrison with him. They're planning a foray to capture you.'

Fulke set aside his food and began donning his chausses. 'Excellent,' he said, grinning fiercely.

'Excellent!' Maude cried, looking at him in horror. 'They're planning to take you and you say excellent!'

Fulke finished dressing and came round the bed to give her a smacking kiss. 'Of course. Gwyn FitzMorys has split the Whittington garrison. While he chases himself up his own backside, I'll be paying Weren a visit!'

His step lithe and energetic, he bounced from the room and clattered down the stairs. Maude shook her head. Clinging on for the wild ride was proving more exhausting than she had thought.

CHAPTER 27

In the first light of a summer dawn, Fulke rode out of
Babbin's Wood and entered Whittington at the head
of a host of Normans and Welsh.

Limewashed daub and wattle dwellings grew out of the
grey half-light, smoke rising from newly awakened cooking
fires. A dog howled in warning and set up an answering
clamour from other dogs in the village. Folk peered out of
their cot doors, then slammed them and knelt to pray. But
Fulke's army ignored the settlement, and rode on to the
painted timber keep.

One of the gates was wide open to admit an early
delivery of firewood and the guard who should have been
on the wall walk was slouching on his spear and talking to
the carter. Had he been at his post he would have seen
Fulke's men sooner than he did. As it was, he had time for
just one bellow of warning before three Welsh arrows
brought him down across the open entrance. The carter
fled. Fulke and William thundered forward to secure the
gates.

After that, the fight for Whittington was brief. Caught
unawares, the soldiers of the garrison swiftly yielded and
were herded into a sullen knot in the corner of the bailey.
Fulke commanded his men to shut the gates and take position on the wall walks. William took a detail and searched

the hall and storehouses lest any FitzMorys troops were
hiding, waiting to spring an ambush.

Fulke was elated at how simple it had been. He had
expected to fight hard for the keep. Some of his success
was sheer good fortune, but he owed most of the easy
victory to the laxness of Weren FitzMorys's command. Only
one guard on duty and in the wrong place. Fulke was aware
that even as squire of fifteen he could have done better.

There was a scuffle from the direction of the hall, and
William returned, dragging a woman by her drab-coloured
cloak. At least Fulke thought it was a woman until William
tore off her wimple, revealing unbecomingly cropped hair
and the frightened features of Weren FitzMorys.

'I found this tasty wench skulking in the bower,' William
declared with a wolfish grin. 'Fortunately for "her" my
appetite for rape seems to have vanished.'

Fulke's own mouth twitched and he had to fight not to
laugh as he rode up to the captive.

Weren FitzMorys was crimson with chagrin and fury.
'You'll pay for this!' His attempt at a snarl ended on a
whimper.

'We all get what we deserve in the end,' Fulke replied
coldly. 'If you had set a better watch and been less negli-
gent, you would not be standing before me now in a maid's
dress . . . or perhaps you would?' he taunted.

Weren looked as if he might weep. 'When Gwyn returns,
he'll deal with you!' he threatened in wavering tones.

Fulke raised a scornful eyebrow. 'If you can only issue
threats on another's behalf then indeed you are rightly
attired.' He nodded to William. 'Put him out of the keep
with the garrison . . . and, for decency's sake, give him his
wimple back.'

'My pleasure,' William grinned.

A weeping Weren FitzMorys was marched to the wooden

doors of the keep and thrust out wearing the garments in which he had tried to conceal his identity. The garrison was allowed to depart in a more dignified manner. Any other servants and retainers who desired to leave were permitted to do so unharmed.

Silence fell. Slowly Fulke dismounted. He had an urge to shout his name and hear its resonance bring the timbers to life. He almost felt as if such a cry would break a spell and that former FitzWarin inhabitants would come pouring out of the buildings in welcome, his father leading them.

William, sober now, knelt to kiss the damp earth of the courtyard floor. Seeing the gesture, Fulke lifted his spear, its head adorned by the red and gold FitzWarin banner, and presented it to his brother.

'Go and fly this from the battlements, Will,' he commanded. 'Let everyone know that once again there are FitzWarins at Whittington.'

Fulke brought Maude to Whittington later that morning. She had been waiting for him in Babbin's Wood with an escort of six knights, there to protect her and remove her from harm's way should the taking of Whittington end in disaster. But it hadn't, and his heart was bursting with joy and fierce pride as he kissed her and set her on her mare to bring her home.

As they rode out of the woods, Maude gained her first glimpse of the keep that had engendered so much bitter struggle since the time of Fulke's grandsire – the great-grandsire of the baby growing in her womb.

The castle stood on a low rise, overlooking a crossroads: Oswestry to the west, Chirk and Wrexham to the north, Whitchurch to the east and Shrewsbury to the south. The Welsh border curled in a semi-circle less than three miles distance on all but the southern boundary. There was a palisade around the whitewashed timbers and a ditch surrounding the sharpened stakes. The gates stood wide in greeting, but they were heavily guarded and vigilant soldiers manned the wall walks. Inside the compound were numerous daub and wattle storage and service buildings, and a large wooden hall with oak roof shingles.

Fulke drew rein and looked at her. 'It is not as great as Lancaster or as grand as the Archbishop's palace at Canterbury,' he said with defensive pride, 'but it is mine and one day it will be the finest keep on these Marches.'

She turned her gaze from the castle to him. 'If I had wanted palaces and vast castles, I would have agreed to become John's mistress,' she replied on an admonitory note. 'It is mine too, and it is already the finest keep on these Marches. I desire no other.'

Although he swallowed, he still found it impossible to speak further, but he reached across the space between them and clasped his hand over hers.

A long day turned into a long night of celebration, although no one got particularly drunk. They could not afford to drop their guard. This morning had been a clear demonstration of what happened when vigilance was relaxed even for a moment.

That night, lying in the chamber above the hall, his and Maude's cloak for a groundsheet, a blanket above, Fulke wrapped his arms around his wife. 'Tomorrow we begin to build,' he said, his lips at her throat. 'I will have the village carpenter make us a bed.' He pitched his voice low. Whittington was crowded with his men and others were using the chamber for sleeping space too.

'You could have made do with the one that was already here instead of having it taken out and burned,' Maude commented. 'It was good seasoned oak.'

Fulke grimaced. 'Mayhap it was, but my father always

said that a bed was a couple's private space. I want to begin afresh, not lie with you where FitzRoger and his sons have lain with their women and whores.' He nipped her flesh and cupped her breast. 'I am giving you a clean slate to furnish Whittington as you choose.'

Maude made an interested sound. 'With a marble table for the dais and silver cups and tablecloths of silk damask?' she teased.

'And I always thought you a woman of sound taste.'

She pinched him and he leaped against her with a muffled protest. Their lips met, softly at first, but with a kindling hunger. Mindful of the other sleepers, they made love in silence — intense, fierce, shattering. As they parted and drifted into sleep, secured by the clasp of hands, Fulke pondered on the nature of silence, how much meaning it could hold: from hollow desertion waiting to be filled with noise; to the containment of pleasure that was magnified to a blinding intensity by the very need to make no sound.

And behind her closed lids, Maude imagined Whittington as it would be in the future. The proud baronial *caput* of the FitzWarin family, complete with a dais table of speckled Purbeck marble. Smiling to herself, she snuggled against Fulke.

Gwyn FitzMorys looked at his older brother in furious disbelief. 'You haven't got the abilities of a cracked louse!' he cried. 'How could you have let it happen!'

'They were on us before we knew it,' Weren said miserably. He flashed an accusing look at Gwyn. 'Besides, half the garrison were away with you, flashing their mail at the Shrewsbury whores.'

Gwyn reddened. There was an element of truth in the sally but he was not going to admit it. 'We were meeting with the under-sheriff!'

'Amounts to the same thing.'

Gwyn seized Weren by the throat of the borrowed tunic. Apparently the idiot had been trying to escape disguised as a maid and had been the laughing stock of FitzWarin's soldiers. 'It amounts to more than you ever will!' he spat. 'God on the Cross, all you had to do was keep the gates shut and maintain a vigilant guard on the wall walks. Papa was right when he said that you couldn't organise a drinking session in an alehouse!'

Choking, Weren strove to prise his brother off and could not.

'Papa will be turning in the grave where the FitzWarins put him!' Gwyn snarled and released Weren with a push that sent him reeling against the wall.

'You should have been there!' Weren gasped as he struggled upright.

'Why? I'm not the heir.'

'No, but you know what to do! You shouldn't have taken the best men!'

Gwyn glared. He had taken them because he had been expecting to set out along the Northern March with Henry Furnel in search of Fulke FitzWarin. Instead, FitzWarin had slipped behind his back and struck at the weakest point. Now he had Whittington, and from what the men said, sufficient Welsh mercenary troops to secure the place. Besides, whatever hatred he might feel for FitzWarin, Gwyn acknowledged that the bastard possessed formidable military skills. 'No, I shouldn't,' he said softly. 'It was my fault for overestimating your ability.'

'What are you going to do?'

He felt the anxiety in Weren's stare. Weren might be the elder brother, the one entitled to the land, but he had about as much notion of how to control and govern as a plough ox. Gwyn thought about shrugging and leaving him in the lurch, but for their father's sake and his own pride he could not.

'I am going to stay here and fight on,' he said. 'You' – he stabbed a forefinger – 'are going to John with the news of Fulke FitzWarin's outlawry. Now we have no land, it is your duty to secure a fief to support us until we can regain Whittington.'

He watched Weren swallow. 'And God help you if you fail,' he added, 'for I certainly will not.'

CHAPTER 28

Whittington Castle, Shropshire, February 1202

I n the deep of the night during one of the heaviest snowfalls of the year, Maude gave birth to a daughter. Her labour lasted from the hour of compline until the second matins bell and the midwives had little enough to do to earn their pay except catch the baby in an apron, clean its face and cut the cord. The infant squalled lustily the moment she entered the world, announcing her presence to all and sundry.

'Red hair and a temper to match!' the senior midwife laughed.

'And a red face!' Maude laughed too, and blinked back tears. She was exhausted, sore, overjoyed and overwhelmed. It was almost impossible to believe that this tiny, furious creature was hers. Seeing the ripples and kicks beneath the skin of her belly was one thing; meeting their cause was another. She held her newborn daughter awkwardly in her arms and gazed into the crumpled, bawling features.

'She'll calm in a moment,' the second midwife said cheerfully. 'Shows she's strong. It's when they don't yell that you have to worry.'

Emmeline, who had come for Maude's lying-in, cooed over the baby, tears running down her cheeks. 'Just like her poor grandmother,' she sobbed, wiping her eyes on her blue wool sleeve.

Still bawling, the baby was gently bathed in a ewer of warm water, dried in a soft towel, then tightly swaddled, bands of linen cloth replacing the muscular constriction of the womb. Being wrapped seemed to soothe her and the indignant bawls became little snuffles and hiccups.

The midwives delivered the afterbirth and Maude was helped from the birthing stool to a clean bed, freshly made up with linen sheets and a sheepskin cover. Emmeline went to fetch Fulke while Barbette brushed and braided Maude's gleaming silver hair. It had been un-plaited for the birth in the belief that it would help her push the child from her womb. The infant was placed in Maude's arms and mother and daughter assessed each other. Maude would not have called her daughter 'beauti-ful', still puckered and red from her birth and the ensuing tantrum, but that didn't matter. It was overwhelming love at first sight.

'She has her father's eyes,' Barbette murmured.

Maude smiled and touched the soft little cheek. The baby turned instinctively towards the finger. 'And his voice,' she said.

The door opened and Fulke strode into the room, filling it with his presence.

Maude watched him approach the bed. She knew he had been pacing ever since her labour had begun. Every hour or so he had sent one of the hall maids to enquire upon her progress until the exasperated midwives had returned the message that everything was going as it should, and that the birth would happen when it happened.

'I would rather have fought a battle than waited out these last hours,' he said as he stooped to kiss her. 'I am told we have a girl child.'

'You do not mind that it is not a son?' She knew how much store men set by their heirs, as if begetting a male child was the ultimate proof of their virility. She could remember her father's disappointment as each of her mother's pregnancies had ended in miscarriage or stillbirth, with herself the only surviving offspring and dismissed except as a bargaining counter in the marriage market. And this child was special, the first FitzWarin to be born at Whittington in more than fifty years.

'My only care is that you are both safe.' He looked at the child cradled in Maude's arms and tentatively touched the fuzz on the baby's brow. 'Red,' he said.

'Hold her.'

Very gingerly, as if he had been offered a primed barrel of pitch, Fulke took his daughter in his arms. Maude swallowed the lump in her throat. She had been astounded at her miniature perfection. Now the baby's tiny, delicate size was emphasised by Fulke's own height and robust strength. She watched him extend a forefinger, and saw the look on his face as the baby curled her little fist around it.

'I have heard about women who can wrap men around their little finger, but this is the first time I have seen a man captured by a single clasp,' she jested tearfully.

Fulke returned her smile, his own eyes bright with moisture. 'Even if you were to bear me a dozen sons, no moment will ever crown this one,' he said hoarsely. He gazed down into his daughter's birth-crumpled face. 'What shall she be named? Jonetta for your mother?'

Maude shook her head. 'No,' she said, 'Hawise for yours. What else could she be named with that hair?'

Winter gave way to spring and then the heavy greenery of summer. Fulke deepened the ditches around the palisade, he repaired and strengthened the timbers, and he made himself ready for whatever Henry Furnel and the FitzMorys brothers might throw at him. But the summer passed, the grain was harvested, Christmastide arrived and still they did not come.

'John cannot afford to pay his troops in Normandy,' said Jean de Rampaigne, who was visiting them for the feast season, having spent the last month in Hubert Walter's household. 'He is so unsure of the loyalty of his Norman barons that he has entrusted major keeps to his mercenary captains.'

'If he cannot afford to pay his troops, then surely that is unsound policy.'

Jean shook his head. 'He can't afford to pay them out of the revenues of Normandy, that is true, so he's paying their wages out of England's purse, milking the kingdom for all it is worth.'

Fulke acknowledged the statement with a humourless smile. 'Hubert always did make a good herdsman,' he said.

'Aye, and like a good herdsman he can see when the cow is in danger of running dry.' Jean cut a small spiced chicken and raisin pie in half with his meat knife and put one section in his mouth. He offered the other portion to Maude who sat on Fulke's other side, but she smiled and shook her head.

'It's dry salt sausage or nothing this time.' Fulke grinned at his wife. 'While she was carrying Hawise, it was garlic. I could not approach her for fumes!'

'And see what happened when you did!' Giving as good as she got, Maude patted her belly. It was still flat, but for more than a month she had known that another new life was growing within her.

'Blame me,' Fulke said in an injured voice.

'You would be unhappy if I blamed anyone else,' Maude sniffed.

'I would be more than that.' Fulke felt a tug at his chausses.

'Da,' said Hawise, and clinging to his leg with one hand, held out the other one, demanding to be picked up. The dictate, imperative and tyrannical though it was, melted his heartstrings and he plucked her into his lap. She stared up at him out of huge smoke-hazel eyes and then squirmed around so that she could play with the garnet-set cross hanging around his neck. Those who had not known his mother said that save for her hair she was made in his image, but he knew differently. Her looks were pure de Dinan. In character, she had more than a hint of Vavasour, especially when it came to wanting her own way. Maude said that she was like him, but then she would. He considered Jean's words and their implications for his own life.

'Can John win?' he asked.

'Hubert says that it is only a matter of time and that it has been so since Richard's reign at least. The Normans liked Richard – as we all did because of his luck and his daring and the way he could light up a room like a blaze of candles. John may have the ability, but he lacks Richard's glow. The Norman barons neither like nor trust him. When they see him setting mercenaries above them, the damage is irrevocable.' Jean took a swallow of wine. 'Hubert has even heard rumours that some of the barons with lands in England and Normandy are paying homage to Louis of France for their Norman holdings to protect them from pillage.'

Fulke nodded pensively and looked at the child in his arms, her delicate curls a near match in shade for the garnets in the cross.

'I say good fortune to them,' William said from further down the board. 'And I hope John is torn to pieces in Normandy – let him lose it all and know how it feels.'

'It might avail our sense of justice, Will,' Fulke said, 'but if John loses Normandy it will not bode so well for us.'

'Why not?' William thrust out his lower lip.

'Because as he loses lands across the Narrow Sea, it leaves him more time to concentrate his resources on affairs at home – on the Scots, the Welsh and Irish . . . and outlaws.'

'You're not afraid of him, surely?' There was a sneer in William's voice.

'No. But only a fool would not see the implications.'

'And I am a fool?'

Fulke shrugged. 'We are all fools sometimes,' he said, determined not to enter into a sparring match with his brother. 'All I am saying is that we must watch the situation and be on our guard. Nothing is ever as simple as it seems.'

'Not even you,' Ivo guffawed at William, thereby earning himself a cuff.

Maude rolled her eyes heavenwards and excused herself to visit the garderobe. Fulke smiled at her, knowing their thoughts were in mutual agreement. At least she had the justification of a temperamental bladder to avoid the banter.

Hawise tried to put the garnet cross in her mouth and Fulke gently dissuaded her.

'Hubert still hopes that you and the King can come to peace,' Jean murmured.

Fulke raised his brows. 'Likely the peace of the grave.'

'Yes, if your fight with him continues.' Jean hunched over his wine cup. 'The King needs trained fighting men more than ever now.'

'Then let him come to me and ask for them.' Fulke gave Jean a suspicious look. 'Did Hubert send you here to prepare the ground?'

'Hubert sent me nowhere. I asked his leave to celebrate Christ's mass with you and he gave it willingly. All he said was that it would be a pity if you burned your bridges instead of building them.'

'I have built them . . . and I am very happy to have Prince Llewelyn for an overlord.'

'Dangerous though if John turns his attention to England and decides that the Welsh are making too many inroads on his borders.'

'I'll keep an eye on the matter.' Fulke shifted Hawise in his lap and reached for his cup. 'For the nonce it is Christmas, and John is in Normandy.' There was a note of finality in his voice that warned Jean to change the subject.

Jean licked crumbs from his fingers, then folded his arms. 'You might be interested to know that Hubert has been busy in the matter of the FitzMorys brothers,' he said.

'Indeed?' Fulke's tone was wary.

'He has offered Weren FitzMorys the royal manor of Worfield in exchange for Whittington.'

'And the answer?'

Jean shrugged. 'Weren's the weaker of the two, but he's also the heir if you are speaking of English and Norman law. Of course, by Welsh law, the brothers have an equal say in the disposal of their inheritance. From what His Grace says, he thinks that Weren will accept Worfield and play by Norman rules.'

'Leaving Gwyn disaffected and dangerous.'

'And isolated,' Jean said.

'Sometimes a lone wolf is more dangerous than a pack. I—' A sudden flurry at the far end of the hall distracted Fulke's attention, and then filled him with concern. 'Take her.' Dumping Hawise in Jean's lap, he leaped from the dais and strode towards the door.

A man wearing a heavy cloak and hood was assisting an ashen-faced Maude to sit down at one of the dining benches.

'Maude?' Fulke knelt in consternation before her and took her hand in his. 'What's wrong?' All manner of thoughts flew through his head like spears, uppermost the notion that she had perhaps suffered a fall and was miscarrying.

'I'm afraid it is my fault, my lord,' said the newcomer. He pushed back his hood, revealing the light hair and eyes of Fulke's informer Arfin Marnur. 'I have come from Shrewsbury. Your lady met me outside and bade me give her the news I was bearing and . . .' He gestured to the result. 'I am sorry.'

'What news?' Fulke demanded fiercely. 'Tell me!'

'My lord, Henry Furnel and Gwyn FitzMorys have gathered a force together as you thought they might. Even as I set out to warn you, they were making their preparations. They think you will not be looking for them in the winter's cold.'

Maude had laid her free hand protectively over her belly.

Fulke saw the gesture and inwardly winced. He imagined he saw the host arriving at their gates. Whittington was strong and solid, but it was not impregnable. And both FitzMorys and Furnel were dangerous.

'You have done well, Arfin,' he murmured 'and I am grateful for the warning.' He gestured to the trestle. 'Be seated and take refreshment.'

Maude raised frightened eyes to his. 'Are we to prepare for a siege?'

'We are as prepared as we can be, but that will only happen as a last resort.' He looked at her and his mouth tightened. 'I'm going to take the fight to them. They won't be expecting that.'

If Maude had looked pale before, now she was ghostly. 'Is that supposed to comfort me?' she asked in a choked voice.

'No, to comfort myself,' he said grimly. 'I will not let them within a mile of this place.' He squeezed her cold fingers in his and stood up. 'I need to arm up,' he said.

Maude rose. 'If you make me a widow, I will not forgive you,' she said passionately.

'I will not forgive myself either. I've not come this far, fought this hard, loved this much to lose it all before the feast has even begun.' Regardless of a hall full of onlookers, he gathered Maude in his arms and pulled her close, binding her to him, breast and hip and thigh. She buried her face in his tunic and he felt her shudder. But after a moment she lifted her head and faced him with a resolute expression.

'I will help you with your armour,' she said with a swallow.

Fulke's heart turned over at her frightened courage. He wanted to tell her that it would be all right, but he couldn't, because it might not be the truth.

Fulke's right arm felt as if it was made of molten lead. He did not know how much time had passed, minutes or hours, since he had discarded the broken stump of his lance and drawn his sword. The once smooth edge of the blade was pitted and nicked by dozens of encounters and the blue of the steel was edged with clots and drips of red.

The force from Shrewsbury was much larger than Fulke had expected. He was both flattered and dismayed. There had been no choice. Furnel's men, their numbers swelled by mercenaries belonging to the FitzMorys brothers, had to be prevented from laying siege to Whittington. Breathing harshly through his mouth, he cut at a knight who came at him, aiming for the small space between aventail and nasal bar. The man reined aside with a scream and Fulke spurred forward in time to see Philip knocked from his horse by a knight whose shield was emblazoned with the boar device of FitzMorys. Alain and Audulf de Bracy charged to Philip's defence. For an instant, the fighting was furious. Several

Shrewsbury knights arrived to defend their companion. Alain went down. Audulf was swallowed up by the enemy.

Fulke saw red. His last rational act was to sheath his sword and draw the morning star flail from his belt, a deadly bludgeon for close-in fighting, a weapon not of courtesy and chivalry like the sword, but of the common mercenary and men whose only intention was to destroy.

Maude was pacing the wooden wall walks of the battlements, taking a breath of clean air, when she saw the men returning. At first she was not sure, for it was dusk and the air was murky with a drizzle so fine that it was almost mist. She made out soldiers on horseback, heard the chink of harness and armour, but they seemed to move so slowly and they were bearing several litters, when she knew well that Fulke's troop had none. For a heart-stopping moment she thought that it was the force from Shrewsbury, but that lasted no longer than the time it took to recognise Fulke's banner on the standard-bearer's lance. Then with horror she realised that if they were bearing litters, there must be wounded and dead.

'God have mercy,' she whispered and, whirling round, ran along the wooden walkway to the stairs. She almost slipped on the wet wood, wrenched her ankle, grazed her hand as she clutched the stair rope for support. Pelting down to the hall, she shouted the alarm to the folk gathered around the fire and ran out into the bailey.

'Open the gates!' she shrieked like a harpy to the guards on duty.

They stared at her.

'Your lord is home, open the gates, damn you!'

They ran to do her bidding, wrestling the heavy draw bar back into its socket and swinging wide the massive, iron-studded doors.

Hand pressed to her thundering ribs, Maude watched the horses turn from the road, cross the ditch and fill the archway. Their hides steamed in the drizzle and the men's armour glittered like the scales of freshly gutted fish. Heads down, shoulders slumped with weariness, the troop rode into the bailey two abreast. Maude sought Fulke. She knew his customary place, two horses back from his lance-bearer. He wasn't there and her stomach leaped in fear.

'Where is he?' she demanded of Ralf Gras who was dismounting from the place that Fulke should have held. 'Where's my husband?'

Ralf Gras removed his helm and Maude gasped at the sight of the deep clotted cut beneath the knight's left cheekbone. 'Back with the wounded, my lady,' he said with a jerk of his head. 'Lord Alain's sore injured.'

Maude's lips silently repeated the words he had spoken and suddenly she was pushing frantically along the line, seeking, terrified of what she might find, but knowing she had to find it none the less.

The dead were thrown across spare horses, heads down, faceless and nameless for the moment. Some of the injured were able to ride and were being helped from their mounts by companions. She saw Philip leaning heavily on Ivo, his face contorted with pain. Behind them, Fulke was walking beside a litter, his features drawn with grief and concern.

Maude cried his name and ran to him. His arm swept out, engulfed and embraced her tightly, and she felt the brief shudder he permitted himself before he let her go. 'There were too many of them,' he said hoarsely. 'I could not reach him in time.'

Maude gazed at the unconscious man lying upon the litter fashioned from two spear shafts with a blanket stretched between. 'How badly is he wounded?'

'I do not know. A broken shoulder and ribs for sure. He

took a blow to the head and he has been as still as death ever since.' Maude saw the fear in his eyes. 'He is my youngest brother and he is my responsibility. I cannot lose him.' There was anguish in his voice.

Maude could see that he was exhausted but would not yield because of his 'responsibility'. Taking his arm, she tugged him gently in the direction of the keep. 'There is nothing you can do for the nonce except see him made comfortable. Come within and I'll tend to him.'

Wordlessly he followed her and stumbled.

'You are wounded yourself?'

'It is nothing, mere bruises.' He shook his head impatiently. 'I've no broken bones or cuts to be salved.'

But still, he needed healing and care, she thought as she brought him within.

The first task was to tend to Alain – as much for Fulke's sake as the patient's. Remembering how the monk at Wotheney had examined Theobald when he collapsed, she searched Alain's eyes with a lighted torch to see if the soul still inhabited his body. Both eyes reacted to the flare, their dark centres contracting. When she spoke his name, he gave a soft little moan and his body twitched. Behind her, she was aware of Fulke watching her examination with hawk-like intensity.

'I do not believe he will die,' she said with as much conviction as she could muster. While she was not a professional chirugeon or healer, her position as lady of the keep brought with it the expectation that she would know something of both occupations. Besides, her reputation had been enhanced among the men by the way she had dealt with Fulke's arrow wound. 'If he can be given honey and water off a spoon, so much the better. I would say he is capable of swallowing.'

'I will do it,' Barbette offered.

Maude nodded her thanks to the maid and moved on to examine the other wounded men, Fulke following anxiously at her shoulder. She felt the weight of his need for her to tell him that all would live, but she could not give him that reassurance. Only God had the answer. At least there were no gut wounds. Men could linger for days with such injuries and die in screaming agony. But there were some serious cuts to be stitched and broken bones to be set. She sent for the priest who had been a groom's son and had some knowledge of the latter and set those who were competent to binding the less serious wounds.

Pushing up her sleeves, she set to work herself: washing and stitching, bandaging and comforting. At first Fulke stayed with her, talking to the men over whom she toiled, but at some point he left, and when Maude paused for respite and looked round, he was nowhere to be seen.

Philip had suffered a mace blow to the thigh. The bone was not broken but he was badly bruised. William was applying a cold compress to the area as the brothers sat with Alain.

'Fulke?' William said to her enquiry. 'He was here not long ago to look at Alain. I think he went to the battlements.'

'The battlements?' There was fear in Maude's voice. 'Does that mean you were pursued?'

Philip shook his head. 'No,' he said quickly, 'nothing like that.'

William flashed a humourless grin. 'If they gave us a hiding, we took their hides,' he said. 'They weren't capable of giving chase.'

'Then why . . .'

Philip indicated his comatose brother. 'Alain's friend, Audulf de Bracy. They took him hostage and like as not they'll string him up when they reach Shrewsbury. Jean de

Rampaigne's gone to see if he can save him.' He washed his hands over his face. 'Fulke has taken it hard. So far, he has brought us out of every scrape unscathed. Now he thinks he has failed us, but it's not true.' He gave Maude a troubled look. 'Go to him, Maude; he needs you.'

She collected her cloak and, leaving the chamber, climbed the stairs to the wooden wall walk. Mindful of her earlier near mishap, she trod carefully. Fine rain shrouded the night air, bearing on it the smell of woodsmoke from the cooking fires.

Fulke was standing at the place where the walk over-looked the road, although there was nothing to see. It was full dark by now, and the only light came from the keep itself and the dwellings in the village.

'You should come down and unarm,' Maude said softly as she joined him. 'Your mail will be red through with rust if you stand here much longer.'

He looked at her blankly, clearly struggling to change the focus of his thoughts. 'It does not matter,' he said. 'It can be cleaned.'

'You will not bring them home any sooner no matter where you stand,' she murmured. 'At least come below and let me tend your bruises.'

'They don't need tending.'

'A matter of opinion.'

He rubbed his forehead wearily. 'Maude, let me be . . .'

'So that you can brood yourself into a hole?' She took his hand and saw him wince. The knuckles were swollen where something had struck them. 'Theobald used to say that you could not judge a man by his victories, but by his conduct in defeat.'

That drew an indignant spark. 'I haven't been defeated!' His shoulders squared and his chin came up.

Maude gave a knowing nod. 'Well then.'

He sighed and turned again to the unyielding darkness. 'I bit off more than I could chew,' he murmured. 'And for my mistake, others have paid.'

'They knew the price when they joined you,' Maude said. 'Many times you have seemingly bitten off more than you could chew and then astonished everyone by devouring your endeavour. William says you had a victory.'

'William would.' He bared his teeth. 'We held them off, and hurt them enough that they turned back from Whittington, but at cost to ourselves.' He gazed into the night, as if by will alone he could pierce the night and bring the missing men home.

'They will come,' Maude murmured.

He braced his arms on the wood. 'And I will wait for them.' He cast her a dismissive glance over his shoulder. 'You do not have to stay. This is my vigil to keep.'

Maude eyed him with exasperation. Whatever she said, he was not going to relinquish his position. Short of getting his brothers to carry him down by force and tie him to a bed, there was nothing more she could do. After a brief deliberation, she left him to his brooding, but only for as long as it took to collect a cup, a flagon of wine laced with uisge beatha, some bread and a smoked sausage from the kitchens.

When she returned, he had not moved, except that his head was bowed and more than ever it seemed to her that he was bearing an intolerable burden. She set the flagon down by his feet. 'It is my vigil too,' she said. 'I will not let you shut me out.'

He turned his head, his movement slow with weariness. The rain gleamed along his temple and jawline. Fine droplets quivered on the ends of his hair. 'In God's name, Maude,' he said hoarsely, 'do you never give up?'

She gave him the smile of an adversary. 'You should

know better than to ask. My stubbornness is easily a match for yours.'

He made an inarticulate sound that could have been either agreement or dismissal. Maude tilted her head. 'I won't leave until you do.'

'I was wrong,' he said. 'The only time I bit off more than I could chew was when I took you to wife.'

Maude shrugged. 'You could always seek an annulment.' She withdrew the bread and sausage from the protection of her cloak.

Fulke eyed her and the food. She could see that she had diverted him from his brooding and that for the moment he had forgotten his weariness. 'I could,' he said and now there was bleak humour in his tone. 'However, I would be in just as bad a case, for then I would starve for want of fighting and loving, and instead of you bedevilling me out my mind, I would have nothing but memories and regrets.'

She gasped as he pulled her against the damp linen of his surcoat and the rusting iron rivets of his mail shirt. The pungent smell of salt sausage and bread rose in the moist air. The shape of the former squeezed in her hand caused Maude to glance down and almost burst into irreverent laughter. Somehow, she choked it back. Fulke's gaze lowered to the sausage then met hers. She saw the answering humour spark and then quench. He stepped back.

'I'm not hungry,' he said, but stooped to the wine and took a long drink straight from the flagon. He wheezed slightly as the uisge beatha kicked him on the way down his gullet. Nevertheless, he took another long pull.

Suddenly Maude was ravenous, almost craving, and in moments she had devoured more than half of the sausage.

Fulke returned to his vigil. Taking the flagon from his hand, she filled her mouth with the burning wine.

'Will they regroup in Shrewsbury and come again?' she asked.

He shook his head without looking at her. 'I doubt it. They have lost the element of surprise. John is bogged down with troubles in Normandy. He cannot afford the men or the time to add to the aid he has already given, whereas I have Prince Llewelyn on my own threshold and need but ask him for reinforcements. Come the spring, of course, matters might change.' He rubbed his brow. From his action, she knew that he must be suffering the kind of woolly headache that grew out of exhaustion. 'I dare take nothing for granted.'

Although she doubted her power to succeed, she was about to try and persuade him again to come inside, when they heard the clop of hooves on the road and a shout to the gate guards to open up. The voice was familiar even if the riders were two indistinct shapes in the mizzle.

'They're back!' Suddenly Fulke was imbued with a fresh charge of energy and he pelted down to the bailey. Maude winced as she heard him skid on the wet wood but, like her, he grabbed the rope rail and saved himself from serious injury. She followed him carefully, her stomach queasily replete.

'It wasn't easy,' Jean told Fulke. The knight's slender brown hands were cupped around a mug of wine while Barbette gently tended his battle bruises.

'He made it look as if it was.' Audulf de Bracy's voice was filled with the enthusiasm of a man reprieved from the gallows to whom life is momentarily almost too sweet to be contained – two black eyes, a lopped earlobe and a slashed hand notwithstanding. 'Strolled up to Furnel and the FitzMorys brothers bold as you please and offered to entertain the men with songs and music. Said he was a travelling player out to earn a crust and a bed for the night.'

'Audulf heard me,' Jean took up the tale, 'and cried out that he was a nobleman and that if he was to be executed on the gallows the next day, the commanders should let the minstrel sing some religious songs for him. I was brought to his room and bade to do so. When the time was ripe, I overpowered the guard and Audulf dressed in his clothes. We left him bound and gagged with Audulf's leg bindings. To Furnel's men, it looked as if Audulf was escorting me out. By the time they found their companion, we were well away.' He raised his cup in a wry toast. 'One day I'll compose a song about it.'

'I owe you a great debt for tonight,' Fulke said quietly. Maude had finally persuaded him to remove his armour. He still had not eaten, and there was a feverish glint of exhaustion in his eyes. Sleep was the greatest need of all, but he would not yield while Alain lay in a stupor.

Jean shrugged. 'I did it for friendship. You would have done as much for me. It would have been a sin to waste my skills and let a man die.'

'Amen to that,' declared Audulf, raising his cup.

Fulke paced to the great bed where Alain lay, and Audulf joined him. 'Is he going to wake up?' the knight asked.

Fulke did not miss the note of anguish in Audulf's voice despite the man's striving for neutrality. Audulf and Alain had been bosom companions since small boyhood. The bond of brother to brother was strong with the thread of blood, but the bond of friend was perhaps stronger still because it was of choice. 'He has to,' Fulke said. 'If not for his own sake, then for everyone else's.'

'He will be all right, by and by,' Maude said. 'Indeed, it might even be possible to rouse him if you shake him, but the drubbing he has taken, he needs the peace.' She raised a warning forefinger. 'When he does rouse, he will have a terrible headache and will likely be very sick. It is best if you leave him for now.'

Audulf nodded, reassured if not entirely convinced. Maude took Fulke's arm. 'I have had a hot tub prepared for you in the kitchens and I have told the maids to make you a pallet beside Alain so that you can be within reach. Come,' she said. 'I can see you are almost sleepwalking.'

He did not consciously yield, but let her lead him out of the room and under a covered wooden walkway to the kitchens. A cauldron simmered over a banked fire and there was a steaming bathtub to one side. Through exhaustion as thick and heavy as a pile of woollen blankets he was aware of Maude helping to undress him, of stepping into a tub so hot that it almost scalded his flesh, and then, as he grew accustomed to the heat, of the lapping, exquisite comfort. Maude rubbed his knotted shoulders and, as she worked, the aching band across his forehead eased slightly. She gave him an infusion of willow bark to cushion the pain of his bruises and anointed them with a soothing balm. The tension had been a scaffold, keeping him on his feet. Now, beneath Maude's ministrations, it was demolished and weariness tumbled down on him.

When he left the tub she rubbed him down with a large linen towel and helped him dress in a clean tunic and chausses. Everything became a blur. He had no recollection of returning to his chamber, nor of lying down on the pallet she had made up for him. The darkness took him like a mother and enfolded him in dark, comforting arms.

He woke deep in the night to the sound of a child's crying and a woman softly hushing it. Disoriented, he blinked, not knowing where he was. Memory slotted reluctantly into place from what seemed a far distance. He heard the murmur of voices and sat up. His bruises made him stiff and he turned his head awkwardly in search of the sounds. His brothers were all asleep on pallets arranged around the room. Maude was seated at the side of the great bed, a gurgling Hawise in her arms, and Alain was propped up against the bolsters, his eyes open and lucid. As Fulke stared, Alain managed a weak smile.

CHAPTER 29

Palace of Aber, Wales,
August 1203

'Another daughter,' Fulke replied to Llewelyn's enquiry. 'Born on Midsummer's Eve and christened Jonetta for Maude's mother.' He was here at the Welsh court to perform his obligatory days of feudal service to the Welsh Prince.

'Midsummer's Eve?' Llewelyn gave him a sidelong look.

Fulke twitched his shoulders. 'Yes, I know, the feast of St John and damnable timing,' he said wryly.

'But Maude and the babe are safe and well, or you would not be here.'

Fulke grimaced and took a drink from the cup of mead that Llewelyn had offered him. Eight months ago, Llewellyn's common-law wife Tangwystl had died in childbirth, long enough to dull the edge of Llewelyn's guilt and pain, but the subject remained touchy. 'Yes, sire, both are well.'

Maude had begun her labour at dawn and they had been kindling the evening bonfires when she was delivered. His apprehension had been turning to fear when the midwives placed the damp, howling bundle in his arms. 'I did not care whose feast it was, nor that the child was another girl,' he said quietly, 'only that they should live. I am sorry for your bereavement. If it had been me, I would have gone mad.'

Llewelyn drank his own mead and glanced around the sun-washed walls of the great hall. 'I did and I pray you never have to know such grief.' A harshness entered his voice. 'When she died, I rode a good hunting horse into the ground for no more reason than my own rage.'

'I am sorry, sire,' Fulke murmured, ill at ease. He did not think that the words existed that would comfort Llewelyn.

'Don't be, Fulke.' Llewelyn's mouth curved in a bleak smile. 'If Tangwystl was my heart, then Wales is my soul. I may have lost the one, but I still have the other and I intend to keep it.'

He paced to the hall doorway and looked out on an arch of August-blue sky. Fulke followed him, but held a slight distance, giving him space if not privacy.

Llewelyn looked over his shoulder. 'I have had several marriage offers,' he said. 'Men desiring to console my grief and consolidate their position by offering me their sisters and daughters.' He clenched his fist on the iron-studded oak door.

Fulke made a sound of polite enquiry.

'From Scotland, from the Manx King, from other Welsh princes and marcher lords, including Ranulf of Chester.' Llewelyn's mouth twisted bitterly. 'Do you not wish to join them, Fulke? Offer me one of yours?'

Fulke did not know whether to feel pity, anger, or take the remark as a form of backhanded flattery. 'I know that men frequently find husbands for their daughters while the infants are still in the cradle, but I am not one of them, my lord,' he said in a tone that, although neutral, conveyed reproach.

Llewelyn cleared his throat. 'Pay me no heed. I spoke out of my own ill temper, and I owe you better than that. Your daughters deserve better too.'

Llewelyn left him, making it clear that he desired

solitude. Fulke went to finish his mead and watch the clouds chase each other across the sun as it burned down towards the straits of Mon. His daughters. He tried to imagine them as grown young women, ripe for marriage, but the thought sent such a pang through him that he dismissed it with a shake of his head.

Behind him, he was aware of the bulk of the mountains, Eryri, the natural castles that kept the Normans out of Wales. Wild, beautiful, forbidding. Him on one side, Maude on the other. Watching Ivo tease and cajole a Welsh girl in the shadow of the stable wall, he felt a frisson of Llewelyn's loneliness and it was too much.

It was a wild, November day and Maude had opted to remain in the warm, well-appointed bedchamber above the hall with her embroidery. She was embellishing Fulke's feast-day tunic of blue wool with a border design of running wolves. It was painstaking work, but the finished result was worth it as she could tell from the length already completed.

Needle suspended, she paused to rest her eyes and studied her daughters who were playing on a large square of stitched sheepskins near the bed under Barbette's close supervision.

Hawise, at almost two, was a robust child with Fulke's eyes and a profusion of auburn curls. She was sturdy rather than graceful, but quick of movement and temper. Five-month-old Jonetta was a pea from an entirely different pod: placid, swift to smile, indolent and easily placated. What hair she possessed was FitzWarin black. She had beautiful feathery eyebrows and eyes that were turning from the kitten blue of birth to a lucent agate-hazel.

Maude's gaze softened. Her love for them was so strong that sometimes it almost brought tears to her eyes. She would remember her childhood and her own mother's weary indifference, and she promised herself that never would her daughters suffer for want of affection.

The curtain rattled on its pole and Fulke entered the chamber, his hair windblown and his stride energetic, as if imbued with the motion of the blustery weather. In a twinkling of legs, Hawise was off the rug and at his side, clinging to his chausses and clamouring to be lifted. Jonetta rolled over and squealed at him, showing her two new teeth.

Maude laughed. 'I am reminded of your jousting days, when women would throw themselves at you without shame,' she declared as he lifted Hawise into the crook of his right arm and bent to scoop the baby into his left.

He grinned. 'You kept a tally then?'

Maude pretended to put her nose in the air.

'I still have your ribbon in my pouch,' he said. 'The one Theobald forced you to give to me. You do not know how much it irked me that the only woman I wanted was the one who kept herself aloof.'

Maude's face flooded with warmth. 'And now that you have me?'

He gave a playful shrug. 'I do not know. Certainly it has not eased the wanting one whit.'

Her blush deepened and her glance flickered to Barbette who was pretending great interest in the fleece she was spinning. Maude thought about sending her out. It would not be the first time they had scandalised the household by drawing the bed curtains at midday.

Hawise had been fiddling with the ties on Fulke's cloak. Now her small fingers found the package tucked inside the wool.

'What's that?' Maude asked, seeing the edge of it as their daughter tried unsuccessfully to wrest it free.

Fulke shifted his grip on the baby and reached awkwardly

into his cloak. 'A letter from your father,' he said. 'The messenger's wetting his throat in the hall.'

'My father?' Maude repeated. Leaving her embroidery frame, all thoughts of dalliance flown from her mind, she came to him and took the package. Her father's seal, impressed in red wax, secured its privacy. She turned it over in her hands as gingerly as if it contained a snake. He seldom wrote, although he had sent a christening gift of a silver cup at Jonetta's birth and an exhortation to Maude to do her duty and bear a son next time. 'Did the messenger say what it's about?'

Fulke shook his head. 'You know your father. It's more than any servant's life is worth to ask his business.' He swung the girls in his arms until they shrieked, then sat down with them on the rug and drew them into his lap. 'You won't know unless you open it,' he said with a shrewd glance.

Gnawing her underlip, Maude broke the seal. Her father's writing was an untidy, barely legible scrawl. That he could read and write owed more to his determination not to rely on a scribe rather than to any desire to be educated. He had only seen fit to give her the power of literacy to increase her worth in the marriage market.

Frowning, she scanned the lines, rereading them to make sure that she had understood.

'Well?' Fulke said. 'What does he want?'

'It's a wedding invitation,' she said in a slightly stunned voice. 'He's getting married.'

Fulke stared at her. She held out the letter to him. 'To Juliana de Rie.'

Fulke took the vellum sheet. 'Do you know her?' His eyes narrowed in concentration as he tried to decipher the lines.

Maude shook her head. 'Only what he says, that she's Thomas de Rie's widow.'

Fulke snorted. 'Likely she's rich and of child-bearing age.' He read further down the page, pulling it close, holding it away. 'The wedding's at Christmastide,' he deciphered at last and, passing the letter back, rubbed his jaw. 'Do you want to go?'

Maude thought of the reasons to stay at home: the discomfort of travelling the roads in winter; the danger from John and his minions; the tepid relationship between herself and her father. Weighed against them were the burdens of guilt and family obligation – and curiosity concerning her new stepmother. She hesitated. The answer to Fulke's question was both yes and no.

'It would be politic to do so,' she said at last. 'Even if I have quarrelled with him in the past, I am still of his flesh, and he has never set eyes on his granddaughters. In truth, I do not want to go, but I feel I must.'

Fulke nodded. 'Politic – and there you have it in a nutshell, sweetheart. There are bound to be some powerful barons present, and it never does any harm to mingle with them. It's a foolish man who burns all his old bridges without building new ones – as Hubert Walter is always lecturing me,' he added with a grimace.

'A foolish woman too.' Her smile was pensive. 'I wonder if I will like my stepmother.'

Juliana de Rie was nothing as Maude had imagined. She was perhaps about thirty years old, a woman of diminutive stature with straight brown hair, heavy-lidded blue eyes and ordinary features. Her voice was quiet, her manner unassuming, but certainly not brow-beaten. Nor was she particularly in awe of her bluff, overbearing husband.

'Your father likes to think that his bite is as frightening as his bark, but it is not true.' She smiled at Maude as the women sorted through the wedding gifts on the day following the marriage. The men were out hunting the forests of Wharfedale, hoping to bring fresh venison to the table.

Maude looked at a collection of silver-gilt goblets that had been a gift from Earl Ranulf of Chester. Her reflection was distorted in the surface until it was no more than a blur of coloured shapes. 'Even so, it is not pleasant to be on the receiving end,' she replied and thought of her father's greeting on their arrival.

He had kissed her on either cheek, embraced Fulke and scrutinised his granddaughters with a critical eye, remarking that red-haired girls were less favourably regarded in the marriage market because the colour was indicative of a hot and unruly nature. Then he had berated her for producing female children instead of the necessary male heir. Fulke had replied in a tone of deadly calm that Hawise's red curls made her all the more precious since they were a reminder of her grandmother and that, sons or daughters, he valued his children on their merits, not their sex. Her father had given a disparaging grunt, but mercifully said nothing more.

Juliana clucked her tongue. 'He does it because he thinks that to praise or show pleasure is weak. He is a very proud man, your father.' She folded her arms and considered Maude. 'I think perhaps he is a little afraid of you also.'

'Of me!' Maude raised her head from the goblet's reflection and gazed at her stepmother in astonishment. 'Whatever gives you that impression!'

'The way he speaks to you, the way he circles you from a distance without approaching too close. And the way he looks at you when you are unaware. I think he can hardly believe he has begotten you.'

Maude gave a mirthless laugh. 'Indeed, that is true!'

'Do not be so awkward,' Juliana said impatiently. 'He is daunted by your beauty.'

Maude stared at her.

'Oh, come now. You must have seen your reflection in a gazing glass, the envious looks cast by other women. The way men follow you with their eyes.'

'I pay such things small heed,' Maude said stiffly. 'Besides, I have neither the time nor the inclination to stare in a gazing glass or notice men other than my husband.'

Juliana ignored the rebuke. Instead, her rather thin lips twitched in amusement. 'With a husband like yours, small wonder,' she said, then brought herself back to the subject in hand. 'By all accounts your mother was a beauty too, and some men are afraid of such women. They feel they do not have the strength to hold on to them, except by "keeping them in their place".' Juliana smoothed her hand over a bolt of wine-red silk that had been a wedding gift from Fulke and Maude. 'One of the reasons for his interest in marrying me, apart from the suitability of my dower, is that I am no beauty. He can look at me across a room and not feel intimidated.'

'I intimidate my father?' Maude's voice rose. When she saw some of the other women guests glancing her way, she ducked her head and lowered her tone. 'How can you say that?' she hissed. 'All my life he has tried to intimidate me!'

'You are not listening,' Juliana said impatiently, her own voice low but equally as vehement. She gestured at Maude. 'Look at you. Strong, wilful, the kind of looks to dazzle men's eyes. Your husband is a rebel, an outlaw, and one of the most talked-about and secretly admired men in the country. Of course your father is intimidated. And because it is unmanly to show weakness he blusters and belittles you.'

'So it is my fault,' Maude said, her face setting like stone.

'No, of course not, it is his, the fool.' Juliana gave an exasperated shake of her head as if dealing with a dull-witted child. 'Perhaps he will never come to terms with it. He is not the kind of man to look inside himself and make changes. But if you know his reasons, then perhaps you will find it in your heart to be more forgiving.'

Maude swallowed. 'As you say, my mother was beautiful,' she said bitterly. 'He used to beat her and belittle her in front of everyone. I was ignored because I was a girl child and not the longed-for son. I cannot do as you suggest. It is too late, and I have learned not to shoulder the blame for the weaknesses of others.'

Juliana eyed her sombrely and Maude felt that she had to say something more. She was never going to be fond of Juliana, but that did not mean they had to be on bad terms. 'I wish you both well of this marriage,' she said. 'Although perhaps you will understand if I am not a frequent visitor.'

'Yes, I understand, although I am sorry.' Juliana sighed and folded her hands in the hanging sleeves of her blue wool wedding gown. 'A rich man's widow is never a widow for long – as you have cause to know yourself. The match may seem strange to you, but I believe I can live in amity with your father, and he is comfortable with me, whatever has happened in the past.' She gave a little shrug. 'Some marriages are disasters from the beginning; some burn like fire; and others are as comfortable as an old pair of shoes.' She gave a small, introverted smile. 'I count myself most fortunate to have the last.'

From the corner of her eye, Maude saw Hawise reaching to the tail of Lady de Vesci's snappy little lap dog. By the time Maude had dived to the rescue of both, and laughed about the near incident with the other women guests, the moment of intimacy had passed and Chester's wife, the Countess Clemence, was engaged in conversation with Juliana. Maude tried to imagine marriage to her father being as comfortable as an old pair of shoes and gave up.

However, it was easy to equate herself and Fulke with the image of fire.

The forest of Wharfedale reminded Fulke of Wales with its wild, deep greenery, the fern-clad chasms and gullies of rushing white water and outcrops of lichened rock. Wolves still roamed in its heart and the wild boar was not as rare as it had become in the south. It was King John's forest, but Robert le Vavasour had the right to hunt and take game within its bounds, a privilege recently granted by John on his return from Normandy.

'I was in two minds whether or not to invite you to my nuptials,' said le Vavasour as the huntsmen paused between trails to dine on bread, spiced ham and small chicken pasties washed down with watered wine. The dogs milled around the kennel-keepers, the alaunts and wolf-hounds standing as tall as ponies, the terriers, wiry and red of coat, snuffing at shin height.

Fulke shrugged and bit into a pasty. 'In truth I was in two minds whether or not to attend. With King John back in England, it would have been safer to remain at Whittington.'

'Then why didn't you?'

Fulke eyed his father-in-law. There was the faintest hint of Maude in the straight line of his nose and the set of his jaw. 'For Maude's sake,' he said. 'Because you are her father.' He chewed and swallowed. 'And sometimes you have to take risks.' He glanced across the clearing towards two men who had just arrived and were dismounting from their horses: Ranulf of Chester slim, dark-haired and Fulke's own age; de Vesci a little older, florid-faced with a petulant crease between his brows. Men with whom he had much in common. John had seduced and slept with de Vesci's wife to the Baron's fury and chagrin. Chester was a neighbour;

his sister had once been betrothed to Llewelyn and Fulke had set about courting his friendship.

'You will not conduct rebellious talk under my roof,' le Vavasour warned sharply.

Fulke reached for another pasty. The hunt had made him ravenous and they were very good, just the right blend of spices to meat. 'Weddings are traditional places to discuss politics and cement alliances, as well you know,' he said. 'If you invited me here, it is because you desire a foot in either camp.' He licked his fingers. 'Don't worry. I won't talk treason behind your back. It would not be good manners and, whatever your opinion of me, I do have a certain sense of decorum.' He helped himself to a third pie.

'If you had a sense of decorum, FitzWarin,' Chester said, joining them, 'then you'd leave some of those pasties for others.'

'All's fair in love and war where these are concerned, my lord.'

Chester grinned and seated himself at Fulke's side, resting his spine against the rough bark of an ancient oak. 'Do you say the same about our King?' He took two pasties, tossing one to de Vesci who remained standing.

Fulke shrugged. 'I say nothing beyond what has already been said. I hold Whittington of Prince Llewelyn now.'

De Vesci looked at Fulke. 'Are you not afraid that someone here will hand you over to John for a mess of silver? You are outside your own territory and there is a price on your head.'

'Of course I am afraid, but more for my family than myself.' Fulke took a gulp of watered wine. 'But if I paid heed to that fear, it would stifle me. I watch my back; I heed my instincts.' He raised an eyebrow at the three men. 'I make alliances with those I trust, or whose interests run with mine.' He knew that Chester had a pact with

Llewelyn. He also knew, however, that Chester was loyal to John, and the Earl's dealings were concerned with securing his own borders rather than striking out in rebellion against the King. De Vesci had a grudge against John, was unlikely to do the King any favours, but he was not yet an open rebel. His father-in-law Fulke trusted after a fashion. Le Vavasour was forthright, arrogant, bigoted and frequently insufferable, but he did have his own peculiar code of scruples. If he intended giving Fulke to John for a payment of silver, he would announce it loudly and do it openly, not through the postern door of his own wedding feast.

'But still, it is dangerous for you to be abroad with John back in the country,' said de Vesci. He put Fulke in mind of a terrier, snapping and dodging, looking for an area into which he could sink his teeth.

'I agree, but I have gone too far down the road to turn back.'

Chester rubbed his neat black beard thoughtfully. 'If you were willing, I could speak to John on your behalf – broker a truce between you. You need the security of the King's peace. He needs experienced fighting men.'

Fulke grimaced. 'You would be treading old ground. Hubert Walter has tried before and been refused in the shortest of terms. Besides, I hold Whittington for Llewelyn and I would rather serve him as a liege lord than John.' When Chester said nothing Fulke gave him a look through narrowed lids. 'What makes you think that I would be willing to negotiate?'

Chester arched one eyebrow. 'Common sense,' he said. 'Self-preservation. At some point, the King must either negotiate or fight with Llewelyn. Welsh dominance is always at its height when a ruler is occupied elsewhere in his kingdom. Once John turns his gaze on Wales, Llewelyn will be wise to retreat behind his mountains.' He gestured between himself and Fulke. 'We both know that Llewelyn is the better man, just as we both know that John has superior resources. If you are caught in a border war, then God help you. All that will be left of Whittington is a smoking ruin.'

Fulke reddened beneath the Earl's scrutiny and jumped abruptly to his feet.

'I am sorry, but it is true,' Chester continued relentlessly. 'And I would be no kind of friend or neighbour if I did not point it out.'

'Then why did you agree a pact with Llewelyn?' Fulke challenged.

Chester sighed. 'Because it was sound policy to do so. Because keeping a Welsh dragon from my door is just as important as serving an Angevin leopard.'

Frustrated, Fulke swept his black hair off his brow. 'John is in the throes of losing Normandy and Anjou to France,' he said. 'It may be that he will lose England too.'

Chester quietly shook his head, underlining the fact that he thought Fulke was clutching at straws. 'John may be many things, but a fool is not one of them.'

Le Vavasour had been watching the exchange in shrewd silence. Now he rose to his feet and dusted crumbs from his hunting tunic. 'I would think seriously on what my lord Chester says,' he told Fulke. 'At least let him speak to the King on your behalf. John cannot afford to ignore the word of one of his greatest earls, especially if it is added to the opinion of Hubert Walter.'

Fulke gazed at his father-by-marriage. Robert le Vavasour did not speak out of concern for either him or Maude, but out of anxiety for his own lands and privileges. This right of free warren, for example. And who could blame him? A man with the ability to tread the thin line between the factions and not put a foot wrong would reap a fruitful harvest.

'I need to think on what you have said.' Fulke went to untether his courser's reins from the branch around which they were wrapped. The horse champed on the bit and butted at him, seeking a tid-bit. Fulke rubbed its soft, pink-snipped nose. 'Once I played a game of chess with John.' He looked round at the others. 'Doubtless you all know the tale, it's common knowledge. We were boys and he was angry drunk, wanted a scapegoat, someone to trample. I wouldn't let him trample me. He and I, we are still playing that game of chess. He wants the satisfaction of triumph and I will never give it to him while there is breath in my body and my heart still beats. He knows it; so do I.'

The hunt resumed, the men chasing their prey through dappled sunshadow, the horn blowing its trespass into the deepest, most secret parts of the forest. Usually Fulke enjoyed the exhilaration of the chase, the powerful feel of the horse beneath him, the twist and turn of manoeuvring between trees and through bramble-clad undergrowth. But as they hounded their quarry, a fine, eight-tined stag, through the forest, he found that his heart was bursting with the deer's, rather than singing a hunter's paean to the joy of the kill.

A week after the wedding, Fulke and Maude set out for Whittington and, at the Earl's invitation, broke their journey at Chester. Ranulf still wanted to persuade Fulke to make his peace with John.

'Let him grant me my hereditary due and I will do him homage,' Fulke said with the grim determination of oft-repeated rote. 'But not until then.'

Maude enjoyed the sojourn at Chester. The wedding and the celebrations afterwards had been an ordeal that she wanted to forget. She was glad that she had attended her father's nuptials, but relieved that the duty was over. Juliana might be able to see the good in le Vavasour's nature, but Maude's view of her father was tainted by the past and she could not regard him with affection or any sense of empathy. Certainly she had been surprised by the way he seemed to warm and relax when Juliana was near, the expression of a well-fed cat settling on his features. Smiling and solicitous, Juliana was swift to attend to his comfort, hanging on his words as if they were pearls of the utmost wisdom, and doing his bidding as if it were a genuine pleasure. Maude had felt slightly nauseated, but she had recognised how well they suited each other. A pair of comfortable shoes, as Juliana said.

Fulke laughed aloud when she told him of the comparison her stepmother had made. 'I would not like to wear either one,' he declared with mirth as they lay in bed on their first night in Chester's great keep. 'I'm sure that one or the other will find a pebble at the end of their toes.' Outside a heavy snow was falling, but they had the heat of their bodies to keep them warm, and coverlets of lined fur.

'You would rather play with fire?' Maude flicked back her hair and rose on her elbows to look at him. The dim glow of the night candle emphasised the declivity between her breasts.

'What?'

'She said that some marriages burned like fire – but that old shoes were better.'

Fulke grinned. 'Not from where I'm looking,' he said.

By the morning the snow was piled as high as Fulke's waist and any thoughts of journeying on were curtailed. He and Maude indulged in a silly snowball fight which became a free for all with half the castle joining in. Indoors they played merels and fox and geese, hoodman blind and hot cockles, sporting with abandon like children, aware that this was a rare and magical respite from the knife-edge on which they lived.

Fulke took Maude around Chester's thriving booths and stalls. She waited patiently for him, feet quietly freezing as he enthused over swords and helms, spurs and horse harness, and he tucked his hands beneath his arms, made vapour patterns with his breath and tried not to let his eyes glaze over as she chose hair ribbons and small feminine fripperies for the bower.

The morning after their expedition around the town, the weather began to thaw and, on rising, Maude was sick.

Fulke eyed her as she staggered back from the garderobe, heavy-eyed and wan. He knew the signs by now and was filled with a mingling of anxiety and pleasure. Anxiety because he feared for Maude's wellbeing, pleasure at a masculine sense of virility and the hope that this time she might bear a son for Whittington.

Maude pulled a face at his scrutiny. 'I ate too many honey comfits yesterday at that sweetmeat stall by the west wall.' She clambered back into bed and swallowing, closed her eyes.

'Liar,' he said lightly and ran his hand over the slight curve of her belly. 'When will the new child be born?'

She shrugged. 'Likely it was conceived under my father's roof, so the autumn I would hazard.' Her voice took on a slightly aggrieved note. 'If it is a boy, he will claim all the credit for urging me to my duty, and if it is a girl, I will be to blame.'

'If he opens his mouth,' Fulke growled, 'I swear I will cut out his tongue and tack it to my whetstone. The credit or blame is mine. I own responsibility full measure.'

A smile softened her lips and her eyes opened, green and clear, drawing him in. 'I will hold you to that,' she said.

'But still, you cannot start a fire without striking a spark on a steel.'

They kissed tenderly for a moment, and then Maude drew away. Her nose wrinkled mischievously. 'Since you acknowledge your blame, you had best find Barbette and send her for dry oatcakes and mead, else I shall be abed and puking until compline.'

Earl Ranulf's wife Clemence proved to be convivial company and she and Maude spent many hours in the bower gossiping over their embroidery and weaving while the men took themselves off to look at horses and live-stock, or hunt game with hawks and hounds.

In Clemence of Chester, Maude found a kindred spirit, bright, eager and strong-willed. They shared similar tastes and opinions and although there was a gulf of power between Fulke and Ranulf, their husbands were men cast in the same mould. Indeed, the women had so much in common that their friendship developed a depth far beyond the short span of its existence.

A new style of gown was becoming popular: a sleeve-less, full tunic with loose armholes that was worn over a tight-sleeved underdress. It was a boon for women in preg-nancy. Maude expressed interest and Clemence immedi-ately had her sempstresses fashion one for her in soft, blue linen trimmed with matching braid.

'I do not believe I will ever use one of these gowns for such a purpose,' Clemence sighed as Maude tried on the finished garment and declared that it was ideal. 'You are more fortunate than you know to have the joy of children.'

Turning, Maude saw Clemence gazing wistfully at the two small girls, the baby robed in a smock, Hawise in a green tunic that was a miniature replica of adult garb. The child's auburn curls were caught back in a braid ribbon, exposing the delicate nape of neck, rounded cheek and sweeping eyelashes.

'Surely such a gift may yet be granted to you,' Maude said in a tone of gentle concern. 'You have not been married to your lord for long.'

Clemence shrugged. 'Almost four years. How long were you wedded to yours before you conceived?'

The answer being a week, Maude said nothing.

'Ranulf was married to Constance of Brittany before me and there was no issue from their marriage either,' she said. 'I doubt in my heart that it will ever fall my lot to mother a child, although daily I pray.'

'I am sorry,' Maude said softly, 'that must be a grief to you and your lord.' She ran her hand over the folds of blue linen and felt the slight swell of her fecund womb. 'I would be honoured to have you and Ranulf as godparents to my next child.'

'And I would be happy to oblige.' Clemence's soft grey eyes misted with tears of pleasure and pain. The women embraced. Not wanting to be left out, Hawise came to join in and Jonetta let out a protesting squeal. Laughing, tears running down her cheeks, Clemence swept the smaller infant into her arms and gave her a longing cuddle. And Maude realised how fortunate she was; that, whatever the obstacles of daily life, she still had everything she wanted.

CHAPTER 30

In the summer, Fulke and Maude attended another wedding, but this time unalloyed pleasure shared their sense of obligation. Barbette was to marry a young Welsh nobleman: the son of Madoc ap Rhys who had halted Fulke and his brothers on their first foray into Wales in search of Llewelyn.

Despite her advancing pregnancy, Maude insisted on escorting Barbette to the nuptials at Dolwyddelan Castle. After all, she declared, it was only mid July and the child was not due until late September.

They took two days over the fifty-mile journey, so that Maude was able to rest along the way. There was time to gaze at the grandeur of the Welsh scenery, the purple darkness of shadowed hills and the narrow cascades of white water cutting paths down the precipitous slopes of the mountains. It was not a gentle land, but it was beautiful and filled the mind with awe at God's creation.

Maude's new maid Gracia stared open-mouthed at the sight of the slopes of Moel Siabod lowering over the keep at Dolwyddelan. She had been born and raised on one of Hubert Walter's East Anglian manors and this was the first time that she had seen mountains.

Fulke was amused at her awe. 'The further you go, the higher they get,' he told her. 'The Welsh have a mountain called Yr Wyddfa that stands with its head in the clouds. Eryri they call it. The place of eagles.'

'I prefer Whittington,' Gracia said in her flat, forthright accent and scowled at the mountain as if she expected it to come tumbling down on her.

'I am glad to hear it,' Maude said. 'You won't be tempted to go off and leave me for a Welshman like Barbette then.' She gave her senior maid a smile to show that she was teasing.

The wedding was celebrated with joy and laughter, feasting and revelry. Three days later, Maude and Fulke set out again on the homeward journey to Whittington. It was an emotional farewell. Maude embraced Barbette and Barbette wept on Maude's neck. They had been close companions for eleven years, had grown together from girls into women and parting was a wrench.

'I will send word when the child is born,' Maude promised.

Barbette nodded and smiled through her tears. 'God speed you, my lady . . . my lord.' She reached up for Fulke to kiss her cheek.

The weather was kind and the roads firm. Fulke and Maude made good progress and it was only a little after midday when they stopped at Corwen to seek refreshment and rest the horses. Indeed, Maude was glad of the respite. For the last mile, she had been in discomfort with nagging backache and a heavy feeling in her loins but when Fulke asked her if she was all right, she nodded and forced a smile.

There was a hostelry in the settlement and they were served mead and yeasty golden ale with barley bread and ewes' milk cheese. They dined outside beneath the low-spreading branches of an apple tree in the garth. Maude was not particularly hungry but she made a token show of eating. Hawise, as usual, devoured her portion with almost masculine gusto and Jonetta nibbled daintily as if she had been receiving lessons in etiquette from the women of the court.

Fulke watched them with amusement. The princess and the peasant, he called them. Hawise left her father and clambered determinedly into her uncle Philip's lap. The match of hair colour and the family resemblance had led more than one person to think that she and her uncle were in fact father and daughter. 'Her appetite puts me in mind of Richard,' Philip grinned.

'Let us hope she never attains his girth,' Fulke said wryly. His two youngest brothers and Ivo were at Whittington, guarding its walls. Only Philip and William had accompanied him and Maude to the wedding. Given his bulk, Richard was a better custodian than he was a traveller and Ivo and Alain rubbed along well together.

Maude pressed her hands to her abdomen, tautly swollen beneath the concealing sweep of her blue surcoat. At least Richard's girth was spread around his body, she thought, and caught the landlord's eye on her again. He and his wife had been watching them covertly throughout the meal. At first Maude had thought that it was the natural reaction to having noble guests descend on them but now she was beginning to wonder. Even if their clothes were fine and the men made a show with their mail and weapons, the scrutiny was a little too close for comfort.

The wife murmured to her husband. He shook his head and abruptly returned to the alehouse. Arms folded ready for a fight, she followed him.

'Whoever says that men rule the roost is not a married man,' Fulke grinned. 'I would not wager on the poor soul's chances.'

'I would not wager on yours, either,' Maude said tartly.

Whatever the altercation taking place, there were no raised voices. Moments later, the wife emerged clutching a besom and proceeded to vigorously sweep the area before the alehouse door. There was no sign of the husband.

'Likely she's belaboured him to death,' Fulke commented.

'If she has, then he must have deserved it,' Maude snapped, feeling irritated.

'Men always do,' Fulke said ruefully.

The alewife ceased brooming, glanced over her shoulder into the dwelling, then walked briskly over to Fulke and his troop.

'My lord, you should know that there were armed men here earlier,' she said quickly, her Welsh accent running the words together. 'From their talk as I served them, they intended laying an ambush across the road about a mile from here. It might be better if you were to take another path.' Her gaze went from the two infants to Maude and her expression made Maude lay her hand protectively across her womb.

Fulke sat up, all trace of humour leaving his face. 'How many?' he demanded. 'How long ago?'

'More than an hour and at least a dozen of them,' the woman said. 'They were speaking of a party of travellers with small children amongst them whom they were expecting to come this way from Dolwyddelan. My husband says it is none of our business.' She darted a look towards the hostelry and then back to Fulke. 'Mayhap it isn't, but it would be for ever on my conscience if I let you ride on without warning you – for the babies' sake. I got two young grandchildren of my own, see, and my daughter's carrying again.'

'Thank you, mistress.' Fulke gave her a silver penny from

his pouch. At first she refused it, saying she had not told him for a price, but he insisted. 'For your grandchildren if not for you.' At last she accepted the coin, and returned to sweeping her spotless threshold over-vigorously, her lips compressed.

'Doubtless one has been tracking us and the others lying in wait,' Fulke said grimly. 'They'll put themselves between us and Whittington and spring an ambush at some likely place.'

'We can take them,' William said with a fierce gesture. 'There are fifteen of us.'

'Fifteen fighting men,' Fulke nodded, 'two laden pack-horses, two women, one of them great with child, and two infants.'

'They could stay behind.' William jerked his chin at the hostelry.

'With men to guard them, of course,' Fulke said, 'which would bring our numbers down. And do not say there is no need for a guard. It would be worth any man's while to take my wife and daughters captive.'

William scowled and gnawed at his thumbnail.

'Take Stephen and Ralf and ride scout for me,' Fulke said. 'I need to know their whereabouts and movements . . . and who they are.'

Maude watched William and his companions mount up and ride off. Suddenly she felt very close to tears. Her back was hurting abominably and all she wanted was a quiet haven where she could lie down and rest without worrying about danger or pursuit. For the nonce, it was a prospect as distant as the moon.

Fulke laid his hand over hers and squeezed her fingers. Then he rose and went to fetch their horses. She watched him, her heart aching with love and fear.

* * *

Instead of taking the road to Llangollen and an evening's rest, Fulke led them north-east along the Afon Morwynion. Maude gritted her teeth as her mount bumped along the narrow track. The dull ache in her back had become a sawing pain. She told herself that it would go away if she ignored it. She sang songs to the girls and rocked Jonetta in her arms to stop her from grizzling. Her womb tightened like a drum, and the pains grew steadily worse, causing her to bite her lower lip and grip the reins with whitening knuckles.

A horseman came galloping up fast from behind. Fulke's hand tensed on his sword hilt as the sound of hooves came closer, then relaxed as he recognised Ralf Gras.

'What news?' he demanded, drawing his horse round.

'They've gone to ground in a thicket off the Llangollen road, my lord,' Ralf announced, his eyes gleaming beneath the banded browline of his helm. 'And they're being led by Henry Furnel and Gwyn FitzMorys.'

Fulke swore softly, although it was no less than he had expected. Any opportunity they got they would try and bring him down. He looked narrowly at Ralf. 'Where's William?'

The knight's gaze shifted from Fulke's. He cleared his throat. 'He thought that a few spare horses would not go astray, so to speak, my lord. He says he will join you with them at Whittington on the morrow.'

Fulke groaned. 'He will never change,' he said to Maude. 'He doesn't just spy on them and come away, he steals their horses.'

Maude had small interest in William for the nonce. 'How much farther must we travel before we're safe?' she asked distractedly as she rubbed her back.

His eyes sharpened. 'What's wrong?'

'Nothing. I'm just saddle-weary and the child is pressing against my spine.'

He continued to look at her and she wished she had not spoken as she saw his anxiety deepen. 'We'll head for the grange at Carreg-y-nant,' he said. 'Then on the morrow we can double back to Whittington. It isn't far.' He took Jonetta from her, bounced her a couple of times to make her laugh, and then handed her to Gracia.

The name of the grange meant nothing to Maude, and she knew that 'not far' to Fulke, who was accustomed to riding at a pace twice as fast as this, could be an interminable distance to her.

The party set off again, but within a quarter of a mile, Maude knew that she could not go on. The pain in her belly was becoming deep and unbearable. As her mount picked its way along the riverbank, it stumbled slightly on a hidden mouse hole and Maude was unable to catch her cry in time.

Fulke swung round from the head of the troop and was immediately at her side. 'What is it?'

The contraction tore through her and, for a moment, she could do nothing but cling to the reins, blind of anything but the pain. 'The baby,' she gasped as her womb relaxed, briefly releasing her. 'I am in travail!'

Fulke looked at her in horror. She saw him struggle with panic and even through her predicament felt a moment of bleak humour. He could fight his way out of anything, but a woman in childbirth was enough to turn him as pale as whey.

'Carreg-y-nant is less than five miles,' he said.

'You might as well say five thousand miles, it is too far.' She set her teeth as her belly tightened again.

'But the girls took more than half a day to be born. Can you not wait?'

Maude would have laughed had she not been in such

extremity. 'I can wait,' she gasped with a last thread of reason before the pain tore into her, 'but the baby will not.' As if in confirmation, at the height of the contraction, she felt a strange rending within her body and suddenly her gown, her saddle and the horse were soaked in birthing fluid as her waters broke.

Fulke swore blasphemously. Dismounting, he thrust the reins at one of the other knights. 'Take the men aside,' he said. 'Make a fire and boil some water from the river.' Turning to Maude, he lifted her gently from the saddle.

She heard him speaking to Gracia, was dimly aware of being carried to the waterside and laid down on a blanket.

'No,' she panted, 'save the blanket. You'll need it later.'

Fulke removed it. Gracia pushed up Maude's soaked skirts and looked at Fulke. 'Kneel behind her and hold her, my lord. She has no birthing stool so you must suffice. It is not seemly, but there is no help for it.'

Through the redness of pain, Maude was aware of him doing as Gracia instructed him. She felt the support of his arms, the power of his body bracing hers. She put her hands behind her, sought him and gripped for dear life.

Gracia was no midwife, but at least as the eldest of ten siblings she had attended at a birth before and knew what had to be done. However, both of Maude's girls had been born at their allotted time in a warm chamber with many attendants. This one was coming two months early into a rough wilderness and, if not stillborn, would likely die within hours of birth.

The urge to push was overwhelming. Pain squeezed her loins and she screamed through her teeth. Behind her, Fulke was rigid as she gripped him.

'Jesu,' he said shakily, trying for humour and failing. 'It's worse than a battle.'

'It is a battle!' Maude groaned. A woman's battle that men rarely got to see, with no ransoms taken, no mercy for the weak.

She cried out as another contraction surged over her.

'Push!' cried Gracia, peering between Maude's parted knees. 'I can see the head!'

Maude swore, her shriek rising like a vixen's and her nails digging into Fulke's flesh, branding his forearms with deep half-moons. Tears of effort, anger, and pain ran down her face.

'Why is Mama screaming?' demanded Hawise's high, frightened little voice from the place where the men were making camp. Someone gave a soothing murmur.

Maude bit down on her lower lip. Now she was not even permitted the relief of a scream. The next contraction rose and surged with the violence of a wave at high tide.

'Push!' urge Fulke and Gracia. She imprisoned her voice in her throat and concentrated on releasing the child from her womb. It came in a sudden, hot, slippery gush and a thin wail filled her hearing. Alive then, she thought, as she slumped against Fulke, gasping with effort.

'A boy,' Gracia declared tremulously as she uncurled the cord from between the baby's legs. 'You have a son.'

Compared to the state of her daughters at birth, Maude was shocked at how scrawny and small this new addition was. His wail was weak and querulous with a slight hiccup between breaths.

'He looks like a skinned coney,' Fulke said, and taking the blanket Maude had bidden him save, wrapped the baby in one of its corners. The wails quieted to snuffles. Father and son considered each other nervously.

'If I might have your knife, my lord, I can cut the cord,' Gracia said.

In a daze, Fulke handed her the weapon. The maid probed beneath the blanket and snicked off and tied the cord.

Fulke returned the infant to Maude. She took him gingerly. He was so light, so small. It was indeed like handling a skinned coney. 'He ought to be christened,' she said and swallowed against the tightness in her throat. 'If he . . . if he dies, I want it to be in the grace of God.'

'He's not going to die,' Fulke said forcefully, as if the strength of his voice would make a fact out of uncertainty.

Gracia bit her lip. 'There is no priest, my lady, and I do not have the dispensation of a midwife.'

'I want him christened . . .' Maude's voice cracked. It was the most and least she could do for him. She drew him close, pressing him to her body warmth. He was covered in a waxy grey substance that made him look as pale as a corpse. Tears of exhaustion blinded her eyes. Her womb contracted painfully and, between her legs, she felt the slither of the afterbirth.

'Roger de Walton was trained for the priesthood, but he never took his vows,' Fulke said. 'He is the nearest we have to a priest.' He left the women and approached the fire, returning moments later with the young knight in question. Rather clumsily, de Walton took the baby in his arms whilst Fulke filled a drinking horn with water from the river.

'How is he to be named?' de Walton asked, worried lines furrowing beneath his mop of blond hair. He looked like a man holding a pig's bladder balloon that might burst at any moment.

'After his father,' Maude whispered.

Fulke nodded and gestured to de Walton.

The baby's wail became a fractious roar of sheer indignation as the cold river water was trickled over his forehead. Roger de Walton rather self-consciously murmured the words of baptism and bundled the baby back into Fulke's arms.

'With a yell like that, he's going to cling to life,' Fulke reassured Maude. 'Look at him, he's strong.'

She heard the pleasure and pride in his voice. The power of the baby's cry and the fact of his baptism had calmed her fear. She knew that she must have miscalculated the time of his conception, for although he was small and scrawny, he was still too vigorous for a child born two months early. To Fulke, she managed the semblance of a smile, but only a semblance. They were still under threat of pursuit in the middle of nowhere and several miles from shelter. Out of the deepest part of the woods perhaps, but not yet clear of the trees. And she was so tired, so very tired.

On the morrow, they brought Maude in slow stages to the grange at Carreg-y-nant. They made her a litter out of cut saplings and blankets for it would have been too dangerous for her to ride astride a horse or even sit pillion. Although her labour had been swift, she had bled considerably and was as pale as bleached linen, her eyes dark-ringed and bruised with exhaustion. It was impossible that she would be able to move on to Whittington the next day as Fulke had intended. Looking at her as they rode through the gateway of the grange, he was filled with apprehension. She had been very quiet for most of the journey, responding to his attempts at conversation in monosyllables. The baby had suckled from her a couple of times and although scrawny and small, was tenaciously holding his own. It was Maude who worried him. He could not bear to think of losing her, but he knew that women often died bearing children, if not at the birth, then soon after.

At the grange, the monks furnished Maude with a pallet and a brazier in their tiny guest room. She was given hot mead to drink and a nourishing mutton and barley broth, after which she fed the baby again and fell asleep.

'She will recover, my lord,' Gracia reassured Fulke softly as he stared down at his sleeping wife and unconsciously gnawed on his thumb knuckle. 'Peace and sleep are what she needs.'

'Peace!' Fulke uttered the word as if it were a curse. 'I doubt she's had that since the day Theobald died.' He cast his gaze around the stark, limewashed walls, bare of all decoration save a simple wooden crucifix and an aumbry cupboard with a studded wooden door. There was peace for her here. The monks' only visitors were shepherds. It was a rare occasion indeed when they received travellers such as themselves. 'If I have killed her—' He spoke very low and broke off abruptly.

'In God's name, Fulke, stop belabouring your conscience,' Maude muttered without opening her eyes and scarcely moving her lips. 'It would take more than you to kill me. I knew what I wanted when I consented to wed you. Now go away, you great ox, I'm trying to sleep.'

'See,' said Gracia, spreading her hands palm upwards.

Reassured, if not at ease, Fulke leaned over to kiss his wife's brow and returned to his men in the small refectory, discovering that in his absence more guests had arrived. If the place had been full before, now it was as packed as a barrel of herrings, the glint of the mail like so many fish scales enhancing the comparison, not counting the nose-catching aroma of so many unwashed, hard-travelled bodies.

'My lord.' Fulke bent the knee as Prince Llewelyn shouldered forwards, a mead cup in his hand.

'Get up,' Llewelyn said. 'There's little enough room to breathe, let alone to kneel.'

'No, my lord.' Fulke wondered with a sinking heart if he and his troop would have to move out to accommodate the Prince's entourage. Maude would have to stay. However brave she was, she was not fit to travel even another hundred yards.

'Fortunate then that we are only tarrying to dine and water the horses,' Llewelyn said. 'I understand that congratulations on the birth of a son are in order, Fulke.'

'Thank you, my lord.' Fulke did not miss the slightly wary expression in the other man's eyes. Something was either afoot or amiss.

'Maude is well?'

'Tired, my lord. The birth was swift but rough. The child came early, but he has taken no harm from it.'

'I am glad to hear it.' Llewelyn's tone was stilted and Fulke began to feel decidedly uneasy.

'It is fortunate that I have seen you,' Llewelyn continued, thus confirming Fulke's concern. 'It saves me the task of summoning you. Certain changes have come about and we need to discuss them.' He glanced around the packed room, grimaced, and pushed his way to the door. 'Outside might be better,' he said.

With deep misgiving, Fulke followed him. 'Certain changes' had an ominous ring about it.

The air was fresh and clear compared to the sweaty fug inside the small refectory, although there was still a pungent smell of sheep from a pen of ewes gathered for milking.

Llewelyn drew a deep breath, held it, and exhaled. 'You know that I have been negotiating to marry with Rhannult of Man?' he asked.

'Yes, my lord.' Fulke could see nothing to affect him in Llewelyn taking the Manx King's daughter to wife.

'Well, it has come to naught because I have received a better offer – better for me that is, and one that I cannot refuse even if it does take a very long spoon to sup with the devil.'

The short hairs at Fulke's nape began to prickle. John, he thought, and stopped himself short. It was impossible. John did not have any unmarried sisters and his wife was too young to breed. But he did have a bastard daughter.

'King John has offered me his daughter Joanna to wife,' Llewelyn said. 'She is of an age to marry and he has offered me the lordship of Ellesmere as her dowry. The wedding is to take place in Shrewsbury before Martinmas.'

'Congratulations, my lord,' Fulke said woodenly, the words emerging as if they were choking him just by being in his mouth. Llewelyn was right. It was an opportunity that no sane man would refuse whatever the length of spoon required. It would mean security for Llewelyn and for Wales. It would also mean his own position at Whittington would become untenable.

Llewelyn looked at him sombrely. 'I have been in negotiation with John's representatives for some months. There is to be a truce between us. I will not raid his lands and he will not seek to encroach on Wales – for the moment at least.'

Fulke swallowed. 'And what of me, my lord? I do not suppose that I will be a welcome guest at your nuptials?'

Llewelyn sighed. 'I wish I had better news for you,' he said, 'but I do not. John has asked me not to succour his enemies at my court. He even said that he would increase the size of his daughter's dower if I were to present him with your body.'

The prickling at Fulke's nape extended down his spine. 'I have served you with loyalty, my lord,' he said, his voice husky with the effort of controlling his fury. 'I have given you my trust. Are you going to betray that loyalty and trust at the whim of a man who has never kept a promise in his life?'

'Fulke, it is not as simple as that.' Llewelyn made a gesture that asked for understanding. 'I would hope to keep the loyalty and trust of my men because I return that loyalty in full measure. But this is different. I cannot afford to sacrifice the peace and security of my entire people for one marcher holding that lies on the very edges of my jurisdiction – for one man.'

'I thought you were different,' Fulke said, the bitterness swelling and surging in his chest.

'I am. I refused to arrest or kill you. I told John that it was his dispute, not mine. But beyond that, I cannot help you. My hands are tied.'

'By John,' Fulke snarled. 'You speak of freedom and then you hold out your wrists to be bound!'

'Fulke, enough,' Llewelyn warned. 'I have given you my reasons and they are sound. Raging will avail you nothing.'

'The same as serving you then. Nothing.' Fulke bared his teeth. 'I need not renounce my fealty since you have renounced yours in my enemy's favour. You will live to regret it, my lord. You are not entering into an alliance, but a trap!'

One of Llewelyn's attendants opened the door and looked out, obviously drawn to investigate by the sound of raised voices. Fulke swallowed and held his fists down at his sides. He could feel the pressure of his sword hilt against the inside of his wrist and it was all he could do not to draw the weapon.

'You are right,' he said in a voice gritty with the effort of control. 'You have given your reasons, and raging avails me nothing.' He strode away, putting distance between himself and the temptation to lash out.

In one fell swoop, he had again become a landless outlaw. Llewelyn would yield Whittington to John and the Welsh mountains would no longer offer succour and safety. He would have to take to living in the forests again and relying on the support of sympathisers to his cause, or enemies of John. There was a bitter taste at the back of his throat. On the day that his son was born, he had lost his patrimony. The fight had to begin all over again, and he had no stomach for it.

It was a full hour later that he felt sufficiently calm to return to the guest house and join Maude and the children. She was asleep on her pallet, her braided hair gleaming on the coarse, bracken-stuffed pillow. The swaddled baby lay at her side in a makeshift cradle fashioned from a willow gardening basket. Fulke gazed upon his wife's face, the dark shadows beneath her eyes, the delicacy of brow and cheekbone and jaw. He knew that most of that delicacy was false, that Maude was usually as robust as a horse, but the bearing of three infants in swift succession and the circumstances of her last travail had drained her strength. How could he ask her to live an outlaw's life now when she needed rest and comfort? How could he trail three small children in his wake, the youngest a baby prematurely born? It would be irresponsible and likely end in tragedy. He gnawed on his thumbnail, already bitten down to the quick, and turning from the bed looked at his two daughters who were playing in a corner with Gracia. He had engendered them. Now it was his responsibility to give them a proper life.

CHAPTER 31

Canterbury, November 1204

The light was fading and Maude could no longer see to set the tiny stitches into the new smock she was sewing for the baby. She had strung a row of painted wooden beads across the cradle and he was hitting them with his fists and gurgling with the pleasure of accomplishment. Maude could almost feel his tenacity. Despite the handicap of being born on a wild Welsh riverbank, her son had thrived. There was still very little meat on him compared to her daughters at this stage in their lives, but he was formidably strong. Like rawhide, she thought with a half-smile, rather than plump, soft leather. She was not unduly concerned about his health, for he had the voracious appetite of a wolf cub.

The great pity was that Fulke could not see his son's development, the small daily changes that marked an evolving and strong-willed individual. The girls were growing and changing too, although not as swiftly as the baby. Like her brother, Jonetta was too young to miss her father, but it had affected Hawise. Not a day passed without her demanding to know when her papa was returning. She had become naughty and attention-seeking, and seemed to think that her father's absence was her tiny brother's fault because he had been born and then her papa had gone away. It was impossible to explain politics to a two-year-old, no matter how bright.

With a heavy sigh, Maude put her sewing aside and rose to close the shutters against the gathering dusk. The cathedral bells tolled the hour of vespers. For the last four months she had lived her life to their sound, counting the time, fixed in a limbo of waiting and wondering.

After Prince Llewelyn's declaration of his betrothal to John's daughter, Fulke had brought his family to the sanctuary of Canterbury and put them beneath Hubert Walter's wing, knowing that John would not dare touch them. Then he and his brothers had left England for exile in France: jousting, hiring their swords, spending the winter where John could not reach them. Maude had thought about crossing the Narrow Sea to join them, but it went no further than wishful thinking. A sea crossing at this time of year was always dangerous and never comfortable. She would have to leave the sanctuary of Canterbury to reach a port and would be game for capture. And the children were too small and vulnerable to risk such a journey. So she remained at the Archbishop's palace under the auspices of her former brother-by-marriage and waited.

Come the spring Fulke said he would return, but to what? An outlaw's life hounded from pillar to post? She bit her lip and drew the iron bolt across the shutters. Each time she thought in that direction, she was frightened by the uncertainty of the future. What was going to happen to them?

'Play with me, Mama,' Hawise demanded, tugging at Maude's dress. 'Play clapping.'

Maude had no inclination to do so, but for her daughter's sake she forced a smile and held up her palms so that the child could smack her own against them and chant a simple rhyme.

'Me too,' said Jonetta, toddling up.

'You're just a baby. Go away, I'm playing with Mama.' Hawise gave her sister a violent shove. Jonetta toppled over with a thump and set up a mighty howling – although more from shock than injury.

'Hawise, you wicked girl!' Maude shouted with exasperation as she reached to pick up and comfort Jonetta. The way Hawise flinched from the raised voice immediately added guilt to Maude's anger.

'I'm not wicked, I'm not!' Hawise stamped her feet in frightened defiance and her pale skin turned an alarming shade of beetroot. From the cradle, there came an indignant wail as the baby's voice joined the mélange. Gracia, whose hands had been occupied with some intricate braiding, dropped her work and hastened to scoop up the roaring infant. Her action increased the size of Hawise's rebellion to a full-blown tantrum that even King Henry in his heyday would have been hard-pressed to equal.

The door opened and Hubert Walter stood on its threshold, his expression one of pained astonishment. Clutching his hand was a little girl, her eyes huge as she took in the scene.

'I have come at a difficult time, Daughter,' Hubert said. 'I'll return later.' He began to turn away.

'Oh no, your grace, please come in,' Maude implored, grimacing at the prospect of being abandoned to the mercies of three screaming children and wishing she was the one who could walk away. Perhaps Fulke had known what he was doing in more ways than one.

The sight of the Archbishop and the other little girl took the force out of Hawise's tantrum. Her screams diminished, her colour eased, although she continued to cry and ran to press herself against her mother's skirts. Maude's free arm enfolded her in a tender if exasperated embrace.

'Celibacy does have its rewards,' Hubert observed dryly.

'So does motherhood,' Maude answered with a pained smile. She looked at the child Hubert had brought with him. She was obviously ill at ease, but stood her ground doggedly. Maude thought she must be about seven or eight years old. Her ash-brown hair was bound in two neat, shining plaits twined with red silk ribbons and she had a solemn, pointed face, dominated by wide eyes the grey-gold of coney fur. 'Who is this?' she asked.

Hubert glanced down at his charge and squeezed the small hand engulfed in his great paw. 'My cousin and ward, Clarice d'Auberville,' he said. 'She has but recently come into my charge after her father's death.'

Maude knew that he did not literally mean that the small girl was his cousin. The relationship would be at least once or twice removed. She remembered from her marriage to Theobald that he had had a girl cousin who was married to a d'Auberville. This could not be their daughter. The age gap was too great, but a granddaughter was likely. If she was in Hubert's care, then probably the mother was dead too. 'I am sorry to hear such sad news,' she murmured.

'She was not close to him, and her mother died in childbed four years ago,' Hubert said as if the girl was deaf. 'You know how it is in a great household when there is no mistress to rule it. She has spent her time with different nurses and the wives of her father's knights. Now she has come into my care and I have to find a niche to suit. While she is at Canterbury, I would ask of you the boon of caring for her.'

'You think me capable?' Maude asked wryly.

Hubert smiled. 'I know you are,' he said, sounding more confident than she would have been in his position.

Maude tilted her head. She felt deep sympathy for the child, whose circumstances sounded similar to her own as a girl. No mother and an indifferent father. 'Of course I will take her.' She smiled reassuringly at the little girl.

Hubert relinquished his grip on his charge and stooped to speak to her. 'This is Lady FitzWarin. You'll be staying with her for a while until more permanent arrangements are made for you.'

'Yes, your grace,' Clarice said, her childish treble aping the response of someone much older. She curtseyed to Maude, her manners beautiful. Maude ached for her, remembering herself as a child, weighed down by her grand-mother's lectures on propriety.

Satisfied, Hubert nodded and left, closing the door behind him.

There was a moment's silence. Before Maude could decide how to break it, Hawise leaped into the breach. One fist still clutched in her mother's skirts for safety, she took a step towards the newcomer.

'How old are you?' she demanded.

Clarice looked at her solemnly. 'I was eight at the feast of St Anne,' she said.

Hawise's mouth became a circle of awe and admiration and Maude fought not to smile. Hawise viewed adults as giants who could be either kind or cruel according to their whim and her behaviour. Older children, however, were worshipped because their position was not so far above her own. 'When I'm a big girl', was Hawise's constant refrain.

'I'm nearly four,' Hawise lied. 'Can you play clap?'

Within moments Clarice was seated on the rug of stitched sheepskins, playing a finger game with Hawise, all awkwardness forgotten. Hawise demanded; Clarice gave, her expression grave and sweet.

That first meeting set the tone of Clarice's presence in Maude's household. Gracia jestingly referred to the child as 'St Clarice' because of her unfailing good humour and patience. Unlike Hawise, whose moods were as volatile as her hair, Clarice was placid and gentle. She loved sewing and spinning. She adored the baby and playing big sister come mother to Hawise and Jonetta. Her clothes were never dishevelled or dirty, but, although fastidious, she was never prim. Maude sometimes wished that she would act more like a little girl of eight than a grown woman, but came to accept that it was Clarice's nature. She also began to love her and dreaded the day that Hubert would come and take her away when he sold her wardship or arranged her marriage. But she could not shut that love away. To deny affection to the child because of what might happen would be a sin, even though she knew that she was storing up heartache.

'When is Hawise's papa coming home?' Clarice asked her one raw morning in late February the following year. She and Maude were sitting companionably together at the embroidery frame in the window embrasure and Hawise and Jonetta were out with Gracia.

'When he can.' Maude forced steadiness into her voice. When indeed?

Clarice bent over the needlework and made several dainty stitches. 'Is he dead?' she asked.

'No, of course not!' Maude gasped and crossed herself. 'Whatever makes you say that?'

'When my mama died, they said that she had "gone away",' Clarice said. She set the needle precisely in the fabric and left it there. 'I waited and I waited for her to come back, but she never did because she was dead and no one would tell me about her.'

Her composure was such that Maude felt an over-whelming surge of pity and grief. She put her arm around the girl's narrow shoulders and drew her close. 'Hawise's papa quarrelled with King John and had to leave England,' she said. 'I promise you that he is still very much alive.'

Clarice nodded and pursed her lips. 'Then when is he coming back?' She slanted a challenging glance at Maude who realised that Clarice would not believe until she saw with her own eyes.

'I cannot be sure of that . . . I am going to be honest with you and say that I miss him and I only wish that I knew.' It sounded as if she was deluding herself. Maude swallowed and began sorting through the tapestry silks, but all the colours blurred and ran together before her eyes, making it impossible to find the colour that she needed.

A warm May breeze rattled the halyards and flapped the clewed sails of the vessels in the harbour at La Rochelle. Fulke watched a herring gull wheel overhead and then settle on the spar of a sleek galley.

'Get you to England in a day and night,' said the ship's captain, whose name was Mador. 'Swifter than a cormorant skimming the water.' He clapped his hands and rubbed them together whilst eyeing Fulke from shrewd, weather-seamed eyes. 'What do you say?'

Fulke considered the vessel. Any ship plying its trade across the Narrow Sea would do if he were being practical. That old wine hulk down the wharf, or the fishing galley with the red sail that had just put off a cargo of Kentish oysters. But Fulke did not feel like being practical. He wanted to make a noble gesture, the reason he was looking at the largest galley along the length of the moorings, her new, clinker-built hull gleaming and her prow decorated with ornate carving. If he were going home, it would be in style. He would not skulk ignominiously into some obscure harbour aboard a poxy little boat stinking of shellfish or stale wine. Of course, he could have sailed last week with Hubert Walter and the Bishop of Norwich, but it would have been on their terms and he had not been sure at the time that he wanted to accept them.

'I say that if we can agree a price I'll take her,' Fulke said.

They repaired to a wharfside tavern where they drank tart red wine and dined on hot fritters filled with goat's cheese. After some hard bargaining, a fee was agreed and half the money paid over.

'They say that prowess in the joust makes men rich,' Mador said as he tucked the pouch of money into his leather mariner's satchel. Between his lids, his eyes were glints of bright sea-blue.

'What makes you think we have been jousting?' Fulke asked.

'You wear it as plain as your clothes,' the ship's captain said. He nodded at William who had just joined them. 'Half your teeth missing at a young age and one ear resembling a lump of pease pudding. There's a man who takes risks with his body.'

William looked indignant.

'And you, my lord.' Mador gestured at Fulke. 'You have a mark high on your nose that has marred what was once fine and straight. Mayhap where a helm was forced back into your face?'

'A chessboard, actually,' Fulke said, touching the healed bone.

'Whatever.' The mariner shrugged. 'I know the look; I've seen it oft times in mercenaries before. God knows, I am one myself.' He drank a mouthful of wine. 'It is no coincidence they call outlaws wolf's heads. They bear the same hunger in their eyes as such beasts – lean and prowling and ready for the kill.'

'So now we are outlaws?'

Unconcernedly, Mador reached for a fritter and bit into it, hollowing his lips and blowing at the scalding heat of the cheese inside. "'Oo 'ell me,' he mumbled.

Fulke exchanged glances with William. He turned his cup on the board, and the dripped wine from its rim made a wet pattern on the scrubbed oak. 'My name is Fulke FitzWarin,' he said.

Mador managed to close his mouth on the fritter. 'Aye, I've heard of you.'

Fulke made a wry face. As usual, the ballads were doing the rounds of the taverns and winehouses.

'Heard you jousted in front of King Philip of France hisself.' Mador chewed noisily and swallowed. 'They say you defeated his champion and the King offered you lands and riches.'

'Not precisely.' Strange how tales enlarged with the telling, Fulke thought. He had indeed fought a French knight one to one under the eye of the King of France, and won, but there had been many such individual bouts. King Philip had sent one of his mercenary captains to offer Fulke a position, but the daily wage of a household knight, while generous, barely constituted lands and riches. Besides, even if offered, he would not have taken them for he had seen how fickle such gifts were. Philip was at war with John. Fulke could have had free rein to waste towns and villages throughout Normandy, but he had no stomach for such warfare.

Then Hubert Walter, John de Grey, William Marshal and Robert of Leicester had arrived at Philip's court to negotiate a truce between Philip and John. Hubert had exhorted Fulke to return to England and promised to do all within his power to end the quarrel between him and John. If only Fulke would surrender and mollify John's pride, Hubert would guarantee the restoration of Fulke's lands.

'Including Whittington?' Fulke had asked in a voice heavy with cynicism and distrust.

'Including Whittington,' Hubert had said as if his confidence was total. 'John needs experienced fighting men as never before. And he needs loyalty too. When you take an oath, you are not the kind to abandon it on a whim.'

Fulke had been flattered but not drawn in either by the air of certitude or the praise. It was not as simple as that, never had been, and trust was a coinage so adulterated as to be worthless. He had promised to think on the matter and Hubert had sailed home alone.

The sea captain's voice broke through his introspection. 'So you're returning to England with a laden purse?'

Fulke smiled without humour. 'You have the laden purse now,' he said. Nearby the tavern-keeper's three children were rolling like puppies. They were all girls, the eldest about seven, he reckoned, the youngest little more than two. He thought of his own daughters and ached at the memory of feeling little arms clinging tightly around his neck. Hawise with her bounce of red curls and incessant chatter. Jonetta with her solemn dark eyes and peeping smile. Their new brother, little more than a blanketed scrap in his arms when Fulke had bade his family farewell in Canterbury. Likely sitting up and crawling by now. And Maude. The thought of his wife sent a pang through him. She had borne the journey to Canterbury with stoicism even though she was not fit to travel. They had carried her on a litter and she had not complained. Not once, although he had seen the teeth marks in her lower lip where she had bitten down to avoid crying out. She had agreed with him that his leaving England for a while was for the best, had not clung and wept, but he had seen the effort it had taken and he was still haunted by the look in her eyes. He had sought oblivion in the bottom of a cup and in the brutal competition of the tourney field, but even through the drunkenness and the gut-surge of the fight, he had remained aware. The longing, the bitterness, the frustration had only increased.

'But why to England?' Mador demanded, refilling Fulke's cup and tilting more wine into his own. 'What is there for you in England?'

Fulke's eyelids tensed. 'The rest of my life,' he said bleakly. 'Or my death.'

CHAPTER 32

Fulke opened his eyes. He had been dreaming that he was on the deck of the ship and for a moment fancied that he could still hear the roar of the ocean and see the green swell parting beneath the surge of the ship's bows. The roar resolved itself into the surge of the wind through the trees of the Andreadswald and the green swell into the fluttering of new summer leaves. It was a little past dawn and the small clearing was filled with the smell of barley cakes sizzling in bacon fat as Richard turned them over a charcoal fire. Other members of the troop were grooming their mounts, breaking their fast, stretching their sleep-stiffened limbs.

Fulke rose and entered the trees to ease his bladder. It was two days since they had landed at a small cove along the Dover coastline. Sailing into the port itself would have been suicide for a Breton ship with outlaw passengers. They had spent the first night in a shepherd's hut on the Downs and the next day buying horses before setting out for Canterbury. The pilgrim road would have been the quickest, but also the most populated and therefore dangerous. Instead, they took to the smaller tracks and the deep shelter of the forests. Yesterday Fulke had sent a messenger to Hubert Walter, and now they waited.

Returning to the fire, Fulke speared one of Richard's

barley cakes on the point of his eating knife, and blew on the crisp brown crust. The camp was strangely quiet and after a moment he realised why.

'Where's Will?' he demanded. 'And where are Alain and Ivo?'

Richard kept his eyes on the greased iron of the frying pan as if it was of great fascination. 'They went hunting,' he said.

'Hunting?' Fulke said sharply. 'Where?'

Richard shrugged and looked uncomfortable. 'They did not say − just that they would bring some meat for the fire.'

Fulke cursed beneath his breath. Meat for the fire might mean hare, deer, or coney from a wild warren. It might also mean supplies from a raided barn − a risk they could not afford. 'Why did you not rouse me?'

'They said to let you sleep, that they would be back soon.'

'And you did as they bade you. Christ, have you no judgement of your own!' He glared at Richard, exasperated but knowing he should have expected as much. Richard was a follower, not a leader, and William's character could be overbearing.

'Fulke, it's nothing. They've gone hunting. They'll be back before we've struck camp.' Richard's brow furrowed. 'You take too much of a burden on your shoulders.'

'Because others have no notion of responsibility.' He ate the barley cake without tasting it and gave orders for the camp to be dismantled, one ear cocked for the sound of returning hoofbeats. Perhaps he was jumping at shadows that did not exist. What bedevilled him was knowing that the control was out of his hands and all he could do was wait, like a mother anxious about a child, or a wife pacing out the time between her husband's leaving and his return.

As a younger man, he had paid no heed, but he understood that anxiety now.

Richard was preparing to kick out the fire and Fulke was cinching his saddle girth when they heard muffled hoofbeats and the jingle of harness. Fulke turned to the sound, and even though he knew the guards he had posted would not let an enemy through, long instinct drew his hand to the hilt of his sword.

The colours of horses flickered through the leaf dapple: oak-brown, copper-chestnut and autumn-leaf dun. Harness winked in a flash of sunlight. So did armour and the tips of spears. Fulke drew his sword and his heart began to pound. Perhaps the guards had been ambushed and unable to sound a warning. He grabbed his shield from the tree against which it was leaning and thrust his arm through the leather straps, signalling his men to draw their weapons.

The first riders into the clearing were two knights wearing plain surcoats of blue linen over their mail. Because he was a warrior, Fulke's attention was first for them. The one on the near side wore an open face helm that revealed a portion of his narrow, handsome features.

'Jean?' With relief and pleasure, Fulke sheathed his sword.

'Never mind me, what about greeting your wife?' said de Rampaigne, twisting in the saddle to indicate the other riders.

Fulke followed Jean's pointing finger to the small chestnut cob in the midst of the soldiers and the figure sitting astride. It was not obviously a woman on first glance, for a brown, hooded cloak covered all overt signs of gender, but once his attention was fixed, he did not know how he could have been so blind.

'Maude!' Breathing the name, he strode to her. She kicked her feet free of the stirrups and came down into his arms, her own winding tightly around his neck. For a moment the world went away as he embraced her, his nose filling with the sweet herbal scent that she used to perfume her clothes. Sage and lavender and bergamot. The curves of her body, the pale sea-green of her eyes beckoning him to drown as they filled with tears. Everything he had missed and wanted.

A throat was loudly cleared and a voice said wryly, 'Delighted though I am to see such marital harmony, the conception of your fourth child should be a private matter, FitzWarin.'

Maude blushed. Fulke raised his lips from Maude's, and turned to bend his knee to Hubert Walter of Canterbury. The Archbishop was watching them from the back of his dappled mule with benign good humour.

'Your grace,' Fulke murmured.

'Get up. You can't help me from this nag in that position.'

Fulke hastened to aid Hubert from the mule. The saddle-cloth was emperor purple, stitched with small crosses in thread of gold and must have cost a fortune in itself. Hubert was wearing plain robes by his standards, with only a bare trimming of metallic braid and embroidery, but the linen of his vestments was of a heavy weight and fine weave. The Archbishop had always been a robust man, fond of his food but muscular beneath the flesh. Now that muscle tone was sagging and the flesh was taking rapid command. Hubert's breathing was stertorous as he flicked dust from his robes and leaned on his staff.

'Your children are safe at my manor of Malling,' Hubert wheezed. 'I thought it best to leave them there for the nonce. No one will dare to touch them beneath my juris-diction and, as Maude can attest, they are all flourishing.'

Fulke nodded. His cup would have run over if he could have seen them now, but he knew the limitations as well as Hubert. 'Thank you, your grace.'

'Hawise made this for you.' Maude produced a plaited loop of brightly coloured scraps of wool. Attached to it was a wooden cross fashioned of two oak twigs, the pieces bound together with strands of strong, red hair. 'She says you're to wear it around your neck.'

'Made me bless it too,' Hubert said gruffly. 'She has your will of iron.'

'She has mine,' Maude contradicted. 'Fulke is merely stubborn.' There was a tremor in her voice.

Fulke swallowed the ridiculous lump that came to his throat as he looked at the offering. Very carefully, he placed it around his neck. 'For this, if nothing else, I have to make my peace with John,' he said and, cradling the cross, looked at Hubert. 'Do you have tidings?'

Leaning on his staff, Hubert walked heavily to a nearby tree trunk and sat down in ponderous stages. 'My knees,' he said ruefully. Rubbing them, he regarded Fulke sombrely. 'The King says that if you come to him at Westminster and lay down your arms in surrender, he will deal with you leniently. If you continue to play the outlaw, then he will hunt you down like a wolf in the forest.'

'How leniently?' Fulke demanded.

Hubert Walter screwed up his face. 'He would not be drawn, but both Salisbury and Chester believe that he can be brought to see sense in restoring Whittington to you – as do I,' he added, spreading his hands to show the fleshy palms, criss-crossed by deeply imprinted lines.

'So, he has not been brought yet.' Fulke narrowed his lids.

'No, but he will.'

'You were confident that my father would have Whittington too,' Fulke said bitterly. 'You were confident that you would make a truce of Philip of France and it came to naught.'

Hubert Walter gave an exasperated sigh. 'And for that reason the King needs you as much as you need his pardon. Both of you must compromise.' Leaning forward, he emphasised the 'must' with a thump of his staff.

Fulke tightened his jaw. 'I will surrender to him, but I will not compromise on Whittington. That remains immovable. It was the reason that I turned outlaw. Let him give me what is rightly mine and I will serve him to the best of my ability all of my days. If not . . .' He shrugged and glanced down at the crude little cross between his fingers. 'If not, then what hope do either of us have? It's nigh on twenty years since he struck me with a chessboard and I rattled his skull against the wall in recompense. In God's name, Hubert, you must find an end to this for all our sakes.'

'That is what I am trying to do.' Hubert pinched the bridge of his nose and rubbed his lids with forefinger and thumb. 'If you will but attend the King at Westminster, I will guarantee your safety. So will William of Salisbury and Ranulf of Chester.'

Fulke frowned. He had lived so long without trusting that it was difficult to grasp an olive branch without fearing that it might turn into a snake. But then why else was he here?

'None of the other barons will lay a finger on you because whilst you might be a vicious thorn in John's side, you are not a threat to them. Indeed,' Hubert added with bleak humour, 'many of them sympathise with you. You are striking a blow for their interests as well as your own. The King cannot touch you lest it be with his hired men and you have proved yourself twice the worth of them. John needs you.'

'I will come,' Fulke said after a long pause. 'But only with my full complement of men and an escort provided by my guarantors.'

'As you wish.'

Fulke's eyelids tensed slightly at the soothing note he heard in Hubert Walter's tone. The Archbishop was a renowned diplomat and statesman, a manager and manipulator of men. It was one of the reasons he was so favoured by John. But behind Hubert the diplomat, Hubert the politician and Hubert the Archbishop, lay Hubert the brother of Theobald Walter. Fulke latched on to the thought.

'I doubt that you can give me "whatever I wish",' he said with a grim smile, 'but I do thank you for what you have done . . . for keeping my wife and children safe.' He squeezed Maude's waist.

'I could do no less for my brother's memory, and even an Archbishop must have a conscience tucked somewhere about him.' Hubert heaved to his feet. 'I leave it to you to escort your wife back to Malling. Jean will travel with you as my representative.'

Fulke inclined his head. 'Thank you, your grace.' Hubert was playing a delicate game. He had not actually said before witnesses that he was granting Fulke the succour of the manor, but the implication was there to be taken up. Kneeling, Fulke kissed the Archbishop's sapphire ring of office, then rose as a knight brought forward Hubert's glossy dappled mule.

Hubert rode away, his escort following, all save Jean de Rampaigne, who clasped Fulke's arm and slapped him on the back in camaraderie before going to greet Richard and Philip.

Fulke drew Maude into his arms again and rubbed his stubbled cheek against the tender softness of hers. 'I dare not hope,' he said. 'I shut the faintest glimmer from my mind lest it be no more than a false dawn. We have had too many of them, too many broken promises for me to lower my shield.'

At the sound of horses crashing through the under-growth, he snatched his recently sheathed sword from the scabbard. Maude clutched his arm in a reflexive gesture, but recovered herself and stepped back, leaving him room to move.

Ivo burst into the clearing at a ragged canter and slewed his lathered mount to a halt. Blood spidered from a deep cut on the back of his left hand. Behind him came Alain, his complexion the colour of whey.

'Will!' Ivo panted, leaning over the pommel. 'Will's been taken!'

Fulke's heart had been pounding hard in response to the threat of attack. Now it seemed to stop within him. He strode up to the horse and grabbed the bridle in his fist. 'What do you mean he's been taken?' he snarled.

A sheen of sweat glistened in the hollow of Ivo's throat as he swallowed. 'We were following a deer trail, thinking to bring down a hind, but we came upon a poacher instead, butchering his kill.'

'And?' Fulke's tone was like quenched steel.

Ivo bared his teeth in anguish. 'An ambush had been set for the poacher by the royal foresters, and we rode straight into it. They knew we were not legitimately in the forest, for we were not blowing our horns to tell of our presence and we were carrying bows. We should have run' – he gasped as Maude bound his wound with a strip of linen torn from her wimple – 'but you know Will.'

Fulke needed little imagination to see the scene for himself. It would not occur to William to retreat. Always, someone more responsible had to haul him away by the collar and Ivo and Alain were not of that ilk. He was furious. At William. At the men who had taken him. At the whole Godforsaken mess of fate.

'They'll hang him for a traitor,' Alain said hoarsely.

'You should have thought of that before you went adventuring,' Fulke said. His voice was husky with the effort of control and he spoke softly because once he raised it, he knew that the sheer volume of frustration and rage would fell every tree in the wood.

He turned to the staring, dismayed men. 'Saddle up,' he said with a terse sweep of his arm. 'We'll ride after them. Jean, will you do me the courtesy of returning my lady to Malling.'

'No,' Maude declared as Jean began to nod in agreement. 'I'm not returning without my husband.'

Fulke turned to her, his body as tense as a wound trebuchet. 'I will come to you as soon as I can, I swear.'

Maude laughed bleakly. 'If I had a penny for every time you have said those words to me, I would be the richest woman in the world. As it is, they beggar me!'

'Maude . . .' He held out his hand to her, not knowing if he intended to remonstrate or reconcile. 'Don't be awkward . . .'

She took a step away from him in what could be either a gesture of release or rejection. 'Go,' she said with glittering eyes. 'Go and save William from a bed of his own making, but remember, you make your own too, and this is the last time that I will lie in it and wait for you.'

Fulke could hear the hammering of blood in his ears, could feel the tension tighten within him until every nerve and sinew was whining with the effort it took not to break loose and lash out. He could sense the men watching him, waiting to see how he dealt with a woman who spoke so boldly.

'Jean.' He almost strangled on the word.

The knight nudged his horse forward. 'My lady, shall we go?' he said to Maude with polite neutrality.

With a narrow glare at Fulke, she stalked to her mare.

Refusing the aid of a boost into the saddle from Philip, she swung astride with the ease of a squire and gathered up the reins. Then without looking round, she turned the palfrey and rode out.

For an instant, Fulke stared after her, then, exhaling harshly, strode to his own mount. 'Come,' he said brusquely. 'We are wasting time that we do not have.'

John had sat on the bench throughout the morning, presiding over the court sessions of the forest hundred with unwaning concentration. Richard's love affair had been with the sword and the machinery of war — occupations that had drained the Angevin treasury to a husk. John's fascination was with the judicial process. How it could make and break, how it could be applied to create revenue and bring order, and how, in his own case, it could be manipulated and side-stepped to further his will.

This morning he had presided over several breaches of the law from the petty to the serious. Damage to property, thievery, murderer, abduction. The usual gamut. One foolish man had beseeched him for justice and been carried away screaming to face the gibbet. It might have been different had he asked for mercy instead. Salvation or damnation: it all came down to words.

John lightly brushed his beard with a beringed forefinger and signalled the next case to be brought before him.

'Caught in the great forest, poaching deer,' said the official as the bruised and beaten prisoner was ushered forward, the shackles clanking on his wrists. 'Won't give his name.' The official's tone implied that it didn't matter; this one was fodder for the gibbet.

John eyed the man, judging him to be in his early thirties. One eye was almost swollen shut. Dried blood was caked beneath his nose and joined the clotted mess of his split lip. He would not have been recognisable to his own mother, and yet John felt a glimmer of familiarity. It was the way the eyes held his in defiance, the knife-slash brows and heavy black hair. He knew those characteristics. No common peasant would return his look so boldly. No common peasant would wear a padded gambeson or sport such fine embroidery at the cuffs and hem of his tunic. John hunted his mind, searching thickets of memory until one sprang a reply like a startled quarry, and he began to smile.

'He might not give you his name, but I will,' he said, 'He is William FitzWarin, brother of Fulke, and a valuable capture indeed. Tell the men who caught him I will give them the same payment that I give to those who bring me the hides of wolves.'

'You'll gain nothing from having me,' William snarled and was immediately clubbed to his knees by the guard standing over him.

'Show more respect for your King!' the man warned.

'I'll give it where it's due,' William gasped, a bruise beginning to swell on his temple.

John gestured sharply to stop the soldier from clubbing William again. 'I want him alive,' he said and stroked his beard. 'For the moment.' He slanted a glance at William. 'It all depends on how much your brother values your life.'

'Fulke will never yield to you!'

'Then you will hang from a gibbet for outlawry and poaching the King's deer,' John said indifferently and waved his hand. 'Take him away.'

William of Salisbury, who had been witnessing the cases with John, cleared his throat. 'I understood from the Archbishop and Ranulf of Chester that you were going to negotiate an honourable agreement with FitzWarin,' he muttered. 'I thought it was understood that you were going to restore his lands in return for his expertise as a battle commander.'

John eyed his half-brother. 'I never said that I would, only that it was a possibility.' He looked at his fingernails. 'Now it is less of one because I have better means to bring FitzWarin to heel; I have a hostage.'

Salisbury frowned and looked discomforted. 'But men will not see the fine shade of meaning,' he protested. 'They will only believe that you have gone back on your word.'

'It is the difference between justice and mercy.' John shrugged. 'Men should know the boundaries and what they are truly asking for before they open their mouths.'

Salisbury beckoned a squire to bring him wine. 'Why can you not give FitzWarin the land he asks for? It is not as if it is the size of an earldom, and if he swears his loyalty, I know that he will abide by it.'

John said nothing. He rubbed his forefinger back and forth across the smooth cabochon sapphire in one of his rings.

'It's about that chess game when you were youths, isn't it? You still haven't forgiven him for that.'

'Why should I forgive him? He never apologised,' John said, and then, as he saw the look on Salisbury's face, waved an impatient arm. 'God's bones, of course it isn't just about that chess game. It's about everything that has happened since.'

'But there has to be an end somewhere. John, give him the land.'

'As a favour to you?'

'If you like, but to yourself also.'

John scowled. He was aware of a griping sensation in the pit of his belly that had nothing to do with his digestion. It was a feeling that had often been present in his young manhood as he watched the way men reacted to his brother Richard. Coeur de Lion. That said everything. Richard's courage; Richard's rugged golden beauty; the way his charisma alone could light up a room and inspire its occupants with hero worship. Fulke FitzWarin did not have a golden blaze about him, his magnetism was more subdued, like the gleam of steel, but it existed and men were drawn. John hated Fulke FitzWarin, but few others shared his sentiment. They hated him instead, calling him Softsword for the loss of Normandy, as before, as an adolescent, they had scathingly called him Lackland because he did not have an inheritance. Making laws, hearing common pleas, strengthening the administration meant nothing to barons who wanted a magnificent warlord on a destrier.

Fulke FitzWarin had the glamour of the tourneys about him, but what galled John most was knowing that if set to the task, Fulke could administer and account with thorough competence. John's gut was seething because he knew that Salisbury was right. He would be doing himself a favour by making peace, but he did not know if he could bring himself to do so.

'John?' Salisbury was leaning round to look at him, his indignant features, so much like their father's, screwed up in concern.

'The matter of FitzWarin is not open to negotiation,' John said tersely. 'Bring forward the next plea.'

'But—'

John glared. 'Not another word, Will, I'm warning you.'

Salisbury subsided, but John could tell from the tension in his half-brother's jaw that he was far from happy. He was fond of Will, would do more for him than most, but he was angered by Salisbury's determination to champion FitzWarin's cause.

'I am the King,' he said, the words emerging with force and containing a hint of petulance.

The presenting of the next prisoner did not quite drown out Salisbury's mutter, but John chose to ignore it. 'And a king is accountable for his deeds.'

The charcoal burner's coarse woollen robes chafed Fulke's skin and he suspected that he had picked up lice from the greasy cap. Charcoal dust smeared his face and hands and he carried a large iron fork – a weapon masquerading as the tool of his trade. The charcoal burner had been delighted to exchange his own garments for a fine linen shirt and woollen tunic edged with blue braid, not to mention a payment of a shilling for his load of charcoal and the hire of his donkey and cart.

Fulke clicked his tongue and led the cart towards the hunting lodge. Outside, a group was gathering for a day's sport. Greyhounds, lymes, brachs and alaunts milled in the courtyard, some held on leashes by kennel-keepers, others roaming free, their noses eagerly snuffling the ground. The bright rich garments of the riders proclaimed their nobility. Fulke's borrowed robe had once been leaf-green, but weathering and charcoal tending had reduced it to a murky shade of sludge.

Fulke saw John among the company, wearing royal purple on sapphire blue. His horse was a spirited dappled gelding and John was smiling as he wheeled the horse and spoke to William of Salisbury. The latter shook his head, fumbled in his pouch and handed something over. Salisbury had been gaming and losing again, Fulke thought, narrowing his eyes the better to focus. But then Salisbury had always allowed John to get away with cheating.

John signalled to the senior huntsman. Decked in forest hues of brown and green, a longbow and quiver at his shoulder, the man unslung a decorated horn to blow the advance. The dogs began to bell with excitement and the courtiers urged their mounts forwards. Fulke drew his cart to the side of the road and leaned on his fork as the King and his retainers set out to hunt.

Fortunately, the donkey was so old and placid that it was almost dead, and scarcely paid any heed to the tumult of dogs as they loped past. A wire-haired terrier investigated the delightful smell of Fulke's chausses and cocked its leg. Fulke restrained the urge to kick the little shitbag into the following week and maintained a patient expression on his charcoal-blackened features.

The nobles rode past. Doffing his cap, Fulke knelt, hiding his features by gazing at the ground. 'God save you, my lord King!' he cried, thinking that no one else would.

John was diverted by the shout, and pleased. 'And God save you!' he responded, reaching to his cloak.

There was a glitter and a gentle thud. The grey trotted on. Fulke stared at the ring brooch that had landed in the soft earth at his knees. It was made of silver, with the names of the three kings who had visited Jesus's birth engraved around its perimeter, a sure protection against the falling sickness. Fulke knew that John always had a couple of spare brooches pinned to his cloak for such occasions. Whatever his faults, no one could accuse the King of personal parsimony towards his lower subjects.

William of Salisbury had lingered behind to adjust his stirrup and as Fulke stood up, the brooch in his hand, their eyes met and recognition dawned in Salisbury's. The Earl shook his head in warning.

'You fool, what are you doing here?' he hissed. 'Do you not know how dangerous it is?'

'Would you not do the same for your brother?'

Salisbury glanced towards the hunting party. 'I am not sure that I would,' he said.

'Where's Will? How closely is he guarded?'

'You expect me to tell you?'

Fulke shrugged. 'I'll find out anyway.'

Salisbury grimaced and looked up the road to the riders as if by thought alone he could will himself back among their number. 'They're guarding him in one of the bailey stores near the kitchens,' he said. 'I cannot help you more.' Jerking on the reins, he spurred his mount to catch up with the others.

Fulke pinned the brooch on his ragged tunic where it shone with rich incongruity. 'You heard that?' he said.

The mound of charcoal moved slightly as if a mole was at work beneath. 'I heard,' came Philip's muffled voice. 'What was all that noise?'

'The King is going hunting.' Fulke went to the head of the cart and clicked his tongue to the reluctant donkey. 'There's never going to be a better moment.'

Fulke brought his cart of charcoal into the courtyard and, beneath the bored eyes of a couple of guards, took it round to the kitchen buildings. Charcoal was used to heat the braziers of the private rooms, but it also had its place in the kitchens where a steady heat was required within the fireboxes to cook sauces and more delicate dishes.

The servants were busy preparing food for the return of the hunting party. A huge picnic had been taken, but appetites were always made voracious by a day's sport. The guards sat down to watch the road and play a desultory game of dice. A woman brought them a jug of cider and a wooden platter of bread and cheese. One of the kitchen attendants gave Fulke a hot cheese fritter and filled his horn cup with ale.

'Where's Osbert today?' she asked. She folded her arms, obviously preparing to settle down and gossip.

Fulke mentally grimaced. 'Business elsewhere,' he said gruffly. 'I offered to take his place.' He took a large bite of the cheese fritter.

'What's your name then?'

'Warin,' he said around the mouthful and changed the subject. 'Saw the King a moment ago, riding out to hunt. He gave me this brooch.' As he showed her the trinket, his gaze flickered towards a low, thatched shed a little to one side of the kitchen buildings. A guard dozed on a bench outside the door, leaning on his spear. 'Got something important to protect in there – the royal treasure?' He grinned to show that he was jesting and finishing the fritter, wiped his greasy hands on his tunic.

She shook her head. 'No, only a poacher. The foresters caught him yester morn south of here.'

'There'll be a hanging then?'

She shrugged. 'They say he's important.'

'Oh?' Fulke took a drink of ale.

She shrugged. 'Supposed to be a dangerous outlaw, but he didn't look very dangerous to me after the way the foresters had beaten him.'

Someone called from inside the kitchens and she went back inside. Fulke breathed out on a soft oath of relief at her going and anxiety for William. He hoped his brother was not so badly beaten that he would be a hindrance. He gazed past the door through which she had disappeared and down the muddy track leading past the pig pens and midden to a wattle-gated back entrance.

The guards on the main entrance were still facing outwards and absorbed in their game. He heard their good-natured laughter and prayed that he would not have to kill them.

'You can come out,' he said, returning to the cart, 'but keep your heads low. There's a guard to disarm outside the prison, and two on the gate whose lives will be sweeter for not seeing us.'

The mountain of charcoal moved again, revealing a layer

of horse blankets and, beneath them, half a dozen of Fulke's men, armed to the teeth.

Fulke rapidly outlined his plans to the men crouched in the cart. 'There's a back entrance down by the midden pit and the pig pens. We'll use that to leave.' Instructions given, he strolled over to the dozing guard.

'I hear you've got a prisoner, friend,' he said conversationally.

'What's it to you?' The soldier raised his head and Fulke's black, dusty hand clamped down across his nose and mouth, shutting off air. There was a brief struggle. Philip arrived, whipped the keys from the guard's belt and unlocked the prison door. Then, as Fulke dragged the guard inside, Philip snatched the man's helm off his head, jammed it on his own, and sat down on the three-legged stool, leaned on his spear and pretended to snooze. It would not fool the other guards if they came close, but as long as they did not look too hard, the deception would hold.

Fulke kicked the door shut and dragged the struggling guard's eating knife from his belt. 'I will kill you if I must,' he warned, laying the edge against the man's unprotected throat. 'And that would be a shame for your wife and children when you do not have to die.'

The man continued to struggle but with less conviction. Fulke nicked him with the dagger. 'A last warning,' he said. The door opened again and Alain slipped inside. With speed and silence, he unlatched the guard's belt and bound his arms with it. A gag was made of the man's rolled-up leg bindings and tied securely in place.

William, who had been sitting on the bed bench and staring in astonishment as wide as his blackened eyes would permit, rose to his feet and extended his shackled wrists. 'Get me out of these damned things!' he said hoarsely.

While Alain sat on the guard, Fulke took the keys from

the floor where they had fallen in the scuffle and unlocked the wrist shackles. These he secured around the guard's ankles.

'I knew you would come,' William cried. 'I knew you would.'

'I wouldn't have had to if you had shown more sense in the first place,' Fulke snapped. 'Are you fit to travel?' The sight of his brother's bruised and battered visage filled him with fury at the perpetrators and worry at William's physical condition.

'Fit or not, I'll endure,' William nodded. A fierce grin split his injured lip so that it began to trickle with blood. 'Can you imagine John's face when he finds out that you've broken me from his clutches?'

'Is that all it is to you? Another daring escapade?' Fulke glared at William. 'Another deed to show that I can run rings around John if I choose?'

William reddened 'I—'

'Christ, Will, you speak like a child, not a grown man. It is time that you discovered responsibility.'

'I don't need lectures from you,' William snarled.

'God alone knows what you do need then. You said you knew I would come. Perhaps I should have left you to stew!'

'Go on then!' William made a vigorous throwing gesture, exposing a chafed ring of skin on his wrist. 'Leave me. Let John hang me and then you won't have to bother!'

'This isn't the time to quarrel,' Alain pleaded urgently. 'We shouldn't delay.'

With an effort, Fulke swallowed the anger, frustration and relief that were roiling within him and nodded brusquely. 'You're right, of course,' he said. He looked at William, at the swimming glitter in the other man's eyes, at the red banners of pride and chagrin on either high cheekbone. 'Come here.' He set his arm around William's shoulders and engulfed him in a hard hug. William hesitated briefly and then responded, his hands gripping Fulke's grimy tunic until the knuckles showed white. A stifled sob wrenched in his throat.

'Enough,' Fulke said after a moment, his own voice ragged with emotion. 'It's a long road home.'

It was a full hour before the alarm was raised. At first, the gate guards paid no attention when they saw that the stool outside the prisoner's hut was empty. Since the kitchens were close by, they thought their companion had slipped away to eat and drink, or perhaps to relieve himself. By the time they did go to investigate, it was too late and their quarry long gone.

John returned from his hunt in a jovial mood. They had brought down a ten-point stag after a fierce chase. Two hounds had been killed, but not favourite ones and they were easily replaced. The other dogs had been rewarded by the deer's heart and liver and entrails, steaming and red from the slit body cavity. Four bearers now carried the kill, its hooves bound to an ash spear shaft, its mighty antlers bobbing at the ground with each stride the men took. John was flicking bits of broken twig from his mount's mane and animatedly discussing the day's sport with Salisbury as they rode into the courtyard.

'The best chase in a long while,' he said. 'I thought he was going to evade us in that thicket.'

Salisbury murmured agreement, his manner slightly pre-occupied. He looked rapidly around the compound and rubbed the back of his neck.

A groom came to take the horse and John swung down from the saddle with exuberance. He clapped his hands and rubbed them together, revealing the pleasure and energy that the hunt had germinated. Salisbury dismounted beside him and handed his reins to his squire. John looked almost fondly at his brother. A flagon of wine chilled in the well and a game of dice would occupy them before the dinner hour, and afterwards, there was the prospect of hunting more tender prey among the women who had accompanied the court to the hunting lodge.

It was not until he entered the long hall that he realised something was amiss. Two knights hovered near the threshold, looking miserable. A serjeant was on his knees, head bowed in more than just deference. John knew abject fear when he saw it and some of his pleasure evaporated.

'You have something to say, Jacques?' he said to the more senior knight who had been in his service for several years.

The man swallowed and his look darted between John and Salisbury, before settling on the floor rushes. 'Sire, William FitzWarin has escaped.'

John stared. 'What?'

In hesitant detail, the knight told him what had happened, now and then asking the serjeant to corroborate.

'A charcoal burner?' John's complexion whitened. In his mind's eye, he saw the ragged individual standing at the side of the road. He heard the shout and saw himself casting a silver brooch to the bastard.

'We saw no harm in him. Who searches a charcoal burner, especially when he is expected?'

'The whoreson,' John whispered. 'The stinking, gutter-begotten, leprous whoreson!' Shoving the knight aside, kicking the serjeant in the ribs so that the kneeling man lost his balance and fell, John strode down the hall. Rage made tiny spots dance before his eyes. His chest rose and fell so rapidly that soon it became hard to breathe and he staggered. Checkmate. It was checkmate. Once more, he had been punched in his royal dignity.

Salisbury caught his arm and drew him to a bench. A snap of his fingers summoned wine. 'Now you see why you need him fighting for you, not against you,' he said vehemently. 'Think of the damage he could do to the French. It's not as if he has lands in Normandy to safeguard. He would be as good as, if not better than your mercenaries.'

John closed his eyes and swallowed. Salisbury pressed a goblet into the King's hand. John set his lips to the cool silver-gilt rim and gulped the rich, dark Burgundy. Sometimes he had a fancy that he was drinking his own blood.

'John?' Salisbury leaned over him.

He opened his eyes and gazed into the worried, lugubrious features of his brother. There was not a single thread of Angevin temper or selfishness in William's nature – a source of both relief and exasperation to John.

'Very well,' he said and drained the wine to the sediment. 'Let FitzWarin be pardoned for his crimes against me and let his lands be reinstated. But I do this for love of you, Will, not for love of FitzWarin.'

The look of delight in Salisbury's eyes made John want to kick him. The words were out, but never had he wanted to revoke them more because it was admitting defeat. Even knowing that FitzWarin would have to kneel before him in surrender was no consolation. He raised his hand as Salisbury's joy prepared to translate itself in speech. 'Do not say anything else. You have pushed me to drink from a cup I would rather abjure. Do not make me renege on my acceptance.'

Salisbury's face fell. 'But you will sign a safe conduct if I have the scribes write it?'

John rose to his feet. 'What's wrong, Will, don't you trust me?'

'You know I do.'

'Either you're a fool, or you're lying.' The expression on Salisbury's face immediately filled John with guilt and a fresh spurt of anger. 'Oh, do what you will, you purblind fool,' he snarled. 'Write what you want and I'll put my seal to it.' Snatching the flagon from the squire, he stalked away in the direction of his private chamber.

Salisbury bit his lip and stared after him. He even took several paces forward, then stopped himself. Turning on his heel, he went to order the scribes, then went in search of reliable witnesses.

CHAPTER 33

It was late dusk when the raiding party arrived at Malling. The Archbishop's manor was smugly prosperous, with tile shingles on the roof instead of thatch or wood, and a frame of seasoned oak. The honey-scented glow of beeswax candles beckoned from the open shutters, as did an appetising savoury aroma.

As the horses clattered into the yard and the men began dismounting, the manor's heavy, iron-studded door swung open. There was a sudden blur of motion and a little girl with a sheaf of hair like red silk shot down the wedge of light and launched herself at Fulke.

'Papa, Papa!' she shrieked.

Fulke grunted as the child struck his thighs with what seemed like the weight of a small pony. Stooping, he swung her up into his arms and the cool, silky tips of her hair whipped his face. He did not have the heart to scold her for running in amongst so many horses. Lessons could come later. The clutch of her arms almost choked him but he didn't care.

'Mama said Uncle Will had got into trouble again and you had to rescue him.'

'Well I did, and now I'm here,' Fulke said, studiously avoiding William's gaze. There were not enough grooms and each man was taking care of his own horse. Without a word, William took Fulke's and led it away with his own.

'Are you going to stay for ever and ever?'

Fulke winced. He could not risk staying at Malling above a couple of days. The hunt would be on again with a vengeance and he could not afford to abuse Hubert Walter's hospitality. 'No one can stay in a place for ever, sweetheart,' he fenced. 'I am here now. That is what matters. Now, where's your mother?'

Maude appeared in the doorway. Her right hand held Jonetta's, keeping the infant from toddling after her sister, and her left cradled the baby. Her expression was impassive, but when Fulke strode over, the mask crumbled and her face contorted as she struggled not to weep in front of her children.

'You have William safe?' Her voice choked and wobbled.

He nodded. 'No harm to any of us. I'm sorry, sweetheart, I had to go.'

'I know you did.' She compressed her lips. 'I'm . . . I'm sorry for what I said. But I meant it,' she added fiercely, 'every word. I cannot bear to dwell in this living widowhood.' Then she was in his arms and they were embracing awkwardly around their children. Need burned up in Fulke, stronger than love, more powerful than just desire. Had they been alone he would have taken her straight to bed and submerged himself. As it was, because of duty and propriety and external concerns, he drew away with a shuddering gasp and wiped his eyes on the cuff of his gambeson. Maude looked at him with luminous eyes, her complexion flushed and her breathing swift.

Hawise tugged at his chausses, demanding attention. He squeezed her plump little hand and, drawing another deep breath, bade her lead him inside the manor like the grownup girl she was.

The main room had a central hearth with enough space

for two cauldrons and a griddle. Oak benches were neatly arranged around the perimeter of the chamber and the walls were decorated with bright embroideries, the colours overlaid by a patina of red and gold light from candle flame and hearth fire. He felt the sense of domestic order and neatness flow over him, bringing with it a powerful evocation of nostalgia. He was like a traveller returning to something that he had once experienced and loved, knowing that he could not stay.

His absorption in the hall's atmosphere was disturbed by the arrival of another child, a cup of wine carried carefully in her hands. She had ash-brown hair divided into two neat, glossy braids, wide-set grey-gold eyes and a sweet expression. Dipping him a respectful curtsey without spilling a drop, she presented him with the cup.

Fulke accepted it from her with a word of thanks and a puzzled look at Maude who was watching the girl with affection.

'This is Clarice d'Auberville, the Archbishop's ward,' she said. 'She became part of our household in Canterbury before Hubert brought us to Malling and I hope he will let her stay, since she is kin of a sort.'

Fulke raised his brows.

'Her father was related to Theo.'

Fulke looked at the girl and she looked gravely back. There was a slight resemblance to Theobald in the eyes, and in the proportions of brow and nose. What a strange, serious little creature, he thought. In responding to one of his daughters he would have crouched to be on a level with them, or lifted them to his own height, but beneath the quizzical restraint of Clarice's stare, he did neither.

'I am pleased to greet you, child,' he said formally and took a drink of the wine.

She dipped another curtsey and folded her hands

demurely. 'My lord.' Her voice was small but clear, acknowledging him with deference. Fulke almost spluttered. It was
too much.

'Clarice, perhaps you could help fill more cups with
wine,' Maude said. 'We are to have a houseful tonight and
I'll need your help.'

Fulke gazed in bewilderment as Clarice murmured assent
and walked with brisk decorum to the oak sideboard to
begin arranging cups.

'Jesu,' he said. 'I don't know whether to pity or envy her
future husband. How old is she?'

'Nearly nine years old.'

'She acts more like a grandmother!'

Maude smiled. 'She does have a way about her,' she
admitted, 'but you'll find it impossible not to grow fond.
Hawise adores her.'

The noise and flurry of men entering the hall behind
them curtailed all further conversation. Maude greeted
William with a cool kiss on the cheek and words of
welcome that were slightly forced. If William noticed, he
kept it to himself. So did Fulke. Maude went to take
command of organising food and sleeping places for Fulke's
men, and Gracia whisked Jonetta and the baby away to bed.
For a moment, Fulke stood like an island amid the chaos
and bustle.

'Do you want some more wine?'

He looked down. Clarice was offering him a fresh cup
while reaching to take the empty one from him.

Fulke laughed. 'Child, you will make me as drunk as a
May reveller,' he said, but took her offering rather than
slight her.

She fixed him with that solemn gaze. It was almost like
being scrutinised by a nun or a stern maternal aunt and he
had to struggle not to laugh at the incongruity. Christ alone

knew what she would be like when she was an adult.

'I did but jest,' he added kindly. 'You are being helpful.'

'I like to help.' She accepted the compliment as her due and, taking his empty cup, wove her way through the throng back to the sideboard. Thoroughly diverted, Fulke gazed after her until Hawise, who had not been put to bed with the others, yanked at the hem of his tunic.

'Pick me up,' she demanded. 'I can't see.'

Fulke scooped her into his arms and perched her on his shoulders. 'High enough?'

She giggled and pulled his hair and the ghost of loneliness evaporated.

'How long?' Maude's voice was a whisper. She and Fulke had retired to the curtained alcove of their bedchamber. Beyond the heavy woollen hanging, the floor was occupied by the pallets of sleeping men, servants and children. There was scarce an inch of free space in the entire manor and she knew that everyone had needle-sharp hearing. 'How long do we have?'

Fulke was sitting on the bed. He had earlier removed the ragged clothes of the charcoal burner and with a grimace she had set the garments aside to be cut up and put in the latrine for arse wipes. They were useful for nothing else. He had washed the charcoal dust from his body in the stone horse trough by the stables. Maude would have liked to prepare a hot bathtub, but there had been neither time nor space. Besides, it would have been unfair to the others and so the horse trough had sufficed. 'How long?' he repeated as he removed his clean tunic and shirt. Despite his ablutions, the smell of smoke and a tang of sweat still clung.

She could tell that he was hedging for time and that therefore the reply was not good. Not that she expected it to be. He had trespassed at the King's hunting lodge; he had broken William free and in doing so run yet another ring around John. 'Tonight? Tomorrow night? Next week?'

He rubbed his palms over his face. She looked at his hands and remembered the jolt they had sent through her at the time of her marriage to Theobald. She had fallen in love with Fulke on her wedding morn, had danced on the gossamer lines of a web and now she was stuck fast.

'Sooner rather than later,' he said, taking his hands away and regarding her, his eyes dark as black water in the light of the weak cresset-lamp flame. 'I dare not risk antagonising Archbishop Hubert. This is a sanctuary for you and the children, not for me.'

'Then it is no sanctuary at all.' She unlaced the leather thongs at the sides of her shoes and pushed them off her feet, resisting the urge to throw them. 'I cannot bear it.' Foolish words. She had to bear it because there was no other solution. She might be able to run through the woods after him, up hill and down dale, but the children could not, and they were what mattered.

She met his eyes and her breathing quickened. 'Would you give up Whittington for me and your offspring?' she asked. 'Would you surrender one thing in order to have the rest?'

'My principles and pride, six years of my struggle and fifty of my family's?' His voice was neutral, but she was not fooled.

'Is it worth it?'

'That depends on the value of honour. Dross, or gold.'

'So, your honour is priceless and because of it your life is dross.'

'Because of it, my life is honourable,' he said. 'Without it *I* would be dross.'

'Then there is no more to be said.' Maude bit her lip,

tears of frustration filling her eyes. She knew that if she asked him outright to yield, if she pleaded and wept, he might do so for her sake, but it would be a hollow victory. As he had just said, he would feel diminished in his own eyes. Likely he would grow to resent her for making him yield when it was against his will. If she damned his honour, then she damned him. Yet the alternative of a life in exile, seldom together, always listening for pursuit, was just as unpalatable.

Tomorrow he would go. All they had of each other was tonight and she did not want to waste it in recriminations and quarrelling, each of them chasing their own tails to nowhere.

Tears sparkled on her lashes and rolled down her cheeks. Her throat ached with the effort of containing her grief. She fumbled with the side lacings of her gown, catching the waxed ends on the eyelets. Fulke laid his hand over hers.

'If I could do it, I would,' he said.

'I know,' she choked. 'Don't speak.'

The lace knotted and she could not see through her tears to unravel it. Fulke tried but his hands were trembling, and in the end he had to cut the cord with his knife. Maude struggled out of the gown, no mean feat given the yards of material in the skirt and the small space of the alcove. Flushed, panting, tearful, she knelt on the bed and faced him, drinking in his scent and filling her eyes with his harsh, masculine beauty. She was parched with wanting, yet knew that to drink from the cup was only to want more and to be denied. Setting her hands to the hem of her chemise, she pulled that off too, and in the beat of heart and breath while discipline still held, she unfastened her braids and shook them out, clothing herself in the ashen silk of her hair.

'Holy Christ,' Fulke said softly. He reached out to touch its sheen, then brushed it gently aside so that his hand was on her skin. Her throat, her shoulder, her breast. Maude gasped. She met his eyes, saw the heaviness of desire and the effort of control. But tonight it didn't matter. Not the first time.

She pushed his hand aside and threw her arms around his neck, carrying them body to body on the bed. 'Now,' she demanded fiercely, 'take me now.'

It was almost an echo of their wedding night: the enclosed space giving the illusion of privacy; the proximity of others that lent the intensity of silence to their lovemaking; and the knowledge of the danger in which they stood increasing an urgency already built by months apart. It was a white-hot conflagration, swift, profound and shattering.

Washed up on the shore, lapped by small after-ripples of sensation, they lay half drowned in each other's arms, gasping like swimmers newly surfaced from a wild tide. She pressed herself against the damp, salt taste of his body, unwilling to relinquish her hold, her craving only increased by the moment's satiation. She felt the rise and fall of his chest, the thunder of his heart like galloping horses; her own beat hard in rhythm. Tonight was all they had, and the memory might have to sustain her for a long time.

Their second lovemaking was slow and languorous, like the gentle curling of surf on the beach, and afterwards they slept shoaled together, surfacing again somewhere near dawn to join again in the poignancy of need and pleasure on the verge of parting.

They lay in the aftermath, reluctant to rise, drawing the closeness out to the very last grain. The sound of voices came to them through the curtains. A whispered argument was being conducted as to whether they should be roused or not.

Fulke made to part the curtains. Maude stopped his arm with an instinctive motion, and then withdrew its restraint. Time, unlike wine, could not be sealed up in a flagon and kept, much as she wished it could. Sighing, she sat up, reaching in the dark for her chemise.

Fulke opened the hangings a chink. 'What is it?' he said brusquely. 'If it's petty I will kill you. If not, then you are wasting time.'

Philip and William exchanged glances. The latter's face wore the colourful hues of the beating he had received at the hands of his captors and he stood slightly hunched, favouring his kicked ribs.

'The watch has sighted riders approaching,' he announced. 'Philip said it wasn't an army and not to disturb you, but I said you needed to know.'

'Banners?'

'Salisbury and Chester.'

'Admit them. I'll be down as soon as I'm dressed.'

William gave Philip a triumphant look, which Philip accepted with a smile. 'Perhaps you're learning at last,' he said, and received a two-fingered salute by way of reply.

Fulke closed the bed curtains and reached for his shirt.

'I heard,' Maude said over her shoulder. She was rummaging in a narrow clothing coffer that had been squeezed between the foot of the bed and the wall. There were folded garments within, layered with dried rose petals and sticks of cinnamon bark. She withdrew a gown of green linen with deep side gores. The dye was beginning to fade slightly in the creases, but it was suitably decent to greet a couple of earls – certainly better now than the one she had worn last night. God knew where she was going to house Salisbury and Chester. Malling was already packed as tight as a barrel of salt herring. 'What do you think they want?'

Fulke shrugged. 'Could be rags, could be riches. Let's go and find out.'

Salisbury and Chester were in the great hall. Clarice had seen to their refreshment as attested by the fact that both men held brimming cups of wine and were looking with bemusement at the grave, sweet-faced child who was now enquiring as to the merits of their journey.

'Not one of yours, Fulke?' asked Salisbury as the men clasped hands and Maude gently directed Clarice to go and look after the other children, channelling the girl's nurturing instincts in a different direction.

'How did you guess? No, Maude's fostering her at the moment. She's related to the Archbishop.'

'She'll make someone a formidable wife.'

'Yes, it's frightening.' Fulke smiled for form's sake, but his eyes were wary. Although the social formalities were being observed, this was far from a social visit. Maude returned and, taking the place of the juvenile hostess, ushered the men to a quieter corner of the hall where a cushioned bench and two chairs were arranged around a brazier.

'I suppose you are here as a result of what happened yesterday?' Fulke asked.

Salisbury cleared his throat. 'It would be foolish to pretend otherwise.' He crossed his legs and stared at the embroidery down the mid-seam of his shoe. 'My brother has authorised myself and Ranulf to seek you out and offer you terms.'

Fulke's heart jumped. Behind him, he was aware of Maude's utter stillness. 'Terms.' He nodded and bit the inside of his mouth. 'What sort of terms?'

'Yield to John, acknowledge him your liege lord and he will restore your lands.'

'Including Whittington?' Fulke raised one eyebrow and

was unable to prevent the note of disbelief in his voice.

'Including Whittington. I have his word on it.'

'I am sorry, my lord, but the King's word is not enough.'

Salisbury flushed slightly. 'You cannot blame him for imprisoning your brother. Anyone in John's position would have done the same with such an opportunity.'

'Mayhap they would, but that does not alter the fact that I would not trust John further than I could throw him.'

Sighing, Salisbury delved into the leather satchel at his shoulder and produced a sealed scroll. 'I have here a safe conduct from the King for you, your brothers and all your men so that you may come to Westminster with impunity and make your peace. It is witnessed by myself and Ranulf and the Bishop of Norwich.' He held the scroll out for Fulke to take. 'John's as weary of this conflict as you. He acknowledges that there has to be an end.'

Fulke took the scroll and, drawing his meat knife, broke the seal. 'A pity he did not acknowledge it six years ago,' he said grimly and unrolled the vellum to look at the neat brown script of one of John's army of professional scribes. The signature was John's though, and below it were the names of the all-important witnesses. 'Is this the only copy?'

'John de Grey has sent a copy to Norwich and one to the Chancellor,' Ranulf said. 'You might not trust the King, but you can trust his intent this time. He needs your loyalty.'

Fulke smiled without humour. 'And that he could have had six years ago too.' He wafted the scroll at the two Earls. 'Then it was just me. Men were scrambling over each other to please the new King, offering him all kinds of bribes for favours. Selling their souls. Now there is more discontent. John is losing Normandy. He is, some say, losing his grip on England. I do not believe that, but I know there is a cauldron of discontent.' He leaned forwards to emphasise his point. 'All it takes is someone like me to give it a more vigorous stir – mayhap inveigle my father-by-marriage and the northern barons into a revolt, draw in the Scots and the Welsh, and John would have a full domestic war on his hands. I may be a minor cog, but it is the minor ones that turn the larger ones, that turn the mill wheel and grind the corn . . . for better or worse.'

'You will not get a better offer,' Salisbury said somewhat stiffly.

'Oh, I know, my lord, I know. And I do not pretend to have the luxury of the upper hand, but still, there is a certain sweetness amongst the bitter in having two Earls bring me the King's terms in person.' Rising to his feet, he went to Maude and handed her the letter. 'Our son's inheritance, and our daughters' dowries,' he said to her.

'Then you accept?' Salisbury asked.

Fulke set his arm around Maude's shoulders. 'You may tell the King that I will come to London and surrender to him as he requires.' He looked at the two men. 'You can also tell him: stalemate. He will know what you mean.'

The summer sky was a deep manuscript-blue, reflecting in the River Thames as it wound past the palace and abbey in a glittering ribbon towards the city further downstream. Fulke gazed out on a traffic of galleys, cogs and rowing boats, swans, cormorants and restless geese. It was said that the geese laid their eggs at sea and so, being related to fish, could be eaten on Fridays with impunity.

Fulke inhaled deeply. Watching the geese, pondering on their mating habits was, he knew, procrastination. Before him, the palace of Westminster waited, and within it, like the beast in its lair, was John.

It had been sixteen years since Fulke's last visit to Westminster. Then he had been a youth of nineteen, the glamour of knighthood veiling his eyes. He had watched a king crowned, had received the blow of accolade in the chapel, had encountered a little girl in a dishevelled blue dress, her eyes brimming with indignation, never thinking that one day she would be the mother of his children. And before that he had played chess with a drunken, vindictive braggart who was now a king.

'Are you ready?' Salisbury asked.

'As ready as I will ever be,' he said, and received a reassuring thump on the shoulder from Ranulf of Chester.

'On the morrow you can go home to Whittington, or Lambourn, or Alberbury – wherever you choose,' said the Earl at whose town house on the river strand Fulke and his family were lodging.

Fulke nodded and unconsciously grimaced at the prospect of yielding to John. The only consolation was that in his turn John would have to yield to him and grant him Whittington – the reason for, if not the root of the quarrel.

Fulke and his men had donned their finest garments. Fulke wore his mail, burnished until the steel glittered as if it was fresh from the armourer's workshop, and over it his surcoat of red and gold silk appliquéd with the wolf's teeth device. His brothers were all similarly accoutred. They looked professional and formidable, as was Fulke's intention.

The marks of violence on William's face had faded to background hues of pale yellow and dull, muddy purple. He gave Fulke a tight smile. 'One last time pays for all,' he said quietly so that the words did not carry beyond the space between himself and Fulke. 'And if he reneges on his promise, you will not stop me from killing him.'

Fulke looked at him sidelong. Salisbury had custody of Fulke's sword which was to be given to John in token of surrender. None of Fulke's men had so much as an eating knife on show, but he knew quite well that William had a blade concealed inside his boot. 'No, I will not stop you,' he said. 'I promise.'

Salisbury led them into the great Rufus Hall where John was holding court. The room, despite its great size, was packed with officials, administrators, courtiers, supplicants and servants: a seethe of humanity all drawn here at the will of the stocky, dark-haired man seated on the throne at the far end. Fulke was put in mind of a nest of ants or a bee skep. There was that same sense of purpose and industry. Despite his antipathy, Fulke was impressed, but there were too many dark memories for comfort. The chess game in that winter's dusk; the confrontation at Castle Baldwin when, in front of the entire court, John had given Whittington to Morys FitzRoger. Although Fulke was here under the guarantee of a safe conduct, he did not trust John, and never would.

Salisbury sent his herald to announce their arrival to the King. John dipped his head to listen to the messenger, then sat upright and stared down the hall, his hands resting on the lion's head finials on the arms of the throne.

Fulke met John's gaze. From a distance, he could not see what the eyes held. Hatred, resignation, weariness? Or perhaps like his own, distaste and a desire to have the episode finished. Time to turn a new page, even if the awareness remained that a previous page existed.

John crooked his forefinger and beckoned. Fulke drew himself up and, Salisbury on his right, Chester on his left, walked down the hall, followed by his men. All he saw was John, although he knew at the back of his mind that a corridor of officials and courtiers watched his progress. They were a blur. The only items in sharp focus were the throne and the man seated upon it. John, by the Grace of God, King of England, lord of Ireland, Duke of Normandy and Aquitaine and Count of Anjou. He was not wearing his crown, and as Fulke drew closer he saw that the once black hair was salted with grey and lines of care were beginning to deepen between nose and mouth. The dark eyes were heavy lidded; since their last encounter, John had learned to conceal his thoughts, for they gave nothing away.

Reaching the foot of the dais, Fulke paused. Salisbury and Chester both knelt. Fulke drew a deep breath like a man about to dive into deep water, and then knelt beside them, bowing his head, exposing his neck to the symbolic blow of the sword. Behind him, he heard the rustle of cloth, the clink of mail as his brothers and his men followed suit. And then he waited, his gaze upon the thickly strewn rushes and the fresh herbs that had been scattered upon them to add perfume and sweetness.

The silence stretched as John drew it out. Fulke forced himself to relax, to clench neither his fists nor his jaw. He could feel William's tension, strung like the rawhide on a mangonel pulley.

Mercifully, Salisbury broke the tension. 'Sire, I have brought Fulke FitzWarin into your presence so that he may surrender himself to your clemency and that you may give him the justice of his lands,' he said.

Salisbury must have been awake all night thinking up that clever turn of phrase, Fulke thought, still looking at the floor. He heard the whisper of fabric as John moved on the throne.

'Well then,' John said, the hint of a purr in his voice. 'Let Fulke FitzWarin speak the words of surrender from his own lips.'

Fulke swallowed against a stubborn constriction in his throat. This was the most difficult thing he had ever had to do: submit to the man whose injustice had turned him outlaw. He raised his head and now looked straight at John. There was a waiting smile in the dark eyes, a smug curling of the lips. You bastard, Fulke thought, and a sudden spurt of anger broke through his calm. The knot in his throat vanished and he lifted his voice so that it rang with strength and pride and men turned their heads.

'I, Fulke FitzWarin, do yield myself and my men unto the judgement of John, by the Grace of God King of England. I acknowledge him my liege lord and swear to serve him honourably to the best of my ability from this day forth. In token of my surrender, I yield to him my sword to break or restore as he will.'

William of Salisbury stepped forward and presented John with Fulke's scabbarded sword, the leather cared for but worn, the sword grip bound with strips of overlapping buckskin.

John grasped the hilt and, rising to his feet, approached Fulke where he knelt at the head of his brothers and his men. The hair on Fulke's nape prickled. He could sense William preparing to whip the concealed knife from his boot and launch himself at the King.

Slowly John drew the sword. Having been forged for Fulke who was above two yards in height, it looked unwieldy in John's hand. The shorter arms, the stocky body looked incongruous against the length of the blade and the deep handgrip.

'To break, or restore,' John murmured, considering his reflection in the mirror gleam of the cherished steel. Salisbury made the smallest sound in his throat and John glanced briefly at his half-brother. 'The choice is mine.'

He held on to the moment, advancing at last to Fulke. 'Some here would say that I should have given you Whittington when you first came to me, but I had already been asked by a man with a claim of common possession at least the equal of your claim to hereditary right.'

Fulke's said nothing, determined not to rise to the bait and give John a way out. The ground, despite the cushioning of rushes, was hard beneath his knees. He willed William to hold his tongue and stay his hand.

'You have no reply?' John paused before Fulke, the sword raised.

'No, sire,' Fulke said impassively. 'Unless you want me to repeat my oath of surrender. Each of us knows why the other is here.' He glanced around the hall, reminding John that the scene had witnesses. 'And so does everyone else.'

John compressed his lips. 'I wonder if they do,' he said. Abruptly, he gestured to Fulke. 'Rise.'

Fulke almost staggered as his aching knees bore his weight. It was no mean feat to stand up in a mail shirt on legs numbed by kneeling.

'Gird on your sword.' John handed Fulke the belt and the weapon as if casting a crust to a beggar. Then he stalked to his throne, and sat down. 'Now come to me and kneel and do homage for your lands – including Whittington.'

Fulke's heart was hammering. Suddenly his fingers seemed enormous and it was all he could do to latch the buckle of his swordbelt and secure the scabbard lacings. Advancing to the throne, he knelt once more, his knees screaming protest, the long muscles of his thighs trembling with reaction. John leaned down and took Fulke's hands in his. There was a moment when both men almost flinched from the touch and the revulsion could clearly be seen in each of their faces, but the clasp held. Once again Fulke raised his voice and in a loud, if slightly shaking, voice proclaimed his homage to John. And John in his turn declared, although not as loudly, that he accepted Fulke's homage and granted his entitlement to all his lands, and specifically to Whittington.

John leaned further to give Fulke the kiss of peace. 'And may it bring you naught but grief,' he whispered as his bearded lips brushed Fulke's cheek.

Fulke rose and, stepping back, saluted the King. 'Thank you, sire. Whatever you wish for me, may I return twofold as a loyal vassal.'

John made small chewing motions, his jaw thrusting forwards and back. 'You may go,' he said. 'The Justiciar's office will see to your needs.'

Fulke bowed again, deeply, then turned and walked from the King's presence, his head held high and his hand on his sword hilt. He had given his surrender and his oath of fealty. John had restored his lands. Now they were bound in a pact, lord and vassal, and it seemed to Fulke that like many an arranged marriage, the bride and groom had been forced into a match that neither desired, but which, out of duty, they would fulfil. It was, as he had said to Salisbury, stalemate.

CHAPTER 34

Whittington Castle, Spring 1206

D usting her hands, Maude eyed with satisfaction and disgust the pile of winter floor rushes that now occupied the midden heap at the far end of the castle ward. All morning the maids had been sweeping, the men shovelling and barrowing to remove the successive layers of detritus laid down between November and March. The winter had been so bitterly cold that when the rushes needed changing it had been warmer to throw a fresh layer on top than get rid of the old. By April, it had been like walking on a springy, soft midden layer. The sight of maggots this morning had finally galvanised her into acting.

The yard fowl were gorging themselves on the unexpected windfall with greedy disbelief. At least there should be a glut of eggs out of this, and a good supply of meat for the table, she thought with a grimace at the rank mound.

The floor of stamped earth had to be purged with ashes and lye before a new layer of fresh green rushes was laid and scattered liberally with toadflax to keep away the fleas, and lavender to improve the smell. At least the hall would be pleasant to welcome Fulke's return − whenever that might be. He had been inordinately busy since the spring thaw, visiting their own manors far and wide, dispensing justice, receiving reports from reeves and stewards. Occasionally letters would arrive, written in his own hand, which was bold but difficult to read. They were hardly the stuff of troubadours. For a man who could wield a sword with such rare artistry, he had very little skill with the pen. He was well. He hoped she was well. He hoped that the children were well. The last such missive had arrived three days ago from Wiltshire and left Maude torn between fury and amusement.

An infant's shriek of delight made her turn to see Hawise pushing her little brother in one of the empty barrows. The sunlight made a flaxen nimbus of his hair and sparked Hawise's curls with fire.

'Have a care!' Maude cried, shading her eyes.

Hawise looked towards her mother and the barrow tipped over, spilling its occupant. The shrieks of delight became roars of shock. Maude ran over to them and snatched little Fulkin into her arms.

'I didn't mean to.' Hawise looked anxiously up at her mother.

Maude suppressed the urge to shout at the child. Hawise grew more like her uncle William every day. She was impulsive, stubborn and frequently in trouble. You couldn't just sit her down with a straw doll like Jonetta or a piece of embroidery like Clarice and expect her to behave quietly.

'I know you didn't,' she said, forcing a calm voice through clenched teeth. Apart from a bump on the head, Fulkin appeared to be all right. She pushed his hair off his brow and kissed him. He twisted in her arms, the fall forgotten, and clamoured to be put back in the barrow.

'Hawise push,' he commanded fiercely. Short on vocabulary he might be, but already he had his priorities.

Maude restrained herself. It was foolish to cushion her children in a fleece of maternal devotion so thick that they smothered. Her father's wife had borne a son last year and so great was Juliana's pride and anxiety in the child that she coddled and cooed over him beyond Maude's bearing. So did her father and that was almost worse for Maude who had endured his indifference during her own miserable childhood.

Sighing, she turned from the midden heap and tramped back to the hall where the maids had begun brushing the floor with the powerful soap mixture, the smell so pungent that it made the eyes water. Clarice, as usual, was in the midst of the proceedings and thoroughly enjoying herself.

'Child, you astonish me,' Maude said as she took up a broom and began sweeping beside Clarice. If you were going to ask the maids to work hard at such a task, then you had to show willing yourself even if you loathed the toil. Besides, every pair of hands made the purgatory shorter. 'Why do you take such a delight in these chores?'

Clarice puffed a stray wisp of light brown hair out of her eyes and gave her serene smile. 'I like to make things better,' she said. 'I like to mend and make good. The hall was becoming horrible. When we've finished it will look lovely.'

A saint in the making, Maude thought, although Clarice did not have strong religious leanings. She was wearing a large cross on her breast at the moment, made of silver and set with garnets, but that was not the result of a particularly devout nature. The piece had been willed to her by Hubert Walter who had died of a seizure not long after Fulke had regained Whittington. Maude had been left a similar item, set with amethysts, and a Psalter with an ivory cover. She always bore it to mass and said prayers for Hubert . . . and for Theo. She and Fulke owed both men a debt they could never repay. Not that Theo would ever have acknowledged that a debt existed. And Hubert would have brushed the suggestion aside with an avuncular, if cynical laugh and the statement that no one ever did a good turn for nothing. She and Fulke were helping to assure his place in heaven through the charity he had shown to them. But still, in her heart, she acknowledged their generosity, and made a point of special prayers for their souls.

By noon, the floor had been thoroughly scrubbed and left to dry while everyone dined around the cooking pot in the courtyard. The cook and his attendants had prepared a vegetable pottage thickened with barley and copious amounts of bread. Everyone was ravenous and the food disappeared in short order. Then it was back to work. Rushes that had been cut the previous week and spread to dry, were carried into the hall and strewn on the floor in thick swatches. Maude set the children to scattering herbs, even little Fulkin, who thought it was great fun to grasp pudgy fistfuls of dried leaves and throw them on the floor.

Leaving the children under the watchful eyes of Gracia and Clarice, Maude went in search of the dairy maid to confer with her about cheeses, but stopped short as she entered the courtyard and saw the troop of horsemen riding over the ditch. The glitter of mail, the dried lines of salt on the necks of hard-ridden horses. The panting wolfhounds either side of the leading bay stallion.

'Fulke!' The word was a soft gasp. She felt herself dissolving with pleasure, then was suddenly aware that she was wearing her oldest gown and that her hair was bundled out of the way in a tatty kerchief.

He drew rein and dismounted in the fluid motion that she knew so well and handed the reins to his waiting squire.

'Fulke!' This time her cry was louder and, lifting her skirts, she ran to him. He caught her in his arms and swung her round. They kissed and were almost knocked down by the dogs. A grinning Ivo seized their collars and hauled them away.

'I wasn't expecting you, why didn't you send word!'

Maude gasped as their lips parted. Her kerchief had slipped. She began to adjust it, but he was quicker, plucking it from her head. Her braids tumbled down, heavy as sun-whitened barley.

A rueful expression crossed his face. 'It was easier to ride than write,' he said. 'Besides, I had but recently sent you a letter.'

Maude's own expression mirrored his. 'Is that what it was?' she sniffed.

Fulke reddened defensively. 'I'm no Jean de Rampaigne, I have no skill with a pen,' he said. 'I thought you would know already what was in my heart.'

'Knowing is not the same as being told,' she said.

Fulke's lips twitched. 'If you promise to cease scolding me, I promise to make up for lost time.'

Maude narrowed her eyes while she decided whether or not she was in a mood to be cajoled. 'I will promise nothing,' she said, 'at least not until you have washed away the stink of your journey.'

The amusement was in his eyes now as well. He looked her up and down from untidy braids to smirched hem of gown. 'Does not the bible say that before you criticise you should examine your own faults?'

'Oh, come within,' Maude snapped, niggled that he had got the better of her, and self-conscious about her state of dishabille. 'We have been laying new rushes in the hall. There isn't much to eat above pottage and bread, but at least the surroundings will be sweet.'

He followed her, lips compressed to conceal a grin. Maude told two menservants to fill a tub and Fulke went to greet the children who were industriously herb-scattering. Immediately he was engulfed, excited shrill voices clamouring for his attention.

One ear cocked to the noise, Maude spoke to the men,

enquired after their health, saw to it that their cups were filled with wine and that those who were hungry were at least offered pottage and bread with marrow jelly to stave off the worst pangs. Of Fulke's brothers, only Ivo and Richard were present. The others had been given castellan duties at various FitzWarin holdings. William had the responsibility for the estate at Whadborough in Leicester-shire and that was literally keeping him out of mischief. Alain was with him, serving as his deputy, and Philip had the care of their estate at Alvaston.

Once the tub was ready, Maude left the replenishing of goblets in Clarice's more than capable hands and rescued Fulke from the bombardment of his offspring. When Hawise wanted to follow them into their chamber, Maude turned her away. 'Even if you have all the tantrums of hell, it won't make a whit of difference,' she said as her daughter inhaled to scream. 'Your papa will play with you later.' Gesturing Gracia to take charge of the child, she drew the curtain firmly across.

Fulke unlatched his belt and laid it on the coffer, then stripped off his woollen tunic. 'You say she is stubborn like me, but I know from where she gets the will to drive that determination,' he murmured.

Maude placed a dish of soap scented with mint and rose-mary at the side of the tub and, pointing to a stool near the tub, she bade him be seated so that she could unwind his braid leg bindings.

'So,' she said, 'are you going to tell me everything that you did not in your "letter"?'

His fingers lightly brushed the side of her braid. 'Later,' he said. 'If I tried to talk to you now, I doubt I would make much sense. I want you too much.'

Maude looked up, somewhat surprised. She had been anticipating declarations of love, need and desire. They were what had been missing from his written words. But now her curiosity was piqued by the hint of something more. She opened her mouth to ask what he meant and he took immediate advantage.

Maude's body decided that the question could wait. Curling her arms around his neck, she tumbled into the molten sweetness of lust. He cupped her buttocks; she pushed her hips against his and felt him already as hard as a quarterstaff.

Kissing, fondling, they feverishly stripped each other's garments. The thought of someone drawing aside the curtain and discovering them added a spice of fear and urgency to the moment. There was no bed in the room, only a narrow bench that was totally impractical, and the floor, garlanded in prickly rushes. But there was the tub.

'There's room for two,' Fulke murmured. 'If you sit in my lap.'

Laughing, Maude eyed his groin. 'Are you sure?'

Fulke stepped into the tub, sat down in the hot water and held out his hand. 'Why don't you join me and find out?'

Giggling like an adolescent, Maude took his hand and stepped into the tub, but it was as a knowing woman that she straddled Fulke and eased slowly down.

'Well?' he asked somewhat breathlessly, 'was I right?'

'Only just,' Maude replied. However, she still pressed forward, upon and against him, and heard with gratification his hiss of pleasure. The angle might be tight, but it only served to enhance the sensations. Their position also meant that she had the control, and could hasten or prolong at her whim. A carnal smile on her lips, she began to move with infinite, exquisite slowness.

★　　★　　★

What bathwater remained was almost tepid by the time they emerged from the tub. Maude sat on the bench, robed in a clean shift, gently patting the wet ends of her hair. Fulke, heavy-eyed and fumble-fingered, attempted to fasten his chausses to his braies.

'I doubt,' he said, 'that the most accomplished Southwark bath girl could equal that performance.'

Maude gave him a look through her lashes. 'How do you know about Southwark bath girls?'

'I don't – well, only by hearsay. William Salisbury has one for a mistress, but I've never met her. He and his wife don't see eye to eye and it's seldom that any other body parts meet either.' He snorted. 'Besides, you leave me neither the energy nor the wherewithal to be of the remotest use to the wenches of Southwark.'

Maude raised her brows. 'I am glad to hear it.' She tilted her head to one side and eyed him. 'Are your wits clearer now, or have I made you lose them?'

'What?' He blinked at her.

'You said that you would tell me later what you had not said in your letter – that you wanted me too much to talk sense.'

'Oh yes.' He finally managed to secure the last hook and looked at her with a smile. 'You are right. I do feel as if my wits have been dragged through a fine sieve . . . not to mention other parts.'

Maude made an indignant sound. 'Stop japing. Tell me.'

'I have to ride out again,' he said, 'although not for another month at least.'

She eyed him suspiciously. 'Where to?'

'Ireland.'

'Ireland!' She looked at him in surprise. She had been envisaging Lambourn, Devon, or Yorkshire. That was the summer gone, and likely half the autumn. The cold Irish Sea. Dull tones of green and misty grey. Theobald's grave. A sense of danger coiled in the back of her mind like a wet Irish fog. 'Why?'

He donned a clean shirt of linen chansil and topped it with a fine woollen tunic. 'Because of the lands you had in dower from Theobald. William Marshal, as their over-lord, has asked me to go since he is occupied at court and John will not release him yet. Because they are my respon-sibility as much as any other part of my lands.' His head emerged through the neck opening of his tunic, his hair standing up in rumpled black spikes. 'It is an obligation I cannot shirk. Nor can I deny the request for a favour from William Marshal.'

Maude swallowed. 'Surely your English lands need you more?'

'Not for the moment. I have been busy and, besides, my brothers can care for them.'

'Can you not send them to Ireland in your place?'

'No,' he sighed. 'Not unsupervised. It has to be me.' He picked his belt off the coffer.

Maude set aside her comb and threw her hair over her shoulders, the gestured equivalent of clearing the ground for battle. 'If you must go then I am coming with you,' she said.

Fulke opened his mouth.

'And do not tell me that it is dangerous and no place for a woman. I know the first, I was in Ireland with Theobald when he died. As to the second – well, if Irish women dwell there, then so can I.' She had a sudden, clear vision of a woman with eyes the colour of harebells and a moist, red mouth, a woman who had visited Theobald on the day before he died – like a harbinger of ill fate. The feeling of danger increased.

'I . . .'

'I won't be dissuaded,' she added fiercely.

He shook his head and laughed as he latched the belt at his waist. 'Jesu, Maude, you are priceless! You're still the little girl with a stolen ball in your hands, determined that you are going to play whatever the cost. You attacked me with your blade of a tongue before I had a chance to speak. I was going to say that if you can bear the journey and the damp and the mists, there is nothing I desire more than to have you by my side.'

'Oh,' she said, torn between anger at being patronised and chagrin that she had indeed leaped down his throat before he could make his meaning clear. Partly she was fighting her own fear in insisting so vehemently that she accompany him.

His lips twitched. 'Perhaps I would rather be bedevilled out of my mind than bored out of my skull.' He pulled her into his arms. 'Don't scowl. Life is too short to sulk.'

'I'm not sulking,' Maude said, not quite truthfully. Sometimes the line between wanting to shower him in kisses and wanting to belabour him with her distaff was very blurred. 'I'm just packing chests of cloaks in my mind.' Then she smiled. 'Although if you are by, they won't be necessary to keep me warm.' She kissed him, nipped him with her teeth to show that he should still be wary, and, mindful of the array waiting in the hall, went to finish dressing.

CHAPTER 35

Limerick, Ireland, Summer 1206

Maude and Fulke knelt side by side at Theobald's tomb in Wotheney Abbey and prayed for the repose of his soul, although neither had any doubts that he was at peace. The quiet wilderness of the place, the soft chanting of the monks were lullabies to soothe the most troubled slumber.

The only regret, Maude thought, in the midst of her prayer, was that they had not brought their children to lay their small hands on his effigy and light their own candles in his honour, if not his memory. Theobald would have liked that, would have liked to know that she and Fulke had offspring.

Not knowing what he would find in Ireland, Fulke had insisted that the children remain in England where they were safe from harm. Besides, the journey across the Irish Sea was a trial for adults, let alone infants of four, three and two. Clarice might have managed, but there was no point bringing her without the others. They were staying in the household of Ranulf of Chester, and while they might be missing their parents as much as their parents were missing them, they had the maternal cosseting of Clemence of Chester to compensate. Maude would not countenance sending her children to their grandfather. Le Vavasour might have mellowed since his marriage to Juliana and the birth of their son, but, remembering her own childhood, Maude would not trust him with her own offspring even though he was their grandsire.

She had not told Fulke yet, but her flux was more than two weeks late. She had suffered no queasiness, but her breasts were tender and she suspected that she was again with child. However, there had been a couple of false alarms over the past two years and she was not going to say anything until she was certain.

Together they lit candles and left the chapel, escorted by a young monk, tall and handsome, with the powerful bones of a Viking rather than an aesthete. Maude felt that she ought to know him, but it was not until Fulke was helping her into her saddle and the monk looked up to bid them farewell that recognition dawned. It was the eyes that nudged her memory, almond-shaped and of a startling cornflower-blue.

'You entered the noviciate here just before Lord Walter died,' she said as she gathered the reins.

'Indeed I did, my lady.' He bowed and seemed pleased that she had remembered. 'I had a vocation and my mother said that it was fitting that one of her sons should pray for the others.' His French bore a lilting Irish accent, soft as rain. 'She remembers Lord Walter with affection. I know that she would be pleased to receive your visit.'

Maude murmured a polite response and clicked her tongue to her mare.

'Your mother?' Fulke asked, looking intrigued.

The young monk nodded and smiled. 'The Lady Oonagh O'Donnel. De Chaumont was the name of her second husband, my father. She's a widow now. Her third husband died last autumn, God rest his soul.' He crossed himself. So did Fulke.

Maude rode on without waiting, her spine as straight as a lance. It was a few minutes later than Fulke came trotting up to join her, the look on his face one of keen interest and curiosity.

'I did not realise that you knew the Lady Oonagh.'

'I don't know her,' Maude answered, tight-lipped. 'I only met her the once when she came to bring her son to the monastery. Theobald died just after so my mind was occupied with more important matters. Certainly I am not well enough acquainted to go visiting, or even to want to go visiting.' She twitched her cloak into place like a bird smoothing ruffled feathers and eyed Fulke sharply. 'You are not considering doing so?' In her mind's eye she saw again the slanting blue eyes, the lush, red mouth, and heard the feline purr of the voice.

His gaze slipped from hers and focused somewhere in the region of his mount's pricked ears. 'She is widowed,' he murmured, 'and her late husband's lands at Docionell border ours at Glencavern. For reasons of polity if not compassion, I ought to go.'

'For reasons of polity, I see,' she repeated, nodding vigorously. 'It has nothing to do with the lady herself then?'

'You're not jealous, surely!' he teased.

'Not in the least.' She tossed her head. 'I don't want you to make a fool of yourself, that is all. I met her when she brought her son to Wotheney shortly before Theo died, and I saw what she was like. The troubadours have a word for such women: *Belles dames sans merci*. Beautiful women without mercy.'

'Ah no, I've only met one such in my time.' He reached across the space between their mounts to grasp her hand.

She snatched it away. 'You need not try and cozen me,' she snapped.

'I wouldn't dare,' he said wryly. 'But I think that for "reasons of polity", and to protect me from myself, you had best accompany me.'

'I would rather beat myself with nettles.' She narrowed her eyes at him. 'I have been trying to remember what she said to Theo, but it is several years ago. Something about you being a fine young stag that she was tempted to go after and bring down. That she had always regretted letting you get away when you were a squire.'

'I'm older and wiser now.'

'Not as old and wise as Theo, and even he was hard pressed to hold her.'

'She will be older too.'

'And likely more desperate.'

Fulke made an exasperated sound and rode off in front for a while. Maude looked at his broad back, protected by a gambeson thickly padded with raw fleece. Did it matter, she wondered? Either she trusted him or she did not. Either he had the wit to see beneath the surface, or he was a dupe. Not once had she questioned his fidelity during their months apart. Why now? Because she had seen Oonagh O'Donnel and the glamour she exuded. Because the woman had spoken of Fulke with husky amusement and the lingering regret of a lioness that had declined to feed and was now hungry.

She kicked the mare's flanks, urging her forwards in a trot to join Fulke. 'Go if you wish,' she said on a more placatory note, but with shadows in her eyes.

He looked at her. 'I think I have to,' he said, 'but not out of longing or lust. I outgrew those pangs years ago – except where you are concerned.'

She smiled briefly. She couldn't call him a liar on that score, but she could call him a flatterer. 'Then out of what?'

'Curiosity.' He shook his head impatiently. 'No, it's more than that. It has to do with laying the past to rest. With standing before her as an equal, not some patronised squire.'

'But she will only patronise you as a grown man now. If you had seen how she treated Theo . . .'

He shrugged. 'Even so, if I do not face the challenge I will always wonder.'

Maude eyed him narrowly. The penchant for facing challenges was one of the strongest elements in Fulke's nature, but not always to his advantage. 'Just have a care,' she said.

'And you will not accompany me?'

Maude shook her head. 'I will be cutting nettles,' she said.

'Does it never do anything but rain in this Godforsaken place?' Jean de Rampaigne grumbled, drawing his hood over his ears and grimacing at the low grey sky. On Hubert Walter's death, he had left the Canterbury household and become one of Fulke's permanent retainers.

'It's what makes the grass green,' Fulke answered. 'And I'd hardly call it Godforsaken, the number of monasteries and convents that have sprung up.'

'Under our Norman influence.' Jean guided his mount around a deep wheel rut in the muddy track.

Fulke grinned. He wondered if Oonagh would make any impression on him. The thought of her irritated like an itch he could not reach. He knew that Maude was against him paying her a visit, but if the itch was to let him be then it had to be treated, and the only way of doing that was to confront it. Not lust, not longing, but unfinished business that needed closing off.

'So what are we going to do when we arrive? Sit and talk about the state of the weather?'

Fulke snorted. 'I doubt it,' he said with a touch of apprehension in his eyes. 'She's a recent widow – by misfortune rather than design this time,' he said wryly. 'As her neighbour, I need to know her intentions – find out if she's intending to remarry and, if so, whether it's to someone likely to start a war with his neighbours.'

'Then you had better hide behind your shield while you're asking her,' Jean said. 'If she could arrange a "hunting accident" for de Chaumont, she won't balk at dealing with anyone else who stands in her way.'

'And I won't balk at dealing with her.' Fulke glanced over his shoulder at the solid troop of men at his back, their mail silver-sleek in the rain. Although his voice was filled with confidence of authority, he could not prevent the twist of tension in his gut. Oonagh O'Donnel was unpredictable and ruthless.

They crossed the boundary between Docionell and Glencavern, the only evidence of this being a boundary stone, lichened over and covered with thinly grooved lines, coiling like a spider's web. There were many such stones adorning the wild greenness of Limerick, some standing in circles like huddled old women, others lone sentinels, leaning as if blown by the wind.

As they drew nearer to Docionell, the lush smell of greenery and soft drizzle was overlaid by the more acrid scent of woodsmoke. The men became aware of a billowing cloud that did not belong to the blanket-grey sky. Fulke and Jean exchanged glances.

'Seems as if we're not the first visitors to pay our condolences,' Fulke murmured and slid his shield from its long carrying strap to the shorter hand grips, bringing it round on to his left arm.

'Could just be a barn fire,' Jean said, but not as if he believed it.

'It could.' The Irish, like the Welsh, were always conducting fierce clan wars and smoke from one burning settlement or another was almost as endemic as the rain. When a lord died, mayhem often followed, usually created by the lord's own relatives, all keen to grab their share.

Fulke and his troop approached cautiously. They were of a sufficiently large number to defend themselves, but there was no point in taking risks.

The stockade gate and the posts on either side were ablaze and the attackers were on the verge of breaking through. Barelegged, they brandished spears and hurled insults and missiles at the defenders who were desperately trying to douse the flames with cauldrons and buckets of water.

Fulke drew rein on the crest of a ridge overlooking the struggle which appeared to be very one-sided in favour of the attackers. He gnawed on his thumb knuckle. 'Either ride away or become embroiled,' he murmured to Jean. 'Do you have a coin to toss?'

'When you go to visit a lady, it's unchivalrous to turn away your respects unpaid,' Jean said.

Fulke looked sidelong at his friend.

'I've been waiting twenty years to see Oonagh O'Donnel again,' Jean murmered.

Fulke was unsure if Jean was jesting. The regular, olive-skinned features could wear any expression at a whim and the dark brown eyes were inscrutable. 'Then we had best go and join the mêlée,' he said, and urged his mount down the slope towards the fighting.

It did not take long for a scout from the attackers to notice them and cry the alarm. As Fulke and his troop came on towards the battle, shields forward on their left arms, horses lined up stirrup to stirrup, a herald galloped out to meet them, a spear brandished in his right fist. About ten yards from their line, he yanked his Hibernian pony to an unruly halt. 'I greet you in the name of Padraig O'Donnel, rightful lord of Docionell,' he declared in passable Norman French. 'What is your business?' His undertunic was of Irish plaid but he wore a good Norman helm and short mail shirt.

'And I greet you in the name of William Marshal, over-lord of Glencavern,' Fulke responded. 'What is your business that you should be assaulting this place with fire and sword? Where are Lady Oonagh O'Donnel and her sons?'

The scout's gaze flickered along the line of horsemen and he moistened his lips. 'This land belongs to Lord Padraig,' he reiterated.

'He can prove his right to it? He has sworn an oath of homage for it?'

'This is none of your business. I'm warning you to leave while you still can.'

Fulke's smile was humourless. 'No, I think I'll stay. Besides . . .' Running his hand along his belt, right to left, he drew his sword and contemplated the blade. '. . . it's a while since I used this. I would hate to think of it rusting in the scabbard. Tell that to Lord Padraig.'

The scout licked his lips again, then abruptly whirled his pony and lashed the reins down on its hairy neck. He galloped up to a mail-clad knight who was directing operations with a mace, and gesticulated towards Fulke's troop.

'Now the fat is in the fire,' Jean murmured, drawing his sword.

Fulke narrowed his eyes the better to focus. At the Irish knight's left shoulder stood a man kitted out in the mail and surcoat of a professional mercenary. He towered head and shoulders above everyone else. A bushy black beard jutted on his chin, and a fearsome Dane axe rested casually over one shoulder. Fulke had seen the destruction of which such weapons were capable. A single stroke could shear a man's arm or split him skull to sternum like a bacon pig.

Fulke studied the besiegers. 'It is obvious that we are not

here to aid them. Either they must fight or yield. They've had enough time to make up their minds. If they're going to fight, I do not want to give them space to organise.' He signalled the men to prepare to charge. He hoped the attackers would run, but if they stood their ground, then at least the power of the charge should do serious damage.

Jean cast off his cloak and levelled his lance, his banner fluttering from the socket beneath the spear. Down the line, harness jingled as men adjusted and waited the final cry. Below them, pinned on the flat ground between the burning stockade and the ridge, the men of Padraig O'Donnel dithered, and were rallied by the bellow of their leader to stand firm on the stockade slope.

'*Fitz Warin!*' Fulke roared, and spurred Blaze. Through his body, he felt the powerful motion of the horse and the shudder of the ground as twenty destriers surged forward. He fixed his gaze on Blackbeard. Bring him down and Padraig O'Donnel was naked. Uttering a yell, he spurred in to engage.

Blackbeard whirled the axe, a weapon that Fulke's great-great-grandfather had faced on the field of Hastings. Light glittered on the blade, and its motion made a song of the wind. The action was so slow that Fulke could see the fragments of upward air it sliced, and the smooth effort of the arms that wielded it, and yet so fast that the terrifying delivery was inevitable.

Down it came, decapitating the accurate thrust of his lance head, shearing, slicing; on into muscle, sinew and bone. Fulke heard himself roar a denial. He tore on the reins and Blaze responded through a fountain of lifeblood, galloping on, forelegs still reaching for the ground ahead, back legs creasing, buckling.

Fulke flung himself from the saddle, hit the ground and felt his ribs crack. Someone stabbed down at him and the sharp silver edge of a spear pierced his flank. There was the whump of a sharpened sword blade and his attacker toppled, ripping the spear out as he fell.

'No!' Fulke gasped through near blinding agony, as Jean de Rampaigne stood over him protectively. 'Lead the men. We need to drive them off!'

Jean hesitated briefly, then with a grim nod bellowed a rallying cry.

Fulke crawled to the dead spearman, and taking the weapon from him used the ash shaft to lever himself to his feet. Strange shapes swam before his eyes. Red fish, black stars. He staggered and fell. Figures came running through the smoke and voices chattered in urgent Gael. He tried to defend himself, but they brushed his efforts easily aside as if he had no more strength than a child, and between them they carried him through what he could almost fancy were the burning gates of hell.

'Well?' Jean de Rampaigne enquired. 'Is he going to live?'

The woman who had been tending Fulke rose to her feet and washed her bloodied hands in a copper ewer. She wore no wimple as a widow should have done, and her hair, still as black as Jean remembered, hung down her back in a single heavy plait. Her gown was suitably sombre, but it clung to her figure, outlining the curve of breast and hip. More than twenty years on, tired and bloodstained as she was, Oonagh FitzGerald, now O'Donnel, retained her allure.

'He is lucky,' she said. 'The spear missed his vitals, but it is still a nasty wound and he has lost a deal of blood. Also he has broken several ribs.'

'You haven't answered my question.'

She fixed him with a stare the colour of harebells. 'That is because I do not know. For the moment he is safe and

I have given him a sleeping draught so that he may help his own body to heal.' The slightest of smiles touched her lips. 'As I remember, he was not one to remain still unless forced.' She glanced over her shoulder at Fulke's form, lying in the great chamber bed.

Jean looked too. Fulke was so still, so composed, that he might have been a dead man. Fortunate that the black-bearded giant had struck down a hundred marks' worth of destrier rather than the man riding it, and used the moment to make his escape. Fulke would not have survived a sustained attack.

'If he does not take the stiffening sickness or wound fever, then he will be no worse for his injuries,' she said. 'But they will take more than this day to show themselves. He must rest . . . and we must pray.' As she drew Jean out of the chamber he had to step over the enormous wolfhound guarding the threshold.

'You still keep the dogs then?'

'I value loyalty and I have found no creature to match,' she said.

'Not even your husband?'

She shrugged. 'A dog gives love unconditionally.' She led him into a small private solar annexed to the bedchamber. Assembling two cups, she poured him a measure of Irish mead. 'I miss Niall, God rest his soul, and I curse him for dying and bringing his bane of a brother down on me in my vulnerability.' Handing him the drink, she studied him. 'What brings you so timely to Docionell?'

'Business, my lady,' Jean said, being as frugal with the truth as Fulke had been to Maude. 'Through marriage, Fulke has lands in Ireland, held of William Marshal of Pembroke. Since you are Fulke's neighbour, he deemed it a courtesy to pay a visit – particularly when he heard from your son at Wotheney that your husband had died.' He took a drink of the mead which was powerful and sweet, redolent of heather and clover.

'Courtesy,' she smiled. 'You would be more truthful if you said self-interest.'

'Rather call it concern for Docionell. You should be glad of it, my lady. Without our timely arrival, you would not still be mistress here, would you?'

She conceded the point with a lifted forefinger. 'So you came to make sure that I was not going to marry a warlord spoiling for a fight? Am I right, or has my siren song lasted down the years?'

Jean's eyes filled with humour. 'Not for Fulke,' he said. 'He only has eyes for his wife.'

She considered him with mutual amusement. 'What about you?'

'Me? I have no wife.' Still smiling, he wandered to the embrasure and looked out. The smell of smoke hung in the moist air, heavy as dark cloth, and the people were toiling by torchlight, aided by some of Fulke's troop, to mend the broken gate.

'They will be back.' She joined him at the window's arch, and leaned against the wall. 'Padraig wants this land.' Her face contorted. 'He claims that Niall promised it to him before he died, but that is not true. He claims that he should rule it since Ruadri is a monk promised to celibacy and Collum but thirteen years old. It would have been different had my eldest son not been killed whilst hunting. Adam would have seen him off.' She gave a shrug and the way she held herself dared him to extend sympathy or pity. 'As it is . . . Padraig knows how vulnerable I am.'

'Fortunate that you have good neighbours then,' Jean said laconically, pity the last thing on his mind. He was intensely aware of her presence, could almost swear that he felt the heat of her body in the small, chill space between them.

'Indeed it is,' she said. He heard the whisper of fabric as she moved away to replenish her cup. 'But how long will you stay? You did not come today with the intention of becoming embroiled in a battle. That was merely fortuitous for me and unfortunate for you.'

'We will stay as long as needed,' Jean said.

'Do not say things that are not true just in order to keep the peace of the moment,' she said scornfully. 'False promises are worse than none at all. As soon as Fulke is well enough to travel, you will make your excuses and go.'

'I would stay.'

She looked at him, suspicion in her eyes now. 'Why would you want to do that?' she asked scornfully. 'A polished Norman knight, a courtier. What is the lure?'

Jean smiled. 'I was ever a man for new challenges, and if you remove the veneer, what lies beneath is not so polished.'

'Is that so?'

'Indeed it is, my lady.'

'Well then, you are no different to the rest.' Oonagh paced restlessly to the door arch and looked through it at the sleeping man. 'His wife,' she said, 'has he left her behind in England?'

'No, my lady. She is at Glencavern and I have taken the liberty of sending for her.' Her back was turned on him so Jean could not see her expression, but he thought her spine stiffened.

'Tell me about her,' she said.

'Mayhap you know her. She was formerly married to Theobald Walter.'

Oonagh turned. There was a gleam in her eye. 'Thin and pale as a stalk of winter grass,' she scoffed. 'Yes, I met her once.'

'Fulke has moved heaven and earth for her,' Jean said.

'When he was an outlaw he risked his life to ride into Canterbury and snatch her from under King John's nose. It is a love match the like of which most of us never see.' He could tell that it was not what she wanted to hear. Her expression was tight with displeasure, the full lips slightly pursed.

'He is no longer the untried squire whom you could twist around your little finger,' Jean warned softly. 'Then he was malleable. Now you will find forged steel.'

Her lips curved. 'That may be, but he came to visit out of more than just duty. And I am no longer the young widow. Then I was malleable too.'

'What drew him here was his duty mingled with the slightest tinge of curiosity, nothing more. It would be dangerous to think otherwise, and it seems to me that you are in enough danger already.'

'You would threaten me?'

'Never, my lady. Just advise.' Jean inclined his head. 'Now, if you will excuse me, I have the men to oversee in Fulke's place.' He strode briskly from the room and, although he was tempted, neither hesitated nor looked back. She wanted Fulke out of pique, out of a whim to continue what she thought was unfinished. Out of a desire to have the security of a strong protector at Docionell – out of need itself, he thought with a grimace as he entered the smoky great hall. Well, there was need and there was need, and he intended to show her the difference.

CHAPTER 36

'Injured!' Maude shot to her feet and the messenger took several hasty steps backwards. 'How badly?'

'I do not know, my lady. Sir Jean said to tell you that Lord Fulke is in no danger, that he is being well tended.'

'I am sure he is.' Maude ground her teeth. There was a horrible space where her stomach had been and it was rapidly filling with terror and rage. If Fulke had not ridden home, then his wounds were more than superficial. Either that or they were an excuse. The latter thought was so unworthy that she quashed it with shame. 'Did you see his injuries yourself?'

The soldier gnawed his lip and looked at the wall as if it was of great interest.

'Did you? Answer me!'

'I saw them bearing him to the lady's chamber,' the messenger said uncomfortably.

'And?'

'Forgive me, my lady, he could not walk and there was more blood than I have ever seen – although it could not all have been his. Sir Jean asks that you come, and bring a strong escort with you.'

Maude nodded. Somehow she rallied herself, managed to thank the man for delivering tidings that were none of his fault and dismissed him.

Within the hour, she was on the road to Docionell, her heart thundering in tune to the pounding of her mare's hooves. When one of the soldiers cautioned her about riding so fast, she rounded on him like a she-wolf and snarled that she could outride any man.

'I do not doubt that, my lady, but your horse cannot sustain the pace,' the knight said neutrally.

Swallowing her rage and anxiety, she eased the mare to a gentler pace and murmured an apology. A part of her was terrified that Fulke was dying. She kept reliving the messenger's words about blood. She kept thinking of him in Oonagh O'Donnel's chamber. Holy Virgin Mary, let him be safe, she prayed. Let him come to no harm. And as they passed the weathered grey boundary marker, the mare's hooves began to drum again in a hard, fast rhythm.

They came to Docionell, descending the ridge as Fulke and his men had done, and at an almost similar pace. Dusk was falling, but it was still sufficiently light to see the shored-up damage to the keep gates, and it would take days for the stink of charred wood to dissipate. Half a dozen men were occupied in digging a large hole – a grave, she realised, as she saw the corpses of three horses lying beside the mound of new earth, their legs stiff, bellies swelling at the sky. One of them was a liver chestnut with white markings. After a single glance, she turned her head away, unable to look.

The guards on duty saluted and passed her through. She recognised one of them and leaned from the saddle to ask him about Fulke.

'I could not say, my lady,' he replied. 'We have not seen him today, but Sir Jean says that he will make a good recovery.'

Her anxiety eased, but only a little. It was like a violent toothache that had subsided to a throb. She would not be comforted until she had seen for herself. She rode on into the courtyard and swung down from the saddle without waiting for one of her escort to dismount her. Travelling satchel over one shoulder, bow and quiver over the other, she headed straight towards the low timber building of the main hall.

Men looked at her askance as she stalked into the room. Flushed from the exertion of her journey, wisps of hair escaping her wimple and her bow in her hand, she was the image of the goddess Artemis. Fulke's men bowed in deference; the Irish, looking startled, followed suit.

'Maude?' Jean de Rampaigne pushed his way forward, his expression full of concern. 'You must have ridden like the wind.'

She embraced him and stepped briskly away, knowing that if she did not, she would cling to him and weep floods of tears. She searched his face, seeking clues and finding none. 'Where is he, Jean? What happened? I saw . . .' She bit her lip. 'I saw them digging the graves to bury dead horses, and Blaze was one of them.'

Jean drew her arm through his and spoke in a reassuring tone. 'Blaze was killed by a single blow from a Dane axe. Fulke took a spear in the side – it's a nasty wound but unlikely to kill him. He suffered some broken ribs too when the horse fell.'

'Take me to him, for God's love, Jean, before I go mad. I knew that there was danger in his coming here. I could feel it like a great dark hole.' She caught back a sob. Much good it would do her to play the hysterical wife. It was not as if she was unaccustomed to tending injuries and Fulke, by the very life he led, was frequently exposed to danger.

Jean brought her to an oak door at the end of the hall, set his hand to the latch and ushered her within a handsome solar. There was an embroidery frame by the window with a basket of bright silks nearby. A brazier smoked softly, giving off a dry scent of peat and herbs, and candles of heavy yellow wax burned on wrought-iron prickets. A maid sat in one corner, industriously preparing retted flax to be spun into linen thread, the fibres spread out in a white-gold fan of angel hair in her lap.

'Where's your mistress?' Jean demanded.

The woman nodded towards the closed off curtain between the rooms. 'Tending my lord, sir.'

Maude saw Jean's jaw tighten. Her stomach fluttered with anger and resentment. 'That is my place now,' she said and started towards the heavy woollen hanging. She reached to rattle it aside, but before she could lay her hand to the fabric, it was drawn back on a soft clacking of rings and she came face to face with Oonagh O'Donnel.

The woman was clad in her undergown of bleached linen. Her surcoat, of the latest fashion, Maude noticed out of the corner of a jaundiced eye, was draped over a curule chair near the brazier. She wore no wimple either, and her hair shone with the gloss of rare ebony wood. A large silver wolfhound rose from the foot of the bed and padded to the woman's side.

Maude met Oonagh's clear blue stare, frigid as a pale spring sky. 'I am Lady FitzWarin,' she said, 'and I have come to care for my husband.'

The other woman smiled almost mockingly. 'I know who you are and why you are here, my lady.' She gestured to the bed. 'He is a strong man, your husband.' Her voice was smoky and imbued with languid double entendre. She looked as if she had just risen from the bed of a lover rather than the tending of a sick man.

'And I am a strong woman,' Maude answered coldly, 'so that makes myself and Fulke two halves of one whole.'

Oonagh O'Donnel raised one eyebrow, the smile remaining, as if she doubted the veracity of Maude's words but was too polite to say so.

'He is mine now,' Maude said and thrust past the other woman to the bedside. 'Fulke?'

He was lying on his back and a little to one side. His dark hair was damp on his brow, but from the bathing of a herb-infused cloth rather than the sweat of fever. The scent from the bedclothes wafted across her nostrils. Musky, perfumed, as if Oonagh O'Donnel had wrapped her body in the sheets. Perhaps she had. His eyes were open and lucid.

'Maude? Thank Christ.' His hand went out to her and she gripped it possessively, meshing her fingers through his and feeling the pressure of bone on bone. Behind her, she felt the draught of the curtain settling into place as Oonagh drew it across.

'Was she worth it then?' Maude leaned over to kiss him and then recoiled, for the smell of the Irish woman was on his skin. She could taste the perfume on his lips. What had Oonagh O'Donnel said about him being strong?

'What's wrong?' He looked at her with puzzled eyes, the pupils large and dark in the deepening shadows of dusk.

No, Maude thought, angry with herself. Oonagh was wrong. Fulke would have to be very weak to succumb. She had never known his eyes fix on another woman except in the heat of a young man's lust in the days when he was unwed and she belonged to Theobald. 'You smell of her,' she said with a grimace. 'You taste of her. I cannot bear it . . .'

'You don't think . . .' He looked so alarmed that she was both amused and chagrined.

'Only for a moment, then I put it from my mind. It was what she wanted me to think.'

'She said that she would shave me.' He darted her a glance then looked away.

Maude was not such a fool as to believe he had not been tempted. Likely he had and most sorely. She could imagine Oonagh discarding her fine tunic to avoid getting it splashed or soapy. Could imagine her kneeling in the bed and provoking him. Wounded he might be, but that did not mean his entire body was incapacitated. 'Providing that is all she did, I will let her live,' Maude murmured, lightly patting her bow and quiver.

'Maude!'

She lifted her brows. 'I mean it. If I am not a jealous wife, it is because you do not give me cause. But if you ever did . . .' She left the rest of the sentence to his imagination and rolled the bedclothes down. 'Now, let me have a look at your injuries.'

Despite her feelings of antipathy towards Oonagh O'Donnel, she had to admit grudgingly that the woman had made a fine job of cleaning and binding his wounds. But then she was attracted to Fulke and he had, after all, saved her life and her livelihood.

'How long before you can travel?' she asked as she replaced the bandages. 'Another two days – three?'

'Depends on Padraig O'Donnel.' He looked thoughtful. 'I cannot leave Docionell without a strong garrison. The moment I ride out, I know he will be back.'

'You are not intending to stay here!' She was unable to keep the revulsion from her voice.

'Of course not.' He took her hand and kissed her finger-tips. A tired smile creased his eye corners. 'I have a thoroughly able deputy whom I know will relish the task – although he doesn't realise it at the moment.'

*   *   *

Jean stared contemptuously at Oonagh. 'You're a bitch,' he said softly so that his voice would not carry beyond the thickness of the curtain she had just dropped. 'A conniving, jealous bitch, and it will avail you nothing. Go back in that room in quarter of a candle notch and you will indeed find them two halves of one whole. It will take more than your petty scheming to split them asunder.'

'I do not know what you mean.' She tossed her head, making her black plait ripple like a newly tugged bell rope.

'You do,' he retorted. 'God's love, my lady, but you do. You must have heard the horses arriving; you must have known she was here. But instead of coming to make a formal greeting, you arrange to meet her on the edge of the bedchamber with your hair exposed and your surcoat removed. I am neither blind nor stupid, so do not treat me as if I am.'

Anger flashed in her eyes and he saw the slap coming even before she launched it. He caught it halfway to its mark and forced her wrist round and down until she gasped, tears of pain glittering. The maid at her flax-spinning made a soft sound of distress.

'Out!' Jean commanded, and turned such a glare in her direction that the woman gasped and fled.

'All men are blind and stupid!' Oonagh tried to wrench free, but Jean tightened his grip, feeling her flesh grow hot and bruised beneath his fingers.

'Not me,' he panted.

Her free hand dived towards the knife in his belt. His other got to her first and he swung her round and against the wall, pinning her there with the weight of his body. His breath matched harshly with hers. Lust and violence crackled between them like the air around a split of lightning. The dog made a bored sound and padded off to flop down across the outer door.

She arched towards him, sinuous and supple. 'Are you going to beat me?'

He imagined her white flesh with the reddening sting of a horsewhip or the hard imprint of his fingers. He knew of men – and women – who played such games. You did not cross the Bosporus and see Constantinople, nor dwell at the royal court and remain ignorant. He supposed it had its appeal, but not for him.

'No,' he said grimly, 'I'm not. But I am going to put the notion of bedding with Fulke FitzWarin out of your mind for ever.'

'And just how are you going to do that?' she mocked. 'Men brag of their prowess between the sheets, but their deeds never match their boasting.'

'Mine do,' Jean said, and lowered his mouth to hers.

It hurt to sit up, but propped on a backrest of several down-stuffed pillows, Fulke could manage. Maude had disappeared to inspect the kitchen arrangements and find him a bowl of stew. The lady of the settlement was momentarily absent about her duties too. Jean de Rampaigne, looking somewhat the worse for wear and at the same time full of himself, was sitting on the edge of Fulke's bed.

'Well, what do you think to my proposition?' Fulke enquired with a straight face. 'Do you want to stay and tame the Irish?' Certainly, Jean looked as if he had made a start, and if the muffled sounds in the antechamber had been any indication, it had been a hard-fought battle.

Jean did not rise to the bait. 'You are offering me the fief of Docionell as your tenant vassal, and the supervisory care of Glencavern?'

'Subject to Marshal's confirmation but I cannot see that he will object!' Fulke permitted himself to smile. 'I understand that to a man considering marriage, the lady has some fine dower estates with good grazing and an excellent harbour. And, of course, until the youngest son comes of age, he will need a warden to oversee his interests.'

Jean nodded. 'I suppose it comes to us all,' he said.

'What does?'

'Settling down. Governing land. Raising children.'

'If it's not to your taste . . .'

Jean showed a flash of white teeth. 'Oh, it's very much to my taste. That's how I know I'm growing old.'

'Well, if that is the case, then I must be in my dotage.'

'You are,' Jean laughed, but almost immediately sobered. 'No, it has been different for you. Since birth, you have had an obligation to your family, to Whittington. I was raised without expectation of land. I pledged my faith to the Walters in return for food and shelter and a daily wage. The same for you until now and in return I have given my services, whether they be of sword or diplomacy. When I was younger I had my duty to my lord, but no deeper responsibility and it suited me well.' His smile flashed again. 'Girls were for tumbling and adventure was my lifeblood. I am not saying that I have lost either of those interests, but time does not stand still. I am almost two score years old. The only knights over that age who go adventuring are desperate ones.' He gestured around the room. 'No, I think I will have adventure enough keeping hold of Docionell and its chatelaine.'

'It is what you desire? I do not want you to take it out of faith to me and in doing so be unfaithful to yourself.'

'It is what I desire,' Jean said firmly and folded his arms as if gathering the offer to his breast. 'I do not believe that I will hanker after new adventure or women to tumble for a long time . . . if, of course, she will have me.'

'Do you doubt that she will?'

Jean pondered for a moment then shook his head. 'No,'

he said. 'She is like me. She cannot afford to dance on the edge for ever, no matter how exhilarating. Besides, she needs a protector for this place, and you are clearly spoken for. I believe I have brought her to see the benefits of changing allegiance.'

'Good,' said Fulke wryly. 'Perhaps you ought to go and tell my wife before she does your future wife an injury.'

Jean and Oonagh were married two days later in the small wooden chapel adjoining the hall. Fulke was well enough to be on his feet, if a little slow of movement. He had vacated the lord's bedchamber so that Oonagh and Jean might have it for their wedding night – although, as he observed to Maude, the couple had managed very well on the solar floor thus far.

Oonagh wore a gown of simple blue linen, bound at the waist by a girdle of silver braid. In deference to the sanctity of the chapel, she had covered her plait with a light veil of silk, bound in place with a bridal chaplet of myrtle and roses. She pledged herself before the witnesses in a loud, clear voice, making it clear to all that she had not been forced into the marriage. Jean presented her with a gold besant in token of endowing her with his wealth, and a ring as a symbol of the bond between them.

The priest blessed the couple and gave the Church's sanction to the union. Bride and groom kissed, their hands bound together by the priest's stole of office. With smiling eyes, Oonagh stood before Fulke and Maude to receive their congratulations. As Fulke stooped to kiss her cheek, she mischievously turned her head so that their lips met, and then she set her arms around his neck and made sure that the kiss was a full-blooded salute. 'In memory of the past,' she said with a coquettish flutter of her eyelashes as she released him.

Fulke inclined his head. 'May it be put behind us.'

Beside him, Maude quietly seethed. While she had made her truce with Oonagh, the women were never going to be outright friends. There was too much suspicion and jealousy on both sides. They would tolerate each other for the sake of the bond between their husbands, but no more than that.

Maude murmured her congratulations and the women kissed the air above each other's cheeks. When Jean stooped over Maude to receive her tribute, she embraced him in the manner that Oonagh had embraced Fulke, but with slower deliberation.

'For all the times I have asked and you have been there,' she said. Fulke looked shocked, but also reluctantly amused. Oonagh's brow, irritatingly smooth for a woman of her years, wore the tiniest furrow of irritation. Good. Let her realise that she was matched.

'If I had known you would do that to me,' Jean jested, 'I would have got married years ago!'

They were sitting down to the wedding feast in the hall – a hastily arranged affair of spicy meat ragout and bannocks, when the alarm horn sounded on the stockade and one of the guards on duty came running with the news that Padraig O'Donnel had returned with more men and siege ladders.

Cursing, Fulke eased to his feet. Jean finished his mouthful of ragout, washed it down with wine, and, tearing a piece of bannock off the large round in the centre of the trestle, headed for the wall walks.

Oonagh stared at the ruins of her wedding feast and cursed fluently in Gaelic. Fear snatched Maude's appetite, already fickle in the first weeks of pregnancy. Suddenly the spicy scent of the stew was nauseating. She pushed her bowl aside. 'We need to prepare for the wounded.' She rose to her feet, taking refuge in motion, one hand instinctively going to her belly. 'And help the men on the walls. Where do you keep the cauldrons for laundry and dyeing? No one will climb a ladder into a faceful of boiling water.'

'In one of the bailey stores, still ready from last time.' Oonagh was on her feet, her expression bright with anger. 'I'll show you.'

As the women worked to fill the cauldrons with water, to build fires beneath them, to prepare lengths of linen bandages, needles and thread, their truce gave way to a grudging respect for each other's skills.

'You're not a dainty Norman lady after all,' Oonagh said as she watched Maude pump the turves with the bellows to fan the flames and increase the heat beneath the cauldron.

'Is that what you thought I was?' Maude wiped her brow on her forearm, leaving a sooty smut. Beyond the wall walk, they could hear a cacophony of howls and insults as O'Donnel's men prepared to put up the siege ladders.

'When I saw you with Theobald Walter, for sure,' Oonagh said. 'So pretty and meek and neat; the sort of woman that you hear French troubadours praise in their songs.' Her tone emphasised that she was not passing a compliment. 'I could not imagine Fulke being besotted by such a wife unless he was attracted to her lands.'

'He was.' Maude began to gasp. It was hard work, but worth it. The flames were fairly licking beneath the cauldron now. 'No man marries for love alone – and few women get the choice.'

'Did you have a choice?'

'Oh yes.' Red-faced, Maude stopped and wiped her brow again. 'Him or King John.'

Oonagh stared, then suddenly she began to laugh. 'And therein lies the difference. I had the same choice, and I chose John.' Sobering, she took the bellows from Maude and attacked the fire. 'I wouldn't make the same mistake again. Not that he was a bad lover, you understand, far from it, but he did not keep the promises made between the sheets.' She grimaced. 'But then I was naïve enough in those days to believe that he would.'

'John only keeps his promises when forced to them,' Maude said grimly. 'Whether between the sheets or in full view of the Curia Regis.'

Oonagh looked at her curiously.

'It is a long tale. Ask Jean to tell you, it calls for the skill of a troubadour.'

Oonagh's look of curiosity increased. Within the cauldron, small bubbles began to rise in the steaming water. Whether or not she would have pursued the subject became a moot point as the women saw Fulke walking slowly towards them, constrained by the wound in his side. Maude could see that he was hurting and she hurt with him. Pray God that he did not have to fight.

'Your former brother-by-marriage has brought mercenaries from Limerick to support him,' he said. 'Dregs and gutter-sweepings, hired on the promise of rich pickings.'

Oonagh whitened. 'Are they strong enough to break through?'

He rubbed the side of his jaw. 'I . . .'

'The truth.' Oonagh bared her teeth. 'I don't want false reassurance.'

Wintry humour glinted in his eyes. 'Nor would I give it to you. There are plenty of them, but rudely trained. There is a possibility they will overwhelm us by sheer weight of numbers. We have managed to get a messenger away through their ranks to Glencavern. That is all I can tell you. I am sorry that it is not a precise answer, but warfare never is. Just now they are drinking uisge beatha in huge quantities for courage and working themselves into a rage by hurling insults. Keep the water ready, we are going to need it.'

'You will not fight on the wall walk?' Maude said unsteadily, imagining him slowed and weakened by his wound and made the prey of a howling Irish spearman.

'Do I look like a madman?'

'No, but that means nothing. You didn't look like one when you rode into Canterbury to take me, nor when you went after Will when the royal foresters captured him.'

He took her by the shoulders. 'Even if I desired to fight, I would not, because I am a liability to the other men. Grant me some leeway of common sense.'

'I know you. You will not sit still and watch others fight unless I tie you to a bench with ten yards of rope.' Tears of worry glittered in her eyes and she forced her hand up between their bodies to wipe them away.

'Of course I will not sit and watch. There are other things to be done: organising a second line of defence for one. If they break through, they need to be contained. The best fighting men are on the wall, but that does not mean that those left are incapable of defending themselves.'

Maude compressed her lips and nodded. At least he would not be leaning over a parapet with a sword in his hand – unlike Jean. She glanced at Oonagh, but the Irish woman's expression was controlled, her emotions tucked away until it was safe to bring them out.

'Where's your lad?' Fulke demanded of Oonagh.

'In the hall.' She jerked her head and a glimmer of fear escaped to spark in her eyes. 'Surely, for God's love, you are not bringing him out to the battle?'

'I would not dream of endangering him, but the people need a rallying point. It is him they are fighting for, not a group of Normans upon whom none of them had set eyes a seven-day since.'

'Very well then.' Oonagh swallowed. 'Do as you see fit,

but if anything happens to him, I will kill you myself.'

'You won't need to,' Fulke said grimly, 'because I will already be dead.' And on the comfort of those words, left the women at the cauldron and moved on.

Fulke sought in the hall for Oonagh's thirteen-year-old son and found only the women industriously cutting strips of linen into bandages. No, they had not seen the young lord. Hand pressed to his aching side, Fulke searched every corner and crevice of the room, checking the bedrolls for sign of the slender, dark-haired youth. The bedchambers were next, but there too he could find nothing. Fulke cursed. He went to the boy's bed bench and picked up a discarded linen shirt. It was old and beginning to fray: a garment that the lad wore at night. Bundling it up, Fulke took it back into the hall and moved stiffly over to the two huge silver wolfhounds dozing by the fire.

'Seek,' he commanded, thrusting the shirt beneath the questing damp noses and pitching his voice high as if playing a game.

The bitch hound lunged to her feet. 'Seek,' Fulke said again, wafting the shirt under her nose.

The wolfhound cast around the floor, burying her nose in the rushes, licking them. Then with a whine, she trotted from one side of the hall to the other, zigzagging almost as if on the trail of a hare, before shooting out of the door into the bailey. The younger dog followed, gambolling, half copying, eager but unsure. Fulke gritted his teeth and, ignoring the pain from his chest each time he expanded his ribs, did his best to run after the dogs.

The bitch snuffled the bailey, the grass trampled to a clay-like mud by the passing of too many feet. She circled, and Fulke was beginning to wonder if she had lost the lad's scent among the confusion of so many others, when she set off again at a straight run towards the wall walks. Now Fulke did curse. God in heaven, the most dangerous place that the lad could be, and without armour too!

From the ditch below the stockade, there came a sudden, concerted howl of voices, followed by the slamming sound of wood on wood as the siege ladders struck the top of the defences. Missiles sang through the air, egg-sized chunks of stone hurled by slingers, pots of powdered lime that smashed on impact and blinded the eyes. Arrows fired from on high, curving and plummeting – not many of those, thank God, but then it only took one to wreak the damage.

A lime pot exploded on the steps above him, filling the air with choking white powder. Fulke threw his sleeve across his face and stumbled up the last few steps. The dogs fled, yelping.

'My lord, you should not be here!' cried Ralf Gras. His shield was down on his left arm, his sword drawn. In front of him, a group of soldiers had hooked grappling irons around the top of the ladder and were attempting to cast it and its cargo of rapidly climbing men down into the ditch.

'The lad!' Fulke gagged. 'I've come for the lad!'

'What lad?'

'Collum O'Donnel, who else?'

'He's up here?'

'Well, he's certainly not anywhere else!' Fulke snarled.

Ralf suddenly lunged and slashed. There was a yell and the Irishman at the top of the ladder crashed down, taking with him several of the climbers beneath. Two serjeants dislodged the ladder, pushing it sideways until it fell away with its cargo and hit the ground with a jarring crash.

Fulke drew his sword and eased along the timbered wall walk. The boy was standing near the entrance to the next stairway. Transfixed, he was gripping the pointed tips of the stockade stakes and leaning over to watch the attacking swarm. No helm, no armour. Just a wedding tunic of bright red wool and a cloak of a colour only a little less dark, making of him a wonderful target.

'You little fool!' Fulke roared. 'What in the name of God's ten toes are you doing!'

The boy looked up, startled. 'I was just—' he started to say and then his eyes widened in shock, giving Fulke a split second of warning. Through instinct and years of training, he ducked and at the same time, swiped low with his sword, connecting with unprotected flesh and bone.

The mercenary screamed and fell. Fulke struck again to make sure that he stayed down. The boy began to gasp, his breath sawing in his chest in a high-pitched whine of shock. Fulke felt the trickle of blood down his side. His mouth was dry, his heart pounding in great hammer strokes.

'I thought I could help,' the boy said through chattering teeth. 'I didn't want to stay in the hall.'

'That doesn't mean you have to endanger yourself and everyone around you by climbing the wall walk!' Fulke grabbed his arm and bundled the lad back down into the bailey. The heat of the moment was holding his pain at bay but he knew he would pay for it later. Behind him, he could hear the clash of hard-fought battle as more of O'Donnel's men gained the walk boards.

'I can fight, I've started my training.' Pride rang in the boy's voice and, beneath it, an undercurrent of trembling fear. Fulke suspected he had forced himself to take the greatest risk of all because of the shame of that fear.

'You have courage, lad,' Fulke said grimly. 'What you need to accompany it is common sense. You'd not last a heartbeat against one of those mercenaries, and I doubt that your uncle Padraig would much care if one of them "accidentally" spitted you on his spear. Stay close to me. You're of more use being seen by your people than standing up there as a target.'

The boy flushed, but bit his tongue on a retort and followed Fulke. There were injured to be passed down the line and brought to the hall. The cauldrons of boiling water had to be hoisted to the battlements; the people needed to be encouraged to hold their guard. If the mercenaries took the compound, it wouldn't make any difference who had surrendered and who had fought. They would all be treated the same. Fulke took the boy everywhere, except into the thick of the fighting, ensuring that his red tunic was seen by the defenders.

Fulke and Collum were in the hall with Maude and Oonagh when a party of mercenaries led by Padraig O'Donnel broke through the walk defences and gained the compound. Maude was bandaging a soldier's arm wound and Oonagh was tending another man who had taken a blow to the skull from a slingshot stone when Padraig burst into the hall, his huge, axe-wielding bodyguard at his side.

A woman screamed. Fulke drew his sword and pushed Collum behind him. Maude lowered her patient's arm and groped on the trestle.

Everything became a sudden chaos of flashing weapons, battle cries and savage motion. Fulke parried the blows launched at him, using his mail-clad body to shield the boy. In terror, Oonagh backed behind the trestles trying to keep them between her and the warrior who desired to run her through.

Blackbeard loomed, his teeth bared in an ursine snarl. Fulke saw the axe blow descending and knew that even if he did manage to parry in time, it was useless against the cleaving power of the Dane axe. But instead of a heavy shearing edge separating his head from his body, there was a different singing in the air and a blur of motion. The bodkin head of a hunting arrow drove Blackbeard violently backwards. The goose-feather shaft protruding from his mail shuddered once and stopped in tandem with the heart it had pierced. Blackbeard's eyes were wide open from the shock of impact and they remained that way, glassy with death.

Fulke stared, then he turned his head and saw Maude in her archer's stance. At ten paces, there had only been one outcome. Jean burst into the hall with several Docionell men and set upon the mercenaries who had broken through. There was a vigorous skirmish, sharp but short. Without the protection of his mighty bodyguard, Padraig O'Donnel was no match for Jean's blade.

In the silence that followed the destructive whirlwind of battle, the boy knelt beside his uncle's corpse and uncurled the fist from the hilt of the bloodied sword. 'It's mine,' he said as Fulke looked at him askance. 'As it was my father's.'

'Your father's?'

'My uncle Padraig stole it from his body.'

Breathing hard, Fulke looked at the body of Padraig O'Donnel and pressed his hand to his ribs. His fingers came away red and sticky.

'It's over,' the boy said, his voice filled with a new maturity despite its childish treble.

Maude pushed to Fulke's side. 'Let me see,' she said.

'What?' He looked at her nonplussed, thinking for a moment that she wanted a good look at the corpse.

'Your side, you're bleeding again,' she said impatiently. 'Let me look.'

'At least I know I am alive,' he said ruefully. 'It is a good thing your aim is so true. I doubt you would have the skill to stitch my head back to my body.'

'Do not jest!' she said sharply.

He swallowed. 'Christ, if I did not, I would weep, and

there's too much to be done. Besides, there are others in worse case than me.' He indicated the surrounding bloody shambles. 'Tend them first. I can wait.'

She clucked her tongue at him, but turned to the table and picked up a length of bandage. Although her hands were perfectly steady, she kept her head averted from the body of the black-bearded mercenary and her complexion was white. Fulke issued a terse command and three soldiers bore the hulk from the room.

Oonagh came to look upon the corpse of her brother-in-law. 'God rest his soul,' she said, making the sign of the Cross but speaking the words as if they were an insult. 'Now perhaps I can celebrate my marriage as it should be celebrated.' Stepping delicately over the body, she went into Jean's arms.

CHAPTER 37

Whittington Castle,
November 1214

On the feast of St Andrew, Fulke's daughter Hawise was betrothed to William, heir of neighbouring Baron Robert Pantulf of Wem. The lands of FitzWarin and Pantulf marched side by side and the family had interests in common.

Hawise and William knew each other socially, although their contact had not been great thus far since William Pantulf was close to thirty years old, a handsome man of the world, and Hawise, although precocious, was not quite thirteen.

'Perhaps we should have had a wedding today instead of a betrothal,' said Robert Pantulf to Fulke as they watched the betrothed couple dance to the music of pipes and tabor in Whittington's decorated great hall. He was an elderly man, beginning to stoop, but his eyes were full of life.

'Hawise is still too young.' Fulke shook his head and watched his daughter, an ache in his heart. It hardly seemed a moment since she was a small, curly-haired infant sitting in his lap and demanding his attention. Now she was practising the steps of a mating dance with the man who would be her husband. Her hair, loose in token of her virginity, rippled like autumn leaves to her waist and she was wearing a laced gown the colour of peacock feathers that showed the swell of developing breasts. She was caught in the narrow space between child and woman, innocence seeking knowledge and more enticing than she realised. The realisation would be another step on the path.

'I was the same age as her when I was betrothed to Theo,' Maude murmured softly, joining the men and wrapping her arm around Fulke's.

'As I said, too young to wed,' Fulke repeated. 'She still has much growing to do before she is ready to be a wife.'

Pantulf smiled slightly at Fulke. 'Perhaps I detect a desire in you not to let her go?'

Fulke cleared his throat and rubbed the back of his neck. 'She is my firstborn,' he said. 'Of course it is hard.' He smiled ruefully, trying to lighten the moment. 'Her little sister is only three years old and it seems not a moment since Hawise was that age.' He glanced at his youngest daughter. Mabile was sitting on Gracia's knee, her narrow white-blonde plaits braided with gold ribbon in honour of her sister's betrothal. Mabile would never marry. He would always have one daughter at home, but that was tragedy, not a source of pleasure. Her birth had been difficult for she had been born feet first and it had been a long time before she breathed. At first she had seemed like any baby – perhaps a trifle more fractious, but as time passed, it became obvious that she was different.

Seated at a trestle beside their uncles William and Philip were Fulke's two sons. Fulkin, a coltish, graceful ten, butter-haired and blue-eyed, and Ivo, conceived in Ireland, now seven, and dark like his sister Jonetta. For the nonce, beneath the sharp gaze of the adults, they were behaving. 'With boys it is different,' Fulke said. 'They make your heart fierce with pride; they don't melt it.'

'Aye,' Pantulf said gruffly and looked towards his son and heir. The two men watched the couple weave in the steps of the dance. William Pantulf moved with an athlete's grace.

Fulke had seen him in the tiltyard and at swordplay. He handled himself well and, although lightly built, he knew how to make every stroke count. He also had patience and the ability to see humour in most situations — traits that were a necessity when it came to dealing with Hawise. His age had made Fulke pause for thought, but reflection had shown that although there were younger men aplenty, there were none he would trust with his daughter's happiness and the control of the lands that were her marriage portion.

Pantulf gestured towards two dancing, giggling young women. 'What about the other lass? Have you anyone in mind for her?'

'Which one? Oh, Jonetta. I've opened tentative negotiations with de Pembridge's lad for her,' Fulke said. Jonetta sparkled like a dark jewel. By contrast, her companion looked drab, which was not really true. Clarice's glow was softer and less easily seen from a distance.

'I forgot that the other one was your ward,' Pantulf said. 'Had any offers for her?'

'One or two, but none that suited.' Fulke did not elaborate. Clarice, gentle, biddable Clarice, was twice as stubborn as either of his daughters. Hawise could be persuaded by flattery and attention, Jonetta by the promise of a new gown, little Mabile by the sticky bribe of a sugared plum. But nothing worked on Clarice. Neither threat nor cajolery, bribery nor bellowing. She did not wish to marry; she was happy as she was. Her proposed husband might be a paragon of manhood, but she did not want him. There had been no tears, no pleading, just an implacable determination. Since the offers in question had been merely good rather than excellent, it had been simpler for Fulke to abandon the issue.

'Aye.' Pantulf gave him a knowing smile. 'While she stays unwed, her revenues are yours and you have an extra nursemaid and helpmeet for your household.'

'That is true.' Fulke nodded, thinking how good Clarice was with Mabile. 'But I would not keep her from marriage deliberately. Rather it is her choice.'

'You give her a choice?'

'You do not know Clarice,' he said wryly. 'My daughters can be contrary to the point where it is a wonder I have not torn my hair out by the roots, but with Clarice it is an art. You would not believe unless you saw.'

Pantulf raised his brows and looked with renewed interest on the unremarkable brown-haired girl swirling and turning with the other dancers.

'The strange thing about Clarice,' Fulke murmured, watching her too, 'is that she has been an adult ever since she came to us – and that was as a child of barely eight years old. I can remember once when Maude and I were having an argument over something petty and she fixed us with a look that the sternest Mother Superior would have been hard pressed to duplicate. I felt about this tall.' He raised his thumb and forefinger in illustration.

Pantulf grinned. 'Even more reason to find her a husband.'

Fulke shook his head. 'I think,' he said, 'that when the right man does appear, it will be Clarice who chooses him, not anyone else.'

'Papa, Papa, come and dance!' Hawise flourished up to him, her cheeks flushed with exertion and happiness, her peacock gown swirling. She tugged at his arm. 'You've talked enough, come and dance!'

'Then again,' Fulke laughed to Pantulf, 'perhaps I'm not strict enough with my womenfolk. You see how they order me about?'

'I see how they respond to you,' smiled Robert Pantulf. 'God grant my son the same grace.'

*   *   *

'I am watching my children grow into adulthood,' Fulke said to Maude much later that night as they prepared for bed, 'and I feel more than ever that I am standing in my father's shoes.' His voice was a little slurred. You couldn't drink good Rhenish wine all night and expect to keep a clear head. 'I can remember when I was their age, and my father was mine.'

'You are feeling your years?' Maude looked teasingly at him. She was a little giddy herself. With a flick of her fingers she dismissed the maid and plumped down on the bed.

'I am feeling the passage of time.' He stooped to remove his shoes. 'Yet everything seems to stand still. My father had no daughters for whom to provide betrothal celebrations, but I can remember Christmas feasts when we danced like that with relations and neighbours. I was one of the youngsters then, exhorting everyone to join the jigs and carols, and my father was the amused adult. Now we have changed places. Am I his ghost? Or is he mine?'

'You're drunk,' Maude said, thinking that she was not so far off that condition herself. 'First comes pleasure, then sadness.'

'Well, that's true,' he said and cursed as his leg binding became knotted beneath the fumbling of his fingers. 'I'm glad to see Hawise happy, I'm glad her marriage is settled, and I'm sad that I'm beginning to lose her. Already she looks to William Pantulf as if she draws her sustenance from him . . .'

Maude came and knelt before him to help with his leg binding. 'That is as it should be,' she murmured.

'Yes, I know, and I'm glad of it, but it still cuts me like a knife.'

'You still have two more daughters.'

'Promise of more wounds. What sort of comfort is that?' He gave a broken laugh. 'Jonetta will wed soon enough and Mabile . . .' He shook his head and swallowed.

'Oh, Fulke.' Maude unwrapped the second binding and moved up his body, pushing him back on the bed. She painted his face with the end of one of her braids and kissed him softly. 'You still have a wife too. What sort of comfort is that?'

He threw his arms around her, enveloping her in a hug that almost crushed her ribs. 'Where would I be without you?' he muttered.

'Likely in the hall with your brothers still drinking to old times,' she said flippantly, but stroked his hair with tender affection. In a moment, she would have to push him away so that she could breathe, but understanding his need, she pressed herself to him.

'Melusine,' he muttered, his breath sodden with wine fumes. In moments, he was snoring. Maude gently extricated herself, took a gasp of air, and looked at him in the faint flicker of the night candle. She thought he had been troubled of late, but it was more of an inkling on her part than anything he had said or done. Perhaps there were difficulties with the estates. Since returning from an expedition to Poitou with John in July, he had been poring over the accounts with his stewards and had been on several whirlwind visits to various FitzWarin manors. Occasionally he had been into Wales too. The cordiality that had existed between him and Llewelyn during the outlaw days had lost its robustness. They were polite with each other. Fulke had forgiven but not forgotten Llewelyn's withdrawal of support and Llewelyn did not trust a marcher lord who had made his peace with John. Fulke was still a dangerous warrior, and some of the border lands were in dispute. Courteous but barbed words had been exchanged over the manor of Gorddwr which had a FitzWarin tenant as lord over a settlement more than three-quarters Welsh.

Maude yawned. The morning would bring what it would bring. Perhaps drink had made her maudlin too, that and the realisation that her eldest daughter was almost at an age to wed. And soon her sons would leave to begin their training in the household of Ranulf, Earl of Chester. First pages, then squires, then knights. But not yet, she comforted the surge of panic within herself. There was still some small space of time to nestle her brood, and the glory was in seeing them fly and knowing that she had given them the wings to do so . . . all except Mabile, whose wings were of fragile, damaged gossamer. Everything came so slowly to Mabile and with great effort. At three, Hawise had chattered ceaselessly like a magpie from the moment she rose to the time she lay down to sleep. Mabile, however, had not even begun to grasp the intricacies of language. Sometimes, as if raging against her inability to communicate, the infant would throw spectacular screaming fits that were only comforted when she was held tightly and soothed like a swaddled infant. Most of the time she was silent. She would sit for hours, staring at images only she could see, and softly rocking herself to a heartbeat rhythm. It was eerie and disturbing to watch her. A heart-breakingly beautiful faery child, perfect and yet irrevocably flawed.

Maude found that she had been silently weeping and, knuckling the tears from her eyes, took herself to task. Curse the wine for exposing her vulnerable underside when she was always so careful to keep it hidden. She curled her body around Fulke's insensible form, taking comfort from his solid warmth, and, closing her eyes, sought the panacea of sleep.

Next morning, nursing the remnants of a vile headache, Fulke wandered into the bailey and groaned as he saw his father-in-law riding into Whittington. Rain was threatening in the wind. The trees beyond the timber keep fluttered their final rags of colour on winter-black branches. It was no day for travellers to be abroad, but Robert le Vavasour was a contrary bastard at the best of times.

Fulke's wolfhound bitch thrust her moist nose into his hand, seeking affection. He patted her head absently and watched le Vavasour dismount from a handsome bay cob – the sort of animal for long journeys when comfort was the requirement rather than hunting speed, or the fire and strength of a destrier. His father-in-law was dressed for a long journey too, well bundled up in a thick cloak and hood, with tough, cowhide boots rather than the softer goatskin, and the leather well waxed against the weather. An escort of knights travelled with him, but not his domestic household. Not a social call then.

With a forced smile of welcome, Fulke went forward to greet le Vavasour. After all, he told himself, the old devil might finally have come to give him the manor of Edlington over which they had been in dispute for many years. It was supposed to be part of Maude's dower, but le Vavasour insisted it wasn't.

'Christ.' Le Vavasour's gaze roved disparagingly over the timber battlements and walkways. 'It always astonishes me that a man of your standing would turn outlaw for the sake of a place like this. Why don't you build in stone? Surely it cannot be safe with the Welsh so close?'

Fulke abandoned the pretence of a smile. 'Aside from the fact that stone costs money that I do not have,' he said curtly, 'King John will not grant me permission to strengthen the fortifications.'

'A pity, but understandable.' A narrow, almost furtive look entered le Vavasour's eyes. He pushed down his hood and stripped off his gauntlets. 'Are you not going to invite me within?'

'Since you have ridden all this way to see me, it is the least I can do,' Fulke said dryly. 'A pity you did not arrive yesterday. You could have celebrated your eldest grand-daughter's betrothal to William Pantulf of Wem.'

'I might have done if I'd been invited,' le Vavasour growled.

'It's only a betrothal, not a wedding. We would not omit you from that in spite of what you have to say about red-haired girls.' Fulke beckoned to a couple of grooms and they hurried to help with the horses.

Le Vavasour grunted. 'I speak as I find,' he said and followed Fulke's open-armed gesture towards the keep.

'How are Juliana and Thomas?'

'Better for the distance,' le Vavasour said. 'You know women and children. All right in their place, but not too close to yours.'

Fulke's headache increased.

Once inside the keep, le Vavasour swept his eyes around the limewashed walls decorated with banners and shields, and repeated that it was a pity the place was constructed mainly of timber. He grimaced at the central hearth, remarking that castles these days were being built with chimneys. Maude he greeted with a perfunctory kiss on the cheek. Her own greeting was equally tepid.

The children were summoned with dragging feet to greet their grandsire. Robert examined Hawise like a horse-coper studying the points of a brood mare at a fair and said that he hoped she would develop the hips for childbearing before her marriage. Jonetta was given a cursory glance and Mabile was ignored, le Vavasour making it plain that as far as he was concerned, she did not exist. The boys were poked and prodded and told to speak up, and when young Fulke did, asking why his grandfather was so rude, was promptly informed that he was a mannerless whelp and that a whipping would mend his tongue.

'I suppose,' Fulke said thoughtfully, as if pondering the notion, 'that mannerless whelps then turn into mannerless old men, and that it runs in the bloodline.' Gently, he tousled his son's barley-blond hair.

The children were dismissed and Maude made her escape by muttering an excuse about talking to the cook and making sure the bed linen was aired. 'Do you want me to prepare a bathtub?' she asked on her way out.

'And dilute my juices?' Le Vavasour waved her away. 'King John might indulge himself every fortnight like a Byzantine, but I'm northern bred and made of sterner stuff. Away with you, woman.'

'Yes, Father,' Maude said meekly, her green eyes filled with unspoken fury. Head high, she left the hall.

'You are staying the night?' Fulke enquired.

'No point in riding on now, is there?' Le Vavasour plumped down in a curule chair near one of the braziers that augmented the heat from the despised central hearth. 'I suppose I could continue to Shrewsbury, but I do have family obligations after all.' He spread his knees and hitched the fabric on his chausses.

Fulke inclined his head and quietly gritted his teeth. 'So, what kind of family obligation brings you to Whittington?' he asked. 'Have you finally decided to hand over Edlington?'

'Edlington was only Maude's in dower while I did not have a son. You know that. Now that Juliana has borne me an heir, it goes to him.'

'I know of no such clause,' Fulke retorted.

'Well, that's the blame of your ignorance,' the older man said firmly and shook his head. 'I didn't come here to give you Edlington, nor did I come to argue. As it happens, I am on my way to a council of barons at St Edmunds, and I thought you might be interested in accompanying me.'

'And why should I be interested?' Fulke looked at his

nails. He knew all about the council because it had been mentioned in certain corners while he was serving John in Poitou. He had kept his head down, but that had not prevented his ears from hearing the talk, or his mind from mulling over the details.

'Because it might be to your advantage, and although you serve King John, I know that there is no love lost between you.'

Fulke considered his father-in-law. 'Would I be right in thinking that the council will be attended by such men as Eustace de Vesci and Robert FitzWalter?' They had led a group of disaffected barons who had been levelling complaints against John and fomenting rebellion for the past three years. Fulke had tremendous sympathy for them, but he distrusted de Vesci and FitzWalter almost as much as he distrusted John. Their rebellion was as much about feathering their own nests as it was about justice. His father-in-law had de Vesci for a close neighbour, but had never seemed particularly keen to join the protest.

Le Vavasour drank his wine. 'Yes,' he conceded, but raised a forefinger as Fulke snorted down his nose. 'It is not what you think. The Earl of Winchester, the Earls of Clare and Essex will be in attendance.' He counted the names off on his fingers. 'And Bigod and Mowbray and de Stuteville. Half the noble families in England and . . .' Here he leaned forward for effect and fixed Fulke with a bright stare. 'Stephen Langton, Archbishop of Canterbury.'

Fulke folded his arms as if rejecting the overture, but his stomach had leaped at the words and he could feel the old exhilaration rise and quiver like tiny bubbles in his blood. His had been a voice in the wilderness when he conducted his own rebellion against John. Now, more than ten years later, there was a concerted movement. 'And their purpose?'

'To make the King acknowledge the rights of his vassals.

To make him realise that he cannot force them to serve him in wars across the Narrow Sea or fund those wars. To bind him to the promise that no free man shall be arrested, imprisoned, or ruined except by fair judgement of his peers. And that no widow shall be forced to remarry or to pay a ruinous fine to maintain her widowhood.' He waved his hand. 'And more besides. It is all to be written down in a charter of liberties.'

'And you expect John to agree to it?'

'I expect him to be brought to agree to it, or risk civil war. These taxes and scutages he continues to levy to play his games abroad are bleeding us dry. I know that you owe him more money than you can hope to repay. The only reason you went with him to Poitou was to be excused the fine you would otherwise have had to pay. Look at what happened to William de Braose when he could not pay his fines and taxes. Hounded out of his power and his wife and son imprisoned in a dark hole to die of starvation.'

There was genuine indignation in his father-in-law's tone, but not, Fulke knew, out of any sympathy for the wife and child. What did worry le Vavasour was the fact that authority could be removed at the merest snap of the royal fingers. William de Braose had been no minor lordling, but an earl of great stature and influence. 'William de Braose was hounded for being too powerful and a party to John's darkest secrets,' Fulke said.

'Do you believe John murdered his nephew?'

'I am scarcely the man to ask,' Fulke said. 'I may have a truce with John, but that does not make me impartial and I have Breton relatives. Arthur was their Prince and he had a strong claim to England's throne . . . until he became John's captive and that was the last anyone heard or saw of him.'

'Then you do believe it?'

Fulke shrugged. 'I believe that Arthur is dead. If not, John would have produced him to stop Philip of France from using Arthur's disappearance as a goad to war. As to whether or not John murdered him ... well, that is a matter between John and God.'

Le Vavasour pulled a face. 'I have no sympathy for de Braose, never liked the man, but if John can destroy him, he can do the same to any of us on a whim. He must be curbed.' He looked at Fulke. 'Will you ride with me to the council?'

'I'll think on it,' Fulke said evenly. A pity the voices were only challenging now instead of fifteen years ago. But then fifteen years ago, John had been new king and the barons had been courting his favour as much as he courted theirs. Now the goodwill was threadbare on both sides.

Although Fulke had answered his father-in-law in a tepid fashion, his gut told him that his decision was already made.

'You are mad!' Maude cried when he told her of his intention in their bedchamber that night. 'You fought tooth and nail for your inheritance and now you are risking it by jumping into a stew of rebellion!' Her eyes flashed and she set her hands on her hips.

Fulke shook his head. 'It's not a rebellion, it's a meeting to discuss a charter of liberties, and your father would not be attending unless he deemed it necessary and safe. You know what he is like.'

'I know exactly what he is like,' she snapped. 'And that is why I am angry. Are you so filled with the desire to go playing at war that you do not see through his ploy?'

'Maude ...'

'He wants you to go with him because his standing will be vastly increased when he arrives at St Edmunds with his son-in-law, the legendary Fulke FitzWarin, who made an art of being an outlaw and finally brought the King to capitulate. That is why he wants you to join him – to bask in the reflection of your glory.'

'That is likely true, and of no consequence.'

'Of no consequence!' So great was her fury that it made her vision shimmer. 'And I suppose this jaunt to St Edmunds is of "no consequence" too! You are a vainglorious fool! You see your youth slipping away and instead of bidding it grace-fully farewell, you're trying to recapture it in senseless rebellion!'

'It's not a rebellion!' His voice began to rise and she saw that she had touched a raw nerve.

'But it soon will be!'

'If we can get John to sign a charter of liberties – a code of honour, if you will – it means that never again will he be able to withhold land from a man on royal whim. Never again will a woman be constrained to marry against her will, or an heir pay more than he should to inherit his father's lands. It is for the good of all.'

'If this "charter" is so laudable, why haven't William Marshal, Ranulf of Chester or William Salisbury put their names to it?' she demanded.

'That's obvious. Marshal swears allegiance then follows it unquestioningly like a dog follows a master. Chester's waiting to see which way the wind blows, and William Salisbury is John's own brother – another dog.' He held out his hand to her in a gesture that asked for acceptance. 'I know that many of the lords who want this charter have their own axes to grind, but there is a core of truth worth fighting for.'

'Worth fighting for,' Maude repeated stonily. 'There you have it.' She flounced away and began unbraiding her hair. 'I sometimes wonder if all you want is the fight. Perhaps you have been warring for so long that you cannot live without it.' She tugged her fingers jerkily through the plaits, untwining the strands. 'I can see it in you. You talk of John's followers being dogs, but you are twitching like a leashed hound at the start of a hunt.' She flung round to look at him. 'Even if you do bring John to agree, he will not love you for it. Why stir up old hatreds?'

'Because they have never been resolved. Mud might sink to the bottom of a pool, but it does not disappear.'

'No, but at least it cannot be seen!'

'And that makes it all right?'

Maude clenched her teeth to dam the scream that rose within her. It was obvious that whether she raged or not his mind was set. 'Do as you will,' she said stiffly. 'I will not argue with you more.' She drew her comb through her hair with rapid strokes, snagging the strands, wincing slightly but receiving the snatches of pain as part of the moment. 'Go and play the knight errant, just do not seek my approval for your game.'

'You could use your tongue to carve a side of beef,' he said. 'I come away bloody from any encounter. I'm as sick of fighting as you are.' Striding to the door, he banged out. Moments later there was a curse as he tripped over one of the sleepers in the antechamber, and then silence.

Maude bit her lip and continued to comb her hair, smoothing and slowing the motion to try and calm the hammer of her heart and the churn of her thoughts. Was she wrong to castigate him? Should she have smiled and said he was doing the right thing? John had many damning traits, and it was true that checks on his abuses of power would be of benefit to all, but surely others could carry the torch. Fulke had done more than enough. The difficulty was that Fulke felt there were still scores to be settled and a resolution to be reached. He could see himself as one of many rather than a man alone. Oh yes, she could understand the seduction, but that did not make it any the more reassuring.

She removed her gown, her shoes and hose, but retained her chemise for warmth as she climbed between the sheets. The bed was cold without Fulke's solid frame to warm her back and her icy feet. Maude curled up, drawing her knees towards her chin, and stared at the night candle, waiting. They had had arguments before – theirs was no milk-and-water marriage – but always the bed had been a source of reconciliation with passion redirected and channelled through flesh. Even if one of them stormed out in a rage, they always came back.

Her eyelids drooped. She woke with a sudden start, thinking that she had been asleep only moments, but the night candle was guttering on its pricket, the bed was cold, and it was obvious that Fulke was not returning to lie in it.

'Women,' said le Vavasour as he poured another generous measure of wine into Fulke's cup – he could afford to do so, since it was Fulke's wine, 'best not to give them ideas beyond bedding and breeding. Any man who does is storing up trouble for himself. Take my Juliana. She never questions my actions. I've made sure she knows better.'

Fulke drank the wine and sank in its cool red poison. 'She goads me beyond bearing,' he said. Somewhere in the wine fumes skulked the knowledge that he had walked out because Maude was far too perceptive. Perhaps all he did want was the fight, and because it was against John that made it seem right and reasonable.

'The buckle end of your belt would teach her to mind her tongue.'

Fulke looked at le Vavasour with distaste. 'I do not need to prove my manhood by beating my wife.'

'A man who beats his wife is master in his own household,' le Vavasour said with scant patience. 'She wouldn't cavil at your decisions then.'

'No,' Fulke agreed, thinking that it must be a desolate life when it contained neither affection nor concern, merely fear and in all likelihood loathing. 'She wouldn't cavil at my going because she would be glad to see the back of me.'

Le Vavasour rolled his eyes. 'You're in thrall, man,' he said. 'It isn't healthy to be tied to a woman's skirts.'

'I'm not.'

'Well then, stop looking towards those stairs as if you're ready to run back up them at any moment. Let her wait. If you go back, she'll know that she's won.'

Le Vavasour's words roused a spark of male belligerence in Fulke. He imagined her lying waiting for him. He would climb into bed, curl his arm around her body and whisper into her neck that he was sorry they had quarrelled. And she would turn into his arms and reply against his mouth that she was sorry too, but he would be the one to make the first move.

'Let her come to you,' le Vavasour said, watching him with narrowed eyes. 'You have to be lord in your own household.'

Fulke nodded. His father-in-law was right. If he went to bed now, it would be admitting that he was in the wrong, even though he still intended riding out in the morning.

Thus he remained where he was, and when the time came to sleep, he stretched out on a pallet in le Vavasour's chamber and let the excess of wine lure him into a deep slumber.

When Maude came down at dawn, she found him there. Misery and anger flowed in expanding rings from her core. She hated her father, she hated Fulke, but she loved him too, and the more she loved and hated, the angrier she became.

With calm deliberation she saw to the breaking of fast and the preparing of rations to eat on the journey. She made sure that Fulke had clean raiment in his pack. When he sat to break his fast, bleary-eyed and unshaven, she greeted him with frozen courtesy and saw that his trencher and cup were placed before him and filled.

'See,' said her father, nudging Fulke, 'I told you that you have to show them who is master. All it takes is a little discipline.'

Fulke said nothing. Feeling a twinge of guilt, he gave Maude a circumspect glance from beneath his brows, but as her eyes threatened to meet his, he looked away and hardened his resolve.

His gut was rolling and he did not feel like eating, but with a long journey ahead, knew that he must. With grim determination he chewed and swallowed.

With no comprehension of manners or discipline, little Mabile wandered up to him and tugged at his knee. He scooped her up and sat her in his lap.

Le Vavasour frowned; Fulke ignored him and curled a protective arm around his smallest and most vulnerable daughter. Mabile sat for a moment then with a squeal pushed herself out of Fulke's embrace. Clarice had entered the hall and it was to her that Mabile trotted. The young woman hoisted her up in her arms and kissed her cheek, while bidding a polite good morrow to the men.

'Discipline,' le Vavasour growled, his expression censorious. 'You need to begin while they're still in the cradle.'

'Spare me your advice,' Fulke said savagely. 'Do I tell you how to order your household?'

His father-in-law shook his head. 'The sooner we're on the road, the better,' he said sourly, his implication being that Whittington's atmosphere was unhealthy for any male in his right mind.

Fulke spared time to strip to his braies and bathe. He chewed a liquorice root to freshen his breath but decided to let his stubble remain. It was December and wearing a beard would prove considerably warmer than going bare-chinned. If he caught lice, he could always shave. His sons loitered, helping him roll his hauberk in a bundle of oiled leather to keep it dry, watching enviously as he girded on his sword.

When he mounted up in the courtyard, Maude came to his stirrup and, in the traditional manner, presented him with his shield.

'Have a care, my lord,' she said.

The breeze wafted her veil away from her face, and the cold December sunlight made her eyes as light and clear as green glass. Fulke's gut swooped with love and desire. He wanted to fling from the saddle and crush her in his arms, but, constrained by the presence and scowl of his father-in-law, and by a last vestige of pride, he stayed where he was. 'And you,' he murmured. 'I promise, everything will be for the best.'

She lifted her chin. 'Then keep your promise.'

Unable to resist, he removed his gauntlet and leaned from the saddle to touch her cheek.

Hawise had dutifully presented her grandfather with his shield which he had accepted with his usual arrogance. 'Come,' he said, nudging his horse with his heels. 'We should not tarry.' He gave Fulke a hard stare.

Fulke reluctantly took his hand from Maude's cheek. She looked at him steadily and replaced his fingers with her own, tracing the echo of his touch.

He kicked his mount and followed le Vavasour out of Whittington's gates, somehow feeling as if he were being tugged against his will.

CHAPTER 38

Whittington Castle, Shropshire, March 1215

C larice sat at her embroidery frame, industriously stitching a border of floral scrolls on to a linen cloth intended for the high table. Her manner was calm, her movements precise but containing an almost water-like fluidity. Press the needle into the linen, pass it through, pull away, creating an image of intricate beauty through a simple act of repetition. Sometimes she imagined herself as one of the goddesses of pagan times, weaving the life stories of mortals with her enchanted silks. There was even a certain dark thrill in taking her small sharp sewing shears and snipping a thread. King John had already died several times that way in the depths of her imagination.

Fulke and Maude had been arguing again. Although the walls were thick, their voices still carried. Clarice had never understood how two people could love so deeply and yet quarrel fit to bring down the rafters. Of late, their disputes had been of a pattern. Maude would call him a fool for staying with the rebels; he would call her a shrew. She would retort with growing impatience, so would he, until Clarice was sure they could be heard at the other end of the village. Bursting with rage, they would tumble into bed and fight each other to exhaustion. A couple of days of besotted, heavy-eyed peace ensued and then it would begin again until finally he would ride away to join his fellow barons, leaving Maude to stamp and fume. They were currently at the midway stage in the latest bout of conflict. Fulke had been home for four days and the second argument had erupted with some spectacular blasphemies a short while since. Now there was silence.

Clarice snipped the end of her thread and, unconsciously pursing her lips, began another lifeline in blood-red silk. The pattern was one of green scrolls, curling into small red flowers reminiscent of tiny scarlet pimpernels. Outside it was a raw March day, full of gusting clouds with the occasional spatter of rain. Seated by the window to gain the benefit of the light, her left side was cold but her right was warmed by the heat of a brazier.

The door opened on a gust of air then banged heavily shut. Fulke strode into the room, the hem of his tunic flaring with each vigorous step. Muttering beneath his breath, he paused, dug his hands through his heavy black hair and sat down moodily at the small gaming table occupying the other embrasure. He abandoned his hair-raking and thrust his head between his open palms.

They had not taken each other to bed then, Clarice thought. Matters must have degenerated and tempers were still likely to be white-hot.

'Would you like some wine, my lord?' She rose quietly from her sewing and went to the flagon standing on the oak sideboard.

He looked up, his expression slightly startled as if he had only just registered her presence in the room. 'Do you see that as your reason in life, to be a cup-bearer?' His tone was savage.

The jibe hit Clarice in the soft space beneath her ribs, but she kept herself from flinching. 'No, my lord. I was offering comfort.'

'I doubt I'll find it in the bottom of a cup beyond a few hours.'

With a steady hand, she poured a small measure for herself and returned to her embroidery frame. Taking her needle, she began to sew, letting the flow of the motion restore her balance. She had entered the FitzWarin household as a child of eight, was now a young adult and by the rights of custom should have been married with at least one child in the cradle. But custom did not take the heart into account. She loved this household deeply and to think of leaving it was so painful that she avoided the subject. The FitzWarins were not her family – except vicariously through Theobald Walter, but she felt as if they were.

Fulke sighed and rose from the seat to pace the room again. He stopped at the sideboard and poured his own wine, then came to look at the embroidery.

'That is a very fine piece of work,' he said by way of apology.

Clarice flushed slightly at the compliment. 'Thank you, my lord.'

'You make it look so simple.'

'The stitches are not difficult.'

'But the pattern is.' He was standing behind her. She could not see his expression but she heard the wry note in his voice. 'Rather like life,' he said. 'Ah Clarice, I have woven a design I am not sure that I like, but it has its fine points so I do not want to unravel it and leave the linen blank as it was before.'

'It would not be as before; it would be full of needle holes,' she said practically, and was rewarded with a snort of humourless amusement. He wandered away, but only to fetch a three-legged stool so that he could sit by her and watch.

Clarice took a steadying drink of her wine and tried to concentrate on her work.

After a moment, he said, 'Do you think I am wrong? Do you side with the other women in my household by calling me a lack-wit?'

'I side with no one, my lord,' Clarice murmured tactfully.

'So you have no opinion?'

'I did not say that.' She bit her lip and decided that she had better turn the tables of interrogation before it was too late. 'Why should you want to unravel what you have sewn? What disappoints you?'

He shook his head. 'You know about this charter of liberties that many of us want King John to acknowledge as the law of the land?'

'Of course I do.' She could not avoid knowing about it when it was the reason for Fulke and Maude's quarrelling.

'The demands are sound; indeed, they were first proposed by the Archbishop of Canterbury, not the barons. But they will limit John's powers and his ability to raise revenues for the Crown. Instead of extorting silver, he will have to abide by a set of fixed fines and codes. He will not be able to force his barons to pay for his foreign wars; he will not be able to play the tyrant with a man just because he dislikes him.' His tone had grown vehement and Clarice could both hear and see that he passionately believed in the rights encoded in this charter. So would anyone, she thought. That was the part which he was reluctant to abandon.

He drank his wine, rose to replenish his cup and returned to the stool. His eyes were quartz-bright with fervour. 'The King sees our demands in a different light. He views them as a curb to his power, an infringement on his royal authority to govern. He says that the men proposing these curbs are mischief-makers who want to bring him down.'

Clarice snipped off the crimson thread and, to rest her eyes from the colour, selected a twist of green. 'And is that true?'

'In part.' He rubbed the back of his neck and looked slightly uncomfortable. 'I know that you only came to live in this household at the end of my quarrel with John, but you must know about it. And certainly there is no love lost between John and our two spokesmen, Robert FitzWalter and Eustace de Vesci.'

Clarice poked the thread through the eye of her silver needle and frowned. 'Didn't de Vesci's wife . . .'

'Bed with King John,' he finished for her. 'And not voluntarily. She was forced, so it is said, in order to keep her husband in favour at court – or at least to stop him from being persecuted by John's officials. John being the lecher that he is, I do not doubt that the rumour is true. So, yes, de Vesci does have an axe to grind, and FitzWalter – I would not give him house room.' He spread his hands. 'The difficulty is that the charter has the backing of many malcontents and trouble-makers. John has the support of some very decent men who have turned a blind eye to his excesses and abided by their feudal oaths. If only those men could be persuaded to stand for the charter, then all would be well . . . but it isn't.'

He sighed as he watched her set the needle in the fabric and expertly weave the new thread into the background. 'So now Maude is angry with me because I am risking all that I have fought to gain and keeping the company of dubious men.'

'It is true that you could lose your lands?'

'Oh yes,' Fulke said. 'Especially now.'

'Why?'

He looked down into his cup and grimaced. 'Just before I came home, John announced that he intended to take the Cross.'

Clarice raised her head from her embroidery. She had grown up on tales of John's cruelty, cunning and perfidy, had lived through the papal interdict a few years ago during John's dispute with Rome over the appointment of a new Archbishop of Canterbury. Despite John's reconciliation with the Pope, taking the Cross seemed excessive for a man who gave little more than lip service to his faith. 'He is going on crusade?' she asked.

Fulke laughed and shook his head. 'If only!' he declared with vehemence. 'No, I doubt that Constantinople need worry that he'll follow in his brother's illustrious footsteps. It is all done in the name of politics. He thinks that he can weasel his way out of this charter by taking the Cross. The Church protects a crusader's lands for a period of four years. Any man making war on another who has taken a crusader's vow is at once excommunicated. Once John was at war with the Pope. Now they are allies.'

Clarice nodded and continued to sew. 'So, what will you do?'

He sprang to his feet, almost tipping over the stool. 'I am caught in a cleft stick,' he said in frustration. 'I can withdraw and see my principles damned, or I can stay and my soul be damned and my lands declared forfeit.' He fixed her with a fierce stare. 'What would you do, Clarice? And do not say that you side with no one, or it is not your place to offer advice. I am asking, and I want you to answer.'

She swallowed and stopped sewing. What would his wife do? Likely snap at him that wanting did not mean that he was going to get. But she wasn't Maude, did not have her appetite for battle. It didn't mean, however, that she was a weakling.

'I would have to decide which was more important,' she said slowly, 'and probably it would be my principles. After all, I would have suspected when I first set out that there would be obstacles put in my way and they might involve forfeiture of land.'

'And the excommunication?'

She pursed her lips. 'I would hope that God would still be merciful. It seems to me that the Pope often uses excommunication as a weapon of policy, not true religious concern, and if that is blasphemy, then *mea culpa.*'

The fierceness had left his expression. Instead, it was charged with amusement and surprise. 'You look,' he said, 'like a little brown mouse. You move around the place as quietly and unobtrusively as a well-trained maid, with seemingly no thought but for the comfort of others. Getting you to express an opinion beyond the fact that rushes need changing or there's not enough salt in the food is like drawing a tooth.'

She flushed and gave him a reproachful look.

'But worth it,' he added with a sudden smile. 'You're not a mouse at all, Clarice d'Auberville. You're a lioness in disguise.' He brushed her cheek in salute and left the room.

Clarice stared at the pattern of her sewing as if it had become a meaningless jumble. Her stomach churned with queasy pleasure. She pressed her cheek where his fingers had touched. Suddenly she was glad that she was alone, to savour the moment, to recover herself, to make a memory and lock it in a secret, gilded box at the back of her mind where no one would ever find it.

The sun was setting over the Thames, spreading a copper patina across the surface of the water. Boatmen in small craft and clinker-built barges plied their trade between the businesses and dwellings lining the river bank, or rowed across the river to the suburbs of Southwark where the city's brothels and bathhouses were concentrated.

Despite having visited London many times, Fulke had

never been to the Southwark side. Now he looked around with interest as he was ushered from the boat and up some wooden steps to a limewashed cruck-frame house facing the river. The buildings standing either side were similar and of prosperous appearance with spacious garths. At the end of the street, a cookshop was doing a roaring trade in meat pies and hot fritters. The smells wafted towards him in appetising, greasy waves, reminding him that he had not eaten since a noon repast of bread and cheese, consumed as he went about his business.

The door was opened by a cheerful maidservant who ushered him into a well-appointed downstairs room. The floor rushes were new, thick, and scattered with dried thyme and rose petals. There was glass in the windows, secured within a removable lead fretwork. Enamelled coffers and solid oak benches lined the sides of the room; the walls were decorated with bright, woollen embroi-deries; and there was even a mirror in an ornate ivory frame. Fulke stared, his jaw dropping slightly. Another woman came forward to take his cloak and offer him the obligatory cup of wine. She was of about Maude's age, with two braids of dark-brown hair framing an attractive, heart-shaped face.

'Ah, Fulke, welcome.' William Salisbury emerged from a curtained off chamber beyond. His receding hair, damp from bathing, was brushed sleekly back from his forehead. He wore a tunic of red wool, loosely belted, and looked more at ease than Fulke had ever seen him. 'This is Richenda.'

'My lady,' Fulke said tactfully, not sure that this was the right form of address. William was married to Ella of Salisbury — a match of convenience that was kept within civilised bounds by the expedience of separate households. Fulke knew that Salisbury had a mistress, but this was the first time he had met her, or been to the house that Salisbury had bought for her, the Earl being more than discreet on the matter.

She inclined her head and smiled, murmuring that she was pleased to meet him, then retired to the chamber that William had just vacated.

'You do not know how that woman has saved my sanity these past few months,' the Earl said, his expression heart-felt. 'I swear, if I did not have this retreat, I would have thrown myself in the river long ago.' He gestured to the trestle table in the corner of the room. A heavy wax candle illuminated a cold repast of spiced chicken breasts, a mush-room frumenty and small wastel loaves made with good white flour.

'It is a difficult time,' Fulke agreed as he took his seat and looked at the food. 'What I would give to be at home now, and at peace, with myself and my family.'

'You know the answer to that.'

Fulke smiled bleakly. 'So do you,' he said.

Salisbury gestured to the meal. 'Let us not spoil our appetites with our differences,' he said. 'You are the guest, will you say grace?'

Fulke nodded and murmured the words of the blessing, signing his breast as he did so. They ate companionably and discussed other matters – family, the weather, hunting – observing the conventions but also renewing friendship as the world outside darkened to a soft, sapphire blue, and the occasional flashes of gold on the river were of reflected torchlight instead of the broad sweep of the setting sun.

Finally, they sat back with a flagon of sweetened wine between them and, with a certain reluctance on both sides, came to the point of their meeting.

'I was disappointed to discover that you had joined the rebels,' Salisbury murmured with reproach. 'I thought you had put the past behind you. I know that you and my brother will never be bosom companions, but I truly believed that you had come to an understanding.'

'Oh, we understand each other well, that is not the difficulty,' Fulke said. He took a fig from the dish of dried fruits in the centre of the trestle and nibbled on the sweet, dark flesh. 'John restored my lands because he needed my sword on his side of the fence and I was costing him too much. Even then, I doubt he would have acted without the pressure brought to bear by yourself, Ranulf Chester and Hubert Walter. I surrendered to him because I knew the opportunity would not come again and I was desperate. It was a compromise and one that was bound to strain at the seams.' He wiped his fingers on a napkin. 'I couldn't not support this charter, Will.'

'It is a list of impossible demands, made by malcontents and troublemakers.'

'So is it wrong to demand that a man cannot be arrested and flung in prison without due cause? Or that a widow should remain in her widowhood or remarry as she pleases without having to pay a massive fine for the privilege?'

'It is wrong to demand that a select group of twenty-five barons should share powers with the King,' Salisbury snapped. 'Such a clause is unworkable.'

'But you see what happens when John has sole governance. Look at what happened to de Braose. In the name of God's pity, look at what happened to his wife and son.'

Salisbury's eyes slipped from Fulke's. 'That was unfortunate, I'll agree,' he murmured, 'but John was provoked.'

'And that makes it all right to starve a woman and child to death?' Fulke said with disgust. 'To leave them in a dark oubliette until the boy died and his mother gnawed on his corpse to try and keep herself alive?'

'No, of course it doesn't.' Salisbury's complexion darkened

until he reminded Fulke of old King Henry when one of his famous rages was imminent.

'It certainly adds fuel to the rumours that he murdered his own nephew and cast his body in the Seine, weighed down with a stone.'

Salisbury looked as if he might choke. 'You sail dangerously close to the tolerance of friendship,' he said hoarsely.

'So do you,' Fulke retorted. 'It is our friendship that has brought me to you tonight and it is because of the value I set on it that I have not walked out. I know what John means to you . . . and you know what he means to me.'

Salisbury took a deep gulp of wine, swallowed and sighed. 'Every man has his demons. John may have more than most, but he is not wicked through and through. If only he were given a chance, he could prove his worth – and I am not just saying it as his brother.'

'He is being given a chance – this charter.'

'Thrust under his nose by his enemies.'

Fulke shrugged. 'How did they come to be enemies, Will?'

'All I am saying is that it is not entirely John's fault, and if you will not join the lords that are backing him, I hope you will look on the negotiations with a degree of common sense.'

It was the nearest Salisbury would come to pleading for John by asking Fulke to be moderate. He could hardly make the request of FitzWalter and de Vesci who were determined to press forward with a vengeance. Last week they had taken the city of London without a finger being lifted against them. Salisbury must be worried too that many of the uncommitted barons were inclining towards the rebels' side rather than John's.

'I will bear your concerns in mind, Will.' Fulke rose to take his leave. 'I need this to be ended too.' He made a rueful face. 'And I want my wife and daughters to stop scowling at me.'

'You should find yourself a house like this,' Salisbury said as the maid lifted Fulke's cloak from the peg. 'Home comforts without the drawbacks.'

Fulke laughed. 'I have enough trouble coping with the women I've got, without adding to the burden. I will see you at Windsor.'

In a marshy meadow called Runnymede, on the road between London and Windsor, rebels and royalists met beneath the shade of striped awnings and King John put his seal to the charter of liberties. There was forced civility on both sides, and the atmosphere was rife with tension. John met the rebel lords with loathing in his eyes and found his black looks reciprocated.

When his gaze lit on Fulke, his lips pursed as if he just drunk from a cup of vinegar. Fulke returned the stare, jutting his chin, planting his feet wide, as if preparing to resist a blow. He knew that Salisbury's hopes were dust in the wind. There was a saying from the bible that a leopard could not change its spots. And Christ, it was true – of both himself and John.

When the King had put his seal to the great charter, thus agreeing to its terms, the tenants-in-chief came to kneel in turn before him and renew their oaths of fealty. Fulke swallowed as he watched fellow barons go forward and bend the knee, putting their hands between John's, swearing their allegiance. His father-in-law was rubbing his hands together, looking both nervous and triumphant – like a small child caught up in the worrying exhilaration of a grown man's game. Only it wasn't a game at all. FitzWalter and de Vesci had attended the negotiations, but had not remained to see the charter sealed. Now Fulke realised that he should have gone with them.

He knew he could not do it. He could not go forward and put his hands between John's again. The contact would poison him beyond recovery. He felt physically sick. Turning on his heel, he pushed his way back through the witnesses, heading for his canvas campaign pavilion and his horse line.

Le Vavasour stared in blank astonishment, then hastened after him, ignoring the growls of protest as he trod on men's feet. 'Where do you think you're going?'

'To join de Vesci,' Fulke said grimly. Damp patches of sweat darkened his pale linen gambeson. He wrenched his banner out of the ground and cast it down. 'Get the tent down,' he commanded his wide-eyed squires.

'But you' – le Vavasour gestured back towards the crowd and the King – 'haven't given your oath of fealty.'

'Because it would be as false as John's promise to honour that charter. You can see it in his eyes. The moment he is quit of this place, he will go to the Pope and demand that it be annulled because he was forced to agree to its terms under duress.'

'He has sworn he will not do so.'

'John would swear on his mother's soul to get himself out of a scrape.' Fulke threw his eating bowls and two cups into a coffer, followed it by two candlestands, and began to dismantle the bench on which they had stood. 'You do as your conscience bids you, Father, and I will attend to mine.'

Le Vavasour gnawed his thin underlip. 'John has sealed the charter, I can do no other but swear for him,' he said.

'Good, then go and do so.' Fulke kicked the bench legs viciously out of their sockets. When he looked up, his father-in-law had gone.

'I do not believe it!' Maude stared at her father in growing dismay and rage.

'You must, because it is true. Fulke would not give his fealty and now he has an outlaw's price on his head.' Le Vavasour shook his head. 'I could not persuade him to give his oath and he rode out as soon as he had packed his tent. Now John will have him excommunicated and his lands declared forfeit.' He spoke with a certain gloomy relish.

'If he does, then I hold you to blame as much as Fulke,' she snapped. 'You were the one who came to him, full of this talk of a charter.'

'And a good thing it has been, only now it has gone far enough and it is time to call a halt. I'll not have you talking to me in that tone, Daughter.'

Maude clenched her fists. She wanted to do more than just talk. Making an effort, she controlled herself. 'And where is Fulke now?' she asked hoarsely.

Her father looked at the ceiling and then at the floor. 'Do you not have hospitality in this household?' he demanded.

'Where is he?' Maude shrieked.

Le Vavasour made a throwing gesture. 'If you must know, he's gone to a tourney in Oxford.'

'A tourney!' Maude saw red. 'Our lands are forfeit, I could have royal officials in the bailey at any moment and he's gone jousting without so much as a message to me!' She felt sick, she wanted to weep.

'The barons who had refused to swear are keeping an army in the field. It is just a way of honing their skills.'

'Honing their skills!' She nodded with vehement fury. 'And what of other duties and obligations? What of me, what of his children? Has he no thought for us?' It was not a question she gave her father time to answer, even had he possessed the wit. She stabbed her chest with her forefinger. 'I am no Maude de Braose to be cast into an oubliette with my offspring for nourishment. When you set out for the north on the morrow, you will take me with you. It is time I paid a visit to my dower lands.' Turning on her heel, she left him standing in the hall, a stunned expression on his face.

Clarice brought him wine, sat him in a chair by the hearth and sent his two grandsons to entertain him. Then she hurried after Maude.

Maude hurled back the lid of a travelling chest and felt pleasure amidst her rage to hear it crash against the keep wall. She tossed in two shifts, two gowns, a sleeveless overtunic and several rectangular wimple cloths. 'A tourney!' she spat as Clarice entered the room, breathless from her run. 'Did you hear him, a tourney!'

Clarice dipped into the travelling coffer and carefully folded the gowns that Maude had hurled within. 'I heard,' she murmured. 'Perhaps it is necessary for him to remain with the other lords.'

'About as necessary as it was for him to go with them at the start!' Maude snapped as she dug a pair of shoes out from beneath the bed.

'You cannot expect to make a hearth dog out of a wolf,' she said. 'Nor would you want to, I think.'

In that moment, Maude came very close to loathing Clarice. The composure, the gentle expression. She itched to slap it from her face. 'Allow me to know Fulke and myself,' she seethed. 'You hide in your corner and pretend you know more about life than anyone else when you know nothing.'

The girl looked at her steadily, without flinching, although the grey-gold eyes were wounded. 'Mayhap because I sit in a corner, I am overlooked and I see and hear more than most. I know that despite what you say, you love him beyond measure and that he would give his life for you.'

'Would he?' Maude flung a braid belt into the chest. 'I no longer know. I cannot reach him across the void that is John.'

'You truly intend to go then?' Clarice asked softly.

Maude compressed her lips. 'I will not be taken for granted,' she said. 'Let him know what it is like to be deserted.'

Autumn winds were stripping the branches of leaves when Fulke rode into Whittington. The estate pigs foraged among the beech mast in Babbin's Wood where the villagers were out gathering kindling to store for their winter fires, and hunting among the tree roots for fungi to augment their diets. Fulke found himself envying them their lives, but quickly quashed the notion. If the winter was bad then they faced the threat of starvation. If there was war, they risked being burned out of their homes or slaughtered. Their wealth was measured in one cow, three pigs, five chickens, not in acres of land and numbers of manors. Doubtless they envied him his fine horse and fur-lined cloak.

The castle gates were open to admit him; smoke twirling from the louvres and giving an extra pungency to the autumn air. His brother William came to greet him as he dismounted. Fulke had written to him, asking that he should come from Whadborough and take the position of constable at Whittington until the dispute with John was settled.

'It's good to see you,' Fulke declared and clasped his brother's taut, wiry frame.

'And you,' William said wryly. 'Llewelyn's young men have been growing restless. We've had more than one raid since the summer. It doesn't matter that you're supposed to be on the same side.'

Fulke gazed at the fabric of the keep. From a besieger's viewpoint, it was a gift. He was glad that the fighting between John and his opponents had not spread to this part of the Marches. But if Ranulf Chester should take it into his head to descend on Whittington, its capture was a foregone conclusion, no matter the skill of its commander. Llewelyn did not have the sophisticated siege equipment, but fire would do just as well for a timber keep, especially if the summer had been warm and dry.

'He's raided Pantulf's lands too, although the Corbets have escaped. I carried out a couple of counter-raids – drove off some herds. It's been quiet the last two weeks.'

Leaving his horse in the care of a groom, Fulke headed for the hall. 'I've agreed a truce until the spring – although my promise was given to William Marshal. If I'd given it to John, I wouldn't be here now.'

William strode at his side. 'Llewelyn won't like you signing a truce.'

'Llewelyn wants what is best for Wales,' Fulke said shortly. The back of his neck was cold, as if someone had just blown upon it. Entering the hall, he stared around. It was a bachelor's mess, the floor rushes soft and greasy, old candle wax overflowing the sconces, crumbs and spill stains on the trestles.

'Has Maude not returned from Yorkshire?' he demanded, although the evidence of his own eyes told him that she had not. He had received a curt note from his wife on a trimming of parchment no larger than the size of his hand to say that she was going to their northern estates. From the brevity and tone, he knew that she was angry, but he had thought it might have worn off by now.

Richard glanced up from toasting a heel of bread over the open fire. 'Not yet,' he said uncomfortably.

'No word?'

His brother shook his head and looked away.

Fulke glowered and kicked the rushes. 'This place is a pig sty!' he growled. 'You might not care about living in shit, but I do. Go and do something about it!'

Richard knew when to make himself scarce. William had already vanished to oversee weapons practice for the garrison. Cursing, Fulke collected a flagon of cloudy ale from the sideboard, a none too clean cup, and mounted the dais to survey his domain with a jaundiced eye.

That night disgruntled, irritated, Fulke rolled himself in his fur-lined cloak for warmth and comfort, but still he was cold and Whittington seemed not so much a haven and a home as a desolate, haunted place. Finally, unable to sleep, he rose. Fetching ink, quill and vellum, he penned a brief letter to Maude, sealed it with the gold ring from his jewel coffer and bade a messenger ride to find her at first light.

Ten days later, with no word from Maude, Fulke left Whittington to visit the Welsh court at Aber. Llewelyn greeted Fulke courteously enough, but with an air of reserve that Fulke reciprocated.

'Wales reaps a bitter harvest when England is at peace,' Llewelyn said, 'for then all her ambition turns to the conquering of her neighbours. Why should I be delighted that you have sealed a truce with John?'

'I am not asking you to be delighted,' Fulke answered. 'Do you remember when you sealed your own pact with him by marrying his daughter, and forced me to leave Whittington?'

'A fair point, but much water has flowed beneath our bridges since that time.'

'I agree,' Fulke said shortly. 'I have not consented to this truce in order to make war on Wales. All I am requesting is that you curb your young men from raiding my lands.'

'In the time of your grandfather, those lands were Welsh.'

'And before that English, then Welsh, then English again. It is a game of push and pull. But if you raid, then my men will retaliate, and so it will go on.'

'Llewelyn has changed,' Fulke said as he rode home with William from their parley. 'He has grown more bitter, more cynical.' Hearing his own words, he winced. So do we all, he thought. When trust was broken and broken again, there came a point when it could not be mended – like a cracked tile underfoot that made the foot step awry and the body lose its balance.

'Do you think the raids will stop?'

Fulke shrugged. 'It is likely for a time, unless the winter is hard and their hunger fierce. I have served Llewelyn warning that I will treat the raids as acts of war, not the peccadilloes of hot-blooded young men, but I have kept the pathways between us open.'

William smiled faintly. 'You have the diplomacy that many do not,' he said. 'The ability to show your fist and talk like a courtier at the same time.'

'I wouldn't call it diplomacy.'

'Then what?'

'Needs must when the devil drives.'

They arrived at Whittington to find travellers' horses in the stables: a powerful dappled cob and two smaller mounts. Fulke recognised his daughter's chestnut mare and Clarice's small brown gelding. There were also several saddle horses probably belonging to an escort, but there was no sign of Maude's favourite cream-coloured palfrey.

His heart leaping, Fulke almost ran into the hall. Tall and whipcord lean, William Pantulf was warming his hands at the fire in the company of the two girls. As Fulke entered the hall he looked up, and his glance alerted the others. Hawise turned.

'Papa!' She ran to him, her red braids snaking. He caught her up and swung her round, hugging her close in delight and pain and then holding her away to look at her.

'Holy Mother, you've grown again! Last I saw you, I could tuck you beneath my arm, now you reach above my shoulder!'

Hawise giggled, sounding so much like her mother that it was almost like an arrow in his heart. To look at she was pure de Dinan, her gaining height and ripening curves the legacy of the grandmother for whom she was named.

'Are you home for good now?' she demanded.

'For the winter at least. Did my letter not reach you and your mother?' His arm around Hawise, he went forward to the fire to greet Will Pantulf and Clarice.

Hawise stiffened against him. 'Yes,' she said. 'We were at Edlington and Will was visiting so he offered to escort us to Whittington. I couldn't come on my own, so Clarice accompanied me as a chaperone.' Her voice was slightly breathless and Fulke did not miss the look that two young women exchanged.

'Is your mother following later?'

A brief silence. Will Pantulf cleared his throat and looked embarrassed, as if wishing himself somewhere else.

Hawise shook her head. 'No, Papa.'

'Why not?' Fulke's stomach turned over. There was a look in his daughter's eyes, a mingling of anger, sadness, and compassion, which contained a feminine wisdom far beyond her years.

Hawise lifted her chin. 'She says that if she is going to be a widow while her husband is alive, she will dwell on her dower lands as befits her station.'

'What!' Fulke demanded, incredulity and anger starting to build.

Hawise's composure slipped. 'Why did you go to a tourney, Papa, instead of coming home to us?'

He shook his head, trying to grasp what she was saying, trying to make some sense of the morass.

'My grandfather said that you had gone to a tourney.'

'It wasn't just a tourney,' Fulke snapped. 'It was a gathering of all the men who felt that the spirit of the charter was not going to be honoured.'

'Mama said that if you wanted to chase your dream as well as your own tail, then well and good, but that you should not expect her to wait at Whittington for you and become another Maude de Braose.'

Fulke's frown darkened and he clenched his fists, furious that Maude should use Hawise as a pawn in their battle. 'She sent you with that message, did she?'

'No, Papa.' Hawise shook her head miserably. 'But I heard her say it. Go to her, please. I cannot bear to watch you destroy each other.' She made a small, helpless gesture.

Fulke kissed her broad white brow and smoothed the curly red wisps that had escaped the tight braiding. 'I'll ride out on the morrow,' he said gently, but his eyes were hard.

A servant brought hot wine and William joined them from outside, hugging his niece, nodding to the others, bringing welcome relief.

'No Maude?' he enquired.

'I'm going north tomorrow to fetch her,' Fulke said, managing for his daughter's sake to keep his voice neutral.

'Well, and what should I say to my wife?'

Clarice looked at Fulke where he stood before the hearth, drinking a last cup of wine before he retired. 'Only you can know that, my lord,' she said, picking up her cloak. Hawise and Will Pantulf had gone outside to admire the stars and each other. In her role of chaperone, Clarice was slowly preparing to follow them out.

Clarice had felt the anger and anxiety coming off Fulke in waves almost as hot as a brazier throughout the evening. Now he was brooding, and although he was far from drunk she could see that the wine he had consumed had made him melancholy rather than mellow. 'One thing I can tell you: she will not come to you.'

'Why?'

'You are asking to hear her words from my mouth. I cannot do that.' Clarice fastened the cloak.

'I don't see why not. Everyone else seems to know her reasons. She must have discussed the matter with you.'

Hearing the growl in his voice, Clarice mutely shook her head. Turning from him, she hurried from the hall, and did not answer when he shouted her back. She had no intention of becoming a grain of corn between two grind-stones, or of putting herself through the mill of facing him and speaking for another woman when all she really wanted was to . . . Clarice gave a terse mutter of self-annoyance and banished the thought before it could develop coher-ence at the front of her mind.

Outside it was a night for lovers, crisp and star-frosted. A time to embrace within the shelter of each other's cloaks, sharing warmth. Clarice's breath whitened in the air as she climbed the wall walks and joined Hawise and Will, standing breast to breast, their lips so close that their own breath mingled as one. She felt no envy; indeed she was wary for she had seen both sides of a coin that evening. Nevertheless, a wistful pang clutched her heart as she looked on the couple and knew that such an innocent love would never be hers.

CHAPTER 39

Shipley, Yorkshire, Autumn 1215

Sleeves pushed back to the elbow, one hand steadying the beechwood mixing bowl, Maude dug her other into the glutinous mixture of salt, bay salt, saltpetre, ground black peppercorns and honey. On the trestle before her lay two dozen thick hams. She could have left the work to Dame Guldrun, who had been making York hams every autumn for the past twenty-five years, but she wanted to learn. Besides, it kept her occupied and prevented her from falling into a bleak mood. There were only so many hours of the day that could be spent at embroidery or archery or tending her children. The boys were too old to need her constant supervision. They wanted to be off with the grooms and dogs, testing their skills, being young hunters, playing at warrior knights. Mabile was in the hall under the watchful gaze of the steward's wife and Jonetta, who had refused with a shudder of revulsion to come out to the cold salting larder and help cure hams.

'Tha hast to rub 'em all ower wi' this mixture twice a week for a moon, turnin' 'em every time,' instructed Guldrun, 'then tha hast to soak 'em for a day and a night and hang 'em up to dry.' Her own pink forearms resembled the hams into which she was vigorously smearing the mixture. 'And when tha's done, tha must always cover t'knuckle wi' ground-up peppercorns to stop the wick things from gettin' at t'meat.'

Maude nodded. That made sense. Pepper might be expensive, but losing a ham to maggots in the winter months made it a false economy to skimp on preservation. She had a tiny cut on her knuckle and it stung ferociously as salt met raw flesh. She coated a ham in the mixture, following Guldrun's example.

'Thass right, my lady.' Guldrun gave a gruff nod of approval. 'You can tell you're a Yorkshire woman, born if not bred.'

Maude laughed with delight at the compliment. The dour folk of these parts had no love for the Normans who had all but wiped out their great-great-grandparents during the harrying when the Conqueror brought fire and sword to England's North Country. There had been few people left to carry the memory, but that had only emphasised rather than diluted its power. To be praised by a matriarch such as Guldrun was accomplishment indeed.

She found herself thinking that it was a pity Clarice had gone to Whittington. With her delight in all things domestic and her dexterity, she would have enjoyed this. The thought of Whittington crept like a worm into the apple of her mind. Perhaps she should have gone with the girls. In truth, it had been her duty to do so, but she had ignored the voice of conscience. Pride and pique and anger: all were justified. In her mind's eye she carried a vision of Fulke jousting in summer sunshine, laughing in masculine camaraderie, flirting with women.

'Ye need not be so hard, mistress,' Guldrun warned with a look askance. 'T'pig's already dead.'

Maude murmured a startled apology. No, she would not think about Whittington or Fulke. Good thoughts obviously made good hams.

An hour later, she and Guldrun finished smearing and turning the legs. Now they could be left for three days until the next application. Wiping her chapped red hands on a scrap of linen, Maude stepped outside the salting larder into a bitter late morning. The wind cut through her thick woollen dress as if the fabric was the sheerest chansil and the sky was overcast, suggesting more rain. Straw had been thrown down in the courtyard to soak up the results of the last torrential downpour. Whereas Ireland's rain was soft, almost green like the land, Yorkshire's came down unforgivingly in hard steel bolts.

Two riders were entering the courtyard, their heads tucked into their hoods and shoulders hunched against the wind. A man and a youth. Her heart began to thump as they neared. A travelling knight and his squire.

Guldrun followed her out of the salting larder, wiping her own hands. 'I'll tell t'steward we've got visitors,' she said and waddled off, her large buttocks rippling magnificently.

Maude nodded without looking at her, all her attention given to the man dismounting from the chestnut cob. The grey sky and the dark blue hood tinted his eyes with those brooding colours and emphasised the dark shadows beneath them. The lines between his nose and mouth were graven more deeply than she remembered. But then it had been a difficult few months.

Turning to the squire, he bid the lad take the horses and find them stabling, then see to the travelling packs. Then he pivoted to Maude.

'Is it not the coward's way out to send your daughter as your messenger?' he asked.

Maude clenched the cloth in her hands. 'I did not send her. She came to you of her own accord.'

'But you chose not to accompany her.'

The first drops of rain spattered from the darker skirt of

cloud edging over the settlement and a sudden ruffle of wind tore at her wimple, sending the fabric billowing into her eyes. She clawed it down and looked at him through wind-stung tears. 'I chose not to,' she agreed.

'Will you tell me why?'

'Is it not obvious?'

'Would I ask if it were? Or do you expect Hawise to do your work for you?'

She saw the spark of anger in his eyes and answered it with a flash of her own. 'I do not know what she has said to you, but I gave her no "work". Jesu, do you think I would put words against her father in our own daughter's mouth?'

'I don't know. Would you?'

The rain slanted down in sleek silver rods. 'If you think that, then you had best recall your squire and ride back to Whittington because there is nothing for you here.' She left him and hurried towards the hall, changed her mind and direction, and made not for the central door, but for the stairs that led up to the small solar and bedchamber above. She was in no doubt that he would follow and whatever had to be said, it was better stated in privacy than providing a meal for the occupants in the hall, including their daughters.

The cold dread that she had misjudged him began to grow on her when he did not immediately follow. She steeled herself, pouring wine into two cups, adding charcoal to the brazier, dismissing the maid who was seated at a sprang frame by the window. Of course he would follow. Why travel all this way in order to ride out again? The horses would need resting even if he did not.

Taking the woman's place at the frame, she looked out on the courtyard. Fulke had gone. She could hear the thud of the rain on the straw. Hens fluffed out their feathers and

huddled in the corner by the midden where a withy parti-
tion fence offered some small degree of shelter. Torchlight
wavered to life in the kitchens across the way, casting a
yellow glow over the darkening afternoon.

The door opened, as she had known it would, but until
he walked into the room, she did not let out the breath
she had been holding.

'I don't know,' he said, as if there had been no break in
their conversation, 'because I no longer know you.
Somewhere I have lost the woman I married, my helpmeet
and soulmate, and in my darkest moments I fear that I will
be unable to find her again.' Pushing his hood down, he
came into the room and stood before the brazier, extending
his hands to the warmth.

'Mayhap because she no longer exists.' His words made
her throat tighten and tears gather behind her eyes. 'I fear
that I have lost the man I married, or that I mistook him
for something that he was not.' She looked at him across
the space that separated them, the heat of the brazier and
the chill of the air. Half rising, she closed and latched the
shutters against the growing inclemency of the weather.
'Why did you go to a tourney?' she demanded. 'Why didn't
you come home?'

'Is that what has rankled with you?' he demanded. 'That
I went to a tourney?'

Maude pushed down the latch and looked at the pressure mark on her index finger. 'That you had more care
for your new rebel friends than you did for us,' she said.
'That you could not leave the matter of John alone.' She
met his gaze. 'I thought you had settled your differences.
You said that all you wanted was justice. All you wanted
was Whittington, but once you had it, it wasn't enough.
John was still there and you wanted to bring him down,
whatever the cost.'

He flushed. 'That's not true. If John were a king in the mould of his father, I would not have stirred an inch from Whittington.'

'Not so, because it was Henry deprived your family of Whittington in the first place,' she retorted.

'Look, this charter is important,' he said impatiently. 'It protects men's rights; it gives them freedom from John's tyranny. He has been forced to dismiss his Poitevin mercenaries who would commit whatever evil he commanded. Hawise said you did not want to be another Maude de Braose; well, the enforcing of this charter ensures that you never will be.'

Maude shook her head. 'Those words are mine, but I said nothing to Hawise; I would not tear her between us.'

'No,' Fulke said grimly. 'She says that she overheard you.'

She bit her lip. Out of the frying pan into the fire, she thought with dismay. 'I was overwrought,' she said. 'I vented my opinion on Clarice.'

She waited for the explosion of anger, but he was silent, his jaw clamped. Feeling cold and shaky, she went to the wine she had poured earlier and handed him his cup, not as an olive branch, but as a way of continuing the communication.

'It's not some boyish jape, Maude,' he said in a less harsh tone. 'If anything it is more important than Whittington itself.'

'Than your family?'

He frowned. 'It doesn't have to be a contest.'

'No, it doesn't,' she agreed. 'And that is why I do not understand why you walked away from the signing. My father told me that you left the place of truce and rode away to join the company of de Vesci and FitzWalter.' Her lip curled. 'That is why I say it is John you want, not peace and justice.'

'Christ, Maude, John has no intention of sticking to the laws of that charter unless he is forced. Do you believe me so petty and vindictive that I would pursue him for an old grievance?' He looked at her with anger, and she saw the pain in his expression. 'You do, don't you?

'I believe that it is not finished between you,' Maude said unsteadily. 'And I cannot help but feel like a widow when you put all your energy into fighting him.'

'I'm not fighting him now; I have sworn a truce.'

'To last how long? Until the spring grass grows beneath your mount's hooves and you can be off to war again?'

'If John abides by the charter, that need not happen.'

'But it will. I can see it in your face. Do not seek to pull the wool over my eyes with bland words.'

Abruptly he set the wine cup aside. 'Enough of this. I have ridden far, I'm weary, and likely I'm making a pig's ear of stating my case. I came to ask you to return to Whittington with me. Its soul is missing without your presence.'

'And if I say no?'

He scooped his hands through his hair and it gave her a pang to see the glitter of silver strands amid the heavy sheen of black. 'I had considered tying you across a packhorse like a sack of cabbages and forcing you to come home, but where would be the point? Likely you would make your escape at the first opportunity or put a dagger between my ribs as I slept. I know it cannot be as it was before – as you say, we have changed, but . . .' He looked at her sombrely, seeking the words. 'But I want us to grow together, not apart.'

Maude felt herself begin to melt, but she stood her ground. 'You will still go off to war against John, though,' she said.

'Whether you come or stay, that cannot be changed,' he

murmured, 'but because of it, I need you more, not less.' He spread his hands. 'Who else will keep my feet on the ground, take me to task . . . accept me for what I am?'

She narrowed her eyes. 'If he were not in Ireland with that vixen wife of his, I would think that you had been taking lessons from Jean de Rampaigne.'

'I swear to you, these are all my own words – although, truth to tell, I do not know from where they came,' he added wryly. 'All the way to Edlington I was coddling my anger, rehearsing what I was going to say to you about obligation and duty.'

'Were you?' Maude's tone was barbed. 'Well, it seems to me that you have had your say indeed.'

'And so have you,' he retorted, 'and we have both said the same thing, so that makes argument fruitless.'

She folded her arms across her breasts but it was not a defensive motion, rather one of assertion. 'Very well,' she said, 'I will return, but you have to promise me one thing.'

He eyed her warily. 'What?'

'That you will not go to another tourney unless you take me with you.'

'I have always worn your favour, you know that.' He patted his pouch. 'I still carry the hair ribbon you gave me on that first occasion.'

'I want to be there to tie it round your lance. I won't be your grass widow ever again. No. You have to promise . . .' She took a step back as he took one forward.

He unfastened his pouch and drew out the strand of green ribbon. The colour had faded, the silver was tarnished, but it still sparkled in places. 'On this token I swear,' he said. 'Bind me as you will.'

Maude took it from him and wound it carefully around her fingers and his, meshing them together, hers red from ham salting, his hard from grasping sword and rein. Their flesh touched, cold from the cold of the room, but heat kindling in the blood. His free arm curved around her waist, hers around his neck. He spoke her name, his grip tightened.

Their lips met, first in tenderness, then in fire. Fuelled by two seasons of chastity, kindled by his touch, Maude was consumed by a rush of need so strong that not only did her loins melt, but the bones of her spine were immolated and her knees buckled. From the unsteadiness of his breathing, she knew it was the same for him. Whatever their quarrels, whatever their differences, in this they were as one. It was a battleground and a place of peace-making, of yielding and assertion, of passion – and love.

Later, lying on the floor, she gently untangled the jousting ribbon from their bound fingers and trailed it lightly across his closed lids. He smiled, and, with eyes still shut, trapped her hand and kissed its palm.

From the courtyard, the sound of children's voices and the barking of dogs came up to them, muffled through the timber walls and the tightly closed shutters.

Maude sat up. 'That will be our sons, home from their ride,' she said. 'We had best find them before they find us.'

'And why shouldn't they find us?' Fulke pulled her back down to him, kissing her thoroughly. 'They need to know about love as well as war.'

'Mayhap, but I would hate your heir to get the notion that the solar floor is the customary place to learn.'

Fulke laughed and let her go. 'I suppose so,' he said as she scrambled to her feet and cast around for her wimple. There was the sound of footsteps scuffling up the stairs. 'You start with a bed and work your way down.'

The door burst open and two boys accompanied by a large wolfhound hurtled into the room to find their mother filling two cups with wine and their father seated on the

bench, his legs outstretched in a casual pose. Being boisterous boys, unconcerned with outward appearance, neither
noticed for one moment the tell-tale stalks of straw adhering
to their parents' clothing.

CHAPTER 40

Whittington Castle, Shropshire, Summer 1216

Four months after her fourteenth year day, Hawise was married at Whittington to William Pantulf of Wem. It was a huge gathering with guests from both sides of the baronial divide arriving to celebrate and use the opportunity to discuss their differences, arrange pacts, choose loyalties. Llewelyn declined to attend, but sent his congratulations and the gift of a small brooch fashioned of Welsh gold for Hawise.

The young men held a mock tourney on the sward behind the keep and the older men joined in, lured by memories of their youth. Looking on in the June sunshine, the women laughed and chattered among themselves, exchanging gossip, commenting on the play. Matrons considered matches for their daughters, and daughters considered too, giggling behind their hands, fluttering their lashes like wayward moths.

In the evening there was dancing in the keep, and on the torchlit sward for the air was as warm as new milk and the dusk lingered in a translucent green-blue gloaming behind the flutter of the firelight. Adorned in a wedding gown of teal-coloured silk, her red hair unbound in token of her virginity and crowned with a chaplet of white dog roses, Hawise was a stunning bride. Smiling with obvious delight, resplendent in blue wool, William Pantulf did her justice and guests agreed that it was a fine match.

Maude and Fulke had received several offers of marriage for their sons. A Welsh lord, Madoc ap Griffin, who already had marcher relatives among the de Laceys, had proposed a union with Fulkin and his daughter Angareth, an engaging black-haired moppet of five years old. The notion interested Fulke. Llewelyn might be the greatest lord in Wales, but he was not the only one and alliances across the border were always useful, especially when there were connections with the powerful de Lacey family. He had agreed to consider it, but bearing in mind the ages of the children and the fluid political situation, would take his time.

Maude smiled and curved her arm around Fulke's. She thought he looked very fine in his court tunic. The dark crimson colour suited him and the gold braid edging cuff and hem added richness. Her own gown was of oyster-coloured silk with a trim of sage-green embroidery. There had been compliments aplenty for the bride and groom, and that was how it should be, but there had been compliments for herself and Fulke too. Some of the shine of Hawise's wedding day had rubbed off on them, and she could feel the magic glowing in the air.

Fulke had come to Edlington in late October, had brought her home to Whittington in November, and stayed. It was now June and the truce was still holding. While the rebels had continued their fight, Fulke had remained at Whittington, tending his own concerns, his ears cocked to what was happening, but not actively taking part. Sometimes she had felt the strain in him, had seen him rise from their bed and prowl the keep like a caged wolf, and she had felt like a gaoler. Prince Louis of France had landed on English soil six weeks ago and was going from victory to victory as the rebel barons rode into his camp. Maude was aware that Fulke had been considering joining them. He had not said as much, but she knew him well enough to recognise the signs.

This wedding had been good for him, she thought. He had been able to invite guests from both sides, to meet them on his own ground and discuss the situation. While he wanted to see John acknowledge the charter and stand by its terms, he did not want Prince Louis to claim the kingdom, set up his Frenchmen in positions of authority, and make the terms of the charter completely impossible. And while he hesitated, Maude prayed.

Fuelled by drink, the laughter was developing a raucous edge. 'Time, I think, for the bedding ceremony,' she murmured. 'If you go and fetch Will, I'll take charge of Hawise.'

He nodded, but did not move. She watched him rub the back of his neck and was filled with amused tenderness.

'I know,' she said softly, 'it doesn't seem a moment since she was a babe in arms.'

'She is still that to me,' he said.

She saw him swallow and knew that he was remembering the times Hawise had clambered into his lap and fallen asleep against him. Her squeals of delight as he took her up on his saddle. Her small hand engulfed in his. All that care, all that protection was now to be yielded into the hands of another, and because Hawise was so confident in the love of her parents, she had run joyfully to her bridegroom and not looked back.

Maude touched his arm. 'She will be all right,' she murmured. 'You chose well when you chose Will Pantulf.'

Fulke wriggled his shoulders as if the words were heavy raindrops. Maude could guess that just now, he was wishing he had not chosen anyone for her. That the thought of seeing his daughter, his 'babe in arms', getting into bed with a man and coupling with him was difficult to bear, although he knew it was a necessary rite of passage. She felt a shudder go through him.

'Come,' he said with sudden gruffness. 'If we don't do it now, they'll all be too drunk to bear witness, and I will lose whatever courage I have.' Drawing a deep breath, he plunged amongst the merrymakers, adopting the mask of affable host and parent.

Smiling through a sudden sting of tears, Maude went to fetch the bride. She arrived at Hawise's side just as Fulke, Will's father and the senior male guests surrounded the groom and took him away to disrobe him. Jests flew thick and fast from wine-loosened tongues, although the presence of the senior men kept them just within the bounds of decency.

Hawise was laughing, her eyes a little over-bright because she had drunk too much wine, but she showed scarcely a sign of fear or nervousness as she was ushered into the main bedchamber. Garlands thick with May blossom decorated the walls and the bed had been draped with new hangings of thick Flemish cloth.

While helping Hawise to remove her bridal chaplet and the heavy, embroidered wedding gown, Maude used the moment to ask her daughter if she was all right.

Hawise wrinkled her nose at her mother in an unconsciously copied mannerism. 'I know what to expect,' she laughed.

'You do?' Maude lifted her brows and tried not to look worried.

'Oh, Mama.' Hawise gave her a nudge. 'You'll have the proof of my purity to hang on the wall behind the breakfast trestle.'

Maude grimaced, remembering her own wedding morn and the young knight with the flint-hazel eyes who had looked anywhere but at the bloody sheet, hanging like a victory banner for all to see.

'I know you're virgin still,' Maude said, 'if not quite as pure as the driven snow.'

Hawise looked sidelong at her mother. 'Did you and Papa bed together before you were wed?'

Maude shook her head. 'No,' she said. 'We had the opportunity once, but I was still another man's wife and we both held back.' She smiled and stroked her daughter's hand. 'Your wedding night will be different to either of mine — I wish you well.'

'How different?' Hawise asked curiously.

Her mother's lips twitched. 'My first husband was more than thirty years older — a good man, but I was very young and he was not my choice, although I came to love him dearly. With your father . . .' She gave a small shrug and her smile deepened.

'Mama?'

Maude laughed and felt warm colour flush her cheeks. 'Wildfire,' she said. 'He snatched me from beneath King John's nose and took me into the woods. I became an outlaw's bride and our wedding bed was a bower of bent-over saplings under the stars. It sounds the stuff of a troubadour's tale — indeed, it was, but we were living on a blade's edge. I knew that every time we parted it might be the last time I would see him alive.'

'And nothing has changed,' Hawise said.

'No,' Maude said wryly, 'and that is why your wedding night is different and you are perhaps even more fortunate than I. Fear might lend a spice to pleasure, but too much seasoning destroys it.'

Their murmured speech was curtailed as Clarice arrived with a silk bedrobe to arrange around Hawise's shoulders. The way the young woman's glance flickered between the two of them revealed that she had overheard the tail end of their conversation, although she said nothing except to murmur that Mabile was sleeping and one of the maids keeping an eye on her lest she wake.

Maude studied Clarice. She was wearing a gown of rose-coloured linen, the skirt made to flare by the insertion of several gores. The colour suited her. Her features were ordinary but she had flawless skin, glossy hair, and the loveliest eyes. Several looks had been cast her way during the feast and more than one enquiry made.

'I saw you in the dance with Rob d'Uffington.' Hawise smiled and wagged a playful forefinger. 'And it wasn't your cheek that he kissed at the end.'

Clarice flushed. 'He was wine-merry,' she said. 'It meant nothing.'

'Well, what about Simon de Warren? He was watching you all night.'

'Simon de Warren has so high an opinion of himself that there is no room for anyone else,' Clarice said shortly, making it clear that she did not appreciate being teased. 'I am happy for you, truly I am, but do not try to find me a mate from among your husband's companions.'

Hawise opened her mouth but before she could launch into an argument, there was a loud thump on the door, announcing the arrival of the bridegroom's party. Maude hastened to open it and bid them enter while the other women hustled Hawise over to the bed and placed her in it. Will, attired in a chemise similar in style to that of his bride, and topped with a cloak, was pushed into bed beside her with much laughter and bawdy jesting. The latter subsided as Father Thomas advanced to bless the bed and its occupants, sprinkling them with holy water, but resumed as soon as the priest had pronounced the final amen. There was much military innuendo concerned with thrusting spears into targets, shooting arrows and oiling scabbards.

Fulke let them have their sport: it was all part of the ritual, but it was one of the hardest things he had ever had to do. At least the Pantulf family had agreed to forgo the part of the ceremony where the couple were displayed naked before witnesses. Each family was content with the bargain without citing that particular ritual. Gritting his teeth, Fulke endured for as long as he could. 'Enough!' he finally roared, spreading his arms and ushering the revellers away from the bed. 'Time to leave them in peace.'

More loud, good-natured jests followed that statement, as he had known they would, but the guests allowed themselves to be herded from the chamber and back to the trestles where food and wine still waited to be consumed and the musicians continued to play. As the chamber door closed at his back with a soft thud Fulke felt as if a part of his life had closed with it.

Since the newly-weds had been given the main bedchamber, Fulke and Maude intended sleeping in the hall with the other guests, but no one was ready to retire just yet. The evening was warm, spirits were high and folk were reluctant to abandon their revelry. With a fixed smile Fulke performed his duty as host, and wished himself far away. William and Ivo were busy emptying a flagon between them and carousing in true bachelor fashion. Although both of them had manors and lands to tend on the FitzWarin estates, neither had chosen to settle in marriage. Richard ambled up and joined them, partnered by a squire of William Pantulf's and four venison pasties. Fulke's gaze wandered further and found Philip seated at a trestle with his wife, Joanna, who was the daughter of a Leicestershire knight. They had been wed for less than six months, but in true FitzWarin fashion she was already round with child. Alain was courting a ward of Robert Corbet's and they were dancing with others on the sward, using the opportunity to draw close to each other and hold hands in the movement of the carole. Fulke's smile was poignant. How well he remembered. How swiftly time seemed to plunge through the neck of the hourglass.

Maude arrived at his side, wrapping her arms around his. 'Come,' she murmured softly, 'they will not notice if we slip away for a while.'

'I could think of nothing better,' he murmured. With a last glance at the guests to reassure himself that no drink-fuelled quarrels or fights were about to break out, he followed her tug.

Together they walked around the perimeter of the keep, Fulke's wolfhounds padding at heel. Maude paused at the wattle fencing that bordered the herb garden, and with sudden decision opened the gate and stepped within. The beds were illuminated in hues of silver-grey with the faintest tinge here and there of natural colour. Bidding the wolf-hounds stay — Maude's herb garden was banned territory for the dogs ever since one had vigorously dug up the tarragon roots whilst burying a bone — Fulke followed her into the garden.

'I was thinking of our own wedding night,' she said as she wound her way past the beds of sage and betony, hyssop, tansy and marigold, towards the vine arbour at the garden's end.

'Were you?' He slipped his arm around her waist.

'How it was.' She turned so that she was facing him and traced his jaw with her forefinger.

The sounds of laughter and music came to them, slightly muted by distance, making of them watchers on the banks of a river rather than swimmers in the tide. He pushed her back into the shadows cast by the vine leaves. 'How it was?' he said indignantly.

Her smile was teasing. 'Why do you think I brought you here?'

'To look at the plants? For the delight of a stroll?' he teased in return, and was aware of a pleasant shortening of his breath. She tried to pinch him and he grabbed her hand, trapping it against his breast. 'Or perhaps to remind me of my misspent youth when I have been feeling my years . . . to remind me that I am a husband as well as a father?'

Maude pressed against him. Her free hand went around his neck. 'I am hoping,' she said huskily, 'that you do not need reminding of anything.'

It was three days later that the messenger arrived from William Marshal. Hawise and Will Pantulf had left for the keep at Wem that morning, which was to be their home. Most of the wedding guests had departed too; only a few lingerers were milking the last dregs from the celebration.

Fulke broke the seal and unrolled the sheet of vellum. It was a scribe's neat writing, but Marshal's blunt words that leaped from the page, brutal as the blow of a club.

'What is it?' Maude came anxiously to his side, her head tilted to read the script.

'John has confiscated my lands at Alveston because he does not believe I will hold to the letter of the truce,' Fulke said furiously. 'Apparently it's a warning to keep me loyal — a hostage for my good behaviour.'

'What does Marshal say?'

'Entreats my patience! Says that John trusts no one just now because even Salisbury has deserted him.' Fulke laughed harshly. 'Whatever patience I had, the last grains have run out like sand through an hourglass. John has just drawn a sword and cut me loose!'

Maude compressed her lips. She did not weep; she did not argue. The time for all that was over. 'Wherever you go, I go too,' she said and, without giving him a chance to argue, went to pack the baggage chests.

Fulke joined the rebels, but when the first glut of his fury wore off, he found himself discontented. He had no burning desire to fight for the King of France or see French lords acquire English lands by right of conquest. William Salisbury, after a minor toying with the rebels, had clearly thought the same and returned to his brother. There was a siege at Lincoln where the castle was held for the King. John descended on the city, raised the siege, and scattered the rebels.

Fulke was not at Lincoln. He joined neither side, but spent the time coddling a severe and serious bout of ague at his manor of Whadborough in Leicestershire. It was mid-October, a damp day, the leaves whispering from the trees and clothing the ground in slick brown and yellow patterns. Braziers burned in the main chamber, fragranced with aromatic herbs, and Maude had dosed him with horehound syrup and a tisane made from blackcurrants, honey and wine.

She saw his malaise as one not so much of the body as of the mind. Unable to see a way out of the vicious circle in which he was bound, having loyalty to neither Philip, nor John, nor for that matter Llewelyn, he had retreated into a feverish state where he did not have to think about any of them. Maude left him to sleep for the best part of the day, finally taking him a bowl of meat broth and two wastel loaves as the mid-afternoon began to descend slowly towards dusk. A maid replenished the candles and the braziers and quietly left the room.

Maude gently nudged Fulke awake. He pulled himself upright and leaned against the bolsters. His eyes were hazy with sleep, but the glazed look of fever seemed to have diminished a little. His chest still rattled like a coffer of rusty swords, though. He was not on the mend yet.

'I'm not hungry,' he croaked.

'Just drink the soup then.' She broke the bread, dipped it, and ate a morsel herself, feeling rather like a mother trying to cajole a picky child.

After a moment, he raised the bowl to his lips and sipped in a desultory fashion. 'I have been thinking,' he said. The deep power of his voice had been constricted to a smoky whisper. 'There is something I have been meaning to do for a long time – since my mother died.'

'What?' Maude eyed him cautiously.

'I want to sponsor a religious foundation on my land. At Alberbury, where my mother and father are buried.'

She felt a jolt of queasy fear. She wondered if he thought he was dying and wanted to make provision for his soul. Her fear must have shown on her face, for he shook his head and found a smile.

'I am not sick unto death, I hope,' he whispered. 'But matters such as Hawise's marriage and the fact that I have taken to my bed at all lead me to realise that I should set my affairs in order.' He paused to cough and Maude took the bowl of broth so that he would not spill it on the sheets.

Her anxiety abated somewhat as she remembered Theobald's preoccupation with his monasteries in the latter part of their marriage, a growing need for the spirit to be comforted rather than the body.

'Yes,' she murmured, 'I think it is a good idea.' Perhaps if he went home and threw himself into the building, his discontent would ease. That was part of it too, she thought. While temporal leaders failed, God was a constant.

'I have thought also to make provision for Mabile,' he said, taking the broth from her again and cupping the bowl in his hands. 'Without a miracle she will never be fit to wed and she cannot enter the Church because she does not comprehend the meaning of worship. If – God forbid – anything should happen to us while she lives, I need to know that she is protected by law.'

Maude nodded and folded her arms. It was a defensive gesture and one that she immediately reversed by unfolding them again and sitting beside him. She often wondered if she had done something during her pregnancy to cause Mabile's condition. It was said that women who gave birth to babies deformed by a harelip had been startled by that animal during their pregnancy. However, she could think of nothing to account for Mabile's misfortune unless it was the difficulty of her birth. Mayhap it was God's punishment for her parents' sins. Either way, the guilt and uncertainty gnawed at her. 'What do you intend?'

He sipped the broth and set it aside. 'I am going to give Lambourn and all its revenues to maintain her for as long as she lives.'

Maude stared. It was his richest manor, the plum of his de Dinan inheritance. It was guilt, she thought, like her own, for which he was over-compensating. Then again, not all the riches in the world could compensate for their daughter's tragedy.

'It is the least I can do,' he said, as if reading her thoughts. 'That and a chapel for prayer.'

In the morning Fulke was well enough to leave his bed and sit before the brazier, wrapped in his warmest tunic and fur-lined cloak. He had developed a harsh, rattling cough, but he was bright enough to be considering plans for his religious house.

He dictated to the scribe in a hoarse, scratchy voice. Another three or four days' rest, he thought, and he would be well enough to think about leaving Whadborough, but for which destination was a question he did not want to consider. Home to Whittington, or south to rejoin the rebels? He had no idea. Last they heard, John had been at Lynn, organising supplies for his army of mercenaries, but where he was now and what his intentions were, Fulke did not know.

It was obvious now that John would never honour the charter he had signed at Runnymede. It was the same problem, grinding round and round in Fulke's head until it ached beyond bearing. John or the French. The price demanded was too high to support either. Look to God instead. He smiled with grim humour.

The quill scratched across the vellum. Fulke could have written the missive himself, but a formal letter demanded formal writing, and Fulke's hand was apt to sprawl and lean alarmingly to the right. He rubbed his forehead and Maude brought him a cup of spiced wine. Earlier she had massaged his chest with aromatic herbs and goose grease. The smell was revolting but it had eased his breathing.

There was a thump on the door and Fulke's squire, Walter, poked his head around to announce that a messenger had arrived from Earl Ranulf of Chester.

'Admit him,' Fulke commanded.

Maude's expression had frozen. 'What do you think he wants?'

'I know not, but for him to send a messenger here, it must be important.'

Maude bit her lip. He could imagine the scenarios racing across her mind because they were doing their best to gallop through the wool occupying his own. John was on his way here with an army, squashing resistance as he went as he had squashed it at Berwick by butchering everyone in his path. The royalists had seized Whittington and were holding their children hostage. The French had retreated and John was demanding surrender of all rebel barons.

The messenger was ushered into the room and bowed to Fulke. He was a florid man of middle years with a thatch of grey hair and a full moustache.

'You look as if you have ridden hard,' Fulke said in greeting and gestured the man to rise.

'That I have, my lord, and with momentous tidings.' He gratefully took the wine that Maude gave him and drank deeply.

Fulke was aware of Maude's hand returning to his shoulder and gripping. 'Yes?' he prompted.

'The Earl of Chester bids me greet you and deliver the news that King John is dead at Newark Castle of a grievous flux of the bowels.'

'Dead?' Fulke repeated blankly. The word rang in his ears but seemed unable to pierce further.

'Aye, my lord. He took ill of the gripes on the morning he left Lynn and they worsened.' The messenger licked his lips. 'He was making for Swineshead Abbey and sent his baggage train the short route across the estuary. It was caught by the tide and all the gold with which he was going to pay his soldiers was lost. When he heard that news, it worsened his plight. My lord rode with the King to Newark and sent for the Abbot of Croxton when it became plain that he was mortally ill. But there was nothing to be done.'

Maude crossed herself. 'God rest his soul,' she whispered.

Fulke followed her lead, responding by rote as he struggled to assimilate the news. John had loomed over most of his life. He had expended years fighting him, pushing at him as if he were an insurmountable object in his path. Now suddenly there was nothing, and he was free to go forward, except that the removing of the object seemed to have brought him to his knees.

'Earl Ranulf has been named an executor of his will and co-guardian of the young King with the Earl of Pembroke. They ask that you come and swear your fealty as soon as you may.'

Fulke rubbed his jaw and felt the prickle of stubble like small needles against his palm. John's son and heir was a boy of nine, so in effect his guardians would rule the country. He had every respect for Chester and Pembroke. 'And the Great Charter, what said they of that?'

'That they will honour the terms, my lord,' the man said.

Fulke thanked the messenger and dismissed him to seek food and rest. Rising to his feet, he walked haltingly around the room until he came to a chess set arranged near the window. Suddenly he felt incomplete – as if half the pieces were missing. 'I should be leaping for joy,' he said to Maude, 'but I feel naught but emptiness. All these years . . .' He swallowed. He was not going to weep because John was dead. He was not! But against his will, the tears came anyway.

She put her arms around him. 'A freed prisoner has to grow accustomed to the daylight,' she murmured.

'There are only two years between us in age.' He continued to gaze at the chess pieces through a blur of moisture. 'I thought . . .' He swallowed. 'I thought he was going to be my enemy for ever.' He blinked hard. It was as though his hatred for John was a skeleton around which the flesh of his life had been modelled. Now, without that solid backbone, he was dissolving. Perhaps he should have died of this ague even as John had died of the flux.

'Game's end,' Maude said. Leaving their embrace, she picked up the heavy wooden chessboard, pieces and all, and, carrying it past the astonished scribe, she threw the entirety on the fire.

Fulke stared through a brilliance of tears. Billows of

smoke rose towards the roof vents. The flames siezed the edges of the board in avid, fiery claws.

'Finished,' Maude said with a brusque nod. 'Neither black, nor white, but mingled ashes. Now we can go home.'

CHAPTER 41

Alberbury, Shropshire, Summer 1222

A smell of powdered stone dust filled the air, mingling with the sound of a mason's hammer chipping on stone. Alberbury Priory was growing out of the land cleared for its birthing, stone by mortared stone. It was to be a house of Augustinian canons when completed; Fulke had already negotiated with Lilleshall Abbey for the provision of a prior and monks.

Fulke watched the toiling labourers and artisans with a mingling of pleasure and irritation. 'Pleased as I am to see this working going forth to the glory of God,' he said, 'I cannot help but think that I could put these masons to better use at Whittington, strengthening the defences.' He folded his arms and frowned.

'Can't you just send them, sir, and set them to work?'

Fulke glanced at his son and namesake. The lad was almost eighteen with a nimbus dazzle of fair hair and dark grey eyes. Coltish, still growing into his limbs, but promising the athletic strength to balance his height. He was serving as a squire to Ranulf Chester and his leave was short: a couple of weeks to visit his family during the long days of midsummer and attend his sister Jonetta's wedding to Henry of Pembridge.

'It isn't as easy as that, son,' Fulke said wryly. 'I cannot strengthen Whittington unless I am given a licence from the King. If I build in stone without his yeasay, then he is entitled to command his sheriff to see that all the work is destroyed. Also I would be levied an enormous fine and we are already in debt to the Crown.'

'Well, why won't he give you permission?' The youth picked up a chip of stone and lobbed it across the grass.

'Because I was one of the rebels who took against his father. Because it is forgiven but not yet forgotten. Young Henry and his advisors could grant me permission to strengthen my keeps and then find that instead of using them to keep the Welsh at bay, I was fomenting another rebellion.'

'They don't really think that,' the young man said. 'Earl Ranulf would be happy for you to build in stone. Look at me, I'm his squire and his godson. He wishes you nothing but well.'

'Earl Ranulf may have a say in governing the country, but his word is not the law and there are others who are more cautious.'

'William Marshal, you mean.' The lad screwed up his face. 'He's almost in his dotage.'

Fulke cuffed his heir, not entirely in play. 'I hold William Marshal in high regard and so should you,' he growled. 'He may not be correct to be cautious, but his reasoning is sound.'

'Well, it doesn't seem sound to me to forbid you to strengthen Whittington. What if Llewelyn strikes?'

Fulke laughed without humour. 'Whittington will burn,' he said. Turning from the industry, he strolled back towards the keep. It was a slow process, regaining trust, he acknowledged. Slow and often frustrating. In the six years since John's death, the country had slowly settled back to normal, like a pool clearing after the throwing of a stone. Fulke remembered kneeling at the feet of John's nine-year-old son to pledge his homage. The child had been fair, with his mother's pale complexion and long, fine bones. The crown upon his yellow hair was a circlet belonging to his mother since John's regalia was somewhere in the murk of the Wellstream estuary. Henry's responses had been given in a clear voice, high-pitched as a bell, almost feminine. The eyes were Isobel's, the features thin and fastidious. There had been nothing of John to see, thank Christ, in any of the child's features or mannerisms. Fulke could not imagine playing chess with Prince Henry except on the most excruciatingly polite of terms. The sort of man he would make remained to be seen − as it remained to be seen with his own sons.

'I think, then, that I would strengthen and be damned,' said his heir.

Fulke's lips twitched. 'Yes, I used to think that way too. I must be getting old.'

Maude watched Clarice's silver needle fly in and out of the Flemish linen. The weave was so fine and tight that it did not seem possible that human hand had been involved in its manufacture. The quality had been reflected in the price, but since it was to be an altar cloth for the family chapel when the new abbey was consecrated, expense was not an issue. They were in Alberbury's garden, sitting together on a turf seat.

'I do not understand why you turned Hamelin Fitz-William away,' Maude said irritably. The day before, Clarice had refused an offer of marriage to William of Salisbury's bastard son, Hamelin. It was true that the young man was only eighteen years old to Clarice's five and twenty, but good marriages had been made with a much wider age gap. He was a friend of young Fulke, pleasant, personable and mature for his years. 'Every match we have proposed, you have rejected.'

'I am content as I am.'

Maude suppressed the urge to throttle Clarice. The words were spoken serenely and the face remained smooth and untroubled. It was like talking to a nun who had such a powerful vocation that it was unshakeable. The same words every time, like a litany. The slight, sweet curve of the lips. Maude longed to shake that composure and see what lay beneath.

'If you had been raised in another household – my father's, for example – you would have been forced to the altar long before now,' she said darkly.

'I know, and I am thankful beyond measure that you have put no such pressure on me.'

'I think you are afraid,' Maude said sharply. 'You have such a comfortable nest with us that you don't want to fly away and feather your own.' She had thought that Jonetta's marriage the previous week to Henry of Pembridge would put Clarice in a receptive frame of mind, but apparently not.

Clarice set her needle neatly in the fabric and rose, hands pressed to the small of her back. 'Perhaps you are right,' she murmured, 'but I do not see why it makes you angry. While I remain unwed, my lord can avail himself of my revenues.'

Maude gritted her teeth. Arguing with Clarice was as futile as pummelling a bolster. 'I am not angry, merely concerned.'

'You need not be.' Clarice stooped to pluck a small clump of weeds from the soil. 'I have said I am content . . . unless of course you want to be rid of me?'

'Don't be foolish,' Maude snapped defensively. 'We have raised you as one of our own and we love you dearly.' She met the perceptive grey-gold gaze for an instant, then looked at the embroidery. Clarice was as sharp as a needle and there was an undercurrent of truth in her observation. Maude sometimes found Clarice's presence annoying. Her air of serenity and her unfailing good nature could be as wearing in its own way as petulance and tantrums. Moreover, now that Clarice was a woman grown, there were frictions – unspoken but potent.

Clarice said nothing, but strayed further up the bed, pulling a weed here, deadheading a flower there. It was always her way. Arguments never went anywhere with Clarice because Clarice, quite simply, refused to argue. The docility was indicative of either a truly bovine nature or control beyond belief. Maude was still not sure which, she only knew that it was becoming increasingly difficult to live with it. Cut Clarice and likely she would bleed pure honey.

A shadow covered the sunlight on the embroidery frame. Looking up, she met the frightened eyes of one of the younger maids.

'What is it, Nesta?'

The girl dipped a curtsey, holding the folds of her gown with shaking hands. 'My lord sent me to fetch you, my lady. There's been a Welsh raid at Hilfrich . . . they've torched it. There are some villagers in the bailey – several sore wounded.' She swallowed.

Maude was immediately on her feet. 'Dear Jesu. Nesta, take care of Mabile.' She indicated her youngest daughter who was sitting in a corner of the garden, playing with a heap of shredded petals and singing in a strange, high-pitched voice. 'Clarice, come with me.'

Together the women ran from the garden to the keep. The first thing Maude saw was Hilfrich's reeve, Sion, his hand heavily bandaged and the wrappings brown with dried blood. Lying at his feet was a child of about Mabile's age, her fair plaits matted dark-red around a terrible wound in her skull. Fulke was crouching, his hand on the man's shoulder, his expression one of fury and grief.

'She's dead.' Sion said, looking numbly at Maude. 'One of them rode her down and she took a kick . . .' He didn't finish the sentence. His eyes were glazed and dry, looking inward to the horror of what he had seen. He was a Welshman. His wife was English, but there was no sign of her among the gathering of shocked, dazed villagers.

'What happened? Who did this?' she asked Sion. Clarice had found a blanket and she laid it tenderly over the dead child, covering the awful wound beneath its woven softness.

'They came without warning,' Sion said. 'Out of nowhere on horses they came.' His voice was as blank as his eyes.

'Who came?' Maude took his bound hand and gently unwrapped the bandages.

'The Welsh,' Fulke answered for the reeve, the word harsh with rage. 'Hilfrich is a border village. They claim it theirs.'

Maude was appalled. 'But why burn it to the ground? Always before they have raided for crops and cattle, not . . . not like this.' There was a deep cut across the back of the reeve's hand, exposing a glisten of tendon and bone. She winced: even with stitching, he would likely lose the use of the limb.

Fulke shook his head. 'I know not,' he said grimly. 'Llewelyn and I . . . we have had our differences ever since I made peace with the King and renewed my oath of fealty, but this . . .'

'Llewelyn? You think it was Llewelyn's men?'

'Who else could it be?' He moved on among the villagers, stooping to talk and console, promising them that he would deal with the matter. Young Fulke followed in his footsteps, white-faced but resolute.

Maude applied herself to tending the wounded. Earlier

she had been irritated with Clarice but now she could do naught but bless the young woman as she moved efficiently among the villagers, her calm, competent manner visibly easing their distress.

'They are all telling the same story,' Fulke said later to Maude. He had ordered the horses saddled and was grimly donning his mail. 'No warning – just armed riders pouring into the village, torching the houses, driving off the live-stock, riding down anyone who got in their way.'

'What are you going to do?' Watching him put on his armour, she felt sick with fear. For six years, there had been peace; seeing him in mail again made her realise how fragile that peace was, how complacent she had become, and now, caught off guard, how vulnerable they all were.

'Look at the damage,' he said.

'What if the Welsh are still there?'

'They won't be.' He gave her what she had long ago christened his wolfish look. 'And if they are, I'm no untrained farmer armed with naught but a hoe. They won't run with their tails between their legs because they won't be able to run.' The last word ended on a grunt as he laced his scabbard to his swordbelt.

She gnawed her lower lip. The thought of him caught up in a fight chilled her but so did the notion that the aggravation between English and Welsh had taken a new and vicious turn for the worse. 'Why did they do it?'

'I would guess that Llewelyn is serving me notice of a full border war,' he said grimly. 'Henry won't let me strengthen my keeps and Llewelyn must know this; he has his spies. Hilfrich is only four miles from Alberbury. He's been at odds with Pembroke and Chester all summer.'

'You cannot withstand Llewelyn,' she whispered. 'Not alone.'

'Tell me something else I do not know,' he said bleakly.

'I will go again to the King, demand that he let me strengthen my keeps, for if he does not, the Welsh will overrun the borders.' He pulled her against him and kissed her hard. 'I hope not to be gone too long.'

As he left the chamber, his son stepped out. 'Take me with you, Papa?' he requested. 'I can act as your squire, I know what to do.'

Fulke looked at the lad. He might well need more than a squire at his left shoulder and had no intention of endangering the youth. Give him a few more years of experience and it would be different. He set his hand on the boy's narrow shoulder. 'No, I need you to stay here and guard your mother and sisters.' His fingers tightened as his son's face began to darken. 'And before you complain that I am wrapping you in swaddling, let me tell you that remaining here is just as dangerous. If the Welsh come, the responsibility for defending Alberbury is yours.'

'Yes, Papa.' The youth still looked crestfallen, but accepted the judgement. Fulke nodded brusquely, man to man, and turned to stride for the courtyard, only to find his way blocked by a breathless Clarice.

'Your spurs,' she said, showing him the silver crescents, then knelt to attach them to his boots. Fulke let her. Bending over in a hauberk was uncomfortable and breathing was difficult. He looked down at her bent head. Being still unwed and in her own domain, she wore no veil, and the skin of her parting was a precise white line dividing her glossy, braided hair. A feeling of tenderness flowed through him.

She rose to her feet, her face slightly flushed from stooping. 'God keep you, my lord,' she said and he saw the suspicion of moisture in her eyes. Then she left him, walking swiftly, her spine straight, her head carried high.

Fulke hastened out to the gathering troop in the

courtyard. As he passed the industry at the priory, he crossed himself. '*Ora pro nobis*,' he said to an Augustinian monk who was one of the supervisory party from the Mother Abbey of Lilleshall. 'Pray for us.'

The hamlet of Hilfrich stood on the Welsh border a little over four miles from Alberbury, to which the villagers paid their dues. It was, or had been a small farming community: seven cots with stockades and vegetable garths, housing a total of six and twenty individuals. Now it lay in smoking ruins. Every house had been torched, every fence smashed down, every animal pen emptied and the animals themselves either driven off or slaughtered. Fulke guided his horse through the debris, the drifts of smoke smarting in his eyes, particles of soot floating in the air like black snow. The smell was choking and acrid.

A few bodies sprawled amongst the burning ruins. An old woman too slow to run. A man who had resisted them with a boar spear. He thought of the little girl back at Alberbury, ridden down by a warhorse. And his gorge rose.

'Bastards,' said Richard, riding up beside him, his voice muffled as he held his cloak over his mouth. His eyes were red-rimmed and streaming. 'You think it is Llewelyn?'

'Not in person,' Fulke said, 'but certainly a raiding party and probably of men who are fighting for the pleasure of killing the English as much as for coin.' He grimaced, the taste of ashes in his mouth. 'I know Llewelyn well but old friendships count for little in the wider scheme of a prince's ambition. Besides, I am allied to Pembroke and Chester and my keeps are the weakest link in that chain.' He looked bleakly at the smoking remnants of what had been a thriving hamlet. 'I think that this is the warning of the blaze to come and we are standing directly in the path of the fire.'

* * *

There had been pleasure in torching the buildings, in seeing the people run and scream. In watching the smoke rise to make clouds in the clear blue sky, trampling the vegetable plots, slaughtering the animals. Gwyn FitzMorys had not smiled for a long time but he was smiling now. He had a war band, he had Llewelyn's sanction to raid along the border, and he had old scores to settle.

CHAPTER 42

Late November was the start of the season when men clung to their hearths, mending implements, telling tales, tending their animals which grazed close to home, the winter grass supplemented by the stores of meadow hay reaped in the summer. The women spun fleece into thread and wove thread into braid. They stitched garments from homespun cloth and stuffed their cowhide shoes and boots with the ram's wool that was too coarse to spin. The older children tended the fire and spun too; the little ones played games with coloured stones and hobbyhorses made from sticks and straw.

This year, along the Marches, however, it was also a time to hone spears and bind new rawhide around the rim of the shield that had been stored in the rafters, to string bows with waxed gut and make arrows from the feathers of indignant geese.

At Whittington and Alberbury, the village men went to be trained by the lord's serjeants and sometimes by the lord himself. They learned how to thrust past a shield, how to protect each other, how to fight when the only weapons they possessed were the knives they used to butcher their pigs in winter.

'You do not seriously think that they will stand and fight the Welsh, do you?' Maude asked as Fulke returned from one such training session and cast his whalebone sword on a bench. Some of the village boys were still practising at the archery butts and their shouts floated up to the solar window.

'No, but at least they can defend themselves should they be cornered.' He paced the room like a caged wolf, pausing only to pour himself a cup of wine from the flagon and gulp it down. 'It aids me to feel less helpless,' he said. 'The King – or his advisors – still refuse to let me build in stone. Christ's wounds, am I so high in prowess that they think I can bring down the monarchy because of a single castle of stone, or hold off the Welsh without one?' He went to the window and looked out, fists clenched.

Maude sighed. She had no answer and knew that he did not expect one. Last week the King had again turned down Fulke's request to strengthen his keeps against the likelihood of Welsh attack, although he had been granted permission to move his livestock into the royal forest at Lyth. Maude wondered if the young King's excessive caution was a way of exacting retribution from Fulke. She would not put it past him and his advisors. God alone knew what John had told his son about the quarrel between the Crown and the FitzWarin family. Perhaps old scores had been passed on, or perhaps the formidable reputation of Fulke's youth was now doing him a disservice.

She joined him at the window, leaning her head against the steel-streaked sleeve of his gambeson. 'You can only do your best,' she murmured.

'Which is likely not good enough.' He set his arm around her waist. 'They raid my villages and retreat into Wales like wraiths. I cannot pursue them and they know it. Nor can I make peace with Llewelyn when he is bent on war with marcher barons who are my allies.'

It was the same ground, trampled so many times that in

her mind's eye, Maude could see the grooves that it had worn: round and round, deeper and deeper until there was no way out. 'Perhaps you should just let Llewelyn come,' she said. 'Let him overrun Whittington. Then Henry will be forced to act.'

He snorted. 'What would that do for my honour?'

'Your honour would not be involved. You have told Henry that you cannot hold against the Welsh if they come in force.' She wrinkled her nose. 'Although certainly it would ruin your pride.'

'If I abandon Whittington to Llewelyn, then that leaves the settlements beyond this open to attack. It's like a creeping puddle of wine on a trestle.' He rumpled his free hand through his hair and sighed. 'I suppose I should arm up and take out the patrol.'

Maude kissed him. Below, on the sward, Clarice and Mabile were watching the practice at the butts. Young Fulke was back with Ranulf of Chester and Ivo was squiring in Salisbury's household. For the nonce, their sons at least were safe. For the nonce too, they were alone, and both in need of distraction. In a moment, as he said, he would don his mail and take out a patrol to scour his borders in search of Welsh raiders. There would be danger, and hours of anxious waiting.

'I suppose you should,' she agreed, twining her arms around his neck and nipping his earlobe. The fire between them was not as bright a blaze as it had been in the early days, but still burned hot at its core. 'Is there nothing I can do to persuade you to tarry a while?'

He smiled and turned to her. 'That remains to be seen,' he said.

It was a long time since they had made love during the day. There was the added spice of knowing they might be discovered, the novelty of daylight, and the spiralling excitement of sudden lust. They kissed and fondled their way to the bed in the next chamber, strewing clothes as they went. Her wimple, his sword belt; shoes, hose, gambeson, gown.

By the time they fell upon the coverlet, he wore only shirt and braies to her chemise. He kissed her nipples through the fine linen fabric, nipping them to taut erection until a cry broke in her throat. She reached beneath his shirt, running her fingers over his ribs and feeling the raised, misshapen bumps of damaged bones long healed. The flat stomach and light fuzz of hair down its centre. And the hard rod of his manhood straining at his braies. It was his turn to gasp as her hand found its way inside and stroked him gently. He pushed her chemise above her thighs and the cold air struck her skin, raising gooseflesh. But so did his touch, feather light, promising, withholding, promising in a rhythm that made her writhe and arch towards him. She increased her own assault and parted her thighs, thrusting against him in wanton demand, positioning him so that the first surge would be sure and deep. He held back for a moment, quivering. 'Stop it,' he panted hoarsely. 'Do you think I am made of stone?'

'It certainly feels like it,' she purred and rubbed her thigh along his flank. Then she manoeuvred and bore down.

An oath of pure lust hissed between his teeth and he thrust up into her. Maude gasped at the force, then stifled a cry against his shoulder as the pressure and pleasure brought the promise closer to the brink. She clung to him, nails digging, breath whining in her throat, felt him gather to withdraw, and pulled him in closer.

'No!' she panted. Her hands moved to his buttocks, her legs clasped around him, forcing him on to the exquisite point of no return, shattering her senses with the force of her climax. She heard him groan, felt the strong pulsation of his own release within her body.

There was a long silence. She was aware of him still taking his weight on his arms in consideration, of his mouth moving blindly against her throat. 'That was foolish,' he muttered.

'Mayhap, but I would not be displeased to hold another babe in my arms.' She stroked his hair. She did not add that because she feared for him, she wanted a part of him to keep within her. For the moment, she had his seed, if not his child.

He played with a loose tendril of her hair. 'Melusine,' he said softly. 'What you want is yours to command.'

She nipped the side of his hand. 'Within reason,' she said. 'If I asked you to stay in bed with me the rest of the day, I know what your answer would be.'

He smiled tenderly. 'Beloved, much as I love you and my flesh rises to attention at the sight of your fair body, another bout like that one would kill me.' He withdrew and sat up.

'You would rather take your chance with the Welsh than with me?'

'Don't be awkward,' he said, tweaking her plait. Stretching luxuriously he left the bed and began dressing. Maude sighed and followed his example, pursuing the trail of her own clothing into the solar.

Still engulfed in the soft afterglow of pleasure, she rode out with him and his troop as far as the swine foraging trails in Babbin's Wood. The trees wore the black garb of winter, mossed with green on the northern sides of their trunks. The wind roared through the branches like an invisible, breathing monster, although the loudness was above them in the tops of the trees. On the forest floor, the main sound came from the creaking of old, strained wood, the jingle of harness and the thud of hoofbeats muffled by a damp brown carpet of leaves.

Maude rode with Fulke for a couple of miles, then bade him farewell and turned back with her escort. She was still within safe bounds, but she knew that when she had gone, Fulke would pick up the pace.

'God be with you,' she said, touching his hand.

'And you.'

She watched him ride off until the glint of mail and colour of shields ceased to flicker between the black trunks. Then she turned back to Whittington with her escort of four soldiers from the garrison.

They were on the edge of the forest, the road to the village in full view, when it happened. There was the sudden, loud groan of a tree in extremis. Maude looked up, screamed and wrenched her horse away, but was too late. The old beech, survivor of storms since the time of the Conquest, was finally defeated and tore from the soil to come crashing down across the small bay palfrey, snapping its neck. The mare buckled and went down, and Maude was partially trapped beneath her.

It happened swiftly; it happened slowly. Maude stared at the sky and at high black branches waving like the arms of a mob. She felt no pain for her legs were numb. 'I'm all right,' she said in a clear, lucid voice to the men stooping over her, their expressions filled with horror and consternation. She fixed her eyes on a large cloud of orange fungus growing out of the bark of the fallen tree. This wasn't happening. It was a dream, a vivid moment of imagination, the kind of hallucination induced by eating poisoned mushrooms. She was aware of thinking that it had happened to her and, because of it, Fulke would be safe. So it was all right.

The four soldiers levered the tree off the horse and dragged the horse off Maude. Once the weight and the warmth were gone, she began to shiver, her teeth chattering beyond control. From the waist down, she could feel nothing. There was no pain when they lifted her on to a horse and bore her the final half-mile to the castle.

'My lady, one of us should ride after your lord and tell him what has happened,' said Ralf Gras anxiously.

'No,' Maude rallied. 'He will not thank you for interrupting his patrol and there is nothing wrong with me that a day's bedrest will not cure.' Her voice rang with determination. If she believed, then it had to be.

Clarice came running, Mabile in tow. Maude smiled and made light of the incident for her youngest daughter and scowled at the knights, bidding them hold their tongues in front of the child. Although Mabile's grasp on reality was tenuous, her detachment was not total.

Clarice hastened to warm the great bed with a hot stone and add fresh kindling to the brazier.

Ralf Gras shook his head at her. 'There is naught broken that I can tell,' he said in a low voice, 'but still there has been much damage done. My lady says that she feels no pain – and that is not a good sign.'

Clarice glanced at the bed where two of the patrol were gently laying Maude. Her eyes were closed and her pallor obvious. 'I do not care what she has told you, Ralf, go and bring my lord. I will take the responsibility.'

He nodded brusquely and strode from the room.

Clarice approached the bed and touched Maude's legs. 'You are sure you feel nothing at all? Can you move them?'

Maude frowned and struggled, biting her lip. 'Not an inch,' she said with frustration and the beginning of fear.

Very gently, Clarice hitched up Maude's skirt, then gasped.

Maude raised herself and stared in dismay and despair at the swollen livid bruising. She had seen men with damage from morning star and mace blows, but nothing as extensive as this. 'And no wonder,' she said, falling back against the bolsters with a small thump. Cold sweat dewed her palms, her armpits and brow. Holy Mary, Mother of God . . .

'I'll make up some cold compresses,' Clarice said. She was clearly at a loss. Such a remedy was totally inadequate and they both knew it. For a moment, they exchanged looks.

'I have sent for Fulke,' Clarice said.

Maude gave an exasperated shake of her head. 'You should not have done. He is burdened enough already and I do not want him to see me like this.' Not three hours since they had lain together in this bed and talked of making another child between them. Now . . . She placed her hand over her belly. 'I will be all right, by and by,' she said.

'Of course you will.'

Again, their eyes met. The voice said one thing, while the mind knew another. Maude threw her head back on the bolster and closed her eyes.

During the night, feeling began to return to Maude's legs, and it came as pain. Hot, crushing, terrible. Clarice gave her willow bark in wine to drink, but although it was an efficacious remedy for a headache, it did little to take the agony from her damaged limbs. The cold compresses eased her a little, but there was pain inside too, a shrieking agony in her lower back that was so bad it made her vomit. By morning, she was so distressed and sweat-soaked that Clarice took the decision to dose her with the more dangerous medicine of syrup made from the seeds of the white eastern poppy. An hour later, Maude fell into a restless doze and the sweating abated.

Leaving her with the maid, Clarice went to break her fast, although in truth she had no appetite. Her eyes were hot from lack of sleep and her stomach queasy with anxiety. She had seen folk recover from injuries more gory, but the areas had been small. As far as she could tell, Maude had broken no bones, but her flesh had been severely macerated. Clarice only needed to think of what happened to an apple or plum when it was dropped from a height to know what the outcome would be. It wasn't fair, and the knowledge that life never was gave her no consolation at all.

Rain slammed against the shutters and every sconce and niche carried either torch or candle to mitigate the gloom. Clarice joined Mabile at the fire and forced down a wastel roll spread with honey and a cup of rosehip tisane.

'Mama better?' the child asked. She was cradling a straw doll, swaddled to look like a newborn infant.

'Yes,' Clarice said, yielding the small truth, withholding the greater one. 'She's sleeping now.'

Mabile rocked the baby and herself. 'Papa coming?'

'Soon.' Providing that Ralph had found him. God pray that he was not too late. Finishing the bread, her cup still in her hand, she returned to the bedchamber with Mabile and a vigil she would rather have abjured.

Fulke returned shortly after. Still in his mail and saturated cloak, he swept into the bedchamber like a whirlwind. Clarice leaped from her seat, a warning finger set to her lips, and he jerked to an abrupt halt. His eyes were wild, his entire demeanour one of suppressed violence. Swallowing, he took Clarice by the shoulders, set her bodily aside and advanced to the bed to look down on his wife.

'Mama sleep,' Mabile said. One small hand was folded around her mother's thick silver braid. He looked down, his gaze so fierce that Clarice thought he would burn a hole in the bolster, then he swung round and came back to her.

'How bad?' he demanded.

'I am not a healer,' Clarice began, before he cut her off in mid-excuse.

'You of all people I expect to be honest. How bad?'

Clarice felt a tightening ache in her throat. She shook her head, making the gesture serve for all the words she could not speak.

The time seemed to stretch for eternity as she watched him take the burden of her meaning and settle it across his shoulders like the spar on a cross.

'I am sorry,' she whispered.

He said nothing. Spangles of rain glittered on his cloak and the wet steel of his hauberk flashed as he breathed unevenly.

'I have dosed her with syrup of white poppy to ease the pain . . .' Clarice said, wondering why there was no such remedy for pain of the soul. And now she had to hammer a nail into his cross. 'But it might be best to send for the priest so that he is here when she wakes.' She touched him when he did not respond. 'Shall I do that?'

His eyes stumbled to meet hers and she saw that they were opaque and glazed. 'The priest,' he repeated slowly, as if they were speaking in a foreign language.

'To shrive her soul.'

His head came up. 'She is not going to die. I won't let her.'

He asked her for honesty and then he rebuffed it. She did not blame him. 'Then to pray for her recovery,' she said tactfully as she took his cloak. 'If you are going to sit in vigil, you must unarm. A sword cannot help you here.'

His look sharpened and focused, and she felt the force of his anger at his own helplessness strike her like a mace blow.

'You cannot hold her hand and drip rain all over the sheets,' she continued.

He gave a graceless shrug of capitulation and she helped him out of the wet hauberk and gambeson, ordering his squire to take them away for drying out. She brought him wine and wastel bread. He drank the former, ignored the latter, and seated himself at Maude's side, his eyes intent on his wife's face as if he would hold her to life with his will. His hand smoothed her hair off her brow.

Clarice hesitated, then left to fetch the priest, taking Mabile with her.

Very gently, Fulke pulled aside the bedclothes and raised Maude's chemise to look at the damage wrought. The sight of the swollen, livid bruising filled him with fury and despair. How could this have happened? If the tree had fallen one moment sooner or later, she would have been unscathed. God's will? How could God have willed something like this? Tenderly he replaced the covers and knelt in a position of prayer at her side. Her breathing was swift and her skin was hot to the touch. After a life of battle, he knew the signs. A man would be crushed by his falling horse, or receive several body blows from a mace or morning star; he might survive the impact, but never live for more than a few days. His urine would flow red, or not flow at all. He would develop a fever and die.

'Maude.' He took her braid in his hand, holding it the way their daughter had done. He felt hollow, an empty space where there had been a fullness of love and laughter, of quarrelling and companionship. 'Maude, stay with me.'

She moaned softly and her head moved from side to side on the bolster. Her eyelids flickered and she looked at him. The clear green was misted as if with fog, and her pupils were small, dark pinpoints.

'Fulke?' she whispered. Her hand groped and he took

it in his, squeezing it as if he would imbue her with his own life force.

'Yes, beloved, I am here.'

'I told Clarice that she should not send for you, that she was making a fuss over nothing . . . but I am glad she did not heed me.' Her voice was a hoarse whisper. 'It happened so swiftly. I didn't even see the tree fall . . . so quick . . .'

'Hush.' He smoothed her hair. 'Save your strength . . .'

'For what?'

'Ah God,' he groaned, swept by fear, grief, and the need to keep her with him. 'Do you remember when we first met? You were the contrary little girl who had snatched my brother's ball because he would not let you join his game?'

Her brow was furrowed with pain but she forced a smile. 'I remember. What of it?'

'Be contrary now for me, Maude. I don't want you to leave me.'

Reaching up, she touched his face and he saw her try to smile. 'I don't want to leave you either,' she said huskily, tears welling.

'We have years yet.'

'Yes. Years . . .' She closed her eyes. Her teeth clenched and he saw the pain tighten the tendons of her throat. He remembered she had looked that way when giving birth to their son on the banks of the Afon Morwynion. He had been helpless then; he was helpless now.

'Where's Clarice?' she gasped.

He cleared his throat. 'She has gone to fetch you the comfort of a priest – not that you need one.'

'I need . . . Jesu . . .' She broke off, writhing with pain and pointed to the flask of poppy syrup on the coffer.

Fulke picked it up. His fingers trembled as he removed the stopper. 'How much?'

For a moment the pain rode her so hard that she was incoherent. He watched her fight her way through it, like a swimmer battling the tide, and drag herself half on to the shore, exhausted. 'Two measures in wine,' she panted, gesturing to a small cup made of hollowed-out bone.

'You are sure?'

She nodded, biting her lip, her features gaunt with suffering.

With shaking hands, Fulke poured the syrup into the measure, then into the cup. Twice. Then added sweet mead to disguise the bitterness. Maude's glance flickered to the door as if fearing an intrusion. Her fists clenched on the coverlet and as he set his arm behind her shoulders to lift her up, she cried out in agony. He tilted the cup to her lips and she drank. Some of the liquid spilled from her mouth corners, but when he would have removed the goblet, she grasped his hand and held him talon-fast, gulping and swallowing until she had drained the cup to the lees.

After she had drunk, she subsided on the bolster and briefly closed her eyes. He thought that she was going to sleep, but her lids rose and she looked at him. 'Fulke, promise me that you will stand firm whatever happens; promise me that you will not break.'

Her gaze was as sharp as glass, piercing him with its intensity. 'I cannot change the habit of a lifetime,' he said with a strained smile, trying to make light of her words and failing. They both knew the meaning. She wanted the security of his oath to take with her on her journey, and although he gave it to her willingly, he did not know if he could keep it. She was not his life, but she was the light in it, and how could he stand firm if he was stumbling in the dark?

'Promise . . .' Her voice was as clear and brittle as glass too.

Somehow, he found the strength to answer without faltering, although his throat was as tight as a wound cord on a siege engine. 'I promise.'

'I hold you to it . . . do not forget.'

The priest arrived with the articles of the sacrament in a small, leather-bound box. Fulke wanted to leap to his feet and roar at the man to get out, for in his dark Benedictine robes he reminded Fulke of the first crow hopping towards a corpse. Maude must have felt his aversion, for she renewed her grip on his hand.

'Let him come,' she whispered. 'I am in need of spiritual comfort.'

Fulke slowly rose to his feet. 'As you wish,' he said softly. He did not look at the priest as he left the room, but back at her. She met his eyes and her lips curved, but he saw the effort it took, and he could not smile in return.

Outside, Clarice was waiting for him.

'Do not,' he warned grimly, 'play the mother hen. If you offer me food, drink or a bath, I will not be responsible for the consequences.'

Clarice, who had been about to do exactly that, turned away and carefully added more fuel to the charcoal brazier burning in the centre of the solar. 'You should send for Hawise and Jonetta and your sons,' she said, taking refuge in a different form of practicality.

He nodded. 'I was about to summon the scribe.'

Clarice's heart ached. She wanted to ease his burden, to give him comfort in order to comfort herself, but knew from his words, from the stiffness of his body that she would be rebuffed. She glanced towards the room where Father Thomas was occupied with Maude. 'When he has finished, I will give her some more poppy in wine.'

'There is no need,' Fulke said with a brusque gesture. 'I have already done so.'

Her eyes widened. 'You knew the dosage?'

'No, but Maude did. Two measures.'

Clarice turned quickly away before her face betrayed her. One measure was strong and only just safe. Two would kill. Maude had taught her the lore, emphasising the strength of white poppy syrup. She pressed her clenched fist to her breast, clutching the knowledge to her heart and feeling as if it would break.

Behind her, she heard Fulke's shaken breath and the rustle of fabric as he moved. 'She knew,' he said hoarsely. 'Oh yes, she knew.' And strode from the room.

Clarice stared into the brazier and felt the delicate surface of her eyes begin to burn and smart from the strength of the glowing charcoal pieces. She could remember her mother dying of the lung sickness when she was a small child, but she had scarcely known her. The bond Clarice had forged with Maude, however, had been everything. Mother, daughter, companion and confidante.

'I cannot bear it,' she whispered, and even as she uttered the words knew that they were an indulgence of the moment. She could and would bear the grief that was coming. She was Clarice the solid, Clarice the dependable, Clarice the gently mocked for her wise-woman ways. That she was also Clarice the bereft and Clarice the lonely were facets that would go unnoticed except by herself.

The November night was dark and cold. A single candle burned on the coffer and the faint scent of hot charcoal and incense filled the chamber. On the bed, Maude lay in the white, marble silence of death and Fulke sat beside her, gazing upon her face. Her eyes, those arresting cat-green eyes, were closed. Her blonde hair glowed loose on the pillow, like that of a virgin or a woman recently in the arms of a lover. Smoothed of pain, her face was young,

the skin clear, the lips curled as if at some inner amusement. But she would never laugh again, and neither would
he, he thought.

After the priest had gone, she had lapsed swiftly into a
deep sleep from which no one could rouse her. Their
farewell had been said on the threshold of the room when
she had smiled at him. He had known, but not wanted to
know. Now, although the knowledge was with him, he had
little comprehension.

'The life I have led, I always thought that I would be
the one to leave you,' he said to the still form in front of
him. 'Wives become widows. Why didn't you permit me
that selfishness?' He touched her hair: thick, heavy, silver-
blonde. Many women lost the glory of their locks as they
grew older, but Maude's had remained abundant and the
colour meant that the first grey of ageing did not show.
Now she would never grow any older, but already he felt
twice his age. He could have stopped her drinking from
that cup; he knew he could, but only to prolong her
suffering. Hers was over; his had begun. The troubadours
who sang the ballad of Melusine had omitted the detail
that when she flew out of the window never to be seen
again, she took her husband's soul with her.

The candle flame guttered as the door opened and
Clarice tiptoed into the room, her gaze huge and dark in
the shadow-light. A cloak hung at her shoulders and she
carried a small oil cresset lamp in one hand and a flagon
in the other. He looked at her resentfully. He did not want
anyone intruding on this last night that Maude would rest
in her own bed with him by her side. It was his vigil to
keep alone.

He was thankful that she did not offer him wine, for
if she had, he would have dashed the flagon from her
hand. She poured a cup for herself and left the flagon

within conspicuous view before seating herself across from him.

'We do not need your company,' he said.

She gave him a steady look, composed and reproachful. 'I know that you do not want to share this moment, but I loved her too.' Then she lowered her head over her clasped knuckles and began to pray, her lips moving silently.

The silence stretched, broken only by the soft sputter of the candle as the flame caught an impurity in the wax. After a time, Fulke reached to the flagon and poured himself a scant cup. There was no sign of the flask of poppy syrup or the small bone measure. If it had remained, he might have been tempted to drink his own death.

He looked at the young woman quietly praying across from him. Candle and cresset lamp illuminated the gleam of moisture on her cheek. How was it possible to cry silently, he wondered, or was it just another sign of Clarice's fastidious perfection? And then he saw that she was struggling not to break the cadence of her breathing, that beneath the cloak she was shuddering with the effort of holding herself together.

He watched, feeling pity, exasperation, and envy, for he was unable to weep. The wound was so deep that it had maimed all his responses. 'Clarice . . .'

She made a choking sound and a gesture of apology. Rising, Fulke came around the bed and awkwardly folded his arms around her. It was the first time he had ever seen her discomposed, and somewhere deep within, his bleeding emotions struggled to respond.

'It's all right,' he murmured. 'Weep if you want.'

She turned her face into his breast and gave vent to her grief, clutching him so tightly that in the morning he would see bruises on his arms. Her voice rang in the darkness of the room, and the force of her breath stirred the light silver wisps of hair framing Maude's brow.

He held her, stroking her braids. His own grief burgeoned within him, but did not break for Maude's death had left too vast a hollow ever to be filled.

CHAPTER 43

Although the snow held off, there was frost that winter, hard as the iron edge of a war sword, and the Welsh raids continued through the chiming cold. Fulke moved his herds from the byres and winter grazing surrounding Whittington and pastured them on the royal lands at Lyth. He took out his troops on constant patrols, riding through the frozen silver landscape, feeling as if he were trapped inside a sorcerer's mirror. Ellesmere Water was a sheet of ice the thick grey-white of loafsugar. Swans huddled among the sedges, breast feathers resembling the fronded delicacy of snowflakes, necks curved round and bills tucked into the warmth of their folded pinions. Everything not dormant endured or died.

Torn between enduring and dying himself, Fulke was in perfect tune with the season. Losing Maude had left him frozen. He could not grieve, because somewhere the connection between feeling and expression had been severed. He lived without enjoyment of life, each day dragging into the next with a dreadful inevitability. His mind functioned on a practical, perfunctory level, but inside there was a void.

The Welsh were elusive. They raided; they slipped back over the border and melted into the hills. The only way to bring them to heel, Chester opined when he and Fulke met to discuss the situation, was to take an expedition into Wales, building castles as they went, in the manner that their ancestors had done to the English after the great Battle of Hastings. But for such an undertaking, royal troops would have to be mustered and the young King had matters more pressing on his trencher. For the nonce, his marcher barons could fend for themselves.

In a way, Fulke was glad of that fending. It occupied his time, gave him a purpose to rise in the morning and see each day through to its close. If he pushed himself to physical exhaustion he knew that he would fall into a fathomless slumber and not awaken until the morning. What he dreaded were the nights when he dreamed that Maude was sleeping beside him. He would feel the warmth of her body, the tickle of her hair, smell her perfume, and would awaken in pleasure only to find himself embracing the bolster. They were the bleakest times, the ones where he thought he would rather die than endure.

His children provided small islands of consolation and warmth in an otherwise barren landscape. Swift to show emotion, Hawise had wept a river of tears at the news of her mother's death. The tragedy had been made more poignant by the news that Hawise was to bear a baby. Now Maude would never know her first grandchild, or the grandchild know her save in memories planted by others.

Jonetta had grieved quietly with fewer outward signs of emotion, but much prayer in the chapel. The boys had wept, but they had not remained long – a few days for the funeral and mourning and then they had returned to the households in which they were squiring. Clarice had taken Mabile under her wing, mitigating the worst of the child's bewilderment and finding her own comfort therein. His brothers had visited him too, riding in from the scattered FitzWarin estates to grieve with him and keep him company, but

Fulke could only bear so much of their concern and had not encouraged them to remain. Richard was the only one who stayed, and that was because he had always been with Fulke, had never evinced an interest in dwelling as other than a hearth knight in his brother's employ.

Drawing rein in the biting cold of a late January morning, Fulke dismounted at the gates of Alberbury Priory. It was still only half built, but the walls continued to rise and there was a small chapel to house the FitzWarin family tombs. One day, he would lie here himself with Maude on one side and his parents on the other. For the moment, they awaited him. He removed his sheepskin mitts and blew on his hands, which despite their covering still felt like blocks of ice. Father Lawrence, the Augustinian Prior, came out to greet him and offered him hot wine in his private solar – at the moment a timber hut in the precincts. The masons had downed tools for the winter and the scaffolded buildings had a deserted air, albeit made beautiful and crystalline by the heavy frost.

'You are welcome, my lord,' said the Prior. His tonsure fitted the surroundings, for it was silver too, thick and heavy. 'You take out the patrols, I see?'

'For what good it does.' Fulke looked around the solar. A charcoal brazier glowed in the centre of the room. There was a large trestle on which stood two heavy candlesticks and a devotional book was open in front of the Prior's oak chair. 'The Welsh will still come and there is no sign of a truce as yet between Marshal and Llewelyn.'

'You cannot make one of your own?'

'Not without breaking my friendship with Marshal and destroying any bridges I have begun to build with the King.' He took the wine that the Prior offered, his hands beginning to tingle and burn as feeling returned. 'The herds at Whittington have gone to Lyth.'

'And the herds at Alberbury?'

Fulke swallowed the wine. 'I am here to remove them, and to take my daughter and my ward to Lambourn,' he said, adding quickly, 'You need have no fear for the priory. Llewelyn would not burn down a church or harm monks. What he wants to destroy is my authority along the March – the keeps that house the men who stand in his way.'

The Prior eyed him. 'Aye, well, there is not so much to burn down here as yet,' he said, 'but it may be different in the future.'

Fulke shrugged. 'Other things may be different too. I live in hope that in the spring the King will give me leave to strengthen my keeps. He must see the necessity by now.' *Live in hope.* The words mocked him. He socialised with the Prior a while longer, then left him to visit Maude's tomb. There was no effigy as yet, and even when one had been chiselled out of cold, Chellaston alabaster, it would be a winter thing, white and stiff, reflecting none of the living beauty that had been his wife. Then again, it was only her mortal remains that lay in the church. Her soul, like her namesake, had flown from the window and was long gone. She rested in peace. It was the living who were in turmoil.

He rode on to the keep at Alberbury. Like Whittington, all movable objects of value had been taken to manors that were not under threat from the Welsh; herds and livestock too. The stables were empty of all save the immediate mounts of the garrison and the patrol.

It was Gracia who came to greet him with the welcoming cup.

'Where is Clarice?' He looked around, seeking her familiar figure, but finding only servants.

'She's gone to see a wise woman over Knockin way, my lord,' Gracia said with disapproval. 'Wouldn't take no for an answer.'

Fulke looked at the maid in dismay. It was totally out of character for Clarice to take off anywhere, and to go in search of a wise woman on the day before a long journey was beyond comprehension. 'The borders are too dangerous for such a jaunt,' he growled. 'Why in God's name does she want to see a wise woman?'

'She says that we have run out of many herbs and simples and that she won't be able to obtain the same in Lambourn. Old Mother Ranild always has them to sell.' Gracia shook her head to show what she thought of the notion. 'I told her she shouldn't go, but she bade me mind Mabile and keep my counsel to myself.' Her voice took on a slightly aggrieved note.

'I doubt we are in such dire need of any supplies that she must take herself off across country when the Welsh—' He broke off, knowing that he should not pile his own anxieties on to the maid. Sighing, he dismounted. 'Doubtless she will return soon enough. Is there any pottage in that cauldron? I'm as hungry as a bear.'

He was too late and Gracia was shrewd. 'And if she doesn't?'

'When I've eaten, I'll take some troops and ride out to find her.'

Despite the bone-chilling cold, Clarice had enjoyed the ride to Knockin. A groom and a serjeant accompanied her for protection. She did not really believe that she would be robbed on the road, or that the Welsh would attack, but her rank made it impossible for her to travel anywhere without an escort. The serjeant rode ahead, the groom behind. Between them, Clarice rode aloof, her dappled grey pony clopping along the frozen earth track.

She knew she was being contrary in visiting old Ranild on the day before they left for Lambourn, but since Maude's death, she had felt restless. There was a need in her to kick against the walls of her ordered existence. Mostly the impulse was contained, but today it had burst forth, fuelled by a huge red sunrise over a glittering world of hoar and rime. It was too strange and wonderful a day to spend at the hearth. Owing to her diligence, the travelling chests were already packed. Besides, they did need the herbs. Syrup of white poppy for one. There was scarcely any left in the flask after what had happened in November and it was an essential part of the medicinal supplies. She could have begged some from the infirmarian at the priory, but she wanted more than just simples and potions. The maids said that Mother Ranild had cures for every malady, including afflictions of the heart and sickness of the soul.

Arriving in Knockin, Clarice was directed to Mother Ranild's house by the village alewife. From the woman's avid expression, Clarice knew that the gossip was about to spread like wildfire.

Mother Ranild lived in a substantial cot on the edge of the settlement, a little apart but not entirely separate. Leaving the track, Clarice rode past a penned gaggle of hissing geese, the male white as a snowdrift, his wives the drab brown of trampled straw, and dismounted with her escort outside the hut's door. A bunch of rowan was tied over the entrance, and several horseshoes had been nailed to the oak of the door itself. Smoke eddied from gaps in the thatch and Clarice's sharp nose detected the fragrant scent of burning pear wood.

She knocked and was bade enter by a firm voice. Signalling her escort to wait, she lifted the hammered iron latch and, suppressing the urge to cross herself, entered the domain of Mother Ranild.

A fire crackled in the central hearth, sending smoke to join soot-blackened rafters. Bundles of herbs were tied to the beams with hemp twine, as were several lengths of dried sausages. The walls were lined with clay jars and even a couple of phials of expensive glass. The beaten earth floor contained baskets of wool and more sheaves of dried herbs. At the far end of the room was a small trestle on which several wooden bowls were stacked. A tall, slender woman was grinding a mixture, using a pestle and mortar of shiny green stone. Looking up, she ceased her work and, wiping her hands on an apron of natural brown linen, came round the trestle to Clarice.

'What can I be doing for you, mistress?' she enquired pleasantly, and gestured the young woman to a bench near the hearth. There was no curtsey, no acknowledgement of Clarice's rank. Indeed, Clarice felt as if she should pay deference to the woman, who had the air of being queen of her domain. The nose was thin and beaked, the mouth wide with teeth that were still white and strong – rare for a peasant woman whose face told a story of at least three score years.

'I came to buy nostrums from you.' Clarice perched on the edge of the bench. 'You are well spoken of by the women at Alberbury.'

The light blue eyes sparkled shrewdly. 'Am I indeed?' Going to the shelves, she took down a jug and poured a bright golden liquid into two cups. 'And you are, mistress?'

'Lady Clarice d'Auberville.'

'Ah, Lord FitzWarin's ward.' The woman nodded as if some puzzle had fallen into place, and handed Clarice the cup. 'Mead,' she said, 'brewed from my own hives.'

Clarice thanked her and took a tentative sip. The taste of summer flowed over her tongue and spread through her in a warm glow. 'Wonderful,' she murmured, wondering how and what the wise woman knew of her. Doubtless the maids' gossip travelled both ways.

'I have a flask to spare if you want to add it to your list.'

'Thank you. It would be most welcome.'

Mother Ranild tilted her head and considered Clarice thoroughly. 'I wonder, though, why you have chosen to come to me rather than the apothecary in Shrewsbury, or the monks of your lord's new priory.'

'Because I have heard of your reputation,' Clarice answered, thankful that she was not prone to blushing. 'They say you are indeed a "wise" woman.'

'A poor show if you reach my age and you are not,' Ranild said with waspish amusement. 'Tell me the things that you want.'

Clarice reeled off her list. Gall–oak ointment and powder, honeysuckle syrup for coughs and agues, southernwood to remove internal parasites, figwort ointment for blemishes. Mother Ranild's eyebrows rose at the request for white poppy syrup, but she made no comment and added it to the collection on the trestle, together with the flask of mead.

Clarice folded her hands in her lap and looked down. 'I am told that you are also skilled in potions to cure ills not of the body,' she murmured.

'Ah, now we come to the crux of the matter, I think,' the woman said with satisfaction. 'Is it a love philtre you want? A spell to bind some man in thrall to you?'

Clarice's gaze flashed indignantly to Mother Ranild's. 'Indeed I do not!'

Mother Ranild chuckled. 'Calm yourself, mistress, I did but enquire since it is the most common reason for young women to visit my cottage – that and procuring a remedy for their growing bellies.'

Clarice tightened her lips. 'I do not need that kind of potion either,' she said curtly.

'Then what do you wish?'

She swallowed, feeling vulnerable beneath the wise

woman's candid stare. 'My . . . my guardian Lord FitzWarin lost his wife two months ago,' she said. 'I want something to ease his grieving.'

Mother Ranild folded her arms and the twinkle in her eyes grew serious. 'I do not bottle time, child,' she said softly.

'Perhaps I said the wrong thing. I want something to help him grieve. It is as if he has become frozen within himself. Not a tear has he shed since she died, and yet I know they gather within him until it is a burden he can scarcely bear.'

Ranild looked at her long and hard. 'Something to make a grown man cry,' she murmured. 'I have no such remedy on my shelves. What you need cannot be crushed in a mortar and scattered in a drink.'

'Then what do I need?'

'You must discover that for yourself. Give me your hand.'

Clarice hesitated, then did as she was asked. The maids said that Mother Ranild could read a person's future by studying the lines on the palm of their hand. Clarice was not sure that she wanted to know, but her curiosity was as strong as her fear.

Ranild scrutinised Clarice's palm for some time, tracing the lines on it with a firm forefinger, narrowing her eyes now and then.

'What do you see?' Clarice was drawn to demand.

'You are like tranquil water,' Ranild muttered. 'Calm and clear but deeper than you seem. People who know you take you for granted when they should not, or perhaps it is that they don't know you at all. You are not afraid of change, but you have no desire to do so. Indeed your desires dwell in other directions.'

Clarice made to tug her hand away but Ranild tightened her grip and her eyes met her visitor's knowingly.

'Nevertheless, I see a husband and child for you in the

time to come,' she said, and frowned. 'However, they lie on the other side of great danger. There is fire and envy and hatred . . . and it comes soon.'

Clarice did snatch her hand away then and jump to her feet.

'You are wishing that you had not come to see me,' Ranild said with a knowing nod. 'Perhaps you are right, child, because in so doing you may have sealed your fate. Go home, and pray that you are in time.'

'In time for what?' With shaking hands, Clarice spilled silver on to the trestle and put the nostrums in the willow basket she had brought with her.

'The rest of your life on this earth.' Ranild swept the money into the purse at her belt of plaited leather, then made a shooing motion. 'Go, child. Hurry.'

Bemused and agitated, Clarice emerged from the hut into the frozen light of early afternoon. It was just under two hours' ride back to Alberbury. What could happen in that time to merit Ranild's warning?

The serjeant boosted her into the saddle. Grasping the reins, she turned the mare on the homeward road and set a pace that caused the groom to raise his eyebrows.

'Ground's too 'ard to run 'er like that, my lady – with respect,' he said. 'You'll make 'er lame for the morrow.'

Clarice eased the mare down from trot to walk. 'I am eager to be home,' she said, 'but I would not lame her.' She patted the palfrey's neck, thick with the silver of her winter coat, and curbed her impatience. Overhead the earlier sunshine was being swallowed by hazy cloud carrying the yellow tinge of impending snow. Perhaps there would not be a journey on the morrow anyway.

Two miles later, they encountered a group of people on the road, driving an assortment of livestock. Women and children, surrounded by wicker cages of assorted squawking fowl, were perched on a cart drawn by two lumbering oxen.

To the groom's enquiry, the peasant leading the group leaned on his quarterstaff and wafted his hand back the way they had come. 'The Welsh are over the border,' he declared. 'You're going to ride straight into them.'

The serjeant gave Clarice a worried look. 'We can either head round to Shrewsbury, or go north to Whittington and Oswestry.'

'Which is safest?'

The man grimaced and squinted at the heavy sky. 'Neither, my lady. If the Welsh are over the border, they'll be straddling the Shrewsbury road by the time we reach it, and likely the road to Oswestry. One way or another, we'll have to slip through.'

Clarice had a brief vision of Mother Ranild examining her palm and then bundling her out of the door. 'Oswestry's nearer,' she said. 'We'll find succour there.'

Snow began to fall, deceptively gentle in its slow, twirling progress. But the ground was so cold that where it landed it stayed, building in soft, powdery layers. Perhaps it was the hypnotic effect of the flakes, perhaps the reduced visibility – whatever the reason, both the serjeant riding slightly ahead of Clarice and the groom failed to see the Welsh patrol on the road until it had seen them, and by then it was too late.

Riding into Whittington, Gwyn FitzMorys felt uneasy, for it seemed to him a haunted place in the bitter January afternoon. The silence was of a village deserted. Neither human nor animal moved amongst the thatched houses and vegetable plots. Not a single wreath of smoke eddied skywards, nor was there the customary aroma of cabbage pottage wafting from cooking pots. The occupants of Whittington had left their houses to fate.

Gwyn sat astride his warhorse in the main street, his sword bare in his hand lest there were any stragglers to catch and knowing in his heart there would not be. The icy light glittered on his mail coat. His breath emerged on white puffs of vapour and his horse steamed too as if he had ridden it straight from the cauldron of hell.

'No one, *fy arglwydd*,' said one of the bowmen whom he had sent to probe amongst the houses for occupants. 'They have all fled before the news of our coming.'

'Then let us announce our own arrival.' Gwyn bared his teeth. 'Burn them to the ground.'

He watched as a torch was passed from hand to hand and finally thrust into the thatch of the nearest cottage. No one came raging out of the keep to stop the destruction as fire spread from house to house like a contagion and the smoke that had been missing now curled in choking abundance to meet the snowclouds.

The castle was as quiet as the village. Gwyn rode through the gates into the courtyard, his sword still ice-bare in his hand and his shield held high in case the open gates should be the jaws of a trap. They were not. He stood in the courtyard where once he had stood as of right and knew that Whittington was his to claim, but not to hold. If Fulke FitzWarin had seen fit not to defend it when its possession had once been his *raison d'être*, then it was impossible for a minor Welsh knight to do so. Once it had been enough to build in wood. Now stone was the order of the day if a man wanted to keep what he had.

Snow fluttered; black and grey smuts of woodsmoke infiltrated the stars of glittering white. Gwyn tasted the grit of ash and the purity of meltwater on his tongue. Dismounting and tossing his reins to a companion, he went among the buildings of his childhood and gazed on the changes wrought by FitzWarin's hand. The murals on the plasterwork in the hall, the partitioning of the chambers. The new kitchen building and bread oven; the improved well housing. The Normans had stripped the place to the bone before they left and there was not a single item of wealth or furniture to be plundered. Only the keep's fabric remained, soaked in more than a hundred years of bloody conflict.

'Give me a torch,' he snapped at a footsoldier who had followed him into the keep.

He had just gripped the knotty shaft of the pine pitch brand when two men from the troop he had ordered to block the road arrived with a captive.

Gwyn found himself confronting a young woman in rich Norman garb, her blue cloak lined with coney fur. Her face was flushed with cold and fury and her grey eyes burned with the gold reflection of the torch in his hand.

'Making for Oswestry, my lord,' said one of the guards in Welsh.

'Alone?'

'No, she had a groom and a soldier escort.'

'Had?' Gwyn raised his brows.

'Yes, my lord.' A glint of vicious pleasure flashed in the soldier's eyes. 'They were Fulke FitzWarin's men, and the lady is his ward, Clarice d'Auberville.'

Gwyn looked at her through the sooty ripple of smoke from the brand. 'Indeed?' He stroked the sides of his moustache. 'Welcome, Lady Clarice,' he said, switching to Norman French. 'Your guardian is foolish to let you ride abroad in these troubled times.'

She bared her teeth at him. 'Your men killed my escort for no other reason than they served Fulke FitzWarin. I thought that the Welsh were civilised, but I was wrong!'

'We are more civilised in the matter of war than your own countrymen,' Gwyn retorted. 'Be glad that you have not been raped, and that you still have your life.'

'What are you going to do with me?' She regained a degree of control, breathing hard but rapidly retreating into an icy dignity.

'Take you to Prince Llewelyn. You will be welcomed at his court until your ransom can be agreed.' Gwyn smiled wolfishly and looked her up and down. 'Who knows, you might even find a Welsh husband to your taste.'

She stared at him with loathing. 'Not on present re-commendation,' she said and rubbed her hands together, shuddering as if at some deeply unpleasant notion.

Gwyn smiled. 'A woman with claws is always more inter-esting between the sheets.'

She did not rise to the bait.

'Since you are Fulke's ward,' Gwyn said, 'you can be his proxy and witness to the burning of Whittington.'

She clasped her cloak at her throat and looked at him like a queen. 'It will avail you nothing.'

'On the contrary, it will give me great pleasure and satis-faction.' He strode from her side to a heap of dry straw and kindling that his men had piled up inside the doorway of the hall. Thrusting the torch into its heart, he watched the fire blossom from its core like a hatching egg. Other piles lay at strategic points within the compound and soon Whittington was ablaze, ragged turrets of fire crenellating the dusk, staining the falling snow with red shadow-light. It was beautiful, eerie, tragic.

Clarice watched the FitzWarin pride blaze heavenwards in surges of fierce heat and energy, as if the stored conflict of the years were fuelling the flames. It was a release too, she thought, and tilted her head to gaze upon the highest flames leaping from the timber wall projections. Snowflakes landed on her lashes with cold delicacy, making her blink, and despite the wafts of intense heat gusting off the burning timber, she shivered. Behind her, she heard Welsh shouts of approbation and pleasure.

The man beside her studied the destruction with a strange smile playing about his lips. At last, a sigh rippled through him. Turning, he commanded their horses to be brought. Clarice's grey mare balked and snorted in alarm at the roar of the flames. It took two men to hold her while Clarice gained the saddle. She drew the reins in tight and tried to soothe her mount, but it was not until they were clear of the burning keep and heading for the road that the mare ceased to prance. A notion to gallop off in the direction of Babbin's Wood and lose herself amongst the trees was swiftly dispelled by Gwyn FitzMorys, who attached a leading rein to the grey's bridle and wrapped it firmly around his saddle horn.

'It would be foolish to run, my lady.'

She shrugged. 'I do not think so.'

He smiled bleakly and kicked his mount. 'Tonight we sleep at Ellesmere. You will find a bed there more comfortable than one in the snow.' Digging his heels into his horse's flanks, he urged the animal forwards. Clarice glanced back at the keep. Through the falling snow it burned and spat like a beast consuming itself . . . or mayhap it was a phoenix, beating its great wings, fanning the flames of its death pyre and preparing to rise from the ashes of its own destruction.

The snow was falling swiftly now, the flakes still soft as a caress, but more of them, whirling and dancing, settling now to the depth of the horses' hooves. Through the screen of white, riders appeared like wraiths on the road before them, blocking their path in a jingle of harness and mail.

'Fulke!' Clarice's lips formed the name without uttering a sound. Exultation and fear coursed through her.

Gwyn FitzMorys drew his sword. 'You are too late, FitzWarin,' he snarled. 'Whittington is burning to the ground and by my hand.'

Clarice could not tell what expression Fulke wore behind his helm. All she could see was the grim line of his mouth, the taut jaw, but she could imagine the look in his eyes and she could feel his tension like a wall of heat. Surreptitiously she freed her feet from the stirrups.

'It is you who has misjudged your timing,' Fulke said harshly. 'I care not if Whittington burns, and for all that the Welsh army is across the border in force, your troop cannot withstand mine.'

'You say you care not for Whittington,' Gwyn sneered, 'but that's a lie.'

'I said I care not if it burns,' Fulke said bluntly. 'Like a tide, Llewelyn will retreat, and when he does, I will build in stone. You have cleared the ground. Indeed, perhaps I should thank you.' He inclined his head in a mocking gesture.

'And your ward, do you care for her in a similar wise?' Gwyn gestured to Clarice. 'Would you see her destroyed too?'

'Do what you will; her lands are still in my keeping.' Fulke's stallion plunged and sidled, until he was forced to draw in the reins' full measure.

In a flash of motion Clarice kicked her feet from the stirrups, flung down from the saddle and ran across the space between Gwyn's troop and Fulke's. The startled mare bucked and kicked out at Gwyn's horse, which reared and skittered. She heard Gwyn's curse, followed by the thud of hooves hard in pursuit. Fulke spurred forward and his sword cut across the downward stroke of Gwyn's. Clarice tripped over her skirts and sprawled in the snow, winding herself, losing her wimple. Strong arms scooped her up and she was hauled across Ralf Gras's saddle.

'You're safe my lady,' he said, but she barely heeded him, her eyes wide and wild on the struggling, fighting men. In the gathering murk of dusk, it was difficult to pick out detail. Everything was a blur of snow and steel, whiteness and darkness blending to create spangled shadow shapes that broke and re-formed. The battle cries, the screams of the wounded, the thud of destrier hooves. Blood staining the snow. The name, '*FitzWarin!*' howling out like the cry of a wolf. She clenched her fists and prayed. Fulke's shield flashed. He was fighting like a demon hot from hell with no care or thought to his own safety. A horse galloped past, dragging its unseated rider whose spur was caught in the stirrup. He had lost his helm and as a shod hindhoof caught his skull, she heard the sickening crack of breaking bone. Awkwardly, Ralf caught the beast's trailing reins. A long smear of blood stained the churned new snow, leading to a black, shining puddle in Gwyn FitzMorys's hair. His arms were spread wide, his sword lay several feet away, and his dark stare was fixed in death.

When the Welsh realised their leader was dead, they beat a hasty retreat, melting away in the direction of the woods beyond the village. Clarice bade Ralf set her down and walked the skirmish site, seeking out the wounded. Dusk was fully upon them and the wind was bitter. If any man was seriously injured, Clarice knew he would not live the night. At least, she thought grimly, she had syrup of white poppy to ease the passing of any bound from the world.

'I've given the order to make camp in the castle courtyard,' Fulke said as she comforted a soldier who had taken a spear through the shoulder. 'The fires will last until the morning at least.' His voice was flat and hard, the battle tension still shining in his eyes.

She nodded and swallowed. 'There are two dead, but none mortally injured.'

'There would be none dead at all if you had not been taken with the folly of going to visit a wise woman,' he growled. 'What in God's name possessed you?'

'We needed things that I could not be sure of obtaining at Lambourn.'

'Things that were worth dying for?' he demanded icily, then cast his gaze around the battle site. 'Yes, I suppose they were.'

'I was not to know the Welsh would come over the border,' she snapped, stung at his tone, but knowing he was right.

The soldier with the shoulder wound quietly rose to his feet and made himself scarce.

'You knew there was a likelihood. Christ, Clarice . . . I thought you more responsible!'

'Then you thought wrong. And it was for your sake that I went to see Mother Ranild at all.'

'For my sake?' His voice rose. 'You think that going to see a cracked old hag will do something for me?'

'She's not a cracked old hag! She's a wise woman and I wanted her advice.'

'About me?'

Clarice avoided his gaze. 'I wanted her to tell me how to help you through your grief.'

'God on the Cross, do you have to meddle in every part of my life!' he exploded. 'First it was wine and a clean robe. Now it's nursemaiding my head!' He pointed to his skull. 'And your desperation to coddle me almost got us both killed, you foolish wench!'

'It was caring that sent me, not coddling, but you are right. I should not have gone!' Clarice blazed. It was not just the reflection of the flames that suffused her face with colour. 'And I'm not a wench!'

He swore through his teeth and stormed off towards the

burning keep. She stood alone in the road. At the first sign of trouble, everyone had made themselves industrious elsewhere. Snow whirled down, the flakes as large as swan feathers now and falling rapidly. Clarice thought about mounting her mare and riding off, but it was no more than a thought. The heat of rage and chagrin might be sustaining her now, but she would need more than that to last the deep winter's night. Besides, there were wounded to be cared for, and whatever Fulke thought about her nature, her sense of responsibility held her impulse in check.

Drawing her cloak tightly around her body, pulling up the fleece-lined hood, she turned through the snow-laden dusk to the red pyre that was Whittington.

The Welsh had been beaten back but they had accomplished their objective. There was no saving Whittington from being razed. Fulke narrowed his eyes against smoke and snow and kept vigil. He could not roll himself in his cloak like the other men and let the heat of destruction warm him through the night like a common bonfire.

He walked between the burning buildings and thought of the fight to gain this place. The struggle, the sacrifice, the determination and pride. Sparks showered as part of the hall caved in upon itself. He watched the golden specks dazzle away into the night, taking the opposite path to the falling snow. Here his younger children had been born. Here he had slept with Maude on a bare wooden floor and talked of the future. It was as if each spark was a memory fleeing into the night, never to be seen again, and suddenly he felt utterly bereft. All that would be left by morning were the charred black remnants of the structures, smoking gently, and nothing of his former life.

Suddenly he could not bear it. Everything was gone; he ought to be part of the fire too. Like a drunkard, he staggered towards the remnants of the great hall, drawing his sword as if to challenge an enemy in its red depths.

There was a movement to one side; he spun, the weapon raised and streaming with firelight. Then he lowered it. 'Go away,' he said raggedly, and felt a pressure growing within him. 'I do not want or need your company. Damn you, woman, leave me alone!'

Clarice ignored his command, putting herself between him and the fire. Her eyes were wide and dark, and her fists were clenched in the fabric of her mantle. 'You want Maude,' she said gently. 'You need Maude, I know that. I wish she were here too. I wish she could bolster my courage and tell me what to do because I am lost on my own. I wish she was at your side to comfort you, but she isn't. She's dead and in God's keeping. Let her go.'

He saw his own hand swing the sword, saw the fear blaze in her eyes, but she stood her ground. The steel glittered an inch from her throat before he reversed his grip on the hilt and with a roar of anguish, hurled the weapon into the heart of the fire where he had been going to leap. And the storm broke, driving him to his knees in the snow as he wept for Maude, for himself, for all the wasted years, both past and future.

Clarice knelt with him and encircled him with her arms. Through the wrenching, tearing shudders of his grief, he felt the softer tremors of her crying, and on a distant level heard her whispering that it would be all right. Not the same, not unchanged, but all right.

CHAPTER 44

Whittington Castle,
Summer 1224

The quarried stone had travelled up the Severn to Shrewsbury, then by ox cart and pony pannier to the site of the new keep. From his saddle, Fulke watched the loads arriving and felt a strange mingling of pleasure and poignancy. His horse tossed its head and the bells attached to the scarlet ribbons plaited in its mane jingled musically.

The debris of the burned timber keep and stockade had been raked aside and a new keep with rounded gatehouse towers was rising on the site of the old fortress. Already the memory of the former building was fading. He could not picture the precise position of the kitchens or recall whether there had been five or six window embrasures down the length of the hall. But then how much did it matter except to the corner of his mind that yearned with nostalgia for a time that perhaps had not been as perfect as now it seemed?

The fire that had burned down the former keep had been like the fire of his marriage to Maude. So fierce it was an immolation, leaving naught but charred ruins beyond the white-hot glory. He would never experience that heart-searing conflagration again, and he was glad, for he knew that he would not survive it. But there were other paths of loving that grew out of a gentler caritas.

The soft clink of a mason's hammer carried to his ears and the cheerful shouts of the craftsmen as they toiled. Many of them had come from work on the priory at Alberbury, now finished – in its first stages at least – with a chapel dedicated to St Stephen as the final resting place of the FitzWarin family. As a place too, for other rituals.

On this thought, he tugged lightly on the rein, and turned the horse in the fresh dew of the early summer morning. A little way back, Clarice was waiting for him, giving him time alone to collect his thoughts. There was a smile in her grey-gold eyes, the luminous flush of youth to her complexion. His heart, scarred and patched as it was, turned within him at the sight of her. If not love, if not lust, the emotions engendered ran as close as sun shadows.

It was a year and a half since Maude's death. He still grieved; there would always be a hollow place within him, but it was no longer a yawning cavern. Yet he was wary, unable to put his complete trust in the sensation of almost fulfilment.

'By summer's end, it will be habitable,' Clarice said. 'And the truce with Llewelyn means that even if there is another war with Wales, Whittington will stand as a rock against the tide.'

'The amount it is costing, it had better.' He smiled at her optimism. It was what he needed to draw him out of his darkness. She was right, of course. He had made his peace with King Henry too and had received his authority to rebuild the border keeps of Alberbury and Whittington. He had also received several small gifts from the royal hand: a waiving of a fine; a present of venison; and, ironically, a beautiful inlaid chessboard with a casket of carved ivory pieces.

The Marshal family had granted him the right to hold a fair each year at Wantage in recompense for what had happened to Whittington because of his support for them. The previous June, Hawise had borne him a small grand-daughter, with Maude's silvery hair and green eyes. If not exactly his heart's desire, he had what he needed.

'You are sure?' he said to Clarice for the third time that morning. 'There is many a younger man who would be pleased to call you wife.'

Her expression lost some of its serenity. 'What do I have to say to persuade you?' she demanded, an exasperated note entering her voice. Reaching across the space between them, she laid her hand over his, her flesh white and smooth over his scarred and tanned. 'I know that with my dowry, I could have the pick of a dozen younger men. Indeed, you have paraded most of them before me on other occasions. I do not want them; I want you. And if you ask why, or say that you are old enough to be my father, I will hit you.' Her complexion flushed beneath the onslaught of her words. If he had learned to grieve at Whittington, she had learned to speak out.

'You have more understanding than a husband of my own years would ever have and you still have your strength. I have seen you at your best and at your worst, and I know that I can trust you.' She lowered her eyes. 'I ... I can never replace Maude, nor would I want to. She was everything to you and such love only comes once ... but I would be your life companion now. Don't shut me out, or doubt me.'

He swallowed, moved by her words. 'I do not doubt your integrity,' he said huskily, 'but I have to justify my own by giving you the opportunity to change your mind.'

'Thrice given, and thrice refused,' she said, the smile returning to her eyes. 'I will not change my mind.'

Capturing her hand, he turned it over in his and rubbed his thumb across her palm and fingers. In that she was like Maude, he thought. Once a notion entered her head, it was impossible to dislodge. 'Well then,' he said, his own lips curving, even though his gaze was more grave than hers, and perhaps a little sad. 'If you are ready, let us go.'

In the early summer morning, the dew still wet on the grass, they left Whittington to the masons and took the road to Alberbury Priory and the waiting priest.

Author's Note

I first came across the story of Fulke FitzWarin in a book by Glyn Burgess entitled *Two Medieval Outlaws*. At the time I was researching Eustace the Monk for his role in *The Marsh King's Daughter*, but reading Fulke's story, I realised that here was a novel bursting to be written and I decided to make Fulke my next project.

So, how much of *Lords of the White Castle* is truth and how much is fiction? Rather like a plait, there are three strands to the story: the facts that are verifiable history; the facts that are massaged by the 'tabloid journalist' skills of Fulke's chronicler; and my own interpretation of the two with a seasoning of personal imagination.

Fulke FitzWarin was born somewhere around 1170 into a Shropshire family of obscure origins but high ambition. His father was known as Fulke 'le Brun' – The Brown – suggesting that he was dark of hair and eye. Incidentally, Fulke's brother Philip was known as 'The Red', thus I have given him auburn hair in the novel.

The tale about Fulke and Prince John quarrelling over a game of chess may be apocryphal, but some scholars, notably J. Meisel in the book *Barons of the Welsh Frontier*, believe that it is probably true. What is certain is that from an early age John and Fulke had no fondness for each other. John did give Whittington Castle to Morys

FitzRoger for the sum of fifty marks and rejected Fulke's petition even though Fulke had been granted the right to have the castle in the Curia Regis court. Fulke turned outlaw as a result and for three years wreaked havoc up and down the borders until John pardoned him and restored his lands. Fulke seems to have had a powerful supporter in Hubert Walter, Archbishop of Canterbury, who at one time was also the Justiciar, the Chancellor and the papal legate. It was said by some that he wielded more influence than John himself. It seems very likely to me that Fulke's connections with the Walter family began during his youth when the chronicle says he was a companion to Prince John. The Prince was being educated in the household of Ranulf de Glanville, whose nephews Hubert and Theobald Walter were. Although the evidence is circumstantial and cannot be proven, I also think it likely that Fulke was acquainted on a social basis with Maude Walter before their marriage.

The union of Fulke and Maude is where Fulke's unknown chronicler takes history into his own hands and, in the interests of a good story, shifts the timescale slightly. While Fulke's marriage to Maude is not in dispute, it did not take place until after Fulke's rebellion, whereas the chronicle puts their marriage during the period when Fulke was an outlaw. It is also the chronicler who supplies the details of Maude being lustfully pursued by King John and of enduring the perils of childbirth in the Welsh wilderness. The chronicler makes no mention of Maude having two children by Theobald Walter, but it seems likely that she did and that they were given into foster care when her first husband died. I have gone with the chronicle on this particular issue since taking the other option would have tangled the strands of the story to no purpose.

During the periods when Fulke was not doing anything spectacular, the chronicler keeps the readers enthralled by having his hero fight dragons and giants and embark on a Ulysses-like adventure. In the interests of maintaining reader belief, I have had to weave my way around some of the more improbable happenings, or find my own interpretations!

Fulke was one of the barons involved in the Magna Carta rebellion, although there are no firm reasons for his support. He could have been driven by a natural taste for making trouble, or by the fact that he was deeply in debt to the Crown at that time. And perhaps old grievances still died hard.

Whilst researching, I came across the strong possibility that Fulke's third daughter Mabile had severe mental or physical disabilities. This detail is suggested by J. Meisel in *Barons of the Welsh Frontier*. Mabile never married and she did not enter the Church. One or the other would have been de rigueur for a noblewoman in the thirteenth century, but there is no evidence for either. There is, however, proof that Fulke gave the income of his richest manor to support her in his will, and his eldest son Fulke agreed to abide by the ruling.

Maude died in the early 1220s; the cause is not known. Fulke married again, this time to Clarice d'Auberville who, from the circumstantial evidence, I believe to be a relative of the de Glanville family and of Hubert and Theobald Walter. Either with her, or perhaps with Maude before she died, Fulke had another daughter, Eve. The chronicle says that Eve went on to marry Llewelyn the Great, Prince of North Wales. This may or may not be true. Again, there is circumstantial evidence supplied by Eyton in his twelve-volume *The Antiquities of Shropshire*. Hawise's husband William Pantulf died in 1233 and Fulke took on the guardianship of his daughter and two small granddaughters.

Fulke outlived Clarice and was in his early nineties when he died. By all accounts, he was active until his mid-eighties when his eyesight failed and his son took the baronial responsibilities upon his shoulders. Fulke's heir and namesake only outlived his father by about six years. He drowned in a stream at the battle of Lewes in 1264 while fighting on the royalist side against Simon de Montfort. For a time the Montforts took custody of Whittington and Fulke's small grandson. The land was restored when King Henry regained control of the kingdom, but young Fulke, my Fulke's grandson, did not come into his inheritance until 1273. The FitzWarin line continued until 1420 when the eleventh Fulke FitzWarin died without a son to succeed him.

After Llewelyn's men burned Whittington to the ground, Fulke rebuilt the castle in stone. The gatehouse still stands today in testament to the events of more than seven hundred years ago. And if you are fortunate and go there, perhaps on a day in June as I have done, you may see a company of reenactors bringing a past reality to life.

For anyone wishing to read the truth and the myth of the story of Fulke FitzWarin I can recommend Glyn Burgess's *Two Medieval Outlaws*, published by Brewer (ISBN 0-85991-438-0) as an excellent starting point. For a more detailed examination of Fulke and his environment, I suggest J. Meisel's *Barons of the Welsh Frontier: The Corbet, Pantulf and FitzWarin Families 1066–1272* published by the University of Nebraska Press. I also found R. W. Eyton's *Antiquities of Shropshire*, published in twelve volumes by John Russel Smith 1854–60 very enlightening – but probably difficult to obtain. My local library had the collection, but in their rare books room and I was only allowed to read it under the strict supervision of the librarian!

I welcome comments and feedback on my novels. You can reach me via my website at:

http://www.btinternet.com/~elizabeth.chadwick

or e-mail me at elizabeth.chadwick@btinternet.com.

The Conquest

Elizabeth Chadwick

When a comet appears in the sky over England in the spring of 1066, it heralds a time of momentous change for Ailith, a young Saxon wife. Newly pregnant, she has developed a friendship with her Norman neighbour, Felice, who is also with child. But when Felice's countrymen come not as friends but as conquerors, they take all that Ailith holds dear.

Rescued from suicidal grief by Rolf, a handsome Norman horse-breeder, Ailith is persuaded to become nurse to Felice's son, Benedict, but the situation soon becomes fraught with tension. Ailith leaves Felice's household for Rolf's English lands and, as his mistress, bears him a daughter, Julitta. But the Battle of Hastings has left a savage legacy which is to have bitter repercussions, not only for Rolf and Ailith but for the next generation, Benedict and Julitta.

From bustling London streets to windswept Yorkshire Dales, from green Norman farmland to the rugged mountains of the Pyrenees and the Spain of El Cid, this is an epic saga of love and loss, compassion and brutality, filled with unforgettable characters.

'An author who makes history come gloriously alive'
The Times

'The best writer of mediaeval fiction currently around'
Historical Novel Review

The Marsh King's Daughter

Elizabeth Chadwick

England 1216: Dissatisfaction with King John has bred a civil war which threatens the social order.

Unwanted and unloved, rebellious Miriel Weaver is forced to a convent by her violent stepfather. Her plan to escape from the harsh life of a novice nun crystallises with the arrival of recuperating soldier of fortune, Nicholas de Caen. Miriel sees in his pride and self-sufficiency a kindred spirit and, once he is well enough to leave, a way out.

The two part in Nottingham on bad terms which are to blight both their lives. When they meet again by chance, they agree to call a truce – but the truce becomes first friendship and then a dangerous passion. Almost too late, Nicholas and Miriel realise that the chain of events triggered by their first meeting could now ensure they never know the pleasure of living . . .

'One of Elizabeth Chadwick's strengths is a stunning grasp of historical detail. Her characters are beguiling and the story is intriguing and very enjoyable'
Barbara Erskine

Other bestselling Time Warner Books titles available by mail:

☐ The Conquest	Elizabeth Chadwick	£6.99
☐ The Winter Mantle	Elizabeth Chadwick	£6.99
☐ The Falcons of Montabard	Elizabeth Chadwick	£6.99
☐ The Marsh King's Daughter	Elizabeth Chadwick	£6.99

The prices shown above are correct at time of going to press. However, the publishers reserve the right to increase prices on covers from those previously advertised without further notice.

———————————— sphere ————————————

SPHERE
PO Box 121, Kettering, Northants NN14 4ZQ
Tel: 01832 737525, Fax: 01832 733076
Email: aspenhouse@FSBDial.co.uk

POST AND PACKING:
Payments can be made as follows: cheque, postal order (payable to Sphere), credit card or Switch Card. Do not send cash or currency.

All UK Orders	**FREE OF CHARGE**
EC & Overseas	25% of order value

Name (BLOCK LETTERS) ....

Address ....:...

....

Post/zip code: ....

☐ Please keep me in touch with future Sphere publications

☐ I enclose my remittance £ ....

☐ I wish to pay by Visa/Access/Mastercard/Eurocard/Switch Card

☐☐☐☐☐☐☐☐☐☐☐☐☐☐☐☐☐☐

Card Expiry Date ☐☐☐☐   Switch Issue No. ☐☐